EX LIBRIS

The Great Wide Open

DOUGLAS KENNEDY

HUTCHINSON
LONDON

1 3 5 7 9 10 8 6 4 2

Hutchinson
20 Vauxhall Bridge Road
London SW1V 2SA

Hutchinson is part of the Penguin Random House group of
companies whose addresses can be found at
global.penguinrandomhouse.com.

Epigraph from 'Antilamentation', *The Book of Men* by Dorianne Laux
(W.W. Norton & Company, 2011)

First published by Hutchinson in 2019

www.penguin.co.uk

A CIP catalogue record for this book is available from the British Library.

ISBN 9781786331694 (hardback)
ISBN 9780091953737 (trade paperback)

Typeset in 12.5/14.3 pts Adobe Garamond
by Integra Software Services Pvt. Ltd, Pondicherry

Printed and bound in Great Britain by Clays Ltd, Elcograf S.p.A.

Penguin Random House is committed to a sustainable future for
our business, our readers and our planet. This book is made
from Forest Stewardship Council® certified paper.

For the ever-amazing Amelia Kennedy

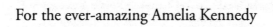

Man is not what he thinks he is, he is what he hides.

— André Malraux

You've walked those streets a thousand times and still
you end up here. Regret none of it, not one
of the wasted days you wanted to know nothing,
when the lights from the carnival rides
were the only stars you believed in, loving them
for their uselessness, not wanting to be saved.
You've traveled this far on the back of every mistake,
ridden in dark-eyed and morose but calm as a house
after the TV set has been pitched out the upstairs
window. Harmless as a broken ax. Emptied
of expectation. Relax. Don't bother remembering any of it.
Let's stop here, under the lit sign
on the corner, and watch all the people walk by.

— Dorianne Laux, 'Antilamentation'

All families are secret societies. Realms of intrigue and internal warfare, governed by their own rules, regulations, boundaries, frontiers. Rules which often make no sense to those outside its borders. We prize the family more than any other communal unit because it is the essential cornerstone of social order. When the external world turns harsh and unforgiving – when outsiders who have intersected with our lives disappoint and even maim us – the family is supposed to be the shelter toward which we are magnetically pulled. The repository of comfort and joy.

Given how we venerate this essential primitive construct, idealize its potentiality, crave it to be the one place to which we can turn for the possibility of unconditional love, is it any surprise that the actual reality of 'family' is usually such a destabilizing one? All the flaws in the glass of the human condition are refracted one-hundred-fold within our next of kin. Because family is the place where all our grievances with the world begin. Because family is often internecine. Because family frequently becomes a source of confinement and ever-magnifying resentments. To grow up in a family is to discover that everyone has a talent for the surreptitious; that, for all the talk about being among the people who know you best, and who will always watch your back, you are all harboring secrets.

I reread that paragraph twice over, the words ricocheting around my psyche like some out of control pinball, a ding-dong cascade of distressing truths. I lit up another cigarette – my eighth of the day so far, and it was only 3.20 p.m. I crumpled the now-empty packet on my desk, buzzed my assistant Cheryl and asked her to run downstairs to the machine in the lobby and pick me up another pack of Viceroys, as I'd be working late on this manuscript tonight. Last night had been a particularly excessive one on the nicotine front, owing to my distress that we'd re-elected our B-movie actor president for a second term. Staggering in late from a party I'd been invited to in some Gilded Age townhouse off Gramercy Park, I discovered, among the many messages on my answering machine, one from C.C. Fowler. He's the chairman of the publishing house where I ply my trade. And he sounded like he'd had four cocktails too many as he informed me:

1

Hello, Alice. A quick thought: we need a fast book on Reagan as political game-changer – because he is now about to become, for better or worse, the most influential president since FDR. Can we discuss this over lunch Thursday?

C.C. always did have his eye on the marketplace. But I couldn't help but think: who would want to buy a book on a president whom we'd voted back into power with such a thundering second mandate? He won forty-nine of the fifty states last night, letting it be known: his brand of patriotic sentimentality and *making money is everything* spiel plays big time in mid-eighties America. I hit the button on my phone that put me in immediate contact with Cheryl, telling her to phone C.C.'s assistant and suggest lunch this Friday – 'as you know I will be leaving early Thursday'.

Cheryl – being someone I could totally trust (and believe me, in a publishing house, someone who keeps a secret is as rare as a happy alcoholic) – already knew why I had to duck out of work at 1 p.m. tomorrow: I was visiting my brother in prison. The fact that he was locked up in a federal facility an hour north of Manhattan was hardly a state secret. His arrest and trial had been major news everywhere.

I'd been paying him weekly visits ever since his incarceration a month or so ago. I got a letter a few days before the election, asking if I might be able to get up to the prison this week as 'I really need to see you and talk something through'. He was vague about what topic this 'something' happened to be, alluding to the fact that he'd been thinking through so much. 'Soul assessing' was the curious term he used. His recent letters to me were now peppered with the redemptive language of the newly converted. Maybe I'm being too harsh here. Maybe I am still getting my head around the idea of My Brother the Felon. Maybe his newfound conscience since being sent up the river smacked of convenience ... especially since finding God in the joint strikes me as one of those de rigueur outcomes of felonious American life.

Still, he is my brother. And though our world views are seismically disparate ones – how can a family produce, when it comes to basic sense and sensibility, such radically different children? – my stubborn streak of loyalty has made me stick by him. Especially as familial fealty usually comes with a big subtext of guilt.

I called the prison and put my name down on the visitors' list for Thursday at 4.30 p.m. As before, the official I was speaking to reminded me to bring some form of photo ID and warned me that I could, at the discretion of the prison, be body-searched – and he read me, as before, the list of proscribed items (guns, knives, prescription and illegal drugs, pornography, and that dangerous substance known as chewing gum). When asked by the official if I understood what was not permitted I told him:

'It's my fifth visit, sir. I always play by the rules.'

'I don't care if it's your twenty-fifth visit. We always have to read you this list. Are we clear about that?'

'Yes, sir.'

'See you Thursday, Miss Burns.'

On the train north through the suburban somnolence of New Jersey I continued work on the manuscript I'd just bought from a Harvard Med School professor and psychoanalyst on Families and Guilt. It's a subject which just about everyone sentient can relate to; a book that might just break wide on the bestseller lists if I can curb Dr Gordon Gilchrist's tendencies to veer into hyper-shrink vocabulary. Transference is something we can relate to – especially when it comes to all the fun stuff bequeathed to us by dear old Mom and Dad. But start hitting the reader over the head with *cathexis/decathexis*, or *Signorelli parapraxis*, or the wonderfully labyrinthine realm of *counterphobic attitude*, and you have them feeling intellectually cowed and overwhelmed by terminology that can only be understood with an *Oxford English Dictionary* to hand. I've spoken to Gordon about this – and how, if he can scale back his cerebral gymnastics, he has a good shot at being next season's must-read *So You Think You've Got Problems?* tome. But even though my red pen was boxing out big chunks of far-too-technical text, I felt a sharp stab of *objective identification* when I happened upon the paragraph that started:

All families are secret societies. Realms of intrigue and internal warfare, governed by their own rules, regulations, boundaries, frontiers. Rules which often make no sense to those outside its borders.

Was my brother now musing on the secrets that had so underscored our family life and helped create the culture of secrecy that eventually landed him in jail? We are not just the sum total of everything that has happened to us, but also a testament to the way we have interpreted all that has crossed our path. The music of chance intersecting with the maddening complexities of choice – and how, in the wake of bad judgment and self-sabotage, we so often rewrite the scenario to create one that we can live with.

'Prisoner's name and number?'

The distended voice crackling through a small speaker mounted in Plexiglas at the entrance to the federal correctional institution in Otisville, New York. A brick gate, lightly barbed-wired. Concrete walls. A hint of low-lying dormitory buildings within. Beyond these features – and the sign informing you that, verily, this was a prison – there was little very oppressive about the look of the place. Bar the fact that you were incarcerated there for as long as the criminal justice system had decreed you deserved to serve your debt to society.

I spoke his name. I also had a little notebook open and ready in my left hand, and read out the number he'd been assigned when first processed through here: '5007943NYS34.'

'Relation to the prisoner?' the voice crackled back.

'Sister.'

Moments later there was a percussive, telltale click and the heavily reinforced door opened. I entered and walked down a short open-air corridor: no roof, the gray November sky above clearly visible, two seven-foot-high breeze-block walls keeping you on the straight and narrow route toward a second security checkpoint. Here I had to show identification, and wait as all the contents of my bags were emptied out and inspected. I also had to submit to a pat-down by a woman officer. Once it was determined that I wasn't armed and dangerous, that the two bags of Oreos my brother had asked me to bring were, indeed, those honest, humble schoolroom favorites, and there were no hidden razor blades in the jars of peanut butter also accompanying me, I was directed into a waiting room. A bleak place, painted state-hospital green, with gray plastic chairs, fluorescent tube lighting, cracked ceiling tiles, scuffed linoleum. Even though this was one of many recent pilgrimages up here I still found the place unsettling. A prison is a prison – even if your brother has been offered the opportunity of piano or Spanish lessons as part of the rehabilitative process.

'Alice Burns?'

My name was being called – by a compact Hispanic gentleman in a blue prison officer uniform just a tad too large for him. I stood up. Another further inspection of my bags, then I was ushered into a small room, fitted with a desk and two upright steel chairs. How I wanted a cigarette right now. How two or so Viceroys during the fifty minutes I'd be allotted with my brother would make the agony of it all a little more manageable.

I sat down in one of the hard chairs, awaiting the arrival of Prisoner Number 5007943NYS34, my eyes slammed shut for a moment's respite from such institutional creepiness.

'Hey there, sis.'

My eyes snapped open. My brother was in front of me, looking around three pounds lighter than when I'd seen him last week. I stood up. We exchanged an awkward hug, as I couldn't match the enthusiasm with which he gathered me up in his arms, and embraced me as if he was passing on some spiritual life force.

'That's quite some hug,' I said.

'Pastor Willie told me I'm the biggest hugger he's ever encountered.'

'And I'm sure Pastor Willie knows a thing or two about forgiving hugs.'

'You going ironic on me, sis?'

'Seems that way. How'd you lose the weight?'

'Exercise. Better diet. Prayer.'

'Prayer can make you shed pounds?'

'If you start looking on high-calorie stuff as the Devil's temptation ...'

I hoisted the bag of goodies that I had brought him.

'Then why did you request all this highly un-nutritious junk food?'

'A little treat every day is no bad thing.'

'Whereas eating ten Oreos in a row is the work of Satan?'

'You're getting that tone again.'

'Didn't sleep much last night – and I find this all rather stressful.'

'As you should – given how badly I behaved. I ruined many lives. I brought shame down on us all.'

I held up my hand, like a cop directing traffic.

'You've apologized enough to me.'

'Pastor Willie says you can never apologize enough for past sins; that the only way you can redeem yourself is by walking the walk of righteousness and atoning for the past.'

'A lengthy prison stretch strikes me as plenty of atonement. Did you vote on Tuesday?'

'Can't. One of the many downsides of being a prisoner: you lose the right to vote. You lose the right to do just about everything.'

He started pacing up and down this narrow room – that old anxious habit of his which he repressed for years until he was marched away in handcuffs and forced to do the perp walk in front of the assembled media. Seeing him now I understood a painful truth: despite all this born-again talk of newly acquired inner harmony and redemption, despite putting a brave face on the sentence imposed on him, despite being assured by his lawyer that he would be out in three years, my poor brother was still coming asunder inside these low-security walls. Putting myself in his path I took hold of his two hands and led him back to his chair as he intoned:

'I'm so sorry, so sorry, so … '

That was another side effect of his out-of-body stress: his need to repeat, over and over, the same phrase. I gripped his hands tightly.

'Stop apologizing. What's done is done. And I am glad to hear you angry.'

'But Pastor Willie tells me anger is toxic. And until I practice forgiveness … '

'Pastor Willie has not lost everything. Pastor Willie is not locked up in a prison. Pastor Willie wasn't made a public example of by a district attorney on the political make. What the fuck does that evangelical know about *your* anger?'

'Pastor Willie told me last week, during our private prayer session, that you are a shining example of "sisterly solidarity".'

'I would appreciate it if you didn't mention the unfortunately named Pastor Willie again. It's natural that I'm here for you.'

'Would that my brother had been so charitable.'

His brother. My other brother. Now in hiding, a morass of guilt and stubborn moral superiority. Incommunicado to us.

'He's not a happy guy about all of this,' I said.

'Bless you for sticking by me, and not writing me off as scum as he did.'

'You're hardly scum,' I said.

'Mom said the same thing to me last week. You guys still not talking?'

'I haven't slammed the door, but she is still blaming me ... '

'I've told her to stop doing that. It wasn't your fault.'

'In her eyes it's always *my* fault. I was always the daughter she never wanted, as she told me on three too-many occasions.'

'We all need a great deal of healing.'

'Oh please ... '

'I know you think this is all touchy-feely. It's time we start becoming honest with each other.'

'That must have gone down well with Mom. Imagine if you'd said that to Dad ... '

A long silence ensued after my comment. My brother stared at the floor, his distress evident. Eventually he reached over for a bag of Oreos, tore open the top, and grabbed three of the cookies, wolfing them down quickly.

'I've wanted to talk about Dad with you for a while,' he said.

'I'm sorry I brought him up.'

'Never be sorry about bringing up Dad. But ... '

He hesitated for a moment before saying:

'I now need to discuss with you some truth I've never told you before.'

'I'm not sure I want any truth this afternoon.'

'But this is something that needs to come out.'

'Why now?'

'I have to share it.'

'I hear the voice of Pastor Willie behind this need to *share* . . . '

'He did tell me that until I confessed this transgression –'

' "Transgression" is a big, loaded word.'

'Will you hear me out, *please*?'

Silence. A very long silence. My brother kept his back to me, his gaze fixed on the wall. Finally he started to speak. And when, almost a half-hour later, he finished recounting his tale I found myself in vertiginous territory; the ground beneath my feet brittle, about to give way.

'So . . . fifteen years after this event . . . you decide to lay it all on me,' I said. 'In doing so you're insisting that I share your secret – and keep it just that: a secret.'

'You can tell the world if you want.'

'I'm telling no one. You've brought enough trouble down upon yourself over the past few years. But I have to ask you: who, besides Pastor Willie, knows about this?'

'No one.'

My eyes scanned all four corners of this grim little room, checking to see if there were any cameras or microphones in sight. None on view. But I still dropped my voice down to a choked whisper as I said:

'Keep it that way. Don't listen to that evangelist about sharing this story with anyone. Do you think Pastor Willie can keep quiet?'

'He's always telling me that everything we talk about is confidential; that he is a great keeper of "eternal secrets".'

And I bet, like so many men of hyper-piety, he has more than a few dark secrets of his own.

'Well, your secrets are profoundly *temporal.* From this point on . . . I am going to forget that I heard this story.'

'You're sounding like Dad now,' Adam said.

'I am anything but our father.'

'Then why are you conspiring with me, the way he did all those years ago?'

'Because, alas, we are family. And one of the truths accompanying that statement is the fact that I am going to have to live with the knowledge of what you just told me.'

'Even though, a moment ago, you said you were going to forget that you ever heard it.'

'That was me being far too facile. I'm never going to forget that story. I'm also never going to talk about it again. And I now truly regret you telling me.'

'You had to know. Because it's so about us. Because it's what we are.'

But then, after casting his eyes up toward the cracked ceiling tiles and fluorescent lights above us, his gaze turned back to me, eyeing me like a sniper who'd just found his target.

'And now you're implicated,' he said.

Days after that blindsiding prison visit the gravity of what my brother did – and my father's immediate complicity in it all – was underscored by something that continued to haunt me: my acceptance of the secret he'd just dropped in my lap.

My brother was right: by telling him to shut up about it all – to keep this terrible crime permanently concealed, to insist that he take an oath of silence, of *omertà* – I had colluded with him.

All families are secret societies.

And a secret uttered is no longer a secret.

When that secret is shared with a parent, a sibling, it can become a cabal, a conspiracy. If, that is, you engage with the secret.

'*You had to know. Because it's so about us. Because it's what we are.*'

Us. The Burns. Two parents born in a time of 1920s abundance that quickly collapsed into hardship and national despondency. Three children latterly arriving amidst all that mid-century peace and plenty. A quintet of Americans from the upper reaches of the middle class. And a testament – in our own disparate, tortured ways – to the mess we make of life.

My mother, repetitive to the core and always reaching for a bromide with which to band-aid the pain, did say something recently that showed a flash of hidden wisdom:

'Family is everything … which is why it hurts so much.'

I consider all this from an uneasy perch – peering over the insouciant precipice of youth into my fourth decade, the personal

9

landscape around me littered with much inherited and self-generated debris. Making me wonder: when did the sadness start? When did we all opt for it?

I stared down at the manuscript again, reaching for my still glowing cigarette. I took another steadying drag, then picked up my pen.

All families are secret societies.

To which, had it been my book, my words, I would have added the following lines:

And if there is one thing that the past two decades has taught me it is this salient truth: 'unhappiness is a choice'.

PART ONE

NOSTALGIA IS THE domain of conservatives. All that talk about the good old days when life was simpler, moral and ethical values clearer, and people knew the rules – it's the lingua franca of anyone who is ill at ease with the shifting mores of now. But anyone who invokes 'back then' is also engaged in a picture-postcard vision of history, as airbrushed and golden as one of those cover illustrations on a Mormon brochure depicting Heaven.

Mormons. I remember my first encounter with one of those Latter-Day Saints. It was September of 1971, early one morning before heading off for my first day of my last year of school. My mother was cooking my father breakfast while the *Today Show* blared on the tiny 12-inch Sony Trinitron, strategically placed on a countertop to allow her visual access to it while 'destroying food.' That was Dad's ongoing comment about his wife's culinary skills: the fact that she had no talent whatsoever in the cooking department, rendering meals bland, tasteless. I concurred with Dad – so much so that I had recently started to cook my own dinners, even going down to the A&P on the Old Greenwich main street to buy food with the babysitting money I earned most weekends.

I was heavily into doing my own thing, which that week included wearing a wooden peace symbol on a braided rope that bounced just above my chest. I'd found it the previous weekend on a trip into the city with my boyfriend of that moment, Arnold Dorfman. He was one of the few Jews in this corner of Connecticut; a fellow unhappy transplant from Manhattan. The moment Dad saw the peace symbol around my neck he'd let off a tirade about the 'pinko' influence of Arnold's father, who had made the mistake, a few weeks before, of questioning Nixon and Kissinger's sideshow bombing of Cambodia at a local cocktail party to which my parents had also been invited. While they were out my boyfriend Arnold came by for an hour of study and fifteen minutes of sex. Arnold being Arnold he had calculated that the party would break up by eight thirty so he was gone from my room by eight ten ... exactitude being one of Arnold's quiet obsessions. Sure enough the front door opened around eight thirty-five. My parents were back home. Within moments they were arguing, my dad sounding as if he'd downed four vodka martinis too many.

'Don't tell me how to think out loud,' I heard him shout.

'I've told you once, I've told you a thousand times, when you drink you start shooting off that big Irish mouth of yours.'

This was my mother – the former Brenda Katz of Flatbush, Brooklyn – with her voice raised in the tone of denouncement which she used on each of us whenever we displeased her. Not that I could blame her for castigating my father. Ever since the United States had started careening down unforeseen new 'radical' paths – Dad had become increasingly furious about the domestic disorder of the country he'd sworn to defend as a *Semper Fi* veteran of the United States Marine Corps. Mom, meanwhile, had spoken out repeatedly against our bombing of Southeast Asia.

'I don't need that peacenik Hebrew doctor giving me a lecture on war.'

'Stop calling him a Hebrew.'

'Hey, it's better than "Jew-boy".'

'You sound like your father.'

'Don't speak ill of the dead.'

'Even though you hated him.'

'I can speak ill of him, you can't. Dad being Dad "Jew-boy" would have been too polite for him. "Kike" – that was more his style.'

'And now you're just trying to show me how anti-Semitic you are.'

'How can I be anti-Semitic? I married you. But maybe that's what turned me anti-Semitic.'

'My daddy will hear what you said.'

'*Daddy ... daddy!* You're forty-four years old and still sounding like some recently bat-mitzvahed JAP. Your daddy and I happen to agree: you are a spoiled child brat. And he knows he and your yenta mother did the spoiling.'

'Go on, tell me you hate me while you're at it.'

14

Before my father could answer in the affirmative, I heard the crashing of glasses and the slamming of a door and my mother sobbing. I went over to my record player and put on my favorite album of the moment: Joni Mitchell's *Blue*. How I wanted to be like her: the independent, poetic, passionate hippie chick who had the heart of a true romantic, but could see through all the bullshit of men and the conformist cant of American life (even if she was Canadian). How I wanted to be on a lonely road, traveling, traveling, traveling.

I frequently envied my brother Peter – six years my senior and now in his first year at Yale Divinity School. Peter was always the star student. He won a full scholarship to Penn, then put fear into my mother by announcing that he was taking a year off after college to work as an organizer for the American Council of Churches in the Deep South. My dad also voiced concerns about Peter's safety – 'because there's nothing more stupid than a Southern redneck with a gun'. That was one of the intriguing contradictions about Dad. He might have been an arch-Republican – and a great supporter of Nixon – but on the civil rights issue he was surprisingly nuanced, declaring on several occasions that rights were rights, 'whether you are white, black, yellow or just an all-American asshole'. I remember him actually being deeply affected when Martin Luther King was assassinated in April of '68 ('That was a good man'). Just as he wanted the FBI to throw every black militant into solitary confinement.

'There's a big difference between peaceful protest and trying to change things with a Molotov cocktail,' he said during a Thanksgiving dinner last year when Peter actually showed up, as did my other brother Adam with his not-so-bright girlfriend Patty – whom he'd been dating since starting business school (at Dad's insistence) at SUNY New Paltz. That had been a surprise choice. I had no idea if Adam was even interested in going into business. What I did know was that he really wanted to play hockey. But ever since a car accident two years ago when he was twenty, and in which one of his teammates – a black guy named Fairfax Hackley – died when he fell asleep behind the wheel, the professional sport dreams had vanished. Adam had emerged from the car badly concussed and bruised. Physically he had recovered well enough to play again. But that didn't seem to be an option for him.

Sitting across the table from Adam I saw the haunted look in his eyes, how he was all false enthusiasm, agreeing with my father way too often and laughing blithely at Patty's inane jokes. I couldn't help thinking how little I know this brother of mine. Ever since the accident he had struck me as reduced, a shadow of himself. Apart from telling me 'It should have been me', he never spoke of the car crash. For Adam it became a room he would not let anyone enter. Every time I mentioned it I was shot down by my dad or mom. As such I had learned not to ask any more questions about it. But I couldn't get to the bottom of why Adam was suddenly so complicit in a complete change of personal direction – of doing everything ordered by Dad. He seemed desperate for paternal approval; of looking upon our father as the ultimate voice of authority that he needed to placate ... even though he also knew that he would never totally please the man.

Peter, on the other hand, had now made it his life's work to fly in the face of anything that our father demanded of him; to counterbalance Adam's obsequiousness by playing the liberal provocateur at any opportunity. On his return home from three harrowing months in Montgomery, Alabama, he quietly related how he'd received a death threat from the local chapter of the KKK after he brought five elderly African American women over to the local courthouse to register to vote, and raised all sorts of legal objections when the clerk on duty tried to subject these women to a civics test.

'The clerk was an old cracker, a real nasty sonofabitch ... '

Patty shifted uncomfortably in her seat. Our father noticed this.

'Language, son,' he told Peter.

'Did I offend you?' Peter smiled thinly at Patty. 'As I was saying, this cracker sonofabitch was demanding that these three very genteel, elderly women pass a citizenship test by naming the fourteenth president of the United States.'

'Franklin Pierce,' I said.

'How did you know that?' Adam asked me.

'He went to Bowdoin,' Dad said. 'Which is where Alice is heading.'

'They haven't let me in yet, Dad,' I said.

16

'We used to play Bowdoin in hockey,' Adam said. 'Bunch of pretty smart preppies.'

'Well, now they want to jazz the place up,' Mom said, 'which is why they're after your beatnik sister.'

'Beatnik is a rather fifties word,' Peter said.

'Well, she ain't no hippie,' Dad said.

'*Isn't a hippie,*' Mom said.

'You think I don't know English grammar?'

'I think our daughter turned into a beatnik because you broke her heart when you moved us all out of New York,' Mom said. 'Just as you broke my heart.'

'Then move back to the frigging city,' Dad said. 'And don't call me up when you get mugged by a couple of 'Ricans with switch-blades, or lose your lunch when you see some black junkie whore wiping her twat on Eighth Avenue . . . '

'Jesus, Dad!' Adam said, putting a protective arm around Patty.

'And when your sister here runs off with some *schwarzer* jazz musician –'

'That is so out of line,' Peter said,

'Hey, I didn't use the N-word,' Dad said. 'But on your mother's side of the family, *schwarzer* is their N-word.'

'Can you give me the jazz musician's number?' I asked.

'That's not funny, young lady,' Mom said.

Across the table Patty was looking as if she had just walked into a Tourette's convention. Peter smiled.

'Welcome to the family,' he said.

Half an hour later, Dad – well into his third martini – announced to everyone that he understood why most of the Southern states were maintaining the Confederate flag. The entire point of that comment was to infuriate Peter. My brother played it cool, reminding Dad that his grandfather – William Silas Burns – was one of the founding members of the Ku Klux Klan in Georgia.

'Don't you dare call me a fucking racist,' Dad shouted in response.

'But, Dad,' Peter said, 'you gave me all sorts of shit when I showed up here my junior year at Penn with Marjorie.'

'That's because she started in on the Black Power thing.'

'You also asked me – when she was out of the room – why I couldn't get some nice white girl ... like Patty here ... to go out with me.'

'Typical of your father,' Mom said, 'to play the racist card ...'

'How many times do I have to tell you assholes: I'm not a fucking racist!'

'Dad, please,' Adam said.

'I'm sure Patty would agree with me,' Dad said, 'that the problem with this country today is that all this radical talk is the whining of the spoiled elites ...'

'Tell that to some unfortunate eight-year-old black child in Montgomery, still being told she has to use a segregated toilet for "coloreds only",' Peter said.

'Better than Mr Radical here bragging about getting blown by some Black Panther chick on the way to the revolution,' Dad said.

At which point Patty fled the table, crying. Adam followed.

'You ignoramus,' Mom said. Dad just smiled and threw back the rest of his martini. Peter, meanwhile, shook his head.

'You try so hard to be an asshole, Dad – but you're nothing more than an attention-seeking little boy throwing all your toys out of the crib.'

Bullseye ... to which Dad's response was to reach for a glass of water and toss it in his eldest son's face. There was a moment of shocked silence. Peter stood up. Keeping our father in his ferocious gaze – Dad now looking very much like a tipsy adolescent just caught doing something very naughty – he picked up a napkin, dried his face and simply shook his head again.

'Goodbye,' he said.

Then he went upstairs. As Mom turned the full voice of her invective on Dad, congratulating him 'on ruining another Thanksgiving', I fled.

Secure in my room, I put on an album. *Music from Big Pink* by the Band.

As I dropped the needle on the vinyl, there was a knock on my door. Peter was outside, a small Army-surplus duffel bag over his shoulder, his gray duffel coat already buttoned around him.

'Don't go. Don't leave me,' I said. He came over to the bed and sat down next to me.

'Sometimes the only response you can make is hitting that door marked "Exit",' he told me. 'Keep that in mind, Alice.'

'Believe me, I'm counting down the days until I am out of here,' I said.

'At least you haven't got too long left ... and since when have you had such good taste in rock?'

A song called 'The Weight' was playing. We listened for a moment, united in our confusion as to why our family never seemed to gel; why it was always such hard work.

'As the song implies,' said Peter sadly, 'everybody's got a weight that they drag behind them.'

Giving me a hug he picked up his bag. 'And now, excuse me while I disappear.'

After he headed down the stairs I stepped out onto the little balcony off my room, and saw him hurry toward the fifteen-year-old battered Volvo that he'd bought for five hundred bucks when he started Yale Divinity; the sort of small European car that everyone considered the height of cool. Peter. How I wanted to emulate his intelligence, his bookish knowledge, his independence. How I now watched, with jealousy, him backing out of the driveway and zooming off. Meanwhile, my father was standing under an empty tree on the front lawn, a cigarette on the go, his head lowered to avoid eye contact with the son he had just shamed with that dinner-table dousing. As the Volvo hurled down the avenue Dad put a hand against the tree and shut his eyes. Was he feeling guilt, remorse, shame at lashing out like that – and ending Thanksgiving on such an explosive note? How I wanted him to pound on the fender of the Volvo as Peter drove by, begging him to stop, then throwing his arms around his son and making it all better. I knew Dad to be someone who never apologized – especially when he knew he was wrong.

Now here I was again on the same balcony, months later, after yet another family explosion, watching the Dad I both loved and dreaded leaning up against the only tree on the quarter-acre we called our own; the moonlight framing him as he pulled on a cig-arette, his shoulders slumped, the sense of world-weariness – of being trapped in a life he just didn't like – consuming him.

I'd come out onto the balcony with a pack of cigarettes that I kept hidden behind some books on a shelf in my room. I was taking a second deep drag as Dad suddenly turned around and glanced up in my direction, surprised to see me. I dropped the cigarette, crushing it out with my foot. But Dad was motioning, in true military fash-ion, that I report to his side immediately. Grabbing my jacket from my bed, I tiptoed down the stairs, not wanting Mom to be part of the dressing-down that I was about to receive. But I could hear the small television booming in the kitchen – and Mom watching *Marcus Welby, M.D.* as she cleared up the kitchen mess. I snuck out the front door and walked over to the tree. I expected to be shouted at, told that I was grounded for the next month. But instead he reached into his shirt pocket, pulled out his pack of Lucky Strikes and offered me one. I took a cigarette and watched as Dad tapped out a fresh one for himself, lifting the pack up so he could pull it out with his lips. Then, in a flash, his Zippo appeared and he lit us both up. I was so thrown by this that I took a few little half-puffs.

'If you're going to smoke,' he said, 'you've got to look like you know what you're doing. Right now you're coming across as a dumb kid who's trying to play the grown-up ... and failing. Here's how you inhale a cigarette.'

For the next five minutes Dad taught me how to smoke, showing me how to draw the smoke properly into my lungs; how to hold the cigarette between my fore-and middle fingers (I'd had it between my thumb and forefinger, making me – in Dad's gentle words – 'look like some girl faggot'); how to gesture and wield a cigarette with confidence. I was so taken aback by this impromptu lesson that I worked hard at ignoring the harshness of the unfiltered Lucky Strikes, and the way they scorched my throat. After a couple of fur-ther deep drags I was able to inhale without spluttering, something Dad noticed with approval.

'When did you start smoking?' he asked me.

'I only have one here and there.'

'You're not answering the question.'

'About a year ago.'

'Well, you're turning eighteen any moment now – at which point it will be your constitutional right to drink and smoke as much as you like. But had you come to me last year we could have had this lesson back then. Instead you wanted me to catch you smoking ... which is why you dared to light up on your balcony with me down below. Here's a little piece of advice that my dad gave me when he caught me smoking at the age of fourteen and rewarded this discovery with a slap across my kisser: *Never get caught.* Then he sat me down and did what I just did with you: taught me how to smoke like a grown-up.'

Dad smiled at the memory – one of the few times I'd ever seen him smile when mentioning his father.

'Your grandfather was a two-pack-a-day man. He paid the price with the emphysema that got him.'

An image crossed my mind: Grandpa Patrick visiting us in Manhattan the year before we moved to the burbs, looking wizened and leathery, accompanied by a rather blowsy younger woman who seemed just a little tipsy but still wheeled in the oxygen canister that now had to accompany Grandpa everywhere.

'If Grandpa Patrick died of cigarettes,' I asked, 'why are you encouraging me to smoke?'

'I'm hardly telling you to start, as you're the one who's been smoking for some time now. And yeah, the papers are recently full of all that press stuff about cigarettes causing cancer. But your yenta grandma puffed away until the emphysema got her at seventy-nine. Not bad going for a two-pack-a-day old broad – though her lasting so long makes total sense, given how her God-given role in life was to drive everyone fucking nuts. You can go to the library and look at the back issues of the *New York Times* and read all the Surgeon General's warnings and decide for yourself if you want to puff away or not. Just don't hide this kind of stuff from me. Don't hide anything from me.'

'*Don't hide anything from me.*' These echoed the words Mom had said when, a few months previously, in a rare burst of mother–

daughter solidarity she took me to her gynecologist and had me put on the pill, right after there had been two pregnancies in my class at school.

'We didn't have this option when I was your age,' she'd told me. 'Then again, when I was your age Roosevelt was in the White House and nice girls from Flatbush never did such things. The world's a changed place, and I don't know what you and Arnold get up to. But I do know that I'd rather you be safe than sorry.'

Truth be told Mom herself was always safe *and* sorry; fearful prudence being her modus vivendi. But I was very grateful when she made me an appointment with Dr Rosen – especially as Arnold and I had crossed the 'going all the way' line just two weeks earlier, the first time for us both. After Mom and I left the doctor's office in Stamford (and went to a pharmacy nearby – as there was, in Mom's words, 'no way I'm letting the pharmacist in Old Greenwich know that you're on the pill'), she took me for a grilled-cheese sandwich and a cherry Coke at the lunch counter in the drugstore, telling me:

'Under no circumstances can your father ever know about this,' she warned me. 'Like every damn Irish Catholic, he believes that sex is a male prerogative – and that pure females, like his beloved daughter, don't do such things. Keep his illusions intact, and know you can come to me with any problems in that department. Don't hide anything from me.'

Hearing Dad repeat that line while handing me another Lucky Strike I found myself wondering: do all families have such webs of intrigue? Do parents often try to win favor with their children by informing them: they are the one to be trusted and, in turn, letting it be known that there is no such thing as a united front in this household?

'Your mom would kill me if she knew I was encouraging you in a habit she hates,' said my dad, lighting up another. 'So keep the cigarettes out of her sightline, and pop some of these before going inside.'

Tossing me half a roll of peppermint Life Savers, he watched as I took a deep drag of my cigarette, nodding with approval as I slowly exhaled all that smoke.

'Know how I survived Okinawa?' Dad asked. 'I was the only one of six who got out of there alive.'

'Because you got lucky?' I asked, thinking: this was the first time Dad was ever talking to me about any of this.

'Because I realized, two days in, that we were all going to die. So I asked Gustavason, our captain, if he was in the market for a runner to go behind the lines between officers, getting orders and logistics back and forth. I told him I could run a hundred-yard dash in fifteen seconds. It was about six in the morning and there was a lull in the fighting. We were in a trench behind which were two other trenches, filled with our soldiers. It was the rainy season, so the ground was completely sodden. It must have been a quarter-mile between where we were standing and the rear trench. Gustavason pointed to it and told me he was giving me ninety seconds to get there and then back to him. If I succeeded, I would be his runner. If I didn't, by even two seconds, I'd be back on the front line. When he said "Run!" I ran like a lunatic. Splashing in mud, dodging ditches and crevasses and men, scrambling across the field of trenches, then turning right back, hell for leather, toward the forward trench. It was the longest minute and a half of my life. "Ninety-four seconds," he said as I fell to my knees in front of him. Reaching down he grabbed my shirt and got me back on my feet. Then he told me that the two guys who'd tried out for the position the day before did it in 106 and 110 seconds. So I was twelve seconds faster, which, he said, in the height of battle, could be the margin between life and death.'

Dad lit up another Lucky Strike. I motioned for him to give me another.

'Of course, after that, all the Prospect Heights guys in my platoon hated me. Told me I was a fink, a rat, for copping out of the front line. Cut me off from that moment on. Wouldn't say a word to me, wouldn't even nod in my direction or acknowledge my presence. Then, one by one, they all started to die. Rocco went first – stepped on a land mine during a late-night patrol. Severed his legs, medics couldn't get to him before sun-up, by which time he'd bled to death. Buddy O'Brian got bayoneted by this crazed Jap who managed to sneak into one of the trenches before dawn when everyone was trying to get two hours of sleep. Buddy was the first soldier he saw. Gutted him. His screams woke Gustavason who blew off the Jap's head with his service revolver. By the end of the first month, all my pals from the neighborhoods were gone. Even the captain bought it – hit by a sniper's bullet. And me? I just kept running. Eighty-two days later the battle was over. I had survived. I even got promoted to Staff Sergeant after we'd secured the island.'

A long silence followed. I tried to think about what I should say next, but didn't know how to process all that my father was telling me. As he raised his hand to have another pull off his cigarette I could see that it was shaking. Instinctively I reached out and put my hand on his shoulder. Dad's entire body stiffened.

'I never knew you went through all that,' I said.

'Don't know why I told you,' he said, his voice almost a whisper.

'But it's an amazing story. You survived all that when you were just a year or so older than I am now, I mean, that's crazy brave stuff, Dad.'

He shrugged my hand off his shoulder and turned on me.

'Never ever fucking try to make me feel good about myself by calling me brave,' he spat at me.

'But, Dad –'

'I ran. Do you get that? *I ran.*'

'But you were running between officers. Under fire. Dodging snipers. You didn't run away from –'

'What do you know? You're just a little girl.'

'I was just trying to say how heroic –'

'I was the coward. They died, I didn't. Because I ran.'

His index finger punched my shoulder as he uttered that last word. It hurt, that use of his finger as a physical exclamation point. I burst into tears, overwhelmed by the vehemence of his reaction, the fierce anger unleashed at me, his rage at having figured out a way to survive when all his comrades went over the top and died.

'I shouldn't revisit that stuff,' he said, reaching for me. 'It may have been twenty-six years ago ... but in here, it's like yesterday. Like a runaway movie which keeps screening all the time, and where the projectionist is a nasty fuck who refuses to turn the damn picture off.'

Many years later, when I recreated the scene for each of the four therapists I saw at varying stages of adult despair, I found myself articulating one strange thought: as unpleasant and upsetting as my dad's response was when I tried to comfort him, it was nonetheless the moment I felt closest to him. Because it was also one of the few junctures when he took me into his confidence and showed me the immense pain within.

'Maybe, one day, it won't haunt you so much,' I told my father.

'Yeah, maybe when I'm dead.'

'Don't say that.'

'You don't have to be so nice, Alice. I don't deserve it.'

I put my hand on Dad's shoulder again. This time he didn't shrug me off. Instead he hung his head, stifling a sob with another drag off his cigarette.

'Try to forgive me,' he said. Then, giving me a fast hug, he headed back into the house. I stood there in the cold, finishing my cigarette, thinking how little I knew about so much. And how, for all their proximity and omnipresence in your life, a parent is still such an unknown country – with realms completely closed off from you. And how sad my mother and father were. Especially when they were together.

As soon as he went inside I heard Mom raise her voice. In an exhalation it all started again: Mom castigating Dad, him calling her the worst mistake of his life. I finished my cigarette. I crept back inside, unnoticed. I went up to my room, shut the door and put on the great Joni Mitchell.

Sleep arrived finally, followed by first light and a voice shouting from downstairs:

'Alice! Will you get the front door? ... and shouldn't you be in school?'

Mom. Followed by more banging on the front door. And the subsequent sound of my parents exchanging loud words in the kitchen. I glanced at the bedside clock. Seven forty-one. Shit, shit, shit. The first day of school was due to start in just over twenty minutes ... and if you showed up at 8.05 a.m. you were rewarded with an afternoon detention. I was out of bed and dressed in five minutes. Meanwhile the knocking on the door grew louder … as did the familiar angry voices. I grabbed my book bag and raced down the stairs. Pulling open the front door I found two Mormon missionaries, all smiles. They couldn't have been much older than me, both clean-scrubbed with very blond hair and very white teeth, dressed in identical black suits, white shirts, striped ties, plastic name tags adorning their lapels. They took my bewilderment in their stride, the taller of the two broadening his smile.

'Good morning there, young lady! And do I have good news for you!'

'What good news?' I asked.

'The best good news imaginable! You're going to be able to live with your family for the rest of eternity!'

I stared blankly at Elder Amidon, trying to gauge whether I heard that correctly. His pal chimed in:

'Just think: heavenly Paradise forever with your mom and dad.'

'That is *my* idea of Hell,' I said.

And I ran off to start my last year at school.

2

THE MYSTERY PHONE calls began coming the next night. Around 8 p.m. I was upstairs writing an essay. The phone rang. I heard Dad pick up the upstairs extension, then put it down moments later when Mom shouted from the kitchen:

'Who's calling this late?'

'Wrong number,' Dad said.

The next morning, over breakfast, the phone rang again. Dad grabbed it. After hearing who was on the other end he spoke tersely in the receiver:

'You have the wrong number.'

Mom was scrambling eggs. I watched her face tighten as Dad put down the phone.

'The same wrong number as last night?' she asked.

'Different voice,' Dad said, lighting a cigarette. 'If it happens again call the phone company.'

It did happen again. The phone was ringing as I came in from school. Mom had left a note on the kitchen counter – *Tutoring, home around 5.30.* During the last year she had volunteered as a part-time reading comprehension teacher in Stamford's black and Hispanic area. For Mom – who complained frequently that most of the stay-at-home wives in Old Greenwich passed the day playing tennis, planning meals, doing amateur dramatics, driving their kids everywhere (until at sixteen they all started driving themselves), gossiping over sangria and WisPride cheese on Triscuit crackers – the twice-weekly trip to Stamford was her opportunity to bring a little liberal social consciousness into her life.

I came home from another bad day at school, dodging the attention of the Cruel Ones, a clique of girls in my class who made life hell for anyone they considered not like them. The phone was ringing.

'Burns residence. Who is this?'

A decisive click on the other end of the line.

I was pouring myself a bowl of Cap'n Crunch when Dad walked in five minutes later. I was surprised to see him home at four in the afternoon.

'Got to pack,' he explained. 'Heading back to Chile tonight. Can't be helped. The assholes are talking about nationalizing my mine again.'

The 'assholes' were the government of Salvador Allende: democratically elected Marxists who had won a surprise, narrow victory in the Chilean elections in 1970 and were already beginning to take over all foreign-backed companies, of which the country's copper-rich mines were a big target. For the past ten years Dad had been employed as an executive by the International Copper Company which had interest in mines in Haiti and Algeria and assorted locations in South America. It was Chile that had caught Dad's imagination and he'd begun travelling there around five years before when ICC were exploring the possibility of a mine up in the Atacama Desert. Dad took to it from his first visit. 'Best place in the world,' he'd said, showing me pictures of himself on a donkey with a local guide, exploring a wide-open stretch of sand. He was spending a lot of time in Santiago, even trying to learn Spanish and remarked on several occasions that a local cocktail called the Pisco Sour had become his new drink of choice.

'If I had my way I'd move there tomorrow.'

He always made comments like this in earshot of Mom – who would frequently snarl back: 'Just throw me the keys to the house, turn over what little money you've got put aside, and go. You're adding nothing to our lives here.'

'How long this time?' I asked.

'Maybe a week, maybe two.'

'But I've got my Bowdoin interview next week.'

'I'll get Peter to drive you, sparing you the fun of having Mom in the car with you for six hours. Sorry, kiddo, but this is business – and a lot depends on it.'

I sensed that the real reason why Dad feared they were going to take his mine away was because, once it was gone, he'd no longer have the excuse to be away half the month. That was another of my complexities vis-à-vis my father: part of me so wanted him around; part of me understood why he needed to flee Mom: the endless fights; the sense of ongoing permanent discord together.

'There was another weird phone call when I came in from school,' I told him.

'Anyone on the other end?'

'Don't know. I answered it. When they heard my voice they hung up.'

'Gotta call the phone company,' he said, and disappeared into the den at the end of the hall. I heard the rotary dial of the phone whirring. I heard Dad whisper: 'I told you not to call me here.' I heard the door to the den close. I thought: my father has a secret. I knew that I'd never ask him what it was.

Dad stayed in the den a very long time. When I heard tires on the gravel in the driveway, and the front door opening and slamming shut, I went down to ask Mom if I could go out with Arnold. But before I could ask that question I heard her screaming:

'You're not fucking leaving.'

'It can't be helped,' Dad said.

'I won't allow it.'

'You won't *what*?'

'*Allow it.* If you leave you don't come back.'

'If I stay I lose my job. Because, like it or not, this mine is my baby. And if they take the baby away –'

'Listen to you: "*my baby, my baby*". Do you ever say that about any of your children? About *me*?'

'Stop being pathetic.'

'You're the pathetic one here. The little boy who has to run away ...'

'You want to call time on this fucking marriage go right ahead.'

'Maybe I will,' Mom screamed.

'Be my fucking guest.'

More tires in the driveway, more crunching of gravel. Dad's car to the airport was here.

He headed down the corridor. I tried to turn and get upstairs, not wanting him to know that I'd been listening in. I was too late. He saw me trying to scramble upstairs and held on to my arm.

'You hear all that?' he whispered.

'Kind of.'

'Ignore it. Just the usual marital crap. I'm going nowhere. Neither is your mom. We're wedded to all this – which is the wrong side of tragic. But there you go.'

The truth was, I always feared Dad leaving. Even now, with college just under a year away, I was afraid that, were he to vanish off to South America, Mom would turn into her own mother and begin to hound me constantly.

That was one of the most unsettling things I was beginning to realize about my mother: she was still very much a little girl, and one who could not get away from her own mother. My grandmother Esther lived in Manhattan right up until her death last year on the eve of Yom Kippur (which, according to Peter, was some sort of Jewish poetic justice). She was always old to me, always crabby. She met my grandfather Herman when she was twenty-one and he was just back from World War I, where he'd served first in the infantry, then in bomb disposal. He was a guy from the Yorkville section of Manhattan who volunteered for the Army at eighteen and, on his return, started learning the diamond business. He dressed like a 1940s dandy. When he married Esther her more well-to-do family thought he was beneath them. From what Dad told me the marriage was a disaster from the outset. But this was the start of the 1920s, when divorce was something that only the jazz-age rich ever contemplated. Seven years after they were wed, their one and only child, Brenda, was born – giving my grandmother, who never worked at all in her life, a reason to be.

Mom was endlessly indulged as a child and endlessly crowded, never left alone by her mother. She had little or no independence from the get-go. After graduating from an all-women's college she returned home to her parents' apartment on the Upper East Side and lived there until she married my dad. She was never encouraged to think of the possibility of an independent life. She got a job as a production assistant at NBC through someone Grandpa knew. For three years she worked with the likes of Abbot and Costello, Sid Caesar, even the opera tenor turned popular crooner, Ezio Pinza.

Men flirted with her, took her out to dinner. A dentist named Lenny Mailman wanted to marry her – 'but what was I going to do as a dentist's wife?' Then Brendan Burns came along. They met at his sister Martine's wedding. Lenny didn't want her to go to the wedding. He had his nephew's bar mitzvah that Saturday. Imagine if she'd played dutiful girlfriend with the dentist and ended up out on Long Island watching Lenny's nephew declare: 'Today I am a man.' I wouldn't be here right now. That's the way life works. You're in a certain place at a certain time. There's a look across a room, an introduction made, a conversation simply struck up, and the entire trajectory of your life changes.

Mom had often rued out loud about going to Martine's wedding – especially as her future sister-in-law later turned into a mean drunk who made her disdain for Mom very much known. But the main reason she regretted meeting Dad was because, when she fell pregnant with Peter, that was the end of her career at NBC. Though as I found out from Peter himself, who'd been told many times by Mom that he ruined her professional prospects, she had been politely let go by the network just before she found herself a mother-to-be. It was Grandpa who told Peter all that, after hearing from Peter the guilt trip that Mom had laid on him over the years. Grandpa even called her up, informing her that saying such things to her children was shameful. Mom berated Peter for going to her father with all this. Dad then berated her for berating Peter, blurting out in front of us the shocking truth: Mom had been fired from NBC 'for neurotic incompetence', at which point she bolted from the table in tears, running upstairs and crying uncontrollably until Peter went to her bedroom and said something that made her stop.

Ah, Peter. Mom could intimidate Adam. She could make me feel as if I was engaged in an endless power struggle with her. But with Peter she was cowed by his sense of tranquility, his righteousness. Mom. Who could never sit still for more than five minutes. Who threw open my bedroom door and barged in. Once I caught her reading my diary when I was fifteen, telling me: 'I have a right to know what you're thinking.' Mom – who had to interfere in everything, as if she were terrified of discovering some hidden truth about the way her three children saw her: as a woman in thrall to her many overwhelming, despotic pathologies. Mom – who told me on several occasions when we recently clashed:

'You know I love you ... but I've never really liked you.'

That comment hurt like hell the first time it was landed on me. Mom saw that and just shrugged, saying:

'The truth is not always nice.'

The second and third times she blurted out a comment about my lack of likeability I couldn't help but think: *her viewpoint toward me will never change.* Just as she often had to undermine my confidence with nonstop criticism. When, last term, I received a B minus on a term paper about Sinclair Lewis she told me, after picking up the essay on my desk at home (when I was out of my room):

'I think the teacher has a point here when he says that your thoughts on *Babbitt* aren't very original.'

'Why did you go into my stuff again, Mom?'

'Because this is my house – and while you're under my roof I am allowed to look at your schoolwork.'

'Not if it is an invasion of my privacy.'

'You're just angry because you know that what the teacher told you is right: you have a limited way of thinking about important things ... like a great novel.'

I stepped back from her, as if slapped.

'Why are you so cruel, Mom?'

'I'm just reiterating what the guy wrote. The fact that he still gave you a B minus ... he's clearly generous.'

At moments like this I so understood why my father was always happy to be on his way to the airport. As he was tonight. After Dad's taxi drove off in the direction of JFK and his flight to Chile I hid upstairs, James Taylor playing away. A few minutes later, Mom knocked on the door, then immediately threw it open.

'Why didn't you wait until I said you could come in?' I demanded.

'You going to give me a hard time too?' she asked. 'Tell me what a bad person I am? How I can't do anything right. Unlike your cherished Cindy Cohen, right?'

She choked back a sob. A stab of guilt sideswiped me. Cindy Cohen was the mother of my best friend, Carly. Mom knew that I looked upon Mrs Cohen as a stable *fellow New Yorker-in-exile* maternal figure. Someone who I could talk to about all the problems of my little life without fear of reprobation or merciless denouncement. I found myself immediately hunching my shoulders – an instinctual reaction when I am made to feel as if I were a very bad little girl. Mom saw this. Game, set, match to her.

'You finish your homework?' she asked.

I nodded.

'Want a drink? Dubonnet. My favorite.'

'Really?'

'No – I'm saying that to test you, to see if you have a thing for booze, then scream at you for being a teenage alky.'

'I'm not,' I said, all defensive.

'I actually know that. Which is why I am offering you a drink. Come on downstairs, okay?'

'Okay,' I said, surprised by this nice turn of events, a nice hour with Mom. I followed her into the kitchen.

'Your father thinks Dubonnet is a girlie drink. But I gather it's really popular in Paris. Someday, before I'm too old or dead, I am going to spend a month there, even though I may not be able to speak the language. Paris is, for me, a symbol of everything I've denied myself.'

She picked up the stainless-steel tongs and plopped a couple of cubes of ice into a glass, then added a slice of lemon and poured me a cautious half-glass of Dubonnet. We toasted each other, I sipped my drink. It struck me as slightly sweet, but with a subtle kick. I smiled, thinking: *I had a Lucky Strike with my dad and now I am having a real drink with my mom.* 'Here's some news,' Mom said. 'Next year, when you go off to college, I'm insisting that your father moves the two of us back to the city.'

'What has Dad said about that?'

'He doesn't know yet.'

'What do you think he'll say about all that?'

'He'll tell me that, to buy us a decent apartment, it'll cost around eighty thousand ... and this place will only sell for fifty, fifty-five grand. He'll put up all sorts of arguments. But I don't care. I've done my time in White Bread Purgatory. I've spent a decade with all the Gordys and Bobbis and Chips in this damn town. I'm also planning to go back to work. Train as a realtor.'

'I thought you'd want to teach. Continue what you've been up to in Stamford.'

'Yeah, but that's remedial reading stuff. To be a real teacher – that takes years of training. As a realtor I can make actual money. Even though the New York market is terrible right now. But when a market's low you can, if you're shrewd, do really well. The thing is: I want to be back in the city.'

'That's fantastic, Mom,' I said, wondering: was this just more of the same sad edgy talk about getting out of Dodge that we'd all been hearing for years?

'Trust me, I'm only hanging on here to get you through the last year of school. Once you're off at college I'm out of here, away from the likes of that stupid Silly Quinn.'

Silly (that was her real name) Quinn was the mother of Bobbi Quinn, the Queen of the Cruel Ones. Bobbi was the daughter of the captain of the local fire department which, in her mind, gave her a degree of small-town prestige. She and her second in command, Deb Schaeffer, were constantly targeting my friend Carly Cohen, in part because her dad wrote non-fiction pieces for places like the *Atlantic* and *Harper's*, and because her mother was a psychologist with a private practice who also worked at a mental hospital up in Stamford. 'My mom says your mom spends her day hanging out with psychos and retards,' Deb would spit out whenever Carly was in her sightlines, though it was Bobbi who came in for the kill, always calling Carly 'the fat dyke'. Because, yes, Carly was a little chunky and a little butch. Carly tried to fight back, one time telling Bobbi that she was going to end up married to a used-car dealer, living in a trailer park. But Bobbi just ran off to the coach of the women's volleyball team (of which she was the captain), in tears, relating this 'horrible insult'. Immediately Carly was called into the principal's office and reprimanded for making such an unkind, class-oriented comment. When she tried to explain that these girls had been calling her far worse, the principal – who went to the same Catholic church as Bobbi's parents – actually told her that her 'clothes created problems for her peers'.

As it was the early seventies you would never dream of going public about being gay. You lived a secret, and although Carly confided in me, there was no way she could come out and announce her lesbianism ... especially at her age and in a place as obedient and unadventurous as Old Greenwich. Nonetheless she did make a stand through her fashion. Blue overalls, work boots, a white T-shirt and hair that was so closely cropped it almost resembled a crew cut. For Bobbi and Deb and their fellow Cruel Ones this was a gift which Carly had given them. And the boys they hung out with – the jock fraternity, the big-teethed knuckleheads whose fathers ran the local Ford and Chrysler dealerships, or the seriously preppy guys with names like Bradford and Jason and Ames who were already serious golfers or killer tennis players – also turned their scorn on Carly. As they did on me and Arnold.

Arnold. Tall, weedy Arnold. Whose mother dressed him always in chinos and tan or maroon crew-neck sweaters, with button-down shirts and moccasins. Arnold – who hated these sartorial choices, but didn't feel empowered enough to fight them. Arnold – who told me, around a week after we started seeing each other, that his ambition was to eventually become a Supreme Court justice. Arnold the very articulate, very self-conscious boy who'd just spent the summer as an intern at a big law firm in New York – commuting in five days a week in the same tan Brooks Brothers suit that his mother had bought him on sale. Arnold who never complained about Old Greenwich and used his coolly diplomatic/adversarial skills to shrug off their comments – all of which targeted his Jewish geekiness and Coke-bottle-thick glasses, with expressions like 'nerd rabbi' or 'Hebrew four-eyes'. We made an interesting trio – me and Carly and Arnold. Though Carly often found my boyfriend just a little inelastic and 'someone who seriously reads all the footnotes in every text book' – and Arnold, in turn, considered Carly to be 'a militant in a closet' – we still formed an island of New York Jewish quirkiness amidst all that rigid WASP suspicion of anything not within their country-club playbook.

I'd had the pleasure – a few months back, right before school ended for the summer – of watching Arnold playing head-games with one of the bigger bullies of our class, after Jason Fensterstock called him 'Mr Yiddy'. Quick as a flash, Arnold asked Jason if his German ancestry meant that he was a Nazi by temperament. Arnold kept quietly pressing home this point in front of a group of people in the school dining room, cross-examining him in a perfectly logical, calm voice. Posing questions like: 'So does your dad – whom everyone around town knows to be something of an anti-Semite – keep a private collection of swastikas around the house? Does he have a thing for the 'Horst Wessel Song'? Did you ever see him eye up muscular young men because he too is Master Race inclined?'

Fensterstock – a nasty piece of work, with that mixture of bully-ish flippancy and uptightness – responded by dumping a glass of chocolate milk over Arnold.

The next day in school Carly got up at morning assembly and told her fellow students that she was organizing an anti-war protest in front of the local draft board office in Stamford the next weekend. Though a few of us applauded – there were even one or two shouts of 'Right on!' – there was a loud chorus of derision led by the Cruel Ones. Later that afternoon, after classes ended, Carly and I decided to take advantage of the heat of the day and bicycle down to Todd's Point. It was our local beach, always kept clean and free of hot-dog and hamburger stands. During midweek it was usually empty – though today, when I showed up with Carly, we discovered that Deb Schaeffer and her knucklehead boyfriend, Ames Sweet, had gotten there before us, along with six others from their jock/cheerleader clique. Seeing me and Carly walking onto the sand, he immediately signaled to Deb and the others to follow him. Within moments, Carly and I were surrounded.

'We don't let dykes and lefties on the sand,' said Ames.

All of the girls now encircled Carly, leading a cheer that went: 'Lessie, lessie, lessie.' I tried to march forward, but the others blocked me. Carly also tried to break free, but the quartet hemmed her in.

She was in tears. Then, out of nowhere, the local lifeguard, Sean, was on the scene. He was a dude in his early twenties who always struck me as a spacer: sandy-haired, somewhat pumped, with an inability to look you in the eye; a 'yeah, man, it's kinda happening' deadhead. But he was also a serious swimmer, an early exponent of skateboarding, and someone who wasn't afraid to speak up if he saw stupidity happening in front of him.

'What's, like, going on here?' he asked.

Carly was now crying too hard to say anything.

'They're telling us we can't come onto the beach,' I said.

'She's lying,' Deb Schaeffer said.

'Then why is my friend here crying?' I asked.

'Because we found the two of them kissing,' Ames announced.

Carly was suddenly furious.

'You liar. You pathetic fucking liar,' she screamed.

'So the fat dyke can speak,' Ames said.

There are moments when people cross a line which can best be described as the point of no return. As soon as this comment was out of Ames's mouth, Sean said:

'That's it, dude. You're barred from the beach.'

'You fucking shitting me?' Ames said.

'Shitting you I am not,' Sean said. 'Not only are you barred from here, but all your friends are as well.'

'Fuck you,' another of the guys, Ronnie Auerbach, said.

'You're all leaving now,' Sean said.

'Or what?' Deb demanded.

'Or I'm calling the cops.'

'On what grounds?' Ames asked.

'Cruelty.'

Sean put his hand on Carly's shoulder, trying to steady her. Then looking at me he said:

'Why don't you guys go for a swim?'

'Thanks, man,' I said, leading Carly by the arm toward the shore.

'Hey, just doing my job. And on this beach, *my beach*, we don't tolerate stuff like that.'

'Fag lover,' Deb Schaeffer said.

'Faggot,' Ames added.

Conveniently, a police car showed up moments later, the beach being part of the cops' beat in Old Greenwich. I had my feet in the water when I saw one of the local officers – a large Italian named Proccaccino – get out of his black-and-white. As we walked back up the beach I heard him tell Sean:

'If we arrested everyone in this town for name calling ... '

'This wasn't name calling,' Sean said, 'this was sick bullying.'

'It was the bitch who called us names,' Ames said.

'You're the lying, evil bitch,' Carly said. 'I said nothing to you.'

'She's right,' Sean told the cop. 'I was here. I heard her say nothing.'

'She called us names at school,' Deb answered.

'I can smell little-girl bullshit a mile off,' Sean said. 'And you're just two feet away.'

'Sounds like schoolyard stuff to me,' Officer Proccaccino said. 'And none of our business.'

'Except that this gang of bullies tried to stop those very cool girls from coming onto my beach.'

'It's not your beach,' Proccaccino told him.

'I'm the guard on duty. It's my beach. They're not coming on it.'

Proccaccino looked flustered.

'Is what Sean saying here true?' he asked.

'They called me "a fat dyke",' Carly said, the received slur repeated by her with a mixture of defiance and anguish.

'She's lying,' Deb Schaeffer said.

Proccaccino turned to Sean.

'It's "she said this, she said that". You gotta let 'em all on the beach.'

Ames stepped in front of Proccaccino. 'You let him keep us off the beach my dad's going to hear about it. And you'll be back on the nigger beat in Stamford. Understand?'

Proccaccino understood. Ames Sweet's father, Gordon, was both a big-shot lawyer on Wall Street and a town alderman who (according to Arnold) liked to throw his influence around, especially as he was chummy with Connecticut's Republican governor. He also had

Old Greenwich's mayor in his pocket. Which meant that if his little boy Ames was going to make a complaint against one of the police officers, trouble would follow. Sean also realized the trouble that might follow – because, like Proccaccino, he too had been raised here, albeit on the wrong side of Route 1. That was the gasoline alley side, with small split-level houses and the roar of the road nearby; the place where all the working-class people who serviced Old Greenwich lived in unspoken resentment of all the folk like us who lived east beyond Byrum Park, the big green space where most of Old Greenwich High went to smoke dope (and where dealers from the ghetto beat of Stamford came down to sell grass and LSD). Everyone at school knew that Ames Sweet was also in cahoots with the guys in Stamford; that he'd been dealing drugs among his fellow students for them. I'm sure Officer Proccaccino knew all about that too. Just as he knew his hands were tied by Gordy and Sally Sweet who lived right on the beach on McKinley Drive in one of those big waterfront Cape Codders which spoke money and status.

Old Greenwich may have been seriously white bread, but its children were just as susceptible to all those big city vices that were less prevalent in Manhattan – because the kids there my age had so much more to do. Back in New York a punk like Sweet might have eventually walked out of legal trouble, but not before the cops scared the shit out of him by threatening to throw him into a precinct cell for the night (until Daddy and his lawyers showed up to bail him out). Here, in suburbia, an Italian American wearing a blue collar found himself intimidated by an Ames Sweet – and the pathetic power he represented.

Proccaccino blanched, furious and daunted. I could see him trying to make a decision amidst the pressure suddenly exerted on him.

'I can show you the clause in the Connecticut State Lifeguard Manual,' Sean said, 'which reads: "The lifeguard on duty has the legal prerogative to ban any persons from the beach he is monitoring, should he feel said persons are a threat to the safety or order of his beach." I've got the manual at my stand over there. That's the law, Officer – and I'm enforcing it.'

Proccaccino now looked like he wanted to be anywhere but here. He turned to Ames.

'Sorry, Ames ... '

'My name's *Mr* Sweet ... '

'Sorry, *Mr* Sweet. But the law's the law, and Sean here has the upper hand in this case. If he says you and your friends have to leave the beach, my hands are tied.'

'This time next week,' smirked Ames, '*you'll* be elsewhere, Officer. And there'll be a new lifeguard on duty.'

Deb Schaeffer glared at me and Carly. But just when she was about to say something Ames put his hand on her wrist, stopping her from coming out with a vindictive comment which the police-man could hear and which could be possibly used against her and the rest of her little cabal. He signaled to his gang that they call it quits. But as they all walked away Ames swiveled around. With a smile as menacing as it was sadistic he outstretched his index finger and pointed it directly at Carly. Then turning on his heel he flipped us the bird before grabbing Deb Schaeffer by the buttocks. As he drove off in the mustard-yellow Mustang that his daddy had bought him last year when he made captain of the lacrosse team, Proccac-cino turned on Sean.

'Do you know what the hell you've done, son?' he asked.

'He's a bully, Officer. And I have this thing about not tolerating bullies.'

'You don't got a couple of kids to support,' Proccaccino added. 'As for you, young ladies, your parents will be hearing about all this.'

Proccaccino was absolutely right about that. At seven that night the phone rang. I tried to grab it first, thinking it was another mystery call. But Mom beat me to it and got a shrieking earful from Sally Sweet, accusing me of trying to land her beloved Ames in trouble with the police and being in cahoots with 'that creepy little girl Carly Cohen – who is clearly not normal'. Fortunately, as soon as I'd got back home I'd told her all that had transpired on the beach. When Sally Sweet called, Mom motioned for me to run upstairs and listen in on the tomato-red Princess phone on her side of the bed. For all her craziness Mom could, when necessary, come out swinging, especially if she felt her children were under unfair threat. That night she was in complete 'take no prisoners' mode.

'Explain to me, Sally, what you mean about Carly Cohen being "not normal"?' she demanded.

'She's clearly someone who hates men.'

'And what made you deduce that?' she asked.

'Oh please,' Sally Sweet said. 'You know she has no interest in boys.'

'If that is true does that give your boy the right to attack her and my daughter in such a repugnant way?'

'*Repugnant? Repugnant?*! How can you say such things?'

'Because your son has a reputation around school and around town for being a shit par excellence.'

On the other end of the line, Sally Sweet took the sharpest intake of breath imaginable.

'How dare you –'

'And how dare you allow your little bully to intimidate our children? And how dare you make a comment like you just did about lovely Carly Cohen?'

'You would feel that way about her.'

'You mean, because we're both Jewish?'

'I didn't say that.'

'Of course you didn't. Let me guess your next line, Sally: "I was only following orders."'

Click. The line went dead.

I think this was the moment I loved my mother the most – because I got to hear her play the tough, take-no-crap New Yorker who was going to stand up for basic decency and a love of diversity amidst all the suburban rigidity around us.

I phoned Carly to see how she was holding up. Mrs Cohen answered, telling me that she was expecting a patient in a few minutes and didn't have time to talk, but said that, after coming home, Carly headed out to debate club at school. Before I had time to ask if she had informed her what had transpired on the beach she said she had to go – but told me to drop over tomorrow after school. As soon as she hung up I was dialing Arnold's number, briefing him at length on all that went down with Ames and his gang of anti-Semites.

'We should definitely report this to the school tomorrow,' he said, mentioning that I could go with Carly to the principal, 'and if you want me to be there I can deal the legal card when Mr O'Neill starts acting as if we are some Jews United front against Connecticut WASPdom.'

'I'll check with Carly in the morning before our first class. But I'm pretty sure she'll want you there to play the Bad Cop.'

'This has all got to stop,' Arnold said.

'But we both know that, this being Old Greenwich, it won't stop.'

Early the next morning there was loud banging on my door, followed by Mom throwing it open and bursting in.

'What did I tell you about knocking?' I yelled at her.

'Shut up,' she yelled back. 'Something terrible's happened. Carly didn't come home last night.'

3

THE SHOCK WAS considerable. So too the guilt. Carly missing? Vanished from view since heading out last night? Why hadn't I told Mrs Cohen immediately: 'There's no way that she would have gone to the debate club after what happened on the beach'? Why hadn't I done more for my friend?

Though it was only seven forty-five Mom seemed to have all the forensic details of the case: how Carly returned home after that bullying incident on the beach and hid in her room. Her mother was on the phone to a patient then had to meet her husband in the city that evening: dinner and a play. When they got home around eleven, Carly wasn't in her room. Or anywhere in the house. Her father got into his car and scoured the town, looking everywhere for his daughter. When he couldn't find her – and Mrs Cohen had been simultaneously working the phones, desperately calling the parents of everyone in the debate club – they rang the police. They also called Mom around 11 p.m. She confirmed that I had been at home all night, that Carly had never dropped by here.

'She's really been missing all night?'

'At six this morning the police found Carly's bike abandoned in Byrum Park. She'd never made it to debate club.'

'She'll come back,' I said, fear edging into my voice.

'How can you be so sure?' Mom asked. 'Do you know where she might have run off to?'

'No idea,' I said, knowing that if I told the truth I would be breaching the huge trust that Carly put in me, and also knowing that the longer she was missing the harder it would be for me to sit on this knowledge.

'You'd better not be lying,' Mom said.

Arnold showed up on his bicycle two minutes later, sparing me more cross-examination.

'Have your parents been called by Mrs Cohen?' Mom asked him.

'Of course. My mother's over there now with her.'

'Then I'm going too.'

'I'm sure Mrs Cohen will appreciate that,' Arnold said in that serious way of his which masked all irony, intended or not.

When we were outside the house, he put his arm around me.

'If there's anything you think I should know ... ' he said.

I buried my head in his shoulder and started to sob.

'If I tell you ... ' I finally said.

'Lawyer–client confidence,' he said. 'Unless it interferes with due process of the law.'

'I'm not your client, Arnold,' I hissed. He smiled at me in that learned-judge way of his, then leaned over and kissed me on my head.

'You know what I'm saying here. It's better if I know.'

I couldn't help but agree with him. I motioned for us to start biking. We made our way to Main Street and the one coffee shop that was open early (and where there was a booth right at the back, out of earshot of everything). Ordering us two cups of joe and two plain doughnuts he made sure the waitress was elsewhere before indicating that I could now unload on him. Which I did. Telling him what Carly had confided in me. His eyes never once went wide when I detailed everything I knew. When I finished he stared into the dirty brown surface of his coffee for a good minute, considering his judgment, his words.

'Alice, you need to tell Mrs Cohen – but only if Carly isn't back home by 6 p.m. tonight. If she walks in the door before then you are sparing her and someone else a lot of potential misery. My feeling is: she's fled there ... and will probably be convinced to return to her parents. It's the logical place she ran to.'

'Will you come to the Cohens with me if I have to go tell them what I know?'

'Absolutely.'

'I feel so bad not telling Mrs Cohen now. That woman has been so nice to me.'

'The mom you always wanted?'

'I can't say that.'

'I can,' Arnold said. 'And yes, I will be there with you if you have to tell all to Carly's mom. Meanwhile ... let's go to school and get those assholes in trouble.'

We biked off. As soon as we pulled up the long drive to the entrance of Old Greenwich High we discovered a welcoming committee in place: Mr O'Neill the principal; his deputy Miss Cleveland (a tall, weedy woman who always struck me as an updated version of Emily Dickinson without the poetry); a man I didn't know in a suit; and Officer Proccaccino. In the past Mr O'Neill and his number two had always been very dismissive of anti-war, flower-child, bookish me: 'the girl who reads', as Deb Schaeffer once hissed in my direction. Today they treated me as if I were one of the Nixon daughters paying the school an honored visit.

'Alice, I am so, so sorry about what happened,' Mr O'Neill said.

To which Miss Cleveland added: 'We've already heard from Officer Proccaccino here how you took a very principled stand against the abuse heaped on poor Carly.'

'Is there any lead on her whereabouts?' Arnold asked the man in the suit.

'Who are you, kid?' the suit asked.

'He's my lawyer,' I said.

'Arnold doesn't need to be part of this,' Miss Cleveland said.

'I'm not talking unless Arnold's here,' I said.

'Anyway,' Arnold said, 'I too have been on the receiving end of the bullying from Sweet and Schaeffer and Fensterstock and Bobbi Quinn: all your preferred athletes and cheerleaders whom you have allowed to abuse us ... resulting in this calamity for which I am holding you and your entire staff personally responsible.'

'That is so way out of line,' Mr O'Neill said.

'Let the kid speak,' the suit said, then reached into his jacket pocket and pulled out a very official-looking badge. 'Detective Paul Stebinger, Stamford Police.'

'Why don't we all go inside?' Miss Cleveland said.

Once we were in the principal's office Detective Stebinger asked me to run through exactly what had happened on the beach. I took him through it all, event by event, word for word. Officer

Proccaccino seemed shamefaced when I related how Ames Sweet threatened him with trouble from his father if he allowed Sean to bar him and his cohorts from the beach.

'The kid actually said that?' the detective asked Proccaccino. When the officer nodded yes, Stebinger shook his head, then turned to Arnold.

'Okay, Counselor, since you seem to be in the know about so much at the school, has this sort of bullying been going on here for a while?'

Arnold's response was fluid and to the point. He outlined how the school turned a blind eye to the way in which a coterie of athletes and their female fans were allowed to push around anyone who didn't fit in with their world view, and how repeated complaints to 'those in charge at Old Greenwich High' fell on deaf ears. O'Neill and Cleveland tried to intervene, but were told to hold their comments by the detective. I really had to admire Arnold's sense of moral righteousness, and the way he pulled no punches. All I was doing was reporting what went on in the sand, and the verbal abuse rained down on poor Carly. Arnold, on the other hand, was playing the *j'accuse* card: taking apart the entire culture of silence that characterized the school administration – and it was clear that Detective Stebinger was quietly appalled at the disclosures being made. I watched Miss Cleveland's face as Arnold recounted coming to see her at the end of the last semester, complaining about the anti-Semitic comments that Fensterstock had been making, and the deputy principal telling him that it was just playground silliness, nothing more. I saw the terror in her eyes, the realization that her career was suddenly in jeopardy. Just as I knew that Arnold was possibly jeopardizing his college recommendations by attacking the school ... though Arnold being Arnold he'd probably assessed in advance 'the risk/gain differential' and decided that the stand he took would play in his favor.

He was right about that. When he finished his spiel Detective Stebinger looked impressed.

'Remind me to call you eight years from now when I need a lawyer. Of course, I am going to write up all that has been reported to me and pass it on to the State Board of Education. And I am afraid, sir ... '

He turned his steely gaze on O'Neill.

' ... you have a lot to answer for. As do you, Miss Cleveland.'

She was about to say something, but Stebinger stopped her, saying:

'I need you to call Ames Sweet and Deb Schaeffer in here then. I want this done discreetly. No loudspeaker announcements.'

'Are they going to be charged with Carly's disappearance?' Arnold asked.

'That's *sub judice*, young man. I want to thank you and Miss Burns for all your help today.'

'You're most welcome,' Arnold said.

'I need to have your word that you will not discuss any of this with anyone ... not even your parents,' the detective said. 'If your folks have any questions tell them to call me.'

He handed both of us his official card and signaled that we were – as they say in the military – dismissed.

Outside the school, the sky had clouded over. As we walked to our bicycles Arnold said:

'It looks bad.'

'I now really need to talk to Mrs Cohen. Tell her what I know; what Carly never could.'

'And if you do that, and if she comes home tonight ... you will have breached many codes of friendship. Do you know the name and address of the person with whom she might have sought refuge?'

'Only that it was someone in the city. Carly was secretive about that stuff. I just knew the bare minimum. But it's still a lead for the police and her poor parents.'

'We will be at Mrs Cohen's on the dot of 6.01 p.m. If our friend is back we will express happiness and withdraw. If she has yet to show her face you can spill all the beans – not that you know that much.'

'And the cops will ask why I didn't tell them all this when they questioned me this morning.'

'I will run defense for you. Trust me, I will not let them engage in reproach. They didn't ask you *that* question this morning. Had

47

they done so and you'd obfuscated that would have been a different matter.'

Obfuscated. In the midst of all this drama and fear the thought came to me: *my first boyfriend,* the first guy I ever slept with, was someone who used that word with an ease that was almost technical. Can vocabulary be a turn-on? Arnold may not have been a hunk – I never was in the market for some Ames Sweet beefcake – but his smarts were sort of sexy. And I really needed the escape hatch of sex right now. I laced my fingers through his and asked:

'Is your mother definitely in the city today?'

Twenty minutes later we were having sex in Arnold's narrow single bed, under a poster of Oliver Wendell Holmes. Sex: it was an unknown territory for us both. Arnold being Arnold he researched the subject very thoroughly after our first fumbling attempts at lovemaking. Finding his parents' copy of *The Joy of Sex* – which was, with *I'm OK, You're OK,* the book that everyone's mom and dad seemed to be reading that year – Arnold learned all about various positions, the mysteries of the clitoris, and the secret to prolonging the male orgasm. I was rather grateful to Arnold for this crash course in intimacy. As we both gained confidence, a certain actual passion developed. With Arnold's somewhat professorial approach to it all, we became accomplished at it. We never exchanged romantic words, never declared love for each other. Like Arnold, I was prudent about such things, not wanting to say something that I knew was not true. But we were also seventeen, awkward in the eyes of the outside world, awkward in our own eyes, both rather isolated, not just in this town into which we had been dropped in our early teens, but also within our respective families. Though Arnold's parents had all the right progressive views, and were supportive of Arnold's studies and ambitions, they were also remote and distant, very much caught up in their two high-powered careers, rarely showing him any affection. That morning after Carly disappeared, lying next to me on his monk-like bed, still holding me tightly amidst the postcoital fog, he said this:

'I hope Carly's parents know that she wasn't running away from them; I know her dad was a bit awkward but at least they always told her she was loved.'

'Don't your parents tell you that? Even my insane mom and dad do that once in a while.'

He fell silent, looking away from my questioning gaze.

'Not part of their vocabulary,' he finally said. 'I get the feeling that, as long as I am successful, I'll be tolerated by them.'

'I'm sure it's not that bad.'

He clutched me tighter, saying:

'It's that bad.'

Then he changed the subject, saying:

'We really should go looking for Carly. Let's head to her usual hangouts – just to tell ourselves that we are doing something to find her.'

We biked to a diner on Route 1 where I knew she hid out to study and write in her journal. No sighting of her for two days. We moved quickly on to a bowling alley where Carly frequently burned off aggression and anger by knocking down ten pins. I brought Arnold to a corner of the public library near Byrum Park where Carly had a favorite chair tucked away in an alcove behind the 'American Fiction' section, and which was another of her preferred hiding places. And, of course, we went back to the scene of the initial hate crime: Todd's Point Beach. Neither of us truly expected to find Carly concealing herself behind a sand dune, or bowling with the local firemen. But, as Arnold noted, it gave us the illusion of being engaged in the search for our friend. And it chewed up the hours. Around four o'clock it struck us both that with all the desperate hunting around we'd eaten nothing.

We headed to the drugstore on Main Street, where there was a luncheonette and a grumpy woman with a pencil holding up her bun-like hair. She had big rouged lips and chewed gum nonstop. After taking our order she asked:

'You kids from Old Greenwich High?'

'That's right,' Arnold said.

'Why aren't you at school?'

'We've been given the day off,' Arnold said, sounding a little testy as he was about the last person in the world you'd accuse of truancy.

'Is that because of the kid who went missing?'

'Perhaps,' I said.

'Well, I just heard that they arrested two students today on suspicion that they had something to do with it.'

Arnold and I looked at each other, wide-eyed.

'Did you hear what evidence the police had against them?' Arnold asked.

'It seems the girl's bike was found in Byrum Park – and the two kids they arrested were seen there around the same time as the missing girl. And I heard they had a thing against her ... '

We finished our grilled-cheese sandwiches and iced tea, jumped on our bikes and raced over to Mrs Cohen's. When we knocked on the door we were just a little surprised to find my mother behind it.

'What are you two doing here?' she asked.

'We heard about Carly's bike being found in Byrum Park,' I said.

'And we wanted to give Mrs Cohen support,' Arnold said.

Mom glared at me – letting me know that she knew I considered Mrs Cohen's house to be a refuge.

'This isn't a good moment,' Mom said.

But behind her came the voice of Mrs Cohen.

'Let them in, Brenda.'

My mother reluctantly did as requested. We followed her into the kitchen where Mrs Cohen was sitting at the breakfast table, her eyes red from crying. Immediately Arnold was professional kindness itself. He pulled up a chair and sat down opposite Carly's mother, putting a hand on top of hers.

'Mrs Cohen, I just want you to know that I am all but certain Carly will return home to you.'

My Mom came in here:

'How can you be so certain, Arnold? We just heard from the detective – who I gather interviewed you and Alice this morning – that they're holding Ames Sweet and Deb Schaeffer on suspicion of her disappearance.'

Carly's Mom came in here.

'It seems Deb Schaeffer confessed to the police that they came across Carly in Byrum Park around 7.30 p.m. last night ... '

'What was Carly doing there?' I asked.

Mrs Cohen shrugged and lowered her head.

'She didn't tell me what'd happened,' Mrs Cohen said. 'She was home for two hours after the beach business ... and she never opened her mouth once about it.'

She started to sob again.

'If only I had talked to her, asked her if something was wrong.'

'But if she didn't seem to indicate anything was wrong ... ' Arnold said.

'I had a goddamn phone call I had to take when she got home. A patient in the city who just had to talk, talk, talk for almost ninety minutes. Because of her I didn't have time to see if Carly was all right. All because of this woman who was depressed after her Pekinese died. Then I had to hop a train into the city to meet Josh at the theater. Why didn't I put off seeing the play?'

'Because Carly didn't hint that something bad had happened to her,' Arnold said.

Mrs Cohen put her face in her hands.

'What happened to Carly in the park?' I asked my mother.

'Bad things,' she said, then looked at Mrs Cohen, silently asking if it was all right to tell us these bad things. Mrs Cohen nodded her assent. Mom continued:

'It seems that Ames Sweet was meeting some guy from Stamford who supplied him with the drugs he peddled around school. Deb Schaeffer was there too. Carly came upon them, the guy from Stamford scattered, Ames grabbed Carly and told her that if she said a word about any of this he'd get his friends in Stamford to rape her and cut her throat. When Carly struggled he pinned back her arms and told Deb to pull up her T-shirt, rip off her bra and write *Lessie Snitch* in lipstick on her breasts. Which Deb dutifully did. Ames also said that if he saw her face in school tomorrow she was ... '

' "Dead meat",' Mrs Cohen said, her face now hard, the anger showing through the grief. 'That's what that little shit said to my daughter: "dead meat".'

'Deb told all this to the police?' Arnold asked. Mrs Cohen said:

51

'Detective Stebinger told me that, in the course of a rather tough interrogation – with her mother present – he informed Deb that it was best to come clean about everything now, especially as Ames was going to be charged with some very serious crimes, and she was not just an accessory, but also someone who could be charged with assault and even kidnapping. That's when Deb broke down and confessed everything.'

'Did she indicate what happened to Carly after they attacked her?' I asked.

'According to Deb Schaeffer, when they let her go Carly was quite hysterical and fell to her knees in the grass. They got on their own bicycles and rode off, leaving her there, traumatized, crying uncontrollably. They left her there, the little shits.'

Silence – which Arnold broke.

'I'm sorry to bring this up – but what does the detective think happened next to Carly?'

Mrs Cohen bit down on her lip, fighting the urge to break down again.

'The cops don't know. No one at Old Greenwich Station saw her board a train – but it was late and maybe she sneaked on, sat in the toilet until it got to Grand Central.'

'Or she could have gone up to Route 1 and thumbed a ride somewhere,' I added.

'Or those little monsters are lying, and did something more to her,' Mrs Cohen said.

'But if Deb Schaeffer broke down while under interrogation by Detective Stebinger,' Arnold said, 'it strikes me that, God forbid they did something worse to Carly, she wouldn't have been devious enough to cover that up; that the reason she spilled her guts to the detective is she was so frightened of this whole business escalating into the sort of crime where she could end up doing serious time.'

Mom shook her head, saying:

'I know you don't want to hear this, Cindy, but I worry that Deb Schaeffer is smoke-screening things. I mean, why would Carly run away, knowing you and Josh would protect her?'

'But she never talked about all the stuff that was happening to her in school. Maybe she felt we were always too preoccupied.'

Mrs Cohen was no longer crying. Her voice sounded flat, strange – as if she was now in permanent shock. I glanced over at Arnold. With a grave nod he signaled that the moment had arrived for me to say what I didn't want to say, but which I knew I had no choice but to say.

'Carly told me she was in love with somebody.'

'What?' Mrs Cohen whispered, now on her feet.

I repeated what I'd just said. My mom came in here.

'What's his name, where does he live, and why haven't you told us or the police before now?'

'*She* lives in New York. I don't know *her* name, *her* address. And the fact that it's a *she* – and that Carly swore me to secrecy about that detail ... '

I broke off, unnerved by the fury now in my mother's eyes. My boyfriend attorney stepped in here.

'In missing person's cases there is usually a twenty-four-hour window where everyone waits and sees if that individual comes home. It was me who advised Alice not to say anything until that twenty-four hours had passed. Which is what she is doing now.'

'Why did you advise that?' my mother barked.

But I wasn't going to let Arnold incur the wrath of my mother now.

'Because it was a secret,' I barked. 'A secret which Carly entrusted me with. And I am someone who keeps secrets.'

4

HER NAME WAS Gretchen Ford. She was a fact checker at *Time* magazine; a woman in her late twenties, originally from Indiana who came to New York for college at NYU and never left. I gleaned all these details from an article in the *New York Times* which came out two days after I had revealed all to Mrs Cohen in the presence of my mother. Of course Mrs Cohen called the police immediately – and Detective Stebinger was on the scene within the hour, taking down what little I knew, and also telling my mother to stop acting like I had just been discovered spying for the Soviets.

'Your daughter was asked to keep a trust,' the detective told her. 'And yeah, this information might have been useful this morning. But as she doesn't know the name or address of this woman ...'

'You still should have said something,' Mom hissed at me.

'No need to be so harsh, Brenda,' Mrs Cohen said. 'I agree with the detective. Alice did the right thing by not betraying Carly's secret. Just as she did the right thing by coming to us now.'

Detective Stebinger turned to Mrs Cohen.

'Did you have any suspicions that ...?'

He left the sentence hanging there, unfinished, sparing himself the need to utter the word that no one wanted to articulate back in the early seventies. But Mrs Cohen didn't sidestep the question.

'Yes, I sensed that my daughter had lesbian inclinations. Did I discuss it with her? Not really ... and I will admit this ... part of me didn't want to know. When she went into the city most Saturdays and Sundays, telling me she was hanging out with friends there, I chose to buy that storyline. Even if I privately wondered ...'

She lowered her head, grief washing over her again.

'If I'd only not been afraid to confront the truth ... if only I'd told her: it doesn't matter who or what you are.'

Arnold put a steadying hand on her arm.

'Carly always told us what a wonderful mother you are.'

More sobs from Mrs Cohen – and I watched my own mother's face tighten. It couldn't have been easy for my mother to hear this. I also knew that Arnold was playing fast and loose with the truth right now – because Carly often complained to us that, for all her seeming 'goodness', Mrs Cohen could be something of an absent presence in her life. The irony wasn't lost on me: my friend had a mother who was frequently preoccupied with matters other than her daughter, while simultaneously welcoming me in like the daughter she always wanted. And now I was wondering: was this because, unlike her daughter, I was straight?

'So Carly never even gave you a hint where her "friend" might be living in the city?' Detective Stebinger asked me.

'None at all.'

'Or what she did, where she worked?'

I shook my head.

'And you never thought about asking her this?' Mom asked.

'I'm posing the questions here, ma'am,' Detective Stebinger said.

'It's an obvious question,' Mom said, 'and one that needs an answer.'

I ignored that comment and faced the detective.

'I let Carly tell me what she wanted to tell me. I didn't push for details. All I knew was: her friend was older and, according to Carly, very nice.'

'Then why hasn't she come forward and said something by now?' Mom asked.

'Because I asked for an initial one-day press embargo on Carly's disappearance,' Mrs Cohen said, 'in case she came back.'

'And we agreed to that embargo,' Detective Stebinger said. 'Until now.'

The next morning the story was everywhere. By that evening Gretchen Ford had come forward and contacted the police, informing them that Carly Cohen had indeed fled to her apartment in the Murray Hill section of Manhattan in the wake of being brutalized in that Old Greenwich park, showing up on her doorstep late that evening. But when she suggested to Carly that she call her parents to tell them she refused. Gretchen Ford herself admitted to the police that she had made a grievous error not calling them herself. Or letting the cops know that Carly was at her place. But as she told the *New York Times*, when Carly showed up she was just her younger 'friend' who had run away for a night after a bullying incident. Carly begged her to let her hide out at her place. Gretchen Ford, not wanting to get further implicated in all of this, insisted that Carly go home to Old Greenwich – and actually walked over to Grand Central Station the next morning and bought her a ticket for the 9.03 a.m. train north. Then she escorted her directly onto the train and waited until it pulled away. After that . . .

Carly never showed up in Old Greenwich, leaving the police to believe that she skipped off the train at the next stop, 125th Street. Of course, in the wake of her 'clean breast' statement to the cops, Gretchen Ford's life was rapidly ruined. The press helps dictate the court of public opinion – and they had decided that she was worthy of public crucifixion. Arnold – who in the wake of all these revelations, was now buying copies every morning of the *Daily News* and the *New York Post* to track how 'the low-brow press' (as he called them) were handling the case – kept me informed of her terrible downfall. So too did my mother – who was glued to television coverage of Gretchen Ford's undoing. Eviscerated (Arnold's word) for having a secret lesbian relationship with an underaged girl, she was then even more damned for trying to cover up this fact . . . and, as such, not calling Carly's parents immediately. Or not escorting her back home personally to Old Greenwich. And, of course, there was the whole public distaste at the homosexual element . . . and the way the press delved into Gretchen Ford's background and dis- covered that she was ejected from her strict Baptist family back in Indiana for an 'inappropriate relationship' with a young woman she'd 'cruised' at church. The *Daily News* found out that she had met Carly at a gay bar in the West Village four months earlier – only ten days before Carly's eighteenth birthday. But the very fact that the relationship started when she was still officially seventeen made many people scream 'statutory rape' and 'abuse of a minor.' The *New York Times* and *New York* magazine did point up the fact that Carly had been over the age of consent a week and a half into the start of the relationship. Just as the reports from people who had met Carly together with Gretchen Ford and noted how happy they seemed; how supportive and patient the older woman was toward her younger, frequently troubled lover. As my mother, in her usual take-no-prisoners way, noted:

'Of course all those "friends" who reported what a great gal this Gretchen was were just *like* Gretchen.'

'Jesus, Mom. You sound like Dad.'

'I've got nothing against lesbians. The tragedy here is that this one could have done the right thing and saved your friend.'

'She panicked because she knew she would be exposed,' I said.

'Thank God she never told you the woman's name or address. You would have been pulled into the vortex of all this,' Mom said.

The vortex deepened a few days later – when Carly's knapsack containing her Old Greenwich High student ID was found on the beach at Far Rockaway. A homeless man, interviewed later by the police, said that he saw a young woman matching Carly's description sitting on the sand, crying, anguished, around sunset the day before. He tried to talk to her, but she was far too distressed and screamed at him to go away. The guy headed off to panhandle outside the Far Rockaway subway station. He managed to scrounge a dollar from someone, ate a hamburger in a diner and returned to the beach with his bedroll, only to find the young girl's bag and her jacket left down by the water's edge. As he told the reporter from the *New York Post* – from which myself and Arnold learned all – he immediately found a cop and informed him that he thought that 'the girl had thrown herself into the ocean and drowned herself'. Arnold being Arnold, he actually called the meteorological office at JFK Airport (which was right next to Far Rockaway) and found out that the water temperature the previous day in Jamaica Bay was around fifty degrees, with an air temperature of forty-three. Then he phoned his doctor uncle – a hematologist in Chicago – to find out how long someone could survive in such cold sea water.

'Uncle Jerome told me: fifteen minutes tops. Also: the current in Jamaica Bay is a wicked one. No wonder the Coast Guard still can't find the body. Poor Carly was probably swept way out to sea.'

This news landed like a devastating slap across the face of Old Greenwich. Mrs Cohen was far too grief-stricken and traumatized to speak to the press. Her husband issued a short statement, asking for privacy and pointing fingers at the powers that be at Old Greenwich High 'for not curbing the culture of bullying that resulted in my daughter living in a state of daily fear, and being assaulted by two of her classmates so severely that she ran away from home and is now feared dead; an apparent suicide which could have been prevented had the principal and teachers of Old Greenwich High intervened earlier'.

In the wake of Carly's presumed death by drowning, Gretchen Ford was immediately fired from her job at *Time*. Her fellow tenants in the apartment building where she lived in Murray Hill signed a petition calling for her eviction. She beat them to it, disappearing completely from New York and going into hiding at an undisclosed location. Like Carly she too vanished. Unlike Carly they found her body two months later in a car parked on the side of a frozen road in northern Michigan. There was a hose attached to the exhaust pipe and all the windows taped shut. But the people who started this nightmare walked away from it all. Though he spent a night in the cells of the Old Greenwich police station Ames Sweet's dad used a top New York criminal lawyer and his political connections in the state to get him out. Once it was clear that he hadn't murdered her in Byrum Park, Ames's father called the whole business 'the unjust ravings of a clearly unstable young lady'. I also heard how his lawyer and Deb Schaeffer's attorney managed to get Deb to retract many of the damning statements she'd made to the police, accusing them of strong-arming her into a confession. The Sweets also pressed the families of the other bullies to talk up about Carly's 'provocative behavior', and how she had allegedly cruised two of the girls in their gang (an outright lie). The school still needed to show that it was doing something about all this, so there were three assemblies on 'being kind to each other'. Miss Cleveland was also let go – though as my mother noted, 'they needed a sacrificial lamb and decided: better that it's the woman who gets to take the fall'.

As it turned out Miss Cleveland ended up being quickly hired by an elite private girls' boarding school in Massachusetts – what Mom called 'failing upwards'. And though Mr O'Neill assured the local press that he was cracking down on in-school cruelty, several weeks after Carly vanished, Ames Sweet walked by Arnold in a corridor and hissed at him:

'Heard the Jew didn't get into Yale.'

The fact that Arnold had been turned down by Yale just a few days earlier was well known around the school (where such things got broadcast on the jungle drums almost immediately). Arnold had been gutted by the news; his parents even more so. Fortunately, there was a quiet, stoner kid named Matt Sheehan standing nearby who was stunned by this comment. When they both went to Mr O'Neill, Ames was called in and, acting all contrite, said that Arnold had misheard his comment, and what he really said was: 'Heard *you* didn't get into Yale' ... and he was sorry for saying something like that. But when Matt told O'Neill that he indeed heard Sweet use two words – 'the Jew' – O'Neill suspended Sweet on the spot. Three days later, Sweet was back at school, which is when Arnold's sense of moral righteousness turned into indignation. That night, he wrote a long letter to a well-known investigative reporter on the *New York Times* named T.M. Reynolds. He told him about Carly's disappearance after a sexual assault that followed months of being victimized; how the central perpetrator had been sprung from jail, how his co-accused had changed her story, how parents had been cajoled, phone calls made to the governor's office, strings pulled, a whitewash administered and bullying within the school still contin-ued today amidst a culture of fear. Meanwhile poor Carly was still missing, presumed dead. Arnold assured him that he could drum up several students who would openly talk about all that had recently gone down at Old Greenwich High, and that he was reasonably certain Carly's parents would want all this widely publicized. Just as I wanted those monsters who had caused all this to pay a price for their abuse. Because they had so ruined the life of my friend. Her disappearance haunted me. And I couldn't help but constantly think: I should have done more to help her ... even though Arnold kept telling me, in his lawyerly way, that my guilt 'was not grounded in fact'. But guilt is still what I felt.

Meanwhile the Coast Guard continued to search for a body in and around the coast of Queens. As she hadn't been officially registered as dead the FBI put Carly on their Missing Persons List. And much to my surprise, T.M. Reynolds paid a visit to Old Greenwich.

It was the first of several trips that he made north into the burbs. Arnold spoke with him. I spoke with him. He was quiet but very thorough. He saw how nervous I was talking to a famous reporter and having to revisit everything that I told the police. He put me at my ease and seemed more interested in the constant harassment that I and my friends had to deal with on a daily basis at the school. Mrs Cohen agreed to speak with him (despite having withdrawn from the world). My mother spoke with him. I sent him to seek out Sean and Officer Proccaccino. He, in turn, interviewed O'Neill and several key teachers at the school. In the first week of 1972, a four-part T.M. Reynolds investigation – 'The Price of Silence: How Old Greenwich High's Culture of Whitewash Engendered Bullying and a Student's Disappearance' – hit the streets.

These *New York Times* articles were a sensation. Reynolds was quite the stylist, and he caught, with lethal accuracy, the price of conformity that was so much a part of life in our town. Cindy Cohen was particularly poignant, showing Reynolds all of Carly's considerable artwork (she was a terrific illustrator) and the drawing that her mom discovered after her disappearance which depicted, with surrealistic flair, the horror of being picked upon by blonde, blue-eyed, highly orthodontured high-schoolers. There was a wonderful moment in part two of the series where Reynolds spent a Saturday at the Greenwich Country Club with Gordy Sweet – who, having surmised earlier that Reynolds played varsity tennis (my mom said that Gordy Sweet probably got an assistant to go to the library and pull all he could on the *NY Times* man), asked if he'd like to play a friendly set or two. As it turned out, Gordy was very much still a serious competitor in his mid-forties, and Reynolds in the article detailed how the guy blew him off the court. Having established his tennis superiority, Gordy then took him to lunch in the club dining room and proceeded to tell him that his son was contrite for his actions, but that the police had no proof (other than the recanted testimony of Deb Schaeffer) that he had threatened and assaulted Carly. He also talked about how Miss Cohen (as he kept referring to her – and Reynolds noted that Sweet placed heavy vocal evidence on 'Cohen', as if accentuating its Jewishness) had been 'fast and loose with her strange sexuality', and that 'outsiders who come into our community should think twice about trying to impose their values on ours'.

The story was picked up by the big three television networks, who dispatched reporters and crews up to Old Greenwich for a segment on their news programs. ABC interviewed the police detective who informed them that Deb Schaeffer had indeed confessed to being part of a sexual assault with Ames Sweet on Carly. Just as they also followed up on the way that the governor's office put pressure on the cops to back off. But most devastating was an interview that NBC's *Today* program did with Mrs Cohen, who broke down on camera, saying out loud that she was now pretty certain that her daughter had killed herself in the wake of all the bullying – and how the school and the state had conspired to turn Carly into the guilty one here.

And then there was Arnold – quoted in the *Times* and looking like a junior law clerk on television – solemnly telling the nation:

'It didn't matter that poor Carly Cohen was picked on for being different and Jewish. It didn't matter that I was referred to as "the Jew" by many of my classmates on repeated occasions. The school allowed it to happen. Even after a young girl was victimized, assaulted, they still let it pass.'

Heads quickly rolled thereafter. O'Neill was fired (later finding another headmastership in Ohio). Ames Sweet was expelled from school. Deb Schaeffer's parents pulled her out before she too could be ejected. In the midst of all this the search for Carly's body continued. Without any success. Mrs Cohen phoned me one day after school and asked if I could drop over. Ten minutes later I was at her house. She was in a bad place: deep black rings beneath her eyes, her face tight with permanent grief. She gave me a hug and told me

61

she was going to make me a proper English tea – with scones and little sandwiches and real lapsang souchong tea from a shop called Fortnum & Mason in London.

'Carly loved my English teas. And I loved making them for her – but I was never home when she was home after school –'

She broke off the sentence on the verge of tears again.

'Carly never complained about you being absent,' I said.

'You don't have to lie to me, Alice.'

I knew I had to do just that, remembering something that my grandfather once told me: 'Don't believe all that Girl Scout stuff about never telling a lie. Sometimes a lie is the biggest kindness you can bestow on someone else.'

'I'm not lying, Mrs Cohen.'

Now she began to weep, reaching out and grasping my arm.

'You're too kind. You don't really think she's dead, do you?'

I lied again.

'Maybe she left everything on the beach to throw everyone off her trail.'

'But if that's the case – if she really couldn't face coming back to Old Greenwich again, if she'd decided to become one of those hippie runaways I read about all the time in magazines – why couldn't she just let me know that she was still alive?'

I had no answer to that sad question. Of course I had hoped that all the coverage and publicity of her disappearance might have made her come out of hiding. But there was never a single word from her.

'I hate to say this,' Arnold noted a week after the segments aired, 'but she's probably dead. A single postcard to her parents saying she saw all the press about her, and that she was alive, could have changed everything. It would have been so easy for her to do. Which is what leads me to surmise she is no longer with us.'

I argued otherwise. I did so because I too feared the worst but didn't want to articulate it. It was more of a comfort for me that the Carly case was in a holding pattern, with Old Greenwich High keeping a tight lid on things. Fascinating, isn't it, how Ames Sweet, who had virtually gotten away with it all simply couldn't stop scratching that malevolent itch, and had to test the limits of tolerance again.

Had Ames never made that crack to Arnold about being the Jew rejected by Yale, Arnold wouldn't have gone to the *Times* and Ames Sweet's life might have turned out much differently. We really do shoot ourselves in the foot with a machine gun, pausing twice to reload.

Meanwhile Mrs Cohen kept inviting me over at least twice a week for afternoon English teas. I had to keep these visits hidden from my mother – whom, I feared, would have become jealous if she knew how much time I was spending with Carly's mom, but I had to do it. I knew that it somehow brought her closer to Carly. As Arnold noted when I told him about spending a few hours with her two or three times a week:

'What you're doing is a *mitzvah*,' he said, using the Yiddish for 'a good deed'. 'You being with Mrs Cohen helps her believe she still has a daughter.'

Three months after Carly's disappearance I received a letter from Bowdoin College beginning with the words I so wanted to read: *You're in!*

I was relieved. The tense psychodrama of college admissions was behind me. I had been accepted to a prestigious college. I had gone up for the interview with Peter in the driver's seat of his Volvo (as Dad was still in South America). Upon arrival in the town of Brunswick we agreed that the campus was beautiful. The Maine sky was a hard blue that day. Even the foliage was putting on quite a spectacular floor show (it was early October after all). The student who showed me around before I faced one of the deans of admission told me that, though the place still had a preppy/jock vibe, 'there are enough arty types here to keep the smart ones at the college not feeling as if they are in Siberia'. Her name was Shelley. She looked reassuringly like a younger version of Grace Slick (which pleased me, being such a Jefferson Airplane fan). She was from Chicago. She said that her father was a civil rights attorney, and that she probably should have ended up at a truly alternative school like Bennington or Antioch, but her dad – for all his left-wing, liberal bias – still had old-fashioned views of the virtue of the liberal arts, and wanted her to have a proper quasi-classical college education. Bowdoin pursued her – and yeah she did like it here. Her religion and philosophy professors were especially good. She loved the coastal Maine vibe, and she'd found enough like-minded urban exiles around the college, along with many suburbanites turned counter-culture subversives.

'You have to put up with the fraternities and the hockey players,' she told me as we walked around the grounds, 'and the fact that this is just the second year where women have been admitted – which, on one level, gives you a lot of choice when it comes to guys, but on another level means that the men are kind of desperate. I mean, one woman for seven men … well, do the math.'

Peter and I were the only two people on Shelley's tour that morning – and I could see she had an eye for him. Before we parted company, she handed him a slip of paper with the phone number of the off-campus apartment she lived in, telling him if we were still around tonight she would be having some friends over around 9 p.m.

The interview went more smoothly than I'd dared imagined. It was with a recent graduate of the college. He'd clearly read from my application, as his first question was: how did I feel about heading up to the sticks for college? I was ready for this one, telling him that I saw myself as the eternal Manhattanite, but one who also knew that there was time ahead for me to live back in a big city; that for college I wanted to be somewhere beautiful, yet worldly, away from metropolitan temptations. I talked about being a fanatical reader and he told me that Bowdoin had always had a very strong English department.

As soon as I left the interview I saw Peter in the waiting room, studying my face, gauging how it had all gone. I gave him a fast thumbs up, so wanting my big brother's approval, knowing that he was the one person in our family who would always watch my back and never betray me. We walked outside into the ravishing autumn afternoon. I filled him in on what had gone down with the admissions guy and Peter told me he was certain I would get in. What did he know that I didn't?

'I hear there's a good diner in town here,' said Peter. 'Want to eat at a greasy spoon?'

The diner was called the Miss Brunswick – and it was, indeed, a classic dive. Inside there was a long counter covered in green linoleum, metal stools, around six booths (more green lino), jukeboxes in every booth, a waitress in her late fifties. Peter ordered us two beers. The waitress eyed me over.

'You want ID, I've got it,' I said.

'Didn't say I did,' she said in a flat Maine accent. 'We got two types of beer here: Schaeffer and Carling Black Label.'

'Both are bad,' Peter said with a smile.

'Then don't order them.'

'Two Mabels,' he said.

'You got 'em,' the waitress said.

When she headed off Peter smiled again.

'What I like about up here is that it is so no bullshit. They've got a naval station just outside of town. And the Bath Iron Works, where they build all the big battleships for the Navy, is just ten miles up the road. A real blue-collar town, with a great college thrown into the mix. This being Maine they have an independent frame of mind. They may not agree with the way you see the world, but they will defend your right to say it.'

'We might get a president from Maine come next November – if Muskie wins the nomination. I so want McGovern to be the Democrats' candidate.'

'So do I. And I'm going to work for him. But the Democratic establishment is against him. Because he's such a dove – and because Vietnam was their war. You know what gets me all the time? The fact that if Bobby Kennedy had lived, not only would the war be over now, but we'd also have right now the most progressive president since FDR.'

'We're a crazy country.'

'We're a great country with a crazed violent underside to it.'

Our beers arrived. The waitress asked if we were going to eat, as we couldn't drink here without both ordering food. She also mentioned that the chili was pretty damn good – and they did it with or without melted cheddar cheese and chopped onions. We both ordered the full-works chili. Then we raised our Mabels.

'To bad beer and diner chili, to you getting accepted at Bowdoin, to peace in our time, and the unraveling of the Secret State which runs everything behind our backs.'

We clinked our bottles together and I smiled at my brother, happy we were together.

'You still off the Viceroys?' I asked Peter.

'Nearly a year and counting.'

'Dad doesn't care that I smoke. He even taught me how to do it properly.'

Peter hoisted his beer and took a deep swig.

'Dad is a man of many hidden parts,' he said.

'What do you mean by that?'

'He says one thing, acts another way. He fabricates things about himself. Know that big scar on his right arm?'

'You mean the wound he got in the war?'

'It was no wound,' said Peter harshly. 'It was a tattoo of the Marine Corps emblem with the words *Semper Fidelis*. Mom refused to marry him if he didn't have it removed. So it was sandpapered off. Left him with that terrible scar.'

'But he told me he got that on Okinawa, when he was hit by "Jap flak" – his exact words.'

Peter shook his head, almost laughing.

'Dad is such a piece of work. And such a liar.'

'That's not fair.'

'Fair? *Fair*? That man's never played fair his whole life. Only you can't see it.'

'That's because he's always been a good dad to me.'

'If only you knew ... '

'If only I knew *what*? He may not approve of your radical credentials, but –'

'I never knew you were such a daddy's girl.'

The comment landed like a left hook.

'I'm my own girl, asshole,' I hissed, grabbing my cigarettes and storming outside. Once there I lit up a Viceroy, squinting in the declining sunlight, watching the cars and trucks roll by, trying to blink back tears, wondering why everything to do with my family was so damn hard, and why Peter – the smartest one of us, the most caring – had come out with such a nasty comment. I took several deep steadying drags on my cigarette, feeling very much alone. A minute later Peter was out the door. I turned away from him, shrugging him off when he tried to put his arms around me. But he persisted, pulling me close to him, saying:

'That was such a jerk move. I am sorry.'

I buried my head in his shoulder and let go, the tension of the interview, of Carly's disappearance, of all the crap at school, at home, suddenly flooding out. At that moment I felt like such a scared kid, overwhelmed by the hardness of life, the hardness of others. I broke down.

Peter suggested we go for a drive. He'd read of a beach not far from here. There was still, he estimated, around ninety minutes of light. Popham Beach turned out to be a good half-hour by car – a trip that brought us north to Bath, then down a two-lane blacktop, then across a small bridge, and deep into backcountry Maine.

We were in luck: it was low tide at Popham. Apart from a couple out walking their dog we had the beach entirely to ourselves. The sign at the front gate informed us we were in a state park. What it didn't tell us was just what an amazing beach was awaiting us beyond the dunes. Even for a city-girl-in-exile like myself – who cared little for, or knew little of, the great outdoors – Popham was a total revelation. Several miles of unbroken sand. High dunes. No food stands or bumper cars or roller coasters or any of that other seaside junk. A true state of nature: wild, empty, with the Atlantic pounding the sand, the percussive *boom-boom* sounding like kettledrums. Having been in floods of tears a half-hour earlier I now found myself smiling.

'This works,' Peter said.

We started to walk.

It took us almost an hour to reach the northern end of the beach, hiking past summer cottages and a couple of big weathered New England homes, as empty and stern and forbidding as the darkening sky above. We didn't talk for a long time. I broke the silence.

'You're right, Peter. Dad's a complicated guy, I know that. But he seems to love me more than Mom does.'

'She does truly love you ... in her own crazy way.'

'But she doesn't like me.'

Peter's silence spoke volumes. And he knew it.

'What can I say? She has all this intelligence and wit, but the problem is: she hates her life, hates herself for it. And you being the daughter ... well, you get the brunt of her anger. Because you represent everything she could have.'

'Like what?'

'Like "possibilities".'

'Mom isn't even fifty. She still has time.'

'Except there's a problem here: she blocks herself. Stops herself from moving forward. She should have a job, a career. She should be back in New York. And what happens when you flee the nest come September? She will continue to stand still and not escape all that has made her so unhappy – which is not just her bad marriage and life in the burbs, but the big disappointment which is herself. That's the real reason she remains so angry. And why she will continue to take her frustration at herself out on you.'

'In the same way that Dad turns on you?'

'And on Adam.'

'But he can control Adam. He can't control you. Which is why he needles you all the time. You still so want our father to like you, right? And his problem is: he envies your personal independence, and the way you think so differently from him. He's always been programmed into a certain life: from being an altar boy to joining the Marines to doing the American corporate man and suburban Dad thing. You are the rambling free spirit. He kind of hates you for that.'

Peter abruptly stopped walking, turning away from me, looking out at the sea.

'You're far too perceptive for someone so young,' he said.

I could see him fighting tears. I linked my arm into his.

'It's okay,' I said.

Peter kept his face turned away from mine.

'No it's not.'

'So let's vow never to make it hard on each other.'

Peter nodded. Many times. Then drying his eyes with his fingers, he leaned over and kissed my head.

'Agreed,' he said.

We walked back to the car. By the time we reached it darkness had fallen. We returned to the hotel. I had an essay due on Monday for a writing class and still had a few pages to go. I told Peter I was going to work for an hour. Mom had given me a great birthday gift: a tomato-red Olivetti portable typewriter, which struck me as the height of Italian cool. I loved it and prided myself on being the fastest two-finger, self-taught typist on the East Coast. Having let go of all that pent-up anger and distress after our exchange in the diner I felt very ready to work.

I was sharing the room with Peter – and he stretched out on his bed for a while with a book. After a few minutes he sat up, looked at his watch and announced:

'I checked out Shelley's address. It's on Federal Street – and we're on Federal Street right now. So why don't we head on up there? I mean, it's not even 9 p.m.'

'You go. I'm going to keep on with this.'

'You've had a big day. Surely you need a break.'

'I've nearly cracked it.'

Peter stood up, grabbing his jacket. Then he came over to the desk, picked up the hotel notepad and pencil and scribbled something on it.

'When you've finished, here's the address.'

An hour or so later, wired after all that concentration, I decided to head to Shelley's place. It wasn't hard to find: a mere three minutes' walk up Federal Street. The closer I got to number 263, the more I heard the Grateful Dead. There were four buttons by the front door, but when I turned the handle it opened automatically. Ah, Maine – a place where people still didn't lock their doors. I went up the narrow, scuffed stairs and walked into a small living room with beat-up furniture, bookshelves made of concrete blocks and wood planks, rock and anti-war posters covering the walls (there

69

was a big one of Jim Morrison – with the words *An American Poet* next to his spaced-out eyes, but someone had scratched out the word *Poet* and written something above it, so that it now read: *An American Fuck-Up*). I smiled. I approved. There must have been around thirty Bowdoin students in the room. The whiff of grass was everywhere, intermingled with a lot of cigarette smoke and the reek of beer. There were two kegs going in a corner. A guy with a ponytail was pouring out foamy beer into large plastic cups. I was immediately intrigued by the mix of people here. Some serious hippies and freaks. Some arty types – black turtlenecks, granny glasses, bell-bottom corduroy jeans – smoking smelly French cigarettes and looking a little bit above it all. A few preppies – button-down shirts and cream crew-neck sweaters – drinking heavily and trying to hit on any available women. And a dude with Jesus hair, a black tunic, loose black pants, seriously thick black glasses, and very bare feet. He was in the midst of a very intense conversation with a woman dressed almost exactly the same, with equally long hair and lips painted purple. I liked the strange mix in the room: the sense that the freaks, the geeks, the Bradfords and Chips from the WASP brigade all mixed here. Just as I also felt very intimidated and young among all these college students. Still, no one was looking strangely at me. Someone passed a bong over. I took a big hit, coughing up a lungful of hash smoke, and the tall thin dude acting as bartender immediately handed me a plastic cup of beer, saying: 'This might help.' I thanked him, glugging it down to quell the hash burn in my throat, immediately feeling very stoned.

'You look lost.'

That was the voice of a guy who'd sidled up next to me. I figured he must be a sophomore or junior. Good-looking in a kind of Jack Nicholson way. Someone with a few days of stubble, a cigarette in one hand, a beer in the other, and big come-on eyes that were looking me up and down. I sensed immediately he went to one of the better boarding schools but had decided to create a role for himself as the perennial bad boy.

'I'm looking for my brother.'

'And who might your brother be, sweetness?'

'His name is Peter.'

'There are a lot of Peters here. You got a name.'

I told him.

'Well, mine's Phil – and why don't we go over in a corner and get to know each other?'

'I'd rather find my brother.'

'You can do that later, sweetness.'

'Please stop calling me that.'

'Would you rather "sweetass"?'

I tensed, part of me wanting to lash out, another part thinking: don't make a scene; it might get back to the people at the admissions office. So I checked my anger and simply said:

'Did you see my brother?'

'So my charm didn't work on you?' he said, suddenly reaching out and stroking my face. I jumped away, horrified. The guy moved in on me again. I glanced around, really nervous. Then, out of nowhere, the barefooted fellow with the Jesus hair was between us.

'Hey, Phil, let's be cool here,' he said.

'Stay out of this, Kreplin.'

'My name is Evan – as you well know. And you're a bit shitfaced, and about to do something which you may regret in the morning.'

Kreplin was getting through to this guy. Phil, looking flummoxed, reached into his shirt pocket for a pack of cigarettes, shook one out, fired it up, took a deep drag and spat smoke out in Kreplin's direction. Kreplin suddenly pulled the cigarette out of Phil's mouth and dropped it in his beer.

'That might have played at Exeter, it doesn't work here.'

'Fucking faggot,' Phil said,

'That I am not,' Kreplin said mildly. 'But you are a total asshole.'

Phil looked like he was about to throw a punch, but stopped himself, the small part of his brain that wasn't full of drunken aggression realizing he might just do something with bad consequences. So he simply fished out another cigarette, lit it up, and blew a cloud of smoke toward me.

'Is your brother a really tall guy?' Phil asked. 'A Yalie? Hanging out with Shelley?'

71

'That's him.'

'You want to find them, next floor up, second door on the right. No need to knock – as a bunch of people are up there too.'

I nodded, then turned to Kreplin.

'Thank you,' I said.

'Might see you next year,' Kreplin said with a small smile, then turned back to the woman he was with. I headed upstairs, wondering how this Kreplin guy had worked out I was still in high school. Did I come across as that young and clueless? – though I also thought: if I did get in here next year I could definitely use a friend like Evan Kreplin.

When I reached the next floor I heard loud music – Procol Harem – coming out of a room in which a whole bunch of people were sitting on the floor, passing a bottle of Jim Beam and a joint. The door next to this scene had the words 'Shelley's Crash Pad' scrawled graffiti-style on its chipped door. I threw the door open ... and immediately wished I hadn't. For there on the bed was Shelley, naked, her legs spread wide, and my brother on top of her, thrusting in and out. I froze, shock hitting me. The loud music from next door, and the fact that Peter seemed oblivious, made me recoil. I immediately closed the door – but not before Shelley turned her head and caught sight of me. There was no embarrassment or shock; she simply smiled at me – a smile which I have never been able to forget.

I raced down the stairs. I saw that Phil guy standing near the beer kegs. I turned on him.

'Thanks for sending me up there, asshole.'

Phil favored me with a malignant grin.

'Welcome to life, sweetass.'

Resisting the temptation to throw a glass of beer in his face – I fled.

Back at the hotel, my heart still pounding, I lay on the bed. I stared at the ceiling. I thought: you never can really know anybody. Even the person you feel you know the best. I smoked a cigarette. I got up and read through my essay, using a pencil to make corrections. There were many things I wanted to change. Then, around 1 a.m., I started retyping it all.

An hour or so later I heard a key in the door. My brother walked in, looking like he'd just thrown his clothes back on and was still under the influence of grass/booze/sex. I glanced up as he entered, then went back to typing.

'You're still up,' he said, his voice hesitant, wary.

'Looks that way.'

'Couldn't sleep?'

'Maybe.' Though my back was to him I could sense him hovering nearby.

'Someone at the party told me you were there,' Peter said.

'Briefly. Didn't see you.'

'You sure?'

'I'd know if I'd seen you or not,' I said.

'Then there's nothing to discuss, is there?'

I stopped typing. I turned and faced my brother. I wanted to scream and shout and tell him that what he'd done had really fucking hurt me. Instead I did what I always did when someone in my family disappointed me. I let him off the hook. Saying:

'There's absolutely nothing to discuss at all.'

5

COME DECEMBER OF that year everyone in Old Greenwich was hoping for a Christmas miracle. Even my mother – who still insisted on having a menorah in our front window and thought that 'miracles were for dumb Catholics like your dad' – told me she was quietly praying for that 'wonderful surprise which would end everyone's collective pain'. Around school it was clear that Carly Cohen's disappearance still haunted the place. I found myself crying at random, waking up late at night unable to sleep, frequently closing my eyes from fatigue during the day and seeing Carly's dead body floating out at sea. Whenever I ran into the Cruel Ones they regarded me with a mixture of fear and contempt – but never dared to utter a nasty word in my direction. Ames Sweet's expulsion and Deb Schaeffer's hurried departure had forced their nasty little gang to temper their ways – especially as the new headmaster, a man named Thomas Fielding, had let it be known that he would not tolerate any further incidents of bullying. He was an ex-Marine (which pleased the hell out of my father), albeit one who had now rather progressive ideas about how to run a school in what he called 'a time in American life when all the rules are being rewritten'.

Mom went to synagogue with Mrs Cohen at the start of Hanukkah – and even acted gracious when Carly's mom told her during the evening that I'd been keeping her company three afternoons a week.

'Of course you wouldn't dream of letting me in on this detail,' she said when confronting me about this some hours after her visit to *shul.*

'I thought you'd get angry at me.'

'For doing something nice to a woman suffering the worst tragedy imaginable?'

'You're not jealous?'

'Jealous of *what?*'

I said nothing. I didn't need to. Mom finally broke the silence.

'I'm glad you're being so supportive.'

Carly never came home that Christmas. Nor did Peter, who chose to spend his holiday break from Yale in Liberia where a college friend was working for the Peace Corps. We'd hardly been in contact since that visit to Bowdoin, though I did receive a postcard from him after I received the acceptance letter. It featured that great vaudeville anarchist Groucho Marx, on the back of which Peter had written: *I told you so! Bravo! Love ...*

And he signed his name.

I didn't reply. When Peter phoned on Christmas Day from Monrovia and Mom handed me the phone my conversation with him was pretty basic: me answering him with simple yes/no responses, making certain that he understood how angry and disappointed I still was with him. Adam was right nearby (he did dutifully come home for Christmas). When I handed the phone back to Mom he motioned to me that we should step outside. I grabbed the Army greatcoat I'd bought a week earlier on a trip to New York – finding it in a great thrift store on Sullivan Street in the Village – took a pack of cigarettes and my Zippo. Snow had fallen the night before, it was an actual white Christmas – and I was planning a winter walk on the beach later on (especially as my parents inevitably began to combust during Christmas lunch – and why should this year be different from all the others?). Adam had driven down from the upper reaches of New York State the night before. Dad celebrated his arrival by drinking him under the table ... to the point where he was fighting a major hangover this morning.

'What's up with you and Peter?'

'Nothing.'

'Come on, sis, I know a problem when I see one.'

Sis. I hated that nickname. Found it cornball. But Adam looked like he didn't need telling off right now.

'How many beers did you down with Dad last night?' I asked.

'At least six. But he insisted that we throw down a shot of Tullamore Dew before every beer.'

'Six beers, six shots of whiskey ... truly impressive.'

'You're still not answering my question.'

'Ask Peter.'

'I can't. He's in Africa, you're here. Please talk.'

'There's no problem,' I lied.

'What are you hiding?'

'Me – a Burns – hiding something? We don't do such things in this family.'

I saw Adam turn a chalky shade of white.

'If you want to know why things are a little weird between me and Peter, why don't you let me in on some of your secrets?'

Adam went even whiter, suddenly walking away from me. Part of me wanted to pursue him. Part of me also thought: he'll never talk about the car accident, and I have to somehow respect that. Part of me also felt: we have so little in common, family blood being the only real tie between us. How can you be so closely related to someone, yet simultaneously so different, so apart?

'I've got some news,' Adam said.

'Tell me.'

'Dad's found me a job after I get the MBA in June.'

'What kind of job?'

'With his mining people in Chile.'

'Wow,' I said, not exactly knowing what to make of this. 'You happy about it?'

'Hey, it'll get me out of the country – which is kind of cool. And it will mean that I either marry Patty and bring her with me. Or ...'

' ... maybe you'll just cut and run?' I said.

Adam smiled.

'You'd like that more for me, wouldn't you?'

'I'd like to see you living the life you want, not what you think is expected of you.'

Adam fell silent for a moment, then said:

'Living the life you want ... what a nice dream.'

'I'm going to live the life I want.'

'You say that now. The truth is: you will probably entrap yourself, just like the rest of us.'

When I tried to say something in reply my brother cut me off.

'Let's end this conversation now, okay? Let's go to the movies, let's get a beer somewhere afterward, let's pretend we didn't discuss any of this. Can you do that for me, sis?'

All I could do was nod in agreement. The snow kept falling. The AM radio kept playing junk music. We both stared ahead into the white void. I decided to break the edgy quiet between us, asking him:

'How many more days will you be staying at home?'

'I'm out of here tomorrow,' Adam said.

'Guess we won't be seeing each other for a while.'

'Guess not. Merry Christmas.'

'Indeed. But I wish –'

'Don't *wish*,' he said. 'It all goes wrong when you *wish*.'

That was the last exchange I had with my other brother for many months to come.

On my third day at Bowdoin, while crossing the quad en route to a late-morning class, I passed by a rather interesting creature: a tall willowy fellow in a paisley shirt, white pants, pale porcelain skin, with a wild mop of curly hair tinged blond and green. His fingernails were painted a matching green. He had a string bag filled with books on his shoulder. He nodded hello as he walked by. The sight of him was both bemusing and rather wonderful: such an out-there flamboyant metropolitan man, cascading across the deep Indian-summer green of this New England campus. But when he saw a trio of jocks in the immediate distance he left the paved path, heading through the grass to avoid them, his head lowered. I'd already got the sense that Bowdoin was a place where the freaks/jock divide was a distinct one. A big beefy type wearing a letterman sweater (with a big B emblazoned across the chest) shouted:

'Hey, Tree Fag!'

The other members of the trio joined in:

'Where's your boyfriend, Tree Fag?'

'Ignore these jerks, Howie,' said a guy walking past. But I also saw that – judging from the sardonic grin on his face – he wasn't stopping the jocks, allowing them to get away with this abuse. I wanted to say something. I was still too cowed by all that was new and strange here – college striking me as a big scary place. But I at least knew his name: Howie.

'Who waters your grass hair, Tree Fag?'

Howie was now all but jogging away from these idiots.

'Great prance, Tree Fag! You one of Santa's elves?'

This caused uproarious laughter. I saw Howie dash into the student union building. I thought: bullies are allowed to get away with it at college too.

On my fifth day at Bowdoin I heard Professor Theodore Hancock give his first lecture of the semester on American Colonial History and I was suddenly aware that here was a wonderful storyteller.

Before coming to Bowdoin I'd been sent an 'Insider's Guide to Classes and Professors' produced by the editors of the college newspaper, the *Orient*. Professor Hancock's American History courses immediately caught my attention, as he was singled out to be 'someone who turns every lecture into an event' and 'never goes dry and academic, but actually makes colonial history into something compelling and very real'.

Before this, outside of reading Hawthorne's *The Scarlet Letter* and learning the usual stuff about how the first settlers in America were 'Pilgrims' escaping religious persecution, I'd had little interest in anything to do with this early portion of our collective history. But after that first lecture by Professor Hancock I was all ears.

Theodore Hancock looked the very role of the New England college professor. He was not particularly tall, and was no doubt destined from birth to wear a Harris tweed jacket, gray flannels, a pale blue button-down shirt, a knitted tie. He had neatly parted light brown hair, a pale complexion, classic horn-rimmed glasses. His voice was always modulated, always reasoned. What grabbed me immediately during that first hour-long lecture was how, in his own quiet way, he commanded our absolute attention.

Great teachers, I came to discover that September morning at Bowdoin, can alter your world view. People often mock educators: 'Those who can't do, teach.' But the truth is: when you are in the presence of a truly remarkable teacher something in you shifts. Maybe, for me, it was responding to something paternal and instructive in Professor Hancock: the sense that he had actual, considered knowledge about something important and that, in the coming months, he was going to get us to consider so much; to make us rethink the origins of America, and how we are still grappling with so many left-behinds from the Puritan psyche. Truth be told, I had an instant crush on Hancock. This surprised me. Because I never felt that sort of magnetic draw toward an older man before. Not that I was instantly envisaging a life with him or anything stupidly teenage like that. He struck me as someone so smart, so thoughtful ... and not riddled with the anguishes or furies that consumed my own dad. He carried himself with quiet Boston elegance. There was a kindness and poise to him, underscored by high intelligence, immense compassion. Or, at least, that is what I was surmising after one lecture. Just as I left that first class with Professor Hancock with this thought: he is an older version of the sort of man I'd always envisaged falling in love with. And that was both exhilarating and unsettling.

After the first week Bowdoin struck me as both brilliant and boorish. My assigned roommate – Connie Lyons from Wellesley, Mass – had gone to a very uppity girls' prep school and had a mother who'd made the US Open in 1952 as a competitive doubles player.

'Mom always said that when I arrived in the world two years later, that was the end of her tennis career.'

This was one of the few personal moments that I had with Connie. She was a redhead who dressed in a very LL Bean style: flannel shirts, hiking boots, pleated plaid skirts. She was bubbly, immediately popular with the other women on the floor of our dorm, very focused on making the junior varsity tennis team, and hooking up with a guy – which she did about ten days after we started college. His name was Jesse Whitworth. He was a member of the most WASP of all the fraternities: Chi Psi, where girls like Connie were most welcomed. During our first week at the college the fraternities – and there were eight of them – had something called 'freshman rush', in which you drifted from one party to another, meeting frat members, seeing if you fit in to their distinctive personalities. Women were a prized minority. Even at the geekiest of the frat houses – Zeta Psi, filled with future high-level cost accountants or professors of microeconomics – women were eyed over with the sort of longing that wasn't far off from that of forlorn souls panning for gold in the Klondike. Only I didn't find myself very flattered by all the attention. I stuck my nose into Chi Psi and Deke – both hyper-preppy and country club. Not exactly my scene, though I did get into an interesting conversation with a Deke about John Updike, which ended when he asked if I wanted to see his library of American fiction in his room upstairs. When I laughed and shook my head he had the presence of mind to smile back and say: 'Last time I use that dumb pickup line.'

Psi Upsilon was the arty house, the hippie house, the druggy house. I wandered into its big green residence on Main Street and immediately found myself in a cloud of weed, with Van Morrison blaring over the loudspeakers and a man who, handing me a bong, told me: 'Welcome to the spaceship.' His name was Casey and, from what I could judge, very much the presiding guru here. Psi U had been in the news last year, as it was the first fraternity in the country to elect a woman president, and had been referred to as a place (as I read in a *NY Times* piece that my mom clipped for me) of 'divine decadence'. But in addition to the bong I found myself being poured a glass of Almaden wine and accepting a cigarette from a gentle guy named Mark.

'We're the alternative house,' he said. 'Everywhere else the frats appeal to a certain type. We take everyone – the wicked smart, the perpetually stoned, the ski bum, the solitary drinker, the truly weird, the jock who does interesting, even a couple of future lawyers who like to walk on the wild side … for the time being, anyway.'

Mark gestured a guy over. He had bare feet, loose black Indian clothes and Jesus-length hair and I liked the look of him.

'I remember you,' he said immediately. 'You were at Shelley's party on Federal Street last October.'

'That's kind of impressive,' I said. 'Considering we didn't speak.'

'Or frightening,' Mark said. 'Evan has the most trenchant memory going.'

'I remember someone interesting,' Evan said.

'I'm flattered,' I said.

'Don't be. I sniff out intelligence the same way I sniff out stupidity – and there's plenty of both at this college. Do you like poker?'

'No,' I replied, strangely drawn in by his off-kilter question, 'but I'd love to learn.'

'I'd teach you in a couple of hours,' Evan said.

'Only if you want to lose money,' Mark said. 'As I found out to my cost.'

'I don't have that much,' I said.

'You should still come along,' Evan said. 'Just as you should join our little circus here at Psi U. We make things interesting.'

Of all the frat houses I visited this was the only one where I felt somewhat at home. But I wasn't someone who wanted to belong anywhere. As I was discovering quickly, college life here could be riddled with social allegiances – and even though Psi U prided itself on its hippie/druggy/arty/left-wing credentials it was still a frat. I couldn't align myself to that world.

But Evan Kreplin became a friend – someone with whom I would frequently play Five-Card Stud. Just as I also began to hang out with Digby Lord – a serious WASP from the Philadelphia Main Line, known to all as DJ, who was fashioning himself to be the Maxwell Perkins of his generation. DJ was a sophomore and had already commandeered control of the college literary magazine, the *Quill*, with his closest associate, Sam Schneider. DJ was a literary snob of immense ferocity. When I admitted to admiring John Cheever he ridiculed me as if I had mentioned a weakness for milkshakes. DJ hated any contemporary writing that was narrative-led. He championed what he called 'meta-novelists', who wrote against the realist/storytelling grain. He spoke about John Barth and Donald Barthelme and Thomas Pynchon with near reverence. I sensed from the outset that DJ was attracted to me. He wasn't conventionally good-looking – which hardly put me off. Tall, lanky, with a tightly curled mop of brown hair, he was also, like me, a cigarette smoker. But whereas I went through ten or so Viceroys a day, DJ was a two-pack-a-day man. He was never without a cigarette in hand – and as you could smoke virtually everywhere outside of the Bowdoin infirmary, he was always inhaling. From what I learned when he invited me out for cheese and wine at the one bohemian cafe in downtown Brunswick, the

Ruffled Grouse, his father – Digby Lord Sr – was a big deal invest-ment banker and a one-time junior tennis pro.

'You should be going out with my roommate,' I told him. 'She's the tennis player of every corporate headhunter's dreams.'

DJ gave me the thinnest of sardonic smiles, then said:

'I would last around five minutes with an *all-smiles-all-the-time* woman like that – and she would last two minutes with me. But you're not exactly hanging out with all those girlie girls around the campus.'

DJ was an observant fellow. To date I hadn't made any close friends among the few women at the college. Either I found them far too preppy and blonde – and, as such, painfully reminiscent of many an Old Greenwich nightmare. Or I was put off by the competitive way they toyed with men – knowing that, owing to their small numbers, they could cherry-pick the fellows they wanted and those they were going to simply tease or keep at arm's length. There was a woman named Philippa – a Brooklynite, Jewish, bookish, pre-med – with whom I occasionally had coffee in the union. There was a touch of the 1950s beatnik to Philippa – someone who might have been more at home with Ginsburg and Kerouac and all the other Eisenhower-era hipsters up at Columbia. Just as she had a decidedly wry take on her full-scholarship exile up here in Maine – and the distance she put between herself and most everyone else up here. Including me. She was always affable and never dismissive whenever I approached her table. We could talk New York arthouse cinemas and jazz joints and why nei-ther of us could read J.R.R. Tolkien ('Too many dwarfs,' she noted). But whenever I suggested we grab a glass of wine some evening down-town she was studying or otherwise engaged ... though I sensed she didn't have a boyfriend nor was actively searching for one. There was something of the loner about Philippa. Just as, within me, there was (I realized much later) an equal sense of concern about having a close woman friend again after the drama of Carly's disappearance ... which still shadowed me and which I still felt I could have prevented.

I mentioned none of this on that first date with DJ, during which I discovered: he was intellectually engaging, he had mostly interest-ing opinions about everything, he was genuinely funny, and he was uncertain of himself in the presence of a woman. His smart talk was a form of flirtation. With a little subtle questioning I also gleaned that his knowledge of women was still somewhat limited. Which made two of us, as beyond Arnold I knew nothing of men. After we drank a bottle of Liebfraumilch – which was the wrong side of sweet, but still gave me a buzz – DJ walked me back to my dorm. When I tipsily told him he could come upstairs with me, as Connie was already hooked up with her tennis god at the frat house and probably wouldn't be home, he agreed. But once upstairs we smoked cigarettes and he browsed through my record collection and told me that I needed to start listening to some jazz, and we played the latest record of The Band, and he sat in my desk chair and I sat on my bed, and I hinted at least twice that he could join me on the bed, and he just sat there, telling me about seeing in New York an amazing Harold Pinter play, *The Homecoming*, and how if he was ever to write plays Pinter would be one of his models. Then he checked his watch and said that he had an eight thirty class in the morning. I took his hands and said, 'I hope we do this again soon.' He gave me a kiss on the head on his way out and said, 'See you around.'

The next day I ran into Sam Schneider in the student union. Sam had already struck me as someone who cared little about flirting. Like DJ, he was all book talk. What I liked about him was that he wasn't at all shy about asserting his Chicago Jewish sensibility in such a largely goyish environment as this New England college. Coming into the union late in the morning after my evening out with DJ I saw Sam at a booth, a pot of tea in front of him. I noticed a volume of Blake amidst three very academic critical studies and a yellow legal pad on which he was scribbling a massive number of notes. He looked up as I approached.

'So: the much-admired Alice,' he said.

'Admired by whom?'

'Guess,' he said, a half-smile crossing his lips, as he pulled one of his books toward him, flipped back to the index and rifled through a few pages. 'Not everyone is a born Don Giovanni.'

Then he started taking copious notes from the book in front of him. End of conversation. I took the hint, heading off to get coffee and an English muffin. But before I moved toward the counter Sam said:

'We're looking for a fourth member of our editorial board. We've never appointed a freshman before. But we might make an exception for you – if you're interested.'

'I'm interested,' I said.

'Then take these away,' he said, pushing a manila envelope toward me. 'New submissions from the usual aspiring writers with, by and large, little in the way of talent. Still we all live in hope, right? Pick out two terrible submissions and two that might just make the grade.'

'By which you mean?'

'You have a degree of taste and discernment. Or, at least, that's what I'm presuming, otherwise we wouldn't be having this conversation and I wouldn't be considering you for the board of the *Quill*. I want a few pithy, smart paragraphs on the four entries you choose. A small hint: DJ has a savage streak when it comes to other people's bad writing. I tend to be a little more critically nuanced, but I also don't suffer fools.'

He tapped the envelope in front of me.

'Off you go. I'd like the reports in three days, no later.'

And he went back to his books.

Seen retrospectively, it is extraordinary how much I wanted to impress DJ and Sam. Just as I also wanted to impress Professor Hancock. I had burrowed deep into Edmund Morgan's *The Puritan Dilemma*, filling up a notebook with a variety of observations and questions, and came into his lecture the next day, waiting for the question period at the end of class to raise my hand and ask:

'Professor, Edmund Morgan points up repeatedly the way that citizenship could be revoked if you questioned the divine judgment of the Puritan theocracy. Might this be seen as an antecedent of McCarthyism?'

Behind me someone whispered: 'Brown-nose.' It was a very audible whisper. So audible that Professor Hancock heard the comment and immediately pointed to the offender – a hungover preppy with deep rings around her eyes and a cream crew-necked sweater that was stained with cigarette ash and what looked like dried-out beer.

'Miss Stevens,' Professor Hancock said, 'might you please repeat your whispered reproach to Miss Burns?'

He knew my name!

Miss Stevens suddenly looked like she wanted to be anywhere but here, especially as all eyes in the lecture theater were on her.

'I meant nothing, Professor,' she said, stubbing out her cigarette in the little tin ashtray on her desk, and coughing a serious hack cough.

'On the contrary, you meant harm, Miss Stevens. And I am asking you again: please repeat what you whispered to Miss Burns.'

Silence. Professor Hancock's lips twitched. I sensed he was someone who never raised his voice, and truly didn't like unpleasantness. Just as I was also learning that he had a strong sense of matters ethical.

'Miss Stevens, we are waiting ... '

She stood up, her face filled with mortification. She grabbed her bag. But halfway to the door Hancock said:

'If you walk out that door I will have no choice but to report you to the Dean of Students for abusive words toward another student. Your choice.'

Stevens stopped in her tracks. Her face still turned toward the door, she said:

'I called her a brown-nose. Sorry. Okay?'

'Back to your seat, please,' Hancock said. 'But not before you explain to us what provoked you to say such a thing.'

Stevens's reply was to dash out the door, sobbing loudly. Hancock stood behind his lectern, cool serenity personified. When a big beefy guy stood up and shut the door Hancock said:

'Thank you, Mr O'Sullivan.' He paused and looked around, taking us all in that one look. 'For those of you new to my classes, I will not tolerate whatsoever hostility or verbal aggression toward one of your fellow students, especially one who has shown a bit of intellectual initiative by reading one of the assigned texts with a certain acuity. Would you mind repeating your question again, Miss Burns?'

But when I began to hesitate, Mr O'Sullivan made a point of looking over in my direction and signaling to me that I shouldn't be scared, but should get the damn question out there again. I did as encouraged, saying again with a slightly hesitant voice:

'Edmund Morgan points up repeatedly the way that citizenship could be revoked on the basis of questioning the authority of the Puritan theocracy in colonial Massachusetts. Might this be seen as an antecedent of McCarthyism?'

'Robert,' he asked, 'might you be able to answer Alice's question?'

He knew my first name as well!

Robert O'Sullivan paused for a moment, then began to say that there were definite antecedents in the need to expel or punish non-believers and the McCarthy witch-hunt.

Hancock then talked for twenty minutes about the ongoing 'conundrum' in Puritan America about fidelity to a God who could never be placated; someone who, according to the theological hierarchy of the colony, considered mortal man to be in a state of fallen grace and largely irredeemable. I thought immediately of my father and his own very Catholic belief that we were all screw-ups – him being the biggest of them all (not that he would ever admit that out loud, but I knew how often he beat himself up about so much). Just as my brother Adam was also silently infused with the sense that he could never meet the high bar set for him by life. Peter too was endlessly feeling judged. Were Mom's pronounced opinions on us all a way of deflecting her own sense of not cutting it, of being an also-ran in the American game of life?

This was one of the more extraordinary things about college: how a lecture like this one could open up so many thoughts about the realities of your own life; how you found yourself finally thinking in a way that was somewhat independent of everything to do with your background, even if you were very much still rooted in it all. And how the big jock whom you had passed by on the way into class – and whom you unfairly dismissed as a lughead – turned out to be thoughtful and smart.

But then there were the other extremes. A week after freshman rush for fraternities was over – and I chose to remain independent – Evan Kreplin invited me over to the Psi U house for dinner. I went up to his room – a small cell under the eaves of the roof, painted jet black – with three of his rather cool friends from the house. A bong was passed around. Evan was playing an English folk-rock group called Fairport

Convention on his stereo and the talk was about an anti-Nixon/ anti-war rally that was going to be staged in three days' time and to which everyone was going, and how the whole house was planning to go out and canvass around town for McGovern, and to hell what Gallup and the other pollsters said: our guy still could be president. Then we all went downstairs for dinner – and two of the ski-bum jocks in the house started a food fight, which everyone joined in. After being hit with a flying plate of baked beans I left, thinking: this school is dumb. Just as I also knew that it was learned and dazzling. Just as I also soon realized that I now had an ally in Professor Hancock.

Our second lecture was on the use of public punishment in the Massachusetts Bay Colony and Hancock related it to our obsession with punitive criminal justice; Nixon had recently declared a war on drugs, and Hancock quietly noted that all this 'war' was going to do was fill the jails with poor people. Toward the end of the class Bob O'Sullivan raised his hand and asked if there was a link between the more retaliatory nature of Puritanism and the same strand of vengefulness inherent in Roman Catholicism. Hancock said that was a most pertinent question and went off on a fast discourse about Jansenism – the bleakest form of Church of Rome thought – and how it so influenced the rigorous, guilt-ridden Catholicism practiced in Ireland.

'And in South Boston,' Bob O'Sullivan said, making everyone laugh, Professor Hancock included.

As we were leaving the class I told Bob:

'My dad from Prospect Heights in Brooklyn once said that the Christian Brothers beat the religion out of him. But what I've learned today is that the Jansenism of his education is still there.'

'My dad was knocked around by the Christian Brothers as well. No wonder he's a cop.'

'Mine's an ex-Marine who's never gotten over Okinawa and his super-disciplined Navy captain father.'

'Looks like we're cut from the same –'

'Not unless your mother happens to be Jewish.'

Bob O'Sullivan gave me a sardonic grin.

'You win that round.'

'Didn't know we were sparring.'

'I'll save the fisticuffs for someone like Polly Stevens.'

'Don't your frat brothers dream of women like that?'

'They do – which is why, beyond football and other sports and who's the hottest babe on campus, the conversational possibilities are limited.'

'And yet you're still a member of Beta,' I said.

'I conform to type. You're a freshman, right?'

'And you?'

'A junior. Might you be agreeable to studying with me sometime?'

I liked the way he phrased that. A definite come-on, albeit one couched in a hint of the cerebral. I regarded Bob carefully for a moment. Long hair, a scruffy half-beard, a blue work shirt over blue jeans. Not in any way fat, but large, imposing. I liked the fact that he wore a pair of thick black glasses which nonetheless looked interesting and ironic on him. I also liked the fact that he was two years ahead of me – and therefore knew his way around college life. But he was still a football player – and that was weird. Especially as the last person I ever considered flirting with was a big Irish jock from Southie, and one who spent a serious amount of time hanging out with knuckleheads. That was the strangest thing about college: how it was already making me rewrite certain rules I had for myself, and the way I had perceived so much.

'Sure we can study together,' I said, trying to mimic in my tone one of those tough dames I'd seen in 1940s detective films.

'Good stuff,' he said ... adding, with another of his wry smiles: 'I'll be in touch.'

'Cool,' I said.

As O'Sullivan walked out into the Indian-summer morning a voice behind me said:

'You clearly have an admirer.'

Oh God, Hancock! I spun around, expecting to be ridiculed for showing my interest in a linesman. But I saw benign amusement in his eyes.

'I wouldn't bet money on that, Professor,' I said.

'I would. One of the many admirable things about Mr O'Sullivan is that there is much going on within. Even though he has to pretend so much of the time that he's just a good fellow who knows how to catch and run.'

Then he handed me the essay I had submitted last week.

'An excellent essay,' he said. 'Really most impressive. Are you thinking of being a history major?'

'It had crossed my mind,' … though, truth be told, I came here thinking I'd be immersed in the world of literature. But again, the way I was looking at the world was shifting.

'We should have a chat at some point,' he said. 'I'm always on the lookout for talent.'

He let that comment land on me.

'Thank you, Professor.'

'I have office hours tomorrow from 2 to 4 p.m. Would that work for you?'

'Of course.'

'Very good then.' Gathering up his book bag he headed off.

I left Sills Hall feeling ever so slightly lightheaded. It was a beautiful day. I walked over to the union, thinking I needed a cup of their joe – which wasn't as bad as so much other institutional drip coffee I was to consume in the years to come. I found myself smiling and befuddled. Could anyone truly see something interesting and perhaps even original in me? I couldn't get my head around that.

Moving downstairs to the student mailboxes, I used the little key to pull out an envelope in which I found a rather cheesy postcard from Valparaiso in Chile, showing fishermen eyeing up local girls in peasant dress, the whole effect looking like Technicolor Carmen Miranda. I flipped the card over.

Sis – in Chile. Doing Dad's dirty work and wondering what I've gotten myself into. Don't show this card to anyone, don't tell Mom, and certainly don't tell Peter, but what's going on here … put it this way: I feel dirty.

I put the card down.

Dad's dirty work?

THAT POSTCARD FROM Adam continued to eat away at me. Especially as I'd written him one back – *Got your message ... tell me more* – but had yet to hear anything further from him.

When Dad showed up a month into the semester for Parents' Weekend with my mom, we had an hour together while Mom went off to buy me new sheets and towels (as she told me that the ones I'd purchased were 'beyond cheap and nasty'). As soon as Mom drove off in the family car I asked Dad:

'How's Adam getting on in Santiago?'

'The boy's doing well. I don't see him that much. He's up in Iquique most of the time. That's where the mine is, so Adam's in the center of the action. Handling some important business for us.'

'What kind of business?'

'Financial stuff you wouldn't understand.'

'Try me.'

'You're suddenly interested in international mining finance?'

'I'm interested in what Adam's up to.'

'Let Adam tell you.'

'But he's five thousand miles away, high up in the desert. And Adam isn't much of a writer.'

'He'll be home for Christmas. He can tell you all then.'

'Why can't you tell me now? Unless he's doing some sort of dirty work for you?'

'*Dirty work?*' Dad said, a dark uneasy laugh accompanying his scornful tone. 'You know nothing about our business down there.'

'But is it dirty business?'

Dad lit up a cigarette.

'All business is dirty,' he finally said, fixing me with a look that informed me: '*and that's the last word I'm going to say about any of this.*'

When I had a moment alone with my mother later that day I asked her if Adam was okay. She shot me a look.

'What do you know that I don't know?'

'I'm just wondering if he's doing all right.'

'My son calls me once every ten days and always tells me he is flourishing. But you're hiding something from me.'

'Mom ... '

'Don't Mom me. Tell me the truth.'

Yet another problem with telling my mother was that she turned into the FBI, refusing to give up until she'd rung all the information out of you. This was the central reason why I confided so little in her, and why even this slightest hint that you knew something of which she wasn't aware resulted in the Third Degree.

'If you don't tell me what Adam revealed to you, I'm telling your father.'

'If you do that it will just cause a fight between the two of you and more bad blood between us all. But go right ahead, Mom. The weekend's been pretty okay so far. No arguments yet – which is some kind of record for this family.'

Maybe she listened to me for a change. But when my parents were leaving the next morning, she took me in her arms and hissed into my ear:

'I'm going to get to the bottom of this.'

That was the absolute last I heard about it from her. Adam never responded to my postcard. In my subsequent weekly Sunday-night phone call with Mom she never went near the subject again, even though I now directly asked her what my brother was up to in Chile. Instead she started to demand why she sensed that Peter and I were no longer speaking. I dodged that one, telling her that all was well with the two of us, that we were back in contact. I had come to understand that, when it came to our family web, the evasion of truth was a necessary strategy. In fact, Peter had been in touch by letter, asking me if I could see a way of forgiving him, as he still regretted what had transpired and seriously missed me. This pleased me. I sent him a postcard of Hawthorne's *The Scarlet Letter* with a simple message: *I will get over this eventually, but you will have to give me time.* So, on a certain level, we were in contact again.

Lying next to Bob that evening, I told him the story of my visit to Bowdoin with Peter. When it became clear I wasn't talking to him because he slept with Shelley, Bob said:

'If you want my two cents on the subject: your brother acted like a typical guy. An attractive younger woman came on to him. He didn't say no. Yeah, it wasn't cool that he did it with the tour guide who showed you around the college, but she invited him over to her place. And he went. It's not like she just tripped and found herself on the end of his penis.'

'That's gross.'

'Hey, that's my Neanderthal side coming out. You need to let go of your considerable anger at so much.'

'I wonder if I'll ever stop being angry.'

'We can work on that together,' Bob said, letting his fingers cascade down my bare back, then leaning in and kissing me at a juncture on the nape of my neck that always made me on the spot amorous. Moments later I was atop him, marveling at the ease with which we moved together; the way our passion built. Bob was ardent and inventive. From our first night in bed together, he'd done something that was beyond Arnold's by-the-book idea of sex: he'd sent my desire into overdrive.

Being with Bob wasn't without its complications. I'd made it clear at the start of our relationship that there was no way I was stepping inside the jock fest that was the Beta Theta Pi fraternity. We had our trysts in my room, my roommate conveniently with her guy in his frat house most nights. We were discreet about it all. This was a mutual decision. I didn't want to advertise whom I was sleeping with. Similarly, Bob knew he would 'get a wicked amount of shit if the frat brothers got wind of the fact that he was sleeping with an 'egghead'. But then, during a discussion about a short-story submission with DJ over a bottle of Almaden Red and many cigarettes at the Ruffled Grouse, he intimated that he knew all about me and 'the Football Letterman'.

'I don't know what you are talking about,' I said, trying to disguise my discomfort and failing massively. A small smile crossed his lips, a smile I didn't like.

'Sure you don't,' he said. 'Because I bet you and the lughead think you've been discreet.'

'He's anything but a lughead,' I said, suddenly angry.

'And you've just revealed all,' smirked DJ.

When I recounted this to Bob, convinced now that if DJ knew everyone would know, he didn't seem the least bit concerned.

'I've heard nothing from anybody in the Beta house – and trust me, if they knew they'd be merciless. You shouldn't worry so much. My dad says arrogance always hides doubt. That's why you've got to simply thumb your nose at the frat boys and cheerleaders of the world. Or the intellectuals who believe you should only hobnob with their elite little group. They all exist to remind you how being different and perceptive places you ahead of the majority of the world.'

I found my arms tightening around Bob as he said all this. When he finished I kissed him long and deep, then said:

'You might be the first person who kind of gets me and I'm falling for you. Falling hard. It's making me feel very giddy and happy – which is a nice surprise, as happy is something I don't do very well. But it's also making me really anxious.'

'Because ... ?'

'Because I fear falling for you and we're so outwardly different, even though when together you are so beyond cool, and because I love making love to you, and because I am scared to be feeling all this stuff. Because ... '

Bob leaned over and took my face in his hands.

'Well, I'm falling for you. Which I think is very cool. Isn't it time we stop this clandestine stuff and are seen together around the college?'

I couldn't have been more stunned. Just as I loved the fact that Bob could be vulnerable with me, telling me later that same night he was always conscious about being 'the blockhead from Southie'; that his mother Irene was hyper-tense and prone to severe episodes where she would take to her bed all day and simply not get up (back in 1972 nobody spoke of depression), and had not been herself for years.

'I'm lucky with my father,' Bob said, 'even if he was disappointed that I didn't take the full football scholarship at Boston College, which is run by the Jesuits. Their team is a feeder to the NFL. You shine at Boston College you could be going pro by the time you're twenty-two. What Dad doesn't know is that I have no interest in going pro. I chose Bowdoin not just because they gave me the full ticket, but because it's academically high-powered. He doesn't know this, but next year I am going to start applying to grad school. I want to get a PhD in English literature. I want to be a professor.'

'But that's wonderful.'

'He'll be proud of me if I keep my grades up and can get the full ticket to an Ivy League doctorate program. But he'll also tell me that I'm letting myself in for a lifetime of being underpaid, and surely with my Bowdoin grades and athletic background, law would be a smarter choice. There's this ongoing belief that we should all be lawyers – because it's the safest ticket imaginable in American life. But I can now see myself, eight years from now, breaking my ass to pass my Massachusetts Bar exams and thinking: this is the last thing I want to be doing with my life.'

'Then don't do it. Be a professor. What would you specialize in?'

'My dream is to study with Harold Bloom at Yale – even though, when it comes to my area of expertise, I'm eventually going to become the guy to go to when it comes to Charles Dickens and the Victorian Novel. If, that is, I can get around Dad's disappointment.'

After this evening, Bob and I allowed ourselves to be seen together around the college. In a small place like Bowdoin word travels fast. Though we were still somewhat circumspect about being in any way affectionate with each other in public, we were no longer playing the clandestine game. As such, people started noticing. After an editorial meeting Sam asked me if I was thinking of becoming the first member of the *Quill*'s editorial board who was also going to minor in cheerleading. He said this with considerable irony. It lessened the cutting nature of this comment, not to mention the subtext that he was disappointed for DJ that I was now 'taken' (an expression I hated). Polly Stevens hissed 'Hello, lovebirds' when Bob and I walked in together for Professor Hancock's lecture. Even when

I met Hancock for an advisory meeting he let it be known that he knew all about my romance with the footballer.

'I'll tell you an anecdote from my past,' he told me one afternoon in his office. 'The summer before I started my doctorate I did a course on Anglo-Irish literature at Trinity College Dublin – a college I would definitely recommend you look into for a junior year abroad. Those two months in Dublin were something of a pleasant interlude for me, a chance to read Joyce *in situ*. Dublin was gray, wet, somber and completely wonderful if you gave in to the sense that you were in something very understandable and totally foreign at the same time. One thing I learned in Dublin was that everyone knows what everyone's had for breakfast. Bowdoin is even smaller – so, yes, word has gotten to me that you are stepping out with Mr O'Sullivan. To which I can only think: you're both lucky to have found each other.'

That was the moment when a certain intimacy developed between myself and Professor Hancock. And when, in turn, I began to confide in him. Much of the time we did discuss matters academic. But he quietly began to draw me out on my parents, my brothers, how I saw the world in all its messiness. He too was keen to share things with me. Such as his love of the piano rags of Scott Joplin, how he'd met his wife, 'the former Maryanne Cabot' – the daughter of a family so upper crust that they put the Brahmin into Boston – and how they married the summer that they graduated. They had three young boys – Theo Jr, Samuel, and Thomas – all under ten. He talked about his sailing boat – a thirty-six-foot yawl on which he escaped most weekends, trawling the Maine coast. It was clear that he'd been raised in a world of quiet, unostentatious privilege and I was amazed at the ease with which the personal began to mark our conversations. Hancock was always exceedingly correct with me. Though he called me by my first name, he never encouraged me to refer to him as Theodore. He was always 'Professor'.

There were hints here and there that he had trouble sleeping. He told me that he was often out of bed around 4 a.m., after only five hours, grading papers, preparing that day's lectures, listening to music. He said that I should become acquainted with the late string quartets of Beethoven and recommended that I buy the recording by the Amadeus Quartet. He was also a great advocate for Bombay gin, telling me that he drank one very dry martini a day, always made with that very English gin. I did borrow the Amadeus's recordings of the late Beethoven quartets from the music department's record library, and found them beautiful in a brooding, troubled way; my roommate asking me to 'turn down that gloomy music' on the rare occasions that she popped back into our dorm.

I was so flattered to be taken in to his quiet, somewhat tentative confidence. Did I see him as the first adult who ever treated me as something close to an equal? Or did that first swoon I felt at the start of the semester persist? The fifteen-year age difference at this juncture in my life seemed huge. I had a boyfriend – and one of whom Hancock approved. On one level ours was a formal friendship – and Hancock was hardly like that creep from the English department, Herb Coursen, who hit constantly on women, was known to turn nasty when turned down, and whose sexual antics seemed tolerated by the administration. By contrast Hancock was an impeccable gentleman – which made him that much more compelling. Did I sometimes think about having sex with him? Indeed I did – and this too tantalized and troubled me. But unlike certain students around the college who openly had affairs with professors I knew that I would never cross that line. Nor did Hancock ever do anything – a light touch on the hand, a casual invitation for a late-afternoon glass of wine – to indicate interest of anything but of a professorial/fatherly nature, even though I sensed he too felt there was an undercurrent between us ... and one which we were both going to dodge exploring at all costs.

'What are you doing for election night?' Professor Hancock asked me the afternoon before we cast our votes. I'd spent the week going door-to-door in Brunswick with Evan Kreplin, handing out 'McGovern for President' leaflets and encouraging the good citizens of Maine to vote for that rare species: an honorable, ethical politician, and one who had promised to end our monstrous, murderous folly in Vietnam.

It hadn't quite gone according to plan. Outside of people associated with the college, a few educated retirees, and a small number of hippies, the vast majority of locals either had long associations with the Naval Air Station or were simply the sort of flinty independent Mainers who were not going to take an individual like Evan in their stride. I was hardly a counterbalance to Evan's sartorial quirkiness and had brought out my wooden carved peace sign – attached to a chain of big psychedelic shaded beads – and draped it around my neck. How little did we realize that our hippie-dippy style would reinforce the belief that McGovern was the 'peacenik candidate', only supported by 'radicals, do-gooders, and pothead layabouts', as a very wizened old lady told us, her vehemence and nastiness catching us both by surprise. But we were both certain that, with just a little convincing, we could turn the tide of things and bring Maine into McGovern's electoral college column.

But when we had the door slammed in our faces by that old lady – who ended her rant with a truly choice comment: 'And another thing, young man – ten years ago, when Bowdoin only admitted upstanding young fellows, a freak like you would have been run out of town' – I realized how far we would have to go to get McGovern in.

'Don't know yet. I'll probably end up pulling the sheets over my head and refusing to leave bed if it turns out as badly as everyone thinks it will.'

'The problem is, Alice,' said Professor Hancock, 'that McGovern, for all his intelligence and probity, is unelectable. Nixon is devious and a man haunted by so much. But there is a realpolitik about him of which I approve. He is effectual – and not as right-wing as the Reagans and the Goldwaters.'

He was backing Nixon! That was unsettling. But when I told Bob about this exchange he wasn't surprised.

'Hancock is from old money. The sort of guys whom my father always considered the Boston ruling class. As much as he probably sees himself as a respectable liberal he's still very much establishment. McGovern is too anti-establishment for his tastes. What Hancock was telling you was: I'm holding my nose and voting for Nixon, as much as I hate having to do that.'

I had registered to vote in Maine – and went down to the local high school to mark the ballot paper for McGovern and every other Democrat up for state and national office. By 8 p.m. that night there was a crowd at the union gathering around a single old television set, listening to Walter Cronkite report that, even before the polls closed, Nixon was about to be re-elected to a second term as the 37th president of the United States, only this time with a landslide of historic proportions.

'Well, my father's probably celebrating with three martinis,' I told Bob.

'And my dad's toasting Nixon's win with Schlitz. It's the triumph of the Silent Majority – who actually believe we are God's favorite country and that anyone who has a dissenting opinion isn't a true American.'

Behind Bob came a voice – and one with a decidedly preppy honk.

'You going to make a speech on that subject in the locker room this Saturday – before you guys get your asses kicked again?'

Bob spun around and found himself facing a tall lanky guy with dirty blond hair, chinos, a red turtleneck, a tweed jacket, a *Nixon/Agnew '72* button in his lapel. I knew him immediately: Blair Butterworth Prescott – he went by all three names – a serious lacrosse player, and a member of Chi Psi.

'We plan to beat Colby on Saturday, Blair,' Bob said with a tight smile, 'and no, I won't be using the locker room the way you use being president of the Bowdoin branch of the Young Americans for Freedom as a way of perpetrating your own Republican agenda.'

'So says the Mick from Southie.'

There was a sudden silence around us. I saw Bob turn febrile with anger. Had he wanted to flatten Blair Butterworth Prescott after that comment, the Irish Jewish girl in me would have applauded. But I also knew that Prescott had the reputation of a provocateur, and prided himself on getting under the skin of anyone he considered fair game. Bob was on to this immediately. Especially as everyone in earshot of this comment was standing back, waiting to see how Bob would react. I could sense Bob counting to ten, taking in a deep steadying lungful of breath, then quietly turning to Prescott.

'The difference between you and me, Prescott, is that I got in here on my own merits, not on account of Daddy.'

Prescott looked thrown by that comment and by the low-level snickers that followed from the group of students huddled around that ancient Zenith television set, with a rabbit-ear antenna just about pulling in the local affiliate of CBS.

'Sore loser,' he said finally. To which a hippie-esque woman turned on him and said:

'Man, we're all losers tonight. Because what this election confirms is: we are so lost as a country that we've given another four years to a man as tricky and negative as Nixon.'

Everyone burst into applause, intermingled with a few cries of 'Right on'.

As Prescott stormed off I nudged Bob and said:

'Let's get a drink.' When we reached a bar downtown we splurged and ordered Michelobs – back then the most upscale of American beers. I drained half my bottle, then raised a subject I'd wanted to raise for some time.

'I'm not going to tell you what to do, who to hang out with, how to live your life. But do yourself a favor and get an apartment off-campus, and get away from those rah-rah guys. They're eventually going to pull you down.'

'Not if I don't let them.'

'The problem is: the herd mentality, the frat-boy mentality allows bad shit to happen – and maybe you'll be present when it goes down. Wasn't there a guy who fell off the roof of your house last year?'

'Yes,' Bob said. 'And he was a good friend. Bradley Mumford. You would have liked him. A swimmer. A bit of a loudmouth, full of swagger, smart as hell. A real brain when it came to the more obscure corners of economics. And amazing at the butterfly stroke. So amazing that the swimming coach was talking about getting him ready, in '74, for the Olympic trials. He decided to drop acid for the first time with a bunch of the resident flower children over at

Psi U. I gather all was cool when he was with them. When he got back to our house some sort of weird paranoia shit set in. He kept telling his frat brothers that some big dark presence was chasing him. They didn't realize he was tripping. Nor did I. He walked by my door, saying he was stepping out onto the roof, as he seriously needed a blast of fresh air. I told him: "It's like way below freezing tonight, man. Stay indoors." His spacey reply: "I need the cold. Because it will help me see clearly. And that clarity might just let me try an experiment with gravity." Stupid fucking me. It was late, it was winter, I'd been drinking and trying to write an essay on Swinburne, I just thought he was talking late-night trash. Ten minutes later I heard this crash outside my window and people screaming. He died on impact.'

I took Bob's hand in mine.

'And you blame yourself?'

'Totally. I was the last person to see him alive. He made that crack about experimenting with gravity ... '

'But it wasn't as if he was suicidal. And you didn't know he was tripping.'

'True – but he did sound a bit wasted. And he did say he was going out on the roof. And ... '

'What did you tell the college, the police?'

Bob hung his head. In a voice that started to crack he said:

'Nothing. I told them I was asleep when it all happened.'

There was a long terrible silence, during which Bob let go of my hand and turned away.

'Who knows about this?' I asked.

'No one ... until now.'

'Why me?'

'Because ... I didn't want this secret to be there, something that I was keeping from you.'

What I thought was: *but now I have to live with it.* What I said was:

'I'm glad you told me.'

'Even though you will now want nothing to do with me.'

'Did I say that?'

'But I let my friend die!'

So did I.

'Kill the Catholic school guilt, Bob. I've told you many times about Carly and how I still feel I could have done more to save her. The guilt for me is still there. Especially as her body was never found – and I have to keep hoping that I am going to get a phone call from my mother one day saying that Carly's been discovered in some hippie retreat way down in Mexico. I understand why you blame yourself for your friend's death – even though you know you too are still beating yourself up for something that you did not cause. Truth be told, you were also right to say nothing – because it would have simply landed you in one of those situations where, even though the only person to blame for Bradley's death was himself, you would have been accused of so much. That's how the world works. *We can't blame the guy who went out high on a roof and fell off, because he's dead. So let's blame the last guy who saw him alive.*'

Bob spun around and buried his head in my shoulder.

'You're amazing,' he said.

'Because I might be one of the few Americans of our age group who thinks that most moral situations can't be defined in black-and-white terms?'

'Or perhaps because you simply *are* amazing. Tell you what: I'll leave the animal house at the end of this semester ... but only if you agree to live with me off-campus. I know what I'm proposing is kind of big. But here's the thing: I get out of the frat house, you get off-campus, which I know you want to do desperately ... and we kind of suit each other, don't we?'

'We do indeed.'

'We have romance, passion, but we also truly like each other. That's the hat-trick.'

'You jock.'

'Guilty as charged. Shut up and kiss me.'

Later that night, clinging to each other in my single bed, I couldn't help but have that ever-present negative neighbor in my head whisper to me: '*Do you really think you know what you're doing here? Rushing in and setting up house with a guy after being together for only a couple of weeks?* The doubts began to ricochet around me. So much so that when I got up to fetch a cigarette and pour us both a little wine, Bob sat up and said:

'Let me guess – you're suddenly thinking: this is all too fast.'

'Am I that transparent?'

'Aren't we all?'

'I want this. But I'm also scared.'

'So am I. But here's the thing: we don't have to treat this as "now and forever". We can simply see how it goes … but still try to make it wonderful.'

'No pressure, eh?' I said. 'Quite an election night.'

'At least some good came out of it. And thank you … '

'For what?'

'For not freaking when I told you about my terrible secret.'

'My mom said something to me when my friend went missing and I kept telling myself that there was something more I could have done to have saved her: "Guilt is like a car out of control. It smashes into everything during its own weird trajectory."'

'Amen to that,' Bob said.

'Let's start apartment-hunting on Saturday.'

The following afternoon, just before his lecture, Professor Hancock motioned me over, asking if I could drop by his office later on. He looked tired, a little sleep-deprived. I wondered if he'd been up late watching the election results. But as the election was called by 8 p.m. Eastern Standard Time that was unlikely.

Hancock went ahead and gave his lecture on the lack of any voting rights in the Massachusetts Bay Colony outside of the Puritan Elect, who were deemed righteous and pure enough to be allowed to mark a ballot paper.

Whatever about the sense of fatigue that I gleaned before the lecture started, within minutes of beginning he had found his usual mellifluous and interesting groove – and we were all transfixed. 'Spiritual purity, a non-dissenting voice, an unblemished life and ingratiating yourself with the colony's theocratic ruling class … this is how you won the right to vote in John Winthrop's Massachusetts,' Hancock noted, adding to widespread laughter: 'No doubt our just re-elected vice president, Spiro Agnew, would fully approve of such electoral methodology. After all, if you do not subscribe to his view of patriotism, his world view, you are a bad American.'

Hancock packed up his briefcase quickly after the lecture and left in more of a hurry than usual. Thirty minutes later I nervously tapped on the door of his office in Hubbard Hall.

He was behind his desk, cleaning his glasses with a handkerchief. Without his usual horn-rims on his face he looked vulnerable, uncertain.

'Ah, Alice, thank you for coming by.'

He motioned for me to sit in the narrow hard-backed chair opposite his desk.

'Does my voice sound harsh, scratchy to you?' he asked.

'I hadn't noticed, Professor.'

'Are you sure about that? Because it certainly sounds harsh and scratchy to me.'

'I really thought you sounded great this afternoon.'

'You're being kind. To me I sounded like some shortwave radio from Eastern Europe, full of static. Last Friday I had to go have a polyp removed from my throat. Yesterday the results of the biopsy came back. The polyp was malignant. I have cancer.'

7

CANCER. THAT IMMENSE, terrible word. Professor Hancock was so quiet and dignified as he explained to me the ramifications of his condition in his office.

'My oncologist told me: when it comes to cancer it's often genetic roulette,' he said, his gaze directly on me. 'Given my age and the fact that I have never smoked a cigarette there is no reason why this polyp should have shown up near my larynx. "Just bad luck,"' the oncologist said. The fact that the biopsy came back positive … the ramifications, I'm afraid, are huge.'

'How huge?' I asked, my voice tentative, anxious – as I didn't know if I should be posing such a question. But Hancock didn't seem thrown by this. On the contrary he clearly needed to talk with me about it.

'The worry is whether the cancer has metastasized.'

'I don't know that word, Professor.'

'Metastasized means: to osmose, to permeate, to spread into other organs and cause death.'

A long silence followed.

'Are you dying, Professor?' I finally asked.

'That is the big question. According to the oncologist a cancerous polyp like this one has a 60 percent probability rate of metastasizing. If it's gone to my lungs, my brain … '

He turned away, looking out at the gray afternoon beyond his office window. 'You won't die, Professor,' I said, my voice no more a whisper.

'That is the hope … '

'You *can't* die.'

Without thinking I reached out and took his hand. Hancock flinched, thrown by this gesture. Then, after grasping it back for a moment – a form of acknowledgment – he withdrew his hand from mine. I wanted the floor to open and for me to disappear.

'I'm sorry, Professor … '

'No need to be,' he said. 'I acknowledge ... '

But he didn't finish that sentence. Instead he lowered his head. Another silence filled his office. One I didn't dare break ... because I didn't know what else to say. Instead he made the next comment:

'I apologize for burdening you with this.'

'I so appreciate ... '

Now it was my turn to not finish the sentence.

'I know I can trust you, Alice. Which is why I know you won't speak a word about this to anyone ... even to your very nice fellow. Nor will we venture onto this subject again.'

'But when you have definite news ... '

'When I have the prognosis ... yes, I will share that with you. Until then ... '

'Don't worry, Professor. I can keep a secret.'

'I know that. Thank you.'

With a quiet nod he indicated that our meeting was over.

Once outside I felt myself sideswiped by all that had just transpired. Professor Hancock dying? Rushing off campus, heading toward Maine Street and then walking directionless into downtown Brunswick, I was fighting tears. This was all too unfair, too cruel. I kept playing over and over that moment, after I took his hand, when he whispered: 'I acknowledge ... ' Was he just thanking me for that brief physical gesture of solidarity? Or was he recognizing that unspoken realm between us; the allure we both felt ... which would never be anything more than that: *an allure?*

I must have walked around Brunswick for a good hour, trying to find a way through the emotional jumble of the moment. I wanted to run to Bob and tell him all. But that would have betrayed Hancock's insistence that this remained between ourselves. Just as I was fearful that, were I to begin to explain to Bob the depth of my distress right now, he would think: she really is in love with him.

So I got my distress under control and met Bob at the union and acted as if nothing had transpired during that after-class meeting with Hancock. Two days later, upon finishing his lecture, Hancock indicated that he'd like a word with me. As soon as everyone was out of the lecture theater he turned to me and said:

'I feel terrible about dropping you into this health crisis of mine.'

'I feel terrible for you, Professor.'

Another of his quiet acknowledging nods. Then:

'For the moment we're going to not speak further about any of this. I'm not saying: let's pretend the conversation didn't happen. It did happen – and you couldn't have been kinder to me.'

'But I did nothing, Professor.'

'You listened. You showed empathy. That is immense. But now ... the matter is closed.'

Because he feared getting too close to me? Because I showed my hand by taking his hand? Because, perhaps, he'd let his New England guard down for a moment and this was now his way of dealing with the nightmare in which he was living?

I had no direct answers to these questions – and I knew I might just spark a breach between us were I to raise any of these thoughts with him. I simply replied:

'I understand, Professor.'

And the matter of his cancer was never raised again between us.

Later that month Bob and I found an apartment on a somewhat ramshackle corner of Brunswick that went by the rather ironic name of Pleasant Street. It was the second floor of a green-shingled house that needed an urgent paint job. The flat was probably no more than six hundred square feet. But the previous tenant – a Philosophy major named Sylvester who was graduating a semester early – had slapped several coats of white paint on its once dismal interior. He was most reasonable when it came to letting us buy all his not bad furniture for one hundred dollars cash. He even offered to leave us his plates, silverware, glasses and kitchen stuff for an extra twenty-five bucks. The monthly rent was seventy-five dollars, utilities about another twenty-five. Bob and I loved the place on first sight, especially as Sylvester had bought an old brass bed and painted it black, not to mention a big couch covered in brown velour. As soon as I saw the bed I was hearing Dylan in my head ('Lay lady lay, lay across my big brass bed'), and seeing me and Bob making love there. Just as I also thought immediately about the posters we could tape to the walls, a couple of Chianti-bottle lamps and a cinder-block and wood-planks bookshelf we could add to the place. Student domestic bliss.

After writing out a couple of checks to Sylvester, Bob and I went to the Miss Brunswick Diner for grilled-cheese sandwiches. We toasted our crazy, wondrous decision to set up life together with a bottle each of Mabel.

'So,' said Bob, 'I told the Beta house last night I was leaving.'

'Wow,' I said. 'How did they take the news?'

'Not well. One of my fraternal brothers called me a traitor. Because by leaving I've resigned my membership, effective at the end of this semester. I think if football season didn't have another two weeks to run they'd have asked me to leave now.'

'So much for all that talk about bonds of brotherhood never being broken.'

'Their point of view is: you're either with us or not.'

'Isn't that how the Mafia works?'

'What's the Mafia?' Bob asked. 'No such group exists in my hometown of Boston.'

I did smile.

Deciding it might be safer to tell my father first about my new domestic arrangement I rang him at his office. He sounded hassled, but accepted the collect-call charges, telling me he was flying out to Santiago again in a few hours, 'and please tell me you've called to say that you voted for Nixon and are overjoyed by his victory'.

'I actually called to tell you that I'm about to save you six hundred dollars next semester.'

'Well, that's nice news! And how are you going to do that, sweetheart?'

'I'm moving off-campus.'

A long pause on the other end of the line, during which I heard the sharp click of my dad's Zippo opening and closing – a sure sign he was lighting up a Pall Mall. Finally, he said:

'Are freshmen allowed to live off-campus?'

'After their first semester they are.'

'By yourself?'

'Actually I'm going to be living with my boyfriend.'

Dad's reaction was somewhat explosive.

'Boyfriend? Boyfriend! Are you crazy?'

'No – because he is wonderful.'

'You are just eighteen, you've just left home, and ... who the fuck is this guy? Give me his address so I can break both his legs.'

'Please, Dad, hear me out ... '

'Let me guess: he's some Weatherman anarchist on the run. Or worse yet a hippie asshole with the hair and the beads and the stoned asshole smile.'

'His name is Bob O'Sullivan, his father is a fireman in South Boston, and he's the starting linebacker on the Bowdoin football team.'

'Now you are bullshitting me.'

'When I bring him home for Thanksgiving –'

'You expect me to welcome this guy?'

'I expect nothing, Dad. What I would like, if possible, is a little bit of understanding.'

'*Understanding*? Your fucking generation is so fucking childish. You make decisions that run contrary to how the rules work, then ask for "understanding". You want understanding. Maybe you think me a "square", not to mention a warmonger, who believes "My Country – Love It or Leave It". I think: an eighteen-year-old girl has no business living with someone outside of marriage. You want to get married now – which I personally think would be screwy – that's another matter. But living in sin ... call me an old-school Catholic, but no, I'm not allowing this. Not on my nickel. Conversation closed.'

And he slammed down the phone.

I was just a little bit thrown by his reaction. Intimidated and scared I went over to the library and put my head on Bob's shoulder, trying not to sob. He stopped work immediately and took me outside, to a bench on a quiet corner of the central quad, letting me clutch his left hand as I smoked one Viceroy after another. All that transpired in that phone call came rushing out. When I finished Bob just shrugged and said:

'I didn't want to bring this up today, but I told my father about our move last night. He essentially said the same thing.'

'Maybe we should get them together, let them drink beer and martinis and trade war stories, and talk about how "the youth of today" are so overindulged, and need a real war and a real Depression to teach them a thing or two about real life.'

Bob smiled.

'No doubt they will eventually meet. No doubt they'll probably like each other. Just as I know my dad's going to like you, and I bet your old man won't disapprove of me.'

'He'll really approve of you, amazed I've hooked up with someone who isn't Jimi Hendrix or Che Guevara.'

'So you're calling me "normal"?'

'Hardly. Just ... I should have told Mom first. She was the one who got me on the pill. Mom isn't all anxious when it comes to sex.'

'Then why didn't you make that initial call to her?'

'Because I knew that the admission I was moving in with you would have caused her to get hysterical. Precisely because you're Irish, Catholic, working class. Everything that Dad is. Mom fell for all that when she was in her early twenties. She's been regretting it ever since.'

'Fear not: your dad will get over this. He won't disown you.'

'He may try to cut me off.'

'Then we'll both get campus jobs, and find some way of making the rent. But he's not going to go there. These Irish, Depression-era guys – they were raised by fathers who believed that good parenting meant "my way or the highway". But you're his one and only daughter. He'll come around.'

It was Adam who came around – showing up unannounced and unexpected that weekend, calling me from a gas station near Lewiston to say that he'd decided to drop in on his sister and he was going to find a cheap motel in the Brunswick area, 'because I don't want to impose on your privacy' (translation: 'I know you're sleeping with some guy, so I'm not going to ask to crash on your floor').

'It is more than a relief to be finally talking with you,' I said.

'And nice hearing your voice,' he said, dodging the subject behind my comment. 'Isn't there a football game tomorrow?' he asked.

'Yeah – we're playing Trinity,' I told him, 'and my boyfriend Bob is –'

'– the starting linebacker?'

'You have been well briefed.'

'Don't worry about Dad. He's just being his usual hard-assed self. And Mom, believe it or not, is onside with you on this one. Told me herself yesterday.'

So that's why Adam was showing up this weekend – to check out whether or not Bob was appropriate for me.

'I thought you were in Chile,' I said.

'Still am – and loving it. Just back stateside for ten days.'

'And you only tell me now? Did you ever get my postcard down there, asking you for an explanation about "Dad's dirty work"?'

'Never reached me. Just for the record: the copper business isn't really a dirty business. I was merely using a turn of phrase.'

'You're a bad liar.'

'Think what you like, sis. See you tonight?'

I fretted considerably about whether I would ever learn the truth about what my father and brother were actually up to in that corner of South America. Just as I was worried what Bob might say about my brother 'just dropping by' on the spur of the moment, and for obvious ulterior reasons.

But Bob was coolness itself about it all.

'Let's get him stoned and drunk, let me bring him over to the Beta house for a few hours after the game on Saturday, and ask him lots of questions about the situation in Chile.'

We dropped in on a Psi U party, all ending up on a waterbed, with Adam a little startled to see his little sister smoking a joint, but also getting into an intense conversation with a New York guy named Carl who leapt in ferociously when he discovered that Adam was working for an American mining company in Chile. I listened with increasing distress as Adam struggled to defend the US presence in the Chilean copper mining industry and to put up simplistic arguments about the socialist government of Salvador

Allende ('Castro came and stayed three months … it's gonna be another dictatorship … they can't run a mining operation like ours without American knowhow'). Carl ruthlessly dismembered his middling statements. When Adam hit him with a riposte – 'Maybe you should stop believing all the Marxist stuff you read in the *Nation* and actually come down and see the place for yourself' – Carl leveled him:

'The truth, my friend, is that I spent all last summer in Santiago, working as an intern in the Chilean Ministry of Trade.'

Then he began to address Adam in fluent Spanish, testing his command of the language. Adam failed miserably. It was clear that, after three months in Chile, he had made no progress whatsoever.

'So let me get this straight,' Carl was saying, all smiles, 'though you know about Milton Friedman you have no idea whatsoever about the Chicago School of supply-side economics that the right wing in Chile want to impose?'

'Stop talking your theoretical horseshit,' Adam said angrily.

'No need to get tetchy, my friend,' Carl said, still smiling. 'Especially as I am simply probing your extensive knowledge of things Chilean, as befits a clearly brilliant man who has gleaned and absorbed so much of the socio-economic dynamic of a culture while aiding and abetting in its exploitation … '

Adam stood up. I thought he might throw a punch but he stopped himself before doing anything crazy. I too was on my feet. So was Bob. I reached for my brother's hand, but he pulled it away, not wanting to appear to need comfort. When I glanced in his eyes what I saw was the sort of hurt and sadness that defined so much about him. How it gutted me to see him vulnerable, defeated, humiliated. He stormed off, Bob in pursuit. I turned on the smug Marxist, sipping his neat vodka.

'You should be in Albania, keeping people in chains. You've got the right cruel streak for that.'

Outside I found Bob, a hand on Adam's shoulder, talking quietly, steadying him. Bob signaled that I should give them a few minutes. I walked to the street, climbed up on the roof of a parked VW Beetle, stared up at the heavy night sky, still fuming at the pitilessness of that super-clever New York smartass, yet also frustrated with my brother weighing into an argument with so little knowledge or assurance to defend his corner. Poor Adam – he showed his limitations far too readily. The truth was, I knew him to be not stupid. But confidence – that key to so much in life, and which he once had in abundance – was no longer something he could muster.

After a few minutes they came over to the car.

'Sorry I couldn't hold my own, sis,' Adam said hesitantly. 'I'm kind of beat after the drive up here. I'll be okay after I crash out.' He gave me a fast hug and then headed off in search of his Buick.

By the next afternoon, in Bowdoin's football stadium, Adam was buoyant, upbeat.

'Beautiful day, right?'

'That it is.'

'For the record,' said Adam as we headed to the bleachers, 'I spoke to the old man this morning. And to Her Royal Yentaness. They have been told, unconditionally, that Robert O'Sullivan is good news; that they should be pleased for you.'

'How did they take it?'

'Terribly, of course.'

I couldn't help but laugh, pleased that my brother's sardonic side was back on show after such a very long time. Especially as he added:

'I told Dad to say a decade of the rosary, that it might make him feel better. His reply was very Irish Catholic. He told me to fuck off.'

I laughed again.

'Come on, the game's about to start,' I said.

We took our seats in the bleachers, me waving hello to several of Bob's friends.

'So you do know some jocks.'

'His pals, not mine. As you've probably heard I've never been across the threshold of the Beta house. Now that he's leaving I'm probably considered Typhoid Mary, the illness that took their frat brother away.'

'You know I was a frat guy at St Lawrence.'

'I remember.'

'We were a bunch of loud, obnoxious morons. To leave that tribe – to go independent as your guy is doing – is essentially telling everyone in your tribe: I can do better. The truth is: he can and will do better out of there. Not that I could have admitted that as Bob has done. But I'm not as smart as Bob.'

'Don't say that.'

'Why not? It's the truth. He's as smart as you are – and that's saying something. Peter's off-the-charts brilliant too. Me: I'm the good-time Charlie. Never the guy with his nose in a book. Never the great achiever. Always wondering what I should be doing in life. Always thinking: I'm not good enough to cut it at much.'

'But you seem to be flourishing in Chile.'

'Flourishing? Hey, it's kind of cool being up in the Atacama Desert. It's right near the Andes, so we're talking high country. Real high country. I've learned to ride a horse. Me on a horse in a desert, six thousand feet up in South America. It's kind of magic. And I've started taking hikes with one of the locals, Alberto, most weekends. He's a cool guy. Kind of our fixer.'

'By which you mean?'

'He's the go-between when it comes to the mine workers and their bosses, the cops and the madams in the local whorehouses.'

'There are whorehouses in the Atacama Desert?'

'It's a mining town. Naturally there are whorehouses.'

'Which you patronize?'

A nervous shrug of the shoulders.

'What can I say except: there aren't exactly a lot of available women up there. It gets lonely.'

'And what exactly is the work you're doing?'

Another nervous shrug. Then:

'Business stuff. Not that interesting.'

'Try me.'

'I'm back and forth to Santiago a lot. Coordinating cash flow, budgets, that kind of thing. Truth be told if I was doing this sort of work in upstate New York I'd find it beyond dull. Down there, in South America ... well, I tell myself sometimes I'm living in a novel.

Especially as no one knows what's going to happen with Allende. Nationalization has started. There's a lot of talk that we could be taken over in a year, tops. Also: the rumor mill has it that he's creating his own KGB: a secret police to weed out anyone who's not for his regime.'

'He won the election, right?'

'With a minority vote.'

'Because there were two other parties running, right? The election wasn't rigged, was it? So that means he was democratically elected. Which also means you can't call his government a regime.'

'Even if they are just that. Give it two years and the place will be exactly like Cuba. No freedom. Travel restrictions. You're either with the Party or you're an enemy of the state.'

'Sounds like Dad has been working on you.'

'Give me some credit for being able to make up my own mind about such things.'

'Sorry. But Dad – do you see a lot of him?'

'He's back and forth between the mine, Santiago and New York all the time. Occasionally we find time to have a couple of Pisco Sours. Otherwise he leaves me be.'

'And the "dirty work" he does?'

'I explained that on the phone.'

'You evaded an answer.'

'Our mine is being nationalized. We have to bribe people high up in the government to keep our hand in. Socialists like money under the table just like everyone else. Does that answer your question?'

'I suppose so,' I said, not at all convinced but also realizing that I was not going to get the straight response I wanted. Instead I asked: 'Are you happy being there?'

'Not a lot of people to hang out with. No TV up there. No movies. Kind of limits my evenings.'

'Try reading.'

'Never really my thing.'

The game started. The subject of Adam in Chile was closed. The football was tense and brutal. The players from Trinity liked to hit hard, and weren't averse to dirty grabs and the occasional under-cut. But the Bowdoin boys hit harder – and when some defensive linesman punched Bob in the solar plexus, a ref saw it and turned a blind eye when Bob slammed his right cleated boot onto the guy's arch. Bob even managed to run back a thirty-yard touchdown from a fumble he scooped up before charging toward the end zone. We were all up on our feet screaming as he made that fantastic play, and it helped push Bowdoin over the top for a 21–17 victory. When we walked toward the players as the last whistle sounded, Adam nudged me and said:

'Your guy did good. Better than good. And who could imagine my bookish little sis cheering a football player on? You look really happy.'

I was ... even though there was still fear of strings attached, ties that bind. At Thanksgiving I agreed to go down and meet Bob's parents. His mother, Irene, was just out of the psych ward at Brigham and Women's Hospital in Boston, and had undergone shock therapy. She was a slight, subdued woman, an apron always over her housedress. The shock treatments had left her vague; placid in a disoriented way. I thought about Mom – and how, for all her craziness, I never wanted to see her subjected to such monstrous treatment. An extreme mother was better than one who had been mentally neutered.

'Do you play on the team with Bobby?' Irene asked me.

'Not yet,' I said, a comment which got a laugh out of his father, Sean. I could see him initially being suspicious of me. Writing me off as an arty type, independent, dressed in a style that he considered unfeminine. At first I thought he was just a large, imposing fireman with a deep South Boston accent, a gold cross around his neck, a substantial beer belly, and a gruffness that belied an evident affection for his son. Outside of the Irish Catholic blowhard stuff he was, I came to discover, a kind, decent man, ferociously proud of Bob, very much up on current affairs and not as closed-minded as I suspected. When he found out I could hold my own drinking Jameson's – and that I didn't get all self-righteous and offended in the wake of his occasional flashes of conservatism – he started to decide I was all right. Driving us to South Station for the train down to Connecticut he turned to his son and said:

'You can forget all those objections I raised about you moving in with a lady.'

'I wouldn't exactly call Alice a "lady".'

'Well, she's not exactly a broad.'

I nearly coughed up a lungful of smoke when he said this, laughing and taking pulls on the bottle of Guinness that he'd thrust upon me before we left the house. Sean himself was downing one as he negotiated us through the empty streets of Boston on the day after Thanksgiving. It was eleven in the morning and we were drinking. I found that kind of cool. On the train south I turned to my boyfriend and said:

'Your dad's kind of okay.'

'He's borderline racist, and sentimental, and trapped ... and I love him a lot. So ... glad you approve. My mom, on the other hand, is off with the fairies. Which, God strike me dead for saying this, is an improvement on the ever-angry, crazy woman she once was.'

'That's the first time I've ever heard you invoke God.'

'Every Irish Catholic boy is taught: even if your mother is an almighty monster – as mine used to be – you can never utter a bad word about her without acknowledging your sin.'

I reached over and took Bob's hand.

'Parents are a killer.'

Unlike Sean O'Sullivan, who didn't object to me sharing his son's bed, my father made it very clear before our arrival that my boyfriend was going to take the guest bedroom when he arrived with me – 'and there's going to be no sneaking around after dark, got that?' Upon arriving, after being shown the other bedroom, Bob assured my dad that he would respect his wishes. Just as he immediately flattered my mother by telling her that, judging from her book collection, she had excellent taste in literature. Seeing that she had a copy of *Rabbit Redux* by the chair in the living room where she did most of her reading, he engaged her in a long, animated discussion about whether Updike was the more impressive short-story writer when compared to Cheever. But then she turned back to me and mentioned that Cindy Cohen would love to see me this weekend – 'but I suppose you're too busy to pay her a call.' I tensed, terrified that this was the moment that Mom would start dealing out the guilt cards, knowing full well that I had backed off contact with Carly's mom because it unnerved me, bringing back all the guilt and horror of my friend's disappearance and apparent death. Bob, bless him, read this immediately (especially as I had told him all about Mrs Cohen's need to contact me constantly in the wake of Carly vanishing). Before I could answer Mom's reproach he mentioned that he was thinking of doing an independent study next semester on Sinclair Lewis. Mom was engaged by all this, bringing up how, when she was at Connecticut College in the mid-1940s, she was obsessed with John Dos Passos's *U.S.A.*

Somewhere in the midst of all this my father nudged me and asked:

'You sure he plays football?'

I'd never seen Mom so charmed by someone. Though not outwardly flirtatious, I could tell that she was just a little blindsided by Bob. Especially as he took her seriously and engaged her intellectually. Dad was even more bemused by this, telling me:

'Your guy knows how to ingratiate himself with the ladies.'

'He's just very smart.'

'So you're serious about him?'

'I am moving in with him, Dad.'

'So I heard.'

'You said you were cutting me off because I'll be living in sin. Which is fine by me. The college library has offered me a job. Twenty hours a week, two dollars an hour. I can make the rent with that. I went to the Student Finance Office. They told me I can get a loan for my tuition for the next two and a half years – and I've got twenty years to pay it off after I graduate. Professor Hancock even told me he will do whatever he can to get me a scholarship.'

'Who's this Professor Hancock guy?'

'Maybe the most brilliant man I've ever met.'

My father flinched.

'That's some statement.'

'He also thinks pretty highly of me.'

'Is he trying to get into your pants?'

'Jesus, Dad ... '

'Just a question.'

'With the implication: if he thinks me smart he must be trying to fuck me.'

'No need for that language, young lady.'

'No need for the sexism.'

'That's not sexism. That's a legitimate paternal concern. So let me guess: he's a totally honorable guy, beyond reproach?'

I felt a wave of self-consciousness hit me, still managing to say:

'That he is.'

Dad smiled a sour smile.

'What I'm hearing is: you've got a thing for this guy.'

'That's not fair,' I hissed, a blush cascading across my face. We were out of earshot of my mother and Bob when this exchange took place. I raised my voice slightly to drive home the following point: 'If my father is going to withdraw financial funding for my education, this professor – who rates my intelligence and that is it – will step in to help. Because, unlike my father, he believes in me.'

Dad hissed back at me:

'No need to tell the world I was being a hard-ass.'

'Here's the thing, Dad. I don't want you to feel in any way beholden to support me. Especially as you think I'm making a morally compromised choice.'

'I never said that.'

I smiled, rolling my eyes heavenward. Dad scowled.

'All right, I did say that. Now I want you to ignore it. Can you do that? Now you have your old man all apologetic.'

'No need to apologize, Dad. No need to pay my way ... '

'You're something, aren't you? Too bad you want nothing to do with law school. You'd be a great prosecuting attorney, making the guy in the stand sweat bullets.'

'That's not my objective here, Dad.' I needed to change the subject. 'When's the next trip to Chile?'

'Tuesday,' he said, and I sensed he couldn't wait to be out of here and back south of the border.

'How's Adam doing down there?'

'Great, as far as I can tell.'

'By which you mean ... more dirty work?'

'You can't stop, can you?'

'Evasiveness brings out the stubborn Irish girl in me. Will he be coming back for Christmas?'

'He might have other plans,' Dad said. 'And your other brother is planning to hang out with his new do-gooder girlfriend up in Montreal.'

'Peter has a new girlfriend?'

'You guys still not talking?'

I just shrugged.

'He must have done something really bad if you're shutting him out like this.'

'We'll get around it all ... eventually.'

'Which is your way of telling me: "Dad, stay out of it."'

'I have something of an unforgiving streak,' I said, knowing privately that I was being too hard on my brother, but still finding it hard to dislodge myself from the thought: he didn't have to run off with the college tour guide ... especially at a moment when, in the wake of all that just happened in Old Greenwich, I was feeling so vulnerable and in need of older-brother protection.

'You unforgiving?' Dad asked. 'I wonder where you inherited that from?'

The two days passed reasonably – thanks, largely, to Bob's ability to put my parents at their ease. How interesting to discover that an outsider of my generation could charm two people who were endlessly combustive and who seemed to suck me into their vortex. Both my parents insisted on driving us together up to Stamford on early Sunday morning for the slow train back to Boston and onwards thereafter by bus to Brunswick. Hugging me goodbye on the station platform Dad whispered in my ear:

'I always knew you'd find the right sort of Irishman.'

Mom being Mom she was even more direct:

'If you lose this guy I'll never forgive you.'

Bob shook hands with Dad, and embraced my mother as she pronounced, in a voice loud enough for me to hear:

'She really doesn't deserve you.'

Then we were in the second-class carriage, watching the Connecticut suburbs roll by.

'That went pretty well,' Bob said.

'Until Mom had to put the knife in with that final comment.'

'The good thing about being at college is that we can largely slam the door on all that.'

Wishful goddamn thinking. Back at Bowdoin we were both very 'heads down' during the highly pressured final three weeks of the academic term. After all exams and term papers were handed in we spent the last few days of the semester packing up our respective rooms and moving everything down to Pleasant Street. Sylvester had left the previous week for Germany – and we discovered rather quickly that, though superficially orderly, he was not exactly the best housekeeper. The refrigerator had congealed food everywhere. There were roaches embedded in the kitchen cabinets ('I thought cockroaches were just a New York thing,' I told Bob), and the sinks and bathtub and toilet were stained in all sorts of disgusting ways. Before we unpacked we borrowed a friend's car, picked up a variety of cleaning materials, and set to work removing all grime while also fumigating the place to kill off the insect population. This took one very long day, after which we celebrated by falling into our freshly made double bed and making mad crazy love, then taking a bath together and drinking bottles of Michelob while clinging to each other amidst the bubbles.

'The last thing I ever expected to do my first year at Bowdoin was to be thorough-cleaning an apartment with my live-in boyfriend.'

'And one who is now officially retired from the game of football.'

'When did you decide that?'

'Just yesterday, when Coach Mattinger called me into his office and asked me why I was leaving the Beta house, and began to tell me that I didn't seem as focused this season as I did the previous two, and he heard I was now hanging out with some "hippie intellectual" – his exact words. That's when I told him to deal me out; that I was done with the team.'

'Just because he made that comment?'

'Three seasons is enough. Leave on a high and all that – not that a 3–7 final season is exactly a high. Still, five touchdowns and eight interceptions during this final autumn season – I can live with that.'

'Why did you wait until tonight to tell me this?'

'Just wanted to find the right moment.'

'Because, *what*? You thought I wouldn't be able to handle it.'

'Hey, what's with the tone?'

'Hey, what's with waiting almost a day and a half before letting me know that you made a crucial decision? I mean, I bet Mattinger told his assistant coaches, and I'm sure you made reference to leaving the team when you had your goodbye dinner with your Beta brothers. Everyone knew about it before me.'

As I was saying this I could see Bob glancing upward at the ceiling, his gaze very much away from mine, as if he were studying the condensation from our bath on the whitewashed wall above us. There was a very long silence when I finished, during which it was clear that Bob was thinking about what to say next.

'Part of me is sad about the fact that an important part of my life is over, and that I've left what I've come to see as a very safe world.'

'Do you blame me for this?' I asked.

'It was my decision, mine alone. But, hey, am I not allowed to mourn it a bit?'

'Of course you can. I understand what's going on – and how it's all a bit of a jolt. And here we are playing house – which I find pretty weird too.'

'You're regretting it already?' he asked.

'Hardly. I love this place – even more since we got rid of the roaches from under the sink and the shit stains from the toilet. And we just made love in that big brass bed. And I'm sitting in the bathtub with you. And I'm trying to get my head around the idea that this is good, that I might be experiencing something close to happiness ... which, coming from my family, is something of a foreign country for me.'

'It's new territory for me as well.'

He leaned over and kissed me on the lips.

'You're right. I should have told you first. Sorry.'

'And I'm sorry if I just got all domestic and marital. Fuck, I sounded like my mother.'

'No you didn't.'

'Now you're being too nice.'

'Nothing wrong with that.'

'I agree. But ... secrets. Keeping things from each other. That's been my life until now. A family always hiding stuff. That's something I can't take anymore. Can we try not to have any secrets?'

Bob stared back up at the ceiling.

'We can try,' he said.

8

THAT JANUARY RICHARD Nixon stood on the steps of the Capitol and took the Presidential Oath for the second time. Days later I got a postcard from my dad in my college mailbox, showing Nixon's recent swearing-in ceremony, with the following message scrawled on its back: *1973 gets off to a great start! Hope you're smiling. Love – Dad.*

I did find myself smiling as I read Dad's card. Too bad he was such a conservative. He had a deep mischievous streak to him.

That January Maine and the rest of New England was hit with cascade after cascade of snow. One morning we woke up to a foot and a half of freshly fallen white stuff, so deep and tightly packed that we couldn't get our front door open. When it was clear that the door was so snowed in that it wouldn't budge – and we both had an 8 a.m. exam that morning on *Beowulf,* and our landlord rarely got his handyman to plow the driveway or clear the sidewalks before noon – Bob ran back upstairs. As I reached our apartment I saw him throw himself out the now-open window. I screamed, completely wide-eyed, racing to the window to see his body in the deeply banked snow covering our front yard. Moments later he jumped up, all smiles. I was furious.

'Are you crazy, fucking crazy?' I yelled.

'Piece of cake!' he said.

'You could have killed yourself.'

'But I didn't.'

He went over to the garage, grabbed a shovel and dug out our door. Ten minutes later we were walking toward the college, in time for our exam. I was still fuming.

'You can take the boy out of the frat, but you can't take the frat out of the boy.'

'Hey, we're going to make our exam.'

'You're not taking this seriously. I mean, remember your frat brother who died last year after falling off the roof.'

Bob fell very quiet, saying nothing all the way to Massachusetts Hall. Before we went inside he said:

'I suppose I deserved that.'

'It wasn't meant as punishment. But Jesus, don't you see what a mad, dangerous act that was? Do you want to break my heart, ruin my life? You're smarter than that, Bob.'

That night, back at home, Bob told me: 'As an act of contrition I'm making you my one and only kitchen specialty: spaghetti with meatballs.' It was a recipe that his home ed teacher at his parochial school had taught him. 'Miss Genovese – totally Italian and totally from the North End. She decided to get the Irish kids in her charge away from the boiled cabbage and pot-roast delights of bad cooking.'

We had most of the supplies for this dinner in our kitchen cabinets, as on a trip down to Portland the previous week we blew our paychecks from the library at the one and only Italian deli north of Boston. Portland back then was a run-down, depressed city, the old center of which was in terrible disrepair. But it did have its quirky attributes, including the Micucci Grocery, where you could find cans of proper Italian tomatoes, real garlic, real Parmesan cheese. We bought them all. Bob also insisted we get seasoned Italian breadcrumbs and a loaf of their bread, and a gallon bottle of proper Italian chianti, which the chunky, friendly woman behind the counter told us was 'pretty drinkable given the price' (four bucks for a half-gallon). After we'd bought all our groceries we sat at one of the little tables at the back of the shop and ate slices of their very good pizza, washed down with cheap red wine.

'Does the New York girl approve of the pizza?' Bob asked me.

'It's really good – and yeah, I am surprised. Just as I am also surprised by all this.'

'All what?'

'Us. This life together. I'm rather astonished how much I've taken to it.'

'Me too. There's an Irish expression I like: "There's a pair of us in it."'

I reached out for his hand.

'A lovely turn of phrase,' I said, wondering: did my parents ever know simple, sublime moments like this together? And if they did was it the arrival of children that led it to going so wrong? Or were they such a bad match from the outset that it was always destined to dispatch them to the unhappy terrain where they now both permanently lived?

The rest of the term was happily devoid of drama, but eventful in terms of so many things coming my way. Such as Bob and I applying to be counselors in a literature camp for teenagers in Vermont. This being a progressive camp, they even informed us that we would have our own room together in the staff quarters, and would each receive, in addition to lodgings and food, $350 each for the month we were there – a small fortune to us. Bob convinced the very irascible Professor Lawrence Hall – a brilliant curmudgeon – to take him on for an independent study on Melville's *Moby-Dick* next year. I received straight high honors in all my courses. And my term paper on the Federal Theatre Project was signaled out by Hancock as one of the best of the year. He called me into his office – our first meeting for some weeks. Since then I'd never ventured a single question regarding the state of his cancer. Nor did Hancock ever volunteer anything about his illness. During our subsequent meetings he kept things strictly to academic business, occasionally asking me about Bob and our plans for the summer. Nothing more than conversational banter. The friendship that was once there – the way he shared with me aspects of his life and drew me out on my own familial shadows – had transformed into a more formal professor/student relationship. Still collegial and pleasant, but with a certain distance now enforced by him between us. A line had been transgressed. Hancock had since reimposed the frontiers.

But this afternoon, after congratulating me again on my paper, he brought out a letter from the head of the graduate program in American History at Harvard.

'I decided to share with him your paper. Here's what he wrote back.'

He handed me the single-spaced typed letter. I read:

This is a remarkably accomplished work of scholarship for an undergraduate, let alone a freshman. When and if she decides to pursue graduate studies I hope you will put her in touch with me.

'I want you to keep that letter,' Hancock said, 'and take it out and read it to keep that doubt gene within you at bay.'

'I don't know what to say, Professor,' I said, wondering how he had discerned all the anxiety in me – especially as I worked so hard at keeping it elsewhere whenever I was in his presence.

'Be flattered that Wendell Fletcher – considered one of the country's leading experts on Roosevelt – admired your paper.'

'I so appreciate this. But . . . '

'But what, Alice?'

'What you said to me some months ago, Professor, about how we all fear being found out . . . that's so me. And I wonder if I will ever shake that feeling?'

'Ultimately that will depend completely on you, Alice. It's just like my writing. Only I can get myself to start, let alone eventually finish the next book. I tell myself I will write in the evenings, after classes, after office hours, after time with my wife and children. But I find excuses to do other things. I tell myself I will write on the weekends, but I bring my boys out sailing. Or I do necessary jobs around the house which I could probably hire a handyman to attend to – but I know they will keep me from the book, so I do them myself. Now that I have tenure I often wonder if I will even start it.'

He broke off and looked out the nearby window.

'But I also know that I need the book – not just for eventual advancement to full professorship in about ten years, but also to keep me stimulated, engaged, feeling as if I am accomplishing something. Then again, the aspirations you have in your twenties – seeing an ever-growing corpus of books you've written, lining a shelf – shift when you become acutely aware of your own limitations.'

Having said that, Hancock suddenly stood up, looking disconcerted, as if he'd overstepped another boundary. I was simply so pleased that he had chosen to show me his vulnerable side again.

'My apologies, Alice. I seem to be in a ruminative mood today.'

'If I may ask, Professor ... '

But before I could pose the cancer question, Hancock began to gather up papers from his desk.

'Must get on with certain other things now.'

I was out the door moments later.

Classes finished the following week. Hancock's last lecture was a moving account of Franklin Delano Roosevelt's final year in office, and how the war economy had finally brought about the economic revival that the New Deal could not deliver, but how Roosevelt had nonetheless conducted the first true experiment in American social democracy, and 'one which has been watered down over the years, but still has immense influence on the national body politic'.

He continued on:

'I know that most Americans today have written Lyndon Johnson off as a warmonger and one who fatally escalated our terrible involvement in Vietnam. I agree that he made a mistake of tragic proportions, and ruined his presidency in the process. But for me the greatest tragedy lies in the fact that, socially speaking, he was the most progressive president since FDR. Look at the Voter Rights Act of '64, the Civil Rights Act of '65, his Great Society policies, Medicare, the Corporation for Public Broadcasting, even the way he has rid our highways of billboards. History will be far kinder to Johnson than we are now. History will see that he was trying to remake America as a true social democracy, and someone who was the great congressional cajoler and backroom arm-twister. When he got the Voter Rights Act passed – an act that fundamentally enfranchised, for the first time in American history, all African American citizens over eighteen who were largely blocked from voting in so many parts of the South and elsewhere – Johnson noted that he had lost the South for his Democratic Party. Nixon's first victory in '68 was proof of this: the first time a Republican nominee won most of the States below the Mason–Dixon line. Johnson changed the entire trajectory of American life with those two key pieces of civil rights legislation, and did so at great political sacrifice. Like all of us Johnson was a deeply flawed man – and one who made several critically catastrophic decisions. But if history teaches us anything, it is that only after the proverbial dust settles do we see the true shape of life's immensely difficult and frequently contradictory narrative. History, as such, might be a survey of the geographic, political, social, economic and theological forces that shape us. But it is also a study of the larger wounds within which we all live. "*He jests at scars that never felt a wound.*" Shakespeare, of course. Wounds define us. Wounds underscore all national destinies. Just as you will discover in your own lives, wounds are an implicit part of your own personal destiny.'

He then thanked us for being such an interesting class and sent us out into 'the pleasures of summer'.

As I was leaving he said:

'Alice, a brief word please.'

Behind me Polly Stevens hissed:

'Lucky you – a private goodbye with Daddy.'

I replied with nothing more than a tight smile. Once all the other students were gone, Hancock closed the door of the classroom. Then, asking me to sit down in a chair near to his lectern, he pulled up one next to me. Looking me straight in the eye he said:

'I am about to put you into a deeply awkward position, Alice.'

'Have I done something wrong, Professor?'

'No – but you might have knowledge of some wrongdoing in my class.'

'What wrongdoing?'

'It's been brought to my attention that someone has been writing term papers for some of my students.'

'Do you know who it might be?'

'No idea. All I know is that two of my students, whom I do not consider to be the most elegant or thoughtful of writers, have turned in papers in this class that are above their usual capabilities. These things are difficult to trace – especially as I gave all of you the option to write a major paper, as you did, or three shorter papers. The latter option would allow the offender to find someone willing to write it for him and not expend too much time on it. I have, of course, confronted the two people I have suspected of cheating. They have both proclaimed their innocence. I turned the matter over to the Dean of Students, who interviewed them both separately. They denied it again. I wanted to press for them to sit a supervised exam. I was overruled – for reasons I won't get into, as it might reveal too much, except to say: athletics count for too much here, as they do in most colleges. In the end I had no choice but to accept the final papers they handed in, even though it remains clear to me that they were not written by the two students in question. My department chairman has told me not to pursue the matter further. But I need to ask you as someone who, I sense, has her ear to the ground: did you know of anyone acting as scribe for any students?'

The anxious, catastrophizing part of me immediately wondered: *is he actually asking – did you write those papers?*

'Hand on heart, Professor, I never heard word of anyone getting another student to write papers for them.'

He scrunched up his face.

'I don't want to press you here. But are you absolutely certain ... ?'

'Professor, if I had overheard something, if I was aware of someone writing a paper for someone else, I truly would have told you about it.'

'I know that, Alice. Which is why I asked you. Because when this came to light a few days ago –'

He suddenly broke off, his voice convulsing, as if he were strangling on the words. His face turned the color of a beet. He pulled out a handkerchief from his trouser pockets, coughing violently into it, then pulled off his glasses and rubbed his eyes. I stood facing him, my own eyes wide at the agony etched across his face.

'There's a water fountain down the corridor ... ' he said, his voice just above a gasp.

Immediately I was racing out the door, first picking up the empty glass on his desk. I was back in less than thirty seconds with the glass now filled, trying not to show my panic and fear. Hancock accepted the glass, downing all of it again. Then he shut his eyes momentarily. When he opened them again his composure was regained.

'Thank you, Alice. I would appreciate it if, as before, all that was spoken here just now was kept completely between us.'

'Of course, Professor.'

He stood up and moved to the lectern, gathering up his books and papers. I decided to take a risk.

'May I ask, sir –'

But before I could finish the sentence he cut off all conversation with two words:

'Good afternoon.'

Then he headed for the door, not turning around to look at me.

I was in serious distress after all this. Distressed by the curt way he wished me farewell at the end of the year, which indicated that he thought I knew more than I was letting on (when I knew nothing). Just as another frightened part of me wondered if he was now going to turn his professorial back to me, refuse to continue being my advisor, reject me like every other important adult had done so far in my life. More than anything I felt as if I had let him down – by not knowing the details he so needed to know.

I broke a promise I made to Hancock: I did tell all to the one person I felt I could trust. Bob was beyond cool. He told me to stop apologizing about never mentioning Hancock's cancer, that I had shown great honor and trustworthiness by keeping this secret. And he too was thrown by the news of the cheating scandal in his class. 'I could ask around, find out who was writing for whom,' Bob said. 'I mean, I'd put one hundred bucks on the reason that Hancock was told by the college to back off on pushing the plagiarism case is because the guys were jocks and very important to whatever team they belonged to. I bet I can figure out who the culprits are by the end of tomorrow.'

But I knew that I would be walking us both into a great deal of trouble if I had Bob pursue this. Just as I also knew that, having broken my vow of secrecy to Hancock, he would never forgive me when he discovered that Bob knew all that he had confided in me. So I said:

'Let's not pursue this any further.'

'You did the right thing. Please don't think that Hancock's distance at the end of your chat today was because he was disappointed in you. The guy had just been very sick in front of you, with that choking fit. He was probably embarrassed and seriously thrown by it all.'

And he enveloped me in his arms – which was exactly the place I wanted to be.

The next day I found the following note in my college mailbox:

Dear Alice – I felt I put you in an invidious position yesterday, and wanted to apologize for doing so. Let's forget that final conversation. You did superb work this term – as will be reflected in your final grade. It has been a true pleasure teaching you. Sincerely ...

When I showed Bob the note that night he said:

'You see, all that worry for nothing. He's decided not to pursue the issue further, and he regrets having involved you. No worries, right?'

'Right,' I said, the worry everywhere in my voice.

We were subletting our apartment for the summer to a music student who had gotten a job at the college's summer music festival. We spent much of the next day packing up our clothes and cleaning the place. We'd promised ourselves pizza and beer downtown after all was done, and were due to leave on the 9 a.m. bus the next morning for Boston. Sean had found us a 1962 Volvo, which he'd gotten from a cop friend who ran a sideline in used cars.

'Hey, it was a steal at six hundred bucks,' he told Bob, who repeated the conversation back to me, mimicking his dad's accent. 'And since the dealer was a cop ... well, we will have comeback if it turns out to be a lemon.'

Bob dug into his savings and paid for half of it, even though his dad offered to cover the whole thing, 'as I've been looking for some way to blow my Christmas bonus'. But my guy was very much determined to cover his share.

'That way he can't say "look what I did for you",' Bob said.

We were both excited about the prospect of finally having wheels, and all the freedom that was going to engender. The plan was: we'd spend a few days with his parents, head out to the Cape, where one of Bob's school friends was spending the summer co-managing a motel and had told Bob that in exchange for helping paint three vacant rooms he could give us a room for nothing for ten days, the work taking no more than three hours a day tops. This sounded like a good deal to us, as the motel was just a block away from the beach. Then, after our sojourn on the Cape, we'd head to the camp in Vermont and were thinking about a drive into Canada afterwards, before heading back to college.

'You going to be done soon?' Bob shouted from the kitchen, where he was finishing mopping the floor. 'Pizza and beer sound very appealing right now.'

'Three more minutes of drudgery and I'm through.'

The phone rang. I got off my knees, glad for the distraction. It was Sam.

'Alice,' he said, his voice laden, 'I just heard something truly bad.'

'How bad?' I asked, completely thrown by his ominous declaration.

'Professor Hancock is dead.'

Have you ever noticed when the worst of news is reported to you – news that you know will change your perspective on everything – it doesn't initially register? It's as if the shock that accompanies it does something to your inner ear, deflecting it.

'That can't be,' I said.

'I'm sorry but it's the truth. Hancock is dead.'

'The throat cancer was *that* advanced?' I managed to say. 'I had no idea. He was so brave.'

'What cancer?' Sam asked, sounding bewildered. 'Professor Hancock was found hanged in the attic of his house this morning. He killed himself.'

9

THE FUNERAL TOOK place a week later. The delay was due to the fact that, as Professor Hancock had killed himself, there was the need for a police investigation. When this was concluded and the body was released from the office of the local medical examiner, the final formalities could proceed.

I learned all this before we were down on the Cape. After getting the news of his death I couldn't sleep, couldn't think in any way rationally. It was as if I had been pushed into an empty elevator shaft. I was in a downward plunge. I called the chairman of the history department at home. Professor Friedlander was something of an eccentric: a tall, gangly man with a shock-white, Whitmanesque beard, and a way of appearing endlessly distracted. He was also known for being a kind fellow, and one whose gentleness belied a scholarly rigor when it came to teaching and writing. I'd yet to have a course with him. I'd yet to declare history as my major, so I had no idea if Friedlander would take the call. But when I rang his home number and told him: 'It's Alice Burns, a student of Professor Hancock. I am so sorry to bother you . . . ', he said:

'No need to apologize, Alice. It's been a terrible day. Theo was someone we all treasured.'

'I'm beyond shocked, sir,' I said. 'I mean, I just saw him two days ago and . . . '

Should I mention the cheating scandal in his class? Surely Professor Friedlander was aware of it. Surely this was not the right moment.

'And I saw him the morning before he took his life,' Friedlander said. 'All seemed fine. He'd been a bit upset about some hockey player handing in an essay that had clearly been written by someone else. But that's happened to all of us at some point of our teaching careers. The thing is – and I've only learned this since seeing his widow Maryanne yesterday – he'd been in a bad mental place for

133

several years. Terrible mood swings, terrible insomnia, a desperate feeling of worthlessness.'

'But he also had the throat cancer to contend with, didn't he?'

'Throat cancer?' Professor Friedlander said. 'What makes you think that he had *that*?'

'But Professor Hancock told me ... '

'That he had cancer?'

'Yes.'

'That makes no sense.'

'It's not something that I'd make up, Professor.'

'I'm not doubting your word, Alice. It's just Theo told me when he had the polyp removed last semester that the biopsy showed it to be completely benign. And Maryanne yesterday gave no indication that the diagnosis was a false one. I'm shocked to hear that he told you that.'

I didn't know what to say. Because I now felt so lost.

'I'm stunned too, Professor. Why did he insist it was cancer if ... ?'

'For all his outward signs of stability and immense professional competence, the man was clearly fighting some terrible demons within. Are you leaving the college for the summer soon?'

'In just under an hour. But I will come back for the funeral.'

'I thank you for all this information, Alice,' he said. 'Just as I appreciate your discretion. And if I raise what you just told me with anyone I will not mention your name.'

'I appreciate that, Professor.'

As soon as I hung up Bob said:

'That sounded beyond heavy.'

I put my face in my hands. Bob came over and encircled me in his arms.

'We have twenty minutes to make the bus ... and it is a ten-minute walk.'

As we were traveling light – a big backpack each, our remaining clothes folded away yesterday and stored in the attic until we returned at the end of August – we rushed over to the depot on Maine Street. We found two seats together at the extreme back of the Greyhound heading south. Looking around and noticing that no one we knew from the college was seated near us I whispered the entire discussion that I'd had with Friedlander about Professor Hancock.

'The way Friedlander was talking, Hancock had definitively told him it was benign,' I said. 'So why did he tell me it was cancer? Professor Hancock was the most rational, level-headed man ... '

'He hanged himself, Alice. He wasn't one hundred percent rational. In fact, it could be argued that he was pretty damn disturbed.'

'But he had it all. That beautiful house on Federal Street. The long marriage. Those three little boys. And he'd just been tenured. I mean if he'd been denied tenure that would have been another matter. But to have finally been granted the permanent job and then to do this ... '

Bob just shrugged.

'As the late great Jim Morrison once noted: "People are strange."'

'That's a little facile.'

'Killing yourself punishes everyone left behind.'

'Not just that. If it's true there was no cancer then he was telling me a lie all along. Why would he do that?'

'For the same reason he killed himself.'

'Which is?'

'That's the mystery.'

Many hours later we were in the Volvo that Bob's father had found for him. Wheels! Freedom. I was happy for Bob. We drove in near-silence to the Cape. The motel was a run-down dump, but our room had a big bed and an ancient air conditioner that rumbled all night, yet still kept the place cool. The painting work did only take three hours a day – and we made a point of getting up early most mornings and having everything finished by noon, at which point we spent the next five hours on the beach. I found being near the water calming as the reality of all that had transpired took hold. Grief sideswiped me. The sense of loss was vast. With it the realization: he was the second person close to me who had committed suicide. Yes, Hancock's death made me finally face the hard truth: Carly was never coming back into my life again. Just as I kept asking myself: why couldn't I have saved him? Bob was right: suicide punishes those left behind. As such it felt not just like an immense betrayal, but a sorrow that was now upending. I discussed only a nominal amount of this with Bob – because I didn't want to bring up how attached I had become to Hancock. But Bob had, I discovered, worked this out a long time ago.

'It's okay to grieve,' he told me one night when we were at some clam shack by the beach, eating fried clams washed down with Heineken beer. 'He meant a great deal to you. He was a big presence in your life.'

'What are you saying here?'

'It's fine by me if you are upset.'

'Sorry, sorry.'

'You don't have to apologize.'

'Yes I do ... because I feel guilty.'

'Why?'

'Because I should have seen the signs.'

'What signs?'

'The signs that Professor Hancock was going to kill himself.'

'You were his student, not his shrink.'

'He didn't have a shrink.'

'You know that?' Bob asked.

'I'm just surmising. If he'd had a shrink he might be still here.'

'Or not. A lot of people who commit suicide have been seeing shrinks, or have been prescribed Miltown and Darvon, which the doctors had my mother on ... and look where it got her.'

I suddenly felt awful – because, of course, Bob had been coping with someone on the edge of sanity most of his life. I also knew I was being defensive because my feelings about Professor Hancock had edged into the romantic – and Bob understood this and had chosen to do the decent thing and say nothing.

'I never slept with him,' I blurted out. 'I'm not that crazy, you know.'

I lowered my head and started to sob. Bob reached for my hand.

'You're hardly crazy. I never thought once that you would have gone there with Hancock ... any more than I thought such an upright old-school Harvard man would have crossed that line – even with his favorite student, whom he clearly esteemed.'

'I'm not worthy of esteem.'

'I beg to differ. So too did Hancock.'

'I can't believe I'll never talk to him again,' I said.

Mom phoned me at the motel late one evening – a 'just checking in' call. But she'd also read Professor Hancock's obituary in the *New York Times*.

'If my memory serves me – and usually it does – your father told me that this was the professor who was kind of sweet on you.'

'Jesus, Mom ... '

'Well ... was he?'

'He rated me, Mom.'

The day before the funeral we made the seven-hour drive back to Brunswick. It was held in the big Congregational Church at the top of Maine Street. It was packed. Given that summer vacation had started ten days earlier I was surprised and impressed just how many other students had come back to say a formal goodbye to Professor Hancock. Taking a seat in a middle pew my eyes were focused on the plain pine coffin. It had been placed on a bier in front of the altar. I hadn't been to many funerals in my nineteen years. My three grandparents. One of my elderly German great-aunts, Minnie, who'd been born in 1870 and emigrated to America after Kristallnacht in 1938. No one else. Until today. But unlike my elderly relatives who'd lived very long lives – Minnie was ninety-eight when she left us – Professor Hancock was still in his early thirties. As I came to discover that oppressively hot morning in Brunswick, the sight of a coffin containing someone only a decade and a half older than you brings about the deepest sort of chill within. I stared at that wooden box, the coffin lid closed (thank God), trying to imagine Hancock within. Wondering if his wife had to bring a tweed jacket, a pair of his gray flannels, a button-down shirt, a knitted tie and his glasses to the funeral home? Were they burying him as if he were dressed for a day of classes ahead? Did they put his lecture notes and a pen in his hand to accompany him into the netherworld? Was there a terrible rope burn on his neck? Did his children view him at the funeral home? Did they see me standing in front of their house this morning after telling Bob that I needed a walk by myself before the funeral started? Did they notice that I seemed lost – as if I had ended up outside their green clapboard Federalist home on autopilot, leaning against their iron garden fence as I found myself lost in grief?

I craned my neck and saw Hancock's wife and his three boys in the front row of the church. How could he have done this to them all? Whatever the crushing despair, the absolute hopelessness, the sense that life must truly end, the aftermath for the survivors – the people for whom you were so important – is beyond monstrous. I kept looking at young Thomas Hancock, his distress so apparent. I identified so much with everything he was feeling, but couldn't show it. An Episcopal priest came to the pulpit. He introduced himself as Professor Hancock's brother and said that today would be, without question, the hardest service he had ever been called upon to preside over. Referring to his older brother as Theo, he recalled how, when they were growing up, their parents had a country place in the Berkshires. And how he, at the age of ten, went swimming in the lake that fronted their home, contravening a direct order from their father not to go into the water without adult supervision. He'd started to cramp up a good fifty yards from the shoreline and had shouted for help.

'My parents had gone off to a friend's house to play tennis. Theo was sitting on the deck of the house, his head in a book – as it always was. He heard my cries, raced to the lake and, stripping off his shirt and shorts, dived in, and swam out to me in record time. He had done a bit of lifeguard training, so he knew exactly what to do, getting me on my back, slowly returning to shore. Halfway there we heard the voice of our father, berating us for having gone against his directive. When we reached dry land I tried explaining it was me who'd been the stupid one here, and that Theo had saved my life. But Dad would not hear any of it, and took off his belt and gave us both three strokes on the backside. What I most remember of this episode was how Theo didn't try to save himself from this whipping – because to do so would have been, in his mind, a betrayal of me.

Which would have been completely against his moral code. That was my extraordinary brother – a man who would rather absorb pain than betray someone close to him.'

His voice cracked as he struggled to keep his emotions in check. He continued on:

'I have, I must admit, been reflecting much on that childhood incident since the horrifying news arrived that Theo had died. What I have felt most profoundly is a sense of guilt. I knew that he had his dark moments. I knew that, like most of mankind, he had known despair. But in the past two or so years, although we wrote occasionally and did see each other last summer at the family cottage for a few days, I had been so busy with my new chaplaincy and my own young family, that we hadn't spoken as often as we should have. Which is why I mention now that July day in 1950 – when Theo took the unfair paternal beating without a word against me. Theo saved me from drowning. Theo gave me the two subsequent decades I have lived since then – with all its attendant wonders. How I wish I could have saved him. How I wish this was all a bad dream, divorced from the harsh reality that we have come here to mark today. How I wish this remarkable man – someone who cared so deeply, maybe too deeply, about so much – could have found that chink of light amidst the darkness. Theo suffered hugely at the hands of life. Just as he took the transgressions of others to heart. Especially when he discovered, at the end of the semester, that a student or group of students had written papers for others in his class – and he saw this ethical infraction as a judgment on himself as a teacher, even though he was blameless. I just wish he had known just how loved he was.'

At that point Thomas Hancock began to sob loudly. His mother put her arm around him, whispering something comforting to him. I was biting down hard on my lip, trying to keep myself in check.

When we all walked out, half an hour and the Lord's Prayer later, all I could think was: *damn you for doing this to all of us. Damn you for destroying the one bit of certainty within me that you were the one rational adult protector I always longed for. Damn you for waking me up to a terrible truth: no one is stable, no one secure. And the perfect life is a lie. Your suicide wasn't a loss of innocence – that had happened already with everything that went down in high school. What your death showed me is we are all so vulnerable. And the frontier between the rational and the unhinged is such a fragile one.*

Back we went to the Cape. We finished our house painting. We drove north to Vermont. We spent a rather civilized month tutoring well-off high school kids who were in danger of ruining their chances of getting accepted at a good college – and had been dispatched by their parents to what Bob called 'a high-priced educational penal colony by a lake' (he was reading Solzhenitsyn's *The Gulag Archipelago* which had just been published in English translation that summer). Many of the kids were the wrong side of bratty. But we both liked a couple of smart, engaged students who were bookish and lonely and didn't seem to fit in with everyone else – attributes which immediately endeared them to me. At the end of the four weeks we loaded up the car with our backpacks and headed north into Canada. It was, for both of us, the first time outside the United States. We fell in love with Quebec City: its cobbled streets; the seventeenth-century architecture; the sense of being in a corner of Europe just a few hours from the American border; the way everyone spoke French and reluctantly answered us back in English. We found a charming old hotel, with a creaky bed and a ceiling fan that belonged in a Tennessee Williams play, for only eight dollars a night – and it was right in the center of the Old Town. We found inexpensive restaurants with French-influenced food. We drank a lot of cheap French burgundy. I grew attached to a Canadian cigarette called Craven A. We made love with abandon. We took long walks along the banks of the St Lawrence. We lounged in outdoor cafes. I wondered out loud if this was what Paris was like – to which Bob replied: 'I sense the ice hockey and maple syrup thing isn't part of the French equation. But the rest of it ... it's a bit like France in Exile.' I vowed to start learning French next semester and to look into a year abroad in Paris come 1974. I also asked out loud something that was nagging me: where would we be a year from now, when Bob had finished Bowdoin and would be heading to graduate school?

'We'll talk about all that,' he said, 'once I know where I've been accepted … if, that is, any English department wants me.'

'Everyone's going to want you.'

'If that's the case, if Harvard says yes, I'd say yes to them – as I'd only be 120 miles away from you, and I'd also make my dad a very happy guy, as he could tell everyone in his station house that his son was a Harvard man.'

'You sure you're going to want to hang out with a mere Bowdoin undergraduate when you're down in Cambridge?'

'Why are you even going down this road?'

'Because I'm so damn happy with you that I fear it will all fall apart.'

'That won't happen.'

'How can you be so sure?' I said. 'I am tying you down at twenty.'

'I haven't noticed any chains attached to my wrist. But I often think I don't deserve someone as smart and clever and cool as you.'

We spent five days in Quebec City, vowing to return, to live in Paris, to avoid all of life's many traps.

We had to cut short our trip by a few days as Bob's mother had a terrible episode where she climbed out on the roof of their house, naked, in the middle of the night, and began to literally scream fury at the moon. Bob's dad called him at the hotel, broke the news to him, and also broke down in tears, telling his son that it was clear the electro-shock treatments hadn't worked, and the state mental health people were suggesting that she be institutionalized. Sean also told him that there was no need for him to come back to Boston – which, as Bob noted on the drive back south, was his way of telling him 'please get your ass down here right now'. I offered to come with him, but Bob felt this was something that he and his dad needed to face together, alone.

'I want to be there for you,' I said.

'But this is going to be grim – and I don't want that inflicted on you.'

'I can do grim.'

'I'd rather do it alone – and I know my dad would prefer that too. He really likes you – but the old guy is also someone with a lot of pride issues, and you being around when Mom is about to be committed ... '

Bob dropped me off in Maine that evening. When he returned four days later, I had imposed order onto chaos, as our subletter for the summer was a slob beyond belief. He never cleaned the place once. He allowed fruit to mold in cabinets. Garbage was rarely thrown out. Breadcrumbs were never swept off counters or floors. Roaches were everywhere. I saw the guy as he was packing up. The shock on my face said it all.

'Hey, sorry if I was a little messy.'

The glassy look in his eyes, and the semi-sweet herbal cloud still hanging over all three of our rooms, said it all: we had sublet to a serious stoner.

'You always leave a place like this?' I asked, trying to keep my anger in check.

'Left you two bottles of Boone's Farm wine in the icebox.'

'You can also leave your fifty-dollar deposit behind so I can hire a maid and an exterminator.'

'But I need the bread.'

'Then you should have had the courtesy of cleaning the place up.'

'That's kind of heavy of you, man.'

'Too bad.'

'I thought you were cool.'

'I thought you were considerate.' And I pointed to the door, telling him I wanted him gone. He hoisted his backpack, on which had been sewn an upside-down American flag. His final words were:

'You belong in the military, man.'

My father would have been so pleased with that comment.

I spent much of the next two days scrubbing the place clean. I also found our landlord and complained loudly about the recurrence of the roach problem (long happening before our crazed subletter) and told him that he simply had to get an exterminator around to give the place a proper fumigation. The man reluctantly agreed. He was an ex-Navy man who'd settled in Brunswick, owned a few properties and hated parting with any money on behalf of his tenants. But when he saw the roach infestation for himself he agreed that he had to do something immediately. I cleared out while the exterminators let loose a cloud of DDT (everything was carcinogenic in the early 1970s), telling me that I needed to stay away for at least eight hours after they were done. I did as ordered, walking to a payphone near Brunswick's wonderful book and record shop, McBean's. Dropping three quarters when requested by the operator, I called Bob at home in Boston.

'You could have called collect,' he told me.

'You know I wouldn't do that. How's it going?'

'Terribly. Mom tried to beat her head in last night at the hospital, slamming her skull against the wall so hard she was unconscious for a couple of hours. They've done X-rays. No fractures, no immediate cranial damage – that's what the head doctor guy told us. But she's now in a straitjacket in a padded cell.'

'Fuck.'

'That's about the right word.'

'I am so sorry. How's your dad taking it?'

'Better than expected. I sense there's part of him that is just a little relieved it is now a state matter and out of his hands. It means his guilt about having her locked away is somewhat reduced. I also found out, by chance, that my father has been seeing someone for the past couple of months – and she happens to be one of my former schoolteachers, Mrs Laffan. Widowed. Husband killed on a tour of duty in Vietnam. Which, according to Catholic Papa, plays well with his confessor, Father Quilligan.'

'He told you this?'

'I'm not exactly inventing it. Anyway I find it kind of cool that he feels he can talk to me about this stuff.'

'It's great your father's got a girlfriend. Is she cute?'

'She's about forty years old.'

'So you didn't have a schoolboy crush ... '

'On Mrs Laffan? Get outta here.'

We both started to laugh, Bob telling me that this was the first time in days that he'd been anything but grim. I informed him about the mess that had been awaiting us, and how it was now cleaned up and even fumigated. I also said how I'd held on to our subletter's fifty-dollar deposit (Bob approved) and didn't hire a cleaner to save money (and also because 'what student ever knows a cleaner?'). But having conserved that fifty dollars ...

'Would it be okay with you if I took half of it and bought a third-hand bicycle? There's a shop off Maine Street that looks like it has some good deals. And if I see a men's bike there as well for around twenty-five bucks ...'

' ... give him a couple of dollars to put it on hold and we'll pick it up when I'm back in a few days. I think bicycles are a great idea. And thank you for playing the washerwoman for us. I owe you.'

'You owe me nothing.'

Later that afternoon, I took my now-purchased Schwinn bike (circa 1967, but in good working order and repainted a funky shade of green) down several miles to Mere Point – a small cove with a boat launch and a lovely panorama of a small corner of the Maine coast. I replayed that comment I made to Bob: '*You owe me nothing.*' Was that a near-declaration of love: the fact that you don't feel you are due something from someone? At home everything was transactional. I was always being told how much I owed my parents, and how their lives had been compromised by the arrival of children. But with Bob there was no sense of 'you have to do this for me because I do all this for you'. We had an ease that I sensed was rare. We were both kids, both trying to find our way in the world, both willing to privately admit to each other that we were, in our own different way, scared of encroaching adult life and all that it implied. But we had also found each other – and had discovered immense strength and trust together. This was new territory for me – and I was surprised at how different, happier, life was within its changed landscape.

Bob returned two days later, looking wan, exhausted. His mother was going to be institutionalized for the foreseeable future. His father had only mentioned Mrs Laffan once during the five days he was back – and she discreetly never showed up at the house while he was there.

'Between us, I think Dad can't believe his luck. He wanted to leave Mom for years – but knew that the Church would never allow it. Now he's been given a get-out-of-jail-free card.'

He admired the absolute tidiness of our apartment, telling me it was wonderful to return to order after such home-front chaos. And we were free of roaches. We took the remaining twenty-five dollars and bought Bob his bicycle. Out at Mere Point, eating sandwiches and drinking the cans of Genesee beer we'd brought along, he reached into the pocket of his baseball jacket (the Red Sox, of course) and handed me a small box. Inside was a 1940s vintage Mickey Mouse watch, which he told me he found in a groovy shop in Cambridge.

'The dude who sold it to me assured me he'd had the movement cleaned recently by some local watchmaker – and that, as long as you didn't swim with it or take it into the shower and remember to wind it once a day, Mickey's left and right hands will keep moving.'

In a time when everyone young and long-haired had fallen in love again with the Marx Brothers, with Bogart in *Casablanca* and with Daffy Duck, there was something *très cool* about being given a Mickey Mouse watch. Irony was an essential part of our lingua franca in a time when everything else around us – the war, Nixon, the distrust between parents and children, urban decay – was difficult.

Two days later classes started. All the talk around campus was about Professor Hancock's suicide, and how it had unnerved everybody. But there was also much discussion about the two hotshot reporters at the *Washington Post*, who had uncovered that the Nixon White House was somewhat implicated in the break-in at the Democratic Party headquarters in Washington the year before. Talking to my dad the weekend I was back, when he surprised me with an early-morning phone call from Chile, he was full of conspiracy theories about why all eyes were now on Tricky Dick and his band of political operators.

'The liberal press has been after that guy for years. So what if there was a break-in? Politics is a dirty business.'

'But the guy has an enemies list,' I said. 'His henchmen have been involved in the cover-up. It's clear Nixon has broken the law.'

'Now wait a minute, young lady, no one's accused our president of any wrongdoing.'

'That will happen. And please don't call me "young lady". We're not living in the Eisenhower era anymore.'

'Ike was a great man. I'll have no bad-mouthing of Ike.'

'I'm not bad-mouthing Ike – even if he did choose Nixon as his running mate twice. But the man did warn us about the "military industrial complex".'

'He was a five-star general, the savior of Europe, not some peacenik.'

'You don't have to be a peacenik to see how the military industrial complex runs everything in this country. The fact that he said that – him being the great military man ... '

'Remind me *not* to discuss politics with you on an international trunk call.'

'You started it.'

'Yeah, yeah. How's things going, sweetheart?'

I could have told the truth – and said that, since Hancock's death, I was still walking around with something approaching shell shock. It was best to say nothing. Best to ask:

'How's Adam?'

'Thriving.'

I heard a certain hollowness behind that statement.

'You don't sound convinced.'

'The kid's doing a great job,' Dad said, even more defensiveness in his voice.

'And how are things in Chile?'

'I can't say much, because everything says the lines are tapped here. Except this: nothing is forever. *Nothing.*'

Three weeks later, at around three in the morning, the phone rang in our apartment. Bob and I both jumped awake. Nothing good ever comes from a 3 a.m. telephone call.

I got to the phone first. It was my brother Peter – out of touch with me for nearly two years. Until now. He sounded anxious, distressed.

'Alice. There's been a coup in Chile,' he said.

'Oh my God. Are Dad and Adam okay?'

'Okay? *Okay?*' Peter shouted. 'They're fine. More than fine. This coup ... they helped engineer it.'

10

THE DATE OF the coup: September 11, 1973. What was known in its immediate aftermath was this: a series of air raids by the right-wing military bombed the Presidential Palace. The head of the military, Augusto Pinochet, also ordered the Army to advance on the center of government while the Navy took control of the crucial port of Valparaiso. By 8.30 a.m. that same morning the Socialist president, Salvador Allende, comprehended the absolute enormity of what had gone down and that he was about to be deposed through undemocratic means. Rather than resign or take safe passage out of the country, he took part in the gun battle against the encroaching military forces. When he realized the game was up he committed suicide.

I heard most of these details from Carl Taylor – the New York Marxist who organized an immediate protest meeting in a corner of the union. Around eight people showed up. Professor Herb Coursen – the notorious sleaze who hit on every woman student in his immediate proximity – was there. He was flying his revolutionary flag for all to see. When I walked in with Bob, the meeting was already under way – Coursen ranting on about how Nixon and Kissinger were the engineers of this coup, seeing the rise of a legally elected Marxist government as further evidence of a Domino theory in Latin America. Carl – smoking nonstop, talking in that rat-a-tat way of his – was telling the group around him how he had managed to get a call through to a friend who ran a radical theater in Santiago. He informed him that intellectuals and artists were being rounded up, and he was fleeing across the Argentinian border that night.

'I don't know if he made it,' Carl said. 'What I do know is that our government has given legitimacy to the military overthrow of a democratically elected president. They are letting Pinochet and his thugs run riot over human rights and, by extension, are authorizing the detention and execution of people whom the junta considers to be dissidents. What I also know is that a member of the student body who just happens to be here today has a father who is deeply implicated in the events currently taking place there. Isn't that right, Alice Burns? Isn't your father – who runs a mine there for the International Copper Company – very much in bed with the junta?'

I wanted to flee. I felt Bob put a steadying hand on my shoulder as he shouted:

'That's not fair.'

Carl shot back:

'Tell that to the family of Salvador Allende, who killed himself rather than be gunned down by the junta. Tell that to the families of the disappeared.'

I found myself cowed by this, but also realizing that I needed to make a response – or live with the consequences of silence thereafter.

'I don't know much about my father's work in South America. And I don't ever recall talking with you about it, Carl.'

'Saying you know nothing about your father's dark deeds is just a little rich. I mean, this is like the daughter of a Dachau guard saying she didn't realize what Daddy was doing all day in the concentration camp just down the street.'

'That is ridiculous,' I said, now furious. 'My father works out of the country. Yes, he runs a mine in Chile –'

'A mine that was nationalized by Allende,' Carl said. 'Surely he told you that he was furious about that happening? Surely you must have known?'

'This is turning into a kangaroo court,' Bob said.

'Let Alice answer my question,' Carl said.

'My father keeps his work in South America to himself,' I said, knowing I was being fast and loose with the truth; that Dad had complained bitterly and on many occasions about what 'those revolutionary Commies are going to do to my mine'. But I never pressed him for details, because, as always with my father, I feared knowing too much as to what he was up to. Just as I decided to open myself up to the proverbial furies and phoned Mom last night, letting her accept the collect call. I decided to say nothing about my call minutes earlier with Peter – but Mom already knew all.

'Was your brother the radical just on to you?' she asked, sounding surprisingly calm.

'Peter called me, yes.'

'First time the two of you have spoken in about eighteen months. He was probably ranting on about your father being a monster, in the pay of the CIA and all that.'

'Were you listening in to our call?'

'Hardly – but I know your brother all too well. Just as I know you're still angry at him for sleeping with that tour guide at Bowdoin when you went up for your interview.'

'How the hell did you know that?'

'Because Peter told Adam what happened – brother-to-brother and all that. And Adam told me – because I can always get him to tell me everything. The girl was legal, right? Over eighteen and all that?'

'Mom ... '

'I'll take that to be a "yes". But you got all moral and Girl Scouty about discovering that your oh-so-ethical brother is just like every other guy when it comes to sex. Get used to it, Pollyanna. Men are dogs. Fidelity is something that only the truly pussy-whipped can adhere to. God knows, if I had made a big deal about your father's flings ... '

'Mom ... '

'Now you're all in shock about this. You're also surprised to find out that Daddy is up to his neck in a *coup d'état*. And that he's brought your brother along for the ride. Know what I think? Allende was a Castro in the making. He had created his own KGB and was already cracking down on his version of dissidents: bankers, businessmen, anyone who didn't support his Marxism. Your father was on his hit list as well.'

'What? How do you know all this?'

'How do you think? Mind-reading? Your dad tells me just about everything – except the name of his mistress of the moment down there. Allende had it coming to him. All he had to do was be a little moderate, a little more centrist, mixing socialism with the free market, and he wouldn't be dead now. The guy overstepped. You can't

149

nationalize mines owned by foreign companies and simultaneously get into bed with Moscow, expecting Washington to sit there and do nothing. He sealed his own fate.'

I was floored by this statement – because Mom was so liberal on so much. Just as I was stunned by the revelations she made about knowing everything about Dad's extramarital stuff. But, as I was beginning to realize, Mom liked to work according to the principal of destabilization – of upending your certainties as a way of asserting her power over you. I realized in this moment that, for all her raving and ranting about my father, she was still wildly protective of him, to the point of turning a blind eye to so much. The Allende regime had taken away something that was, for my father, his *raison d'être*: the mine he always proclaimed that he himself had created. In a life where he often expressed frustration about how things had played out – and where regret was always near the surface – this mine in the Atacama Desert was, for him, his legacy: proof that his time on earth counted; that he'd created something that wasn't there before, and would outlast him. This perception came far later – when I too was thinking about how fast our time here was, and was aware of just how little of what preoccupies us while we have this gift called life lasts beyond our very short span here. But in September 1973 such thoughts were many years down the calendric track. Right now I was just reeling from Mom's directness.

'Welcome to "the way things are",' she said. 'Don't worry about your dad and Adam. They are somewhere safe, waiting for the situation to stabilize. Know this: if it hadn't been for this coup, your father and brother might have been conveniently buried alive in some mine shaft. Or their company jeep might have been forced off one of those switchback roads they have in the Andes. No doubt you'll now join your brother in some protest march against Nixon and Kissinger, screaming about American imperialism and deluding yourselves into believing you can change anything.'

Peter called later with the news that Dad and Adam had resurfaced in Santiago and were being asked by the Pinochet regime to oversee the reprivatization of their mines.

'How did you find all this out?'

'Dad obviously. He called me the other night, wondering how I was taking the news of the coup. I told him that I knew he'd been involved in the American role in it, and that I was ashamed of him. Know what his reply was? Two words: "Sore loser". Then he told me that he was having dinner tonight with Pinochet and would tender my best regards.'

'Why are you telling me this? So I can take your side?'

'Are you on his side?'

'I'm on nobody's side. I just wish people would stop trying to pin me into some sort of political corner.'

'You can't stand on the sidelines as the world detonates around you, Alice.'

Then, telling me he was heading to Washington for a march on the Chilean Embassy, he hung up. Leaving me feeling as if I was the most uptight, prissy adolescent imaginable. Bob said I should stop beating myself up, and stop thinking I should be held accountable for other people's actions.

'What Peter is accusing me of is –'

'Not letting the past go. Your mom is saying the same thing. But that's some advice, given how your family never lets anything go. Nor do mine.'

'Do you ever think that families have to pick on each other in order to maintain a semblance of togetherness?'

'Absolutely. You know what Freud said of the Irish? "This is one race of people for whom psychoanalysis is of no use whatsoever."'

I laughed. And found myself quoting that statement a few days later when I was having coffee with my newest friend, Howie D'Amato. We got talking at a showing of Ingmar Bergman's *The Passion of Anna* – which some New York guy named Duncan Kendall had organized as part of a festival he'd arranged of films by the Swedish master. They were being screened in an auditorium where the big reels of film were fed into two 16mm projectors, and Duncan – being both the festival organizer and projectionist – had to turn on one projector at the exact moment when the other one was about to run out of film. Howie showed up in an electric-blue windbreaker zipped up against the encroaching autumn chill. Most people looked askance at him. But Duncan – being a Manhattan boy and very much an outsider (he wore a tan trench coat, like Bogart in *Casablanca*, and always had a cigarette on the go) – came over and gave him a hug. Duncan was known around the college as the arty guy who got interesting plays on, who organized film festivals of movies that were simply never shown in a provincial place like Maine, and who was mocked repeatedly for that bouncing gait of his. He too was an outsider up here. Which was one of the reasons why he was now giving Howie a hug when he came in to the screening of the Bergman film, and then called me over and introduced us.

'Alice, meet a fellow New Yorker. Howie, ignore the fact that Alice lives with a reformed jock.'

Then he left us as he went over to say hello to a German professor who just walked in.

'So where in New York do you hang your hat?' Howie asked me.

I explained my exile status. Howie said: 'Well, I'm from what Duncan calls the back of beyond: Forest Hills in Queens.'

'How the hell did you end up in Maine then?'

'I wanted liberal arts, I wanted New England, I wanted Hampshire or Bennington, but my dad thought those places would just reinforce my weirdness. Bowdoin was traditional, but inclusive and changing. Or, at least, that's what the admissions people here told me. They offered me a full scholarship, and now ... now I keep thinking about transferring. But my father wants me to stick it out.'

'Italian obstinacy is right up there with their Irish counterparts, isn't it?'

'Oh you are intuitive.'

That was the beginning of our friendship. Howie turned out to be a psychology and art major, and someone who was thinking about doing graduate work in art history with a view to a career in museum curating. He was rare among Bowdoin students as he was outwardly, openly gay. His green hair and flamboyant clothes added to his 'agent provocateur' style. He was also something of a notorious loner. He lived off-campus in a small apartment. He had few friends. Evan found him 'too flighty, too extreme' (this from a guy who lived in perpetual black), while Sam castigated him for 'intellectual sentimentality – he understands his Lacan and his Melanie Klein, but he ultimately seeks solace in Broadway musicals'. Howie also knew that, on every level, he didn't belong here – 'but it is hard to say goodbye to a full scholarship'. His father – a contractor who had a small home renovations business in Queens and Long Island – was reluctant to let his son walk out of such a prestigious school. Over a glass of wine at the Ruffled Grouse one evening – after I ran into him in the library and discovered that he too was up for an antidote to an evening of study – I asked him straight out how his dad dealt with his style and sexuality.

'Weirdly, he's okay with it. I mean, initially, he was completely freaked when my hair went green and I started dressing like a hippie Liberace. But then, at my public school in Forest Hills, a couple of Italian toughies tried to beat me up. I decked one of them. For all my queeny stuff Dad got me boxing when I was about nine years old, and kept me training at it even when I went green. Anyway, when those Italians started pushing me around, calling me a "fagola", and one of them slapped me across the left ear, I let go with two rights to the asshole's mouth. Knocked him to the floor, knocked out two front teeth. The kid's father made a big deal of it. The fact that it happened in the school locker room meant that he insisted I be hauled in front of the principal. My dad came, along with the Italian punk and his electrician father. The moment the other Italian papa got an eyeful of me he started berating his son, telling him in front of the principal: "You get beaten up by a fairy, then you come crying home to me? *Fugetaboutit.*" And he marched his kid out of the office. The principal still had to be stern with me about the assault – but acknowledged that it was self-defense "and maybe the wise guys in the school will now know you are not to be messed with". Dad told me on the way home: "I could not be more proud of you. I will always stick up for you ... though you've shown me and the rest of the world that you can do that yourself without me."'

'Your father sounds like he's good news.'

'I know he struggles with me being so different, so absurd. But I seriously got lucky with my dad. He has transcended so much to be able to deal with me and still shows me such love.'

I found myself all but tearing up when he said that. Just as, having drawn me out on my own family, he knew that my parents did not especially embrace such an unconditional world view.

Howie and I became close. He even liked Bob and his famous spaghetti and meatballs. He was initially a little thrown by Bob's outward jockish style but I watched as they grew easier with each other.

'I could tell you he's dreamy, but you know that already,' Howie said one afternoon as we were walking across campus. 'What really impresses me is how well read and curious he is. He's probably the only member of that fraternity of his who hasn't said shit to me within my general hearing. Which singles him out even more as one of life's better guys. You've got yourself a catch there. Then again, so has he.'

A freak snowstorm hit Brunswick a few weeks later – two inches of the stuff landing on us in the first week of November. It was a true surprise to wake up on the Saturday of a major football game to see the world rendered white. This being New England the teams agreed to still play after the Bowdoin ground staff managed to plow the field free of snow. This being football, I went along with Bob to the game; the only one he'd attended so far this season. Several of his former frat brothers scowled at him when they saw him in the stands with me. The football coach acknowledged his presence with a curt nod. The game was ferocious. With three minutes to go before halftime, an Amherst linesman made a comment to the one black guy on the Bowdoin team – Charlie Smalls – who reacted by executing the most perfect kick in the groin imaginable. The Amherst players tried to subsume Smalls after that, but his Bowdoin teammates blocked them. The referee and the coaches intervened. Initially one of the refs ordered Smalls off the field, but he began to protest, backed up by the Bowdoin coach. Whatever was said had a salutary effect on the referee, who suddenly ordered the Amherst player off the field.

'It's not hard to guess what that asshole said to Charlie,' Bob said.
'I didn't know the KKK were alive and well in Western Massachusetts,' I said.

'Racism is as American as bad diner coffee,' Bob said.

That little incident, with just a minute to go in the first half, seemed to have galvanized the Bowdoin team, who scored a touchdown with around eight seconds left on the clock, bringing the score to 14–7 at the half.

'We've got a chance now,' Bob said, as he accepted a couple of beers from the infamous Casey. He was also passing around a hash pipe while keeping his eyes peeled on the immediate vicinity, as Bowdoin security and Brunswick cops were very much about the field. Bob took several discreet hits off the pipe. The Bowdoin team seemed fired up by the racist attack on one of their own, and became progressively more brutal and skilled at running the ball. Within six minutes the score was tied.

It's amazing how loud you can get when the score is tied at 14–14 with fifty-seven seconds left in the last quarter, and Amherst had the ball on the Bowdoin eighteen-yard line. Things were looking decidedly tenuous when, out of nowhere, the Amherst quarterback got sacked by two Bowdoin guards and fumbled the ball before a Bowdoin tight end scooped it up to run eighty-two yards for a touchdown. The crowd went wild, all of us on our feet, screaming, hugging each other, the sense of shared, out-of-nowhere triumph immense. Is that why we so like sport? Because it lets us believe that this game is a larger metaphor for life's immense struggles and that, occasionally, we can triumph against the odds?

Afterwards I could tell that Bob was feeling a little rueful about not being part of the team that had just pulled off such an amazing win; that in choosing to move in with me he had denied something very crucial within himself. Watching him have a tentative, edgy conversation with his former coach – and seeing how that man kept looking at me as if I was the harpie who had corrupted his one-time star – I started understanding something that I had trouble grasping: the way we all are a mass of forces pulling us in disparate directions, and that we often shut out one side of our character in order

to embrace something new and potentially more positive, but still
hanker after the old ways because they speak to another, essential
side of ourselves. Can we ever truly run away from those locations
within us that we wish were not part of our inner landscape, yet
which we also know are a formative part of so much that we are?

When Bob found himself being handed a beer by some of his
Beta brothers I went over to him, touched him lightly on the shoulder and whispered:

'I think I might head over to a thing at Sam's apartment.'

As I said this, he was being waved over by a couple of his football
chums.

'Cool by me – see you there in an hour.'

Then he went off and joined his friends.

As I walked into his apartment Sam was his usual caustic self.

'Fresh from playing the love interest in *Knute Rockne: All American* ...' he proclaimed as I walked into the door.

'You should go to Borscht Belt with your act,' I said.

'Ah, the old anti-Semitic jibe.'

'Oh please,' I said. 'As my mother's a Jew –'

'But Jews are the biggest anti-Semites.'

'You can hand it out, Sam,' Duncan Kendall said, 'but you don't
like getting flak thrown back at you.'

'So speaks the Manhattan Prince of the City.'

'I come from people raised in Yorkville and Hell's Kitchen,' Duncan said. 'Hardly Edith Wharton territory.'

'You're a Collegiate boy,' Sam said. 'But that doesn't mean you
can write fiction.'

I came in here.

'I liked the story Duncan submitted.'

'You were a minority of one on that score,' Sam said.

'You and your cohort DJ are simply against anything linear,'
Duncan said.

'No – we're just against anything specious and turgid,' Sam said. I
watched Duncan turn white, and try not to show just how hurt he was.

'That is not nice, Sam,' I said.

'Literature is never nice,' he said.

'When I publish my first novel –' Duncan said, all hurt and anger.

'The likelihood of that happening is up there with me becoming an astronaut,' Sam said. At which point Duncan bolted for the door.

'You asshole,' I hissed at Sam as I ran after him.

When I reached the street I found Duncan pacing up and down, a cigarette on the go, talking to himself. He saw me approaching and waved me off.

'No need for sympathy,' he said, drawing deeply on his cigarette, kicking his way through the snow with his LL Bean boots, his trench coat pulled tightly around him against the cold. 'Every time I engage with those guys they pull my chain. Especially DJ – who thankfully wasn't there today because his grandmother or someone like that died, and who has to always go out of his way to make me feel small.'

'He's just as insecure as the rest of us.'

'With all his WASP arrogance that foams out like whipped cream from a can. Sorry for the bad metaphor. Want to get a beer? I could use about five.'

I glanced at my watch.

'My boyfriend said he'd be here about now.'

Duncan tried to hide his disappointment. He failed. I thought fast.

'Tell you what. We live about five minutes from here. I'll go back upstairs, tell them to let Bob know we've gone back to the apartment. Then we could go by Mike's Place and pick up some beer.'

'Let me go back up and tell them,' Duncan said.

'Why walk back into all that?' I said. 'I can handle it.'

'Because I want to show that fuckhead Sam that I can deal with his undermining bullshit.'

Dropping his cigarette out in the snow, he reached into his coat pocket and pulled out a pack of Gitanes, proffering me one.

'Something to keep you warm while I deliver the message upstairs.'

'French cigarettes – I'm impressed.'

'Part of my Upper West Side pretensions. Some people tell me they're so strong it's like sucking on an exhaust pipe ... but it's also the reason I like Gitanes.'

157

Then, with a quick smile, he went back inside, returning less than a minute later, lighting up another cigarette as he came outside.

'Done and dusted,' he said. 'Let's see if Mike has some Molsons in stock.'

'French cigarettes, Canadian beer. You are a Manhattan boy.'

'And one who is going to get as far away from this country as soon as possible.'

'You doing a junior year abroad?'

'Paris. The Sorbonne. Got accepted last week. And you?'

'Thinking about it. The thing is: it depends on where Bob goes to grad school.'

'But even if you stayed here, he'd be elsewhere.'

'"Elsewhere" might be in Cambridge.'

'Oh yeah, that place. They turned me down. So did Yale and Brown and Dartmouth.'

'Does that still bother you?'

'Yes, it does.'

We went to Mike's Place – an all-purpose general store. Duncan's smile grew even wider when he saw they still had two six-packs of Molson's beer left on the shelf. He bought both, along with another two packets of Gitanes.

'Mike gets them in for me,' Duncan said. 'And since I smoke two packs a day ... '

'You're a real addict.'

'I can't think or write without a cigarette.'

'Do you wear the trench coat when you write as well?'

'Only when I am trying to act like someone out of a Jean-Pierre Melville movie.'

'Who's Jean-Pierre Melville?'

'The greatest director of French gangster films ever.'

'Who knows that kind of stuff?'

'Parisians. And peculiar New Yorkers who hide out in cinemas.'

'Which, let me guess, is what you did during your misspent teenage years?'

'Bingo. My parents were unhappy. I loved the education at Collegiate and hated everything else about it. I was always mocked as the guy with the funny walk and the cultural snobbism. When I was thirteen I asked my parents as a Christmas gift to give me a membership at the Museum of Modern Art – because they also have a cinematheque and I could see five movies there on the weekend.'

Over the next four hours, as we drank all twelve of the Molsons and worked our way through an entire pack of Gitanes, and even made a chili together (from some ground beef, onions, tinned tomatoes and chili powder that I happened to have in the icebox and on our kitchen shelves), I discovered that I was in the company of a world-class talker. And an equally world-class neurotic. Duncan had heavily chewed nails and a variety of small nervous tics that reflected a great deal of anxiety and disquiet within. But God did he know so much about so much.

He was seriously well informed about the arts, a bit exhausting, but also interested in me and my interests, commiserating with me about getting yanked up to Connecticut, telling me that his family rented a house in nearby Riverside for eight straight summers during his childhood and 'I vowed after that never to live in the burbs'. He told me that his father, a big-deal white-shoe lawyer at Cravathe, Swaine and Moore, was pushing him to go to law school after college. 'Dad thinks I am this arty loser. It doesn't matter that I am doing so much better in college than my brother Michael. Mike did exactly Dad's bidding. Even though he was a C-plus student Dad pulled strings and got him into Boston College Law School. It doesn't matter that I had straight A's last year. He makes comments all the time to me like: "Why are you taking bullshit courses on electronic music and abstract painting and Weimar literature? You're just a dilettante."'

Listening to Duncan I felt a stab of sadness, of empathy, of kinship. I also found myself thinking: I really love the way his mind works. He talked about wanting to go to Yale Drama after college for the directing program. He saw himself as the next Mike Nichols, though he also could see himself making his way as a writer in France. The thing was, I'd met lots of people at Bowdoin and elsewhere who articulated such dreams (especially the American in Paris reverie) but Duncan struck me as someone who might just do it – if he could get around the doubt and distress that ricocheted within him. Which made him, on a certain level, even more attractive to me.

Suddenly it was close to midnight. No sign of Bob. So much for him showing up within the hour at Sam's apartment. Part of me was annoyed. Part of me was pleased. Though Bob was, on so many levels, far more sound and sensible, there was also that unspoken part of me that felt, in hanging out with his fellow Betas, he had left me here with Duncan. We were now somewhere in that zone between amorous and wasted. So much so that when Duncan leaned over and kissed me fully on the mouth I didn't resist. The feeling of betrayal was counteracted by the headiness of being in Duncan's arms, the sense of romantic and actual intoxication. But when he started edging his hands up my shirt something in me made me step back and tell myself: this is not smart, let alone good. I quickly stood up and said:

'I need to ask you to go now.'

Duncan reached for me again. It wasn't an aggressive move, as he took my hands in his.

'I am crazy about you,' he said. 'And we are so right for each other. And –'

'I am pledged to someone else.'

'Pledged? *Pledged*? This is not some Jane Austen novel. It's 1973. We don't pledge ourselves to anybody. But I've known from the moment I met you last year –'

'That sounds like a pledge.'

'It's a declaration.'

'That's a semantic distinction.'

Moments later I found myself back in his arms, letting him kiss me with a passion and ferocity that I found far too arousing. This time, when one of his hands slipped down the back of my jeans, I didn't pull away. Rather, a shudder ran through me and I pressed myself closer into him. Until, suddenly, we heard the downstairs door flung open and footsteps climbing up the stairs. Within seconds Duncan and I were back at the kitchen table, me smoothing down my clothes, Duncan lighting up two cigarettes for us, and handing me one just as Bob staggered back in. I was terrified that he would immediately suspect what we had been up to. But from the moment he stepped through the door I could see that something was truly wrong with Bob. There was blood everywhere on his jacket – and a look of haunted inebriation in his eyes.

'What's he doing here?' Bob asked, his voice thick with alcohol and South Boston aggression; an anger I'd never heard before.

'Keeping me company until you got back,' I said. 'What happened to you?'

Shaking his head, he staggered off into our bedroom. Stripping off his jacket, he shouted back to me:

'Get rid of him.'

Then he slammed the bedroom door behind him.

Duncan was on his feet.

'That's my exit cue,' he said.

'I'm sorry.'

'For what? It was a wonderful evening.' Then grasping my hands again he whispered:

'You are truly amazing.'

From the bedroom Bob shouted again:

'Is he fucking gone?'

Duncan squeezed my hands tighter.

'I'd rather not leave you with that Neanderthal.'

'He's not like that,' I hissed, sounding so defensive.

I suddenly heard Bob beginning to sob in the bedroom. Duncan went wide-eyed. Then, reaching for a kitchen pad, he scribbled down a number.

'My apartment's a five-minute walk from here. If you need me, if you need a place to run to, call me and I'll be back in a moment. You can crash in my bed and I'll take the couch.'

'You're a gentleman.'

'To my infinite regret.'

Squeezing my hands one last time he whispered:

'Courage.'

The sobs from the bedroom became louder. Duncan grabbed his trench coat and headed down the stairs. I opened the bedroom door to find Bob sprawled on the floor, his face in his hands. Part of me wanted to run over and put my arms around him. But the blood that was all over his button-down shirt and his tears and his evident inebriation also made me think: he has done something truly terrible.

'What happened?' I demanded.

'I've just ruined everything,' he said.

Bob hadn't directly done something terrible. His friends had. But Bob, drunk, stoned, very much in a fog, had stood by while four of his frat brothers beat up Howie D'Amato.

'We were leaving a thing at the Kappa Sig house –'

'What the hell were you doing in that animal house?' I asked.

'What do you think? Kegging. Talking trash. Someone had some speed. Three of the guys I was with did a tab each.'

'And you?'

'No, I just kept drinking, a little grass thrown in.'

'You were drinking a lot?'

'I did some shots too.'

'Of what?'

'Tequila.'

'Great.'

'Yeah, I was beyond stupid.'

'You forgot to meet me at Sam's place.'

Bob hung his head.

'Twice I told myself: "Get out of here now. Get back to Alice." But the frat brothers' pull was too much. Around eleven, a bunch of us decided to head back to the Beta house and weaved our way through the Bowdoin Pines. I was so shitfaced that everything was blurring. But I do remember seeing this thing coming towards us with all that green curly hair of his. One of the guys, Bill Marois, shouted, "Hey, Tree Fag." Though Howie tried to sidestep them, they were suddenly all around him.'

'You as well?'

'Hell no. I was leaning against a tree, completely out of it. Marois and one of the other guys began to taunt Howie, asking him if he was out in the woods looking for a pickup. Howie tried to walk away. They blocked him.'

'And you did nothing?' I asked, imagining the fear that must have enveloped Howie.

'I was so drunk that I blacked out for a moment. When I came to Howie was shouting at Marois: "You're the real faggot here, not me. Because you've tried hitting on me twice in the swimming pool." That's when Marois punched him in the stomach. Knocked him to the ground. Fell on top of him. Pinned him down with his knees and began pounding his face with his fists.'

'You didn't stop it?'

'At that point I did try. Started screaming at Marois to stop. Tried to pull him off Howie. But one of the other guys, Dave Derwin, pushed me away, told me that "Tree Fag had to pay for that accusation". I tried to fight back. Derwin pulled my arm up against my back, threatening to break it. He held me there until Marois tired of slugging Howie. Then when I screamed at Marois, calling him a fucking animal, saying Howie's accusations were probably true, he hauled off and caught me in the solar plexus with his fist. Sent me to my knees. And they all walked off, laughing.'

'And Howie?'

'His face was a mess. Blood everywhere, his nose flattened, a front tooth knocked out. He was moaning, couldn't speak. I somehow got him to his feet. Somehow got him over my shoulder. Somehow got him to the infirmary. The nurse on duty gasped when she saw the condition of his face. Called for an ambulance, called the cops. They were both at the college within ten minutes. The ambulance men told the nurse that Howie's injuries were so serious that they needed to rush him to Maine Medical in Portland where they had a plastic surgeon on call in the ER.'

'And the cops?'

'They took me downtown to the police station.'

'Did you tell them everything?'

'I gave all the names, gave a direct account of what had happened, told them the guys were drunk and jizzed up on Dexedrine, and that I was shitfaced.'

'You didn't mention the grass?'

'I'm not that crazy. But I did tell them I was throwing back shots of tequila. They asked me if I wanted to have a lawyer present but I said no, which they seemed to like. They got a statement from the nurse at the Bowdoin infirmary, saying how I had brought Howie there after the beating and had told her I tried to intervene, but was so drunk ... '

He put his face in his hands again and started sobbing. Any instinct I had about going over and putting my arms around him, telling him all would be well, had gone. I looked at him with something between disbelief and contempt. Even if he did manage to end up exonerated for what had happened the landscape between us had inalterably changed. I was overlaid by another feeling: how your love for someone can be torn asunder in moments.

'Did the police seem to buy your story?' I said.

'They told me that I was still under suspicion until Howie was well enough to make a statement.'

'Any sense of how he's doing?'

Bob shook his head.

'We should call Maine Medical.'

'I did that already – the one call that the police allowed me to make while in their custody. They still took away my driver's license and told me that I shouldn't leave Brunswick without first checking with them.'

'Can they legally do that?'

'I wasn't exactly going to argue with them about that detail. Anyway, when it gets out what happened, how I was too drunk to stop things ... '

'You still tried – and got slugged for your pains. That will win you fans in the court of public opinion. The fact that you got Howie to the infirmary ... that too will count. You're going to get through this – and the college won't expel you. Because you were the good guy in this story.'

But Bob kept shaking his head.

'Is there something else you need to tell me?'

Bob's response was to get to his feet, strip off all his clothes and walk into the bathroom. As the door closed behind him I heard the shower going full blast. I picked up his bloodstained white button-down shirt, his bloodstained white T-shirt. I went into the kitchen. I got a bucket out from below the sink, filled it with hot water from the tap, added a quarter cup of Clorox and plunged his blooded clothes into the bleached water. Immediately a detonation of crimson appeared in the bucket. I suddenly saw Howie's nose exploding as that animal Marois pounded him. Why did Bob revert to type and hang out with those morons tonight? He might not be expelled from the college, but he would have to live with the guilt of all this for some time to come.

I went back and retrieved his jeans and wool letterman jacket, a big 'B' emblazoned on its left breast. They were both drenched in blood. I knocked on the bathroom door.

'I'm bleaching your shirts,' I said. 'But your jacket and jeans … '

'Throw them out. I never want to wear a letterman anything again.'

I grabbed the bloodied clothes and walked right out our front door and down the stairs, oblivious to the November cold. Opening up the trash can by the garage I tossed Bob's clothes away, wondering to myself how I managed to ever get involved with a man who wore a letterman jacket, and then telling myself that wasn't fair on Bob. I lit a cigarette and looked up at the stars and realized that the days ahead were going to be hard ones.

I finished my cigarette, made my way back upstairs and found Bob already crashed out in bed. I followed suit, moments later.

When I came to it was just after midday. Bob was no longer next to me. There was a note on the pillow:

Marois and the others arrested this morning. Heading off to see Howie. I am so sorry for fucking everything up. I love you.

A phone call came moments later. I dashed into the kitchen to get it, naked and cold against the low heat, thoroughly expecting it to be Bob with news on Howie's condition. But it was Adam – on a crackly line from Santiago.

'Hey, sis … thought I owed you a hello.'

'Finally!' I all but shouted. 'Are you alive and well? Are you with Dad?'

'No – he's off at a reception at the Presidential Palace.'

'With his new best friend? I'm sure you're really happy about how all this has played out.'

'No need to get so touchy.'

'You've just been part of a coup and you call me touchy?'

'I didn't call to get hectored by you. I just wanted to touch base, tell you all is good. And to let you know that Peter is allegedly down here.'

'What?' I said.

'Mom called Dad yesterday, telling him that she'd just got a post-card from Peter, saying he'd flown down to Santiago.'

'Fuck, fuck, fuck.'

'Any idea about where he might be right now in Santiago?'

I didn't like the clinical tone behind this question; the way it hinted at Adam's deeper involvement in all that dirty work down there.

'Why are you asking me this? So you and Dad can get him picked up and frogmarched out of the country?'

'So Peter doesn't get hurt in a rather fluid situation down here.'

The coldness in his voice threw me. I'd never heard Adam sound menacing before and this made him sound like a cor-porate heavy, one of those guys who'd been programmed by 'the company' and was fully prepared to stomp down on anyone who was going to mess with their interests. Or was this just me get-ting all paranoid?

'I have no idea where Peter might be,' I told him. 'But I'm hold-ing you and Dad responsible for his safety.'

'That's why you've got to call me immediately – day or night – if you hear from him. Here's my number. You can call collect.'

I scribbled down the many numbers he gave me, then said:

'Tell Dad I want to talk with him.'

As soon as I put down the phone I called my mother.

'So why didn't you call me yesterday when you got the postcard?' I asked her.

'Trust you to immediately begin by attacking me. I'll tell you why I didn't call. Because I was so freaked out to find out that your *meshugga* brother had run off to the revolution –'

'The revolution's over. It's a police state.'

'It's a stable place now. But you know what these crazy Latino types are like. It's all macho theater down there. And if some naive Yale kid starts poking his nose into the coup, or hanging out with the intellectuals –'

'That's exactly what Peter will do.'

'That's exactly why I am scared to death. Peter is my baby, just as you and Adam are too. I would kill for him, claw somebody's eyes out for him. Including your father's. You need to know that. Just as you also need to know that I somehow managed to reach the Dean of Yale Divinity this morning. No one knew where he'd gone. His roommate at his apartment said he got back one afternoon to find a note: "*Out of the country for a while.*" That was it. No further word.'

I then heard something that rarely emitted from my mother's mouth: a distinct sob.

'Are you okay, Mom?'

'Hardly – but thank you for asking.'

'Was there a message on the postcard?'

'"*Down here seeing what's going on and what I can do to help.*" I called your father yesterday after the postcard arrived – and told him in no uncertain terms that I am holding him personally responsible for Peter's safety.'

'What did he say to that?'

'I think it got to him. Because he knows what the junta is capable of. Just as he has friends in all sorts of high places down there, and friends in that agency with the three-letter name.'

'He's working for them, isn't he?'

'Not my business. Nor yours.'

'Yes it is our business. Especially if Peter is now considered a potential troublemaker. You know what those juntas do with troublemakers. And it doesn't matter if he's American or not ... '

I suddenly felt very much overwhelmed by everything that had happened last night and the dreadful news that Peter had flown himself into considerable possible danger. I reached for the pack of cigarettes in front of me, lighting one up, trying to steady myself.

'You still there, Alice?' my mother demanded.

'I'm here.'

'You smoking?'

'I am indeed.'

'It will kill you.'

'So might this family.'

I hung up.

Moments later Bob came staggering up the stairs. I smelled booze on his breath, glimpsed despondency in his eyes.

'How's Howie?' I asked.

'Not great. They have him pretty drugged up, so he can't speak, can't say anything. The good news is that his face looks like it might, in time, heal without the need for anything other than resetting his nose.'

'Lucky him.'

'Have you seen what they've done to my car?'

I went to the window. 'Snitch' had been painted across the front windshield. 'Looks like your fraternity brothers didn't like you telling the cops the truth about Marois and the others.'

'They're all still being held at the police station.'

'On the basis of your testimony to the cops?'

'As Howie can't speak –'

He broke off, shaking his head.

'You hate me now, don't you'?

'I'm just ... disappointed.'

'So am I – in myself.'

'My disappointment isn't in you getting drunk. You came to Howie's aid – and that's admirable. But everyone around the college

168

is going to think the same thing: you were in a frat boy gang on the prowl. Great stuff, Bob.'

'You're going to leave me, aren't you?' he said.

'Why do you say that?'

'Because I know what Marois is going to tell the college.'

He went to the kitchen cabinet where we kept our one bottle of whiskey. He unscrewed the cap, splashed Jameson's into a glass, threw it back. Irish courage. Then, his gaze focused on the floor, he started to speak.

'I ran into the head of the Beta house, Chuck Clegg, this morning as I was walking to my car – which I left last night way over by Kappa Sig. Clegg actually stopped me, did the senior officer routine with me, saying he wanted a talk. He said that, though he didn't at all condone last night, he'd heard from Marois that Tree Fag – I cut him off, telling him: "He has a name: Howie." Clegg looked taken aback, but continued on. "According to Marois, this Howie guy tried to touch him up in the swimming pool." "That's bullshit," I told him. "When surrounded by Marois and his henchmen Howie shouted out that Marois had come on to him." Clegg asked me if I believed Howie. When I said that I did his response was: "Even though he's clearly a fag?" I asked him: "Because he's a homosexual you think he comes on to every beefcake guy?" Clegg said that was how he saw things. I told him I begged to differ. He told me I could differ all I wanted. And yeah, he understood why I broke my fraternal vows – he actually said that – when faced with the law. He also understood why I had to rat out – his exact words – Marois and the others. Because I had told all to the police. Now it seems that Marois was so remorseful about what had gone down, what he'd done, that he wanted to make a clean breast of all past transgressions. So Marois had confessed to the cops, in a breakdown moment, that he had helped cause Professor Hancock's death.'

'Why did he say that?'

'Because Marois went on to tell the police that he had submitted essays to Hancock that were not written by him. And that, on suspecting that cheating was going on in his classes, Hancock went into that dark slide which ended with him hanging himself.'

'So if Marois didn't write his essays for Hancock, who did?'

'I did.'

Those two words landed like a sucker punch.

'Tell me that's not true,' I said.

'It's true.'

'Why?' I finally whispered. 'Why?'

'Fraternal stupidity. Marois was in danger of failing Hancock's course. He'd already flunked one course the previous semester. He approached me in March of last year, flattering me, telling me how I was one of the few smart athletes he knew, and how he just wanted help with an essay, and how no one would know, and how he'd be willing to pay me . . . '

'You didn't fucking accept money, did you?'

'Hell no. But I did help him out by writing the essay. I even dumbed it down a little bit to make it seem more his own voice. Hancock still worked it out. But he couldn't fail Marois because the essay was okay. Without direct proof of the deception, his hands were tied. And that must have fucked up his head, given what you've told me about all his fragilities. So if you're wondering if I feel guilty about all that, the truth is: yes, I do. So guilty it hurts. I don't know what, if anything, I can do to make this all better.'

'There's nothing you can do,' I said. 'It's done. We're done.'

I saw Bob swallow hard, tears welling up.

'Don't say that, please,' he said.

'Where, *how*, can we go anywhere from here?'

Bob snapped his eyes shut. My mind was racing. Augmenting this was my deep, urgent need to scream: *you have ruined everything*. Instead, my voice – as hollow and arctic as a hole cut in the ice – said:

'I think you should find somewhere new to live tomorrow.'

'Okay,' Bob said, his head down.

I stood up, reaching for my cigarettes and my parka.

'Didn't you know how this news would kill so much between us? You know how devastated Hancock was after he found out about the cheating in his class. You commiserated with me about this. How could you have done that, knowing full well that you were one of the cheats? You had such a great academic future. You had me. You chose your jock tribe. You were loyal to them, not to me. Nor to yourself. But here's my ongoing loyalty to you. I'm saying nothing to nobody about what you did.'

After being released on bail Marois was summoned, with his father and an attorney that his dad had brought with him from Lewiston, to a meeting with the Dean of Students, the Dean of the Faculty, the Director of Athletics, and the local district attorney. During the course of the meeting Marois reiterated the story he'd been telling everyone: that Howie had tried to come on to him several times in the past and that seeing him alone in the woods brought back all the shame and horror he felt about being touched 'privately' in the swimming pool by Howie, and he lost it, overreacting completely. He admitted being drunk and jizzed up on speed – because he had been using Dexedrine to keep him awake to study. He truly regretted what had happened. He was appalled that he had acted ferociously. He was beyond ashamed – and wanted to do everything possible to make it up to Howie. But he was reacting to constant harassment from a man who was trying to push his homosexuality on to him, who wouldn't take no for an answer, who was making Marois feel under siege, causing him to eventually explode. To show how much he wanted to make a clean breast of things he was now confessing to cheating in Professor Hancock's class, and in getting his friend Robert O'Sullivan to write an essay for him – which Marois submitted under his own name.

That day word had gotten around campus about what had happened to Howie. Marois's version of events was everywhere. The urban students, the more progressive ones, the arty contingent, were all horrified by the attack. But the college itself was not coming out on one side or the other, using the *sub judice* excuse to keep press coverage of the attack to a minimum. I heard all the conflicting reports – how Howie was obsessed with Marois; how Marois was actually 'that way inclined' and had come on to Howie who turned him down, how the jocks got away with virtual murder at the college because the administration had to keep the old-school male alumni happy by producing winning teams, and how Bob O'Sullivan had gotten expelled on the spot when he admitted to the Dean of Students that he had indeed ghosted not one, but five or so essays for his Beta brothers over the past two years.

That was the wild unfairness of this whole business. Though Bob was immediately told he was no longer associated with the college, Marois was initially suspended with his cohorts, pending further police and college investigations. How could they kick out Bob for a breach of academic trust, yet merely suspend someone who had beaten a fellow student to a pulp and had also instigated the cheating scandal which engulfed Hancock? The college's excuse was that it was still an ongoing police investigation – but as Duncan Kendall noted when I ran into him on the quad the day after Bob left town:

'Bowdoin won the Division II ice-hockey championships with Marois as their captain last year. It caused a flood of alumni money to roll in. Hockey season is just six weeks off. Of course they have to suspend him – because he did several terrible things. But expel the winning hockey player? No chance of that. Your fellow was made the scapegoat here. Had he still been the star football player ... '

'He quit because of me,' I said.

'Looks like he couldn't completely give up the fraternity. Those creeps destroyed his future. Getting expelled from Bowdoin on a cheating charge ... what grad school will look at him now?'

I walked back to my apartment, fighting tears, failing. Returning to the emptiness of my home, however, was a wrench. Bob was gone. His books, his clothes, his record player and LPs – all had been, in the preceding hours, removed. I must say that there was a desperate moment of shock followed by despair when I saw that he'd packed up and left. On the kitchen table was his set of keys and $40 in cash and a note:

I was told by the college to pack my bags. I am feeling too ashamed right now to say goodbye face-to-face. Or maybe it's just too hard to bear. I have no idea where I will be going after this – except home to face the wrath of my father. I have let him down. As I so let you down. As I completely let myself down. Now I don't know what happens next, but I do know that I can't stay here.

I am so sorry.
I love you.

And he signed it with a simple *B*.

I didn't sleep that night. I didn't know who to turn to. Didn't know what I should do next. The next morning I jumped on my bicycle and took a long cold pedal down Maine Street until I reached Mere Point. I sat there on the cold dock, staring out at the water, cursing myself for dismissing Bob like that last night, yet simultaneously knowing that Duncan got it right when he said: 'Bob had it all and fucked it up.' But I couldn't help but feel that I shouldn't have told him to move out right away, that the same judgmental streak which saw me snub my brother had come into play again – and look where it left me. Alone and peering out at the ever-unsettled waters of the Atlantic, not knowing what to do next.

I turned my bicycle back home. Over the next week I went to my classes. I snuck in and out of the library. I sidestepped DJ and Sam when I saw them coming toward me on the quad. I ate all my meals at home. I made myself scarce. The sense of loneliness in the apartment was acute. I missed Bob's arms around me; the way we would cling together after making love; the frequent whispered promises we made to always be there for each other. The week after he left, I took the bus down to Portland, then grabbed a taxi to the Maine Medical Center. I fully expected to be turned away when I asked if I could see Howard D'Amato. The nurse at the reception desk said she would have to ask the family if they would allow Alice Burns to visit their son. She stood up and went into a ward just off the reception area, the swing door flapping behind her. Moments later a large woman in a pink pantsuit and virtually pink hair came out, walking straight toward me. My natural sense of suspicion – coupled with the knowledge that Howie's people were dealing with all sorts of immense things right now – made me step backward.

'No need to be shy, Alice,' the woman said in a thick New York accent. ''Cause I want to give you a real big hug.'

Which is exactly what she did – which is when I also found out that I was being enveloped in the arms of Howie's mother. Her name was Stella. She told me that Howie had told her that I had been a real friend to him – 'which immediately makes you my friend'. Moments later Sal D'Amato walked out. He was tall, slightly pot-bellied, with a shiny bald head and serious muscles. He was wearing a tan suede jacket, tan pants, a red V-neck sweater. He looked exhausted, red-eyed, trying not to appear overwhelmed or furious.

'So you're the sweetheart,' he said.

I didn't know how to respond, so I just said:

'I'm Howie's friend, yes.'

'Alice, right?' he said, now giving me a hug. 'Any friend of Howie's is a friend of mine. Howie's had a lot of visitors the past few days,' Sal said. 'The cops, the college president, a couple of lawyers ... '

'How's he doing?' I asked.

'That bastard flattened his nose and knocked out two teeth. Surgery will take care of the nose – that's scheduled in two days. After that they've got a dental surgeon coming in to install a temporary bridge, with a permanent one to follow in a couple of months. Fortunately, his face – though badly beaten up – suffered no internal fractures. Now my own lawyer is negotiating with the college –'

'Sal ... ' Stella said, her tone indicating he shouldn't continue.

'Hey, I'm not saying anything indiscreet. Everyone's gonna know soon enough we're gonna sue the shit out of the college, and make certain the goon who did this to our boy does serious time in the big house.'

I found myself smiling – not just at Sal's broad Queens accent, but his clear, evident need to defend his son and see that justice was done for him.

'See, Stella,' he said, pointing to me. 'Alice here gets it. She sees what we're trying to do here for our boy. And Jesus, are those fuckers gonna pay.'

Before I was brought in to visit with Howie, I was warned by his mother:

'He don't look his best. But try not to look too thrown when you see him.'

174

I promised that I wouldn't be freaked.

But the truth is: I was freaked.

Howie was in a bed in a small ward. His head was bandaged, as they had to stitch up part of his scalp where the blows had rained down. There were vast amounts of surgical tape on his nose. His face was a mass of bruises and broken blood vessels. There was a wad of cotton in his mouth where his two front teeth once lived.

'Don't tell me I look gorgeous,' Howie said as I approached his bed.

'You don't look gorgeous,' I said, leaning over to kiss him on the forehead.

'You're too kind to come,' he said, his voice thick and muffled thanks to the cotton stuck up in the front of his mouth.

'It's hardly kindness. I was horrified at what happened to you. Like so many people at the college.'

'They still believe his "a faggot wanted to cornhole me" story?'

Sal came in here.

'No need to lay that on Alice.'

'I can handle it,' I said.

'Anyway,' Sal said, 'from what Vinnie Moscone told me – that's my lawyer – this Marois kid's got a little history in that department.'

'Sal . . . ' Stella said.

'Hey, Alice is one of us, right, Alice?'

'Absolutely, sir.'

'She's even a polite kid – and that's rare enough these days. And she understands that everything we say here today is between ourselves, right?'

'You've got my word on that, sir.'

'I'm Sal, not "sir" – but I appreciate your respectfulness. Your mom and dad obviously did a good job with you.'

'I'll tell them that, Sal.'

'Where's Bob?' Howie asked.

'That's another story for another time,' I said.

'He didn't get kicked out because of all this?'

'Not directly.'

'But I told the police and the college that he stepped in, tried to break it up and got slugged by Marois and his goons.'

'It didn't have to do with that, Howie.'

'Now I feel terrible . . . '

'What happened to Bob was Bob's doing, not yours. You need to know that.'

'I'm still sorry.'

'Not as sorry as I am for you.'

The nurse came in, informing us that she needed to get Howie cleaned up.

'I cannot thank you enough for coming down to see me,' Howie said.

'How long will they be keeping you here?' I asked.

'Another week or so. The nose job is scheduled for next Tuesday, followed by the dental work.'

'Then he's coming home with us,' Stella said.

'And buying an apartment before I start NYU in January,' Howie said.

'Is that the plan?' I asked.

'Bowdoin's not only handling the transfer, they are also paying the next two years at NYU. All that and an apartment. It pays to get called "Tree Fag" and have your face rearranged.'

'Enough of that fag stuff,' Sal said. 'You're my son. That's all that counts.'

On the way back to college that afternoon all I could think was: good on you, Howie, for letting your dad and his lawyer squeeze the college for as much as they could. Good on you for deciding to get the hell out Maine and go to a city where your originality and flair will be embraced.

The next morning, I asked for an appointment with the Dean of Students. Christa Marley was straightforward, direct, with a hint of kindness that emerged when she said:

'I am sure the past two weeks are ones you'd rather not have lived through.'

I thanked her for the thought, then asked:

'Do you think there's a way that the college could do me a favor and see about getting me accepted somewhere else for the next semester?'

'As it is only five weeks before Christmas, that is one tall order. Where would you like to go?'

'Trinity College Dublin.'

I saw her face register surprise. Then:

'Interesting choice. Why there?'

'Professor Hancock often talked about it with me. Said it was his dream summer, studying there.'

'Yes, I know how close you were to Professor Hancock. You've really had it hard this semester.'

'No doubt in the future I'll probably look back and say it was formative, that it built character and all that stuff. At the moment I just think I need to be elsewhere for a while. I'm asking for your help in this.'

'Truth be told I have no idea how to get you accepted at such short notice. But let me see if I can get the college to authorize a call on your behalf to my counterpart over there and see if there is any possibility whatsoever. One small thing I do need to discuss with you: the college is very aware of how you raised all sorts of public interest in that friend of yours who went missing at Old Greenwich High.'

'That was my then-boyfriend who contacted the *New York Times*, not me.'

'But you were interviewed by the *New York Times* and also on NBC.'

'Is that a problem?'

'Of course not. It is your right – indeed, your constitutional right – to speak to whomever you want to, to voice your opinion about anything and everything. The thing is: we are trying to limit the publicity about what happened to Howie for Howie's sake, so that he isn't tagged with the label of someone beaten up because of his, uh, flamboyance. Keeping it out of the press will allow him to have a fresh start.'

'I had no plans to go to the press,' I said.

'I am very glad to hear that. I ask that if anyone from the media gets in touch with you, you first call me.'

'But as the college is doing its absolute best to keep everything under wraps ... '

'I can also promise you that, in exchange for your cooperation, I will do everything in my power to expedite your transfer request.'

Because getting me out of the country would also be in the college's best interests.

'I appreciate you trying to move things forward,' I said.

'You absolutely sure that Dublin's the place you want to be?'

I hadn't a clue. But I had read up a great deal about Trinity after Professor Hancock talked so passionately about it. It looked rather wonderful, archaic. And then there was the romance of being abroad, far away from all the mess of everything.

Dean Marley worked fast. She had a long talk with her counterpart at Trinity. In turn I was called into the dean's office the next day so a transatlantic call could be patched in by the operator. I found myself talking with a woman named Deirdre Dowling – who had a gravelly smoker's voice and an accent that was very Irish and highly authoritative when it came to her diction and her sense of formality. She helpfully and clearly outlined the various options and admissions procedures.

I wrote my application essay using a recent Trinity College catalog that was sent via inter-library loan, citing specific courses and professors which made me want to study there. All applications are an exercise in persuasion, in which you are asking the adjudicator: please take me seriously, please let me across the threshold at which you stand guard. I pulled an all-nighter to turn it around in a day, retyped my essay, stuck it all in an envelope and biked the next morning down to the post office off Maine Street. It was a few days before Thanksgiving break. When I handed over the hefty envelope and asked if there was any sort of super-fast airmail to Dublin, the clerk shook her head and said:

'Airmail is airmail. With a bit of luck, it might get there in ten days, at worst three weeks. But it's before the Christmas rush, so ... '

I paid the two dollars seventy cents – a hefty sum for a letter. I decided not to tell my parents of my intention to transfer to Trinity until I received official word from the college that I was in.

I'd heard nothing from my dad since the coup. He came back once to Connecticut, but only later did I find out from my mother that he had twice tried to call me. There was still no news of Peter's whereabouts, but Mom didn't seem overly concerned about her missing eldest child, telling me: 'Your father seems to be keeping tabs on him, so at least I know he's not in danger.'

Did that mean that he'd met up with Peter in Chile, or that Peter was somehow being protected from falling into harm's way?

On the day I received my acceptance letter from Trinity I shared the news with nobody. On that day I also learned that the matter with Howie D'Amato had been settled; that he was receiving a significant settlement from the college. In exchange Howie agreed not to press charges against Marois, or to discuss the matter in public. Marois agreed to write a private letter of apology to Howie, and to understand that any further violent behavior would result in serious jail time.

When it came to leaving Bowdoin, I called my father's office in New York to see if his secretary could wire him in Chile, asking him to call me as soon as possible. I heard nothing. I began to pack up the apartment, trying not to dwell on the sadness and fear within me, as I found myself wondering: what am I leaping into?

Just before midnight, as I was heading to bed, the phone rang. The line was crackly, distant.

'Sweetheart! Sorry I've been so elsewhere for many months. The situation here has been just a little complicated.'

'Is Peter safe?'

'Don't worry about him.'

'So you've seen him?'

'Put it this way – I am ensuring that he is staying out of danger.'

'But if the regime is cracking down on dissidents ... '

'Peter's not a dissident, and he is being protected.'

'Does he know that?'

'I doubt it, as we're not exactly in touch. But trust me, nothing bad will come his way. I have enough serious friends here to ensure that. But that's not the only reason you called me, is it?'

I wanted to press further about Peter, but my father's tone indicated: no further discussion about this will be entertained. I changed the subject, saying:

'I've got some news.'

I expected him to raise all sorts of objections about me going to Ireland, or even having the audacity to apply to Trinity without first having a parent–child discussion on the matter. But instead he heard me out without interruption, though I could tell he was pleased to learn of the financial savings he'd be making once I started there. When I finished, his response was crisp and to the point:

'Well done you for getting into such a fine school. Your mom told me about the business with the boyfriend. You did the right thing there. You've done the right thing deciding to head elsewhere. Your mom won't take the news well. Fear not – I'll smooth it over with her.'

Two or so hours later, when I was fast asleep, the phone jumped into life. I picked it up, fearing the worst.

'You think you can just announce you're moving overseas?'

'Mom, it's two in the morning.'

'You have provoked the worst case of insomnia I've ever had.'

'You'll get over not having me around.'

'Don't you get supercilious with me, young lady.'

'What do you want me to say here? Dad was pretty pleased with the news.'

'That's because your father is forever elsewhere. The two of you are cut from the same cloth. One foot always out the door.'

'And why do you think that is, Mommy Dearest?'

'Because instead of confronting things you run away.'

I thought that one through for a moment.

'Running away is a way of confronting things that you know you can never win. I can never win anything with you.'

'Don't think you'll get away that easily,' said my mother.

'If there's one thing I know about me, you, our family, this fucking life,' I said, 'nothing is ever easy. But an ocean between us … that might just be easier.'

PART TWO

11

NEVER ARRIVE IN Dublin for the first time in January. Unless, that is, you want to live in suicidal gloom. The nonstop somberness, the mildewed chill, is everywhere. Under perpetually clouded skies. The city – downtrodden and bleak most of the year – becomes even more dispiriting at this dark juncture of the calendar.

'First time here?' the chatty cabbie asked me as I loaded my suitcases into his trunk (which he referred to as the 'boot').

'Yes. I'm coming to study at Trinity.'

'Ah, a posh Yank. You are a Yank, yes?'

'I am indeed American.'

'And obviously a smart one, studying at Trinity and all that. Trinity, you know, only started allowing Catholics a few years back,' the cabbie told me.

'Never knew that. So they might have excluded me.'

'Nah, they want the Yanks and their fuckin' money. Anyway, the situation was a bit more complex than what I'm tellin' you. Up until 1970 you had to get special dispensation from the Church to attend Trinity.'

'What "church"?' I asked.

'What fuckin' Church do you think? The Catholic Church. The Archbishop of Dublin had to approve every Catholic who wanted to study there.'

'Then it really wasn't Trinity that was stopping Catholics from going there?'

'Maybe not officially, but their own fuckin' Protestant thing made it very hard for a Catholic within their walls.'

Why did I sense immediately that this man was talking crap? Why did I also sense that it might not be wise for me to point this out to him?

'Well, your timing for visiting us is brilliant. January is the month when the city's a total kip, when even an old blind dog who's lost his reason wants to throw itself into the Liffey.'

'That's quite a metaphor.'

'You takin' the piss?'

'Sorry, I don't follow.'

'You mockin' me?'

'Hardly.'

'I don't need some fuckin' Yank mockin' me.'

'That was not my intention.'

'Sure it wasn't.'

He fell silent. I lit up a cigarette, staring out at the shabby cityscape. We were crossing a square called Mountjoy. Once-stately Georgian buildings in various states of disrepair. Litter everywhere. And grim blocks of modern apartments – very much looking like the low-rise equivalent of the housing projects dotted around New York – just down the street from this near-derelict square. The rain kept coming down. Every time I peered out, the view became even more depressing. And the driver was talking again, now playing nice.

'So where're you from in America?' he asked.

'Originally from New York.'

'Grand town, grand town. You might, by comparison, find Dublin a little on the small side. But the craic here is grand.'

Craic. That was another new word.

''Course, unlike New York, you won't find many of the blacks in Dublin.'

Careful here.

'That doesn't surprise me,' I said.

'Nor should it – because we won't fuckin' let them in.'

He laughed at that witticism, glancing into his rearview mirror to see if I was reacting badly to his provocation. I decided the moment was right to close down further conversational possibilities with this gentleman. Telling him that I was rather tired after the all-night flight, I shut my eyes – and actually passed out. When I woke again, it was courtesy of the driver, tapping me on the shoulder.

'We're here like.'

Did I hear that right? I noticed I still had a smoldering cigarette in my left hand. And that I was in front of a redbrick house, two stories high, with a door painted a bland brown. I looked at the cab meter: eighty pence for the journey, I dug into my wallet, took out a one-pound note and told him to keep the change.

'That 20p will buy my first pint tonight. I'm thanking you now.'

He helped get my suitcases out of the 'boot'. He shook my hand.

'Good luck to yuz,' he said, then got back into his car and drove off.

I hesitated for a moment before raising the door knocker and bringing it down twice. I was on Oswald Road in an area called Sandymount. Two rows of low-lying houses, all narrow and solemn. At the end of the street I got a glimpse of water and a big power station on the immediate horizon. The rain was soft, insidious; a mist with a distinct damp iciness. Part of me wanted to lug my bag back to the nearest main street, find a cab and clear off for the airport.

After a moment the door was opened by a woman in her late sixties, dressed in a housecoat, her face severe, her hair bluish gray.

'So you're Alice.'

This was Mrs Brennan, my landlady. When I was accepted at Trinity I was told that there was no chance I'd be able to live on campus. I had no choice but to be a 'lodger' in somebody's house in Dublin ... 'until', said the Warden of Residences, 'you find a flat share of your own'. The idea of being a lodger, of living with a landlady, struck me as worrisome. But as I knew nobody in Dublin, had no idea how to find a flat, this was my only option.

'Let me help you in with your things,' Mrs Brennan said.

I came into a tight hallway, papered in a faded floral paper. There was a small room off this.

'That's the sitting room,' Mrs Brennan said. 'I allow my girls to read there in the evening, and even watch the telly if I'm around.'

Girls? 'How many "girls" do you have here?' I asked.

'Just yourself and Jacinta. She's from County Laois, doing a degree in education. Plans to teach back in Laois as soon as she's finished. A very nice girl. No problems with her whatsoever. Let me show you to your room.'

I hauled my suitcases up a flight of narrow stairs. In front of me was the bathroom – a plain white box with a toilet, a sink, a bathtub and nothing else.

'Now I suppose you'll want a bath after your flight. I allow my girls one bath a week.'

'Where's the shower?'

'We don't do anything fancy like that. The thing is, to heat the bathwater means putting on the immersion heater. It's rather dear, the electricity. But you'll have enough hot water in the morning and evening to wash your face. And if you tell me which day of the week you'll be wanting your bath ... '

'I usually shower ... *bathe* ... every day.'

Mrs Brennan shook her head.

'We can't allow that. But if you want a second bath per week, the cost will be an additional 50p.'

She opened a door opposite the bathroom.

'Here we are.'

The room was maybe ten by seven feet. Cream paint applied over chip paper. It gave the walls a bubbly texture. There was a coffin-like bed, a rickety bentwood chair, a small table with an old lamp on it which, I suppose, was going to be my desk. A crucifix – replete with a very tortured-looking Jesus – adorned one wall. A Sacred Heart lamp was tucked in a corner above the bed, its red glow the only bit of color in a room that immediately struck me as ideal living quarters for a novice nun.

'Now even though I never make breakfast for my girls after half eight, because you've arrived all the way from America I'll make an exception and have it ready in about fifteen minutes. Do you take tea or Nescafé?'

Instant coffee? No thanks.

'Tea please.'

'Very good so.'

As soon as she was out of the room I put my head in my hands. This was beyond bad. The house was so deeply cold. There was an electric fire in my room, built into the little grate that was there. I tried to turn it on. It wouldn't work. I tried again, the chill starting to get to me. I opened the door, shouting downstairs:

'Mrs Brennan, how do I get the fireplace to work?'

'You have to feed it five pence. That should give you about a half-hour of heat.'

'That's the only heat there is?'

'Yes, that is the only heat.'

I dug into my bag, found some Irish coins, dug out a five-pence piece, placed it in the slot, turned the dial and ... bingo, the electric bars of the fire began to slowly illuminate. By the time I finished unpacking a degree of heat was radiating around the room. My clothes were hanging up in the plain unvarnished wardrobe, my underwear and socks in the small chest of drawers, and my red Olivetti typewriter looked far too modernist and out of place on that rickety desk. I had a stab of sadness. The last time I had set up a place to live it had been with Bob. My Irish guy. Mrs Brennan knocked hard on the door – like a cop demanding entry.

'Breakfast's on the table. Don't want to see it go cold now.'

As I came out the door I saw Mrs Brennan peering into the room.

'What's that thing on the desk?' she asked.

'My typewriter.'

'Quite the color. But I have to tell you: we want no clatter of a typewriter in the evening.'

'You're saying: I can't type here?'

'Not after eight o'clock you can't.'

'Why's that?'

'Because those are the rules. Just as: I expect my girls to be in by 10 p.m.'

'You're not serious.'

'I'm very serious, Miss Burns. House rules.'

I took a deep steadying intake of breath. I held my tongue. I came downstairs for breakfast: two eggs sunny side up, 'rashers', very good Irish brown bread, tea as strong and awakening as any I'd previously tasted.

'Now you'll want a lie-in after your long flight,' she said.

'Actually I think I'll head into the college after I finish.'

This did not please her.

'Suit yourself,' she said.

'Is there a bus nearby?'

'The 7A goes down the Strand and will drop you on the side of College Green. The front gates of Trinity are just there.'

'Thank you.'

'Now Miss Scanlon probably told you that the room and breakfast is seven pounds per week. If you want tea on Sunday – and I usually do a treat like chops or a bit of steak – it's an extra fifty pence. You'll be wanting to go to Mass on Sunday, yes?'

'I don't go to Mass, ma'am.'

Her eyes went wide at that.

'Do your parents know that you won't be going to church?'

'They don't go either.'

'They're lapsed?'

'My dad's lapsed. My mother's Jewish.'

'A Jew?' she asked. 'A real Jew?'

'Just like her two parents. And her two aunts who escaped the Nazis after Kristallnacht. You've heard of Kristallnacht, haven't you?'

Mrs Brennan's face scrunched up and she stared down into her cup of tea. 'If you're heading out you'll need to be back by ten,' she finally said. 'After that I pull the bolt over the door and you'll have to sleep outside.'

As I left the house around ten minutes later I found myself wondering: how do I find a suitable room in a city about which I know nothing?

I walked down to Sandymount Strand. A row of low brick-and-concrete houses facing a beach. The rain was a fine vapor now. I waited on the wrong side of the road for the bus, forgetting again that cars drove on the left here. When a bus arrived with the words Dun Laoghaire across its top, I got on and asked the driver if this would get me to Trinity.

'You mean the college?'

I nodded.

'Didn't you read what it said on the front of the bus: Dun Laoghaire?' – and he pronounced it: *Dunne Leary.*

'Sorry, just arrived from the States. Totally lost.'

'So you are. Other side of the road. Look for a bus that says: *An Lar.* That's "City Centre" in Irish.'

188

Once aboard the right bus I peered out the window, trying to perceive the world beyond the dank wet glass. Much old redbrick. Patches of dereliction. Garbage strewn everywhere on the streets. I kept sucking down my cigarette, telling myself: it will improve when I reach the college.

When the conductor yelled 'College Green' for my benefit, I got off. I found myself staring at high dark walls, black with centuries of soot (or, at least, that's what I sensed), with two statues on either side of the high polished wooden doors. I approached them, noting that the playwright Oliver Goldsmith and the philosopher Edmund Burke were the two bronze gatekeepers out front. The doors were open; a porter in a formal white tie and tails was in a small office just inside the walls. I was going to ask him where I could find the Warden of Residences, but my attention was elsewhere. Just beyond this arching entranceway was the grandeur that was Trinity College Dublin.

Even though I had seen pictures, nothing quite prepared me for its formal elegance – the aesthetic solemnity of its central courtyard, surrounded by stern venerable buildings. In the center of this initial square there was a huge bell tower – known as the Campanile – standing there like a monument to the passing of time (indeed it did chime ominously every hour on the hour). I noticed small doorways everywhere in the buildings that surrounded the square, as well as a long set of steps running up to a somewhat Romanesque structure – which turned out to be the college dining hall. Tucked behind this was a small modern concrete extension: the student union. I ducked inside it, as the rain was now truly slashing down, testing the waterproof limits of my black trench coat. I smelled food. I smelled cigarettes. I also found myself in a fully-functioning pub. It was 11.15 a.m. and already there were many students and several faculty members hunched over glasses of a very black liquid, cigarettes alight, deep in conversation. I went up to the bar – where a woman with a shock of black hair, dark circles beneath very red eyes, was behind the counter.

'What can I get you?' she asked.

'What do you suggest?'

'Are you joking me?'

'I wouldn't know what to order here.'

'Well, as you're in Dublin you should order a Guinness.'

'Fine by me.'

'Pint or a glass?'

'What's the smaller one?' I asked.

The woman cast her eyes heavenward.

'A glass, evidently,' she said.

'Sorry – new here.'

I now watched an interesting bit of local artisanship, as this woman poured my glass of Guinness. Putting it under the tap, she pulled back the lever and let the glass fill up with a swirling brown liquid, stopping it just a quarter-inch or so from the top. Setting it aside, she attended other matters as the liquid began to stop swirling and transformed itself from a mid-brown hue to something decidedly black. In the process, a distinctive cream collar began to form at the top of the glass. Then the barmaid came over and picked up the now-blackened glass, adding a small amount of liquid to the top, ensuring that the cream collar reached the rim.

'That'll be eleven pence,' she said. 'You just arrived today? The name's Ruth. Before you take your first sip here's a little trick to tell whether a Guinness is well poured or not. Tip it slightly to one side ... '

I did as ordered, and noted that the cream upper edge was perfectly intact as I did so.

'We call that the priest's collar,' Ruth said. 'If the Guinness has been properly poured, the collar is always even and firm as you tip it. If it breaks up when tipped then it's shite. But as long as I'm pouring you'll be right.'

I lifted the glass. I took a sip. The Guinness had a viscous texture and a taste that was bitter, but with a strong hint of malt. Though it looked like a pitch-black milkshake, drinking it was a bit like taking in a food substitute with an alcoholic kick. I was immediately partial to it.

I told her about my arrival at Mrs Brennan's, and how I was due back this evening at ten.

'Ah, so they landed you with an old biddy,' Ruth said. 'Give her a week's notice when you see her tomorrow, and get the fuck out of there. There's a noticeboard down the corridor there. Check it out. It's full of flat shares, of people looking for a flatmate. You've got a week to go before term starts. Make it your top priority.'

'Believe me I will. Even my own mother never insisted I was in bed by ten – or, at least, not since I was about thirteen.'

'Well, as long as you are stuck out on Sandymount you're going to have no craic at all.'

'Second time today that I've heard that word.'

'Irish for "good times". Which we need to have in this fucking country, considering how fucked it is.'

I finished my Guinness and went over to the bulletin board. It was crammed with messages and notices, and eight different flat-share offers. I wrote down all the details in my notebook and returned to the bar and took Ruth through the list of places on offer.

'Nah, you don't want to live in Sutton. Northside – and though the water's just there, the area's kind of suburban and dull. Dun Laoghaire is lovely. A beautiful pier, great walks, a couple of good pubs. But it's half an hour on a bus, and too fucking far to walk. Best to keep somewhere near the college ... Ranelagh's a lovely village just about two miles from Stephen's Green ... and that place on Pearse Street ... sounds like a kip, but it's the street right behind us. You'd literally be living just outside of Trinity's walls.'

I liked the sound of that. I asked if there was a phone nearby. Ruth pointed to a black box on the far side of the bar. I had to negotiate its strange operating system: depositing a two-pence coin in a slot, then waiting with a finger pressed up against a button marked A which I had to push when someone answered. The number at the Pearse Street flat rang and rang. No one picked up. Back at the bar Ruth told me that few people had private phones; there was a year-long waiting list for an actual phone line. Most flats just had a public phone downstairs by the front door.

'Take a wander over to Pearse Street and leave the fella a note,' Ruth advised. 'Then you might want to walk down Westland Row and across to Merrion Square – which is still a rather lovely spot.

Get back here before I knock off around four and let me know how you've got on.'

I walked through Trinity's second central courtyard, past the rather ugly modern library imposed on this immaculate Elizabethan campus, past a sports field where, now that the skies had stopped leaking and a hint of sun was fighting its way through the gray gloom, men were passing a ball and dragging each other into the mud. Rugby. Then I left by the back entrance of the college. There was a small railway station at the far end of the street, the place where Westland Row intersected with Pearse Street.

To call it rundown was to engage in massive understatement. Pearse Street had the aroma of dereliction; a place that had no redeeming features whatsoever. Grubby old buildings, a sleazy-looking movie theatre playing a bad Burt Reynolds film (*Fuzz*) that had been released two years earlier back home. Trash on the streets, as I was seeing almost everywhere. The place had a skid row feel – and the building, 75a, was a nondescript three-story brick house with a battered front door and rotting windowsills. It did not exactly engender promise. And it seemed – like Mrs Brennan's grim setup – such a long way away from everything I took for granted back in Old Greenwich and at college in ever-orderly New England.

I walked up the steps, pushed the buzzer next to the name Sean Treacy, waited, pushed it again, waited. I was in the process of scribbling a note, explaining that I had come to see about the flat, when the door opened. A man in his late forties, a shock of curly black hair, wearing a paisley shirt, a cardigan and grubby pajama bottoms, peered out at me.

'Can I help you?'

'Are you Sean?'

'I am indeed. And who might be you?'

I told him – and said that I was here to inquire about the flat.

'Well, Alice Burns from Connecticut – the bad news is that I found a tenant just two days ago. The good news – well, sort of good news – is that I do have a bedsit here. It's not much, it could use a bit of fixing up. But if you were that way inclined ... '

'When could I see it?'

'Come right in.'

The hallway was dingy, papered in peeling paper showing scenes of big country houses. The carpet on the stairs was threadbare. There was a radio playing somewhere. There was the aroma of cooking intertwined with damp. We walked to the top of the stairs where a door flung open and a young woman in a fluffy bathrobe came out, a lit cigarette in her mouth, the accompanying steam further hinting that this was the bathroom.

'Who's this?' she asked Sean.

'A new arrival from the United States,' he said. 'I presume you're a Trinity student, right?'

'That's right.'

'Good luck to you,' the woman said, but in a manner that did not make it sound like a chorus of welcome.

'That's Sheila,' Sean said when the woman had disappeared behind a door at the end of the corridor. 'Trying to be an actress. Not having much in the way of luck. Because the truth of it is: she's no fucking good.'

We reached the third floor of the building, and a scuffed white door with a plain metal handle.

'Now as I told you, the place isn't much to look at.'

He opened the door. What I saw was beyond depressing. A room, perhaps twelve feet by ten, with faded pink wallpaper, an old carpet riddled with stains and cigarette burns, a forlorn double bed with a sagging box spring and grubby mattress, a sink, and a tiny alcove kitchen featuring a fridge, a second sink, a few cheaply made cabinets, and a two-ring hot plate. It was seriously cold in this room. It had felt no heat whatsoever for months. Sean noticed me clutching my arms.

'There's a grate over there in the corner. You can buy peat briquettes or coal at the shop on the corner of Westland Row. I could also probably get you a Kosangas heater. You have to buy the gas canisters for it – but it warms the place right up in a couple of minutes.'

'Is there a bathroom on this floor?'

'Only the one downstairs.'

'How many apartments in the building?'

'Seven flats altogether. But as you're a student, you can probably get in there after most people go off to work.'

'Is it a bath or a shower?'

'Your basic bathtub. But if you do a bit of sport I gather that Trinity has showers next to their pool.'

I shut my eyes, a wave of tiredness and growing despondency rushing over me.

'Would you like a cup of tea?' Sean asked.

'That would be good,' I said.

Sean's bedsit was on the ground floor. I warmed to it immediately. It was full of books, crammed into makeshift shelves, in piles over the floor, and there were papers everywhere, a collage of handwritten bits of verse on the wall. It was the room of a literary man.

'My humble abode,' he said.

'It's wonderful. Are you a writer?'

'A poet,' said Sean. 'Two very slim volumes published here in Dublin. But as being a poet pays nothing, I manage this and two other buildings for a mate of mine.'

I watched as Sean reached into a sink filled with dirty dishes and fished out two teacups and saucers. After a cursory rinse with water he let them dry, turned on the kettle and dumped the remnants of a brown ceramic teapot in the trash can before flushing it clean with water from the tap.

'Back in the States,' I said, mesmerized by this ritual, 'making tea means putting a bag into hot water.'

'Which is why America has such shite tea. Here's how you make proper tea.'

He motioned me to come over to his tiny kitchenette.

'You need to heat the teapot first, then dump in at least four teaspoons of good tea – go to Bewley's on Grafton Street and buy their Irish Breakfast tea – then pour the boiled water over it, stir it twice, cover it and wait at least five minutes for it to steep.'

Having done all that, he signaled to me that I should 'take a pew' on his sofa. I closed my eyes for a moment, waking up with a start to see the tea and a plate of cookies (which he called 'biscuits') in front of me.

'Sorry, sorry, just got in this morning.'

'I'm impressed you're still vertical.'

That's when I told him about Mrs Brennan.

'So you'll be wanting out of there soon. Now I know it's not much to look at ... '

'How much is it a week?'

'Nine quid.'

'That's a lot considering ... '

'The landlord, between ourselves, is a greedy bollocks. But he also won't spend the money doing the redecorating himself. So here's what I might be able to do for you. If you were willing to fix it up yourself, I can point you in the direction of a friend who runs a paint shop and can deliver everything you need. I know someone who can get you a new mattress and fix the bed for about ten quid, all in. I'm sure I can convince His Lordship to not charge you rent for the first two weeks while you get the place in order.'

'But you're saying I have to pay for the paint, the new bed ... '

'That's why you're getting two weeks rent free.'

He poured out the tea, using a strainer over the cup to catch the leaves. When he pushed a jug of milk toward me and I said that I took my tea black he shook his head.

'Tea does not taste right without milk,' he said, pouring some in. I added a white sugar cube to the cup, stirred it twice, took a sip and thought: this might be the best cup of tea I've ever hoisted.

'It *is* better with milk,' I said.

'Told you so. Have a ginger snap. Ireland's finest.'

'The paint and brushes will cost me,' I said, getting back to business. 'Pulling up the carpet and painting the floorboards will cost me. The mattress and fixing the bed will cost me. I need a desk, I need an armchair, I'll certainly need that gas heater.'

'You've done this sort of thing before,' Sean said.

'Indeed I have,' I said, trying to mask the stab of sorrow that came over me as Bob filled my mind's eye and I found myself longing for all that had been lost.

'I can help you with all that,' Sean, said, taking in my moment of sadness but saying nothing about it. 'Maybe thirty pounds all-in.'

Even though I had absolutely no idea how much anything cost in Dublin my in-built bullshit detector told me I'd be spending far more.

'To do it right,' I said, 'will be closer to a hundred pounds. Now the term runs until mid-June. That's five months. About twenty-two weeks. While I'm doing the work I'm going to have to stay at Mrs Brennan's – which is costing me seven pounds per week. Here's what I'm willing to do: two weeks free rent while I fix it up ... but with the option to let me move in earlier, with a reduction of two pounds a week ... which means we, in essence, split the costs of the renovation, even though you're getting my labor for nothing. One last thing – I will want an agreement that the seven pounds per week rent will be maintained until June of 1975 when I graduate. So you're also agreeing to let me have the bedsit for the next eighteen months.'

'And if you leave before then?'

'Then you get a nicely renovated flat which you can charge more money for.'

'So ... a real New Yorker.'

'By which you mean?'

'You believe in negotiation. But I think I could do it for eight quid a week,' Sean said, accepting a cigarette from my open pack of Carrolls.

'Seven pounds – and you get a new bedsit in the process.'

'I'll have to talk with His Lordship. Can you be back here tomorrow at ten?'

'No problem – but I have to know by then. If you can't do this deal for me I will have to start looking for somewhere else.'

'I'll be awaiting you then,' Sean said, 'and will make you another cup of tea, maybe even will have some brown bread and butter to go with it.'

On my way out I lingered in the dimly lit hallway, listening to the music coming from upstairs – someone blaring Irish folk music, and a woman singing what sounded like Italian opera. I sensed immediately: I might not get a lot of peace and quiet here, but there was the college library nearby for that. And while the building was beyond grim, it was right behind Trinity, in the center of the city, a place I had yet to begin to explore. It was a price I could afford, and I would be able, within my modest budget, to create my own little place. I rather liked the idea that the gatekeeper here was a slightly shambolic poet ... and one who, as I was leaving, handed me a thin volume: *The Fare Thee Well*. Its cover was a line drawing of a ferry pulling out of a harbor. The inside back flap had a photograph of Sean looking about ten years younger, his face and eyes full of seductive promise.

I walked back to Trinity and found Ruth, just finishing off her shift.

'Thanks for your advice,' I said. 'I may just have found somewhere.'

I filled her in on the details.

'Sounds like a find – especially as he's letting you fix it up.'

'It's actually a dump.'

'Here's a bit of local wisdom for you – a dump gives you a choice. Accept that it is a kip and live in a kip, or try to change the kip into something a little more acceptable, even comfortable.'

'But don't most people choose the latter option – to slam the door on a dump and live better?'

Ruth gave me the most sardonic of smiles.

'You've got a lot to learn about this place.'

12

As I OPENED my eyes the next morning Jesus was looking down at me from his cross. The Sacred Heart lamp was casting its blood-red glow from its corner position above the narrow bed in which I lay. My body was clammy and damp after a night spent in the polyester sheets. For the first few bemused moments I had no idea where I was – until I caught a glimpse of Our Lord and Savior in crucifixion spread, and heard a knock on the door.

'It's half eight, Alice.'

This was Mrs Brennan's disapproving voice.

'If you want breakfast you best get downstairs now.'

Five minutes later, dressed and feeling very much in need of that weekly bath, I found myself being given a withering good-morning nod by Mrs Brennan, as she placed a plate of fried eggs and rashers on the table in front of me. I also found myself face-to-face with my fellow lodger. She smiled shyly as I came in.

'You must be Alice,' she said. 'Welcome. I'm Jacinta.'

Though she was maybe only two or three years my senior Jacinta dressed and comported herself like a woman well into her thirties. She was wearing a matching cream cardigan and pullover sweater with a small gold crucifix around her neck framed by a set of pearls. She had a tweed skirt, cream tights and heavily rouged lips. I could tell within moments that she was cowed by Mrs Brennan.

'Now, Jacinta, please tell Alice here about the morning tea you have most days with Father Reilly.'

'He's the college chaplain at Trinity,' Jacinta said.

'For the Catholics,' Mrs Brennan added.

'He really is the loveliest man. So interesting and well read and kind. Perhaps you'd like to come along with me this morning.'

'Thank you for the offer – but I have to be somewhere by ten.'

'Another day then,' Jacinta said.

'Absolutely,' I said.

'You hold her to that,' Mrs Brennan told Jacinta, who blushed anxiously in response.

Ten minutes later we were on our way together to the bus stop on Sandymount Strand. As soon as we were around ten paces away from Mrs Brennan's front door I pulled out my packet of Carrolls.

'Can I cadge one of yours?' Jacinta asked. 'I so need a smoke.'

I offered the pack, handing her the box of matches. Lighting up her cigarette she took a deep drag off of it, exhaling with an immense sigh of relief.

'That old bitch really does drive me spare,' she said.

I was taken aback by the bluntness of that statement – and rather pleased to hear it.

The 7A bus arrived. It was marked *An Lar*. We boarded it, heading up to the smoking level.

'Why don't you just leave that biddy and find a flat?' I asked.

'My parents would disown me.'

'The threat is usually greater than the actual action that might follow.'

'My da – he's deputy governor of a big prison. He has a very simple point of view when it comes to me and my three brothers: "My rule of law is absolute." Mammie is even worse. When they found out I was seeing a fella in Maynooth ... '

'He wasn't a priest?'

Jacinta covered her hand with her mouth, caught somewhere between shock and a certain pleasure in the subversive nature of my comment.

'You're a panic, you. His name is Aidan. And his father is a Garda in Leitrim.'

'What's a Garda?'

'The police. My father, being in the prison service, should have approved. But when they heard that we snuck off for a long weekend in Dublin ... well, I am still, in their eyes, a fallen woman. Even though nothing untoward happened.'

'Why's that?'

'Why do you think? You're expected to be a virgin until marriage.'

'I'm sure that's a rule which many people have breached.'

'Not in my family, not in Portlaoise. And listen to me going on like this.'

'Talk away – it's interesting.'

I offered her another cigarette – which she took and lit up immediately.

'Let me ask you something,' I said. 'With this Aidan guy, was it you who stopped it from going all the way?'

'Of course. You know what boys are like.'

'Indeed I do. But let me ask you something else. In retrospect, do you regret not having crossed that line with him?'

'That's a bit personal,' she said, a blush coming to her cheeks.

'Didn't mean to pry. It's just ... '

'Yes I regret it. Especially as I went through such hell afterwards. Neither of my parents would believe me when I assured them I was still a virgin. Know what my Da said: "If you really are then you won't object if we arrange for an appointment for the local GP to examine you and make certain you're telling the truth."'

'Surely you refused to go along with it,' I said.

'I had no choice but to present myself at the doctor's surgery and go through that horrible ... examination. Da told me he'd end my education if I said no. What could I do?'

'And when the doctor reported back to them that your hymen was, indeed, still intact ... ?'

'Not so loud, please.'

I was merely whispering back – but decided not to point that out.

'What did your father say when he discovered you were telling the truth?'

'He still went and spoke to the priest who was in charge of student affairs, and essentially told him that he wanted me back in my rooms every night at nine, as I was a troubled girl who was going to be led into temptation again.'

'Did the priest comply?'

'Of course. I think the sadistic bastard – God forgive me for saying that – actually took pleasure in being my jailer for the last year at uni.'

'A jailer at home, a jailer at school. Poor you.'

'Now you see why I'm stuck for the year at Mrs Brennan's. I am pretty sure my parents let on to her what happened with that fella, as she is often making comments like: "Now I don't suppose you're getting chatted up by the rugby crowd at Trinity, are you?" Drives me spare. And I want to tell the old bitch to mind her own bloody business.'

'Why don't you? While you're at it, why don't you also tell your parents that your life is your life, your body is your body?'

'That sort of thing might play in New York. But here? No way. I'd be shunned, told never to come back.'

'Would that be the worst thing in the world?'

From the startled look on her face I could tell that she had never considered that question before. She blinked and was fighting tears. I put my hand on her shoulder, suddenly horrified that I had so unsettled her.

'I'm sorry, I shouldn't have … '

'No, you're right, of course. But yes, I don't want to be thinking such things. And now I'm talking rubbish … '

'Trust me, I know how hard it is to walk away from crazy parents.'

Just two days earlier, I'd been heading to the departure gates at JFK with my mother in tow. Dad was back in Chile with Adam, shoring up his newly reprivatized mine. He had reassured both of us that Peter was doing fine, even though we still hadn't heard a word from him since he'd arrived there two months earlier and I couldn't help but think frightening thoughts. I'd sent him a letter and two postcards to American Express in Santiago, but silence remained his response. A light snow was falling in New York. All the flights, bar the Aer Lingus one to Shannon and on to Dublin, were delayed. To say that I was anxious was to engage in under-statement. But what was creating the most anxiety was my mother's decision to start weeping as she walked with me to the departure gate.

'I am driving home tonight to an empty house,' she said. 'You have all left me.'

'Mom, nobody's been living at home for over eighteen months now.'

'But at least before I had Peter up the road in New Haven, and you only six hours away in Maine.'

'We all move on.'

'Since when did you become a goddamn philosopher?'

'Since I found out a thing or two about heartache.'

'Why the hell are you smoking?'

'Because I'm a smoker, that's why. Your own mother smoked like a lunatic, and she managed to make it to old age.'

'She could have lived another ten to fifteen years if she hadn't.'

'You spent much of my childhood and adolescence complaining about what a manipulative, nasty woman she was.'

'I can say that, you can't.'

'Why is that?'

'Because she wasn't your mother. And because it's how you feel about me. I know you hate me.'

'That's not true ... even though you make life impossible ... most of all for yourself.'

Mom looked like I'd cold-cocked her with a clenched fist.

'Thank you for unloading this on me minutes before you step on that plane. You won't do anything stupid over there, will you? Like deciding to visit Belfast. There's a war on in Ireland.'

'It's up north, not where I'll be. I'm probably in more danger walking up Eighth Avenue at two in the morning.'

'That's why we live in the burbs – to avoid all that.'

'Actually the burbs bring their own horrors.'

'Tell me about it. I ran into Cindy yesterday. Still no word from Carly, no sign that she might somehow be alive.'

I shut my eyes, thinking about the reason I had had to stop answering Mrs Cohen's letters to me at Bowdoin: because they kept opening up the wound that was Carly's suicide. Now, in the wake of Professor Hancock, I simply had to shut down as many thoughts as I could about these two horrendous, unnecessary deaths.

'Mom, let's not go there, eh?'

'You don't know how fragile Cindy is now.'

'And I bet she's blaming herself for the move to Connecticut,' I said. 'Had Carly been in New York she might not have been picked upon so ruthlessly.'

'The kid was brittle. She could have been victimized everywhere.'

'Why are you defending a place you hate?'

'You know nothing about anything – or, at least, about how people work.'

'What I know is: we all have this one life ... to do with it what we want.'

'Do you know how naive you sound? How naive and completely unschooled in the crap we all swim in.'

'Are you kidding me?' I said, my voice suddenly gaining volume. 'You don't think after what I've been through recently I am somehow naive about life's nasty fucking side?'

'No need for that language.'

'There is a need for it. Because you never listen to me. Because you think you are the only one with pain. Because you're stuck in a life you don't like, but can't do a damn thing to change it. Then you have the audacity to tell me –'

I didn't get to finish that sentence, as my mother suddenly turned and bolted for the exit, leaving me there by the boarding gate, still in mid-sentence, still enraged. I didn't shout out, nor did I chase after her, as I knew that was exactly what she wanted. Instead I just found an empty plastic chair near the gate, stubbed out my cigarette and lit a fresh one, my hands shaking slightly as I felt that usual cocktail of rage and guilt which my mother invoked.

Less than three minutes later Mom was back at my side.

'Don't think you're going to get rid of me that quickly,' she said, putting her arm around me. 'I wasn't going to leave without giving you your going-away present.'

Reaching into her pocketbook she handed me a small, flat narrow box.

'Sorry that I didn't get around to wrapping it.'

I opened its lid – and found myself staring down at a red fountain pen with a red-and-black cap and a gold clip.

'This was your grandfather's fountain pen. It's a Parker Big Red. Dad once told me that his own father bought it for him in 1918, as a "welcome back alive" gift after managing to survive the Western Front in the First World War. I know that Grandfather would want you to have it. Can't we leave on a positive note? *Please ...*'

My mother choked back a sob as she said that. I reached over and put my free arm around my mother and said:

'I do love you.'

She sobbed again, then gave me a fast hug back before quietly extricating herself from my embrace, telling me:

'Do you know my own mother never told me that?'

'That's sad,' I said.

'No – it's just the way life worked back then.'

A woman in a green uniform appeared behind the gate counter. Picking up a microphone she informed us that Aer Lingus flight 107 with service to Shannon and Dublin was now ready for boarding. Mom reached into her purse and pulled out an envelope.

'Another little going-away gift.'

I opened the envelope. Inside were ten fifty-dollar bills.

'Mom, that's crazy.'

'Is that your way of saying "thank you"?'

'Thank you, thank you – but it's so much money.'

'As soon as you get to Dublin go to the bank and put it into traveler's checks – and then you can travel on it next summer. I insist you go to Paris: the one city I am determined to live in before I shuffle off this mortal coil. Maybe you'll find me living there come June.'

I gave her another hug.

'This is too nice of you.'

'I have my moments. Now I have to let you get on that plane. Promise me you'll stay away from war zones and crazy lefties. And please stop smoking. And please call me in a couple of days.'

'If you insist.'

'I insist.'

'*Trust me, I know how hard it is to walk away from crazy parents.*'

But listening to Jacinta's tale of genuine woe and subjugation, all I could think was: Yes my parents were crazy – but not repressively so.

The bus was arriving at College Green.

'Anyway I'll be back tonight by ten,' I told Jacinta, 'because I have to be.'

'Tell you what. We'll wait until the biddie is in bed and then have a natter downstairs. Maybe I could buy us a little naggin of whiskey.'

'That sounds rather promising. Now I've got to go off and hopefully do the deal for the room I'm moving into next week.'

'Surely you're not going so fast.'

'Surely I am. But please – not a word to the old bitch until I give her notice.'

'Lucky you.'

'In what way?'

'You're obviously a lot freer than I am.'

'My older brother Peter said something interesting to me once: "We all complain about being confined, but it is us who do the confining."'

'You're putting all sorts of bad ideas in my head.'

'I'll take that as a compliment.'

'God bless.'

I came to discover 'God bless' was the local equivalent of 'See you around', an ecclesiastical subtext to a simple hail and farewell.

Another gray wet morning. I walked with great speed and determination down Pearse Street until I reached number 75a. This time the door opened on the fourth ring. Sean was there, wearing the exact same paisley shirt, cardigan and pajama bottoms as the day before.

'Why did I figure that, in a city where everyone is at least half an hour late, you'd show up bang on time?'

'Because that's how I was raised – the good girl, always on time.'

'We'll have to rid you of such bad habits.'

'Can I come in?'

'Sorry, sorry, me blathering on like that. Get yourself in and let me get a cup of tea in you.'

I followed him into his room, where Sheila was currently sprawled across his brass bed, dressed only in a man's yellowing white shirt, reading that morning's copy of the *Irish Times* and smoking a cigarette.

I said hello. She didn't reply, let alone look up from her newspaper. Sean went over and whispered something to her. Grabbing her newspaper, she got up from the bed, all attitude and barely suppressed hostility. Heading to the door she doubled back and hissed at me:

'Don't let him fuck you. He's shite.'

After the door slammed behind her there was an embarrassed silence which Sean finally broke.

'Well, that definitely calls for a cup of tea.'

'Looks like you've got a fan there. I read some of your work last night. I liked it.'

Sean stopped spooning tea into the pot.

'Any one in particular?' he said.

'That poem about visiting your father's grave in that town in Wicklow ... '

'Enniskerry.'

'That's the place. And how you made the transference between the guilt of never having been able to get close to him and the ominous tree just outside the cemetery creaking in the wind as you try to find ... what was that brilliant phrase you used?'

'"The endless mystery that is eternal silence".'

'Exactly. And the title poem, about taking the boat train to London and looking back at Dun Laoghaire ... have I pronounced that right?'

Sean nodded.

'You talk about how "a leave-taking is a journey to the edge of the map / far beyond all that defines you". Those lines really stayed with me.'

Sean's eyes brightened. He motioned for me to sit down, hurried over with the tea and a plate of soda bread and butter, and got me talking further about my thoughts on his work. He branched out into an extended monologue about his childhood, his mess of a marriage, his two complicated daughters and the affair that had got him turfed out the family home. I finally had to interrupt him.

'You are interesting, Sean. And you do make a great cup of tea. But I really do need to know ... '

'Yes you've got the room.'

I punched the air with my fist.

'That's fantastic. Did His Lordship agree to all my assorted terms?'

'Every last one of them – with one proviso: if you do decide to leave before June of next year you need to give us two months' notice, otherwise you'll be liable for two months' rent. I sense you can live with that.'

'I sense so too. When can I start the work?'

'Right now if you like. I will need a month's deposit from you. So that's twenty-four pounds. And you'll be wanting to get yourself a jam jar and around five quid's worth of ten-pence pieces, as there's a meter in the room that keeps your lights on. Ten pence should give you about three, four hours if you're not running an electric fire off it. But I'm getting ahead of myself here like.'

Sean phoned his friend who ran the hardware shop nearby. I walked over and chose a plain white matt and white gloss for the walls. When I said I wanted to paint the floors, the owner told me when he delivered the paints he'd have his man see about helping me strip the old paper off the walls and get the moldy carpet removed. 'Give him a quid for his pains.' The fellow who arrived that afternoon with several cans of paint, drop cloths, a roller and two brushes – for which I paid in total eleven pounds – was named Gerard. A quiet young man with a slight stutter and an evident shyness. But he assured me that he knew his way around a paintbrush. Just as he also sized up quickly that the dismal peeling wallpaper in my bedsit hid 'a multiple of sins' and probably needed replastering. When he pulled up a corner of the carpet he assessed immediately that the floorboards were in bad order and needed to be sanded, sealed, and coated with many coats of varnish. He saw my face fall – because he knew that I had decided to do all this redecorating myself.

'Tell you what,' he said. 'If your man Sean is cool with this I could come by after work starting tonight and get the work done for you. I won't be making much in the way of noise, except for the sander which I'll borrow from the shop and try to use Sunday afternoon so I don't disturb anyone's sleep.'

'My budget's kind of limited.'

'Ten quid into my hand, and I'll even repaint all the kitchen cabinets.'

'You have a deal.'

He agreed to start the next night.

Sean was more than reasonable about having Gerard handle the work – 'because, no offense like, but you will probably end up with a better result than if you'd done it yourself'. I went to the bank and withdrew fifteen pounds as Gerard wanted half the cash up front. I met him back at the apartment, paid him, let him know that I really needed to move in six days from now and he assured me that the job would be done in time.

Then Sean told me he could bring me to a friend who ran a furniture place on the quays – the streets running alongside the River Liffey – where a bed and an armchair could be had. I was already fretting a bit about money, thinking: I am handing over thirty pounds, more than a month's rent, to avoid decorating the place myself. A bed, an armchair, a desk, a chair: Sean told me he could score all that for me for around ten pounds tops. Then there'd be sheets and towels and dishes and an electric kettle and the like. Bless Dad and Mom for the money they had given me: it allowed me to do all this. Though what struck me that afternoon, when I found myself in a beautiful inner-city park called Stephen's Green at the top of Grafton Street, was how I had, in just twenty-four hours or so, walked into a whole set of circumstances I didn't expect.

Sitting in that park in Dublin, my Army greatcoat wrapped around me against the cold, I found myself thinking: if I was ever going to have an unimpeded life, children would never be part of that equation. I would never inflict on a son or daughter the sense of being a mistake that had been inflicted on me. Living alone in that bedsit on Pearse Street might just be the right first step toward a sense of proper independence.

I finished my cigarette, the cold making me want to move. I walked out the north end of the park and back down Grafton Street. This was one of two central shopping areas of the city. There was a men's haberdashers, a few jewelers, a posh-looking department store, a bookshop, some pubs on the nearby side streets, a few street musicians, and a cafe to which I immediately gravitated. It was called Bewley's, the one Sean had advised me to get my tea from. As soon as I walked inside I sensed: this was a place in which I would be spending a great deal of time, the perfect place to loiter with intent. The front was a polished mahogany entranceway with etched glass and display windows featuring tea and scones. Inside the sense of Irish Victoriana continued. Shined wood and brass everywhere. Long cases where you could buy all sorts of breads and pastries and a splendid selection of teas and even actual coffee beans (which, I came to discover, were rare items in the Dublin of 1973). Beyond this was a cafe that stretched over three floors. I immediately found myself very much in the whirl of a late afternoon in Dublin – all of the tables crammed with a wide spectrum of people: old ladies huddled together in gossip; a gaggle of Trinity students; two literary types talking in low voices; a priest, wiry, bespectacled, late thirties, reading a newspaper, smoking a cigarette, stealing surreptitious glances at a rather well-dressed elegant woman in her early thirties seated opposite him, a small dog on her lap.

'You seem lost there, pet.'

I swiveled around and found myself facing one of Bewley's waitresses: a woman somewhere in her forties, her hair up in a bun, her cream-colored uniform and apron making her look like a member of staff in some English Big House novel. She was wearing a badge with her name – Prudence – emblazoned in gold.

'I was just looking for a free table,' I said.

'None free, I'm afraid, pet. But you can find a free chair and share a table.'

'That's allowed?'

'Here, if there's a free chair going we don't keep the table to ourselves. Do find yourself a place, and you might want to try one of our sticky buns. They're sinful.'

I took a seat next to the society lady. She smiled tightly and nod-ded when I asked if the chair was free. I sat down and noticed a plate of buns next to the ashtray.

'Do they belong to you or to the table?' I asked the woman.

'They're not mine,' she said, almost recoiling from the thought that she might have a quiet thing for sticky buns.

'I can eat one then?'

'I wouldn't stop you.'

That evoked a smile. Then I reached for a bun. Prudence the waitress came by moments later.

'Ah, I see you've found yourself some very graceful company,' she said. 'Are you going to have a coffee to go with the sticky bun?'

'Sure, I'll try your coffee.'

I opened my bag, took out my cigarettes, matches, and an aerogramme: a thin blue expanse of paper on which you could write an actual letter and then fold it up and discover that the aerogramme becomes an envelope with its own front, on which the address is written. I also removed my red fountain pen, uncapped it and began to write to my dad. The society woman simply sat there, an empty coffee cup in front of her, the Pekin-ese in her lap, a copy of that month's *Cosmopolitan* face up on the table.

My coffee arrived. I sniffed it. I took a sip. It was different from any coffee I'd tasted before – and it was, I should say, much better than I expected. It was served white with heated milk but it had a nice headiness to it. Prudence was right: their sticky buns were addictive. I sat there very happily for a half-hour, writing Dad an abbreviated version of the last thirty-six hours and thanking him profusely for putting that extra money in my account, which was allowing me to set up solo here.

I have really missed our talks, Dad. It has been months since we have sat down and chattered for a couple of hours. I'd really like to hear from you some way. But don't worry about me in Dublin. It's not what I expected: bleaker than I imagined, but also rather interesting.

As my pen moved across the aerogramme I glanced up several times to discover Madame Elegance sitting there, absently stroking the right ear of her dog as she looked off in the distance; a strange amalgam of boredom and pampered despair, as if she were preoccupied with the thought: *I have nothing to do here, nothing to occupy myself, and doesn't that say it all about me?*

But then, as I folded up the aerogramme and wrote Dad's office address on its front, I saw the woman glance down at my calligraphy.

'You from America then?' she asked, her voice clipped, horsy.

'That's right.'

'I went over there once. My nineteenth summer. Worked in a bar in DC. Loved it.'

'Have you been back since?'

The woman lowered her head, then shook it. No.

A moment later she was gone, and Prudence was back at the table.

'Saw you were having a conversation with Her Ladyship.'

'A very brief conversation.'

'I suppose she had to rush back to matters important in Ballsbridge.'

'What's Ballsbridge?'

'How long are you staying in Dublin?'

'I just arrived yesterday, but I'll be at Trinity for a while.'

'Then you'll figure out why Ballsbridge *is* Ballsbridge.'

She presented me with a bill of twenty-two pence for my sticky bun and coffee.

When I returned to Pearse Street, Sean took me down the quays to a shop on the south side of the Ha'penny Bridge, which was a rambling emporium of furniture in varying degrees of decomposition.

'Paddy, say hello to Alice – newly arrived from the States to spend a few years with us, which is why you're not going to do her, right?'

Paddy was a man well into middle age, with long hair that drooped down to his shoulders everywhere, though the front of his head was completely bald. He had a big handlebar moustache, a substantial pot belly, sad eyes. I asked him if we could find a bed and a desk and a little table and wondered if he could find me a big bentwood rocking chair – like the one Sean had in his room.

'Got a beauty downstairs.'

We went down a flight of stairs into a basement display area – where we passed a few dismembered department-store mannequins and a collection of baby carriages that looked like they belonged in a 1940s film.

'Starting a family, Paddy?' Sean asked.

'Don't be a bollocks,' Paddy replied.

We came to a corner of the basement where there was a collection of bedposts. Paddy pulled out a set – brass, somewhat battered and scratched.

'I can sell you these, and get my man to assemble it for you in your flat. I can get him to go down to a lumber yard and get a couple of fresh wood slats cut for the bed, so it will be nice and sturdy.'

'And the price?' I asked.

'Let's talk about that later.'

He then showed me a big roll-top desk, in need of a complete sanding and varnishing – but nonetheless impressive in a Mr Micawber sort of way. It really was Dickensian – and far too large for my small space. But then he showed me a small Victorian writing table – narrow with a green leather inlay that was ink-stained and had two noticeable tears on its surface.

'Once it's covered with your book and papers,' Paddy said, 'you'll never see them.'

He wanted eighty pounds for the lot, delivery and assembly included. I told him I could only pay forty – and that was already stretching my budget (as I didn't want to touch the 500 dollars travel money that Mom had given me). Once I paid for the paint job, the month's deposit, and the furniture I would only have around 180 pounds to last me until 31 March – which meant living on about eighteen pounds a week, of which seven would be handed over in rent. It was, I sensed, possible. Back then you could eat lunch in the student union for around twenty pence. The formal evening meal in the Trinity dining hall – for which you had to wear a black academic robe – was just thirty pence. A pint was twenty pence, a pack of cigarettes around the same price. Theatre tickets were cheap. Which meant going to the movies must also be cheap. I could easily live on £1.70 a day – and not feel like I was starving.

So when Paddy offered to reduce the lot to seventy pounds, I countered with forty-five. And when Paddy, sounding exasperated, said: 'Fifty-five quid is the absolute best I can do,' I agreed, still managing to get him to throw in a mattress as part of the deal.

Afterwards Paddy suggested we repair to a pub off Dame Street called the Stag's Head. Dark wood paneling, a dark-wood-and-brass bar, behind an intricately etched glass door a little sitting area called a 'snug' – and yes, a big stuffed stag's head was mounted on one wall, gazing down glassily at the denizens below. I liked the place immediately – especially taking to the closeted feel of the snug where you could slam the door on the rest of the pub. Paddy insisted on buying the first round. When we staggered out of the place three hours later, not only was I just a little 'scuttered', but also rather amazed by the range and topics of the chat that had decorated the entire afternoon – from the recent 'dustmen's strike' in Dublin ('You do a job like that you have a dim view of human nature,' Sean noted), to whether the current coalition government in Ireland between Sinn Fein and Labour could last. Along the way I was given a fast lesson in Irish politics, and how the enmity between Fine Gael and Fianna Fail could be traced back to the Civil War. I was asked all sorts of questions about whether Nixon would survive, given how the post-Watergate legal noose was tightening around his neck. Just as Paddy wanted to hear all about New York and its jazz joints. I explained how I'd been yanked out of the city as an eleven-year-old and still missed it profoundly.

'No doubt, after university back you'll go,' Sean said, 'and maybe it won't be what you dream of it to be. Because everything changes.'

'Except you,' Paddy said.

'Now who's playing the bollocks?'

The Guinness went down far too easily. Around half nine Sean suggested we head to a little restaurant he knew on Lower Baggot Street called Gaj's where the kitchen stayed open until ten. We piled into a cab, shot up around a bunch of side streets, cruised north of Stephen's Green before heading down past a startling beautiful Georgian square, and then on to Baggot Street. Sean paid the twenty-five-pence fare. We found ourselves in front of a terraced house, and climbed a flight of stairs up to a rather plain pair of rooms, whitewashed walls, a couple of posters featuring Che Guevara as well as a mustached man standing on a soapbox, his clothes very much working man at the turn of the century, proclaiming to an assembled gathering. A very large woman in a pair of overalls came out, eyeing Sean warily.

'Jesus, isn't it my good luck having you walk in here tonight?' she said.

'How are you, Maggie? Still fighting the revolution?'

'Fuck off, you. Who's the nice one there you're corrupting tonight?'

'This here is Alice ... '

'And I'm already corrupted,' I added.

'Go way with you,' Maggie said. 'You look and sound like the American abroad. Don't let this old one near you. He's rubbish in that department.'

'Thank you for the hearty recommendation' Sean said. 'I'll quote that back to you the next time I ride you.'

'The fucking Black Plague will come back to these shores before I let you ride me again.' She turned to me.

'You want the usual, mutton and chips?' she asked.

There was no alcohol served at Gaj's. Just big earthenware pots of tea. Maggie returned moments later with the tea, three cups, milk and sugar. When she hurried off to another table – the place was busy – Sean shook his head.

'I always land myself with the angry ones.'

'You mean, like that Sheila woman you were with this morning.'

'Sheila's not angry. She's just more inclined towards sharing her bed with women. Not that you should ever mention that fact to the little bitch.'

'Are all women bitches to you, Sean?' I asked, hating his sexist tone.

He reached over and squeezed my knee, saying:

'Ah, I love the sisterly solidarity.'

Paddy opened the pot of tea, sticking a spoon into its pitch-dark waters.

'One thing you can say about Maggie's tea – it's so fucking strong you could wake a dead man with it.'

'No doubt she has already,' Sean said.

'You letting us in on intimate secrets, Sean?'

'You see why he's a gobshite, Alice?'

I just smiled, four hours of pints in the Stag's Head still reverberating within me.

'Alice is being a diplomat,' Paddy said.

'Alice needs some food and some of Maggie's deadly tea.'

The tea was as strong as Paddy had warned me. The mutton had been pan-fried in the same oil used for the chips. I watched Paddy put four teaspoons of sugar into his tea and douse his chips with vinegar.

'That's a new one,' I said, wondering if I was slurring my words. 'Vinegar on French fries.'

'Ah yes, the American expects everything to be doused in tomato ketchup.'

'I expect nothing. I was just making a drunken observation.'

'Get this grub into you, you'll be grand.'

We were kicked out of Gaj's around eleven. Paddy said he had to get home as 'the missus is going to raise holy hell that I disappeared for the evening'. It was the first time I'd heard that he was married. As soon as he left us – his goodbye to me was a two-handed handshake and a promise to deliver everything once the room was redecorated and ready for occupancy next week – a sobering realization grabbed me: I was going to be locked out tonight. When I told Sean this his response was to put his arms around me and say:

'You're more than welcome to share my bed.'

He belched slightly as he said this, adding:

'Go on, give us a kiss.'

There are moments when you find yourself on the border between the dumb and the truly stupid. Sean's mouth was open, and all I could smell was the mutton, the vinegary chips, all the now-fermented Guinness we'd drunk hours earlier. I carefully stepped back from his attempted embrace.

Seeing a taxi coming I put my hand out and waved it down. When we arrived at Mrs Brennan's, I staggered to the doorway. I managed to get my key in the lock. I turned it. I tried to open the door. It wouldn't budge. I tried it again. No joy. The door had been bolted. My landlady had, as promised, locked me out for being late. I looked around. Oswald Road was empty, shuttered, as dead as a cemetery. I staggered over to the ground-floor window next to the door. I managed to get my fingers around its frame. I hoisted it upward, thinking she'd bolted it as well. But luck was with me, as the window actually opened. Not as high as I would have liked, but enough for me to scrunch down and push myself through the two feet or so of an aperture that had been created. I went head first. But the room inside was pitch dark. As it was an overcast night, and Oswald Road wasn't the most illuminated of streets, there was no external light to guide me. Being full of Guinness, I didn't judge my entrance in the smartest of ways. Going head first into Mrs Brennan's pitch-black living room meant not noticing a little table positioned in front of the window. Not only did I knock it sideways but I heard several things smash onto the floor. I still had my head on the floor, my feet halfway out the window, when the light sprang on and Mrs Brennan stormed in, her lace robe pulled tight around her, her face in a mask of absolute rage.

'Oh Jesus God, what have you done here?'

'Really sorry,' I said.

'Sorry? Sorry! You smashed Our Lady, you little trollop.'

I looked up just as Jacinta came running down the stairs, also in a robe and furry slippers. She too looked shocked, yet also had to work hard to suppress a giggle. Because there, scattered in front of me, was the decapitated head of Jesus's mother, her gowned body on the far side of the room. Mary's glassy eyes looked up at me with silent reproach.

'I'll buy you a new one tomorrow,' I heard myself say.

'I bought that statue at Lourdes,' she screamed. 'It was blessed.'

'If you hadn't bolted the goddamn door –'

'That's it now. That blasphemy is the limit. You're gone from here first thing tomorrow.'

13

THE NEXT DAY I arrived at Trinity at 10 a.m. with all my suitcases in tow. I went directly to the office of the Warden of Residences, Miss Scanlon. She did not look pleased to see me.

'Ah, the infamous Miss Alice Burns,' she said. 'Mrs Brennan phoned me first thing this morning, telling me of your exploits.'

'I paid her the three pounds she demanded for the broken statue. I gave her the seven pounds she demanded for the full week, even though she kicked me out after two nights.'

'But, Miss Burns, it will take a good fortnight for me to find another lodger for her, so she will be losing some income.'

'Her rules were ridiculous, if you don't mind me saying so.'

'She is a bit strict. Perhaps I should have thought about that first before assigning you to her, you having a different set of rules over on the other side of the pond. The truth of the matter is: you were such a last-minute arrival at Trinity I didn't have much in the way of choice. And Mrs Brennan's last tenant went off to the missions just after Christmas.'

So my bed had been occupied previously by a priest. I decided to say nothing, but I could detect the thinnest of smiles on Miss Scanlon's face.

'Now the problem I have is that I can't find you a flat or anything, and all the college rooms are booked solid for this year.'

'I don't need a flat – because I've found one.'

'That was fast work on your part.'

'The problem is: it was in a truly deplorable state. The landlord has agreed to redecorate it for me, but it won't be ready for another six nights. I need somewhere to sleep now.'

'The only solution would be a commercial B&B. But they charge, on average, two to three pounds a night.'

'I can only afford one pound fifty.'

'That's a tall order.'

'Surely you know someone who'd be willing to accept that price. It's January, after all.'

Miss Scanlon's face tightened. But I could see that she was also thinking: *the sooner I find her somewhere the sooner I am done with her.* She opened her address book, picked up the phone on her desk and asked if I wouldn't mind waiting outside for a moment. I joined the receptionist in the outer room and all my bags piled up in a corner of the office. Just as I lit up a cigarette the door opened and Miss Scanlon came out, holding a piece of notepaper on which was scribbled a name and an address.

'My friend Desmond Kavanagh runs a nice B&B on Lower Leeson Street, not far from Stephen's Green. As it is the quiet season he's agreed to take you in for one-fifty a night, but on the proviso that you are there for seven full nights.'

That was another ten pounds fifty. I was in no position to argue – nor did I want to.

'Thank you so much for doing this for me,' I said. 'I'm genuinely sorry if I made a mess of things with Mrs Brennan.'

'Not to worry, Alice. The good news is that Des will give you a key to the front door, so you can come and go day or night. Being a theatrical he's well used to things bohemian. And I don't think you'll find a statue of Our Lady over at Des's. Good luck to you.'

I headed up to Bewley's for breakfast.

'Looking a little world-weary today, pet,' Prudence said when she saw me at a side table, reaching for a sticky bun.

Ever break a statue of Our Lady while climbing through a window? I wanted to ask her. Instead I said:

'A hard night.'

Prudence smiled.

'That sort of thing is never seen in Dublin. You must have imported it from across the water. I think I might have a few Solpadeine in the back. I'll bring them with your coffee. Make sure to get your beauty sleep tonight, pet. You don't want the drink to be ruining that lovely face of yours.'

I never considered myself at all lovely. On the contrary, I still bought into my mother's view – that I was a quirky little thing,

insisting on a bohemian style, belittling anything old-school romantic. The price you pay for being different – for not being one of
those 'popular girls' who falls into a clique at whatever school or
college she lands in, who always has plenty of girlie girlfriends – is
that you never see yourself as fitting in ... and, by extension, worthy
of love. Was that the inherent problem with Bob? Was there a part
of me always expecting him to wake up one day and wonder what
he was doing with such an oddball girlfriend? Is that why he ruined
everything by playing the frat boy? Because I was too challenging in
my oddness?

This morning was my first meeting with my academic tutor,
Aidan Berkeley. I would be reading English. I was nervous about
meeting him.

'And how are you faring so far?' he asked, motioning me to sit in
an oversized leather armchair – but first having to remove a pile of
newspapers and periodicals from its seat.

'Getting my accommodation situation sorted out,' I said. 'Otherwise trying to work the college out.'

Professor Berkeley got straight down to business, outlining the
four courses I'd be 'reading' for the balance of the year. He told me
that he sensed I'd particularly like the course on Anglo-Irish poetry
taught by Professor Kennelley and a seminar on Joyce by Professor
Norris. Then letting me know that he had other things to be getting
on with, he told me that I should 'pop back if I had any concerns,
pressing or otherwise'.

With time to kill before I was due to check into the B&B, I went
over to the student union for lunch. Ruth was behind the bar, pouring pints, a lit cigarette between her teeth.

'How's Alice?' she asked as I came in. 'You were smart to push that
gobshite Sean away last night. He'd make a pass at a fire hydrant,
that one.'

'Thanks for the compliment. Did Sean himself tell you about the
events last night?'

Before Ruth could reply a voice behind me said:

'In Dublin even the streets have ears.'

I swiveled around and saw a man, narrow and angular.

'Thus speaks the voice of Ulster,' Ruth said, 'where there's no bad word against anyone, no malice aforethought.'

'You're from up there?' I asked him.

'Don't sound like I'm radioactive.'

'Sorry, didn't mean to make such a clichéd comment.'

'It's just ... let me guess, being from "over there" you've never met anyone from Northern Ireland before and expect us all to be wearing a balaclava and brandishing an Armelite?'

'I don't know what an Armelite is.'

'Lucky you. The name's Ciaran Quigg.'

He had my attention: I liked his very full head of black hair, trimmed beard and wire-rimmed glasses. His accent was different – slightly reedy, darkly hued, with a hard cadence on all vowels.

I told him my name and signaled to Ruth to pour me a pint as I sat down in the chair that Ciaran indicated was awaiting me.

'Did you know that Jean-Paul Sartre once went on record to say that Sweet Aftons – a cigarette made in Dundalk – were his favorite smoke?'

'Is that why you smoke them?'

'Perhaps. Try one.'

I accepted, tapping both ends against the table, then stealing a match and lighting it against the tabletop. My eyes watered on the first inhalation of smoke.

'That is one strong cigarette,' I said.

'Which is why it's the existentialist smoke of choice.'

As I raised my glass he touched his pint against mine.

'*Sláinte*,' he said.

'*Sláinte*,' I said back, trying to replicate his pronunciation.

'Not bad for an American just off the boat. So why have you landed in Trinity in the bleak midwinter?'

'Assorted personal reasons.'

'Alice Burns – woman of mystery.'

'I don't show my hand that easily.'

'Alice Burns – woman of *great* mystery.'

'Romantic chaos always seems banal in the retelling.'

'I sense that Tristan and Isolde might disagree with you. She was Irish, you know. Richard Wagner, that old pre-Nazi, knew his Celtic mythology. Still, the man could write a tune – even if most of them last around five hours.'

'What year are in you in at Trinity?'

'Second year.'

'Me too.'

'So we're going to grow old together, Alice.'

'I'm going to ignore that comment.'

'Because it surprised you?'

'Because I sense you're testing me.'

'Testing what exactly?'

'Give me a day or so to figure that out, and maybe we'll resume the conversation.'

'That would be most agreeable,' he said. 'And as my office, outside of lectures, is at this table you'll know where to find me.'

'Indeed I will.'

As I finished my pint and stood up to go, Ciaran stood up as well, and taking my right hand in his he said:

'May we continue the conversation soon.'

In the taxi, with my suitcases, on the way to the B&B on Lower Leeson Street, I found myself running through that entire exchange, telling myself: he's clever, he has a considerable amount of charm and what is evidently a formidable intellect. But after all that's transpired in the past few months the last thing I need right now is a boyfriend … especially one I'd met seventy-two hours after landing here. But I liked his wit and the way he demonstrated his intelligence without descending into the show-off realm that Duncan Kendall often embraced. Duncan. There was someone I hadn't thought about for quite a while – and whom I never managed to say goodbye to before fleeing Bowdoin. Why was it that I was thinking about him now? Perhaps because Ciaran Quigg was his Northern Irish double?

'Stop talking nonsense,' I told myself as the taxi pulled up in front of a Georgian doorway, painted a deep green with a very polished brass knocker positioned in its center. The driver helped me out with my bags. I knocked twice on the door. It opened. A thin man in a brown velour jacket, dark brown tweed trousers and a matching cravat stood there. He lifted his arms in welcome.

'Are you the woman who's been described to me as "trouble"?' he said, smiling.

'I see that my bad reputation has preceded me,' I said.

'Trouble is always welcomed across this threshold.'

Inside I found myself facing a remarkable work of art: walls painted deep greens, with an entrance hall papered in a velour that was not dissimilar from the jacket that Desmond Kavanagh was wearing right now. Beautifully wrought furniture – all heavy oak and mahogany and embroidered upholstery. There were framed photographs – largely from the turn of the century – suspended on long metal wires covering many of the walls. There were manifold portraits from the nineteenth century of regal-looking men and women. There were etchings of big country houses. There was a considerable amount of lit candles. There was an overriding scent of incense everywhere. There was a grand fireplace in the grand front room with a pile of coal enflamed. I felt as if I had walked into a theatre set – and one in which I'd happily live.

It's intriguing how you can spend an entire evening with someone you've never met before and the conversation will never meander beyond small talk or the exchange of essential details about work, family, the business of life, the business of the day. Desmond Kavanagh struck me as a man who was both lonely and naturally talkative. Later in my Dublin time I would hear the word 'garrulous' bandied about quite a bit about the sort of monologist who could 'talk your ear off'. Yes, Desmond was that way inclined – but from that first extended chat in his high-vaulted, rococo 'sitting room' (as he called it), I sensed that, for all his joking about my American directness and the occasional reference to my youth, he also felt I was a receptive audience to selected portions of his life story. I also felt rather privileged that he took me into his immediate confidence about his parents and living with the burden of being regarded as 'different'. I understood it immediately. Just as I also understood I shouldn't let it be known that I understood. We were dealing in code here.

Desmond wasn't just a good talker; he was also an excellent listener. He drew me out on so much – from the unhappiness of my parents' marriage and the conformist horrors of Old Greenwich to all that transpired at Bowdoin which landed me on this side of the Atlantic.

By the time I finished talking it was dark outside, and Desmond – noticing the time – jumped up to use a decorative shovel to top up the fire, then announced:

'I think dinner is in order. Will you join me?'

'But I've taken up far too much of your time.'

'There you go again, thinking that you're an imposition. Anyway, all this talk, all this blather, and it's almost half seven. Tell you what. Let me show you your room.'

Up the stairs we went, finding ourselves on a grand corridor off of which were five doors with name signs. This one was marked 'Oliver St John Gogarty'.

'Do you know who he was?' Desmond asked.

I shook my head.

'The basis of Buck Mulligan in Joyce's *Ulysses*. Quite the wit, quite the dandy, quite the rake. A man who lived as he wanted in Ireland at a time when such personal independence came with a price – as it still does. Anyway, as I am empty of guests right now – a German academic who'd been here doing research for two months left just last week – I thought you might find this room rather suited to you.'

He opened the door and I found myself sucking in my breath. The room – high-vaulted, with green velour wallpaper, had this massive four-poster bed with a green velvet spread, an overstuffed armchair in a matching green fabric with an ottoman, a small mahogany desk that looked like one of those nineteenth-century writing tables I'd seen in films about Victorian misadventures in India, two Tiffany-style lamps on either side of the bed, and a grate with a gas fire that would keep the chill at bay.

'Wow. Can I *live* here?' I asked.

'I'm sure we could come to an arrangement,' he said. 'But wouldn't you miss the essential Dublin student experience of life in a cold, somewhat squalid bedsit?'

'I have signed on for that already' – and told him about the setup I'd landed myself in on Pearse Street.

'Well, there are ways out of such matters. But we can visit that thought in a few days. You said you rushed out of the Reverend Mother's digs this morning without washing. Might you like a bath now? By the way, if you want a bath a day that is fine by me.'

The bathroom was down the hallway, with a wonderful claw-foot tub. Desmond told me to unpack, that he'd run the bath and use some of his favorite bath salts to 'soften the water'. As he left me to sort out my clothes and arrange my desk I could not help but marvel at my good fortune. There was an immediate complicity between us. Fifteen minutes later, as I sat in the bath made aromatic by the lavender-scented salts that Desmond had thrown in, I felt considerable gratitude for all his decency and generosity. And I was starting to wonder if I could possibly get out of my commitment to that tiny flat on Pearse Street.

Later that night – after we'd eaten lamp chops and roasted potatoes and green beans with French wine followed by something for dessert called a sherry trifle – my host made an interesting assessment of my situation.

'Running away in the wake of grief is no bad thing. I wish I'd done that when I'd had the opportunity. Heartbreak only escalates when you're stuck in the same place where the sorrow took place. I admire your courage in voting with your feet, as they say.'

I wanted to know what anguish had befallen Desmond. The way he phrased it – telling me something without letting me in on the actual details – made me realize that I should not push for further information; that this was the elliptical way he wanted to play things, and I needed to let him define the limits here.

I remember getting into bed feeling a little woozy but happy. Putting the blanket over me I looked around the room and thought: life throws you some interesting cards. And happenstance has its upside.

I slept properly for the first time since leaving the States.

'A rare winter's sun,' Desmond said, over breakfast the next morning. 'Have you plans for the day?'

'I was thinking of looking in on my flat – seeing what progress has been made.'

'That can wait. Let me bring you on a bit of a drive.'

Desmond's car – parked round the back from his house in a narrow alleyway – was called a Morris Minor, painted a dark green. To start it he needed to take a large crowbar-shaped bit of metal and groove it into a latch above the front fender, then go back to the driver's seat, turn on the ignition then return to the crowbar and turn it once rapidly. It took about four goes before the engine groaned into life.

'If you're up for a bit of a long day,' he said, 'I thought, given that it's only half nine and we have about seven hours of sunlight, that I'd give you the Grand Southside Dublin tour and bring you out to Wicklow. "The Garden of Ireland" as it's known in Tourist Board speak. But it does have its moments.'

For the balance of the day Desmond didn't stop talking. Not that I was complaining, as what I received was an extensive introduction to Greater Dublin and the countryside immediately beyond it. The Morris Minor did not have the most effective heater going. As it was a particularly cold day my hands remained gloved and my greatcoat pulled around me as I began to discover Dublin's disparate neighborhoods. The elegance and refinement of Ballsbridge. The dreary suburban bungalows of Stillorgan. The mixed bag that was Dun Laoghaire with its workers' cottages, its larger, more established professional-class houses, its rather down-at-heel shopping area, its amazing pier stretching deep into Dublin Bay and facing the ferry port which (according to Desmond) 'has borne witness to far too much heartbreak, as generation after generation of Irish families have put their children on the late-night boat to Holyhead in Wales and a new life in Britain'. He also showed me the Martello Tower in Sandycove – where Stephen Daedalus shared rooms with Buck Mulligan in *Ulysses*. It had the most astonishing view of the bay, but inside, it struck me as ascetic and bleak as a monk's cell. What stunned me, however, was a drive from the village of Dalkey along a clifftop until we reached a view that could be described as majestic: the sweep of Killiney Bay and its rocky strand.

'We call this Dublin's Bay of Naples. Truth be told, it's almost as gobsmacking as that Italian panorama.'

We then passed through Dublin's ever-expanding suburbs, Desmond pointing out housing estates where the sameness of the modern homes called to mind the Levittown developments in the States after the war.

'There's an architectural blight taking hold of the nation called Bungalow Bliss,' Desmond explained. 'That's a style of dreadful modern house which is probably more suited to somewhere like Dallas – not that I've ever been there, but everyone says that it's a shocking place ... and it's also where they killed our John Fitzgerald Kennedy. There's a local word you should know: *gombeenism*. A *gombeen* is a man who will sell out his friends, his family, his community for a few extra shillings. Dublin is now being ruined by property developers who are *gombeens* to the core.'

We were soon out in open country. Green hills, dappled with snow. A mountain – stern, imposing, triangular in shape – which Desmond said was known as the Sugarloaf. The road gained altitude. We were traveling along empty terrain, the occasional lonely house in view, but otherwise open land, harsh, yet epic; a sense of being very far away from the urban world which we'd just left. I was immediately stunned by the discovery that, just twenty or so miles from Dublin, we were in such rugged beauty – with the sense of being cut off from the world beyond. We stopped for tea and sandwiches by the ruins of a medieval monastery at Glendalough. With light still with us we made our way to a place called the Sally Gap. The road was winding, occasionally vertiginous, something of an engineering marvel as it traversed remote, inhospitable terrain.

'This is what's known as a bog – which is also a euphemism for a lavatory. But in this case, it's a wet, muddy ground, too soft to support a body.'

When we were right alongside the Sally Gap I asked Desmond to stop the car. I got out, my shoes crunching into the light crust of snow on the road, the afternoon light now clouded over by a mist that appeared to emanate from the ground itself. There was something truly haunted about this terrain, a sense of the primal and the spectral augmented by the savage grandeur of the Gap itself. Desmond stayed in the car as I walked several paces away from the vehicle, feeling as if I was heading toward some sort of precipice. The veritable edge of the world. No empty beach in Maine, no corner of the White Mountains in New Hampshire, none of the few places to which I had ventured in the great outdoors, had any sense of the harsh wonder that I was enveloped in right now. I turned back. Fog had descended; the vehicle that was my way out of this forbidding world had vanished from view. The silence here was overwhelming. So too the sense that, bar the narrow road on which I was standing, there was no connection whatsoever to life as it was lived now in the eighth decade of the twentieth century. I was both spooked and compelled. I could black out, for a few precious moments, any sense of the past with all its inherent ties that bind. There was the illusion of living in a blank slate in which nothing that I carried with me counted. I felt sleet on my face, a chill encircling me, a howling wind the only sound on the aural horizon. Until there were several distinct beeps of a car horn. I was being summoned back.

When I reached the Morris Minor, Desmond was not looking amused.

'Thought you'd decided to go all mystic and walk off the edge,' he said.

'The place does have that kind of pull.'

'Indeed it does. You trip out here, twist an ankle or the like, and they'll find your corpse months later. Anytime there's some sort of gangster murder in Dublin up here is the choice locale for burying the body – because you walk half a mile off the road and you are in a place you shouldn't be.'

I suddenly felt cold, hugging my arms around me. Desmond cranked up the heater, telling me:

'The one problem with driving a car built in 1957 by the Brits is that it doesn't really want to throw out much hot air. You can now see why I beeped you after your five minutes of communing with nature. Up here it gets bloody frigid. Open the glovebox there and you should find a naggin of Powers.'

'You keep whiskey in the car?'

'I do – and I make no apologies for that. It's there for medicinal emergencies like this one. Now get a dram of that in you.'

I had two fast pulls on the Powers. It did the job. Desmond put the car back into gear. 'Right,' he said, 'back to civilization. Not that I consider much of Dublin to be civilized. And, Alice, I've been thinking: would you mind if I came along with you to Pearse Street, saw what you were getting yourself into?'

'There's really no need ... '

'Away with that now. Let me just look things over for you.'

I found it very hard, given all his kindness and generosity, to say no to him. As we headed back to the city, Desmond drove to Pearse Street.

'Now I don't mean to get all precious on you – but this is no street for a young lady like yourself.'

When I knocked twice on 75a, Sean answered, still dressed in the same pair of pajama bottoms and moth-infested cardigan. He smiled in that ever-hungover rakish way of his.

'The beautiful Alice. And, Oscar Wilde himself.'

Desmond's lips tightened. 'Maybe I should take sartorial tips from you, sir,' he said.

'Always happy to oblige,' Sean answered, adding to me: 'Your man Gerard's hard at work on your place.'

Gerard was anything but hard at work. Little had been accomplished beyond the stripping of the wallpaper and some half-hearted patching of the many holes in the plasterwork.

'Didn't expect to see you so soon,' Gerard said, looking like someone caught out badly.

'But you assured me that all would be ready by the end of the week.'

'Things came up. If you give me another week –'

'Term starts next week,' I said. 'I need to be set up here before then.'

'That's not my problem,' Gerard said, sounding sullen.

'Excuse me,' Desmond said, 'but it is your problem.'

'And who are you?'

'I'm her Dublin uncle.'

229

'Sure you are.'

'You call yourself a painter. Look at the state of this place. A dead-line is a deadline,' Desmond said.

'Who the fuck are you to tell me that?'

Gerard started to stutter as he said that – his inability to get the words out undercut by a genuine menace in his voice.

'How much have you paid this gurrier?' Desmond asked me.

'I was supposed to pay him an additional five pounds today.'

'And I want my fucking money,' Gerard stuttered.

'Who do you work for?'

'What makes you think I'm goin' to answer this poof's questions?'

Out of nowhere Desmond grabbed Gerard by the lapels, pulled him toward him and suddenly backhanded him twice across the face.

'This poof doesn't put up with gobshites. You want another wake-up call now?'

Gerard shook his head, tears rolling down his face.

'So who's employing you?'

'Cafferty's Paints.'

'Finbarr Cafferty?'

Gerard nodded.

'Your boss is one of my oldest friends,' Desmond said, pushing Gerard aside. 'Now away with you.'

Grabbing his coat Gerard vanished down the stairs.

'If there's one thing I cannot stand it's the hard word. Especially when it's aimed at me, and at things that a sad fool like that doesn't understand.'

'Are you going to call up his boss?'

'Indeed I am. And I'm not letting you move into this kip before I've finished painting this place properly.'

'There's really no need for that.'

To which Desmond Kavanagh looked at me steadily.

'Yes there is.'

14

ON THE MORNING that I was due to start classes my bed arrived. So too did an aerogramme with a Chilean postmark, my address written across the front in Peter's spindly penmanship.

I hope this letter finds you in Dublin. I'm lying low on the Pacific coast in a beautiful town in a beautiful country which has been ruined by our government. I think Dad's goons are looking for us everywhere. Adam actually unearthed me in Santiago, offered to fly me back to the States, warned me I was over my head. My response was to go underground. Moving on from here in a few days. Don't worry about me. This is an intricate, fluid situation – but amazingly interesting and important. I ask that you don't tell the family you've heard from me. Let them sweat. Especially Dad – who, I've discovered, is even more complicated than I figured. Have a Guinness for me.

I took a sharp intake of breath after reading this.

'Bad news?' asked one of the furniture delivery men, noting my pursed lips and the aerogramme in my left hand.

'It's too dense to go into.'

'You run off to your first lecture,' Desmond told me, stepping outside the room with me. 'I'll see you back here at 1 p.m., and we can run back to the house and bring your suitcases over and the like.'

'I feel bad, leaving you with all this,' I told him.

'Stop talking rubbish. Off you go to your class. I hear that Professor Kennelley is quite the brilliant lecturer.'

Like so much else, Desmond was spot on about Professor Kennelley. A large, imposing man in his early forties, slightly chubby, with chaotic hair and penetrating eyes, he stood up in the lecture theatre in front of fifty or so of us and began to talk about a poet from County Monaghan named Patrick Kavanagh – who came from

the bog and made his home in the city. He was known to Kennelley
and everyone else in literary Dublin as a cantankerous man, yet one
who had an understanding of the Irish character and the insidious
way that Irish Catholicism and rural isolation create such a toxic
world view. Then he read us the opening of Kavanagh's extraordinary poem, 'The Great Hunger' – which shocked Irish morality back
when it was published in 1942 with its depiction of the isolated,
limited, sexually dead life of an Irish farmer. As Kennelley pointed
out – in an accent that hinted at country roots (he was, I discovered,
from County Kerry) – the poem bulldozed the mid-century 'dancing
at the crossroads' fantasia that the government of Eamon De Valera
liked to propagate as the idyll of rural life. Kennelley himself was an
accomplished poet. When he read the opening lines of Kavanagh's
poem I was transfixed:

> *Clay is the word and clay is the flesh*
> *Where the potato-gatherers like mechanized scarecrows move*
> *Along the side-fall of the hill – Maguire and his men.*
> *If we watch them an hour is there anything we can prove*
> *Of life as it is broken-backed over the Book*
> *Of Death?*

I dropped over to the union after the lecture, running into Ciaran
in the area just outside its entranceway.

'The woman herself,' he said, a sardonic smile on his lips. 'You've
made yourself scarce since we last met.'

'I've been pretty much getting my flat organized.'

'Ah yes, the famous bedsit on Pearse Street. Ruth filled me in on
the details.'

'Really?'

'Yeah ... and it turns out that she knows the man in charge,
what's-his-name, because she once made the mistake of letting the
old boozer between her legs.'

'Sean seems to have convinced many women to make that
mistake.'

'Watch yourself then.'

'Oh, he's tried already – and I think senses he should not try again.'

'You didn't threaten to sue him, did you?'

'Why would I do that?'

'You're American. You lot threaten to sue all the time.'

'Thank you for reducing me to a cultural cliché.'

'Just slagging.'

'Try smarter slagging next time.'

'No need to get all testy with me.'

'No need to talk stupid with me.'

'*Mea maxime culpa.*'

'Congratulations on your Latin,' I said.

I headed into the union and straight to the bar. Ruth was there, pulling pints.

'How's it going?' she said.

'Why are men such idiots?'

'Comes with the territory. The usual glass?'

I nodded.

'Sean tells me you've been adopted by an older fella.'

I said nothing. I sipped my pint and thought: do the jungle drums always beat so loudly here?

I was about to say something defensive along the lines of: 'He's just a generous, decent, lonely man.' But I stopped myself, knowing this was exactly the reaction wanted.

'When I see Sean tonight shall I slip him your phone number? Tell him you're still longing to smell that shocking booze breath of his?' (I had already adopted shocking as part of my vocabulary.)

'Go away with that talk,' she said. 'We've all made the stupidest mistakes when scuttered.'

'There's stupid … and then there's Sean.'

'Fuck yuz.'

There was a touch of dark mischief to her insult. As if she was telling me: *well done, you're learning.*

When I arrived back at Pearse Street I found Desmond sitting in Sean's room, drinking tea.

'Your man here is quite the class fella,' Sean said. 'You should see the job he's done on your flat.'

'No need blowing my horn for me,' Desmond said.

When I went up the stairs I found that Desmond had indeed done something wonderful with my twelve-foot-by-ten space. In the few hours I'd been away, not only had the bed been put together, but Desmond had made it for me – and even surprised me with a green velour bedspread that was an exact copy of the one in the Gogarty room in which I'd been sleeping for the past week. In addition to all the furniture I'd bought, there were plants and a small Victorian-style rug on the floor. The walls were relatively even, the floorboards painted brown and sealed. All my clothes had been brought down by Desmond and unpacked. All the four plates, four dishes, four knives and forks and spoons I'd bought had been put away. There was even a bottle of red wine on the cafe table and a couple of glasses.

'You didn't have to do all this,' I told him.

'Indeed he didn't,' Sean said. 'But he did do a beautiful thing for you. I wish I had an uncle like your man here.'

'I'm not used to such kindness,' I said.

'Maybe we should open the wine,' Sean said.

I loved my bedsit. It was the first place I could really call my own. I learned to deal with making fires with peat briquettes in my room, and using a Kosangas heater, for which I had to buy a little trolley for the canisters that needed refilling every fortnight or so, to dry out the damp that always crept into the walls. As the communal bathroom was always cold – a single electric-bar heater mounted over its doorway providing minimal warmth – I adjusted to having just three baths there a week. All the evident American comforts I'd once taken for granted – central heating, nonstop hot water, proper insulation from the elements beyond – were in short supply here. But I adapted – and surprised myself by beginning to take what once seemed like primitive discomforts as simply part of the scenery.

I was writing an essay on an Ulster poet, Louis MacNeice, on the evening on January 20 when a bomb went off in nearby Sackville Place. The explosion was so violent that my little window shook for a moment. In its aftermath, there was an eerie silence, punctuated by doors on my floor being slammed open. I went out into the corridor and saw Sheila racing down the lower stairs with several other residents. I followed. The front door was open, the cold winter air hitting us. Sean was already there. When I tried to venture into the street, he put his hand on my shoulder.

'You can't go out there.'

He pointed to smoke rising into the sky from a spot on the other side of the Liffey.

'A bomb?' Sheila asked.

Sean nodded. Sirens were now screaming – the emergency services rushing to the scene.

'Fuck,' Sheila said.

From behind me came another voice.

'I've got to get out there. My mammie's over on the Northside.'

This was Dervla – a student from Wexford who was studying fine arts at Trinity and had the bedsit next to mine.

'You can't go, love,' Sean told her, holding her back.

'But Mammie went off to buy me new sheets and towels at Arnotts.'

'I won't let you run into all that,' Sean said. 'Especially as they often plant a second bomb nearby to catch people running away from the first one.'

Dervla seemed to relent, dropping her shoulders, choking back tears. As soon as she indicated that she'd return back inside Sean let go of her – at which moment she sidestepped him and went running off toward the scene of the crime, no coat on her, the rain starting to come down again.

'Fuck,' Sean said.

I dashed after her. Dervla was fast and very determined. I only caught up with her way at the end of Pearse Street. When I finally got hold of her she broke free from my grip and tried to head for O'Connell Bridge. But there was already a police checkpoint up, blocking anyone from crossing over. Dervla lost it, screaming at the Garda. That's when I stepped in, putting my arms around her and letting her sob into my shoulder. I then helped her back to our house. When we reached the front door Sean was there, looking relieved.

'Good on you, Alice,' he said, steering us into his room, pointing to the roaring fire in the grate. 'Warm yourselves there while I make us all something to lessen the chill.'

Sean's idea of liquid central heating was a hot whiskey: two jiggers of Powers in a glass, along with a teaspoon of sugar, a slice of lemon embedded with cloves, topped off with very hot water from the kettle, a spoon kept in the glass to keep it from cracking. As we sat by the fire, we heard the front door open. Diarmuid – who lived in the attic flat at the top of the house and worked over in the library of the National Gallery on Merrion Square – came staggering in, blood running down from his forehead. We were all instantly on our feet.

'Holy God,' Dervla said, pushing him into the armchair in which she'd been sitting. She shouted to Sean to get her some hot water and a clean towel.

'How were you caught in it?'

'Was walking down the end of Sackville Place when this car exploded,' Diarmuid said. 'I must have walked by the car bomb less than thirty seconds before it went off. Fucking madness over there.'

As Sean rushed into his little kitchen to get first aid, I poured Diarmuid a double and handed it to him.

'Bless you,' he said, adding: 'You wouldn't have a fag on you?'

I handed him my lit Dunhill. Dervla meanwhile had pulled a white handkerchief from her pocket and was using it to staunch the blood from what seemed to be a wound just below his hairline.

'Was it the flying glass that got you?' she asked.

'It was some fucking flying thing,' Diarmuid said.

'At least it spared your eyes,' she said.

As soon as Sean showed up with a bowl of boiling water and a tea towel, Sheila poked her head in the room, her eyes wide as she saw Diarmuid with blood now everywhere on his face, his shirt, his jacket.

'Oh Jesus ... ' she said. 'He needs a hospital.'

'Trying to get a cab right now is going to be a little troublesome,' Sean said at the same moment that Dervla pulled away her handkerchief and a small hemorrhage of blood cascaded down. Dipping the tea towel into the boiling water she put it to his wound, causing him to gasp in pain.

'Is that a clean tea towel?' she asked Sean.

'You stuck it in the boiling water. That should kill anything.'

'He needs stitches,' Sheila said. 'I've got my ma's car out front.'

'Then what are we waiting here for?' Dervla said. 'We can get him over to Holles Street in about five minutes.'

'That's a fucking maternity hospital,' Sean said.

'I think they'll accept all comers today, up the spout or not,' said Dervla.

At that moment the phone began to ring. I dashed into the hallway.

'Please tell me that Dervla's there,' came a panicked voice.

'She is.'

'Oh, thanks be to God.'

'Is this her mother?'

'It is indeed.'

I yelled into the next room.

'Dervla, your mom!'

Some hours later, we were recounting all that had happened to ourselves in Mulligan's. Diarmuid, who got his wound cleaned and stitched at the maternity hospital, was being bought drinks by everyone. Dervla, meanwhile, had been reunited with her mother – who'd been walking north up O'Connell Street, not far from Sackville Place, when the bomb went off. She was so rattled she took shelter in another department store for over an hour before the police allowed everyone back on the street, and the queues for the one phone box in the store were so long that she couldn't ring her daughter until she returned to her guest house off Parnell Square. Mother and daughter had agreed to meet for dinner south of the river, so they didn't join us in the pub.

'She was brilliant,' Diarmuid said. 'Thanks be to God that Sheila here had her mum's Mini and drove like fuck to get me as fast as possible to the hospital.'

'I drove fast because you were dripping blood on my mother's precious motor. And my ma gets very fussy about blood on the car seats. We've been pretty lucky so far when it comes to bombings. Just two small ones last year. We still haven't heard how many casualties this one has resulted in.'

'Spoke on the phone to one of my spies on the Northside,' said Sean. 'One dead and fourteen badly injured. He's saying that they think the UVF were behind it for all the usual fucking reasons.'

After Sean's comment the discussion intensified – in low voices, so as not to invite other people nearby in the pub into the argument – about whether it might have been the Provisional IRA who'd staged the attack as a way of galvanizing public opinion in the Republic against the Loyalists, though Sean also wondered out loud if British Army intelligence were also in cahoots with the Protestant UVF. I listened to all this conspiratorial back-and-forth talk, fascinated by how dense and complex and fluid the politics of all this were.

Trying to leave a gang of people in Dublin after nearly five hours of drink and talk was never an easy proposition, especially as eleven on a Saturday night was still considered the early evening and the group dynamic demanded that you stay up for the ongoing jollity and all that. But I needed to phone home to tell Mom not to worry about the bomb.

'Oh my God, a bomb,' Mom said. 'You've got to come home now.'

'It was a small bomb – and I just wanted to tell you that I was nowhere near it.'

'There's no such thing as a small bomb. I'm calling your father in Santiago and telling him to order you home.'

'Mom, you're being ridiculous.'

'That's always your point of view about me. Mrs Ridiculous.'

'I just wanted to tell you: I'm all right.'

'You've been drinking, haven't you?'

'Oh please. Goodnight, Mom.'

Dad phoned the next day. Luckily, I was home writing my essay when Sean shouted upstairs to me that 'the operator from fucking Chile's on the line'.

238

I raced downstairs, fully expecting my father to tell me: I've booked you on the next plane back to New York. Instead he was geniality itself.

'Your mother called me, half hysterical about this bomb thing in Dublin. We get the AP teletype in our office here, so I read their dispatch about it. Bad, but not terrible. I calmed down your mother and told her that there was no reason to order you home. Should this happen on a regular basis, however ... '

'It won't,' I said, thinking: what an absurd assertion that was.

'Your lips to the paramilitaries' ears. How you getting on there?'

I filled him in on the details, then tackled a subject I had to bring up with him.

'Dad, where's Peter, and what's happening in Chile?'

'Peter, to the best of my knowledge, is just fine – even if he is hanging out with questionable company.'

'Have you seen him?'

'Not yet.'

'Have you talked to him?'

'Not yet.'

'Then how can you be certain he's fine? Aren't they rounding up everyone against the regime?'

'It's not a "regime". It's a proper government.'

'An Army coup is not a proper government.'

'I am keeping him safe. And now I've got to get back to the business of running my mine. Have a glass of Tullamore Dew for me. Love you, sweetheart.'

Why didn't I push Dad on that comment which so struck me in Peter's letter: that our father wasn't truly what he seemed? Why didn't I ask him to explain Peter's concern to me? Because I knew that Dad would just be dismissive, along the lines of: *Oh, you know your radical brother, seeing right-wing conspiracies behind everything ... and yeah, I'm supporting Pinochet, but this is just business, nothing more.* But another reason why I was so hesitant to push Dad on any of this was that ignorance about such things was, on many levels, the more comfortable option for me. It meant that I didn't have to face up to all those moral and ethical questions that were thrown up by his activities in such a volatile, shadowy place.

One Thursday afternoon I ran into Professor Kennelley coming out of Bewley's.

'The very clever Alice Burns ... who, like most clever Americans, came to Dublin to be corrupted – and is doing so in the name of Anglo-Irish literature.'

I must say that I rather liked that comment. Just as I favored the lack of striving in Dublin; the way my fellow students never talked about where they saw themselves ten years down the road. Conversations about careers or money rarely emerged. Though somewhat down at heel and isolated, Dublin had a properly bohemian edge – insofar as you could live for very little in less than adequate conditions. Yet the trade-off was that you didn't have to engage in that very American need to achieve. It wasn't all a raffish lack of industry here. I saw a revival, in a small theater, of an extraordinarily bleak and telling play about an Irish family in Coventry called *A Whistle in the Dark*. It pointed up the way writers here were still at the forefront when it came to questioning national myths and the complex local body politic. Just as I discovered writers like Sean O'Faolain who could denounce the Church and the creeping provincialism of Irish life while also showing its urbane qualities.

That was another thing that began to take hold in my consciousness: the understanding that, like most American writing, its Irish counterpart was inevitably grappling with questions of national identity, communal contradictions, the shibboleths and lies and myths that are cornerstones of our collective psyches – though when I posited this thesis in an essay I wrote for Professor Kennelley, his response in a note at the bottom of it was, to say the least, most telling:

I can see how you're looking for common ground between two literary cultures where no writer can sidestep the larger question: what does it mean to belong to such a confounding place?

But you're not considering the way geography also underscores a national literature – and how our island smallness and tribalness defines us. Just as American vastness and fluidity and money is always there in your literature. The boundlessness of your continent provokes thoughts of great freedom and terror back in the USA.

Kennelley had a point, and a more nuanced one than those frequently uttered by the Maoists on the steps of the Trinity dining hall about the way that American imperialism was a pervasive cancer. Then there was an edgy exchange with my neighbor Sheila. When I asked if she wouldn't mind giving the bathtub a quick scrub – with the powdered bleach and sponge left in a corner for the expressed purpose of cleaning up after we washed – she bore into me, saying:

'If you Americans were less concerned with things sanitary than with murdering Vietnamese villagers –'

'Don't blame me for the horrible excesses of Nixon and Kissinger,' I said, somewhat taken aback.

'I'm not blaming you. I'm just asking you to have some fucking perspective about a little ring around the bathtub.'

'What does that have to do with American war crimes? We all clean the bathtub after we use it. Why can't you?'

'Everything you Americans touch has to be so fucking antiseptic. You're afraid of fucking dirt, fucking mess. You want to render everything sterile.'

Before I could shout back a riposte three raps of the heavy metal knocker landed on the front door.

'I'm expecting someone,' Sheila said, pushing by me. I leaned against the wall, not at all pleased with these contretemps, realizing that if I wanted a bath in a clean tub I would have to wash it out myself. Which I was about to start doing. Until I heard the door open and a woman asking if Alice Burns lived here. The accent was a distinctly American one, the voice oddly familiar to me.

241

'You've got a fellow Yank here looking for you,' Sheila said.

I came downstairs and found myself in front of a woman my age. I thought: no, it can't be her.

'That's right, it is me. Back from the dead.'

I was face-to-face with Carly Cohen.

15

SHE HAD CHANGED her hair, dyeing it jet black and growing it so long that it almost touched her waist. Her adolescent chubbiness had given away to immense gauntness. Once inside my bedsit, she took off her pea coat and her sweater; I saw a tattoo of a clenched black fist on her right bicep, beneath which were two words: *Revolution Now*. She told me she got the tattoo during the three years she lived in Oakland and 'got involved in the movement'. What movement? She didn't say just yet. I also noticed the crux of her left arm had noticeable scarring. And she was no longer Carly Cohen. Her new name was Megan Kozinski.

'Kind of weird, the juxtaposition of such an American first name with a Polish last name,' she said. 'But the late Megan Kozinski fit my profile.'

She explained how easy it was to get an identity makeover; how after she disappeared from Old Greenwich she ran off to the West Coast: a five-day bus trip which cost only twenty-one dollars ('I disappeared with all my babysitting savings – around two hundred dollars'). It landed her in San Francisco. She knew nobody, realized she had enough money to eke out life for about a month.

'In Haight-Ashbury, I wandered into a coffee shop with my back-pack. Talked to the guy, Troy was his name, who was behind the counter. He said I could come back with him after work to crash at the place he shared with about five other people. The next morning he told me a friend of his was looking for someone to help run her head shop. So two days after arriving in the Bay Area, I was making one-fifty an hour selling bongs and rolling papers. It was easy to live on six bucks a day. I liked the vibe, liked the whole atmosphere in the Haight, liked the fact that there were a lot of runaways there like me. But there was a problem. Everyone was looking for me. Troy came in one morning with that day's copy of the *San Francisco Examiner*. There was my photo – and they reprinted over a couple of days the whole *New York Times* piece about all the bullying at

Old Greenwich High. You were quoted a lot. I thought that really cool – all the good stuff you said about me. Troy was impressed but said that it was only a matter of time before the cops or the Feds or the private detective whom my parents hired – that little detail was in the *Examiner* piece – came looking for me.'

'Couldn't you have phoned home?' I asked.

Carly's eyes narrowed into a sniper's gaze: hard, clinical, merciless. Her tightened lips held in check an outburst I was certain she wanted to give in to. She reached for my pack of cigarettes and lit one up. After a steadying drag she let out a lungful of smoke in the direction of my face, asking:

'May I finish my story?'

There was almost a menacing chastisement to her tone. I felt myself stiffen. She stared me out. After another long drag on her cigarette she continued talking.

'Troy knew this dude, worked over at City Lights Bookshop, named Sid. He'd been with the Weathermen until they got too violent and crazy. Sid told me how I could get a new identity, and explained how it was particularly easy to score one in Arizona where they were pretty lax about such things. I got the bus to Phoenix, found this fleabag hotel downtown for six bucks a night and spent a whole day in the library looking through the obituary pages of the *Arizona Republic* between 1960 and '65. I hit pay dirt while there: a six-year-old named Megan Kozinski who died when she was in Brazil in November 1960 with her parents. According to the obit her dad was working in Rio, the girl developed some virus and the funeral service was there. Bingo. Back in San Francisco I followed Sid's instructions and wrote to the Department of Records in Arizona, explaining that I was Megan Kozinski, date of birth September 3, 1954, that I had misplaced my birth certificate and could I have another one. The forms arrived. I filled them out, explaining that my parents had been missionaries in American Samoa for the past fifteen years – this was another Sid idea – and enclosing a money order for the six-dollar fee. The way Sid figured it, as there was probably no death cert filed by the Brazilian government with the State of Arizona after Megan's death, and as I also did a check in the Phoenix phone book when I was there and found no listing for her parents, they would not be able to phone the Kozinskis, and would probably buy 'the fifteen years out of the country' ruse as the reason why Megan Kozinski had no Social Security number. After I received an actual official birth certificate for Megan Kozinski, Sid then sent me down to the San Francisco Department of Motor Vehicles. I'd been doing drivers ed back in Old Greenwich, so I just needed a few brush-up lessons which, in exchange for a fuck each time, Sid gave me. Got my license on the first go. As you well know, once you have your driver's license you've got the most important piece of American identity going.'

I raised my hand.

'I need to ask you something: what exactly happened in that park to make you run away?'

'I'll get to that later. Can I crash on your floor tonight? Haven't slept in a day. The overnight ferry from France –'

'What were you doing in France? And how did you find out I was here?'

'The walls have ears. You have any more of that amazing tea?'

I poured her out another cup while watching her butter up another piece of soda bread and all but inhale it.

'Do your parents know you're here?' I asked.

'My parents? Megan Kozinski doesn't have parents.'

'But Carly Cohen does. And from what I've heard, they have been pretty devastated since their only child disappeared.'

'You reap what you sow.'

'What do you mean by that?'

'Like your family, we too were happy in New York. Then Dad got this idea that the city was getting too grim, too dangerous. He had this fantasy of himself going out in his little boat every day on Long Island Sound and coming back to his idyllic waterfront house. My mom, always the appeaser, agreed. They dropped me into Old Greenwich and all that it stands for. They knew that I was going to be the freak in that white-bread fucking world. They knew my life would be hell.'

'So you ran away, allowed everyone to think you were dead, and wrecked their lives in the process.'

'When did you turn into the Girl Scout?'

'Your parents split up after you vanished. Your mother had a nervous breakdown. Your father, last I heard, is something of a drunk.'

'Alice, you weren't picked on, day in, day out. Called "fatty" and "big dyke". You weren't set upon in a park and had nasty shit written on your breasts. Or had that bitch Deb Schaeffer continuing to pin your arms behind you while that sick little boy Ames Sweet pulled out his dick and jerked off on you.'

'He really did that?'

'You think I'd make something like that up?'

'It's just that Deb Schaeffer told the cops the stuff about him writing *Lessie Snitch* on you. But not that he masturbated –'

'Don't dress it up in civilized language. The asshole *jerked off. On me.* Then Deb punched me twice in the stomach. When I doubled over and fell to the ground Ames crouched down by me and forced open my mouth and poured dirt into it and told me if I said a word they'd find me and get me out here again and this time "you might just find out what it's like to have a dick shoved up your ass" – his exact words.'

I sat there, looking down at the top of my little cafe table, not wanting to hear the awful truth of what happened that night.

'Why didn't you go to the police?'

'All I wanted to do after what happened was to have the earth they shoved in my mouth swallow me up. Because I knew the cops would probably treat the whole thing as teenage stupidity – not realizing that there were two black guys there from Stamford who saw the whole thing because they were selling Sweet grass and speed. Even one of them tried to interfere, telling Sweet to knock it off. Know what he said in reply? "Back to your ghetto, shine." The dude at that point drew a gun, his colleague grabbed Sweet and held him while the dude shoved the barrel in his mouth and told him that he was a racist asshole, and the payment for his "shine" comment was going to be allowing them to take back all the drugs without refunding Sweet the hundred bucks he'd handed over ... or Sweet ending up dead. When he withdrew the barrel Sweet begged for his life. The dudes relieved him of the drugs they'd sold him. The guy with the gun then slammed the butt of the gun into Sweet's balls, doubling him over. I bet Deb Schaeffer didn't tell the cops that. Any more than she told me that the dudes asked if they could help me. That's when I told them they could drive me back to my parents' house. They were at some play in the city for the evening. I thought fast, deciding to leave my bike in the park so everyone would believe someone did something to me. The dudes waited outside as I went upstairs, got all the babysitting money I'd saved and left. I grabbed my school knapsack – I figured if I packed a suitcase or removed anything my parents would notice. They didn't know where I kept my money. It was hidden in a shoebox under my bed. Then I left the house and asked the dudes if they would drive me to the train station in Stamford. I knew I was taking a risk, but they were cool. Stamford, as you know, is a busy station – so I was not the only person on the platform as I would have been in Old Greenwich. I got a nine something train to Grand Central Station. As soon as I got into the city I went over to Gretchen's place. You remember me telling you about Gretchen, right?'

'I remember you saying you were seeing this older woman in the city and that I had to keep it a secret.'

'Which you didn't – seeing as how she was ruined after I disappeared. I saw all the press stuff on her.'

'As I didn't know her name or address or anything about her all I told the police – when you didn't return home twenty-four hours after your disappearance – was everything you told me about your girlfriend. Which was nothing. It was poor Gretchen Ford who went to the police after they found your wallet and stuff on the beach. It was poor Gretchen Ford whose life was ruined by her doing the right thing: calling the cops and confessing you stayed that first night at her place. You didn't think about stopping all that – and ending your parents' agony – by letting everyone you know you were alive?'

'Don't you understand? I wanted everyone to think I was dead. That's why I faked my suicide on the beach in Far Rockaway.'

'It killed Gretchen. You know that she gassed herself in her car a couple of months after you vanished?'

She just shrugged, saying:

'That was her choice. Just as it was her choice to let me only stay one night, then march me over to Grand Central Station and put me on the train back to fucking Old Greenwich. Had she accompanied me back, had she called my folks, had she just let me stay a few more days with her –'

'She panicked.'

'Because she was scared of being revealed as a dyke with an eighteen-year-old lover. She could have avoided everything – including her own downfall.'

I couldn't believe what I was hearing: her absolute refusal to accept any responsibility for the chaos she sowed by vanishing – and letting everyone believe that she had drowned herself in the Atlantic.

'Anyway, after putting me on the train back to Connecticut, I worried that Gretchen might finally call my parents and that there'd be a welcoming committee when I arrived at Old Greenwich. So I jumped off at 125th Street and headed to the subway. I hopped the A train, not having any idea what to do next. The last stop is Far Rockaway. Right on the ocean. Before that there are two subway stops straight on the beach. I got out at the first one. I walked over to the sand. I plopped myself down. This homeless guy started hassling me. I told him to fuck off. When he disappeared I stared out at the water and realized that if I didn't die fast, the cops would be looking everywhere for me. And what I wanted to do most of all was vanish. Without a trace. That's when I formulated my plan to leave my bag and wallet there, taking with me just the money I had. The way I figured it the homeless guy would come back, find the bag and the empty wallet . . .

'I figured right. I left everything a few feet away from the water – the tide had just gone in – and hopped the subway right back into Manhattan. Got off at 42nd Street. Walked over to the Port Authority Bus terminal, having to negotiate all the sleaze on Times Square. There was a bus leaving for LA via DC, Norfolk, Nashville, Oklahoma City, Santa Fe, Phoenix, Palm Springs.

They didn't ask for ID when I bought the ticket. Funny how I remember all those stops west, even though I was zonked for much of the journey. I didn't have a change of clothes, let alone a toothbrush. I slept all the way from DC to Nashville. When I got to LA the bus station downtown was so sleazy – and the sky too blue – that I got the first bus north to San Fran. You know the rest.'

I actually knew so very little – except that which she had just told me. Just as I knew that her nonstop talking was unnerving me. I had so many questions and was completely thrown by her presence here in my room, still wondering how the hell she found out where I lived, and why she had made this long overnight pilgrimage from Paris to Dublin to see me.

'You got a bathroom somewhere?' she asked.

'In the hallway downstairs.'

'You've got a shower in there?'

'A tub.'

'I could sure use a bath and about ten hours of sleep.'

I was, of course, going to let her stay. But I was also thinking: my little room is too small for the two of us.

That was the strange thing about all this. I wanted to feel joy in Carly's return from the dead. But all I could feel was a strange numbness, a confusion as to why she had gone out of the way to damage her parents. A simple postcard saying 'I'm alive – don't come find me' would have, at least, let them know that she hadn't been murdered. It might have allowed them to hang together, to not descend into a vortex. I could not imagine punishing my parents in the extreme way that Carly had done. It just wasn't right.

I went downstairs, knocking on Sean's door.

'I have an unexpected visitor from the States. She needs a place to crash for a few nights – and I'm going to put her up on my floor. Is there a spare mattress anywhere?'

Sean said he'd go look in the shed at the back of the house. Meanwhile I went upstairs and ran the bath for my guest. Then I returned to my room and handed Carly – who was already stripped down to her underwear – one of my towels.

'You wouldn't have any shampoo or soap?' she asked. I told her that she'd find them both by the tub. As she was wrapping the towel around her there was a knock on the door. Sean had a single mattress under one arm. He was immediately captivated by the sight of my friend with a towel around her narrow frame, her wildly black hair cascading across her shoulders.

I introduced them, telling Sean she was my friend Megan.

'An old friend from the States?' Sean asked.

'An ancient friend,' Carly said, 'with much ancient history.'

'Well, when it comes to seeing the way history fucks up everything in the present, Ireland is a great spot. Hope we can have a cup of tea soon, Megan. Here's your mattress.'

After she returned from her bath Carly crashed out instantly on the mattress, her clothes and the towel thrown across my bed. I threw her sweaty clothes into my laundry bag and picked up the other dirty clothes she'd tossed into the corner, and brought the damp towel into the bathroom, cleaned up the bathtub, then tiptoed back into my room, grabbed my books, notebooks and the bag of laundry, deciding to head off to the washing machines at Trinity and work my way through some poems by Austin Clarke on which Kennelley had assigned us an essay to be delivered next week.

When I had all the laundry washed and dried I headed up Grafton Street, checking out Neary's, Davy Byrnes and the Bailey, hoping to run into some Trinity friends. Luck was not with me this evening, so I sat in the snug at Neary's, eating a cheese sandwich, drinking a pint of Guinness, wondering what tomorrow with Carly would bring. Finding her hard edge – her anger – more than unsettling. Wondering how my friend – who was always vulnerable, always awash in self-consciousness – had transformed herself into the militant who had just walked back into my life.

Carly, it turned out, had a world-class snore, rumbling and snarling like the belching exhaust of a car. I tried covering my ears with a pillow, but an hour into this aural torture, I sat up in bed unable to sleep. I turned on my bedside light and picked up a copy of the *International Herald Tribune* that had arrived with Carly. It was the only real source of detailed American news on this side of the Atlantic. I was fixated by the ongoing Watergate scandal, addicted to Woodward and Bernstein's reporting. Did I feel a tug of homesickness as I worked my way through the *Herald*'s weekend edition? Reading all this news from home ... I felt both connected with the United States and happily distanced from it all, the source of too much of my recent pain. Is that why the recumbent snorer crashed out on my floor was freaking me out? Not just because she was ruining my sleep, but she was also bringing back everything bad that had made me want to permanently reject that suburban place into which, like Carly, I had been dropped?

Yet here she was: the Eurydice who did return from the underworld.

Sleep finally did overtake me but Carly, having crashed out at seven, was up before dawn, banging around my kitchen. I opened an eye as she asked:

'Morning ... where's the coffee?'

'I drink tea now.'

'Great.'

'There's a place called Bewley's we can go to for coffee.'

Fifteen minutes later we were in Bewley's, the lack of sleep playing havoc with my head. So too Carly's nonstop talkathon. When she raised her voice, telling me that she had been 'some black guy's bitch' in Oakland, heads began to turn. Bewley's was not used to such talk.

'Don't tell me I'm talking too loud?' she said.

'People are looking at us.'

'That bothers you?'

'Yes it does.'

'You always were worried about what other people think. You and that weedy, pathetic boyfriend of yours.'

'Arnold always defended you all the time at school. Just as I did.'

'Did he end up at Yale – as he always thought he would?'

'Cornell.'

'I bet his parents were so disappointed with him for that.'

'Cornell is pretty damn good.'

'But not to Yalie parents. No doubt they made the geek suffer for that.'

'And when you vanished and everyone thought you were dead ... you didn't cause suffering?'

'Let me guess; you sat *shiva* for me with my parents.'

'Everyone who loved and cared about you were devastated.'

'Why do I think: so fucking what?'

'You tell me. Your parents didn't beat you, did they? Your father struck me as a reasonable guy; your mother was a little too worried about keeping everything nice and sane in that shrink way of hers. But unless they were keeping you tied up in the basement, or torturing you, I don't get your anger. Unless you're not telling me something ... '

'Like what? That my dad slept with me?'

'Did he?'

'No. And do you know why I haven't made contact with them? Because, as I told you last night, Carly Cohen is dead. If they had any idea whatsoever that she might be alive they'd come looking for me. This way the trail has gone cold. By the way I'm not stupid. I see that you already regret letting me across your threshold.'

'I didn't say that.'

'You don't need to. It's all over your face. Fear not, I will be gone from your life very soon.'

'Stay as long as you like.'

'How will you sleep?'

'I'll manage. Earplugs ... '

'There you go, trying to suck up to me.'

'I have no interest in trying to make you like me,' I said. 'In fact, I think that task might be kind of impossible. You still haven't told me how you tracked me down, found out my address in Dublin.'

She stubbed out her cigarette.

'As I said earlier: all will be revealed in time. Can I have a key to your place in case I want to go back, have a bath, change my clothes?'

'I washed all your dirty ones last night.'

'You really are goody-two-shoes.'

'You're being mean.'

'Comes with the territory of being angry at the world. In fact, the nicer you are the meaner I'll become. What about the spare key?'

We had to walk all the way back for me to get the spare key. As I was leaving I told Carly to meet me tonight around six at Mulligan's. On the way out the door back toward Trinity I ran into Sean, up early, looking hungover and hangdog.

'How's my beautiful princess?' he asked.

'My friend saws wood all night.'

'She should be sharing my bed then, rather than crashed out on a mattress on your floor.'

As much as I wanted to be rid of Carly I couldn't do anything so unsisterly and bad taste as suggesting that this quasi-charming toxic mess of a man move in on her. I just rolled my eyes and said:

'Good luck convincing her of that.'

The day passed in something of a blur. But I managed to sound moderately cogent during my tutorial with Professor Norris. I worked in the library. I went to the college pool and had a long swim, thereby allowing me to shower in the locker room afterwards. When I turned up on time to meet Carly at Mulligan's I found that she was already ensconced there with Sean. From the way they were laughing, from the many glasses on the table, from the brimming ashtray in front of Carly, it was clear they had been there for a while.

'There's the other American Beauty,' Sean announced, signaling to the bartender that he should pour me a pint of Guinness.

'She's the beauty, I'm the freak,' Carly said.

'That's rubbish,' I said, then asked Sean: 'How did you both find your way here?'

'While you were out being educated I knocked on your door and asked your friend if she would consider having a pint with me.'

Carly came in here:

'I had the bad judgment to say yes.'

Then turning back to Sean she asked:

'Did Alice ever tell you about her friend Carly Cohen – who went missing and was never found?'

'Not at all,' Sean said. 'It sounds like a terrible story.'

I looked squarely at Carly and said:

'You're right. It was a terrible story. It destroyed the poor girl's parents.'

'Alice always sides with the parents.'

'That's not true. And I don't know why we're talking about this.'

'Because I like yanking your chain,' Carly said.

'Yank mine instead,' Sean said, putting his arm around her. Carly rolled her eyes, but didn't shove Sean's arm away. She glared at me. It was unsettling, feeling all this anger, wondering why it was so directed at me, yet also knowing I was the first person she had seen from her Old Greenwich days since her disappearance. Was that why she was lashing out at me? Was this her way of venting all the rage she had at everyone who had picked on her there? I still needed to know who told her where to find me.

When Sean disappeared to the loo I leaned over and hissed at Carly:

'You need to stop treating me like the enemy here. I am nothing of the sort. Just like you also need to tell me how –'

'I need to tell you shit. But I am glad to see that I am getting under your skin.'

'But why?'

Sean returned, putting his arm around Carly again. He noticed the chill between us.

'Now there's no need to bring up the past here,' he said.

'Alice has many skeletons in her closet. And an ex-boyfriend who got thrown out of their fancy college for writing essays for others.'

Now I was totally wide-eyed and just a bit angry.

'How the hell did you know all that?'

'I have my sources.'

Suddenly I wanted to be anywhere but here. Just as I knew, after a mere twenty-four hours, that she might be trouble in my life were she to stay.

Fortunately Diarmuid and Sheila came in, Diarmuid asking in his usual 'Hail fellow well met' way what brought Carly/Megan to Dublin, how we knew each other, and where had she been on her recent travels?

Carly, very much at home with talking at length about herself, got into a long spiel about 'fleeing the fascist repression of Nixon's America, and the apartheid regime imposed on our black brothers and sisters'. She also talked about being at the recent barricades in Paris, and throwing Molotov cocktails at the police before being tear-gassed inside the Gare Saint-Lazare.

'It was fucking amazing,' Carly told us. 'We were shouting "Nixon: Assassin!" – and the world was listening. Just as they listened when a bunch of us radicals staged a protest five weeks ago in Santiago against the Pinochet regime.'

Now I really did feel as if I was in some sort of free fall.

'You were in *Chile?*' I asked.

'That's what I said.'

'You know my brother Peter's there.'

Carly smiled and lit up another cigarette.

'Of course I know that,' she said. 'That's why I'm here. I was with Peter in Chile.'

16

CARLY DID NOT come back to my room that night. By the time I left the pub – shortly after that revelation about Peter – she was sufficiently oiled on Guinness and Powers whiskey not to resist Sean's chubby charm. Free will and personal choice were two concepts not alien to Carly, let alone her reinvented Megan Kozinski self. It was clear she could decide whether or not to sleep with Sean – as rotund and sweaty and unhygienic as he was. Yet the guy also had a certain ruffian allure, a sense of ease, a clever turn of phrase, evident intelligence. I didn't want to speculate what convinced Carly to head to his room that night. I was just relieved that she was not returning to the mattress on my floor and that, as such, I would be able to sleep through until morning without using the earplugs I'd purchased that day at a chemist (another new addition to my vocabulary) on Dame Street.

But sleep did not come easily. I was very much unsettled by that revelation made by Carly about my brother. While still in Mulligan's I pulled her over to the corner of the pub, demanding to know more about Peter.

'We'll talk about this tomorrow,' she said, reaching over and again helping herself to a cigarette from my pack.

'I need to know *now*: is Peter in a dangerous place?'

'When I left him a month ago he was about as okay as anyone can be taking on a military junta.'

'What do you mean by that?' I demanded. 'How did you manage to meet up with him?'

'Stop pushing for info.'

'He's my brother. He's doing dangerous stuff in a dangerous place.'

'Your father is making sure he's not going to get hurt. And Peter's been doing a very good job evading arrest. Because he knows that once they nab him they will deport him immediately – which is what your dad would like to see happen.'

'Did you see my father?'

'Don't be silly. I'm not exactly in the copper business and I don't hang out with assholes who support Pinochet and his vicious goons.'

'My dad's doing business there, that's all.'

'You're now defending Daddy.'

'I'm just not jumping to conclusions without proof of anything.'

'What a good little girl you are.'

That's when I got up and stormed off, cursing myself for taking the bait, for allowing myself to be riled by someone who I had decided was both manipulative and maybe even a little dangerous. Diarmuid, having overheard this exchange, followed me out of the pub.

'Don't be listening to her rubbish,' he said.

'But much of what she was telling me is pretty damn important. Can I trust you?'

'You know you can.'

Diarmuid was, in fact, one of the rare people whom I instinctually trusted. So I unloaded, telling him all about my brother in Chile and how my father was possibly up to no good with the junta. His thoughts:

'Now you know that Megan probably sought your brother out in Chile as a way of getting to you. Why she did that, why she traveled all the way here to see you, why she had to probably get out of Chile and France in a hurry – you'd have to ask her ladyship. My advice to you is: get the info you want from her about your brother, but otherwise let the proverbial sleeping dogs lie. And hope that she takes up with Sean and stays out of your way. I must tell you: she has the air of the perennially troubled to her, and that's just on the basis of less than an hour in her company. You can dismiss my take on her as a premature rush to judgment. But honestly you don't need her disorder.'

Back in my room that night fury overtook me. *When I left him a month ago he was about as okay as anyone can be taking on a military junta.* What the fuck did she mean by that – and why was she dangling the possibility of my brother being in mortal danger in front of me in such a casually sadistic way? All of Carly's things were still strewn around my bedsit. I packed them up, rolled up her sleeping bag, picked up her backpack and piled them by my door. When I woke up – after a bad few hours of sleep – I headed downstairs with all her detritus, rapping lightly on Sean's door. It took three knocks before he answered, his breath a toxic morning-after brew.

'What can I do for you?' he asked.

'Locked myself out. Need my keys back from Megan,' I said, remembering her new name again just before 'Carly' came out of my mouth.

'Hang on a tick,' he said, shutting the door. Moments later he opened it again and handed me the spare keys for the front door and my own flat.

'Brought these down for her,' I said, handing him the sleeping bag and knapsack. Sean's eyes went wide but before he could say anything I smiled and headed out the door.

Later that day, while having my lunch at the union, Carly came barreling into the room.

'What the fuck are you doing, evicting me like that?' she yelled, causing all heads around us to turn toward this high-volume American voice.

'Stop shouting,' I hissed.

'Don't fucking tell me to –'

Carly plonked herself down on the seat next to mine. She reached over and drained almost half my glass in one go.

'I know I am a complete bitch,' she whispered, a sudden flash of sadness on her face.

'You've been vile from the moment you walked back into my life.'

'Would an apology help?'

'It won't get you back on my floor. Anyway, Sean's bed is, I'm sure, more comfortable than the mattress on my floor.'

'There's a fundamental problem with Sean's bed – and that is Sean.'

'I'm sure you'll adapt.'

'You can't stand me, can you?'

'I need to know about my brother.'

'Why should I tell you anything, given how you've evicted me?'

'You haven't left the building; you're just sleeping elsewhere within it. And the reason you need to tell me about my brother is because he *is* my brother.'

Carly scrunched up her face, then lit a cigarette.

'Will you let me crash again on your floor ... ?'

'In exchange for info about Peter? Fuck you.'

My response came out in a furious hiss. Carly smiled.

'I guess we're in what's known as a stalemate.'

'I won't be blackmailed in this way.'

'What are you going to do about it?'

I picked up my stuff and changed tables, pulling out some books and papers and trying to tamper down my anger by lighting up a fresh cigarette. Before I finished the first puff, Carly was seated next to me.

'It was Peter who, on the first night we slept together, told me about you going to Trinity. The next morning, I asked for your address, telling him I might just write you.'

'You were sleeping with my brother?' I shouted, thinking: Peter lost all judgment and reason when it came to the whiff of potential sexual conquest.

'Me and a variety of other women who were part of our little group.'

'What group exactly?'

'*El frente de liberación revolucionaria,* the Revolutionary Liberation Front. An underground movement, with the avowed aim of unsettling the Pinochet regime. We knew we didn't have the resources – militaristic or otherwise – to take on the junta. But what we decided we could do was make their life hell by fucking up centers of communication, fire-bombing after hours at Pinochet Party headquarters, blanketing the city with photos of the leftists who have disappeared and are either being tortured or have been murdered.'

'And how, *why,* did you find your way to Santiago?'

'When things got heavy in Oakland, I got out before I could be linked to any of it. Some of the friends I had made there gave me the contact details of their friends in *El frente*. Trust me, it took some careful sniffing around before I could find them – because they don't exactly have a headquarters or an office. But my Spanish is pretty good and I got a lucky break when I went to this bar in the El Jimineo district of Santiago and told the bartender that I was looking for El Capitán. Naturally the guy thought I was CIA or some American mole working for the junta and told me to come back later that evening to meet the fellow they call El Capitán. When I returned, four guys came for me, threatening to kick the shit out of me, wondering what this *gringa* was doing messing in their politics. Out of the back came this really tall American, who, in fluent Spanish, told his comrades to lay off the heavy third-degree shit. He asked me where I grew up. I told him Phoenix, Arizona, and he started asking me a whole lot of questions about Phoenix, as he'd done time there on a bunch of civil rights marches. When I couldn't answer some basic geographical stuff he told the others to give us a couple of moments, that he wanted to talk privately with me. Once they were gone he introduced himself. Said he was Peter Burns, born in Manhattan, but raised in Old Greenwich, Connecticut. I must be the world's worst undercover operative as I immediately blurted out: 'Oh my God, you're Alice's brother.' Twenty minutes and two cigarettes later he had my entire story. He had a lot of specific questions about the Panthers and really knew his shit when it came to their ideology and operations. He wanted to know exactly who told me about *El frente*. He too was trying to discern if I was some spook operative with the CIA. I must have passed the test because he brought his Chilean comrades back into the room and introduced me as *nuestra hermana revolucionaria*: their revolutionary sister. I couldn't have been more pleased. I soon discovered that *El frente* didn't have a base of operations, that they were moving from place to place, never hanging together, just having the occasional clandestine meeting to decide what move to make next. Me and Peter, we must have slept in twelve different beds over a three-week period.'

She let that last comment sink in. Desperate for her to keep talking, I tried to hide my discomfort.

'Besides sleeping with you, was Peter in any other direct danger?'

Carly smiled thinly.

'Your brother, like me, is committed to the overthrow of the ruling class, the moneyed oppressors. Like me, he was trying to fuck up a military junta. We managed to phone in a bomb scare on the state-run radio station during a broadcast of one of Pinochet's endless speeches. We broke into schools at night and left anti-junta propaganda everywhere for the children to see and read. We kidnapped a well-known pro-Pinochet newspaper editor.'

'You *what*?' I said.

Carly smiled again, pleased how this revelation had landed on me.

'You heard me.'

'What happened to this editor?'

'He was hardly an "editor" the way we might think of one back home: an actual moral arbiter. The guy was a right-wing lackey.'

'Which made it okay to kidnap him?'

'And put a bullet in the back of his head, as we had to do,' she said.

'Don't shit me here.'

'I shit you not, Girl Scout. The asshole was held for around three weeks by *El frente*. We offered the junta a deal – release our second in command, El Teniente, and we will give you your propaganda stooge back. You know how the junta responded? They dumped El Teniente's body in front of the burned-out headquarters of the Chilean Socialist Party. His eyes had been gouged out, his balls cut off, his skull beaten in with hammers and iron bars. What else could El Capitán do but order that Pinochet's favorite apologist be executed? At least they did it cleanly. No torture, no disfiguration. Just one bullet to blow the back of his head off.'

'Don't tell me Peter pulled the trigger.'

'You'll have to ask him that.'

'Tell me now: did Peter kill him?'

Another of her sardonic smiles as she fired up another cigarette. How I wanted right now to smash that smile back into her face.

'I've got you upset, don't I?'

'Yes you do.'

'You evict me from your room, the girl who was missing, presumed dead, who was victimized for years, who comes to you in fucking Dublin, seeking shelter ... '

Part of me felt guilt in the face of this accusation. But it was overshadowed by the thought: she is bad news. Thorny, malignant, menacing. And unstable. I had a choice here: give in to her blackmail and let her return to the floor of my little bedsit in the hope that she might inform me more about Peter. Or stay firm and see what I could still get out of her. Dad once told me: never do a deal with someone who tries to blackmail you. They will always take that to be a sign of weakness ... and one which they have to exploit. I downed part of my pint, then said:

'I don't want you in my room anymore. I don't want you in my life anymore.'

She looked thrown by such directness. It was clear to me now that, in the years since she had disappeared, she had turned her anguish and grief into the sort of hardness that expressed itself best in intimidation and browbeating. Like most bullies she didn't know what to do when her bluff was called.

'Blood is very much on Peter's hands,' she said.

'And on yours.'

'I can live with that.'

'I'm sure you can.'

'Fuck you,' she said, standing up.

'Is my brother okay?'

'You shit on me like that and now you want reassurance?'

'Just tell me: did he shoot that newspaper editor?'

As she snatched her cigarettes, she leaned across the table and hissed:

'El Capitán ordered that Peter do it. Not only that: he ordered that Peter force the gun in Duarte's mouth and pull the trigger so that Duarte would be staring into your brother's eyes in the moments before he died. It was a test – and one which your hard-ass revolutionary brother fulfilled. Perfectly.'

I shut my eyes, thrown beyond belief by what I'd just heard. Not knowing whether to believe it, or to write it off as one of her vicious inventions designed to unsettle me. What I did know in this very instant was that I would never have anything more to do with her. Opening my eyes again I told her just that:

'Stay away from me.'

'Maybe I will, maybe I won't.'

After she left I must have smoked three cigarettes in a row, going over to the bar to order a Powers to accompany the smokes. I never drank whiskey at lunchtime. I certainly needed one right now. Did my brother truly kill that editor? Was there even an editor named Duarte connected to the Pinochet junta? Could Peter have become entwined in matters so radical that he followed such terrible orders? Or was this another of Carly's dark fantasies, put out there in front of me in an attempt to destabilize me further? Clearly she had met Peter – because how else would she have known where I was so precisely?

I needed a walk. It was a rare day without rain, and I had no further lectures that afternoon. I walked down to the quays and hopped on a bus heading westward. Twenty minutes later I found myself in Phoenix Park. It was my newfound refuge, at the far westerly end of the quays; a huge green space with lakes and forests and pathways that led you to believe you were in dense wilderness even though the gray tangle that was Dublin was never more than a few miles away. It may not have had the visual drama of Wicklow, but it certainly allowed me space alone with all the ongoing infernal conundrums playing themselves out between my ears.

Today I found myself walking furiously, my anger acute. How fucking dare she accuse Peter of such things? When it came to matters radical my brother was someone who always sided with the forces of non-violent change, who condemned assassinations or any sort of taking of life in the name of a cause. Hell, all his civil rights work in the South was inspired by Martin Luther King's example of peaceful protest. The last thing he would ever have agreed to do was kill anyone in cold blood.

But why had he decided to drop out of university and head to Santiago? Yes, pissing off our father had something to do with it. Showing the old man that a member of his own family would take the other, more righteous side against a military junta, that too was part of his decision to head there. But to team up with a violent revolutionary group, to do their homicidal bidding, to force the nozzle of a gun into the mouth of a man whose only crime was to play propagandist for a nasty regime, who no doubt had a wife and children ... no, hyper-moral Peter would never have bought into such belligerent extremist insanity. Of that I was absolutely certain. By the time I finished my three hours in the park, getting out of its grounds just as night was falling, I also decided that the worst thing I could do right now was alert my mother about Carly Cohen's monstrous stories. Or contact my father via his office in New York and ask him if, perchance, his 'contacts' in Chile knew that his son was deeply ensnarled in the activities of *El frente* ... if, that is, such an organization even existed.

The next day, after an hour spent with a very helpful woman in Trinity's library, I was able to track down – via copies of *The Times* of London on file there – recent news from Chile. There, in an edition dated March 4, 1974, was a brief story on their 'Abroad' pages about how the body of Alfonso Duarte, the editor of a 'government-backed Santiago newspaper', had been dumped in front of his newspaper's offices two nights previously ... and how 'a Marxist revolutionary group, *El frente*, had claimed responsibility for his murder'.

I slept badly that night, waking once when I heard raised voices. Sticking my head out the door I peered downstairs and saw Carly and Sean stagger in.

'If you think I'm going to fuck ugly old you tonight ... ' she yelled at him.

'Why don't you fuck off to East Germany?' he bellowed back. 'Though the fucking Commie Nazis there would probably boot you out for being a fucking ideological child.'

I shut the door before either of them could catch me eavesdropping. My relief at not having her crashed out on my floor was overshadowed by my fury at everything she had become, and how her rage at the world was a terrifying vortex into which she sucked anyone in her immediate vicinity. When, half an hour later, she banged on my door, demanding to be let in, I remained silent, not daring to move. Her garbled yelling woke everyone up. I heard Diarmuid now also outside my door, ordering Carly to shut the fuck up, and her screaming back, saying that she knew I was inside and wouldn't stop bellowing until I let her in. Sean's voice joined this angry duo, trying to talk sense to her. Diarmuid threatening to call the police finally shut her up. Within minutes, peace reigned again outside my little bedsit. I fell into an uneasy, shallow sleep.

I could have slept on for half the morning, as I didn't have a lecture until after lunch. But at 8.20 a.m. Sheila knocked on the door and handed me a yellow envelope marked Western Union. One thing I knew about telegrams: they were rarely the carriers of good news.

'Thanks,' I said and shut my door before she could ask me what was in it. I sat down on my desk table, fearing the absolute worst: my brother Peter killed by the junta regime. Or Dad – all the stress of his life finally getting to him – dead of the heart attack I always feared would take him from us, leaving me in the clutches of my mother.

I ripped open the envelope.

Can you get to Paris? I'm alive – barely. We need to talk.
Peter

17

I WENT TO THE student travel agency off Grafton Street that morning and found a cheap flight to Paris at the end of the week. Then I crossed over to a post office and telegrammed Peter back:

Coming Friday. What's going on? Carly Cohen is here.

Peter's Western Union reply the next morning:

Don't listen to her. Will explain all. See you at Orly Friday p.m.

My flight was two hours delayed owing to a bad thunderstorm over Dublin Airport. When I reached Orly it was almost midnight. My first sight of my brother threw me. He appeared to have aged around ten years since our last face-to-face encounter many months back. He was rail-thin. His face had an anemic hue. He was smoking a cigarette with disconcerting rapidity, and he looked as if he hadn't slept in days. He attempted a smile when he saw me. He didn't pull it off. We gave each other a cursory hug. An uneasy silence filled the taxi as we made little in the way of conversation during the forty minutes it took to reach the hotel – or, at least, none outside of Peter's desultory questions about how I was getting on at Trinity. I asked him how long he'd been in Paris. His reply: 'Ten days.' I wanted to know why he'd only gotten in touch with me three days ago, whether he'd spoken to our parents.

It was rapidly approaching 1 a.m. I noticed fleeting images from the grimy windows of the taxi: cafes still open, a couple kissing up against a tree, moments of extravagant architecture, the interplay of lamplight on damp streets. I wanted to fall into the evident romanticism of the city. But all I could think about was: how much would Peter actually tell me? Would he entrust me with the truth ... or, at least, his version?

'Don't expect too much,' Peter said as the cab pulled up in front of the hotel. 'It's all a bit one-star here.'

That was a serious understatement. Hotel La Louisiane was shabby *in extremis*. The lobby had a single dangling light bulb, a night man at the front desk who looked like he was in some sort of purgatory of his own making. He snapped his fingers for my passport, took down the details on some official form, tossed me a key and pointed to the stairs.

'So you've decided we should spend a couple of days on the Paris version of skid row,' I said.

'Think of it as an adventure. You ever read Henry Miller's *Tropic of Cancer*? This was the sort of room in Paris where Miller learned how to become a writer.'

'What happened in Chile?'

'Can this wait until tomorrow?'

The wave of exhaustion hit me again. I was with my brother and any confession or otherwise he was about to make could wait. Despite the banging in the radiator, despite the loud verbal fight in the street, despite the guy vomiting in the room next door, I managed to pass out until I heard a knock on my door the next morning. Ten minutes later, after a fast wash in the sink, I was dressed and ready to head out. It was a cloudy, cold day. It didn't matter. Paris immediately had me in its grip. Talk here was loud – especially around the market where Peter brought me for breakfast. At a little cafe opposite a fish stand, where men in thick rubber aprons were using hatchets to chop the heads off very dead *poissons*, the waitress served us *café au lait* in porcelain bowls. We dunked croissants in the milky brew and smoked our first cigarettes of the morning. Peter talked about a couple of little cinemas in the area where he'd been spending a great deal of time, where you could watch old films for very little money and essentially hide indoors from the complexities of life.

'Just yesterday, before you got here, I saw this fantastic film by Fritz Lang called *The Big Heat* where Glenn Ford plays this cop gone crazy after some mob guys kill his wife, and there's this femme fatale played by Gloria Grahame who gets coffee thrown in her face by Lee Marvin, but has her revenge at the end – even if she dies in the process.'

'Isn't that how revenge works? You might get even, but you also screw yourself up along the way. Which is kind of like your bedmate, Carly Cohen.'

Peter shut his eyes, wanting to block out any mention of her. But then he opened them and said:

'Can we first finish our coffee?'

'Whatever,' I said.

After breakfast Peter told me we needed to first stroll at length through Saint Germain des Prés and the city soon took us over. We walked by the Seine. He showed me the Pont Neuf, we loitered in a fantastic bookshop called La Hune – which, had I been a Francophone, I would have lived in all the time. He insisted on bringing me to the Gothic, lofty precincts of Saint-Sulpice, where he pointed out the Delacroix paintings. He also knew of a place near Les Jardins du Luxembourg which was owned by a Breton and therefore specialized in crêpes and the very alcoholic cider made in what he called 'the Maine of France'.

As introductions to Paris go, it was pretty damn wonderful – and far removed from the usual tourist trail. As we sat eating our crêpes, and Peter began to talk about how it was still an ambition of his to crack the language and live here, I could not help but marvel at my older brother's worldliness and sense of curiosity. Along with the fact that, outside of a week spent here during his junior year, Peter had little prior knowledge of Paris, yet in just ten days he had worked out his preferred haunts. 'Do you know anyone here?' I asked.

'A few people,' he said. 'One classmate from Penn who's in a junior position in the Embassy. But under the circumstances I don't think he'd agree to a visit with me.'

'Are you on the run?'

'That's a little melodramatic.'

'So is the fact that you're here in Paris, that you demanded to see me in person, that you've spent the last four hours dodging the subject.'

'I don't want to talk in here. What I have to say I need to say somewhere where we can't be heard. The Luxembourg Gardens are just across the street.'

He settled the check and we headed out. The sun was fighting its way through the dense cloud cover. There were traces of snow in the park. We walked to a place which Peter called his favorite corner of this very formal, exquisitely landscaped green space. Peter pointed to the Pantheon, all the famous French dead interred there. I decided the moment had arrived to speak directly.

'Carly Cohen told me that you were ordered by your revolutionary Capitán to kill a newspaper editor. And that you blew his brains out by shoving a gun muzzle into his mouth.'

That got his attention.

'Oh Jesus fuck,' he whispered.

'Is that a confirmation or a denial?' I asked.

'I didn't kill Alfonso Duarte.'

'Oh, so you know his name. Did you pull the trigger?'

'No.'

'Look at me, Peter – and tell me that again.'

He now faced me directly.

'I did not kill Alfonso Duarte.'

'Then why did Carly say that?'

'Because she is malignant and cruel. I argued hard against it. I was overruled. Duarte was only kidnapped after the Pinochet thugs had arrested a colleague of ours. Picking up Duarte was tit for tat. But he was a bargaining tool. We let the junta know: *you want your mouthpiece released, let go our ten comrades whom you're holding.* We never tortured him. We never beat him. We didn't try to get information out of him. All we did was demand a trade. Do you know how the junta responded? They beat to death our ten comrades. That's when El Capitán had no choice but to have Duarte killed. The junta gave us no alternative.'

'You didn't pull the trigger?'

He shook his head.

'But you were there when he was executed?'

After a pause, he nodded.

'Who pulled the trigger?' I asked.

'Carly pulled the trigger.'

Now it was my turn to be blindsided.

'I don't believe that,' I said.

'But you believed her when she told you it was me who killed Duarte?'

'I never said that.'

'The *lie* she told you ... '

'But why would she do such a thing?'

'*Why? Why?* Are you kidding me? She bragged about doing bank jobs with the Panthers. She bragged about going on midnight runs to score illegal guns for them. Then she shows up in Chile and talks her way into *El frente de liberación revolucionaria* ... '

Peter stood up.

'There's a lot more to say, a lot more to explain,' he said. 'But I am finding all this rather hard right now. I need a walk. I need to think things through.'

'In other words: buzz off for a few hours so I can plot out how best to rationally explain my crimes and misdemeanors?'

'You've really become so judgmental.'

'That's not true. I am simply appalled by what I'm hearing. Don't you feel guilty?'

'The reason I was in Chile in the first place was a woman I met at Yale. A woman named Valentina Soto. I was in love with her. She returned to Chile after the coup to work in the movement against Pinochet. And she was killed by the junta two weeks ago.'

I could see that he was on the verge of sobbing; the tragedy deeply registered in his eyes.

'Were you with her when she was killed?' I asked.

Peter nodded many times.

'If you were there when they killed her, why did they spare you?'

'That's the complicated part of the story.'

He fished into his pockets for a cigarette, lit up, glanced at his watch.

'It's now almost three. Tell you what – see you back at the hotel around six. Is that okay with you? I mean, you won't feel lost or anything?'

'I'm a big girl who was raised for a time in a big city. I'll be fine. Will you be okay?'

'No,' he said.

Then he turned and walked off. I sat on the bench for a good ten minutes, my head swimming. Did Carly really kill the newspaper editor? Was she so twisted, so sick, as to pin the murder on my brother even though she herself carried it out? Was she also thinking that, in the wake of her revelation, I would naturally confront Peter, demanding to know if he had pulled the trigger? Did she figure that his denial would create a river of doubt between us? Was that her game – to drive as big a wedge as possible between myself and my brother?

The cold eventually made me get up and start walking. I spent an hour in the Pantheon, looking at the final resting place of Voltaire, Rousseau, Hugo, Zola. I wondered what it was like to get old, how my grandfather always appeared dapper in an elderly way to me, and how when he died at the age of eighty-two I could only think: that is so ancient. My mother at the time told me: 'One thing you can't understand at sixteen is just how fast your life is going to be. Trust me, when I was your age, I thought a year was huge: the distance from the start of school to summer vacation vast. Now September to June is a blink of the eye. Everyone who has ever lived a life has thought the same damn thing: why is this all passing far too quickly.'

A light snow was falling as I left. Even though it was bitterly cold, I decided to wander with no knowledge of the local geography, to see where my feet would bring me, then somehow find a metro station around five thirty to get me back to our seedy hotel. I deliberately lost myself in back streets. I crossed wide boulevards. I was incessantly looking in shop windows. I stopped and spent ten dazzling minutes in a *fromagerie*, thinking that if I lived here I would exist entirely on cheese, baguettes, red wine, with an unhealthy number of daily cigarettes to keep myself from bloating. I became aware of life going on around me: a well-heeled bourgeois couple in the cafe where I stopped for a glass of wine; a young guy in a thin leather jacket trying to flirt with a woman about my age. My sense of connection with Paris was immediate. I saw myself living in a small apartment – no doubt, a garret – and finding work at the *International Herald Tribune*. I would spend much time in cafes, and spend many an evening in small cinemas, becoming a true film buff. Most of all I would be far away from all the terrible ties that bind – the crazed dance of America, the crazed dance of my family. Even though I also found myself thinking: I was in the city that Mom had always dreamed of calling her own.

Peter had left a note under my door, asking that I knock on his when I got back. I went upstairs to room 312. His place was considerably bigger than mine. It also had an armchair, a larger bed and a simple desk – strewn across which were notebooks, aerogrammes, assorted newspapers, a portable typewriter, and photographs of a dark-haired woman in her early twenties who was lovely.

'Is that Valentina?' I asked. 'She's beautiful.'

'She was indeed beautiful,' he said, emphasizing the past tense.

We ended up at a brasserie near the Sorbonne. Peter ordered us two Pernods, showing me how to dilute it and turn it milky white with a drop of water.

'Did you have a good think on your own, deciding what to tell me, what to keep to yourself?'

'Yes, that's one of the many things which crossed my chaotic mind when I was out on my walk.'

'There's nothing chaotic about you, Peter. You may be the great theologian, the man of ideas, but you are also as rational as they come.'

'You may have a point there. But the other truth of the matter is: I landed myself in a truly irrational situation.'

'Tell me.'

He glanced around him, as if expecting someone to be eavesdropping on us. Then, seeing that the only people near us were an elderly couple, French, and not working for some international intelligence organization, he took a steadying sip of Pernod and lit up another cigarette.

'You act like you're going to the scaffold,' I said.

'Perhaps I am. The guilt I feel is enormous.'

'Tell me about Valentina.'

'She was studying comparative languages. Her father was a big-deal banker down in Santiago – a difficult, complicated man, hugely well connected. Her mother was a socialite, the sort of woman who lived to plan dinners and shop and play tennis at the country club

272

where all the Santiago bigwigs hung out. Valentina had two older sisters who were both married off young. She was the rebel: worldly, convinced that the life her father was forcing on her would be all wrong for her. So she perfected her English, did fantastically well as an undergraduate at the University of Santiago, and when Yale accepted her for their doctoral program, she convinced her father to fund her. The way her daddy figured it – given that she had been supportive of Allende and his socialist government – having her out of the country would be a good thing. Also: I sensed that he was aware of the talk going on in high circles about plans to topple Allende, and he wanted her far away when all that went down. I met her at the start of this academic year. She was coming out of a class, I was racing across the quad to a meeting when I ran right into her. You know the French expression: *un coup de foudre*? That's how it was with us. We looked at each other and almost immediately knew: this was destiny.'

Peter took another long sip of the Pernod.

'Within a week we were inseparable,' he said.

'I don't suppose our father's involvement in Chile had anything to do with your decision not to tell any of us. Especially as he might have known Valentina's father.'

'Yes, I was very concerned about that. Yes, I told Valentina early on. She made some discreet inquiries. Our two fathers were well acquainted, which meant that our dad might have been a little worried about me being involved with such a professed lefty. Then the coup happened. She heard that three of her great friends from university had disappeared and that her father was advising the Pinochet regime. She wouldn't listen to me when I begged her not to go back, telling her the situation was just too dangerous. But she was, in the best sense of the word, a true Chilean patriot. She felt she had no choice but to join the cause against Pinochet. So off she went. There was no news for a month, six weeks. Then, out of nowhere, I got a call one night from someone whose name was Enrico and who told me that he was in the same "movement" as Valentina, and that she had been nabbed by the security forces after a kidnapping she was involved in went very wrong. He couldn't speak much; the line was bad. He said that Valentina had given him my phone number in case anything bad happened to her. It was presumed she was being held in some sort of detention center for the enemies of the regime. I asked if her father had been trying to get her released. His reply was: "Her father wants her locked up." Then he told me he had to put down the phone. The line went dead. Part of me wanted to call our father, ask if he could intervene. But if I finally informed him of my involvement with Valentina, and how desperate I was to learn if she was okay, I feared he might do something like use his contacts to stop me at the airport, have the Chilean police bar me from entering the country. I knew I had no choice but to go there myself, make contact with El frente.'

'Did you really think you could get her out of the hands of the military?'

'I was terrified that the longer I waited for news, the more likely it was that she would be dead. I had that crazed, irrational certainty that if I showed up in Santiago I could somehow put things right. I took out all the money I'd saved over the past five years, bought a ticket for Santiago, and found my way to El Frente. They were suspicious of this *gringo* in their midst. But Valentina had told them all about me. After they grilled me about her they dropped a bombshell. Valentina had been arrested after she and three other comrades from El Frente tried to kidnap a banker whose daughter was married to Pinochet's foreign minister. The kidnapping went wrong, the cops swooped down, and the banker was killed by one of her comrades before he himself was gunned down. Valentina was the only one of them taken alive. What made things about five times worse was the fact that the murdered banker was one of her father's closest friends.'

'So instead of realizing that you were way over your head and disappearing off to the airport and back home –'

'You don't understand. The woman I loved had been seized by a brutal regime.'

'After being involved in a botched kidnapping of a banker who, though tied to the regime, wasn't exactly killing people.'

'He was structuring the junta's finances. I could have simply walked away at that moment. Part of me – the rational part – said:

leave now. But the romantic in me – the person who was longing for some sort of adventure, who wanted to prove to myself that I did have the actual *cojones* to fight a terrible dictatorship – let El Capitán know that I wanted in. And they told me I was now their comrade.'

'When did Carly show up?'

'Around a month later. You can imagine my surprise when she revealed – after a few days – that Megan Kozinski was an alias; that she knew and remembered me from Old Greenwich. She also asked a lot about you. When she wanted your address, saying she was to write you, I saw no harm in giving it to her.'

'You didn't think about convincing her to tell her parents that she was alive?'

'We were in a war situation. We could all have been killed tomorrow.'

'Is that why you also had no problem sleeping with her?'

'I was longing for Valentina. I needed comfort.'

'Why did she say you killed Duarte?'

'You do believe me, don't you?'

'I want to believe you. Whether I can ... '

'How can you believe *her*?'

'I don't believe her. So yes, I'll take your word that you didn't actually pull the trigger. But let me ask you this – how did she get out of the country after the murder?'

'That night, after killing him and helping dump the body, we went back to our hideout.'

'So you helped dump the body?'

'I had no choice. Orders of El Capitán. Yes, I will live with the guilt of that for the rest of my life. Yes, we all went back to the basement hideout we were crashing in for a few nights – we changed address every two, three days – and when I woke the next morning Carly was gone. So too was her bag with her passport and the like. So too was around the equivalent of five hundred dollars in Chilean pesos that I had been given for "operational expenses".'

'She robbed you?'

'My guess is: she got herself to Santiago Airport and onto the first plane out of the country – but again, we're into the realm of *who the fuck knows?* Because it's Carly – and nothing that woman says, as we both now understand, can be taken at face value.'

'And how did you get out of the country unscathed?'

That question caused Peter to flinch. His eyes began to fill up. I suddenly felt terrible. I reached over and squeezed his arm. He hung his head for a moment, then began to speak.

'Two days after Duarte was murdered we headed off to a new hideout, north of the city. We were ambushed by the cops ten minutes outside of Santiago. There were three of us in the car. They marched my two comrades to the side of the road and shot them at point-blank range, leaving their bodies there as they bundled me into a car. The cop in the back seat punched me on the side of my head, his way of telling me I was in deep shit. The punch concussed me and I blacked out for several minutes. The cop slapped me hard on the face, trying to rouse me. He succeeded, then punched me in the head again. This time I went under for a long time. When I came to I was in a tiny windowless room, concrete walls, a dirty mattress, no light, no running water, a bucket as a toilet. I was kept there for two days, my head frequently in agony, my only contact with anyone the three times a day that the door opened, and water and bread were pushed into my room. I screamed. I shouted. A guard came in and kicked me twice in the stomach. I was sick everywhere. They let me lie there, doing nothing. I figured I was going to die there. When the guard came the next day I was ordered to stand up. I was marched to a grubby bathroom and ordered to strip. I was handed a bar of dirty soap and shoved under a cold shower. I managed to wash my body and my hair, almost fainting twice. Then they handed me fresh clothes – loose trousers, a white shirt, a pair of sandals. Once dressed, two guards strong-armed me down a bunch of corridors, pushing me inside a room where there were three men: two Chilean guys in cheap suits and ties, their jackets off, both wearing shoulder holsters with guns, the other in a light khaki suit, button-down shirt, striped Yale tie. He told me his name was Howard Lonergan and he was with the Embassy. Asking permission to speak to me from the detectives – his Spanish was excellent – he came over to where I had been told to sit, crouched down and whispered to me:

'"Peter, I know who you are. I know where you grew up, where you went to school and college, your grad school, just as we have been in touch with your father who – with your brother – is in Chile as we speak and has been apprised of the gravity of your situation. I must inform you that the Special Branch detectives here know you were involved in the murder of Alfonso Duarte. If you tell them what they want to know we may be able to negotiate with them and get you out of the country quickly. As such we advise you to cooperate fully with these gentlemen."

'"Can you guarantee my safety?" I asked him. He shook his head. "What I can guarantee is absolute hell for you if you don't cooperate. I can also guarantee that we won't be able to help you." What choice did I have – given that they shot my comrades in front of me? I had to sing.'

'You told them everything?' I asked.

'Not everything.'

'By which you mean ... ?'

'I said that one of the guys they killed – Gustavo – was the man who pulled the trigger on Duarte.'

'Why the fuck did you do that?' I said, almost shouting.

'I felt that I didn't need to implicate others ... especially as they asked no questions hinting that they knew there was a *gringa* with us.'

'Why didn't you tell them the truth?'

'Was there anything to be gained from that?'

'If she killed the guy,' I said.

'She killed the guy.'

'Then you covered for her.'

'Alice, please try to understand: I'd witnessed the back of a man's head being blown off. I had been forced to watch the summary execution of two of my comrades. I had received two ferocious blows to the head. I had been kept in a black hole for two days, allowed to fester in my own filth. This guy from the Embassy was telling me in no uncertain terms that to not cooperate was to guarantee a long stint in the house of horrors.'

'But you still covered for her?'

'Yes I did. Guilty as charged. But say I had pointed the finger at her? Say I had implicated her? They would have had a field day with that – and undoubtedly would have thought I was in cahoots with her. The guy I said shot Duarte was already dead. Nothing in the cop's lengthy cross-examination of me hinted that they knew a damn thing about Carly's existence. During the eight hours they interrogated me, shouting in my ears, hectoring me, telling me I was a naive stupid *gringo* meddling in their country's business, I sang like a fucking canary, encouraged on by Howard Lonergan – who kept nodding at me as if to say "tell them everything you know".

'After many hours of interrogation I was told that, thanks to my father and his connections with the regime, I was going to simply be deported. But they first needed to know what had brought me down here in the first place. I told them: idealism, wanting to strike out against Nixon and Kissinger. The cop then asked me if, perhaps, a woman had lured me down. I denied that. He called me a liar. He showed me a picture of Valentina, told me they knew we'd been inseparable. Lonergan kept nodding gravely at me, letting me know they had done the research on me and Valentina. The cop opened a file, showed me photographs of the two of us holding hands in New Haven. "Who took these?" I demanded. Lonergan coolly told me: "She was a person of interest to us, given her activities in support of Salvador Allende." What could I do but confess that, yes, we were in love; yes, I had followed her; yes, I had joined El Frente because of her. The cops then left, saying they'd be back in a few minutes. Lonergan told me I had done well – and that I was lucky to be getting out of this entire mess alive. Five minutes later the door opened. But the first person through the door was Valentina. She gasped when she saw me. I gasped too. Her face was battered, as if she'd taken many a beating. She was stooped over, making me think they were keeping her in an enclosed space; her eyes were shell-shocked to the point where they appeared glassy. Her beauty was still there, but she had been crushed by the torture they had subjected her to.

The other cop said something in rapid-fire Spanish to Valentina. She began to cry. When I tried to move toward her, to comfort her, Lonergan grabbed my shoulder, holding me back. Valentina then began to scream at me in English, telling me I was a CIA stooge, that I had betrayed her, the movement, that I was scum. I shouted at the cop: "What the fuck did you tell her?" The cop responded by punching me hard in the stomach, sending me to the floor, doubled up in agony. Valentina was hustled out. Lonergan squatted down by me and told me: "That was beyond stupid." Then he left the room.

Ten minutes later the English-speaking cop came back into the room, told me there had been a change of plans. I was handed over to two armed guards. I was hustled out to a bus on which there were already about two dozen other prisoners. I saw Valentina among them, her head lowered, still crying. When I tried to say something to her one of the guards slapped me across the face. I was shoved into a seat. Two guards with machine guns patrolled the little corridor between seats. We were driven for about a half-hour out to an airfield. We were all pushed along up the gangplank of this big transport plane. Once inside we found ourselves facing five of the nastiest-looking thugs imaginable. All in Chilean military uniforms, all carrying truncheons. One by one they handcuffed us to an iron bar on either side of the plane. They cuffed both hands, the chain around the bar, meaning we were facing the walls of the plane. Once everyone was loaded on, the door was closed and we took off. We flew for about an hour. I was chained up by one of the windows. It was a clear night. I looked down. We were not above land, rather way out to sea. Over the Pacific. The Army men were then back on their feet. They opened the port door of the plane. I suddenly had this terrible premonition of what was about to happen. So did the others, as people began to wail, scream, beg, shout obscenities. The guards had already a plan in play. Two of them would strong-arm one of the prisoners to make certain they couldn't break free of their grip, while a third soldier removed the cuffs. Then he or she was dragged screaming to the port door and thrown out, vanishing into the darkness. One by one they hurled everyone out. The sounds of people begging for their lives, the pleas, the anguish, was

279

beyond anything imaginable. I couldn't believe what was happening, couldn't believe that my life was ending. I desperately tried to make eye contact with Valentina. I needed to see her before I too took that ten-thousand-foot dive into the Pacific. But I was chained in such a way that I couldn't crane my head. Then I heard her cry out my name and two words – *teo amo* – and a final scream. Then silence. A soldier crouched down beside me. I was expecting to follow her. But he put his hand on my shoulder and in bad English, told me: "Someone wants you alive, *estúpido*. Who would want a stupid piece of shit like you alive?" Then he spat on me. They kept me chained to the bar all the way back to Santiago. At the international airport I was brought to an office in some secure area. Two cops stayed with me as I found myself face-to-face again with Howard Lonergan. He had the backpack that was in the trunk of the car when the cops ambushed us, the backpack with the two changes of clothes, my passport and the like. Lonergan told the cops they could leave us. He pointed to the bag, told me to change into my own clothes. Pointing to the Olivetti in its black case he smiled and asked: "Who brings a typewriter to a revolution? A dilettante, that's who." I asked Lonergan why I was spared. His reply: "Your father. He has connections in high places here. And he's one of us."

'*One of us*. So there it was: the admission that our father was, as I always suspected, in the CIA. I decided it wasn't smart to ask more. But I did have one final question for him: "Valentina's father had high connections. He's actually working for Pinochet. Why wasn't she saved?" He deliberately looked away from me as he said: "You'd have to ask her father that." Then he handed me an envelope. Inside was fifteen hundred dollars in cash. "A little gift from your daddy. He wanted to be here tonight. Under the circumstances we all felt it best if he stayed away." Part of me wanted to hurl the money in his face. I did the smart thing – one of the few smart things I had done since arriving in Santiago. I put the money into my backpack and walked.

'"And when I get back to New York . . . ?" I asked Lonergan, thinking that I'd be picked up at the airport by the Feds or the Agency. Know what he said to me? "When you get back stateside you can do whatever you want to do. It's a free country, after all."'

18

WHEN PETER FINISHED his terrible story he lowered his head and began to sob; the crying becoming so uncontrollable that he had to step outside. I threw some cash on the table and raced after my brother, finding him up against a wall, doubled over with grief. I held him until it subsided.

'You tell me you didn't kill that newspaper editor – and I believe you. You tell me you tried to convince your comrades not to murder him – and I believe you. You tell me that Carly pulled the trigger – and I believe you. You tell me that the only reason you joined El Frente was to try to help the woman you loved – and I believe you. You were only guilty of one thing: thinking that a revolutionary movement believes in changing things by sticking to the Gandhi non-violence playbook.'

Peter reached over and squeezed my hand.

'I heard how Duarte was devoted to his two daughters, one of whom was handicapped. And how his wife and girls were destroyed by his murder. I might not have pulled the trigger, but I did aid and assist. How will I ever get over that?'

'Maybe you won't. But here's one thought: you walked into a war. In a war everyone plays by terrible rules. And they were going to kill that newspaper editor no matter if you were there or not.'

'I was still part of the group that killed him.'

'How do you think those soldiers will live with the knowledge that they dragged people screaming to their deaths, throwing them out over the Pacific from ten thousand feet? They'll tell themselves: they were only following orders.'

'I think I need to get drunk tonight,' he said.

'I'm happy to come along for the ride.'

'Thank you.'

'I was harsh on you before I heard the story. Because I felt you had inflicted Carly on me.'

That's when I told Peter in great detail about Carly's crazed behavior since arriving in Dublin.

'Holy fuck.'

'That about says it all.'

'What are you going to do about her?'

'She was hooked up for the moment with the guy downstairs. I sense he's ruing the fact that he let her into his bed. I'm staying away from her – even more so now after what you told me.'

'You must never, *ever* mention anything to her about what I told you. Never tell her that you know she pulled the trigger.'

'And if she starts to publicly accuse you of that?'

'Why would she do that?'

'You know why. Because she's insane. I dread going back to Dublin now, knowing she's just downstairs.'

I asked him a question that had been nagging at me ever since he told me that terrible story: why didn't Valentina's father save her? Surely with his connections high up in the junta he could have stopped her being thrown from the plane.

'The banker killed was one of his oldest friends. He himself is close to Pinochet. To not plead for his daughter's life – especially when she was guilty of a crime against the junta – no doubt strengthened his position with Pinochet and his henchmen. It showed that he was willing to sacrifice his daughter to prove his loyalty. I wouldn't be surprised if good old-fashioned Latin machismo didn't play a part in his decision. She betrayed the family, she betrayed his word of law, she killed one of his closest *amigos*, she deserved the ultimate punishment. But I am also certain he denied any knowledge of her death to his wife and other daughters; that it happened without his okay. Which I am also certain is a lie. His pride let his daughter be murdered by his masters, the junta.'

'Sounds a lot like our dear old dad. His pride has screwed him up royally.'

'With one exception – Dad saved me. I may hate him for his politics, for backing this terrible regime, for being in the CIA. But he did stop them from killing me.'

'Have you thanked him yet?'

Peter shook his head.

'Don't you think you should?' I said. 'A letter or something like that?'

282

'He wouldn't want that in writing. Because that would link him to the Agency. I'll wait until I next see him.'

'*If* you next see him.'

Peter fell silent. I changed the subject, getting Peter talking about the ongoing scandal now consuming the Nixon administration. Peter said that he was certain, given the momentum of things, the president would be impeached before the summer was out. And Saigon was going to fall within the year.

'You know Dad pulled all sorts of strings a few years ago to make certain that Adam didn't get drafted. Getting him to go to that third-tier business school helped. But once he got his MBA he was still fresh meat as far as the Selective Service was concerned – especially as, in the draft lottery, his birth date was number 12 out of 365, which made it a near certainty that he'd be called up. Why do you think I've stayed in graduate school so long? – though now, with Nixon ending the draft, that doesn't matter anymore.'

'Will you go back to Yale?'

Peter refilled our wine glasses.

'When I reached New York, after that one-way flight from Santiago via Miami, I still expected the Feds to be waiting for me and haul me in for interrogation. But as I went through passport inspection in Miami, the only questions were if I was bringing back any booze or Cuban cigars. At JFK I walked off the plane a free man. I went right over to the Air France counter and asked if they could give me a last-minute student deal on a flight to Paris leaving that night. I handed over two hundred dollars. The next morning, I was here. The way I figure it, with cigarettes and some booze and a couple of movies thrown in, I can live in Paris for under one hundred dollars a week.'

'So you're definitely staying here?'

'There's no way I am heading back to the States. Nor do I ever want to see our brother again.'

'Adam didn't have anything to do with Valentina's death.'

'He's working for Dad; he's working for *them*. No doubt he's probably with the Agency.'

'So what if he is?' I asked, trying to tap down the anger. 'Does it matter? Should Adam be held up to account for that? He wasn't on the plane dragging screaming people out to their deaths ... '

'All right, all right – I'm being defensively self-righteous.'

'Something like that. But it's understandable, given how fucking awful all this is. Does Mom know your whereabouts?'

'I sent her a telegram when I got to Paris. The thing is – I figured Dad told her he got me out alive. I also suspected that she'd be waiting for me at LaGuardia. Which is why, when I got to Miami, I changed the flight to New York to JFK. Because I dreaded having to face her.'

I could only imagine her anxiety and fear when she discovered that her first child had been arrested by a bad-assed military junta. Ducking out on her as Peter did – especially after Dad saved his life – struck me as very wrong ... and just a little cowardly. He could have gone back to Old Greenwich with her for a couple of days, made her feel of value to him, given her a little time. Or was this my own guilt speaking? Was I castigating myself for hardly being in contact since crossing the Atlantic, for feeling that I had to wall her out to get away from her?

'I'm not going to pass judgment on you for what you did – but I think you owe her an apology and maybe a phone call.'

'I wrote her the other day – making certain she didn't know the name of my hotel. I don't want Dad looking for me. I'm staying invisible.'

'So when I speak with her ... ?'

'Would you mind simply saying we talked on the phone, nothing more, and that you don't know my exact whereabouts in Paris?'

More lies. More secrets.

'I'm going to tell her I saw you,' I said. 'The reason I will do that is because she is probably frantic about your post-prison condition.'

Next morning, in the day we had left to us, the subject of Chile and everything attached to it was quietly shelved. Peter wanted to know all about Ireland. He told me that I should brave Belfast and judge for myself just how bad it was or wasn't. I had to get an early-afternoon flight back to Dublin's battered beauty. I said goodbye at the hotel and we hugged outside La Louisiane. Peter seemed more than a little sad.

'It's going to be lonely here again, lonely as it was until you showed up.'

'You need to try to meet some people, get connected,' I said.

'Not my priority at the moment.'

I didn't push it further. I held my brother for a long time in front of that dive hotel. I asked him to promise me not to give in to despair; to jump on a plane and get to me if he thought he was heading downward; that he had to find a way of forgiving himself. I told him I loved him. Then I turned and headed back to my Irish life.

Two nights later, back in Dublin, I was jolted awake by voices in the hall.

'Call yourself a radical? – you're a fucking chancer,' Sean yelled.

'And you're a boring fat fuck with a small dick,' Carly countered.

Those were the kindest words spoken between them. I glanced at my bedside clock. 2.08 a.m. Wonderful. Especially as I had a lecture tomorrow at nine – and was still twisted up by everything revealed over the weekend.

As Carly now called Sean 'a half-brain, a talent-free zone' I couldn't help but think: *you have no idea what my brother suffered, what he was put through. And the fact that he didn't shop you to the Chilean authorities ... you'd be on the International Most Wanted List now, on the run, chased by Interpol. You owe him your liberty. Yet you march around, hating everybody, telling hideous lies about others, self-justifying all your malevolence, your bullying, because of all the malevolence you once suffered. You've turned into an even worse version of the monsters who picked on you.*

The next day, crossing Trinity's front square at lunchtime, I heard a booming voice on the dining-hall step declaiming the need for a radical workers' state in Ireland, the end of corporate control, 'the dismantling of all exploitative ruling-class structures'. It was a voice I knew well.

'And right now, *right this fucking minute*, American imperialists are destroying Vietnamese villages and cities. Right now American imperialists are spreading their capitalist creed across the globe – knowing that consumerism is a form of social and geopolitical control ... '

I stopped right by the step and stared up at Carly. She saw me. She flashed me the fastest of vindictive smiles.

'Right now American imperialists are reprivatizing Chilean copper mines and supporting a junta that kills freedom fighters and exploits the proletariat.'

As I turned to go, I heard another voice I knew.

'Surprised to see you're not up there, screaming WOWU.'

I turned and found myself facing Ciaran Quigg. He had three days' scrubby growth of beard and was wearing his usual tweed jacket with a black turtleneck. He looked me over. I liked his interest.

'What's WOWU?' I asked.

'Workers of the World Unite. The usual shite that these would-be Marxists usually scream. Do you know her? Americans don't usually kick with the leftist foot.'

'She was a friend. No longer.'

'Because of all her crazy Commie talk?'

'Because she's someone I don't want as a friend any longer.'

'That sounds severe.'

'It is.'

'Feel like telling me more over a pint?'

'I don't feel like telling anyone more about all that.'

'Understood. But how about the pint?'

Later that evening, as we sat under a taxidermied stag in the Stag's Head, I asked Ciaran what life was like, living in a war zone.

'Ah you know – dead corpses piled up in the street every morning. Little men in camouflage crawling through our back garden. The guillotining of war criminals in front of the Europa Hotel – the most bombed hotel in the world. And the great thing about these public executions is that it's become a great day out for the family. Everyone brings their wee ones along and have a picnic in front of –'

'All right, all right,' I said. 'That's the last time I ask that question.'

'The truth – not that there is such a thing as truth in these matters – is that life just goes on. Where my parents live – right near the university – is rather calm, even bucolic. The chaos from the Falls and Shankill Roads sometimes spills over into us. Just as you do have to be keenly attuned to Belfast's rather tricky sectarian geography. But for the most part you get used to tanks and British soldiers in the streets. You continue to live with the hope and fear that nothing untoward will descend on you and yours.'

'Have you known anyone killed in the Troubles?'

'There you go again, wanting to travel vicariously into the Heart of Irish Darkness.'

'It's just a question.'

'And the answer is: I had a classmate from primary school badly injured in a bombing in London last year. The attack that happened at King's Cross Station. The poor girl. She left Belfast to get away from the madness … and walked right into it in London.'

'God, that's a weird sort of destiny.'

'Or just bad bloody luck. The gods really being nasty buggers. You don't really believe in that "destiny" malarkey, do you?'

'I've come to believe that people write their own destiny – even though they may not do so intentionally.'

'But the unintentional is often that which is wanted – even if the result is a nasty one.'

'Exactly.'

That's when I found myself telling him about Bob and Professor Hancock, and the reasons why I upped stakes and came to Dublin. When I finished he said:

'No wonder you needed to put an ocean between yourself and all that. The fact that you don't wear it all on your sleeve … '

'I tend to be private.'

He lightly touched the top of my hand with his own.

'I guess I am going to have to earn my trustworthy stripes,' he said, lacing his fingers into mine.

'Yes,' I said, withdrawing my hand, 'you'll need to do just that. And Dublin is a city which operates with the vindictive mentality of a small town.'

'So you hate it?'

'Much about it so pleases me. Especially the way that it is both congenial and brutal. I don't trust it. But its contrariness has a weird appeal. Which maybe says something about me.'

On the way back to Pearse Street he told me an absurd story about a priest he knew courtesy of his parents – a relatively open-minded fellow, bookish, thoughtful, worldly, but a world-class drinker who got stopped by the RUC behind the wheel of his Mini scuttered beyond belief. When the officer asked him if he'd been drinking he told the fellow: 'How else do you expect me to live here?' The RUC man had no answer to that and let him drive off.

In front of my door Ciaran remained the complete gent. Just a light kiss goodnight on the lips and the statement: 'Let's do this again in a few days.'

'I'd like that very much,' I said.

The next afternoon I took a walk over to the post office on Andrews Street and made a call home.

'Who's this?' she said immediately, sounding like she was panting.

When the operator informed her that I was on the line, she blurted out 'Oh thank God' and accepted the charges.

'Tell me my little boy is okay,' were her first words. This threw me. How did she know I'd been in Paris with Peter?

'I don't know what you're talking about,' I said.

'The hell you don't. Your father tracked down Peter on Sunday, had a brief conversation with him. He told him you were just over visiting him.'

'How did Dad track him down?'

'How do you think?'

'His CIA friends?'

'I've no idea.'

'You've known Dad was in the Agency for years,' I said,

'Stop sounding like Pollyanna, Alice. We all operate in the hard, real world where everything comes with a price.'

Before making this call I thought at length about how I would handle it, knowing full well that Mom might not know the full extent of the danger that Peter had been in. What had Dad told her?

He was always downplaying so much when it came to everything he related to Mom. With good reason. So all I said was:

'Yes I went to Paris to see Peter. Yes he is doing fine.'

'No he's not. Your father said if he hadn't intervened Peter would have been sent home to us in a box.'

'Thank God he intervened then.'

'God had nothing to do with it. Your father saved Peter. Why did he then stand me up at the airport? Do you have any idea how hurt I was? My child, nearly killed by those crazed leftists, gotten out alive thanks to his father and Uncle Sam – and then he leaves me high and dry at LaGuardia, having driven all the way down to pick him up. It wasn't like I was going to imprison him once I got him home. I just wanted a few days with him.'

'You're right, that was a shitty thing he did.'

'You mean that?' she asked.

'Of course I mean that. I even told Peter he was wrong to do that to you.'

'That's the first time *you've* ever taken my side on anything.'

'I am sorry he hurt you.'

'Can you tell me where he's staying in Paris?'

'Peter needs time to himself now.'

'I'm not exactly going to jump a plane to Paris and move in with him. I just want an actual address. He owes me that much.'

'Then let him give it to you. Why hasn't Dad supplied it, since he knows where to find him?'

'Your dad's being cagey too. You know why I think your father won't give it to me? Because I bet you anything Peter's got some dirt on him. The deal they've made is: Peter will say nothing as long as Dad keeps him from me.'

That 'deal' – had it happened – wouldn't have surprised me. The complicity between father and son here was key. Just as I still had to tread so carefully when it came to not revealing how much I knew, keeping in mind that my father had told her that Peter was almost murdered by 'crazed leftists'.

'Peter is doing well in Paris.'

'You are all in conspiracy against me,' Mom said.

'We're all in conspiracy against each other.'

Mom hung up. A week later I received a letter from her – actually, one of her embossed note cards – with a single sentence written in her careful penmanship.

Read the attached and then reflect on why we all must hang together, love each other, not give up on the family.

Attached to this was a clipping from the local suburban weekly, the *Greenwich Times*: a news story that psychologist Cindy Cohen had been found dead at her home in Old Greenwich, an apparent suicide. She was forty-nine years old. The story went on to say that Mrs Cohen's housekeeper found her on Monday morning, an empty bottle of prescription tranquilizers by the bed. Friends noted that Mrs Cohen had never recovered from the disappearance of her daughter Carly after a series of bullying incidents at Old Greenwich High in the autumn of 1971, culminating with her being set upon by two classmates from her senior class. There was a quote from Mom herself, who was cited as one of Mrs Cohen's best friends and who talked about her bravery in the face of such tragedy, and how it pulled her marriage apart. A local detective from the Old Greenwich Police Department said that, after an autopsy by the medical examiner in Stamford, foul play had been ruled out. 'Mrs Cohen sadly died by her own hand.'

I put down the clipping, feeling beyond awful. Especially as, just an hour earlier, walking into a pub called the Long Bar, I was surprised to see Carly huddled in a corner with several very hard-looking men. As soon as Ciaran saw her with them, he grabbed me forcibly by the arm and spun me around, getting us out the door immediately.

'What the hell's going on?' I asked.

'Maybe you should ask that of your mad friend. Do you know who those men she was huddled with are? Seamus O'Regan is known by every Special Branch officer in Dublin Castle as the unacknowledged head of the IRA in the Republic. One dangerous, scary fucker. And the last person a naive American should be lifting a pint with. For fuck's sake – does she know how dark and bad that man and his circle are?'

I suddenly wanted to tell him everything. But fear silenced me: fear that I didn't know if I could fully trust him to stay quiet about the many people contained within Carly Cohen.

'Do you think she saw us?' I asked Ciaran once we were away from the pub.

'She didn't look up in our direction. Trust me, if those men she was with were suspicious about us somebody would have been on our tail as soon as we were outside the pub. Thank fuck she didn't see us.'

I kept thinking about that clipping I'd received. I decided then and there I needed to confront her with it the next day.

That night I accepted Ciaran's invitation to return to his flat. It was on the top floor of a Georgian building, slightly down at heel.

'It's going to be cold as fuck when we walk in,' he told me. 'But I'll have it warmed in no time. Before then we can seek heat with a bottle of Bushmills I have stashed away.'

I immediately understood why it was hard to heat, as it had high ceilings facing the square. And an old bed that creaked when, an hour or so later, we made love in its confines – after the electric fire and the illuminated peat briquettes in the grate lessened the chill in the room. I knew that by returning to his place I was signaling that I was ready to move us into a different place. What surprised me was the passion that combusted between us. I'd had good sex with Bob. But this was borderline wild. Down and dirty.

Afterwards we lay silent for a very long time. I used my index finger to follow the contours of his chest. He, in turn, took my face in his two hands and whispered:

'I'm never letting you go.'

'I like the sound of that.'

'That doesn't mean I'm a controlling sort.'

'Nor am I – and I run from people who try to control me.'

'I want you as you are. But I want us to share as much as possible ... and, Jesus fuck, I am getting a bit mushy now, aren't I?'

'I can handle such mushiness. Especially as I want all that too.'

We fell silent, teetering right before the precipice in which a declaration of love is made. Later, when we discussed this moment, we both smiled at our timidity in the face of something huge; a sense that we were each other's equal. I loved his quirky, skewed humor. I loved his bookishness. I loved his wordplay and irreverence. Just as I saw earlier, when he steered me right out of that pub before Carly and those heavies could see me, that he had a shrewd protective streak. It's strange the way love often takes you by surprise.

That morning we went to Bewley's for breakfast. Prudence saw us holding hands and waltzed over to me.

'Oh my word! You've found love! And you both need morning-after coffee and sticky buns straightaway.'

Ciaran rolled his eyes, but in a way that showed he was more amused by such an expansive declaration than embarrassed by the publicness of it all. When Prudence moved off to get us our coffees and sticky buns he reached over and took my hand.

'There's a pair of us in it,' he said.

I threaded my fingers through his.

'Indeed there is.'

Prudence arrived with the coffees and sticky buns.

'You'll have to let go of each other for a tick if you want to eat,' she said.

At that very moment I saw Carly come in with the Maoist I'd seen ranting on the Trinity dining-hall steps. Catching sight of me she glared in my direction before heading to a table in a far corner. I thought about the newspaper clipping in my bag, the letter from my mother, the terrible news I needed to impart to her, the fear of even raising such things with her. Ciaran immediately caught the concern swirling around within me.

'Penny for them,' he said.

'Things I can't talk to you about just yet.'

'So there's already secrets between us?' he asked.

'I need to know you better before I spill the beans.'

'Only slagging, my love.'

It was the first time he called me his love. In the past I would have bristled at such a comment just after one night together. I didn't on this occasion. On the contrary, I took his hand again and said:

'My love indeed.'

'Your friend, there,' he said, 'and the fellows she was with last night ... if she gets into bed with them she could find herself in a shallow grave somewhere up near the border with a bullet between her eyes. They are as bad as they come.'

'If they are so dangerous why are they allowed to roam freely?'

'Because they haven't been directly arrested for anything yet. They do the plotting, their henchmen do their dirty work. What I worry about is: should she get caught by the police, Special Branch will interrogate her and they will find out that she's your childhood chum and initially bunked with you when she came to Dublin. Which will throw up all sorts of suspicions about you – and will also mean that the university will be alerted to the fact that you might be a bad political egg.'

'But that's guilt by association.'

'When it comes to paramilitary activity on this island even the most tangential association can land you in deep shite. The fact that she is still living on the same premises as you ... '

'Should I alert the big fool of a poet she's sleeping with?'

'If you intimate to him that you saw her with those IRA fellows you are also letting it be known you know who those gentlemen are. You've got a bit of a dilemma there. Could you call her parents?'

'That's part of the problem – and sorry, I just can't explain why now. I hope you'll forgive my cageyness. It's just ... '

'Complicated?'

'Understatement of the fucking year.'

Across the cafe I could hear Carly and the Maoist in the midst of an angry terse exchange. Suddenly the Maoist stood up and stormed out.

'I need to talk with her,' I said. 'Can you excuse me?'

'Always, my love. Think I'll head over to the library. Meet you at the union at six?'

'Absolutely,' I said, leaning forward to kiss him.

Then I took the twenty or so paces toward Carly. She looked up as I approached.

'To what do I owe this fucking honor?' she asked.

'May I sit down?'

'No.'

I sat down.

'I told you "no",' she said, her voice edging into loudness. Several people at nearby tables turned their heads toward us.

'You have to hear me out. Carly, your mother is dead.'

That statement landed on her like a right to the jaw. Her head jerked backwards, her eyes snapped shut, she looked thrown, disoriented, lost. After a moment her face reassembled into a mask of anger.

'Prove it,' she hissed.

I pulled out the newspaper clipping and slid it across the table to her. She picked it up, again trying to mask her distress as she read the headline and saw the ten-year-old photo of her mother. She scanned the article in silence, then balled it up and tossed it aside.

'You're trying to guilt-trip me,' she said.

'I just wanted to say how sorry I was.'

'I suppose your mother sent you the article?'

I nodded.

'I bet she'll hate you even more when she finds out you had the power within you to save her friend.'

'What are you talking about?'

'You didn't let your mom know that I was alive and well.'

That comment sideswiped me. Especially as I knew what was coming next.

'I didn't think it was my business to blow your cover.'

'And look at the result: you let my mother kill herself.'

'Don't you dare –'

'Don't I dare *what*?'

'Don't you dare accuse me –'

'But had you told your mother, or *my mother*, that I was still alive –'

294

'I had no idea your mother would –'

'You told me she'd been depressed since my disappearance. You told me my father left her. You told me people were worried about her. You could have stopped all this.'

'Don't play head games with me. The reason she was depressed, the reason she killed herself, was because you disappeared and then didn't have the simple decency to let her know you –'

'Typical of you, trying to shift the blame to me. I died. I became someone else. You could have saved her just by calling. But let me guess – you didn't want to get involved.'

'I was stupidly covering for you, stupidly thinking I shouldn't be the one who told your parents –'

'You killed my mother because of your hesitancy.'

The furious part of me wanted to pick up the pot of tea in front of me and smash it in Carly's face. The more rational corner of my brain told me: you can't win this, so walk away from her now before you do something that will make everything so much worse.

Which is exactly what I did. But halfway out I spun back and saw Carly staring down at the table, broken by what I had just told her. I saw her bite down on her lip, fighting tears. Immediately I headed straight to her table again. But when she saw, she was on her feet, grabbing her coat and shoulder bag, racing toward the door, shoving me aside as she stormed past me and out into the damp Dublin morning.

I checked my watch. It was only ten thirty. My head was spinning like an out-of-control top. Her accusations, though completely manipulative and dirty, had nonetheless managed to unnerve me, hitting a guilt chord within. I found myself horrified by the realization: had I told my mother straightaway about Carly's reappearance in my life Mrs Cohen would probably be alive today. I desperately needed to talk to someone about all this – but feared if I went to Ciaran and told all he might back away from me, thinking this was all too complicated, too dark. I wandered up Grafton Street, entering Stephen's Green, lighting up a cigarette, trying to calm myself down, knowing I should be at the library studying, knowing that I could not concentrate on anything else right now, feeling devastated by Mrs Cohen's death, wondering again and again why I was so scared of Carly's possible retribution that I didn't make the phone call that might have saved her mother. Had I been a Catholic I would have gone to the confessional box immediately – though I doubted I would have received much in the way of wise counsel. Yes, I would have been told, after a decade of the rosary and several Hail Marys, that I was absolved of all sin ... even though I am sure the priest would have told me that suicide is among the most mortal of sins and I should have done more to prevent this one. This was the crazed dialogue in my head – all pointing a condemning finger at me. I started tearing up. I felt the wrong side of frantic. I needed a Father right now, but not one wearing a Roman collar. I stood up. I went diagonally across the park, exiting right near Earlsfort Terrace and heading immediately down Lower Leeson Street until I reached the front door of Desmond's house. I knocked twice. No answer. I knocked twice more. I turned and walked down the steps back to the sidewalk.

'Now don't go running away so fast, Alice.'

I spun around. Desmond had an apron on and had a vacuum cleaner in his left hand.

'Sorry, I didn't hear you. I was hoovering.'

'I owe you an apology,' I said.

'For what?'

'For accepting all your hospitality and goodwill, then disappearing on you.'

'You owe me nothing, Alice.'

I started tearing up again.

'Please can I come in?'

'What in God's name has happened?' he asked.

I began to sob. Immediately he dropped the Hoover, put an arm around me, got me inside, got me out of my coat, and settled in front of the fire in the front room. Then seeing that I was still crying he went over to the sideboard and poured me a large dram of Redbreast.

I drained the glass in three large gulps. He poured me some more and set it on the table by the armchair into which he'd parked me.

'Now you can reach for a bit more if things get a little unsettled again,' he said.

And then I began to talk. The whole story – every damn bit of it, starting with Carly's disappearance three years earlier – came tumbling out of me. Desmond's face registered everything I was telling him. I saw his lips tighten at certain moments in the narrative – especially when I got to the Chilean part of the story and told him how Peter said that she had murdered that newspaper editor. When I explained how she showed up on my doorstep, her crazed behavior, his lips tightened again. But as I started talking about her dabbling in far-left activities in Trinity, and me walking into a pub and finding her with Irish hard men, Desmond looked gobsmacked. Then I told him what had transpired just an hour earlier in Bewley's – when she accused me of aiding and abetting her mother's suicide.

'Don't you dare blame yourself for that poor woman taking her own life, God's mercy on her. Her horrible daughter could have spared her the grief that engulfed her. She's a right little bitch. You sure those Republican fellas didn't spot you and your man in the pub?'

'They were all absorbed in whatever they were talking about and Carly never caught sight of us.'

'Thank God for that. This Ciaran fella – he has no political connections, does he?'

I explained that his father was an academic at Queens and his mother worked at the BBC; that he and his family, though Catholic, stayed out of the fray.

'As long as you think he is speaking the truth about all that I can breathe a sigh of relief. The last thing you want is to be involved with someone from up there who is "political".'

'I'm not worried about Ciaran in that regard.'

'In any other regard?'

'He strikes me as very sound,' I said, using a word that was common currency in Dublin; 'sound' being one of the more positive qualities you could have in a city that was so damn shifty.

'You'll have to bring your young man around, let me give him a good look. You know I feel a bit Father Protector towards you – which is also why, if you will let me, I will take care of the problem that is your dangerous friend.'

'My fear is, if you call the police and it turns out that she has done something bad with those "political" gentlemen ... '

'My sense of it is: had she done something more than talk and conspire with those fellows she would hardly be showing her face around Dublin right now. Best to get her whisked out of the country as soon as possible – before she can land herself in real trouble. I have an old school friend who is quite high up in the Special Branch. I'll give him a call, invite him over for a glass or two, and tell him the tale.'

'But say she tells my mother and father that I could have called her mother and spared her?'

'Once she's in custody and en route back to the States you write your parents a letter explaining all to them. I sense, given what a smart and good girl you are, they will understand. Especially if you tell them that the little bitch vowed you to silence about her whereabouts, and she also intimated that she would expose your brother for things he didn't do in Santiago.'

'But that would be twisting the truth a bit.'

'Which is hardly a mortal sin in this case. Anyway, she told you that your brother killed that man, just as she also made all sorts of threats towards you. Given his "connections" your father will, trust me, be very grateful to you that you didn't believe her lies about your brother. Just as I advise you, after the fact, to intimate to them in your letter that you had a hand in allowing the authorities to know about her whereabouts in Dublin. You must simultaneously play innocent if anyone here points an accusatory finger at you. Because my friend will ensure that there's no trace whatsoever that you had anything to do with her being found and picked up. Do be smart now and do sleep at your bedsit the next few nights. If you are elsewhere when she's picked up it will look suspicious.'

'What should I tell Ciaran?'

'Say nothing until after it happens. If he's the good man you think he is, he will be very understanding why you could not tell him anything until now. If he's a bad egg then you will know straightaway. As far as anyone is ever concerned, you and I never had this conversation, even though I am grateful you gave me your trust.'

One of the many good things about unburdening yourself to a friend is the fact that you no longer feel alone with all that is spooking you. But a secret shared is no longer a secret – and though I felt I could trust Desmond implicitly, I also knew that all sorts of questions would still be raised by others. I would have to be very strong and deadpan and seemingly bemused in the wake of whatever way they decided to bust her.

That night Ciaran came back to my bedsit for the first time. We fell into bed, the lovemaking even more passionate than the night before. Around midnight I could hear singing, Sean and Carly crooning 'The Leaving of Liverpool'. Ciaran rolled over. 'Are they always such fucking songbirds?'

'Usually they're mauling each other like a pair of deranged German shepherds.'

'I hate that song,' Ciaran said. 'Sentimental old-sod rubbish.'

'It will stop.'

It did around five minutes later. We both fell into a shallow sleep – and one which ended shortly thereafter when there was heavy banging at the front door. Ciaran was immediately awake.

'Fuck me, that's ominous,' he said.

The banging continued. I heard doors opening. Loud voices in the hallway. Another door opening. Now the voices became even more raised as there were the sounds of a struggle. I was on my feet about to open my own door, but Ciaran grabbed my arm, whispering:

'If that's who I think it is the last thing you want is to be seen taking in what's going on.'

Now Carly was screaming. Other doors were opening. I could hear Sean trying to calm her down, saying: 'You have no choice but to go with them.'

'That bitch upstairs ratted on me!' yelled Carly. 'You hear that, Alice Burns? I know you're the one who called the fucking cops.'

I put my head in my hands. The struggle downstairs ensued for another moment or so. Then a door slammed shut and I could hear the low siren of a police car driving off. Ciaran sat down next to me on the bed, put an arm around me and said:

'If what she said is true I'm sure you had all the right reasons for grassing on her.'

Outside there were hurried footsteps on the stairs, followed by pounding on my own door.

'Alice, Alice . . . ' Sean said, sounding just a little agitated. 'If you're in there you need to come out and explain yourself.'

Despite Ciaran silently signaling me not to answer the door I did just that. Cracking it open, I stared out at Sean with half-awake eyes, playing up the sense that he had just roused me from a deep sleep.

'What's up?' I asked, adding a yawn for effect.

'The fucking Special Branch has just picked up your fucking friend.'

'Wow,' I said.

'Is that all you have to say about it?'

'Uh, yeah. Except: you must be, on a certain level, relieved to be rid of her.'

'What? Can I come in?'

'No, Sean, I've got company,' I said.

'Oh . . . right. Can we have a chat about all this tomorrow?' he asked.

'Sure – but it's you who will have to fill me in on what this is all about.'

'Fuck should I know,' he said.

I closed the door. As soon as it was shut Ciaran reached over and touched my face.

'Am I right in sensing you're now thinking: can I trust the man standing next to me with this story?'

I took his hand in mine. Saying:

'If you're ready to hear it I'm ready to tell it.'

19

THE NEXT MORNING a black unmarked police car pulled up in front of our building on Pearse Street. Two men in bad suits came out and knocked on the door. Sean answered it. They showed him their official ID and explained that they had a few questions they wanted to pose. I overheard all this because Sean had knocked on my door just a half-hour beforehand, asking if I might like to join him for breakfast. Ciaran had already left for one of his early-morning classes. I was sitting in my rocking chair, drinking coffee, stopping myself from lighting up a cigarette, reading Dryden in advance of a lecture that afternoon by Professor Brown, and trying to keep my mind off the events of last night. I could only begin to imagine what Carly was telling the Special Branch and the Embassy people.

All these thoughts and fears were swirling around my head as I found myself unable to concentrate on *Alexander's Feast* and kept expecting an authoritarian knock to come on the door.

When it arrived I almost jumped out of my chair. Hearing that it was Sean didn't lessen my worry, as I was certain he was going to castigate me for ratting Carly out to the authorities.

But Sean was contrition itself. When I opened the door he immediately touched my shoulder and said:

'Sorry about last night. I was just a little unnerved by the cops bursting in like that and carting Megan off to what I hope is the nearest fucking dungeon.'

'Sean, I did not make that call to the police.'

That's when I motioned him inside and said how she'd been seen with the Maoist brigade in Trinity, and how Ciaran and I happened upon her in that pub surrounded by a group of men 'whom Ciaran knew to be Republican hard men'.

'Did he say who exactly they were?' said Sean.

'No, he just knew them by reputation, nothing more.'

'You sure about that now?'

'Absolutely sure of that,' I said, noting how, like Desmond, Sean got very edgy when anything Republican got mixed into the conversation.

'Don't you or your man ever tell anyone that you saw your woman with those fellas,' whispered Sean. 'It never happened. I'm saying this to you for your own protection ... and for mine.'

'Agreed.'

Sean seemed relieved. 'We'll say no more about it. Except: what you told me last night is too bloody true. I am so relieved to have that harpy out of my life. Now then, if you haven't had breakfast I can do a fry-up downstairs. Would you be on for that?'

But following him downstairs all preparations for breakfast were interrupted with the arrival of the Special Branch. Peering out the window and seeing the men getting out of the unmarked car, he shooed me away before answering the door. I hurried back to my bedsit, turning around on the next landing to watch the two Special Branch men enter the house, then closed my door. I only opened it again when I heard the front door slam shut. I waited a good fifteen minutes before leaving my room and daring to venture outside. It was a soft day – a light mist, a hint of spring in the air. I fully expected, as I walked around the corner toward Westland Row and the back entrance of Trinity, to feel a hard hand on my shoulder spinning me around to face a serious man in a dark suit, asking me: 'Are you Alice Burns?'

But I walked on unimpeded. I went to my lectures and classes that day and no such hand arrived, though when I returned that afternoon, I found a note under my door telling me I had '*a call from the American Embassy. Please give Consul McNamara a ring back on ...* ' There was a number scribbled at the bottom of the note.

I went straight back downstairs and knocked on Sean's door.

'I've had a bad morning,' he said.

'What did the police ask you?'

'Lots. They wanted to know everything about me, my politics, my "friends", whether I knew anything about your friend's past and her disappearance. You kept quite a bit from me, Alice. Why didn't you tell me she'd been a missing person for years? You knew she was trouble from the outset. You could have alerted the authorities weeks ago.'

'She swore me to secrecy,' I said, knowing that was an outright lie and feeling the shame and guilt that Desmond told me I should push to one side, but which I knew was going to haunt me for a long time to come. I decided to come clean on one absolute truth, telling Sean:

'She had me intimidated. I know that doesn't excuse my silence, or the fact that I should have warned you she was bad news, but honestly that was, in the end, your decision. The two of you were fighting the night after you took each other to bed. Surely you already knew by that moment that she was trouble. You could have kicked her out.'

'Had I known she was on the FBI's Missing Persons List ... I mean, for fuck's sake, Alice ... '

'Did the police ask you about me?'

'That's all you really care about it, isn't it?'

'We're all trying to limit the personal damage here. Did they ask you about me?'

'Of course they did. And I did the right thing by you – telling them that she had shown up unexpectedly on your doorstep, that you turned her out after one night, that I was foolish enough to take her in, that you had no ties to the radical, dangerous people she associated with.'

'Thank you. The American Embassy left a message from one of their consuls. I sense they're going to want to interview me. I promise you that, if it comes up, I will reassure them you were an innocent party in all this.'

'Know what one of the Branch men told me? That they'd now opened a file on me and would be, in the future, watching me. I truly thank you for all that. You landed me in this.'

'Had you turned her out into the street when she went crazy on you –'

'We're done here, Alice. I will trust you to not implicate me further. As long as you continue to pay your rent on time and cause no trouble you can stay on with us. But don't expect a friendly word from me in the future.'

I left Sean's room, feeling hangdog and castigated, worried he would tell everyone in our building how I had betrayed him. I knew I had no choice but to deal with the Embassy immediately. I found tuppence in one of my pockets and felt it shake in my hand as I fed it into the phone before dialing the number and pressing button A when the Embassy answered. I asked to be put through to the office of Consul McNamara. His secretary answered.

'Ah, Miss Burns,' she said, seeming to immediately know it was me. 'Very pleased you got back to us so fast. You're in Dublin now?'

'Indeed, ma'am.'

'Would you be free to come in tomorrow at 9 a.m. for a bit of a chat with the consul and perhaps someone else interested in all this?'

Might that be a Special Branch man? I wanted to ask. But I knew that would be, under the circumstances, beyond stupid. All I said was:

'Might I come at eleven? I have a lecture at nine.'

'No, nine it must be. But if you like I can call your professor and explain that we need to see you.'

That's all I needed.

'No worries. I'll tell him myself.'

'Very good then. You know where to find us in Ballsbridge?'

'I do indeed.'

'Don't forget to bring your passport with you.'

Why? So you can whisk me out to the airport and get me out of the country before I am attached to more trouble?

'I won't forget.'

'And do be prompt so.'

I put down the phone, beyond panicked. Part of me wanted to go to the GPO, get into one of the private phone cabinets, place a collect call to Dad, tell him all and beg him to use his considerable government contacts to smooth all this over. I decided to count to ten on that plan of action – because once I came clean on everything to my father he then had so much on me, on Peter, on Carly. Since finding out from Peter about Dad's CIA connections I had been more than a little wary of telling him any more than very basic details. God knows what Peter finally let him know about Carly and Chile. I was badly over my head in all this myself – and not by fucking choice.

I slept that night at Ciaran's place. We were up early. He insisted on making me a 'fry-up'.

'The condemned woman ate a hearty breakfast,' he said, placing a heaving plate in front of me.

'Will you bring me a blindfold and a final cigarette before I head out to the Embassy?'

'Better yet I'll walk you there and I'll also wait for you outside – and will begin to stage a protest should they throw you into their dungeon for wayward women who harbored even more wayward women.'

'That's all so reassuring.'

Ciaran walking me the mile or so to Ballsbridge allowed me time to practice out loud what I would tell the consul – as he assumed the role of prosecutor, grilling me on everything to do with Carly. When we arrived at the low, round concrete doughnut that was the American Embassy, he kissed me on the lips and told me: 'Go! You are now one minute late for your interrogation and remember: you're the innocent party here.'

With a gentle tap on the shoulder he got me going up the steps of the Embassy. There was a woman at the reception desk. I explained that I had an appointment with Consul McNamara. I handed over my passport. There were no armed security guards at the entrance, no metal detectors. Just a quiet paunchy man in a suit on a high stool near to the reception desk. He didn't seem particularly interested in me. The receptionist made a phone call. I was motioned inside. Five minutes later I was brought into a small conference room by the same woman with whom I'd spoken on the phone yesterday.

'The consul will be with you in a few minutes so. Glad to see you came in so promptly. Always the best way now. Get this all put behind you.'

I was left alone in the conference room for what seemed like an inordinately long time and I began to think it was a deliberate ploy to unsettle me, make me malleable. Finally, the door opened and two men walked in. Consul McNamara was stocky, all business. I was introduced to Detective Quinlan. He was in his forties with graying red hair. He studied me with professional suspicion.

'Glad you could come in so quickly,' Consul McNamara said, motioning for me to take my seat again. They positioned themselves opposite me. Consul McNamara placed a file in front of him. Detective Quinlan took out a small black notebook and a pen. When the consul opened the file I saw that there was a photograph of me, and several pages of typed reports. He noticed me taking all this in.

'So how are you enjoying Trinity?' he asked, pleasantness itself.

'I'm enjoying it a great deal,' I replied.

'Better than Bowdoin? Wonderful school. Then again, that was an unfortunate business with your football-player boyfriend.'

Oh fuck. Within moments they were demanding to know everything about my involvement with Carly Cohen. I took them through the whole story – from Old Greenwich until her out-of-nowhere appearance on my Dublin doorstep, and how I let it be known that I didn't want her back sleeping on my floor after that first night she showed up.

'So you introduced her to Mr Treacy, and let things take their course?' Detective Quinlan said.

'She came along with me to the pub where I was meeting Sean and a bunch of others. They got together after that.'

'Even though you knew she was on the run, even though you knew her poor parents were still heartbroken by her disappearance, to the point where her mother was on the brink of taking her own life, you didn't think of making a phone call back to the States and saving everyone so much grief?'

I had prepared myself for this question.

'Carly spooked me from the outset,' I replied, maintaining a steady tone. 'She seemed unstable and capable of bad things. I was frightened that, if I did step in and let people know she was alive, she would have retaliated. I realize now what a mistake I made. I will live with the guilt of her mother's suicide for the rest of my life.

I truly wish I hadn't been so scared by her. But she is a very scary woman.'

I was asked many questions about what knowledge I had of her political activities in Dublin. I kept it simple – saying how I saw her with the Maoists at Trinity. Did I know if she was 'a Republican sympathizer'? My reply: we never discussed Irish politics. Quinlan let it be known that they knew I was 'stepping out' with 'a fella from Belfast' – and what were his politics? I replied that Ciaran, like his parents, kept away from the whole fray up north. McNamara then asked me if I knew about Carly's criminal activities while she was missing in the States. I had decided beforehand to deny any knowledge of that.

'You're telling me she didn't share any of her California exploits with you?' McNamara asked.

'She told me she drifted around the Bay area, that's all.'

'She never mentioned her time with your brother down in Chile?'

'We only had one evening together – and she was so strange, so angry, so clearly out of control, I closed down the conversation with her immediately.'

'And when you went to visit your brother in Paris ... her name was never mentioned?'

'That's right.'

'I sense you're not being straight with us here,' McNamara said.

'All my brother told me was that he was in Santiago, that he got caught up in the politics there, and had to get out in a hurry.'

'The very fact that your father is back running a mine there, and has many positive connections with the government there ...'

'I stay out of politics.'

I wondered what they thought they could get out of me that they didn't already know. They weren't hinting whether or not they knew about Carly's activities in Chile, or her involvement with my brother. As such the more naive and clueless I seemed the better.

'She told you nothing about her involvement with the Black Panthers?'

'She talked about running away after that terrible bullying incident in Old Greenwich. She told me about drifting around the States –'

'And working up a new identity for herself?' Quinlan asked.

'No, never heard about that.'

'I don't believe you.'

I directly met his gaze.

'Sir, this is a woman whose disappearance wreaked havoc and major distress on our community back in the States, and who destroyed her parents' lives. When she showed up on my doorstep, she barged into my life with crazy, poisonous anger. You want to know why I really turned her out? Because I told her directly to her face that what she did to her family was monstrous. And her reply was that I was "just a little suburbanite, the good girl".'

'Then why didn't you pick up the phone and let her parents or someone in authority know that she was alive?' McNamara asked.

I was also ready for this question.

'I told Carly I felt morally obliged to call her parents. She threatened to disappear again – or, worse yet, kill herself – if I made such a move. What could I do, sir? *What?*'

Yes, I made certain that I sounded a little choked up as I uttered that last '*What?*' I hated myself for telling such an outright lie. But something had been eating at me ever since I'd heard about Mrs Cohen's suicide, a question that I had raised in bed last night with Ciaran: if my father, through his Agency connections, knew all about Carly's goings-on in Santiago why didn't he let anyone know she was alive? Ciaran's answer was telling and very smart. 'From what you've told me, your father has all sorts of hidden agendas that he will never reveal to anyone close to him. So, yeah, I wouldn't be surprised if his contacts let him in on Carly's activities. He and his masters decided it was best not to let on to anyone that she was very much alive and kicking up trouble. Don't go blaming yourself for staying quiet. Your father did so as well.'

My performance in front of the consul and the Special Branch man seemed to have the necessary effect. They exchanged a glance – and within it I sensed they decided to buy my line about all this. Still, McNamara did ask:

'You're not the political sort, are you, Miss Burns?'

'Absolutely not – and I certainly stay away from everything to do with politics here in Ireland. I'm a guest here. I want no trouble.'

Quinlan looked at me coolly.

'I'm sure you don't.'

They asked me some rather perfunctory questions about the people in my building, and whether I thought that 'this Sean Treacy fellow had a few dark shadows hanging around him or was simply a bit of a fool'. I answered that, from what I could discern, he was definitely the latter. They also wanted to know what I talked about with my brother when I visited him in Paris. I told them: 'Family business.' I sensed they realized they were not getting much more out of me, though I had a question for them.

'Am I going to find Carly Cohen back on my doorstep tonight?'

'By which you mean: is she still in the country?' McNamara said. 'As we speak she is boarding a flight to New York. She agreed to voluntary repatriation. She knows that the FBI will be wanting to have a bit of a chat with her when she arrives back stateside. She knows she could be facing charges back home. But she still chose to return. And her father has been informed about her being found here alive.'

Had he also been informed that she had been living for weeks in the same building as me?

'One last thing, Miss Burns,' said Quinlan, training me again in his sights. 'We were told that an anonymous tip-off brought Miss Cohen to our attention. Who do you think made that tip-off?'

'No idea, sir.'

'I'm not surprised that you have "no idea" – because you allowed a third party to take care of the dirty work for you.'

Heading out to the street I found Ciaran on a bench by the Embassy, reading that morning's *Irish Times*. He stood up as I approached. I put my arms around him and enveloped him in a deep kiss. When we finally disengaged, he flashed me one of his quizzical smiles and said:

'I gather they're not locking you up or throwing you out of the country.' And then he asked me if I wanted to go to Belfast and meet his parents.

The idea of visiting Northern Ireland rendered me uneasy. Every time I turned on RTE on my little transistor radio, there were daily bad-news stories from across the border. Intimidations, bombings, assassinations, bodies found in shallow graves with a bullet in the head.

I didn't tell my mother in our bimonthly call that, the following weekend, I was heading one hundred miles north into a province that was considered a war zone. On the contrary, during our chat I discovered that Carly, upon her repatriation to the States, had been arrested by the FBI on suspicion of aiding and abetting a bank robbery in the Oakland area of California, and that her father had engaged a famous civil rights lawyer, William Kunstler, to handle her case.

'Kunstler is a left-wing big mouth,' Mom said, 'and one who loves stirring the pot. I have no doubt that he is ideal for Carly. There's been loads in the press since her return and arrest. Especially as she could have prevented her mother's suicide.'

I said nothing.

'I take your silence to be a tacit admission that you too could have saved that poor woman's life ... '

'Don't you dare guilt-trip me on that.'

'But you knew she was alive and well weeks ago.'

'As I told the people at the Embassy –'

'I know what you told the people at the Embassy.'

'How do you know that?'

'Guess? Your father has his moles everywhere.'

'So do you know how Dad stopped Peter from being thrown out of a plane in Chile?'

'Naturally.'

'And you approve of Dad's actions there? The corrupt, nasty dictatorship he isn't just supporting, but actively bolstering?'

'You're dodging the subject. The truth is that you were intimidated by that nasty little bitch. That's what you told the Embassy people. That's what came back to your father. His daughter's a coward who –'

I put the phone down. Actually I slammed it down hard. And didn't pick it up again when it started ringing. I was so upset that

I had to go upstairs and collapse on my bed and absorb the nastiness just dropped onto me. I knew that she was going to turn on me in this way. What astonished me was how my father had found out everything from my interview with the consul and the Special Branch man at the Embassy and reported it all to her.

I wasn't totally surprised when, an hour later, the phone rang, followed by a knock on my door and Sheila shouting:

'Alice, it's for you.'

It was my dad.

'To what do I owe this honor?' I said, standing in the hallway, talking in a rather loud voice, not giving two damns who heard me and what I was about to say.

'Sorry to be so out of touch.'

'*Coups d'état* and killing leftists must keep you so busy.'

Silence. Then:

'This is not a secure line,' he said. 'If you continue to follow this pattern of conversation I am putting down the phone and you will not hear from me for a very long time.'

'Your wife just quoted me details from my talk with the US consul here and a member of the Dublin Special Branch. Let me guess where she heard that from?'

'I have no idea.'

'She also told me she knew that you were instrumental to scaring the shit out of my brother by having him put onto a plane with Chilean dissidents and –'

'Alice, I know you're upset. But as I said before, this is not a secure line. And I frankly don't know what you're talking about.'

'Oh really? Your fucking wife just told me I was to blame for Mrs Cohen's death.'

'Mrs Cohen had been in a bad place for years. So don't blame yourself. Still, had you rumbled Carly earlier –'

'What? *What?* The woman wouldn't have killed herself?'

'It might have given her a reason to live.'

'So you are blaming me – even though I told your contacts at the Embassy that I was in an insanely tricky position with that little bitch. Surely your CIA friends told you that.'

The line went dead. My father had hung up. I realized that, for much of the call, I had been yelling. Because as soon as the phone call ended Sean's door opened and his big bulking hulk filled the archway.

'So now I know the truth: you ratted on Carly to the cops, to the CIA man at your Embassy.'

'Think what you like.'

'I will.'

And he slammed the door.

An hour later I was on a train from Connolly Station with Ciaran, heading north to Belfast. It was one of those rare Dublin days when the sun had been at full wattage. As soon as he showed up at my door – I was ready to go with a small weekend bag and my passport in hand – he could tell that I was in a bad place.

'A transatlantic phone call perhaps?' he asked.

'My parents should give lessons in the passing on of guilt.'

On the train a woman came by pushing a cart with things to eat and drink. Ciaran bought us two miniatures of Bushmills and I filled him in.

'Your mother needs to find some way to hurt you,' he said, 'to make you pay for the sin of not needing her anymore. I remember a line from an Irish writer – I think it was John McGahern – noting that mothers will break arms and legs to remain needed. He was talking about Irish mothers.'

'He might as well have been speaking about Jewish ones as well.'

When we reached the border, I kept my eyes glued to the window, expecting something akin to the images I'd seen of Checkpoint Charlie. But there was no wall, no search towers. As the train slowed down I saw several armored cars, discreetly adorned with the Union Jack, in an area that had been severely barbed-wired, with four soldiers in camouflage uniforms, lying prone, with rifles propped up on tripod-like stands, currently trained on our train. This was a proper border check, everyone needing to hand over passports or some form of identification. Ciaran told me that usually happened when crossing by car – but frequently, if the border soldiers thought that you looked reasonable, they would wave you through. Tonight two soldiers came aboard. They were wearing the same jungle-like uniforms and berets as the snipers outside. They each had a pistol on their belts, a large automatic rifle across their chests. I noticed the index finger of one of the soldiers edgily tapping the trigger of his weapon. They walked up the aisle, looking us over. I didn't really anticipate how being in the presence of armed soldiers engendered in me low-level anxiety and that feeling: *I must be guilty of something.* Was this a legacy of a family where, as I had just discovered yet again, to be rendered culpable of so much was the order of the day? I could see one of them – he couldn't have been more than twenty, bad acne, bad teeth, his head close-shaven, an impassive cold look on his face offset by eyes that radiated ease – turning his gaze toward Ciaran, then me. As I made eye contact with him he gave me the smallest of smiles.

'How you doin' this afternoon?' he asked.

I could see Ciaran's shoulders stiffen.

'Can't I talk to your dolly bird, mate?'

Ciaran shut his eyes, then slowly nodded his head. The soldier wasn't going to let the matter end there.

'Didn't hear a reply, mate.'

'Of course you can,' said Ciaran.

'Too bloody right I can, mate. And why are you two heading to Belfast?'

'To visit my parents.'

'Why were you in Dublin?'

'We're studying there.'

'Dublin must be jolly – even if it's a long way from home.'

Ciaran leaned forward.

'You're a long way from home too,' he said.

The soldier didn't react with rage or take the comment to be an affront. Rather, the way Ciaran phrased it – the quiet conversational tone he used – made it almost seem like he was letting the fellow understand: 'I know this is hard for you too.' Seeing the soldier's eyes soften as he absorbed that comment I understood in a flash the fear and the homesickness behind the gruff military manner. Turning away from us I could tell that Ciaran had defused the situation while simultaneously landing a direct punch. The soldier continued scanning the other passengers. After a few minutes I heard a whistle and out the window I could see the soldiers disembarking from the train. A second whistle was blown. The carriages lurched forward. Night had fallen, though there were still heavy searchlights bathing the train and the surrounding land in a strange fluorescent-tube glow. Moments later we were in the dark.

Ciaran signaled to the woman pushing the beverage cart that we wanted two more miniatures of Bushmills and he threw most of his back in one long go.

'Fuck,' he said, his voice just a notch above a whisper. 'I should never cross the bloody border.'

'You handled it well,' I said, taking his hand.

'By which you mean I didn't get myself marched off the train by some fucking British squaddie with a minuscule amount of power in the world which he decided to exercise on me.'

'He's just a scared kid. You won by showing him a little kindness.'

'I didn't want to fucking win. That's the whole problem with this fucking province – everyone wants to win the fucking argument.'

'It's behind us,' I said, thinking I sounded rather Pollyanna-ish.

'Nothing is behind us in the place, Alice,' said Ciaran. 'You know Einstein's comment that insanity is repeating the same thing over and over again with the idea that, this time, the result will be different? That's the dance Northern Ireland has been doing ever since dinosaurs stopped roaming the earth.'

Just under an hour later Belfast loomed in front of us: a semi-lit, low-rise cityscape with a few Victorian towers, many church steeples above endless clusters of small houses and narrow, twisty streets. As I was already preprogrammed to think that we were approaching an ominous place I found my anxiety level rising. Ciaran, as ever sensing when I was filled with unease, reached for my hand and said:

'It only looks like a horror show from a distance.'

Ten minutes later I was meeting Ciaran's double. It was immediately clear that father and son liked each other, that there was a real complicity between them.

314

'I am very impressed that you were willing to defy conventional wisdom and come into our little un-enchanted forest for the weekend,' John Quigg said, looking directly at me. 'No doubt your parents must be dreading this.'

'I decided that they didn't need to know about the trip.'

'That makes me feel trebly responsible for your well-being. As my culinary skills are beyond desperate, and Anne has been at work all day, I thought it best if I got takeaway from the one and only decent Indian in town – if you don't mind the anomaly of eating curry in Northern Ireland.'

I decided that John Quigg was good news. Walking us toward the taxi rank he said: 'My friend Rajiv at the Bombay Palace has assured me he will have an entire Tandoori chicken, three curries, assorted nans, poppadoms and chutneys ready for me to pick up shortly.'

We grabbed a black taxi, John explaining that these black taxis were neutral ones, but that if, for example, you were heading up the very Catholic Falls Road to the Divis Flats, a normal black taxi would drop you at the start of the Falls Road and you would have to transfer to one of the black cabs which only entered that area.

'If you like terrorism tourism the Falls and the Shankill are the Arc du Triomphe of Belfast,' Ciaran said.

The taxi idled in front of the Indian restaurant as John ran inside. As soon as he was gone from the cab I leaned over and took Ciaran's face in my hands and kissed him passionately.

'He's wonderful, your dad.'

'I have my father to thank for you grabbing me like that?'

'Very funny. But seeing how good the two of you are together ... '

'It's a turn-on?'

'I just really want you right now.'

'I'm afraid that's going to be a little difficult right at this moment.'

'I was thinking of later.'

'My parents might just put us into separate rooms. In fact, I know they will – because my mother is a bit like that.'

'A bit like what?'

'Someone who, for all her education and openness, still doesn't want to think of her only child, her little boy, being ravished by a crazed American under her roof.'

'So what exactly have you been telling her about me?'

'Besides the fact that you were raised in a commune run by defrocked priests and recently liberated Carmelites ... nothing at all.'

The cab door opened and John came back in, balancing two brown bags with handles, both steaming.

'Rajiv's best,' John said. 'And I have a bottle of Bulgaria's finest red wine back home to go with it.'

'Bulgaria makes wine?' Ciaran asked.

'Bulgaria makes cheap, drinkable wine,' John said.

The taxi took off. We turned down some side streets and then came into a large green square, beyond which were several Gothic towers.

'The university,' John said.

A light rain had started to fall, making visibility difficult. But I could see that this square was comprised of solid Victorian homes and administrative buildings, the side streets lined with terraced houses, all two or three stories tall, neat, quiet. There was a sense of being in a part of the city that was – as Ciaran had told me – tucked away from all the internecine stuff that defined so much of Belfast. We pulled up in front of a brick house, narrow, with three floors.

'Chez nous,' John said.

What struck me immediately about the inside of Ciaran's family home was that it might have been the most bookish residence I'd ever seen. It was a place of sanded floorboards, nicely yellowed white walls, comfortable Victorian furniture and books, books, books. There were books everywhere – even behind the toilet in the down-stairs loo, piled high right up to the cistern. The entrance hall had floor-to-ceiling shelves, three of the four available walls in the cozy living room were dense with volumes, the kitchen was jammed as well. When I saw Ciaran's room – the walls filled with very eclectic posters of everyone from Oscar Wilde to Jim Morrison to Benjamin Disraeli – I also saw my boyfriend's entire childhood and adolescent reading spread out over numerous shelves. Just as I discovered that he had an even more extensive collection of rock and jazz albums than I saw at his Dublin flat.

And there was Ciaran's mother, Anne – a woman in her mid-forties like her husband; attractive in a severe sort of way.

'The man himself,' she said with a big smile. Ciaran beamed back. She gave him a simple hug – but let her hand rest on his shoulder as she looked her son over, telling him:

'You look like a man who's flourishing.'

'Coming from you that is high praise indeed.'

'My son thinks I have a critical eye for everyone and everything,' she said to me, adding: 'It is a true pleasure to meet you, Alice.'

'And you, ma'am.'

'No need for the Victorian formality. Anne works just fine.'

She leaned over and gave her husband a kiss on the lips.

'I see that John did the right thing and let Rajiv do the cooking.'

'I explained that I was toxic in the kitchen.'

'"Radioactive" might be the more appropriate word – but I didn't marry you for your cooking skills.'

'Nor I for yours.'

A small complicit smile passed between them. This was a first for me, insofar that I had never been with a married couple of my parents' generation who seemed genuinely fond of each other, even hinting in their body language and the way they regarded each other that they were still having sex on a very regular basis (and teasing each other about their respective lack of skill in the kitchen – something my father could never let my mother forget). There was a dining room with an oval mahogany table and chairs just off the kitchen. We all were handed a role to play in setting up things for dinner – mine being told where to find the table mats, napkins and silverware, while Ciaran fed the cats and John found glasses and opened the wine, and Anne organized all the food onto plates and into bowls. John and Anne were hugely engaged people. Anne's work involved producing the early-evening current affairs program on BBC Radio Ulster, and she was ridiculously well informed and articulate about the world out there. There'd been a news item from Chile that evening – the way Pinochet's regime had started targeting intellectuals who had spoken out against the junta. I had a moment of panic, thinking that Ciaran might have said something to his parents about my family's curious involvement in that nightmare. But as Anne went on, talking about how Chile's leading poet, Pablo Neruda, had put himself in grave danger by calling Pinochet a dictator, I felt Ciaran take my hand under the table and squeeze it briefly; a signal that, no, he had not broken my confidence and repeated anything that I'd told him about Dad and Peter down Santiago way. But Anne did ask me how I felt about Nixon and Kissinger's foreign policy 'complexities' – and drew me out with great rigor about my thoughts on the bombing of Cambodia, and whether the president could survive Watergate, and did I think that the new neoconservatism being theorized by Irving Kristol, Midge Decter and 'the rather simplistic, but not to be underestimated Ronald Reagan' might set the tone for the near future? What so pleased me was the way she was genuinely interested in what I had to say, and would – like a brilliant moderator – bring everyone into the conversation. Just as, when John digressed and started asking me about jazz clubs in New York, I discovered just what a fanatic he was about what he called 'America's greatest contribution to the universal language that is music'. And how he and Anne – a year before Ciaran was born – had spent the summer of 1953 in Manhattan, and how he had heard Charlie Parker at Birdland and Bill Evans and Dexter Gordon at the Vanguard – 'and how, in the next life, I am definitely coming back as a New Yorker'.

As it was a Friday night getting to bed at a reasonable hour wasn't a big objective, and we followed the two bottles of wine with a dram each of Black Bush. The conversation turned to the changeover from Wilson to Heath in Downing Street, and why I needed to start reading a brilliant Belfast novelist, Brian Moore.

By the time Anne showed me the guest bedroom – touching my arm again and saying 'It is so good to have you with us' – I was suffering a very private attack of jealousy as I found myself thinking: so this is how a good family is with each other.

Much later that night, after Ciaran knocked quietly on my door, and we made crazed, but verbally muted love in the small double bed in the guest room, I held on to him and said:

'Seeing how cool and good your parents are simply makes me so sad. Because it underscores everything decent I'll never know about family life.'

'Like all of us, they have their limitations. Dad can get, when preoccupied, a wee bit distant and abstract. And you don't want to cross my mother. She has a reserve that emerges when she is uncertain or troubled by something or someone. Outside of that – and especially after hearing all about your relentlessly unhappy ma and da – yeah, I've done pretty well in the parental department.'

'They're also a good model as a couple.'

'By which you mean: they still like each other?'

'Exactly.'

'That's the trick, isn't it? Staying in love.'

'I wonder if my parents were ever truly in love.'

'They must have been ... or, at least, they must have convinced themselves ... '

'That misery loves company?'

'Something my dad said about Northern Ireland recently truly resonated with me. "Whether it comes to a family or a society – unhappiness is always a choice."'

I felt a little shudder come over me.

'Did I say the wrong thing?' Ciaran asked.

'You just spoke an unfortunate truth.'

It was an exquisite early-spring morning when we all woke the next day. At breakfast, when I mentioned that I'd like to see 'the parts of Belfast that tourists don't venture into', John exchanged a look with Anne, while Ciaran cheerily piped up:

'Surely Dad can give Alice his famous Falls and Shankill Roads tours.'

'Why are they famous tours?'

'Because there was an overseas delegation of university chancellors,' Anne said, 'and the chancellor of Queens asked the philosopher

319

king here to do the honors and guide everyone around. Of course, they all wanted to see the war zones ... '

'And yes, I'll show you them too,' John said.

Anne asked if Ciaran wouldn't mind spending a few hours with her over at her late sister's house in Lisburn. She was beginning to sort through the few things she was going to keep and the rest that would be sent to charity.

'My sister Sheila was just two years older,' Anne said. 'We couldn't have been more different. She never left Lisburn, she never married. And she had a fearsome reputation as the local headmistress of a very fine secondary school in the town. We weren't close – but her death from cancer is something that I'm finding hard to bear.'

'Ciaran told me about that. I'm so sorry.'

'This is something that I didn't expect to happen now, when we were all so young. I've been putting off going back to her house since the funeral in February. But with your permission I am going to steal Ciaran for the afternoon. I think I'll be able to face it all with him there.'

'Even though you always told me never to speak ill of the dead, the fact is: Auntie Sheila was something of a pill,' Ciaran said.

Anne burst out laughing. 'You're terrible, did you know that? Sheila wasn't a pill. She was a deadly pill. Which is why the sadness is even harder.'

Over the next few hours, I was given a brief motorized introduction to the sectarian geography of Belfast. We passed the BBC, noting the British Army tanks and armored cars near its highly fortified entranceway. John said that Anne negotiated all that every working day and simply considered it part of her job. We headed up the Shankill Road – low shabby row houses, mostly in disrepair, graffiti and chewed-up streets everywhere. John told me that, given his religious affinity, he probably shouldn't be here – 'but it's a Saturday morning, and Provos don't drive Morris Minors, so if anyone stops us I will ask you to say a few words and show your passport – you do have it on you, yes ... ?'

I nodded.

'Once they hear you're American they will leave us be. Ditto when we head up the Falls Road. But chances are, we will not have any problems.'

'I'm in your hands, sir.'

Turning two corners, we came to a place where armored cars and tanks and soldiers on the street were omnipresent.

'As you might have guessed by now this is the intersection I was talking about,' John said.

There was a small space created between all the armored vehicles through which cars could pass. As we inched forward a gang of Shankill kids behind us began to shout insults in our direction, as if the very fact that we were daring to cross over to the other side marked us as the enemy. A balloon suddenly landed on the hood of the car, startling me – especially as, when it exploded, liquid rained onto the windshield.

'What was that?' I asked, genuinely taken aback.

'One of the little boys back there probably peed into that balloon and was just waiting for the next car to make the crossing. Unfortunately, that was us.'

I could see several British Army soldiers peering in at us. We were stopped by a squaddie – who knocked on the window and asked to see our ID. John handed over his Queens University ID and I gave him my passport. The squaddie was Scottish.

'If you don't mind me asking, why are you bringing a Yank up here?'

'She's working on a thesis for me about the Troubles.'

'You brought her to the right place then. It seems the little shits landed one of their piss balloons on your bonnet. At least your surname should keep you out of trouble on the other side.'

With that he waved us through. Other men crowded in on us but they weren't wearing uniforms or any emblems of officialdom. Rather they were in anoraks, their heads covered by balaclavas, their eyes detached from all facial expressions besides lips that pulled back to reveal bad teeth. John whispered to me:

'Fear not, this is not as bad as it seems.'

One of the balaclava'd fellows knocked on our window. John rolled it down and greeted him politely. We both had our IDs at the ready. The fellow took John's ID, scanned his details, and simply handed it back to him, motioning with his thumb that it was fine to move on. As soon as the car inched forward John said to me:

'The fact that my second Christian name is O'Connell always gets me through without a question.'

'Because they know you're Catholic?'

'And because a certain Daniel O'Connell was known as the Great Liberator for his campaigns at the beginning of the nineteenth century against the Brits.'

'Did you get your second name because someone among the Quiggs was related to him?'

'Not at all – but I am certainly not going to tell them that.'

The Shankill was bad news when it came to a sense of communal deprivation; it looked like a reconstituted early 1970s version of Victorian slums – with an added dose of sectarian tension thrown in. But the Falls Road was something else entirely. The sense of desolation was shocking, with harsh tricolor propaganda everywhere: 'Brits Out', 'One Ireland United', alongside portraits of Republican martyrs, brutalized or killed by 'the forces of occupation'. I noticed many children. It was a Saturday and they were out playing in the streets: girls with toy baby carriages, boys kicking a ball, teenagers of both sexes with cigarettes eyeing each other warily, a group of thuggish young men on the prowl, several with clubs in hand, looking very much like the local enforcers. There were also hard men on every corner – ruffled, grim-faced, with ever-suspicious eyes, noting our passing car with interest, giving off the impression that these were men whom you never wanted to tangle with.

'Are we going to be safe here?' I whispered. John smiled at me.

'They can't hear you on the street outside – and yes, we'll be fine. Because when they let us pass earlier into the Falls one of the lads no doubt used a walkie-talkie to phone the lads up the road to let them know we were all right. Anyway, you did want to see all this. Up on top of the Divis Tower – that's the big tower block over there – is an actual British Army command post. The only way the Brits can get their men in is by helicopter. That's how tight things are for them here in the corner of the city.'

He drove us right up alongside the flats. A group of young toughs – their faces covered by handkerchiefs, like the bad guys in an old western – came up to the car, one of them using what looked like a butcher's mallet to knock on the window. I tensed. John motioned to me not to show fear and rolled down the window..

'What are youz doin' here?' The vigilante asked. Though his face was covered, I sensed he couldn't have been more than sixteen.

'Giving this American student a look at life around here.'

'Our shite is your fuckin' idea of tourism? Get your license over to me now.'

Looking a little on edge John pulled out his wallet and handed over his driver's license.

'The girlie with you, she a fucking Yank?'

'I am indeed a fucking Yank,' I said very loudly. The ringleader tossed John's license back into the car.

'Get the fuck out of here,' he said.

As soon as they were gone, John turned to me and asked:
'Seen enough?'

I nodded. He put the car in gear and got us out of there.

Fifteen minutes later we were back in the calm confines of the university district, at an Italian restaurant. John insisted on ordering a bottle of their house red, telling me:

'I feel like that was a baptism by fire.'

'But I asked for it.'

Silence.

'You must be thinking: why don't myself and Anne engineer a way out of here?' said John.

'I'm not thinking that.'

'Yes you are – and you're right to think it. We should be elsewhere, but there is a stubbornness to us both. This benighted province is where we both grew up, were educated, where we met and fell in love and decided to make a life together. Ulster for us is like that tricky portion of the marriage vow: "for better or worse".'

The wine arrived. The waiter poured it out. John raised his glass to mine.

'Welcome to the family ... if I may say so.'

'You may say that.'

Much later that night, in bed with Ciaran, I told him what his father had said. Ciaran was genuinely surprised – not because he thought his father was in any way meddling with his life, but because it was so unlike his dad to ever put an opinion forward about such things.

'My mother also thinks the world of you – and trust me, she is not exactly Madame-Easy-to-Please. Do you think when I get around to meeting them that your parents will be so accepting?'

'If they're not screaming at each other ... yes, they will like you a lot. My brothers will also approve – Peter especially ... as damaged as he now is.'

'Your father sounds like someone who was pretty damaged himself.'

'Dad was born with this voice of authority in his head, and one which has kept him tied to a life he doesn't really want.'

'Surely his swashbuckling stuff with the CIA has kept him amused.'

'You've never told your parents about all that, have you?'

'If you ask me to keep a secret I keep a secret.'

'Bless you.'

'For what?'

'For being honorable. There's been so little of that in my life – especially when it comes to family.'

And I pulled him closer to me, falling asleep in his arms.

His parents didn't disturb us until noon the next morning. I woke in that small bed, my arms still around Ciaran, thinking: I would never have expected something like this coming my way. While desperate to be with someone who would make me feel loved, there was a significant private part of me who still considered myself unlovable and who feared that, by giving my heart to someone else, I would be inviting inevitable pain, agony. Yet Ciaran, in the few weeks we'd been together, had already shown himself to be fully aware of all my fears. He got me.

As we were boarding the train at Central Station, Anne did something unexpected – she gave me a proper big hug, whispering into my ear:

'Thank you for making Ciaran so happy.'

I whispered back:

'He makes me so happy too. And you are both wonderful. Thank you.'

On the way south Ciaran asked if I'd given any thought to the summer ahead. He'd been offered a possible internship at a barrister's chambers in Dublin – but as this was the last summer before his final year, 'and I will be working for the next forty-five years', he wondered if I would consider bumming around Europe during July and August.

'I've got this friend from Belfast who has this great summer number on the Greek island of Naxos managing his father's bar. There's a little guest cottage attached to the pension which he'd give us for nothing for a fortnight. We could fly to Athens, get the ferry out to Naxos, flop there for two weeks, then see where we want to head next. A summer drifting around the Continent on the cheap, making our way back to Dublin by mid-September, well before term starts.'

'I have absolutely no plans for the summer,' I said, taking his hand, 'and I am certainly not going home to Mom and Dad and Watergate and the war and assorted other American madnesses. I definitely want to travel ... and with you. Sure, I'm in.'

Ciaran leaned over and kissed me.

'I knew I'd have to argue you into it,' he said.

Back in Dublin we both threw ourselves into the business of studying for our exams. There was something genuinely vertiginous about knowing that twelve hours in an exam hall would determine my academic fate for the year. I began putting in eight hours a day at the library and spending most nights at Ciaran's apartment. His flat was absolutely quiet come night, and I got to wake up next to him. Sean continued to cold-shoulder me, and a new arrival on my floor in Pearse Street – a 'headbanger' as Sheila called him – had this thing for heavy-metal music and was blasting Black Sabbath night and day.

I was hardly ever at Pearse Street, just stopping back every few days to see if there was any mail or phone messages. Though there was much-welcomed radio silence from my parents, I received a letter from Peter.

Hi Alice,

Still in Paris, where I have invested 200 francs in a third-hand typewriter with an actual English keyboard. I am attempting to somehow put down on paper all that happened in Chile. Not a novel. Non-fiction. Because the truth is always more extreme than the fictive. Still living in La Louisiane. Just out of nowhere last week I got a letter from dear old Dad in which he told me that he'd been in contact with Yale and they were willing to take me back this coming autumn. Until then, if I wanted to stay in Paris and play the Hemingway expat game for a few more months, here was an international money order for $1000 to keep me afloat. One thousand bucks! That will buy me another four or so months here. Did he send me the money to assuage his guilt? To keep me onside? Who the hell knows? Who the hell cares? I cashed the money order. I've yet to decide about a return to study. But I am determined to finish the book I'm writing at the moment. If I have any cash left over, maybe I'll drift down to somewhere cheap and sunny like Sardinia for a few weeks.

One other bit of news from back home – Mom sent me a letter telling me that Carly had copped a plea with the Feds back in the Bay Area. In exchange for her testimony against her former Black Panther cohorts she's being let off with a slap on the wrist and a bunch of dirty looks. That woman really knows how to wheedle her way out of the darkest corners. There are people like that who are endlessly devious and who wreak havoc on everyone stupid enough to engage with them, and who always seem to get away with malfeasance. I still feel like a fool for having gotten involved with her.

Finally, dear old Mom told me in her letter that you had hung up on her during your last phone call – and all because she dared to suggest that you should have rumbled Carly weeks earlier. If it was you who informed the authorities about her, congratulations on having the guts to do something that certainly needed to be done. Don't listen to Mama's guilt-tripping. She has nothing better to do with her time, alas.

    Come see me again in Paris.
Love
Peter

  Bless my complicated, interesting brother. Threading a sheet of paper into my typewriter I started writing him a letter. It ended up being quite a long letter – five single-spaced pages, in which I told him my big news: I had seriously fallen in love ... and with someone of whom I felt he would approve. I also wrote about how much I felt for him in the wake of his Chilean horrors, and how I knew that we both shared far too much inherited *meshugas* (how I *loved* that Yiddishism), and how he was one of the few constants in my life and I loved and respected him, and wanted him to know that. Just as I also wanted him to know that my studying schedule was now up to ten hours a day, as I was terrified of not making the academic grade.

  I reread the letter, then I walked over to the post office on Andrews Street to mail it before returning to the Trinity library for another long stint with my books. Ciaran was also cramming like mad. We met up somewhere for dinner around six most evenings, returning to our books, and finally retreating to the pub after the library closed at ten. For three straight weeks this was our life. I spent an hour each day in the university pool in an attempt to tamper down the stress that this one-shot-at-getting-it-right event was enveloping me.

  Then, on June 8, exams started. I walked with Ciaran on a particularly wet day from his flat to the back gate of Trinity, hugging him long and hard, and telling him how scared I was. He assured me I would be fine, wondering out loud if the reason I was finding all this so terrifying was because all the judgmental shit in my background had induced in me a fear of failure. As I faced my first paper that day, the fact that Ciaran had articulated for me the ongoing dread that had haunted so much of my life to date allowed me to attack Professor Brown's questions on Sir Philip Sidney with a confidence and relish that surprised me.

Two days later I was a little uncertain about whether I had nailed Professor Norris's complex questions about Joyce's *The Dead*, though I did think I did well when discussing how *Portrait of the Artist as a Young Man* was in the *Bildungsroman* tradition. My papers on O'Faolain and O'Connor seemed straightforward, and I felt relatively confident about discussing the English Romantics with a degree of critical clarity.

But the thing about this crazed eight days – preceded by weeks of work and worry – is that I was too damn immersed in it all to even begin to properly gauge how I had done. Ciaran felt the same way – telling me that he found his conveyancing exam something of an uphill climb, and having 'not a fucking clue if I made good or not'.

Still, when we finished on the morning of June 19 we celebrated by taking ourselves off to the Trocadero for a cheap and cheerful Italian lunch – which went on for about three hours. Hey, we'd come through this torturous process. The summer was going to start in a week's time, we'd found two cheap flights to Athens via Amsterdam and had decided to first spend a few days exploring that Dutch city. I showed up at our lunch with a guidebook I'd just bought for Holland, telling Ciaran about a cheap interesting hotel not far from the Central Station and how we should do a day trip to Delft, and how I also had discovered a place to stay not far from the Pláka in Athens, and –

'Is this hyper-organization your way of coming down from the hell of the last month?' Ciaran asked.

'You know me too damn well.'

He leaned over and kissed me, reaching for me under the table, his hand on my thigh.

'I so want you now,' he whispered, to which I replied:

'As I do you – but time isn't on our side right now.'

I checked my watch. It was now almost four fifteen and we had a train to catch for Belfast at 5.50 p.m., as we were planning to collapse at his parents' house for the weekend. When I pointed this out to my beloved he smiled and said:

'Then we'll order a second bottle of wine.'

I wasn't really up for more booze, and suggested we grab a taxi over to Connolly Station and the 4.50 p.m. train. But Ciaran was in expansive form, saying that we deserved to get a little scuttered before heading north.

'Lead me into temptation,' I said, taking his hand.

'With pleasure,' he said.

At five fifteen we staggered out of the restaurant, making a beeline for O'Connell Bridge, then turning into Talbot Street. I glanced at my watch. Five twenty-seven, and I was craving a cigarette.

'Mind if I duck in here?' I asked, pointing to a corner shop.

'Go feed your addiction,' he said with a grin, indicating he was going to wait outside.

Once in the shop there was a woman in front of me who was having an extended conversation with the big beefy fellow behind the counter, chewing his ear off about something to do with a neighbor in a block of flats nearby who was always screaming at her man, and calling him 'a fucking useless eejit', and how it was ruining her sleep as she tended to turn on her man after midnight ...

'Sorry,' I said, 'but I've got a train to catch ... '

The woman looked at me as if I'd just zoomed in from Mars.

'What the fuck's a Yank doin' on this side of the city?'

'As I said: heading to the station.'

'Well, we don't want to make Her Ladyship miss her train ... '

'None of that now,' the burly fellow said to her, then turned to me all smiles. 'So what can I get you?'

I smiled back.

'Pack of –'

But I didn't get to finish the sentence. Because the world outside erupted. There was a firestorm of smoke, flames, flying glass. I had my back to the doorway of the shop. The blast hurled me forward, landing me head first against a set of shelves. The world went black and when I came to I had no idea how long I had been knocked out, no idea what had happened. What I did know, as I staggered to my feet, was that the shop was in a state of charred ruin, the woman just beside me now on her knees, her face slashed everywhere by the flying glass, the man behind the counter lying motionless on the floor, his chest blown open, blood pumping forth, a reservoir of red enveloping him and cascading into my shoes.

I tried to scream. I couldn't. A cold numbness enveloped me. So much so that when I felt a strange dampness taking hold of my back, and I touched my shoulder and saw my fingers covered in blood, I still had no knowledge of the fact that I was wounded and bleeding.

I tried to scream again. All I could do was mouth one word:

'Ciaran ... '

Then I cascaded forward, my feet giving way under me, but still somehow getting me through the smoking wreckage that was the remnant of this shop and out onto the street.

'Ciaran ... '

I tried shouting out his name. I tried focusing my sight on the devastation before me. But my eyes were stinging, the smoke was thick, and there were bodies everywhere. I looked down. There was a head at my feet. The scream within me now raged forth. I fell to my knees. The world went black again.

Ciaran.

PART THREE

20

NIXON HAD RESIGNED. Gerry Ford was president. Vietnam was crumbling. A mad Frenchman named Philippe Petit had tiptoed his way across the two World Trade Center towers on a tightrope. Turkey invaded Cyprus. You could not walk into a bar or a diner without hearing Eric Clapton's 'I Shot the Sheriff', though everyone smart was talking about Randy Newman and Tom Waits and Steely Dan. And just before autumn arrived in Vermont, our new president sparked outrage by pardoning his predecessor – whose paranoia and need for vengeance had led to his own profound undoing.

Autumn in Vermont. Everyone was saying that this was a classic New England fall, the intensity and coloration of the foliage dazzling. Autumn in Vermont. I was cognizant of its radiance, but in a somewhat distracted way. Just as I did pick up on the radio in my apartment, and through the occasional purchase of a newspaper, the news swirling around my country and the world beyond.

No one in the little apartment building downtown, where I was renting a studio, knew anything about me. Except that, when asked, I informed them that I was a student at the university.

Autumn in Vermont. Every week I had an appointment with an audiologist who was monitoring my hearing, which was still very much compromised. For the first four months there was a constant ringing in both ears. This had lessened, but there was still a problem with any high-register sounds which could bring about momentary agony. I was also having episodes of sonic blurring. The audiologist suggested I consider the use of hearing aids – and said that I would need one for each ear. Immediately I saw myself as some old bat, with cords dangling down and one of those transistor radio packs in each pocket of some moth-eaten cardigan. But Fred the Hearing Aid Guy (as I had dubbed him) was very reassuring, telling me they had just come out with these fully transistorized, cordless, behind-the-ear hearing aids with a discreet earpiece.

Fred was a man in his mid-fifties, with much dandruff on his wide-lapelled check jacket and thick bifocals. My ENT specialist at the University of Vermont Hospital, Dr Tarbell, recommended Fred, telling me with a smile: 'He's a little eccentric, but very much on top of his game. We like eccentrics here in Burlington.'

Fred's practice was in a shopfront of the Main Street arcade. Besides hearing aids, he also fitted prosthetic devices, so his front window was also filled with artificial arms and legs. He ran multiple tests on me, his thoroughness as disarming as his garish clothes and the slow methodical way he did everything. But yes, he did know his stuff when it came to 'auditory aid devices'. As we finished our first consultation he touched me lightly on the arm, saying:

'I heard from Dr Tarbell what caused this loss of auditory capacity. I just want you to know: I am so sorry for you, and all that you've been through.'

Anytime someone brought up 'the incident' (as it was so often called by others not wanting to reference its actual horror) I found myself succumbing to a growing numbness that, mirroring my inner-ear problems, muffled all acts of kindness. Not that I didn't appreciate, on many levels, the decency and benevolence that had been shown to me ever since those two burly Dublin firemen came charging toward me, hunched over on my knees on Talbot Street, staring face down at a monstrosity that I knew would never leave me. The firemen managed to scoop me up just before a nearby parked car, which had caught fire, exploded into flames. Days later, when a Special Branch detective came to interview me in my hospital bed, he told me that, had those firemen not grabbed me, I might have been engulfed in this subsequent fireball. I told him in reply: 'I would have preferred if it had taken me right there.'

Fred the Hearing Aid Guy didn't push me further when I simply bowed my head and acknowledged his kind words with a fast nod. Instead he talked about these two devices and how they were really the most technologically advanced behind-the-ear hearing aids he'd ever come across.

Besides Fred and Dr Tarbell, I had a regular appointment with a general physician – a very firm, proper New England woman named Katherine Gellhorn, also in her fifties, to whom I had gone during my first week in Vermont when insomnia had overtaken me and I went five straight days without sleep. Upon first arriving at Dr Gellhorn's office she eyed me over with a mixture of professional interest and reserved WASP concern.

'So, Alice,' she said, her tone headmistressy yet not unkind, 'you have survived something heinous.'

She insisted on doing a full examination – 'top to toe'. She was impressed with the way the scars on my back from all the embedded glass in me were healing. She was worried about my hearing – and got me dispatched to Dr Tarbell the next day, directly asking why, in the two months I had been at home after 'the incident', I had not been to see a hearing specialist, let alone been prescribed anything 'to help make things easier'.

I met Dr Gellhorn's cool gaze, and said:

'Because I refused to see any doctors. Just as, after two months, I fled to Manhattan and slept for a month on a friend's floor while I waited to hear if the university would accept me. When it did I moved up here, the sleeplessness started, the hearing got worse, and I decided that I now should get medical help.'

Dr Gellhorn thought this over for a few moments, then asked:

'I take it that your family was not exactly supportive?'

'Oh, initially, they were amazing.'

'And then?'

'And then ... the usual bad stuff kicked in again.'

'Alas, that is how many families work,' she said.

Besides arranging for me to see Dr Tarbell she also gave me a drug called Darvon for sleep and Miltown for anxiety. This being the mid-seventies, the acronym PTSD – post-traumatic stress disorder – was simply not part of the medical conversation, any more than the idea that therapy was an essential component of the coping process in the wake of such major psychic injury.

'If you still can't sleep or are feeling wobbly, I will want to refer you to a psychiatrist. But let's see how you're faring in a couple of weeks.'

I was faring terribly. I kept this fact to myself. The Darvon did help me sleep. I stuck with it. The Miltown deadened me, leaving me as blurry and unfocused as my hearing. I put it away, vowing not to use it unless I felt real darkness overtaking me.

Autumn in Vermont. I was sleeping – and once Fred fitted the two hearing aids, my auditory senses were somewhat less clouded. Beyond that ...

I was enrolled as a junior at the University of Vermont. I chose it by chance. The floor on which I lived for four weeks in New York belonged to my Bowdoin friend Duncan Kendall. Smart urban guy that he was he had scored, right out of college, a job at *Esquire* as an editorial assistant, but was already trying to wrangle assignments, seeing himself as a new Tom Wolfe in the making. He had a one-bedroom railroad apartment on 83rd between Amsterdam and Broadway: a rather edgy neighborhood, largely Hispanic. When you walked out onto the sidewalk you had to sidestep used hypodermic needles. You also had to develop a certain street craft when negotiating the block after dark. Duncan had read about me getting caught up in 'the incident' in the *New York Times*. After I was repatriated back to the States – and installed in my old bedroom at my parents' house – he sent me a letter telling me how sorry he was to read about the nightmare I'd been put through, giving me his address and phone number at home and at work, asking if he could visit. I sent back a postcard thanking him, and saying I needed to be alone for the time being. But when things got out of hand at home I decided to walk out one day and not come back. I phoned Duncan from the Old Greenwich train station, wondering if he could provide me temporary refuge. To his immense credit he said:

'If you don't mind sleeping near a bathtub you can crash at my place for as long as you like.'

The bathtub in Duncan's apartment was in a corner of the kitchen, behind which was a little alcove – maybe seven by four – which Duncan had turned into a crash pad for guests, replete with a single futon, paisley sheets, and a poster of Allen Ginsberg overhead, on which had been written that most-quoted declamation from his great poem, 'Howl':

I saw the best minds of my generation destroyed by madness...

What Duncan didn't tell me in his letter was that he had hooked up with a woman in her late twenties named Patricia who painted scenery at the Metropolitan Opera. She was super-tall, with big frizzy hair and a lot of streetwise artist attitude. She lived in an even tougher corner of the city – Hell's Kitchen, on 49th and Tenth Avenue ('Junkie nowheresville, baby,' as she told me in that astringent, New Jersey-accented way of hers) where she had a fifth-floor walk-up studio and had been a little uneasy about her building since an elderly neighbor had been found raped and strangled at the height of August. Since getting together with Duncan she was spending most nights in his bed. But when I showed up and set up life in that seven-by-four alcove, not to mention hanging around the apartment so much of the time, Patricia couldn't have been cooler about my presence in their lives. When Patricia heard me mention one evening that I thought I needed to go back to school and wanted somewhere I could get into fast that was of reasonable academic quality but away from New York and my family, she told me all about the University of Vermont.

'Okay, it's not in the same league as the other colleges you've been to, but I liked my time there. I met some serious people, it's not too rah-rah, and I think you'd take to the Burlington vibe. I even have a friend who works in the admissions department.'

It's strange how the music of chance dictates so much. I'd thought often about how, on our way to Connolly Station, Ciaran turned us into Talbot Street, rather than taking any of the earlier side roads. And how my decision to stop in a shop to buy cigarettes – coupled with that woman talking her head off to the guy behind the counter – delayed us for a crucial few minutes. Had I decided to get the cigarettes at the station we would have been well beyond the epicenter of the bomb when it went off. I would not be here now, sleeping on the floor in an alcove of the apartment of a college friend who probably should have been my boyfriend last year. But the very fact that I pushed him away, stayed with Bob ... the result was me fleeing for Dublin. And the result of that little exploit was ...

A week after this conversation I found myself on the long slow train up to Burlington. Patricia had made a call to her friend in the admissions department and even arranged for me to stay in the home of another Burlington friend: a 'peace activist' named Rachel. She was a tall, ever-cheerful woman with braided hair that stretched down to her waist and perpetually kind eyes. She worked in a local health-food store, was a member of a local experimental dance troupe, and lived in an old Grant Wood-style house that, though divided into separate apartments, had the feel of a quasi-commune. Rachel had evidently been briefed by Patricia on recent events in my life, as she was ultra-quiet and gentle with me, insisting on making me green tea on my arrival, putting a far-too-consoling hand on my shoulder and telling me:

'I am so honored to be in the same room as such a brave, brave woman.'

I wanted the floor to open up and whisk me to the underworld.

'I am hardly brave,' I said, gently shrugging off her comforting touch.

'You are even more amazing to say that. To have survived a war zone –'

'Dublin is hardly a war zone. And I really don't want to talk about any of this.'

Rachel heard my voice crack. She also sensed that I was on the verge of getting very angry.

'Sorry, sorry,' she whispered, guiding me to an armchair and sitting me down. I allowed myself to be seated. I shut my eyes, trying to steady myself, trying to tell myself she really did mean well. At least five times a day since all this went down I kept thinking that maybe Professor Hancock understood something primordial: when the pain had become unbearable, when he felt he'd reached the point of no return, he had no choice but to put his head in that noose and swing himself into oblivion.

But no, I was not going to scream and shout all that at this crunchy-granola good Samaritan with her beatific smile. But I could not avoid grumpiness when she quietly crouched down by me and removed my sandals.

'What are you doing?' I asked.

'Shut your eyes, try to blank your brain, and feel the deep gravitational pull of your breathing.'

I wanted to reply: 'Stop the bullshit.' But she was fast working wonders with my feet. For the first time in months I was having a moment of strange calm amidst endless turbulence. I simply sat back, my eyes deeply shut, trying to keep the screening room within my head void of images, allowing her to momentarily drain the anguish within.

'That was ... different,' I said after she put my sandals back on and whispered '*Namaste*' in my ear, which I learned later was the Tibetan word for 'peace'. 'Thank you so much.'

'Thank you for taking the journey,' she said. 'Please know that the journey you are still traveling on is one where healing will eventually find you.'

She also insisted on giving me 'a healing hug' before sending me on my way to the admissions office at UVM.

My interview there was very straightforward. The admissions officer, a Miss Strang – a quiet woman in her forties – had received my Bowdoin transcript, as well as perusing the Trinity one which I handed over. She too had been briefed by Patricia, as she told me that she knew all about 'what I can only imagine is an ordeal' and that, judging from 'the quality of schools and the grades received', she didn't see any problem with me transferring for the autumn 1974 term. I asked:

'And if I wanted to take a double course load and do the summer semester next year ... '

'Yes, you could complete all the requirements required for graduation in that time. But would that be advisable, given what you've recently been through?'

'With respect, let me be the judge of that.'

'Of course, Miss Burns. No offense meant.'

'None taken. I am sorry if I sounded a little prickly.'

'Understood, understood.'

I felt that encroaching distress when anyone tried to be solicitous toward me – because it seemed to trigger that hidden part of me which was convinced it was my fault that Ciaran died. Just as I also knew that I didn't deserve to have walked away alive, that it was me who should have been blown apart in that blast. But I had not shared this thought with anyone to date. Even though Mom wanted me to see a shrink – especially as we started clawing into each other around three weeks after I was repatriated back to Connecticut – the man she arranged for me to see was notorious in Old Greenwich for being one of those 'Dr Feelgood' types who overprescribed happy pills that deaden everything within you.

It was my brother Adam (of all people) who warned me off Dr Feelgood. Dad and Peter had raced to Dublin after the bombing – my older brother staying in my bedsit during the ten days I was in hospital, visiting me three times a day and dealing with much of the paperwork and administrative stuff needed to get me back home – and eventually securing a $10,000 payment for me from the Irish government. Once I returned to the States it was Adam who stepped in and acted as a necessary buffer between me and my mother. He'd returned from Chile just two weeks before the bombing. I later learned that he had resigned from Dad's company and was now living in a small apartment in White Plains (only Adam would have chosen such a sad little suburb – but as he told me, a studio there was only $52 a month and he was trying to keep his expenses down now that he was out of work). Adam was suddenly a presence in my life, spending part of every day with me, insisting on getting me out of the house. It was also Adam who drove back to Connecticut and packed up another suitcase for me after I did a bunk off to Duncan's. And it was Adam who told me why he wanted me to steer clear of that quack, Dr Feelgood.

'After that accident of mine – when I got thrown from the car and Fairfax died – Mom lined me up with Dr Feelgood. I tell you the stuff he had me on just about did my head in. I thought I was living in some alternative reality. I was numb to everything. So much so that I finally flushed the pills down the toilet in my college dorm. Three nights later I tried to jump out a window. Fortunately, my two roommates were there at the time. They stepped in and stopped me from killing myself.'

'Did Mom and Dad know about this?'

'Fuck no. Nor did I tell them after the fact. But I did go see the college doctor and showed him the empty pill jar. He looked at the prescription and rolled his eyes, telling me never to go near that stuff – or that doctor – again.'

'What did you take to get through it all?'

'Beer.'

That conversation was the beginning of a change in my relationship with Adam. Before now he was always the blocky jock who never dared express an original thought and allowed Dad to call the shots when it came to his life. Nor would he speak much about what when down in Chile, though he did quiz me a great deal about what Peter told me in Paris and did indicate that he knew all about that plane ride over the Pacific.

We were walking the beach at Todd's Point a few weeks after my return home, a juncture when I realized that I was going to have to get away from Mom for the sake of my equilibrium and when I was also beginning to think seriously about killing myself (yes, I know that's two contradictory sentiments in one sentence, but maybe I felt that only by fleeing my mother could I then take my own life for reasons divorced from her craziness). Adam, to his credit, sensed the bleakness of my thoughts. He did something unusual for him – he put his arm around me, saying:

'You must promise me: if you ever feel like you are going to do something drastic you will first pick up the phone, whatever hour of the day or night, and call me. Or get on a train, into a cab, and come over immediately to my place. I know what it's like to feel that sort of despair. I know what it's like to think: I can't bear this anymore. But there is always a way out of darkness.'

'Why did you never tell me or Peter any of this before now?'

'Because ... we never talked this way before. Maybe that was my fault. Maybe I'm also feeling so bad about what happened to you – and that I need to try to do some good for a change.'

I stopped and looked at my brother carefully.

'Did you do bad somewhere?' I asked.

He said nothing, staring down into the sand.

'I made some bad choices.'

'Anything you want to talk about?'

'No.'

'Were you up to dark things in Chile?'

'I was working for a company that – as you probably now know, via our brother – was deeply implicated with the junta. But I didn't do any dirty work for them when it came to things political.'

'But our dad did, right?'

I expected a nervous shrug from Adam – for that was always his style when faced with a question he knew he didn't want to answer. But his response was startling in his directness.

'Dad was indeed working for the CIA. Not as a direct operative in their employ, but as a man whom they could mine for information thanks to all his contacts in Chile, and who saved Peter from certain death.'

'Dad and Peter were there, by my side, at the hospital in Dublin. When I asked him later, Peter indicated things were reasonable between them.'

'You want the truth?'

'Absolutely.'

'Outside of the time at your bedside – and when they were dealing with the police and the Embassy and the Irish government officials – they didn't utter a word to each other. Dad told me that he offered to take Peter out to dinner on a couple of occasions, but he refused. Just as Peter told me that, as soon as they were away from the hospital after seeing you together, they got into an almighty argument about who did what down there, and Dad started accusing him of being a "guy who went to the revolution just to get laid". I gather that Peter started screaming at him in the street, calling him a murderer. Two cops were nearby and actually got between them before they started swinging at each other.'

'Jesus fuck,' I said. 'I had no idea ... '

'Well, after what you'd been through they didn't want to do crazy shit in front of you. I feel bad about bringing this up with you now – but you did ask. You might as well know the truth.'

'But what's the truth here? Dad's version of things, Peter's version, or your own retelling of the story?'

'There's no right or wrong here. Everyone plays fast and loose with the past.'

'My God, Adam – that's elegant.'

'I'm someone who just got tired of living behind many lies.'

'Such as?'

'Please don't push me, sis.'

'Okay, I won't ... as long as you stop calling me "sis".'

That was the last time that any enigmatic mention of past lives was mentioned. Adam never pressed me further on anything – though he was always there to help when I reached out for him. Like collecting the rest of my stuff.

'Wow, your brother is not what I expected,' Patricia said after Adam spent an awkward half an hour with us, accepting a Löwenbräu from Duncan, taking in the bohemian vibe of his apartment and the way that Patricia was dressed only in a leop-ard-skin bra and a rather minuscule pair of shorts. He also turned down the bong that Duncan offered him and so did I (I knew from past experience that Adam was very uncomfort-able with anything to do with drugs). He beat a hasty retreat shortly thereafter, at which point Patricia dropped that com-ment, also noting that:

'Why is it that all the Republican men I've ever met seem to wear the same sort of light blue button-down shirt and khakis and those fucking Topsider moccasins?'

'Decades of sartorial indoctrination,' Duncan said.

'He's still kind of sweet – for a Brooks Brothers stiff.'

'Don't call him that,' I said. 'His style may be a little conservative, but he's got a good heart.'

'Duncan was saying that it's your other brother who's the cool guy.'

'Peter is cool and complicated.'

'Sounds like just my type,' Patricia said, giving Duncan a mocking smile.

'I'm complex, not complicated,' Duncan said.

'Nuances will get you nowhere,' Patricia said.

I found myself choking back a sob. Immediately all eyes were on me.

'Did I say something wrong?' Patricia asked.

I shook my head. I wiped my eyes. I indicated I would love another beer. Duncan moved quickly to the old icebox and pulled out a fresh bottle of Löwenbräu. I thanked him and drained half the bottle in one go. On a mercilessly hot summer day in New York, in an apartment with only an old floor fan for ventilation, and one of those now-constant waves of emotional distress rolling right over me, a very cold beer seemed like the only good antidote to so much dark stuff that, in my more lucid moments, I knew was out of my control. I had also begun to understand that, when the grief broadsided me, it was best not to fight it, even if I was in front of people. Which is why, after the second slug of beer, I began to sob, accepting Patricia's arms around me and the way she held me tight as I buried my head into her right shoulder while my crying raged forth. When I subsided I sank back into the sofa, wiped my eyes with my fingers, downed the rest of the beer, and then heard myself saying things that, up until now, I had kept entirely to myself.

'The blast blew his head off. That was the first thing I saw when I staggered out of the shop, my back all cut up. I walked right into it. Ciaran's head. There at my feet, staring up at me, his eyes wide, his mouth agape, as the flying metal that decapitated him caught the monstrous surprise that ended his life in one explosive flash. I remember screaming. Crazy shrieks. Sounds I never knew I had within me. I fell to my knees, unable to take my eyes off his head. The head of the man I loved, with whom I thought I would build a life. I lost all track of time. I heard sirens. I heard people running toward me. Two big firemen literally picked me up, wrapping me in a blanket, handing me over to two ambulance men. A car nearby, already on fire, exploded into flames. They had to put me face down on a stretcher, my back was so full of glass shards. My screaming intensified. I kept screaming Ciaran's name, saying they had to bring him to me, that we couldn't leave him behind, that ...

'The next thing I knew one of the ambulance men was speaking in a quiet voice to me, explaining that I was suffering from an extreme form of shock, that I had suffered severe lacerations to my back, that he was going to give me something to help me sleep. That's when I felt the dab of something wet on my arm, followed by a fast jab of a needle. Moments later the lights went out.

'When I came to again, I was in a narrow hospital bed, in a ward with about ten other women, a smell of disinfectant and bad food everywhere, the nurses on duty all nuns and largely grim. I was aware that I was lying face down, and that when I moved it was as if all the glass in my back was digging deeper into me. I started to howl. Two nuns were immediately on the scene. The older woman – Sister Mary – was kindness itself, telling me her name, calling me Alice, saying that I was going to be fine, that all the glass had been removed and the pain was just the after-effects of all the stitches that were holding me together, and ...

'I started to howl again, my ears in damaged agony. That's when I made the acquaintance of the younger nun, Sister Agnes. In the movies it's always the older nun who's the bitch and the novice who is still nice, still not all bitter and twisted by all those decades of celibacy and damp convent walls. But at the Mater Hospital in Dublin the roles were reversed, and Sister Agnes showed herself to be an authoritarian who was not going to accept the hysteria of some stupid young American who got herself caught up in a fucking bomb blast. When my screaming went off the charts she grabbed my arm and twisted it, telling me:

'"Now, Alice, we're having none of that. You have to stop this madness right now."

'That escalated my hysteria even more. I heard Sister Mary ask Sister Agnes:

'"Let me handle this please."

'"I'm giving you a minute to get her quiet, otherwise I will take things into my own hands."

'But when I couldn't stop screaming Sister Agnes came back, hypodermic needle in hand.

'"We don't like knocking out our patients, but you give me little choice."

'That's when the needle went in and the world blacked out. When I finally came to the world was completely out of focus. There was a young doctor in front of me. It took me many minutes to discern his face. A soft country accent. He quietly explained that he was Dr Ryan, and that I had been in and out of consciousness for the past thirty-six hours – as it had been decided that, though my injuries weren't life-threatening and I was going to recover from them all, the trauma necessitated that I was "kept quiet for bit". The drugs they gave me did their job. I was in a deep fog – and over the next few days they gradually reduced my intake of tranquilizers – I'm sure that's what they were – so I could be interviewed by the cops, by staff from the Embassy, and spend time with my father and brother Peter.

'Dad was actually wonderful. It turned out that he'd flown the Atlantic the day after the bombing – almost immediately after the Embassy contacted him – and (as I found out later) barred my mother from coming, knowing full well she'd make things ten times worse when she showed up. He also contacted my brother in Paris – even though they were estranged from each other ... I'm not talking about all that today – and told him what had happened. Peter also jumped on a plane. When I finally came around from the drugs there were my father and brother at my bedside. That was fantastic. There are moments when you really need family ... even one as nuts as my own. Dad and Peter put on a great public front, not once showing me the enmity they have for each other, and Dad telling me that he was going to do everything in his power to help put this all behind me, which, in my still-druggy haze, sounded great, even though I knew it to be bullshit. I could still tell that, though he was being very

346

take-charge – meeting with the authorities, organizing that I get flown back to the States as soon as possible – he couldn't handle the awfulness of what I'd gone through. But he displaced all that by keeping busy, issuing orders, being the expert businessman I always sensed him to be.

'Peter, for his part, stayed with me, held me when I was crying, reassured me when I felt myself all over the place, and even convinced my dad to get the doctors to rid me of Sister Agnes. Through my druggy haze I heard Dad blow up at Dr Ryan, telling him that he would not stand for his daughter being kept in a medically induced fog because "some little bitch of a nun can't deal with raw emotion".' That got the doctor's attention. Not only did I get moved to a private room, but Sister Agnes disappeared from my life and Dr Ryan must have made at least four bedside visits a day to ensure that I was okay. Which I was anything but ...

'Then Ciaran's parents came to see me. Ciaran was their only child; their adored son. To say that they were heartbroken by his death, his murder ... that was total understatement. They were beyond devastated. His mother Anne looked like she'd aged ten years. And his father John ... it was as if his entire reason to live had been taken away from him. When they first walked into my hospital room ... '

I lowered my head, my voice suddenly shaky, unable to go on. Tears began to well up. I found that low, internal scream building up in the back of my throat. I did something that had become almost automatic since returning to the States – biting down on a finger until it truly hurt in order to keep the scream at bay. Patricia put her arms around me, but I kept biting down on my finger until it bled. When I pulled it away Duncan went scurrying off to find antiseptic and a Band-Aid. As he staunched the flow of blood from my finger, I started talking again – telling him that, in a bad moment with my mother just a few days earlier, I'd threatened to kill myself – after which she'd gone and flushed down the toilet all the pills that had been prescribed to me in Dublin, and told me that if I had one more outburst at her – I'd taken to screaming at her all the time whenever she got nasty with me – she would have me institutionalized. Then she tried to turn Dr Feelgood on me.

'Which is when I packed a bag and ran here.'

'Well, there's nothing she can do when it comes to touching you now,' Patricia said. 'I mean, you're twenty, right?'

I nodded.

'That makes you an adult. And your brother Adam can vouch for you if she tries to send for the men in white coats. Trust me, we won't let those fuckers through the door here if they show up.'

But nobody ever showed up. Adam dropped by every two days, telling me that he'd gotten Dad onside, calling him down in Chile and filling him in on Mom's craziness and threats, as well as bringing him up to date on my plans to transfer to the University of Vermont. Showing up at the apartment one evening, with a couple of takeout hero sandwiches from a local Italian deli and a six-pack of Carling Black Label, Adam informed me that our father was very pleased to hear I was going back to school and would cover everything. Just as Dad also wanted to remind me that there was the $10,000 emergency payment – which he'd negotiated with some civil servant in Dublin who'd been assigned to my case – on deposit in the Chase Manhattan Bank on East 42nd Street in case I wanted to buy a second-hand car or anything else.

'About the last thing I can see myself doing right now is getting behind the wheel of a car,' I told Adam. 'Because my inclination right now is to drive at around eighty miles per hour into the nearest wall.'

Adam's eyes went wide.

'Did I say the wrong thing?' I asked, my voice reasonableness itself.

I looked over and saw Adam, his face cast downward, brimming with tears. I reached for him, clasping him hard on the arm.

'I'm sorry ... ' I said.

'I want to help you,' he whispered. 'And I can't.'

'You're helping me.'

'Don't lie to me. I can't help anyone. Dad's right: I'm useless.'

'What's that old saying about how being comforted by someone else's distress somehow lessens your own? ... for an hour or so anyway. You are anything but useless. Don't listen to our father. He likes to pick on you.'

'If I drive you to Burlington, will you go to the college nurse as soon as we get there?'

I knew I had to say yes. Because maybe, just maybe, it might make my poor lonely brother – a man I still didn't know or fully understand – feel that little bit less useless; make him believe that he'd actually won a point for a change ... something he'd done little of since giving up his golden sport of hockey.

'Okay – I will go to the nurse.'

On the day after we reached Burlington – we were both crashing at Rachel's place (Adam finding our hostess just a little too 'space cadet' for his comfort zone) – I did present myself at the college infirmary, explaining I was a transfer student about to start class next week. When I told the nurse what had happened to me a few months back, and talked about the insomnia that had been keeping me awake twenty-two hours a day, and – at the nurse's insistence – took off my shirt and showed her the scars on my back, she assumed charge of me. Picking up the phone she called a certain Dr Gellhorn. She agreed to see me that afternoon. Adam drove me to her office. I was with her for well over an hour. By the time I left she had set up appointments with other specialists and had sent me to the pharmacy with two prescriptions to aid the sleeplessness and panic attacks. As I left her office Adam smiled tightly and asked:

'How did it go?'

'She gave me the worst news possible.'

That stopped Adam in his tracks.

'The worst news possible?' he said, stunned. 'What did she tell you?'

'She told me: I'm going to live.'

21

THINGS CAN ACTUALLY fall into place at times of duress. As extreme and weird as you might feel, there can be another part of you which is very determined, whatever the costs, to somehow get through the next sixteen waking hours.

The first time I went back to Dr Gellhorn, she asked me if I was sleeping. I told her that the pills she'd prescribed did the trick – I was virtually knocked out. But when I awoke in the morning it often felt as if my head was like static on a television which didn't have one of those rabbit-eared antennas. She shook her head, 'That doesn't sound good, Alice,' and said she'd like me to try a newfangled drug, Valium, which was a benzodiazepine, and which could be used for sleep and anxiety. Like all such new drugs it was going to be a 'trial and error' introduction.

Part of me wanted to say 'Fuck it' and not go near any further drugs – because even though I appreciated the sleep and the way that Darvon blanketed me in a thick strange cloud of disconnection, I was now a full-time student, taking five courses this first term, and finding my concentration often playing games with me. But the Valium was most effective at night – sending me into a deep sleep and only leaving me half as fogged as the previous medication. Two cups of coffee and a jog would banish most of the murk from my head. But I didn't like the 'mother's little helper' feel of the Valium during the day. So, with Dr Gellhorn's approval, I only reached for a pill in waking hours whenever I felt myself getting rather shaky.

Grief has its own strange trajectory. You think you are having an okay day, okay being something of a triumph for me, then the glimpse of a couple my age holding hands while walking across the quad, or the sound of a car backfiring, or the sight of a certain shade of dark green that put me in mind of that beat-up tweed jacket Ciaran loved wearing (and actually had on when he died) ... a small trigger like that would suddenly send me into a sort of downward swoon which the Valium helped reduce, but which still served as a reminder: *None of this is going to vanish tomorrow. It's part of you now. And it will always be there.*

Dr Gellhorn never suggested that I should talk to someone about any of the internal anguish. Up here in Vermont, a brisk walk along the banks of Lake Champlain was considered the best medicine for psychological distress – and Gellhorn seriously approved of me going out for a daily jog. I even invested seventy-five dollars in a new Schwinn racing bike with five amazing gears. It was Rachel who quietly assumed the role of my big sister, who convinced me to treat myself to the Schwinn bike, as it was Rachel who helped find me a studio apartment in a small apartment building downtown. It suited me fine. It looked over a back alleyway, so it didn't get much in the way of light. But it did have a distinctive retro charm to it and the rent was cheap. I took it. Outside of buying sheets and towels and some basic kitchen stuff I changed nothing in it, putting nothing up on the walls, purchasing a narrow five-tier bookshelf at a junk shop which was completely brimming with books by the time Christmas came.

Holding down five classes required a lot of reading, a good excuse not to have to integrate myself into the life of the college. My class-mates were friendly, a bright and engaged bunch, and I was often invited for coffee, a beer, a party at the weekend. I always politely answered that I had too much going on right now. I tried to keep a low profile, dodging any mention of, or response to, 'the inci-dent'. Maybe it was something to do with not wanting to allow others to partake in my distress. How could I explain that the man I wanted to spend my life with was now deep under ever-damp Ulster ground ... and yet his face loomed everywhere I turned?

Indeed, when one of my literature professors, Jane Sylvester, an Anglo-transplant who wore sensible tweed skirts and fisherman's sweaters, mentioned that she was 'fully aware of the trauma you have been coping with', I snapped back:

'Was a mimeographed memo sent around telling everyone "care-ful, we have an unhinged bomb-blast survivor among us"?'

Professor Sylvester indicated that she had found out this infor-mation from Rachel, as 'I have terrible flat feet and she is the best reflexologist in the area'. I too had succumbed to Rachel's kneading talents and had taken her up on an offer of three reflexology sessions per week at a kindly reduced fee. During my next one, as I accepted her usual welcoming hug and unlaced my boots and removed my socks, I asked her, quietly and with no anger in my voice, to please not talk about my war wounds in public again. She was a touch defensive.

'But I thought your professors would have known all about that,' she said.

'I hardly put it on my college transcript when rushing in my application.'

As she began massaging my feet, searching for the pressure points and entrapments of tension, I relaxed, shutting my eyes. I tried to zone out, hating myself for being even the least bit prickly toward the one friend I had in Burlington. And I had to wonder, given that Burlington was such a small place, just how much everyone else knew about me. Rachel must have been reading my mind as her fingers worked deeper into my feet.

'It doesn't really matter who knows or doesn't know. What you need to *absorb*, Alice, is the fact that what happened to you in Dublin is now part of your being. You will have to accept this – and the changes it has brought to your very essence. It is a big psychic shift – and one which will take you time to integrate into your way of looking at the world. But as horrible as what happened to you is – and to that man you loved so deeply – the other amazing aspect of this tragedy is: you were spared. You got to walk away. You were allowed to continue the gift of life. No, I don't believe in divine intervention, the "hand of God" and all that stuff. But I do believe in karma, in forces in the universe that come to our aid at a certain moment. Something karmic saved you, Alice. You might dismiss that as a bunch of nonsense. But I know that some force decided: *she is not ready to go, she still has work to do, things to contribute. She deserves more time.*'

I pulled away my feet.

'Are you therefore saying, by implication, that Ciaran was ready to go, that these "karmic forces" you are talking about decided he's better off dead?'

'Hardly. But what I do know is that karma can genuinely shield you. Yours did just that.'

'But it didn't shield the man I loved.'

'We are all called at a certain moment to the world beyond – and it is hard to say what triggers that departure, what keeps us here.'

'Apologies – but I actually think you're talking horseshit,' I said, grabbing my socks and walking boots. 'Do you have any fucking idea what's involved when it comes to getting myself through the fucking day?'

Rachel took my right foot in her hand again. Even though I tried to shake it free she held firm and recommended her reflexology. She was a lot more forceful than I imagined and bore down on the area just below the toes with a pressure that made me wince, but simultaneously unblocked a considerable amount of gathered tension. I was more than a little surprised by this – especially as it left me feeling somewhat flighty, as if I'd just drunk two glasses of wine.

'I'm such a bitch,' I said, after Rachel finished both feet and I was experiencing a strange lightheadedness.

'You are what you have experienced,' she said. 'Maybe now you will start looking forward in a different way. I want you now to come back here every other day so I can work on you some more. Just as I also want you to get as much exercise and fresh air as you can tolerate. You need to be doing things that are positive for yourself, and that will help you sidestep negative energy.'

I kept my eyes shut. I said:

'Please forgive me.'

'There is no need to ask for forgiveness from me. Ask it from yourself.'

As hippie-dippy and cosmic as Rachel could be, that statement took hold in my consciousness and served as a sort of positive nag whenever the self-blame game started, and when I began to feel overwhelmed by all the negative forces swirling within me. I also allowed her to talk me into two-weekly yoga classes. I occasionally accepted her offer of dinner at her place, usually in the company of many of her like-minded friends, most of whom would talk at great length – as the days turned darker and the temperature began to head downward – of the imminent fall of Saigon, and the disgrace of Ford allowing Nixon to escape criminal prosecution, and did anyone hear about this rather cool, if somewhat Christian, governor of Georgia named Carter who was an actual progressive and someone outside of the Washington power axis?

I went along to these episodic dinners. I joined a running club and spent most Saturdays jogging in a group of ten along the bike path next to Lake Champlain. I remained responsive and engaged in all my classes. I continued to have my weekly visits with Fred the Hearing Aid Guy, whose auditory aids had made things less clouded. I also saw Dr Gellhorn once a month. I maintained a veneer of sociability – while simultaneously ensuring a polite distance from all other interactions. I spent almost all evenings alone. I worked late in the university library. I was in bed most weeknights by 10 p.m., as my classes usually started at eight the next morning. I gave myself Saturdays off to go running with the group, hunt down books in assorted literary emporiums downtown, shop for food, maybe see an interesting movie or drop into one of the folk clubs and hear someone sing songs of protest or the road to despair. I always bought the Sunday *New York Times* and made myself a proper brunch and tried to go for a long bike ride ... until the snow arrived. I pushed myself hard on the academic front, as I was determined to have all my credits for graduation by the end of the summer term 1975. I had no contact whatsoever with my mother – which was a blessing – and just the occasional call from Dad. In addition to paying my tuition and forwarding me two hundred dollars a month to cover my rent and food, he'd gotten into the habit of sticking a fifty-dollar bill into an envelope and mailing it to me every four weeks. Our calls were brief.

'How you doing, sweetheart?'

Dad really didn't want to know the difficult internal landscape I was traversing, any more than he was at all interested in much to do with my life. He was now spending almost seven months a year in Chile. When he was stateside he'd taken to staying in a big old hotel, the Roosevelt, not far from his company's offices near Grand Central Station.

'Why aren't you coming home for Christmas?' he asked me.

'Why do you think?'

'All right, I know she acted badly –'

'Let's not go there, Dad.'

'All I'm saying is: I will be there, Adam will be there, you can come on Christmas Eve and leave the 26th. To sweeten the offer, I'll even arrange for you to have a room at the Roosevelt from December 26 until New Year's Day. Just think about that – an entire week on me in Manhattan.'

'I don't want to leave Burlington.'

'But you'll be all by yourself.'

'I can handle that.'

'No one can handle Christmas alone.'

'I appreciate the kindness, Dad. But I just can't face any compassion right now. No warmth, no decency. I just need –'

I broke off, unable to finish the sentence. Dad understood.

'No worries, sweetheart,' he said. 'I get it.'

On Christmas Eve, a guy from Western Union knocked on the door. Fresh snow had fallen overnight. The world outside my front door was bleached clean of all impurities – for a few hours anyway. The Western Union man handed me a telegram. I opened it up on the spot.

Just wired you $500 to Western Union Burlington. Wish you were here – but you're smart not to be. Merry Christmas – Dad

I asked the Western Union guy where the downtown office was. He said it was just off Main Street – but I needed to get there before eleven this morning, as they were closing early for the holidays. I was showered and dressed and standing in line with my driver's license by nine fifteen, watching the cashier count out twenty-five $20 notes. I'd been invited over to Rachel's and to Professor Sylvester's house for Christmas Eve and Christmas lunch respectively. Patricia and Duncan also told me I was most welcome to spend the holidays in their Manhattan alcove. I knew I couldn't handle the enforced bonhomie of the season, let alone having to socialize. But I did stop in a wine store and buy a bottle of Asti Spumante and a gift bag, and walked over and put it next to Rachel's door with a note.

Christmas cheer for you. I need to pass the 'festive season' outside of festivities. You are a great friend. My feet thank you too.

Love, Alice

Then, fearing that the wine might freeze in the cold, I rang the doorbell and moved off quickly before Rachel could get sight of me.

After that I bought food and two more bottles of wine, and picked up the new Joni Mitchell album, *Miles of Aisles*, deciding that would be my Christmas present to myself. I counted out my money – I still had $478 left over. I made the bank just before it closed, holding on to $48 – which was enough to cover the next two weeks of life – and deposited the rest in my account. The $10,000 emergency payment still remained untouched. I couldn't bear to use it – and had written a few weeks before to Ciaran's parents offering them the entire sum. I had expressed everything I felt for him; that I had known early on in our relationship that their son was the love of my life and I wondered if I would ever get beyond the pain. I wrote how they were the most wonderful people, an example of what being good parents meant; how I could only begin to imagine the immensity of what they were going through, and I wanted them to have the payoff I'd been given for my injuries in the bombing.

It took some time for John's reply to reach me. It was typewritten. I read it once, then put it away and could not look at it again. It was just too sad.

Dear Alice

I don't get out much these days. Neither of us do. The BBC gave Anne compassionate leave for six months. I finished my last lecture for the term on the day that Ciaran was killed – so outside of grading exams I have not had to face students, and I too have been granted the Michaelmas term off by the university.

To say that your letter touched me and Anne would be to engage in understatement. We both had one of those crying jags that overtake us regularly – and from which little good comes, bar the fact that the next few hours afterwards are a little more tolerable. Maybe that's the process of grief – gradually reaching an accommodation with the horror of it all. But that point of acceptance is still far in the distance. And every day still has its attendant agonies.

Know that we both think the world of you – and had such great hopes for Ciaran's future with you. Your offer of the money is beyond generous – but we want you to keep it for yourself. You have your whole life in front of you – and we both sense you have the strength and rigour within you to get somehow beyond all this. You must use these funds to do something truly interesting and also somehow celebratory. Life is so fragile, so tenuous. Grab it all. Ciaran would want nothing less for you than as interesting a life as you can make for yourself.

Please know that you are constantly in our thoughts. I hope, one day, when the moment is better, we can see each other and no doubt cry about what could have been, but do so without the agony that is still a component of every waking moment.

Courage to you, and love from us both.

John

On Christmas Eve I checked my watch around five and thought it must be 10 p.m. in Belfast. How could they even face the thought of Christmas and all its attendant memories of their boy wide-eyed in front of a glowing tree, laden with presents when he was 'but a wee thing'? I wanted to pick up the phone and call the operator and book a long-distance call to their house in Belfast. I feared that I wouldn't be able to cope with their anguish given the depth of my own. But after a small shot of Black Bush – Ciaran's preferred whiskey; I had a bottle tucked away in the back of a kitchen cabinet – I opened my address book and dialed '0' on the phone and gave the woman who answered the very long number for the transatlantic call. It took about a minute for the connection to be made. After six long rings the phone was answered.

'Yes?'

Anne's voice. Hushed. Broken.

'It's me, Alice.'

She began to sob – and did so for a long time. Eventually I heard John's voice behind her, Anne trying to explain to him that it was me, but unable to finish the sentence. John then came on the line.

'Alice ... you brave wee girl, calling us tonight.'

'I'm sorry. I shouldn't have ... '

'No – this is so wonderful of you. But ... '

He broke off, unable to continue. I could hear him trying to hold back a sob. There was a long terrible silence. Then:

'Bless you, Alice.'

And the call ended.

I sat in my armchair for a very long time afterwards, tears rolling down my face, wondering: will the grief ever end? Will John and Anne ever be able to get beyond it? Will it shadow my life forever?

I phoned home on Christmas Day, expecting Mom to go all cold on me, reproaching me further for my absence. But she behaved as if all was well between us, calling me darling, telling me how much I was missed today, how she hoped I was having a lovely 'solo' Christmas, and how maybe she could entice me down to New York for a weekend soon.

Dad got on briefly. I thanked him for the money. I assured him that I was in a good place. He handed me over to Adam, who was surprisingly upbeat – telling me that he had some 'nice news': he was going to become the new varsity hockey coach at the Rye Country Day School, a rather good preppy academy that was an easy twenty-minute drive from his apartment in White Plains.

'Wow, that is a change of career,' I said.

'I decided to take some time away from the business world,' he said, his voice low. 'It was my old coach at St Lawrence who recommended me for the job – after I contacted him, saying I was thinking of giving something back to society.'

Was coaching a bunch of aggressive prep-school boys in one of the most aggressive of team sports 'giving something back to society'? I decided not to pose that question. All I said was:

'That's very good of you.'

At six that night the phone rang and I found myself talking with Peter. He was in the one all-night phone exchange in Paris. He sounded a little tipsy.

'Guess what I did around five hours ago?' he asked after the transatlantic operator put us through.

'You just got drunk with Simone de Beauvoir?'

'In my dreams. But I did finish the first draft of my book.'

'On Chile?'

'Yes – and I am saying no more.'

'And I am asking for no details. But hey, congrats. That is quite the achievement.'

'Don't say that until you've read it. It could be a disaster.'

'I'm glad to see that, like me, you are sidestepping holiday cheer.'

'Can you blame me?' Peter said.

'Hardly. I just spoke to Mom. She's still puzzled as to why I won't go home. And Adam is giving up the corporate world to coach hockey at a prep school. Where there won't be the possibilities of participating in a *coup d'état.*'

'Just inter-collegiate violence on ice,' Peter said. 'Which was something he was good at.'

'Adam was a thug as a hockey player?'

'You can't play that sport well without being a thug. And that thuggish underpinning is something that you carry with you thereafter into all future endeavors. He's more complicated than he lets on.'

'And when it comes to you, Peter – you are one of life's complicated good guys. And I speak as a rather complicated sort myself.'

'Why don't you jump on a plane and spend the rest of the holidays here? You're not back in school for, what, another two weeks?'

'But coming to Paris would mean having to put on a brave face. That's beyond my talents right now. I am preparing for the next semester – my goal being to be finished with college by the end of summer. And you? Now that you've finished the great *American in Chile* memoir ... ?'

'I've got an introduction to a literary agent in New York. After I polish the manuscript and retype the whole damn thing, off it goes in an envelope to Manhattan. The hope is: he can sell it to a publisher. But as they say over here: *on verra*. We'll see. To supplement what little funds I have here I've been teaching English privately. As soon as the book is dispatched to New York I am buying myself a one-way ticket to India.'

'Searching spiritual enlightenment?'

'Or maybe forestalling the moment when I have to think about actually earning a living, and what I might want to do next.'

'But if the book gets published ... '

'Yes, that might start to change everything. But it's a big "If".'

'Christmas in Paris. Lucky boy. You with somebody?'

'Tangentially. I can't do anything beyond casual right now. And you? How bad is today?'

'Bad, but I am coping. Good to hear your voice, Big Brother.'

Christmas was over a few hours later. I ate a quiche Lorraine, a salad, downed two glasses of wine. I waited the medically stipulated three hours between the two permitted glasses a day and the moment I could take my sleeping pills. I got into bed. I pulled the covers over my head. I gave a small prayer of thanks for having gotten through this most emotionally raw of all holidays, saying goodbye to a year I wanted to forget without the forced cheer and specious optimism of a New Year's Eve party.

In the months that followed I continued to keep very much to myself – but to contribute in an engaged fashion to all my classes. Carrying five courses meant nonstop work. But nonstop work – punctuated by jogging, bike riding, and Rachel's reflexology sessions – also kept the traumatic shadows at bay.

During the winter I received a weekly postcard from Peter. The first – from Paris – informed me that he was about to board a flight that night to Bombay. After that I found myself, almost every week, looking at some glossy image from an exotic address: Bombay, Bangalore, Delhi, Rishikesh, Shimla, Colombo. And during the last big snowfall of the season – on the day of Fools – I found myself staring at a photo of Annapurna, a date mark of Kathmandu, and the following message:

Climbing this unclimbable mountain is beyond me. But I did manage to get an agent – and my book's been bought by Little, Brown! Hope you are reasonable. Back in mid-June.

Love, Peter

My God, this was such good news. I called Adam that night at his apartment. I hesitated in telling him about Peter's excellent turn of events, but also thought: he would not want to find out third-hand. He didn't sound over the moon about our brother's triumph.

'Do you know what it's about?'

'He didn't tell me the content.'

'But the subject is Chile, right?'

'Yes.'

A long silence. Then Adam said:

'Don't tell Dad.'

'Trust me, I won't.'

Especially as I only heard from him every month or so, and I decided to avoid talking with Mom by sending her a letter every ten days, filled with simple news about my work, my studies, what I was reading, my fitness regime. She, in turn, sent back equally banal and neutral missives, talking about her volunteer work, political matters, and how she was so pleased to have this correspondence with me. We were in touch, but at a distance – and that suited us both just fine.

Then it was spring – the final snow absorbed into the earth by mid-April. In mid-May I handed in my final papers and took my last exams. In early June I got a call from Dad – who, being the one who paid my tuition, also received my grades. I did fine, set on a trajectory of graduating in the summer.

'Are you really going to finish college this summer?' Dad asked.

'That's the idea.'

'And then … ?'

'I've got some thoughts.'

'Do you have any thoughts about Peter's book?'

I felt myself involuntarily flinch. I sucked in my breath. I told myself: play dumb here.

'What book? This is news to me, Dad. Did Peter call you from India?'

'Hardly … and I know you're bullshitting me.'

'Who told you then?'

'Who do you think?'

'Mom?'

'Guess again.'

Don't tell Dad. Oh, Adam, I thought, why are you always caving in to that man? Especially when you have it in you to do what the rest of us do: lie. Or just keep your mouth shut.

'I really don't know anything about this, Dad.'

'Sure you don't. Congrats again on the grades.'

The line went dead.

That was the last I heard from my dad for many weeks. I had ten days off between my exams and the start of the summer semester. Duncan and Patricia invited me down to Manhattan. God knows there was a big part of me that wanted ten straight days of big-city life and museums and theaters and jazz clubs. But I also feared some sort of retreat back into the shell-shocked mental cave I found myself last summer. When I checked in with Dr Gellhorn for my monthly appointment and told her that I was fearful of stepping outside the quiet, safe confines of Burlington for the time being, her response was clinical and direct:

'New York can wait for you. Stay put until you are ready to venture elsewhere.'

I did just that. Burlington suited me. Bigger than a town, with enough culture and intelligence and good talk to make it feel like a city. I loved the lake. I loved the encroaching mountains. I loved its left-wing politics, its desire to create a proper social democracy, and the fact that even the Republicans in the state were believers in the common good. And l loved the fact that I had no one here close to me, that I could keep everyone at bay.

Until, that is, one night when, just before the witching hour, the phone rang. I was already in bed, awaiting the sleeping pills to do their magic, so I ignored the first long bank of rings. Eventually they stopped ... only to start again two minutes later. This time I had no choice but to stagger out of bed and over to the phone on the wall of my kitchenette. As soon as I picked it up I heard my mother's voice.

'I knew you were there. Why didn't you pick up the first time?'

'Because I was in bed. Because it's late. Why are you calling now?'

'Because I am in my new apartment in Manhattan.'

'You're *where?*'

'My new apartment. On 74th Street and Third Avenue.'

'How long have you been there?' I said, not certain if I was hearing all this correctly.

'About thirty-six hours. I moved out of the house yesterday.'

'Why?'

'Why do you think? I decided to finally end my marriage. It only took me twenty-nine years ... but here I am, a single woman again.'

22

THE APARTMENT THAT Mom had rented was opposite a famous singles bar, J.G. Melon. Mom pointed this out to me on the weekend I came down to visit her. I decided to stay at Duncan's place. The very fact that I rushed down to see her the weekend after her call surprised her – but it surprised me even more. Her behavior after my return from Ireland had me vowing to keep her far away from me. I'd made good on that vow. It had been over a year since we'd been face-to-face. But upon hearing her astonishing news – the fact that she had finally walked out of a marriage that had rendered both my parents distressed for decades – I knew I had to put my eyes on her and see what had transpired to bring about this momentous decision.

So I called Duncan and booked my place on the futon in his alcove, arriving the night before my rendezvous with Mom. It had been almost ten months since I had been in the city. It was one of those early-summer days when the mercury was punching three figures and the humidity nearing the same intolerable digits. The sidewalks were molten. Five minutes on a subway left you feeling like you'd just done time in one of those Turkish baths that could still be found on many street corners along the Lower East Side.

Duncan was in exultant form when I walked in. After almost a year as an editorial assistant at *Esquire*, during which he'd been consistently pushing the editor-in-chief for a proper assignment – a big 'new journalism' story that would hopefully launch his career – he'd landed, just today, what he called 'a biggie'. It was a profile/interview with E. Howard Hunt, the ex-CIA officer turned Nixon White House 'plumber' (as the former president's henchmen were called) who had been found guilty of assorted Watergate crimes and misdemeanors. He was several weeks into a thirty-three-month sentence in a minimum-security prison in Florida, and had agreed to an in-depth profile by one of the most prestigious and ballsy of American magazines. Duncan would be heading down to Florida

364

in a week's time to begin what would hopefully be the first of four extended conversations with Hunt in prison. Before then, he'd be living for the next seven days in the microfilm and periodicals room of the New York Public Library on East 42nd Street, going through every possible printed word on the wild, crazy ride that was the career of this Ivy League spook turned political felon.

'If I nail this piece, the future is wide open – and I can start writing my own journalistic ticket.'

Patricia, though pleased for Duncan, was nonetheless just a little mocking about her fellow's triumph.

'Now watch him turn into Norman Mailer and buy into all that high-gloss literary New York bullshit. The other night we were in Elaine's and monsieur here was so disappointed when we were sent to a table near the men's room, and George Plimpton simply smiled pleasantly and blanked him when he tried to engage him in conversation at the bar.'

Duncan flinched, looking very much taken aback by this verbal poke in the eye. I glanced over at Patricia. She had a discernibly malignant smile on her face. I decided to step in – but in a somewhat indirect manner.

'How's the painting going, Patricia?'

'Trying to change the subject, Alice?' she asked.

'I am indeed.'

'Why, exactly?'

'Well, since you've asked me directly, I'll give it to you directly: what you just said to Duncan was borderline cruel. Coming on the heels of his very good news it's made me wonder: are you trying to piss on his parade?'

Patricia didn't like this at all – but I saw her stop herself from blurting out something damaging. Instead she put on her most reasonable tone of voice.

'You're taking me far too literally. Isn't that right, Duncan?'

'Yeah, of course.'

'It's great news,' she said, then quickly gave him a very full kiss on the mouth. 'My guy: the future Great American Writer.'

'Don't get ahead of yourself now,' Duncan said.

Patricia had to go off to a dance rehearsal shortly thereafter, and
I offered to take Duncan out for a celebration dinner – as a way of
also thanking him for putting me up. I chose a restaurant all the
way downtown, off Irving Place: Pete's Tavern. It billed itself as New
York's oldest extant tavern, as it dated back to 1864. Its interior was
all wood and beer taps, with a small dining room in the back. The
cuisine was New York Italian. There were better places in town for
spaghetti with meatballs. But I liked going there for sentimental reasons. When I was a kid growing up in Manhattan, it was the place
my dad brought me to for special father/daughter Sunday-night
suppers.

'Now I might not be a shrink,' Duncan said on the subway
downtown, 'but even from my still-limited understanding of
human nature I know that you're making some sort of point about
eating in the place you most associate with you and your father –
appropriately enough on the night before you see the mother, from
whom you've been alienated, and who has just walked out on your
father.'

'Guilty as charged.'

'No need to feel guilty. It's just further proof – as if proof is needed
– that we are all so damn conflicted.'

When we reached Irving Place, Duncan took in the wonderful
brownstones, the locked gates of Gramercy Park, the smell of old
New York money, noting:

'Living uptown in Jungleland and working in midtown I forget
that there are still a few parts of the city which are pure Edith Wharton.'

Once we were seated I asked him if Patricia was still maintaining
her apartment in Hell's Kitchen.

'She's sublet it, and is therefore calling my place "our own". She'd
like us to find a bigger place together.'

'Would you like that?

'Am I discerning a hesitancy in you about her?'

'Listen, she couldn't have been nicer to me when I fled to your
place and you took me in. But I am always a little concerned by
someone who gets competitive with their lover when success comes

his or her way. I am your friend. I don't like seeing you put down. Especially by someone who is clearly frustrated by her inability to get beyond the paint shop at the Metropolitan Opera – not that I would call it a bad job at all.'

Duncan stared down at the red-check tablecloth.

'She's pregnant,' he whispered.

I blinked in shock.

'Oh fuck,' I whispered back, countering it immediately with: 'Unless, of course, you're happy with the news.'

'It's about the last thing I want.'

'Then how did it happen?'

'How do you think?'

'Surely she was on the pill, using a diaphragm, some form of birth control.'

'So I thought.'

'In other words: she tricked you.'

Duncan shrugged.

'Has she had the pregnancy medically confirmed?'

'She told me she did one of those home tests.'

'They're pretty new on the market. Were you there when she did the test?'

'What are you trying to imply here?'

'Even if she is pregnant you aren't morally obliged to have a life with her. You will have to support the child. But –'

'Can we get some more wine?' Duncan asked.

I waved toward the waiter. A few minutes later a liter of house red was in front of us.

'You're drinking most of that,' I said.

'Still on the sleeping pills?'

'I'm afraid so.'

'How is all that going?'

'It's "going".'

'By which you mean?'

'I get through the day by burying myself in work and exercise.'

'As I've noticed.'

'You mean, it shows I've been living in books?'

'And you also look like you've been in nonstop training.'

I lit up a Viceroy.

'I haven't turned into a total health Nazi. I know how bad they are. But they have gotten me through many a bad moment – as they will hopefully do tomorrow, a meeting I am totally dreading.'

'I am not surprised, given what she did when you got back from Ireland.'

'You want to know something? Since telling you about it back in early July – when you took me in – I've not talked about it with anyone else.'

'As it should be.'

'The saddest thing is ... the first couple weeks I was back Mom was nothing less than exemplary.'

From the moment I got off the plane from Dublin, she enfolded me in her arms, told me I was her precious girl, and she was going to get me through the worst of all this. She was extraordinary: patient, kind and very much reasonable when I told her that, outside of trips to a dermatologist, I didn't want any further medical attention. I spent the next few days inside my head, refusing to talk to anyone. I also ate nothing more than a slice of toast, an apple, water. When this continued for two more days Mom called the doctor – without asking me. But the doctor who arrived wasn't our family physician. It was Dr Bruce Breimer – aka Dr Feelgood, the man who nearly ruined my brother's life. When he showed up I told my mother there was no way I was letting him near me. That's when she suddenly lost it, started screaming at me, telling me that since coming back she'd had to put up with my zombie-ness, my weird moods, my need to turn everything into *me, me, me*. I tried to storm out – but Dr Feelgood blocked my path. I started to scream. Feelgood went for his bag and came out with a hypodermic and a vial of something that was probably a very strong tranquilizer, telling my mother to hold me down. When she attempted to grab me, I shoved her hard, sending her into a coffee table. I raced for the front door, Feelgood in pursuit. Fortune was on my side. As I dashed out a police car was driving past, and I knew the cop – Officer Malone, a nice big Irishman.

I waved my arms frantically, screaming at him to stop. He slammed on the brakes and came running out, shouting:

'Freeze – and drop that needle.'

Feelgood did as ordered. I literally ran into Malone's arms, telling him that this doctor was trying to drug me with my mother's consent. Mother was now at the door, shouting that I had assaulted her.

Malone looked at Feelgood – who lived in nearby Riverside and was known in this corner of Connecticut for being the mother's little helper doctor.

'How old are you, Alice?' he asked.

'Twenty.'

'Please go sit in the squad car.'

I did just that. Though I couldn't hear what he was saying from the way he was gesturing at them, I could tell that he was seriously peeved. I saw him point to Feelgood's car parked in the driveway, indicating that he should get in it and drive off. I saw him speak forcefully to Mom, flicking his finger toward the door of our house. Mom tried to explain something but Malone wasn't buying it. Once she was back inside and Feelgood had driven off he came back to the car.

'You don't have to sit in the back seat, Alice. You're not the perp here.'

I joined him in the front seat.

'Now I know why you shoved your mother. I had to ask her if she wanted to bring charges against you as it is technically an assault. But she saw sense and declined because I also told her that she had no right to force you to submit to medical treatment, given that you are legally an adult. And given what you've been through ... '

'Can you please take me to the train now?'

'Why don't you wait until your dad gets home tonight?'

'Because I am not going back to that house. Ever.'

'Where will you go?'

'A friend's place in the city.'

'Tell you what. I'll go inside, ask your mom to stay in the kitchen while you get your things together. Then I'll drive you to the train.'

Fifteen minutes later, an overnight bag and my typewriter in hand, I was waiting on the platform with Officer Malone. At the station I called Duncan, begging him for refuge.

Three minutes later the train arrived. As I got on it I thought: I am never returning here again. When I reached the city I phoned Dad – who had already gotten a call from Officer Malone. He told me that I didn't have to ever deal with 'her' anymore. He also told me that he was in the middle of a crisis meeting at his company, otherwise he'd take me out to dinner. But we'd get together in a few days ...

All that was almost a year ago. Here I was, in the middle of a reverie at Pete's Tavern, trying to tell myself that my recovery in the ensuing months had brought me to a point where I could face my mother the next morning – and do so without fear.

'How do you feel about being in the same room as her tomorrow?'

'Highly anxious. She's always made me nervous and angry. But she's also just done something big in her life. The way I look at it is: it's given me an excuse to finally leave my mental fortress up in Vermont and see if I could cope again in the city. So far so good – and it is wonderful to see you and celebrate your great news.'

'Even if it is overshadowed by that other bad business.'

He reached over and touched the top of my hand – at which point something strange overtook me: the first feeling of desire I'd had for a man in over a year. I touched his with my own, then pulled away, reaching for my glass of wine.

'You want my advice – for what it's worth. This isn't the 1950s. Just because she's pregnant doesn't mean you have to marry her. This woman will ruin your life before it ever starts. Get out now before she overwhelms you.'

Duncan kept staring into his wine, as if he wanted to dive in and vanish into its crimson depths. I sensed that I might have overstepped a mark, articulating a truth that he didn't as yet want to confront. Out of nowhere I remembered my dad once telling me that the day before his wedding to my mother, his Navy father took him aside and told him: 'You don't have to do this.' Had he followed this advice the result would have been: no me. But why do we not heed that voice in our head which says: *this is not right for you* – and then head for the door marked "Exit"?

The very next morning, when I showed up at 175 East 74th Street – and the doorman rang up and got the all-clear and then directed me up to apartment 4D – the first thing my mother said as she opened the door was:

'I walked through the door marked "Exit" ... and ended up here.'

Then she took me in her arms. I gave her a half-hearted embrace back. I wasn't going to pretend all was well between us, that all that had gone down last July had been whited out of my memory. She tensed when sensing my distance, but then carried on as if this was such a happy moment for us both.

'Can you imagine it? Me at forty-eight in my very first apartment!'

The apartment was a sublet; the owner a 'fashion consultant' who had decamped for the City of Angels, and whose decorative taste could be best described as 'far too mod'. There was a red plastic blow-up sofa, a couple of huge floor cushions in pop-art polka dots, and a thick green velvet chair that was suspended from the ceiling by a heavy chain. There were Fillmore East rock posters on the walls, and soft-focus photographic prints of coupling nudes (really tacky – but at least they were deliberately blurred around crucial body parts). The dining table and chairs were clear Plexiglas. There was a canopied bed in an alcove, separated from the living room by a curtain of maroon- and ivory-colored beads; the canopy was made of a diaphanous material, the sheets dark brown. And there was a man coming out of the toilet in a pair of hip-hugger tan flares and a gray silk shirt open to his sternum. He had a gold chain around his neck and a thick gold watch with a deep black dial adorning his left wrist.

Though his presence surprised me – I had arranged with Mom that I would show up at 11 a.m. and expected her to be alone – his sartorial style was in keeping with my mother's newfound mod-squad fashion choices. She had on a zebra-patterned blouse with matching slacks. Silver sandals covered her feet, a large copper skull on a braided leather chain bobbed between her breasts. But the biggest shock of the morning (yes there were a few) was the fact that she had dyed her already black hair even blacker and had it refashioned in a quasi-Afro manner. It looked ridiculous. Like everything else about this setup.

'Hey, beautiful ...'

This was Joe Stud talking. Late thirties, a distinctive Queens undertone to his accent, his very white teeth shining in the morning light flooding in from Third Avenue, him eyeing me up and down in a manner that could be politely described as creepy.

'Who are you?' I asked.

'This is my new friend, Tony. Say hi to my daughter Alice.'

'I think I've already done that. I like your name, Alice. It smells of poetry.'

'What does poetry smell like?'

'Funny kid your daughter.'

'What do you mean by that?' Mom said to him, suddenly testy.

'I was just making an observation.'

'Weird observation,' Mom said.

'Weird kid.'

'That's it, you're out of here,' Mom said.

'What?'

'There's the door – use it.'

Tony looked just a little bemused.

'Like mother like daughter, huh?'

'What a jerk you are.'

'You didn't think that when I was between your legs.'

'If you're not out of here by the time I count to ten I'm calling the doorman and –'

'Hey, fuck you, lady.'

Shaking a Salem cigarette out of a pack in his breast pocket he lit it up, then put his gold aviator shades on his nose and gave us the finger before heading out the door.

As soon as it slammed behind him, Mom sank down onto the plastic sofa and shook her head, looking close to despair.

'I'm such an idiot,' she said.

I said nothing. But I did come over and sit down next to her. Though the central air conditioner was rattling away, keeping the room semi-chilled, the plastic sofa was sweaty underneath. Mom reached over and took my hand. I didn't resist it.

'I know I'm a fuck-up,' she said. 'I know I've been a very bad mother. I know I should have gotten rid of him earlier ... but I didn't think you'd arrive on time.'

'I was taught to be punctual,' I said.

Mom now began to sob. I put my arm around her. She buried her head in my shoulder. I held her as she let go – saying nothing, keeping my contradictory thoughts to myself, wondering if this was the moment I had read about in a bunch of psychological texts when the child became the parent and also thinking: only Mom would have allowed all this to play out the way it just did.

'I take it he was someone you recently met.'

'Last night across the street at J.G. Melon.'

'Have you been spending a lot of time there?'

'What is that supposed to mean?'

'What I just said. Have you been going regularly to pickup bars?'

'I'm a newly single woman on my own in New York. I know nobody here. I'm lonely. What do you expect?'

'I expect nothing,' I said.

'But you deserved more than that welcome.'

Yet the truth of the matter was: Mom was pleased to have me meet her pickup. It somehow validated the fact that, even at her age, she was still able to attract a man.

'Shall we go out to brunch?' I said.

'Great idea,' Mom said, standing up, very much wanting to be free of this entire messy start to our first time together in almost a year. 'They do a great one across the street.'

J.G. Melon's was a speakeasy-style place. Brown wood everywhere, a long bar in mahogany with multiple stools, small tables with bentwood chairs, red-check tablecloths, very good Bloody Marys. We ordered two as well as eggs Benedict.

'Like mother like daughter,' she said.

I checked myself before saying: *it stops with the eggs benedict.*

The Bloody Marys arrived. Alcohol has its uses. And fuck did I need a drink right now. Mom saw this.

'What can I say, Alice? I know I am not the happiest of campers, and that I have let you down very badly. I regret all that. Just as I also wish I could rewrite the past – and not just my stupidity last summer.'

'Has Dad been in touch?'

'You mean, since I walked out? He tried calling twice. But I hung up both times.'

'What happened exactly?'

'Well, as you may have noticed, we weren't exactly in the running for Couple of the Year and then I discovered that your father had someone else.'

'But Dad has always had someone else, hasn't he?'

'Alice! Jesus!'

'It's the truth, isn't it? I remember that phone call from that guy whose wife Dad was –'

'We're not talking about that,' Mom hissed just loud enough for the couple at the next table to turn around and glare at us.

'So there was someone else?' I asked, my voice low. 'Just answer the question.'

'You don't need to know this.'

'On the contrary, I do. Because having tried to have me mentally neutralized by that hack doctor –'

'Not so loud.'

'Why? Because someone might hear that you tried to get your daughter institutionalized after she survived a car bomb?'

All this came out in a loud rush. The guy next to us did indeed hear us. Mom looked at me with something approaching horror in her eyes. I thought she would run for the door. But instead she reached over and took my hand, her voice trembling as she spoke.

'I will never forgive myself for doing that. And I will completely understand if you want nothing to do with me again.'

A pause. I sipped my drink.

'I'm here. That should tell you something,' I said.

'But you can't forgive me.'

I met her gaze.

'Not yet, no.'

Now it was her turn to reach for her Bloody Mary. Mom was never much of a drinker but today she downed half her Bloody Mary in one go.

'There's a woman he's been seeing down in Chile. The daughter of one of Pinochet's senior advisors, Isabella. I hired a detective.'

'Why did you do that?'

'To find out what I needed to know.'

'But did you really need to know this?'

'You don't know what it's like, being cheated on all the time.'

'But you actually *do* know what that's like. As I said earlier, it wasn't as if this was the first time. And, let's be honest here, you just acknowledged that it hasn't been a good marriage.'

'I'm not denying that. But, unlike me, this Isabella woman is twenty-eight and beautiful.'

'You're beautiful, Mom.'

'Now you're lying.'

I laughed. So did Mom.

'I am so pleased that you agreed to see me. I've missed you. I promise you: a new start between us.'

To which I could only reply with a shrug.

Mom took that on the chin, not pressing me for more. In doing so she indicated that she was trying as well to create more open boundaries between us. I got her talking about how she confronted Dad with the evidence of his affair, and how he didn't deny it, telling her that, in fact, it was the first of many. Could she really blame him for straying? When people start stepping away from their marriage it is usually with a certain amount of just cause – or, at least, as the result of years of alienation. Mom said that she couldn't dispute that statement. The only difference was:

'Your father had acted on it in the usual male way – by screwing around. Whereas stupid me had decided, like most women of my generation and before, to suffer in silence. Not anymore.'

I decided not to ask if the dreadful Tony was the first dalliance she'd had since walking out. But she volunteered that information without prompting, telling me that there had been a guy in the public relations game before. It had only lasted about ten days – until he dumped her for a stewardess on Allegheny Airlines.

'Imagine being pushed aside for someone who flies to Buffalo, Harrisburg, Allentown – all the shitholes on this side of the country.'

'Has Dad tried to see if things could be repaired between the two of you?'

'Of course not. That would take guts, and an ability on his part to admit that he was wrong, too.'

'Have you ever admitted that yourself?'

She fell silent.

'You are being very direct today,' she said.

'It's long overdue.'

I lit up a cigarette.

'Still smoking?' she asked.

'Still *seriously* smoking – and even more so since I got blown up. Any objections to that?'

'I just worry about your health.'

'I am ridiculously fit.'

'You clearly eat like a bird.'

'I eat enough.'

'No you don't.'

'If I was chunky ...'

'I wouldn't be so envious.'

I found myself smiling.

'See! I can still make you laugh. Because I can finally send myself up. Dr Davenport told me that one of the reasons he feels I am going to come out of this a changed person is because I also see the absurdity of it all – and am willing to embrace it.'

'Is Dr Davenport a shrink?'

'You're far too fast for your own good. Yes, he's a psychiatrist. Not a strict Freudian. A lot of give-and-take. He's also around forty and kind of dishy.'

'Thank you for that detail, Mom.'

'Oh, come on, you know I'm just having fun. That's what Dr Davenport says: the fact that I can see the humor behind everything has saved my sanity.'

'Lucky you.'

'Don't be hard on me.'

'I am hardly being hard ... and you know that.'

Silence. Our food arrived. Mom stared down at her eggs Benedict.

'It's going to take time,' I said. 'Shall we eat?'

Mom took the hint – and steered the subject away from any thoughts of forgiveness, instead telling me how she had decided to become a realtor and was studying for her exams ('I can't sell anything without getting an NY realtor's license'), but was also starting to train with Cushman & Wakefield – one of New York's biggest firms.

'As long as I get two fast sales I'll be on my way.'

'There's no salary? You're basically working for nothing?' I asked.

'It's all commission. But I'm planning to make it big. I'm going to be the Realtor Queen of Manhattan.'

'Not with that hair you won't.'

Mom blinked and I saw tears. I felt like a shit – that wave of guilt which always hit me whenever she made me feel like the bad daughter, the little girl who ruined everything for her ... and had done so ever since I arrived in the world. Yes, this comment was my form of payback, of letting her know that the landscape between us had changed utterly, that there was not going to be the Hollywood ending reconciliation that she wanted. But watching tears cascade down her face, that other culpable part of me kicked in. The realization that this was all that I had in the world – and how desperate that knowledge made me feel.

'One day when you have children –' Mom said.

'I'm never having children.'

'So you say now. But please, just hear me out: one day when you have children you will work out the fact that you never get it right with them, that all your shit gets churned into their initial innocence and then helps form their own shit, and that you spend much of the rest of your life regretting all that you have passed on. Family is shit and shit is family. And if this is my way of begging your forgiveness ... '

I sat there, my head swimming. I stubbed out my cigarette, immediately lighting another.

'I can forgive the shit. I can't forget the shit. So how do I get around that one, Mom?'

She looked at me, wide-eyed: 'Do you really expect me to have an answer for that?'

Mom tried to convince me to stay with her 'just tonight', but I told her I was going back to Duncan's place. I knew there was still only so much time I could spend in her presence. During the remainder of brunch she did, to her credit, ply me with questions about my well-being. She was impressed I had done so well in my courses.

'Considering what you've been through, it's quite an achieve-ment.'

Part of me wanted to scream back in reply:

'*What I've been through is nothing compared with what I have to face, day in, day out.*'

I kept such comments to myself. I was now almost a year on from the events in Dublin. I knew my equilibrium was fragile. I knew I had no choice but to somehow paddle through the waves of dislo-cation and grief that came at me out of nowhere, almost on a daily basis. We talked about Mrs Cohen. We talked about Carly and how, since copping a plea and testifying against her former Black Panther cohorts, she was living the college-girl life at UCLA (Mom had all the details, telling me: 'I wouldn't be surprised if that destructive little bitch hasn't done an about-face and joined a sorority'). We talked about *Jaws*, the big film of the summer that we'd both seen.

'That shark on screen,' I told her. 'That's the sorrow I'm coping with now. It circles around, menacing, menacing. Then it attacks and removes a small part of me, but still allows me to somehow live. Which is something of a mixed blessing, as a significant corner of my psyche really doesn't want to be here anymore. You need to understand that.'

We were on the street when I told her all this. She stopped, the shock apparent.

'Please don't say that.'

'Are you surprised that I think this way?' I asked. 'Did you expect otherwise?'

She reached out and took my hands.

'The first thought I had when I'd heard that you were in hospital after that bomb was that the bottom was about to fall out of my world. The only reason I didn't rush over to Dublin was that your father forbade it. He thought, given our history, that my presence would simply aggravate things. I should have put my foot down. I should have insisted. I made a mistake. Just as I made an even more terrible mistake when I brought that doctor around. I know that I'm now repeating myself. But what else can I say, except: it's something I'm so ashamed of now. I can understand why you might not want to spend much time with me right now. But please, *please* assure me you won't hurt yourself.'

'I can't promise anything – except that there is also a strong desire to stay here. Among the living. Beyond that ... '

I didn't finish the sentence. Mom – to her credit – pushed no further for details. But as she walked me to the crosstown bus on 79th and Third, she put her arm around my shoulders.

'Give me the chance to make all this up to you, Alice. I know I have a lot of growing up to do now. You can keep your distance if that is best for you – but please don't shut me out.'

My response? I leaned over and gave her a fast peck on her cheek.

'Thank you for a good day,' I said.

Her eyes teared up again.

'I'm always here for you,' she said. 'Don't be a stranger.'

'Okay.'

I stepped onto the bus. Its doors shut behind me. The bus headed west.

The next day, on the Greyhound back to Burlington, I reflected on all that had gone down with Mom. I could feel her isolation, her fear lurking right behind the decision she had made. She could no longer hide from herself under the cloak of a bad marriage. I had no idea whatsoever whether we could somehow reconstruct our relationship into something where all the guilt and anger was diminished. I didn't blame her walking out in the face of another of my father's affairs. Part of me couldn't blame Dad for straying. I was relieved that they had finally ended their long, fractious, ever-unhappy involvement. But I also knew that, for the immediate future, I would continue to maintain a certain distance between us. The same distance that I kept between myself and all others.

Convincing yourself that you are in any way worthy is the hardest thing in the world when everything in your background tells you otherwise. I knew that, like the rest of humanity, I was largely defined by the way I had been raised – by our own singularly unhappy dynamic. Which raised another question: could a family ever be anything but a repository of resentments, grudges, personal gripes and shared griefs? Why were we always being told that happiness – especially as shared by parents and their children, by siblings and by the families they went on to create – was the great ideal, and one to which we should all aspire? Family was a dark business – with occasional moments of luminosity.

Back in Burlington I started the summer term – and was also summoned to Professor Sylvester's office several days after my return. She had a proposition for me. A co-educational boarding school in Vermont was looking for an English teacher starting this September. Would I be interested in the post? The school was located near Middlebury. It was called Keene Academy. Its founder, J.G. Keene, had been a pioneer in New England progressive education: an emphasis on high academic achievement and rigor, with a degree of social informality.

Teaching had, in truth, never been a professional goal. I'd vaguely thought that after graduation I would stay in Burlington and look for a job on a local newspaper like the *Burlington Reader* or take some of the money I received from the Irish state, buy a car, hit the road, get lost in the American Nowhere and see where life would bring me. When I casually raised this thought once with Dr Gellhorn she advised 'a walk before you can run' approach, telling me that my Kerouac fantasies, though admirable, might not give me the necessary anchor I needed right now.

Did I need an anchor? There were moments when I thought: *fuck it, I am hitting the road. I might as well get out of here.* One afternoon I had an urge to go driving. I borrowed Rachel's car and while it was initially good to be on a big open highway, the two front windows open against the hot air of the early-July day, I didn't fare so well. Heading north on Interstate 93, rolling toward Quebec, I was suddenly passed by a large truck with Canadian plates, with the name Bombardier on the side. Moments later I had to turn off to the breakdown lane and wait until I stopped hyperventilating. I felt like an idiot, getting thrown by a word, letting it trigger far too many bad things, like a stupid movie monster who shows up out of nowhere and starts eating the Tokyo skyline. When I could control my breathing again, I managed to get the car back to Rachel's house, knowing that I wasn't quite ready for my coast-to-coast road trip.

I did ask to borrow my friend's car a couple of weeks later for my interview at Keene Academy. Rachel insisted on accompanying me. I didn't take much persuading as I didn't want a shaky moment behind the wheel like the one on Interstate 93. Keene turned out to be a pretty redbrick-and-ivy place, down a back road around seven miles from the village of Middlebury. Everything about the campus was New England Subdued Rustic: the venerable school buildings, the manicured lawns and athletics fields, the tall pines that loomed behind the campus. Approaching it, part of me thought: *oh no, not another ivory tower ... you really need to be out in the big bad world.* As if reading my mind Rachel said:

'Consider it another way station on the way back from the horror you've been through.'

I was interviewed by the acting headmaster, Thomas Forsythe. He was immediately friendly, asking what interested me in literature – explaining that I would be teaching Shakespeare and modern poetry in the fall semester, then twentieth-century American literature and nineteenth-century fiction in the spring. He wanted to know my thoughts on each of those courses. I was relieved I'd done my homework, thinking very much of Professor Hancock and something he once told me during a chat in his office: 'Teaching isn't just a sacred duty; it's also a vast amount of preparation.' Mr Forsythe said that the post paid eight thousand dollars a year, but also came with certain benefits: a rent-free small faculty apartment, free meals in the school cafeteria ('and our food isn't bad'), medical insurance, and almost four months off a year. I told him all that sounded most reasonable. I could live on less than ten dollars a day, which meant I could put aside a considerable amount of money over the course of the year – close to five thousand dollars. Enough to maybe disappear down a cool strip of highway once I was able to deal with open spaces, open roads.

'Professor Sylvester did tell me all about what you suffered in Dublin,' Mr Forsythe continued. 'I apologize for doing so, but I must, for evident reasons, pose this question: do you feel psychologically able for this post?'

I had already prepared for this answer too. I looked Mr Forsythe in the eye.

'I had many physical and mental scars after the bombing. But I sought help with them both – and found that the only way back was by applying myself to my college work, getting very fit and trying to move beyond what has happened. Has it completely gone away? Of course not. But am I able to live, to *function*, with it? I think my final year's transcript from the university answers that question.'

This seemed to do the trick, as Mr Forsythe nodded repeatedly while I delivered my speech. Then he said:

'Well, I can offer you a year's trial. I must be blunt with you. I would truly prefer someone not right out of college – but you've impressed Professor Sylvester and you've impressed me. If you are willing to accept the pay and accommodation package I've mentioned ... '

'It's all fine by me,' I said.

But what wasn't fine was the fact that I had kept my doubts about myself as a teacher very much to myself. Just as I knew that the only reason I was accepting this job was because it had fallen into my lap and answered in a rushed way the looming question of what I would do next with this life of mine.

'Congratulations: you've landed your first real job,' Rachel said on the way back to Burlington.

'I feel like a fraud.'

'Get used to that feeling. It defines most of us, even the truly successful ... or perhaps *especially* the truly successful.'

I finished my term at UVM. I received my BA with no pomp and circumstance. My gift to myself for graduating was taking three of the ten thousand dollars I'd received as compensation and buying myself a car. It was a 1971 Toyota Corolla – third-hand, but in reasonable shape. A week later, after I'd arranged for all the necessary repairs to be done, I packed my car with all my worldly belongings, closed up my apartment in Burlington, promised Rachel that I would stop back every few weeks for a visit and foot therapy, and headed down the road to my first proper taste of the workaday world.

23

MY APARTMENT AT the school was a two-room suite, very neutral and bland: white walls, scuffed floors, dormitory-style furniture. There was a simple living room, a small bedroom, a closet, a sink. A communal kitchen – with a table you could eat at – was at the end of the corridor. Ditto two bathrooms – one for each sex. I arrived before the other staff residents were settled in – all of whom were returning faculty members. I put up posters and artwork. I covered the narrow bed with a linen Indian spread – all patterned needlework in wildly primary colors – which Rachel had given me as a going-away gift. I bought a rocking chair, a floor lamp for reading, and I tipped the guy who ran maintenance around the school to find me a bigger desk. Yes, putting this room together brought me back to Dublin: to the bedsit chez Sean; to sharing my narrow bed there with Ciaran; to his flat on Merrion Square; to everything in our life together; to the hearing aids still discreetly hidden behind my hair; to the impossibility of silencing the anguish that I always felt within.

I made my room very livable and comfortable – and splurged on a decent stereo and more records. David – the music teacher, living down the hall – was obsessed with jazz. He himself was a saxophone player who trained at Berklee in Boston and had taken this job as a stopgap after spending four years knocking around New York, trying to break into the jazz scene there.

David was cute. Ridiculously tall – almost six foot four. Ridiculously thin. He had a great sense of style – wearing distinctive heavy black glasses, narrow black trousers, black shirts, a porkpie hat. He was very funny and could talk jazz patois with a wit and a coherency that I found sexy. When he played his tenor sax . . . well, it just added to my sense of being smitten with the guy. Shame he happened to be gay . . . a fact that he had to keep hidden from everyone at Keene. He had a guy he saw in Boston – a faculty member at the New England Conservatory who was married (which made things even more tricky). To admit that you were homosexual at the time was beyond dangerous (as Howie had found out at Bowdoin). To do so while teaching at a boarding school was to end your career immediately. David knew this. Just as he told me that he had never discussed his sexual orientation with anyone at Keene until I showed up.

'You're the first person here I've felt I could trust. Not that anyone here is so right wing or reactionary – but they also simply don't want to know. Tom Forsythe is, by and large, a good guy – but also someone who has to answer to parents and trustees. He dropped one hint to me around a year ago when he saw that I was driving down every weekend to Boston – and the person who does the mail might have tipped him off that I kept getting handwritten letters with a return address of Michael Bofard from the New England Conservatory. After a staff meeting he asked me to stay behind for a moment to discuss a student who was applying to study cello. He asked if I had any pull at the New England Conservatory and when I replied that I did have a friend there, but he was in the composition department, Forysthe said: "Well, we wouldn't want you to compromise yourself by reaching out to someone who might be seem to be a conflict of interest. We don't accept conflicts of interest at Keene." I got the subtext: I was to continue to keep that aspect of my life far removed from Keene Academy if I wanted to remain employed here. I told him: "Fear not. I will not do anything to bring any conflicts of interest into my work at the school." Nothing was ever said about it again.'

'Well,' I said, 'your secret is safe with me ... but I wish you didn't have to keep it such a secret. You shouldn't have to be so ... '

'"Closeted" is the word I think you're looking for. Welcome to being gay in America ... or anywhere else. Do you know that, up until very recently, you could be imprisoned in the UK for committing a homosexual act? Still, I am so pleased I've told you this. At least there is someone here with whom I can confide.'

I then told David all that had gone down in Dublin. I saw his eyes grow wide as I filled him in on the details, and the long slow recovery that was still very much under way.

'Work is the only way out of it,' I said. 'All that boring physical activity I do also helps keep the demons at bay. So too does reading and burying myself in preparation for my classes. But, please not a word to anyone about what I just told you. Tom Forsythe knows – because he asked me many questions before he offered me the job about whether I was psychologically up to the task.'

There was another teacher on my floor. Mary Harden taught history and had been at the school for almost twenty years. Her apartment was floor-to-ceiling books and records. From my other colleagues I learned she was a hugely dedicated teacher and some-one who had been working – for about ten years – on a revisionist study of the French Revolution which she told me she knew would reinvent her academic career, landing her a big job in some top col-lege or university. Over a glass of wine one evening she admitted:

'Sometimes I think I am writing the epic that never was. I also know that by the time I finish it and hopefully find a publisher I will be in my late fifties at best. Who will want to hire someone that old? Which raises the question: have I left everything far too late?'

The next morning, while teaching my class about modern poetry, I discussed T.S. Eliot and how, in 'The Hollow Men', he talked about the grayness that was at the heart of all human aches and pains:

Between the motion and the act falls the shadow.

Having spent much of the previous night up late, anxiously rereading the poem many times over, trying to formulate my take on it before facing the judgment of my students, I now asked my class:

'So what is Mr Eliot talking about here?'

One student, Rachel Zimmerman – intense, voluble, with rav-aged nails – said that 'maybe he was saying we all have dark stuff in us'. Another of the more vocal members of the class, Alison Maple, commented that 'Eliot was always obsessed with death and *does life amount to anything?* So maybe the shadow was the fact that everyone dies.' But it was Kyle Michaelis who provided the most interesting response. Raising his large hand, keeping his eyes on his desktop, he half whispered in a voice just audible enough to be discernible:

'You're both off the mark here. Eliot was talking about the fact that everyone is thinking one thing, doing the other – and the whole thing about being human is: you don't ever totally understand yourself. That's the shadow: the disaster that is you.'

Bravo, Kyle.

There were moments like this one when I so loved what I did, when I felt as if teaching was not just such surprisingly engaged work, but also something essential. Because you were watching how a world view was formed and reminding yourself that you were having a small hand in the shaping of the perspective. Naturally I was more than terrified my first few weeks of standing in front of a class, trying to engage their easily distracted adolescent selves, attempting to appear confident when I felt unnerved and inadequate and hardly prepared for the massive, profound responsibility that was teaching. When I admitted this to David one evening he just smiled and said: 'In our business there is the daily stage fright.'

'So the fear never goes away?' I asked.

'It's a bit like an actor or a musician. The good ones never totally overcome pre-performance stage fright. They just accept it as part of the deal. And they also learn to use it as a sort of modus vivendi. Fear for a teacher ... it can actually work to your advantage.'

David's words were more than helpful. Though I often found myself thinking, *My God, why are these children listening to such bullshit?*, a hesitant confidence began to inform my classroom style after a few weeks. Just as there were other moments when I threw up my hands at the intransigence of my students, and their inability to escape their adolescent take on just about everything.

That is, with the exception of Kyle Michaelis. Aside from wanting to shout at him to make eye contact with one of us, his answers were always spot on, razor-sharp. Aged seventeen and nearing the end of his time at Keene, Kyle was a little overweight, with not the best personal hygiene habits. He had ended up here in Vermont after not being able to cope with the pressure at Trinity where his chubbiness, his lack of sporting acumen, his strange quirks, made him the target of much bullying at that ultra-elite Manhattan school. I was privy, courtesy of our headmaster, to the fact that Kyle's parents were separating, something Mr Forsythe said that Kyle didn't need to know about while he focused on his applications to college. He also told me that Kyle's father Toby was 'a big-deal book editor' and impressive. His mom, Naomi, was very implicated in New York City politics: Jewish, a motormouth, funny, driven, endlessly edgy. I met her on a parents' weekend and found her to be a more focused and brainy version of my own mother. I could see that she was a little bit overbearing as a parent and a relentless dropper of names. She worked for a famed US congresswoman named Bella Abzug – one of the true early feminist politicians, and someone with a reputation of being super-aggressive and intolerant when it came to general male bullshit. Kyle's mother shared many of Abzug's attributes. I liked her frankness, her wit, her need to impose herself in every situation. She believed that New York City was the absolute epicenter of the universe. When Naomi approached me with Kyle, she let it be known that she'd just been at a charity bash with Richard Avedon and Mike Nichols and, of course, Andy Warhol. She then gushed that:

'My boy says you're the best teacher and someone who really does understand him – which, from where I sit, makes you the most remarkable educator around.'

'But he's a real pleasure to teach,' I said.

Kyle had wandered off to talk to Rachel Zimmerman, who was nearby with her parents and on whom, I sensed, he had a bit of a crush. He was thankfully out of earshot when his mother said:

'You don't have to BS me, Ms Burns [she emphasized the *Ms*]. I know he's the wrong side of strange.'

'Is that a problem for you?'

'Well, put it this way: I can't exactly envisage him having the most normal of lives.'

'What's a normal life?'

'Being able to interact properly with others. Having a conversation like we're having now and not staring at your shoes all the time, as Kyle is now doing with that mousy girl over there.'

'I don't think she's mousy at all.'

'But you think me too New York Jewish, right? You Irish girls always –'

'My mother is New York Jewish. Which makes me as Jewish as you are, ma'am.'

That stopped her in her tracks. I added:

'And I think Kyle has one of the most interesting minds in this school.'

The next day Mr Forsythe slipped a little note in my mailbox, asking me if I would mind dropping by his office. I expected something of a dressing-down for the way I handled Naomi Michaelis. Instead he said that Kyle's mother had told him that she liked 'my sparkiness, and the fact that I challenged her, and was also so committed to her boy'.

'Well … thank you.'

'No, thank *you*, Alice. We all really think Kyle is a special kid – but also one who needs to be handled with imagination and care. Which you do wonderfully. His dad is coming up next weekend – so if you wouldn't mind meeting up with him … '

That afternoon I had my class on Shakespeare and was discussing *The Winter's Tale* – and how it is one of those interesting later 'problem plays' in which jealousy, rage and mistrust prove tragic, destroying a marriage, a family … and then how, like the theatrical magician that he was, Shakespeare suddenly transforms a tragedy rooted in human pettiness into a brilliant morality tale about the power of redemption and forgiveness. Some of the students in my class found the way the play shifted gears to be downright strange.

'It's a fairy tale,' said Jonathan Gluck – a kid from New Jersey whose father was a plastic surgeon who also gave motivational speeches about 'being what you want to be'. David once called poor Jonathan 'a boy with far too much toxic expectation attached to his future – and who knows that his path in life to date has been paid for by nose jobs'. He was a very earnest young man – far too literal and concrete in his way of looking at the world, but also someone who had a certain instinctual intelligence when it came to the nuts and bolts of life. 'All right, Leontes accuses his wife of cheating on him, she dies, he's really sad and screwed up by his mistake – and then, *shazam*, she's restored to life and all is good again? I don't buy it. It's like trying to convince us that the dead can rise again and we can all have a happy ending.'

From the corner of my eye I could see Kyle shifting back and forth in his chair. Finally he shot his hand up, agitated, demanding to be heard.

'Come on, Jonathan!' he all but shouted (a rather uncharacteristic raising of his voice). 'Surely you know that Shakespeare – having been a keen student of ancient Greek theater – understood that comedy is tragedy with a good resolution. Can't you get that? Don't you see what Shakespeare is trying to do here? Show us how, if we find a way of stopping being so caught up in our own ego thing, we might just do things a little better. It's not a fairy tale, Jonathan. It's a *morality* tale. Don't you get that?'

Way to go again, Kyle!

I asked him to come have a hot chocolate with me in Middlebury after that Shakespeare class.

'Have I done something wrong?' he asked.

'If that was the case why would I be inviting you for cocoa?'

He stared off into space, as if he was looking for the nearest black hole.

'Good point.'

We got into my car, him immediately fiddling with the radio, finding an FM station down in the low nineties.

'If you're looking for the NPR station I've already programmed it. Hit button 1,' I said.

'NPR is so new and so cool. Like really intelligent talk and news. Couldn't believe we've got something so good now that is actually *public* – like not for profit and talking up to all of us.'

'I really like your take on things,' I said, thinking: how many seventeen-year-olds have the shrewdness to pick up on the fact that the creation of a smart public radio station nationwide – with affiliates in all states – was a major educational step forward in our country?

'Hey, my dad just got me my first subscription to the *New Yorker*,' he said. 'Cool guy my dad – and he told me just last week on the phone that getting rid of Tricky Dick and his gang paved the way for this new guy from Georgia, Jimmy Carter, who's talking about doing things different in Washington without all the dark bad stuff going on. I like what the peanut farmer from Georgia is telling us about materialism and consumerism and the way we're all obsessed with owning all this stuff and not with larger concerns – like doing good for others. Is that why you became a teacher?'

I thought that one over for a minute.

'I'll tell you the truth: I became a teacher by accident. Because I was offered the job here. But then I discovered that it is genuinely good work.'

'But you're not going to stay here forever, like so many of the faculty. You're a New Yorker. Just like me. And like all New Yorkers you can only take the sticks for so long.'

We pulled up to a little luncheonette on the Middlebury main street. Once inside Kyle lit up a cigarette – having already smoked one in the car – and immediately perused the menu.

'If I order something more than hot chocolate I'll pay,' he said.

'Order what you like, I'll pay.'

'Meatloaf. I really want meatloaf.'

'Then meatloaf you shall have. I've heard it's very good here.'

I stuck to coffee, but watched Kyle run through his substantial plate of meatloaf and a plate of French fries in under five minutes.

'You must have been hungry,' I said.

'Got to fill the hole between lunch and dinner.'

'But dinner back at the school is two hours from now. Surely you're not going to eat another meal then?'

'You sound like my mom.'

'I just think ... '

' ... that I'm fat and ugly.'

'I've never, *ever* thought that. Do you think that about yourself?'

'I weigh one eighty-five – which is about forty pounds more than I should weigh. My mom tells me I should eat less and do sports. I hate sports. Anyway I'm not going to need sports or exercise for what I'm planning to do in life.'

'Which is what exactly?'

'I want to write cartoons.'

'I didn't know that you drew stuff.'

'Can't draw at all. I'm going to write the scripts to cartoons.'
'That's an unusual choice of career ... but kind of interesting too.'
'What you're really saying is: *weirdo*.'
'I don't think you're weird.'
'Everyone else does.'
'Your dad?'
'No – he's kind of cool ... when he's around. He's really into his work, publishing cool writers, dating smart women ... the sort of women who look at me for two seconds and think: fatso with acne. I've seen pictures of him when he was at Trinity – where he cut it big time and I was considered the freak. Which is why I'm here at bizarro prep school. Unlike Dad – who did real well at Trinity, then went on to Williams and did the cool preppy thing, editing the literary magazine, captain of the crew team, all the girls after him ... as they are now. Which is why my mom is leaving him.'
'Really?' I said, surprised that he was in possession of this information, given how his mother asserted that she was keeping 'such tough stuff' from him.
'Don't tell me my mom didn't say something to you last week. She's told anybody who's willing to listen to her. My cousin Geraldine – who's at college at Barnard – wrote me a letter last week, saying that Mom accompanied Bella Abzug – her feminist guru, the woman she so wishes she was – up to a lecture she was giving at the college. And she bumps into her niece, and suddenly comes right out with: "Oh you know I'm leaving your uncle, the adulterous bastard."'
'When did you get this letter?'
'This morning.'
'How do you feel about that?'
'I hope my dad does what he promises and finds an apartment where there's a spare bedroom for me, so I can live with him when I'm not at school or college. But he cheated on my mother. Maybe he'll leave me.'
Strange, isn't it, how an unexpected comment can send your own reflections on your own troubled past down a different path, allowing you to discover an entire different way of considering the

mechanics within. Was that always my greatest fear vis-à-vis my absent father – the terror that he might abandon me, that I might end up in the sole clutches of my mother? Was that one of the damaged bits within me – the part that drove so much within me, just as it clearly did Kyle?

'I'm sure your father loves you very much.'

'He's certainly not critical of me the way Mom is. Your parents still together?'

'Not anymore.'

'Is life better that way?'

'I think my mother is pleased she finally did it ... and terrified at the same time.'

'So you're on your mom's side?'

'Hardly. But I am not taking my dad's side either. If I were you I would take neither side. I would just think about your own life and what you want next.'

'What I'd like next is ... dessert.'

He ate an oversized chocolate brownie served à la mode with an oversized scoop of vanilla ice cream. I watched him again wolf it down, thinking that, like anyone interesting and quirky and outside of the acceptable blah mainstream, he was so damaged within. And unable to reconcile that part of himself which wanted love, wanted to be wanted, with the other part that was doing everything in its power to make that impossible.

'Do you think that Rachel Zimmerman might want me as her boyfriend?' he asked me, a stream of ice cream dripping from his lips.

I knew that Rachel was quietly seeing the very literal Jonathan Gluck – because she told me so after class the previous day when we needed to talk about an essay that she had handed in and which was way off course, and not her style of thought whatsoever. I asked why she had gone down such a colorless track in her thinking on *Macbeth*. That's when she told me that 'my boyfriend Jonathan kept telling me I needed to rethink things – that maybe Macbeth wasn't pussy-whipped but just a bit like an ambitious businessman wanting the big job'.

I had to stop myself from reeling – or from saying something corrective along the lines of: '*I'm sure Jonathan's going to be a very successful corporate lawyer one day – but the guy lacks literary insight, let alone a sense of the poetic.*' Instead I told her:

'In future don't listen to anyone when it comes to your take on a play, a novel, a movie, a work of art, some politician's way of explaining the world. Always trust your own judgment.'

'So do you think Rachel would let me be her boyfriend?' Kyle asked me again.

I chose my next words with care.

'I think she might be "spoken for".'

I chose the wrong words. Kyle turned white. He began to shift nervously back and forth on his side of the diner booth, he began to repeat, over and over again:

'That can't be … that can't be … '

He grew even more agitated. When I reached over and tried to steady him by touching his hand he pulled away, almost screaming, as if he'd been touched by an electrical prod. Immediately, the manager on duty was at our table.

'Some kind of problem here?' she asked.

'It's all fine,' I said. 'He's just a little agitated.'

That was an understatement, as Kyle kept shifting in his seat, taking the fork with which he'd scoffed his brownie, and bending it back so far that it snapped in two.

'Son, you're going to have to leave,' the manager said, oblivious to the distress that Kyle was in. 'And you owe me a dollar for the fork.'

'A dollar! A dollar!' Kyle shouted.

'I'll pay it, Kyle,' I said, suddenly nervous.

'Everyone wants me to pay for everything. *Everyone!*'

With that he suddenly stood up and raced out the door. I dropped five bucks on the table and raced after him. But he was already running down the main street of Middlebury, with me in fast pursuit, heading toward a low-lying bridge. My eyes grew wide as I realized what he was about to do. I ran faster as I dashed for Kyle who, up ahead, had reached the bridge and had one foot on its balustrade and was about to tip himself over and into the river many feet below. But before he could go flying I managed to grab him, hauling him on top of me. Kyle began to roar and struggle against my grip. He became near-violent, shoving me away then jumping up and dashing for the bridge again. Fortuitousness took over here, as two town electricians came running toward this crazed scene and managed to wrestle Kyle to the ground before he could go over into the fast-moving, frigid waters below. They held him down, shouting at a passerby to call the cops. I got over to Kyle, insisting that he stop struggling, telling him all was fine ... even though all was anything but fine.

Then the police arrived.

An hour later Mr Forsythe came marching into the hospital to which Kyle had been taken and placed in a straitjacket in their very small psych ward. I'd pleaded with the attending doctors to treat him gently, but he struggled again when he was admitted to the hospital and they had to subdue him. Fortunately, the cops who'd arrived on the scene first spoke to Forsythe, explaining the scene they came upon, and what I had told them. Instead of being ordered to pack my things and get out of town, Forsythe sat down next to me on the bench in the waiting room and said:

'Thank you for saving Kyle's life. What sparked this episode?'

I explained how it came out of nowhere, and how it all hinged on me hinting that Rachel Zimmerman was already seeing another guy.

'I feel terrible about all this,' I said. 'I had no idea that he was subject to these sorts of incidents.'

'It's the first in a year,' Forsythe said. 'We should have probably warned you to tread carefully with him.'

'But I was treading carefully.'

'Another young woman spurned his interest last year and he went into a big tailspin, trashing his room. His dad pleaded with us to keep him here. But after this incident ... '

'Surely if it only happened once before ... and he only has months to go before graduating ... '

'Say he has another explosive incident like this one and hurts a fellow student? The police told me he knocked you to the ground. This cannot be allowed.'

395

'Surely if he was able to talk regularly to the school psychologist ... '

'He's doing just that. Look what still happened. You didn't even say anything provocative. I can't take the risk, Alice.'

Kyle was being kept in the hospital psych wing until his father arrived tomorrow. Forsythe told me I could, if needed, take the day off.

'There's no need for that. I'm not injured. I'm a little shaken up – and very sad for Kyle. But also very happy that the cops are not dredging the river for him right now.'

'If he had died ... '

He didn't complete the sentence. There was no need. Because we both knew that, had Kyle perished from a fall into the hypothermic waters of that river, the school's reputation would have been upended – with vast repercussions for the future.

'He didn't die – and that's all that matters.'

Back at the faculty residence that night, my colleagues insisted on taking me back into Middlebury for a drink – David saying I certainly needed one, while Mary noted that a prep school in Rhode Island had closed last year when two students hanged themselves in a suicide pact.

I clinked glasses with my colleagues, feeling strangely hollow about all this, especially as I felt so sad about Kyle being locked up in that psych ward for the night. Before leaving the hospital I had entreated Mr Forsythe to speak to the man in charge and get his student out of that monstrous straitjacket. He'd promised me he would do just that.

The next day in class the talk was about Kyle. Word had gotten around and several of my students wanted to know all the details. I had discussed, in advance, how to handle all this with Mr Forsythe. We decided to be direct about the fact that Kyle had had a bad psychological episode and was heading back home tomorrow to New York, but with the hope that he would make a full recovery blah blah blah.

As I was giving the class this official version of what had happened to poor Kyle there was a knock on the classroom door, and

Mr Forsythe poked his head in, apologized to the class for the interruption and motioned me outside.

Once in the corridor I found myself facing a man who immediately struck me as absurdly handsome and exceptionally tired.

'Alice, this is Kyle's father, Toby Michaelis.'

He took my hand. I met his gaze.

'I owe you everything,' said Mr Michaelis.

Little did I know at this juncture: I was soon to owe him so much.

24

MR MICHAELIS ASKED me if I wouldn't mind accompanying him back to the hospital to spend an hour with Kyle. He made this request in Mr Forsythe's office after classes were over.

'They have him on a far too heavy dose of tranquilizers. The resident psychiatrist said it was for his own good – but they've zombied my son.'

Just like they'd zombied me in that Dublin hospital.

'What gave them the right to do that? He didn't break any laws, he just had "an episode".'

'But, sir,' Mr Forsythe said, 'he did try to commit suicide. If it hadn't been for the fast thinking of Miss Burns ... '

'I know that,' Mr Michaelis said, then turning to me, added: 'I will be forever in your debt for that, Miss Burns.'

'Thank you, sir. And you can call me Alice.'

'Only if you call me Toby.'

He touched the top of my hand as he said that.

'I'll be taking Kyle back to the city tomorrow. I've arranged for him to be checked into a psychiatric hospital in Manhattan. He shouldn't be there long.'

He then turned to Mr Forsythe and said:

'I would like to discuss future matters with you.'

I took this as my cue to leave, saying I'd be in the staffroom at the end of the corridor when Mr Michaelis – 'sorry, Toby' – was ready to head to the hospital.

Half an hour later I was in Toby's rented Plymouth as he steered us out of the school grounds and toward Middlebury.

'Why has a smart young woman like yourself sequestered herself up in the Vermont woods?'

'It's a stopgap. I'm not going to be here forever.'

'Piece of advice, if you don't mind – get out as fast as you can. Your twenties should be a blank slate and one in which you avoid tying yourself down, limiting the levels of possibility and experience. By twenty-seven I was married and the father of two children – a nice apartment on the Upper West Side, interesting work, interesting friends – but with no latitude whatsoever. At some point you should vanish. See where life will bring you.'

'I like the sound of that,' I said.

'What's stopping you then?'

I didn't want to get into all that. Especially as I had not talked about Dublin for months now. Toby noted my hesitancy.

'Sorry if I barged into an area I shouldn't have,' he said.

I shrugged and changed the subject, asking him about the writers he worked with. By the time we reached the hospital I had learned all about how he forced the brilliant, alcoholic novelist Stuart Patterson into a fifth draft of a novel which won the 1971 Pulitzer.

'You sound like you love what you do.'

'As work goes ... yes, I am a fortunate man.'

The thing was: he didn't sound convinced of that.

'Then you're lucky.'

'Am I hearing irony in your voice?' he asked.

'Am I hearing an undercurrent of something else in yours?'

We were now in front of the hospital. Toby parked the car, turned off the engine, and turned toward me, looking a little disconcerted.

'Is it that evident?' he asked me.

'Is what *evident*?'

'The fact that I am trying to put a brave face on so much?'

There was a long silence after that, then he said:

'We can come back to all this later ... or not.'

Once inside the hospital, he asked if I wouldn't mind allowing him to have some time alone with Kyle and his doctor. I sat in the waiting room, annoyed that I hadn't brought along some papers to grade. I read a discarded copy of *National Geographic*, admiring its brilliantly crystalline images of marine and coral life on Australia's Great Barrier Reef, wondering to myself how many people in doctors' offices and waiting rooms across America were now looking at this article and thinking to themselves: *there's the world in all its amazing density just in front of me ... and yet so completely out of reach ... because I have trapped myself in all the conventional stuff I promised I would somehow sidestep.*

After almost an hour, Toby returned to the waiting room, looking tense and preoccupied.

'Kyle's not in the best place right now – so his doctor thinks we should just let him rest this evening.'

'I'm so sorry.'

Toby shut his eyes – and I could see him trying to keep his emotions in check.

'If you ever have kids you will discover the great truth about parenthood: it is the ongoing open wound.'

But then, having whispered that statement, he almost seemed to regret it. With a shrug he added:

'Sorry, sorry – a whole compendium of things are jamming up my life right now. Feel like a drink?'

We ended up in a bar and grill in downtown Middlebury. Toby ordered us gin martinis and insisted that what we both needed tonight was good steak. By the time the second Beefeater martini arrived I'd learned much about him – how his father, a distant, remote figure to his children, died in a car accident when Toby was twelve. He had a very religious – Greek Orthodox – mother who matched her late husband for emotional coldness. There was a need on Toby's part to excel at everything and buy into the successful New York life.

'We really do tell ourselves at a certain age that we need this, we need that – as if ticking off boxes on a checklist which subsequently, one morning, we realize is absurd.'

At a later point in the meal, he suddenly stopped and noted that he'd been talking far too much about himself and his world. What about my life?

It's always interesting how much information you impart on a first date (which this had certainly turned into), and the things you keep to yourself. I was sparing about so much that was directly personal but did tell him a certain amount about my father, my brothers and the craziness of my relationship with my mother. But when he started asking me about boyfriends I verbally turned and ran for cover.

'If there's stuff you don't want to talk about, Alice ... no worries. It can wait until another time.'

'Will there be another time?' I blurted out, immediately cursing myself for being so stupidly transparent.

'I'd like that. In fact, I'd like that very much.'

He then went on to explain how, though still officially married, he was seeing someone now in New York.

Did I feel a stab of jealousy as he informed me all about this woman, Emma – whom he painted as so worldly and connected ... everything I knew myself not to be? Did I want that glossy metropolitan sheen, transforming myself into the cosmopolitan know-it-all with fabulous friends?

'Are you what's known as "a scoundrel"?' I asked.

He stared down into his third martini and smiled.

'Yeah,' he finally said.

'That's honest,' I said.

'Or stupid,' he said. Then he called over the waiter and asked if he could arrange a taxi back to the school for me and drop him off at his hotel. When the waiter headed to the phone Toby leaned over and whispered: 'I'm staying at the Inn on Main Street, as it is actually called. I'm not stupid enough to get behind the wheel after three martinis or ask my son's teacher to spend the night.'

Part of me wanted that. Part of me was terrified of the idea of stepping over the line with a man who was still married, seeing someone else and the father of one of my students – even if that student wouldn't be returning to my classroom ever again. Then there were my colleagues – some of whom knew I was heading out to the hospital with Kyle's dad and would have noted my absence in the faculty residence tonight and my arrival back at the school early tomorrow.

'It would be good to stay in touch,' I said.

'That it would be indeed,' he said, reaching into his jacket pocket and handing me one of his embossed business cards. 'The next time you are coming down to New York ... '

'I'll let you know. Will you please keep me up to date about Kyle? He is, in the best sense of the word, a one-off.'

Possibly that was the wrong thing to say, as tears began to run down his face.

'I'm losing him to this craziness of his.'

'You haven't lost him yet,' I said, reaching over and taking his hand – knowing that this was exactly the wrong thing to do if I was planning to take that cab ride back to the school. But as he gripped my hand tightly and fought off further tears, I leaned over and kissed him directly on the lips.

'Let's get out of here,' he whispered.

Many hours later, lying next to a now sleeping Toby, I played through our time together in bed. He was the first man I'd slept with since Ciaran – and the three martinis impeded nothing. His ardor matched my own. In that postcoital moment afterwards, when Toby stood up to pour us each a whiskey and I lit up a cigarette, I came right out with what I was thinking.

'I just want to be clear,' I said looking at him. 'I hope we can do this from time to time. No strings and all that, if that's cool with you.'

He stopped pouring me a whiskey and looked at me with bemusement.

'That's about the last thing I expected to hear from you.'

'You mean you thought I was going to demand absolute commitment and fidelity, and "Oh, Toby, you are everything I've ever wanted in a man ... "'

'Aren't I?' he asked with a smile.

'You're almost eighteen years older than me. You were running your index finger across the scars on my back and wondering what had transpired in my life – what calamity I had suffered – to leave such scars. I'll tell you all about that at some further time. But know this: I really liked what happened tonight and I want more. But you are going to be in New York with your girlfriend, and I am going to be the rube in Vermont, teaching school and living on less than seventy dollars a week. I want nothing more than what I've just proposed. I will ask for nothing more, only that: if one of us decides to end things, we do so civilly. Just as I want your respect and decency. That's it. Are you good with all that?'

He threw back his whiskey, then leaned over and kissed me.

'I'm good with that,' he said.

'I'm good with you,' I said, pushing him back on to the bed.

Thus began a long spell of what I came to call 'freelance intimacy' with Toby. From the moment I returned home, just after dawn, to the faculty residence – and I ignored a somewhat insidious question from David later that morning about dinner with Kyle's father ('If, in fact, you ate at all?') – I imposed a dome of silence over anything to do with Toby. My colleagues knew that, twice a month, I spent a weekend elsewhere – but they never knew it was in Manhattan.

My mother – who was beginning to carve her own lucrative niche in the New York real estate game – always cross-examined me about 'the man I was seeing' whenever we had our bimonthly brunch. Once she got far too pushy – surmising that 'he must be married, otherwise why would you be keeping me and everyone else in the dark about this?' When I quietly asked her to back off she did something unexpected. She told me: 'You're right, I should shut up,' then went on to say: 'I only want happiness for you, Alice – or, at least, to not have to wait until you're my age to find the freedom that eluded almost every woman of my generation.'

'But you've grabbed that freedom now, Mom.'

'You want to know my biggest regret? That I was faithful all those years to a man who never truly liked me. Independence ... it's a foreign country for me. But one which I'm happy to have finally forced myself to.'

Mom might have backed off on 'your secret lover' front, but Adam picked up the scent as well, asking me if I was 'involved with somebody', given my constant trips to the city. And when Peter returned to town – finally having been 'ashramed out of India' – I also refused to acknowledge whose bed I was sharing whenever I was down in Manhattan. Some months into our arrangement I told Toby that I considered what we had to be 'a pleasant sidebar in my life'. Yes, he was still seeing Emma, a junior editor at *Vogue* whom he frequently noted was a little too hyper-ambitious and a younger mirror of his soon-to-be ex-wife. I never commented back. Nor was I ever seen out with him where we could be spotted as a couple. Yes, we went out on the town – but steered away from the 'fabulousness' within which he so lived. I introduced Toby to the world of New York jazz – directing us to the Vanguard where we both heard (and were dazzled by) a young pianist named Keith Jarrett. Or heading uptown to the West End Cafe, where that great boogie-woogie pianist Sammy Price still held forth every Friday night.

Over the next few months I fell into a routine: continuing to teach at Keene Academy, continuing to see Toby, and crashing one or two nights twice a month on the futon at Duncan's apartment. Even when he was out of town on an assignment I had the key to his place and could call it my pied-à-terre. It was easier visiting my friend now that he had rid himself of the dreaded Patricia; her pregnancy ending exactly three nights after he had agreed to marry her (but a week before they were to head to City Hall for the ceremony) when she suddenly began to bleed profusely. Duncan rushed her uptown to Columbia-Presbyterian Hospital. The attending doctor told him that she was simply having heavy bleeding associated with a very heavy period. That's when Duncan bluntly asked the doctor:

'You mean, she's not having a miscarriage?'

To which the doctor said:

'Young man, either you know nothing about female reproductive anatomy or you've been duped.'

Duncan was enough of a gentleman to say nothing until two days after Patricia was discharged from the hospital, at which time he quietly announced that – while she was at work that day – he'd packed up all her things from his place and deposited them with the superintendant at her apartment in Hell's Kitchen. She screamed that her place was sublet – and, as such, she had nowhere to go. Duncan told her:

'Too bad. Next time you lie to a guy about being pregnant, work out in advance where you'll be sleeping when he evicts you from his life.'

When I next spent the weekend chez Duncan, he had gotten over the betrayal part of the romantic equation and was simply relieved to no longer have anything to do with her.

'I think I dodged a bullet,' he told me after I showed up, bottle of Almaden wine in hand.

'I think you dodged three bullets. Your E. Howard Hunt article was brilliant, by the way.'

'It got great play,' he said. 'They even had me on WNYC talking about Watergate. Now *Esquire* wants to send me on the Carter campaign trail. What do you think of the guy?'

'Clean, positive, different – not at all the usual Washington hustler.'

'I take your point,' Duncan said, 'but I worry that Jimmy Carter is going to be like a character in that Frank Capra movie about the small-town boy who ends up in the political circus and discovers that idealism counts for nothing in Washington; that it is all about favor-peddling and deal-making and the usual money-exchanges-hands chicanery. No one will ever totally change the system. We love the noble-minded in America, the clean-hands visionary. The truth is: they rarely come along ... and even when they do, they are rarely effective.'

Yet again I was impressed by Duncan's political erudition, his ability to cut to the heart of the matter, the way he could see the potential narrative twists and turns in the near distance. The more we drank the more I found myself wanting him. He was very much 'on' that night – free of the anxious neurotic edge that undercut so much of his waking life. His was not the sort of ruthless ambition predicated on stepping on the necks of other people as a way of clawing his way to the top. Rather it was rooted in his need to prove to the world – but most tellingly himself – that he was not the rejected child; the eldest of three brothers and the boy on which his mother and father heaped their frustrations and anger.

'Know what my father said to me after reading the E. Howard Hunt piece? "Not a bad effort, but Gay Talese would have done it better. And you are hardly in that journalistic league."'

Hearing this story somehow made me want to reach over and pull Duncan on top of me. I stopped myself, as I knew he was all wrong for me right now. I sensed we would both fall hard, and he struck me as potentially rather needy. I didn't need to be needed right now.

I needed sex and the intimate reassurance it provided. But I couldn't handle the idea of plunging into love, with all its manifold implications – the biggest one being: losing my heart and allowing myself again into the realm of vulnerability. Lighting up a cigarette he told me:

'During the time you were in Ireland, I was with a cellist who was studying at Juilliard. Ann was very talented, very ethereal, very much devoted to me, to us. Someone who told me that she could see building a life with me. What did I do? I panicked. How could anyone seriously love *me*? The uneasy kid who was always told at home and at school that he was too odd to connect with anyone. Here was this lovely woman who saw me for what I was, and just wanted to create something happy between us. Naturally I had to push her away.'

'Stop beating yourself up,' I said. 'You knew you weren't ready for what she was offering. To accept her love was to limit your horizons. Maybe you're right – maybe a part of you buys into all that craziness your parents laid on you. But maybe there's another part of you that wants to wander the planet, having experiences – that thinks true love and all that can wait.'

'But you found it.'

Silence. I lit up my cigarette, pulling hard on it.

'Then it was taken away from me. In an instant. That taught me something – the only fortress we can find is within us. And we all have to accept that everything we do, everyone we connect with, is temporary, impermanent.'

'Is that why you now have this thing going with some married guy – because it's a hedge against permanence?'

'I never said he was married.'

'You don't have to. It's obvious he's married or involved with someone else. Otherwise why would you be crashing here tonight?'

'I'm not talking about any of that.'

'Fine, fine. Didn't mean to pry.'

'You're a writer – of course you meant to pry. The reason I am with him is because the very limitations of what it is – the fact that it will never have any future beyond the boundaries we're both putting on it – makes it possible for me to do this. And I am going to request that you ask me no more, please.'

Duncan honored that request – never once did he ever sniff out the identity of my weekend lover. Nor, to his credit, did he venture a supposition as to his identity.

I'd seen little of my father since Mom had exited the Old Greenwich stage. He'd call occasionally, usually late at night, sounding a little clouded by Scotch and cigarettes, a certain ruefulness entering the conversation. I posed few questions. He told me loads. Such as: the woman whom he'd been seeing recently was twenty-eight; a junior executive in a marketing company. She was now pressuring him to move into the city, find a large apartment for them both and start thinking about having a family with her. I resisted the temptation to quote that word most espoused by teenagers at the moment (as in: most of the kids I was now teaching): '*Gross ...*' But I did speak up after Dad's quasi-drunk revelation that she was dabbling in 'some new religion thing called Scientology'.

'What the hell are you doing with this woman?' I asked my father.

'Love is complicated.'

'This doesn't sound complicated, Dad. This sounds like serious trouble. Remember a piece of advice Peter told me, and that you yourself once gave him: *never sleep with somebody whose problems are bigger than yours.* Why don't you follow that yourself?'

'Because the role of a father is to give advice that he knows he'll never follow. So tell me about your Big Brother's Book.'

'I haven't read it, so I have absolutely no idea what Peter wrote.'

'You expect me to believe that. You're his adored little sister. I know you've read the damn book.'

'Dad, I've actually been pretty straight with you throughout my life so far. Straighter than you've been with me. And I can tell you categorically: I have no idea what he wrote about you, or anything else. Why don't you drop him a line, c/o American Express in Delhi, and ask him to send you a copy?'

'I've fucked it all up, haven't I?'

'I think we've all fucked it up, Dad. You sound lonely.'

'I'm just fine. Remind me not to call you again when I'm feeling a little sentimental.'

Click. The line went dead. I felt miserable for days afterwards, telling myself I was wrong to kick the guy when he was in a vulnerable place. I tried calling him at home. No answer. I called his office in Manhattan and was told by his secretary that he'd returned to Chile.

'Please tell him that his daughter called, and that she wanted to say that she loved him.'

The next night, around one in the morning, the communal phone on our floor rang. I was half awake and ran down the corridor, hoping it might be Dad.

'Person-to-person for Miss Alice Burns,' said the operator in heavily Hispanic-inflected English.

'That's me.'

'Go ahead, señor.'

'Hey, sweetheart ... '

He sounded even more boozed-up this time.

'Hi, Dad, it must be really late there.'

'Did I wake you?'

'No worries, Dad. What's up?'

'That message you left at the office ... it brought tears to my eyes. I just want to tell you how proud I am of you, how you've achieved so much, overcome so much, refused to let some really bad stuff cripple you ... '

I didn't know what to say, not used to my father being in any way effusive when it came to praising me, let alone showing absolute vulnerability. I took a risk. I said:

'Do you miss her?'

'Miss who?'

'Mom.'

'Give me a fucking break. I don't miss her nuttiness. I don't miss the way she always broke my balls.'

'What do you miss then?'

'I'm changing the subject. How can I get a copy of Peter's book?'

'Ask him for one.'

408

To my surprise he did just that, writing to Peter in Delhi. It took my brother a month to reply, as he was in the south of India at the time. But when he got the message from Dad – *I can handle what-ever you wrote about me, I just want to read it* – Peter splurged twenty rupees (about a buck and a half) on a telegram to his publishers, asking them to send a bound proof to his father's office on East 42nd Street. Dad received it in April, a month before the book's publication. Tucked inside of it – next to the standard slip which read '*With the compliments of the author*' – was an invitation to the publication party the following month. Dad rang me in Vermont late one night, positively ecstatic.

'Your no-good, crazy lefty brother has decided that his old man shouldn't be left out of his shared moment of triumph. I'll be at the party!'

'Oh, great,' I said, my sense of caution evident.

'Don't sound so pleased.'

'Mom will be there,' I said.

'I kind of figured that. Will her new guy show up as well?'

'You'll have to ask her that yourself.'

'Yeah, right. What's he like, this Trenton Carmichael?'

'He seems to be making Mom happy.'

'Let me guess why: because he just had a lobotomy. But let me ask you this: what sort of WASP son of a bitch names his son Trenton?'

'Someone with a strange attachment to New Jersey, I suppose. But you're not telling me what I need to know.'

'Which is what?'

'What did you think of Peter's book?'

'Well, it could have been a lot worse, right? I mean, when I first read it I thought – son of a bitch, the guy's painting me as this old-school hard-ass. But then I had one of our junior execs read it – asked him to tell me what he really thought, no holds barred, all that "let it all hang out" shit. Anyway this junior exec – Deke Halligan, great kid – told me: "You should be pleased with what your son wrote about you. Makes you out not to be the villain, but something of a true believer when it comes to Our Way of Life. Yes you do come across as a hard-ass, someone with whom it's difficult to argue a political point, and also a big womanizer. But that also makes you seem cool." He actually used that word about me: "cool".'

'So you're pleased?'

'I've been immortalized, haven't I?'

I had to smile. Repeating the story a few days later to Toby, while in bed, he noted that if he'd been publishing the book he'd get much more coverage on the father/son dynamic – and how Peter's perspective on his dad was rather original in its non-accusatory stance.

'My dad served in the Medical Corps, first in London and then in France after the D-Day invasion,' he told me. 'He never truly got over it. Never talked about it – though, God knows, I tried to get him to tell me all the stories he could. But he kept that memory door shut. The thing was – and I sense this is the same thing haunting your dad – peace was hell for so many veterans. The wife, the kids, the day-in-day-out job, the sense of immense limitation after all that life-and-death drama on foreign soil ... my dad never transcended the boredom of it all. I should have learned from him.'

'But you have. You're no longer married. You've got latitude.'

'You know that's far from the truth. I have two children whom I adore, and who I will be supporting for many years to come – as it is me who will be not only paying child support, but all the school and college tuitions. I'm not complaining. It's just ... there is only so much latitude on a book editor's salary.'

'And Miss Vogue is now pushing you to replicate it all again.'

'We don't have to talk about this, you know.'

'But you've raised the issue. Because it's eating at you. And because I know that you have all these doubts about Miss Vogue, yet still seem willing to start another family with her.'

'Well, she is thirty-one ... and she keeps telling me that reproductive time is running out for her.'

'Why is that your problem? Why do you have to be the sperm bank that fulfills her dreams?'

'Is this your idea of postcoital conversation?'

'You raised it. Part of you still wants the domestic thing. I can't go anywhere near that. In the meantime you're going to fence yourself in even further with a new wife and new kids.'

'Maybe I won't be so stupid.'

'Even if that happens, I'll still want to continue this.'

'So will I.'

And continue we did – in such a discreet way that when he received an invitation from Peter's editor to attend his launch, Toby first discussed the matter with me, saying that he wanted to show up (as he also wanted to cruise Peter for a possible new book) but wanted to make certain I was cool with that.

'Hey, I just know you because I taught your son in school.'

Kyle's mental health had, in turn, improved immeasurably after several weeks in Payne-Whitney and much intensive work with a psychiatrist. He was finishing up high school at a small private school in the city under considerable supervision. I asked Toby once if he wanted to set up a meeting with his son the next time we were both in Manhattan. He told me that Kyle couldn't face up to much that had happened back at the school – and still mentioned his failed suicide attempt with considerable shame.

'Tell him he always has a friend here – and that I truly believe in him. Especially with him being different from his peers, from everybody else. I know what that's like. I saw the nightmare damage that bullying creates.'

He knew all about Carly – especially as her name had recently been in the news again. Still at UCLA, she'd found herself a New York agent and was allegedly writing her 'I was a Black Panther sex slave' memoir, for which she'd been paid (according to Toby) around $50,000: huge money, enough to buy a house in down-at-heel, but still beachy Venice, or a nice, family-sized Upper West Side apartment in New York.

'I promise you that Carly will do nothing as sensible as invest in real estate,' I said. 'She'll go through it all in two years, tops. Unlike Peter I doubt her book will be in any way self-critical or possessing a larger, more nuanced picture when it comes to her adventures among the politically radical fringes.'

'Your brother is about to become a very celebrated writer … if he plays his cards right.'

Indeed, when published in May of '76, *Freefall* had become the most talked about non-fiction book of that spring. It wasn't a huge cultural event as E.L. Doctorow's *Ragtime* was the previous year, or as John Irving's *The World According to Garp* became in 1978. But Peter's beautifully written, frequently unnerving account of his sojourn in Chile was riveting. *Harper's* ran an excerpt. Its content was the source of a debate on William Buckley's *Firing Line* in which the great conservative thinker/showman asked my brother if he didn't accept that the CIA had saved his life. Peter handled himself with considerable agility, telling Buckley that he'd been naive and foolish to wander into the mess that was Chile; that the portrait he painted of his father in the book wasn't of a malevolent secret agent, rather a businessman turned CIA operative who, like so many members of his generation, had fought for his country, was confused and rattled by the radical fervor and fluid sexual mores of the sixties, and had signed up as an intelligence operative out of some Cold Warrior sense of patriotic duty. But for himself and his dad 'it was also a great adult adventure far south of the border, with a brutal junta and their easy-to-seduce women giving it all a Graham Greene tinge'.

Many critics and commentators applauded the fact that Peter had refused to play the self-righteous card, that he portrayed himself as someone who had fled the cerebral piety and ivory tower cosset of the Yale Divinity School and, as an act of rebellion, had gotten himself way over his head with a group of revolutionaries whose good ideological intentions were overshadowed by dictatorial, Fidel-esque instincts on behalf of their leadership. I learned much from the book – most notably the way the women members were treated as common sexual currency, and how two lowly members were shot for insubordination when they refused to torture a police officer that the group had captured during a bank raid.

Then there was the scene in the plane – which had everybody talking. Especially as Peter was unflinching in describing his terror after watching his love and the others tossed out into the great beyond over the Pacific; and how, as much as he so vehemently disagreed with so much about his father, 'at that very juncture, when I thought that maybe I had a minute or two left as a sentient being

– that my time in the world was about to end, and that I would plunge over ten thousand feet downward, to be buried for all eternity within the vast churning, indifferent waters of the Pacific – my father pulled off a remote sleight of hand, forcing the laughing amoral thugs in charge of killing us to spare this insignificant, politically jejune American.'

The launch party certainly hinted that all of literary and media New York was taking a serious interest in Peter Burns. Big-deal writers and journalists were there: Jimmy Breslin, Pete Hamill, Clay Felker the editor of *New York* magazine, Gay Talese, and – oh my God, did Kurt Vonnegut just walk in? Dick Cavett – the brainy talk-show host – made a thirty-minute visit. So too did Gloria Steinem. My mother – seeing all the great and the good here to pay tribute to her boy – was beside herself. Especially when she got talking with David Reuben – who, seven years on from its publication, was still riding a wave of fame on his book, *Everything You Always Wanted to Know About Sex (But Were Afraid to Ask)*. Mom's boyfriend, Trenton Carmichael, was by her side throughout much of the evening. He was – at first sight – a slightly thinner, more Protestant, older, preppier version of my dad – dressed in a blue blazer with brass buttons, a two-tone shirt (white collar and cuffs, deep blue front), a paisley-print tie, gray flannels, polished cordovan shoes. He himself seemed to have a perpetual Scotch and water in hand, and was perfectly pleasant ('Hey, the famous Alice Burns – Vermont's best-loved teacher!'). He even turned on the charm when he was introduced to my father ('You must be so proud of your boy'). Dad didn't look at all happy to be meeting his replacement – and did he get the irony of the fact that he, too, was wearing a blue blazer, gray flannels, et cetera? But to his credit he did give my mother a light peck on the cheek and shook Trenton's hand in that *mano-a-mano* way of his. Then he got pulled away by Peter who wanted to introduce him to Gay Talese. Dad was basking in the general attention – because he was, on so many levels, the other big central character in the book, and one who came across (in Peter's edgy, thoughtful prose) as somewhat larger than life. This was his fifteen minutes of fame – and all thanks to a son with whom he'd had, at best, a complicated relationship. Dad reveled in it. I heard him telling someone: 'I hope George Kennedy plays me in the movie version.' Just as Adam – also dressed in a blue blazer and gray flannels – insisted on gathering us all together (Mom, Dad, Peter, myself) and handing his Kodak Instamatic (replete with a fresh flashcube) to his new girlfriend and joining us for a family snapshot. Peter was wearing a rather cool suit – black, wide lapels (as was the trend that year), a matching black vest, a deep maroon shirt open at the neck. I was dressed like someone just in from the groovy woods – a long flowery skirt, a somewhat diaphanous black shirt (beneath which my black bra was visible), no stockings or leggings, leather sandals, and a pair of half-moon earrings in silver (a gift from Rachel for my birthday). Adam was not comfortable amidst all the New York fabulousness swirling around him. Janet, the woman with him, was his girlfriend of six months' standing. They met as neighbors in the same apartment building in White Plains. She was pleasant, quiet, in her mid-twenties – a nurse working in a home for geriatrics in nearby New Rochelle. Adam had dropped a hint or two about her during our occasional phone conversations. Now here she was, dressed in a cream pants suit, a little too heavily made up, looking as awkward as Adam. Peter and I tried to make her feel welcome. Dad was scathing of Adam's choice, telling me in a harsh whisper: 'What the hell does he see in her? She's the walking equivalent of Levittown: Early Nothing.' She and Adam clung to each other, like wallflowers at the prom. But, when requested, Janet did do the honors behind the Kodak Instamatic: the five of us with our arms around each other, all smiles, all play-acting the happy family. Then, as soon as all four flashcube flashes were used up, we drifted back into our other worlds: Adam's with Janet, Mom with Trenton, Dad with some fortyish woman who had big hair and a cigarette always on the go. Peter, meanwhile, was in deep conversation with Jimmy Breslin – the reigning king of New York journalists. He was chomping on a cigar and gesticulating, while a beautiful, attentive young woman was listening in, her hand on my brother's shoulder.

'Is that your brother's new lady?' Toby asked me, coming over and quickly sliding his hand around me, and kissing me on the side of the head.

'I have no idea ... but she's clearly rather taken with him.'

'As he should be with her – because Samantha Goodings is widely regarded to be one of the hottest young novelists out there. Beautiful and brilliant, with a professorship at Columbia and a major book due out in October.'

'My, my, we really do love high-level achievement in this city. Let me guess: she had a Fulbright to the Sorbonne, and she's going to be competing in the Montreal Olympics this summer as a member of US Women's Polo Team.'

'She had a Keasbey to Oxford and considered going pro for a while as a tennis player.'

'How do you know all that?'

'It's a small world,' he said. 'But I want you to stop sounding jealous.'

'I just feel like an underachiever when surrounded by all this achievement.'

'You could be part of all this.'

'I'm not ready to be her. Or to be here.'

'That's a choice, I suppose. Are you going to be eating with Peter and everyone after?'

'That's the plan.'

'We could meet late then.'

'Emma's away?'

'Obviously. Midnight chez moi?'

'I'll be there. But let me ask you something: is the reason you know so much about the Samantha Overachiever because you've slept with her?'

A small smile formed on Toby's lips which he quickly expunged.

'I shouldn't have asked the question, right?' I said.

'You're learning,' he said.

25

A FEW MONTHS after Peter's launch party I sat with a group of faculty members in our residence lounge and watched as Jimmy Carter won the presidency. A few days before the vote the polls began to unnervingly tighten. President Ford seemed to be gaining last-minute momentum. The idea that, after all the scandalous chaos of the Nixon years, we could be electing his hand-picked successor was just the wrong side of surreal. But the American public saw sense, voting in the moral man from Plains, Georgia.

Someone broke out a bottle of New York State champagne when David Brinkley announced on NBC that Jimmy Carter would be the 39th president of the United States. As we toasted this new political era before heading back to our respective rooms, I told myself that night: *I don't want to be here four years from now, watching the results come in. I want to be seriously elsewhere.*

But I also knew that I still didn't have the will to uproot and re-invent myself. Even when I was down in New York – as I continued to be every other weekend – I still couldn't get my head around the idea of committing myself to life in that ferocious metropolis where the hyper-assertive and the super-pushy flourished.

Peter's book got dazzling reviews and much general atten-tion. He did a thirty-city book tour and told me, in an indiscreet moment some months later, that he'd slept with a different woman after every book event. With the movie money he'd bought him-self a wonderful two-bedroom apartment in an old brownstone in Brooklyn Heights: not much in the way of city views, but high ceilings and great Victorian dimensions. He turned one of the bed-rooms into an office. It had a small balcony and a narrow eastern glimpse of the great harbor into which so many of our forebears traveled.

'I'm calling this my "Melville Vista",' Peter told a reporter from the *New York Times* during an interview in his enviable new place, which he furnished in high modern Scandinavian style, courtesy of

Samantha Goodings. She had moved in with Peter and had taken charge of so much in his life, including promoting them as the young golden literary couple: photogenic, politically progressive, cerebral yet sexy. Or, at least, that was the image presented in *New York* magazine and *Interview*, and that half-page spread in the Style section of the *New York Times*. In the same piece it was announced that Peter's publishers, Little, Brown, had signed him to write his first novel – which he ballyhooed as 'nothing less than a fictional overview of our times; a statement of what it means to be an American in this postwar world'. The fact that he received an advance of $75,000 was also big news. Little, Brown were hoping to publish it in late 1978.

'Your brother made a bad error of judgment if I may say so,' Toby told me one evening in bed.

'How's that?'

'He should never announce to the world that he is writing a major novel.'

'Norman Mailer does that all the time.'

'True – but the difference is: he's Norman Mailer. We all expect that from Norman: the ongoing proclamations of his genius, the way he sees himself as perhaps the greatest scribe since Homer. Peter is nowhere near the stature of Mailer. He's just starting out. And the book, though well received, has not performed as well as his publishers had hoped. Which means they are worried about the Great American Novel he's telling everyone he's writing. He needs to be a little more circumspect about it all. He should also stop going to so many parties and lock himself away to get to his desk, churning out the words.'

'Well, your old chum Samantha is taking him down that "beau monde" line.'

'Stop calling her "my old chum". It was a brief encounter, nothing more.'

'Toby, I know I am not the only person with whom you have this sort of arrangement. I can handle that. But stop acting like sleeping with Samantha Goodings was something equivalent to a sneeze. I saw the way you looked at her at Peter's party. You still have a thing for her. Who can blame you? But the reason I cannot handle New York is because it's full of women like Samantha.'

'You are as bright and beautiful as she is. You could be doing big things here, but you are using Dublin as a shield – a way of stopping yourself from getting beyond all the understandable anguish you suffered. That was two years ago. I am not saying you have to shed it like some sort of reptilian skin. But, if you don't mind me saying so, you are limiting yourself the longer you continue to play the Vermont schoolmarm who keeps telling herself: I'm not good enough to compete in New York. You are good enough to succeed here. More than good enough. But the central question that arises is: can you face that truth yourself?'

The evening after Toby challenged my need to stay in Vermont, I asked Duncan if he thought I was self-limiting. Duncan himself was now hooked up with an entertainment lawyer named Andrea who was always commuting between New York and Los Angeles, and therefore happily announced herself as 'bi-coastal'. She was bright and driven, a little too peppy for my tastes. She also dropped hints that Duncan needed to find a bigger apartment, as the decor was, to her, 'a bit student'. But she was genuinely supportive about his work. He had just returned from an assignment in Algiers where he'd interviewed the Harvard professor turned LSD guru Timothy Leary in his edgy North African exile. Whenever I crashed on the futon and Andrea was also spending the night, I could hear them having loud, robust sex. It was clear that bed was a happy place for them to be together.

One evening at Duncan's – returning home from an afternoon assignation at Toby's apartment – I found myself face-to-face with someone who immediately threw his arms around me and announced:

'I am your blast from the past!'

His once-green hair was now dyed jet black. It was still curly, Afro-like, in style. His tall frame had gotten even leaner. And his very white skin – he was always beyond pale – seemed even chalkier. But Howie D'Amato remained his same effusive self. He seemed genuinely thrilled to see me.

'I didn't know the two of you were in contact,' I told him as Duncan opened a bottle of red wine and poured out three glasses.

'After finishing up at NYU I spent a year or so in San Francisco – *quelle surprise* – but eventually couldn't take being around the word "mellow" much of the day. Naturally fled back east. Forced my way into New York publishing. And I am now working in the publicity department of St Martin's Press. Handsome Boy here is signing a contract with us to write a big book on the decline and fall of 1960s idealism. When his editor walked him into my office, I started to jump up and down, screaming at Duncan: '"You were one of the few people at Bowdoin who didn't call me 'Tree Fag'." He later told me that you were an occasional guest on his floor. I did write you after hearing what you'd lived through. And you don't have to now say a justifying word about why you couldn't see me then. I understood.'

I reached out and took his hand.

'Thank you.'

'But I decided today that I just had to come over and check you out. You do look amazing, girl.'

I told Howie that his talent for hyperbole hadn't left him.

'But I love your late-seventies style. Maybe we can have a really interesting discussion later on about how yams are good for your karma.'

'I see you've hardly changed.'

'Oh, I've changed plenty – thanks to finally landing in New York, slamming the door on the rest of the world, and keeping my horizons focused on Manhattan and Fire Island.'

During my next weekend in the city, Howie insisted on taking me out to dinner at the Magic Flute Cafe on West 64th Street, and then to see Rudolph Nureyev performing on Broadway, spending an astronomical $18.50 each for the seats in the orchestra. Over dinner he got talking about the Son of Sam serial killer stalking New York right now, murdering courting couples as they necked in cars. Just days before I arrived to spend the weekend in the city, a woman student at Columbia University had been randomly shot in the head by a young assailant who escaped on foot. Reading about all this had triggered all sorts of past trauma. When Howie brought it up at dinner it set me on immediate edge. Noting this he reached over and put a steadying hand on my arm.

'Oh God, me and my big unthinking mouth,' he said.

'It's fine, it's fine. It's just … '

'No need to explain. No need at all.'

I reached for my cigarettes.

'I wonder: will I ever get beyond all that happened?'

'Maybe not,' Howie said. 'Maybe you will always be scarred.'

'Are you still scarred by what happened at college?'

'Of course. Sometimes, in quiet moments, I wonder if the reason why I am even more flamboyant now – letting the whole damn world know that I am very out, very gay – is because all that happened in high school and at Bowdoin cut so deep. You know what's the hardest thing for me? Trying to form something longer than a trick or two with anyone. Tonight, after you go back to Duncan's, I'll head down to the Mineshaft and find someone to fuck in one of the toilets there. Then, around three in the morning, I'll go back to my "fabulous" apartment and get a few hours of sleep and pop a Dexedrine in the morning and go to my "fabulous" job. I will talk in a "fabulous" way to everybody and go to a "fabulous" lunch with some magazine editor I'm cruising for an interview with one of my authors, and then will start thinking about the "fabulous" book party I'll be heading to around seven, and everyone I come in contact with will think: "Isn't Howie D'Amato so 'fabulous' and so comfortable in his own queer skin?" The truth is a little more nuanced: I am totally "fabulous" … and lonely.'

Howie became again, after this dinner, a close friend – and someone who, out of nowhere, would ring me in Vermont at midnight and gab with me for two hours. Our friendship deepened and I began to talk more openly about all the turmoil within. What I surprisingly discovered in Howie was a true sense of discretion and what he called 'Jesuitical silence'. The Roman Catholic reference was a deliberate one. Howie wasn't just raised in the Church of Rome. He was also a serious practicing Catholic: one who went to mass every Sunday and believed in the purgative benefits of the confessional box. He even told me of a priest he'd found at St Malachy's, on West 49th Street, who did not scold or condemn when Howie spoke of his gay sins of the flesh.

'Even though he's ultra-circumspect, I have the impression that Father Michael actually finds my sex life rather riveting. He even told me once not to go to any of the other priests for confession, as they might not be as sympathetic and lenient as he is. But it's a church for Broadway Babies and arty types like myself. Which means that all the priests are going to get a sexual earful from their parishioners. Father Michael is, I sense, living vicariously through me.'

Why did I finally tell Howie about my involvement with Toby? Perhaps because it served to cement our friendship. In turn, he informed me that he'd been arrested by the police last year for trying to pick up a man in the toilets of Penn Station before taking the Metroliner to Washington where he was due to shepherd an author through a series of press interviews.

'Lucky me, deciding to accept the advances of an undercover cop.'

'But wasn't that an act of entrapment on the part of the police?'

'Absolutely – and the ACLU lawyer who took my case got all the charges dismissed on the grounds that it was a nasty set-up. My bosses found out about my "crime", as I missed the train and the cops subsequently informed them that I had been arrested for "committing a lewd act" in a public toilet – though, in fact, I didn't even get that satisfaction. The cop showed me his badge around the time I was unzipping his fly. Happily, my boss likes me and smoothed things over with our corporate chief executive, but also warned me that a second brush with the cops would not be tolerated.'

Just like my other New York friends Howie told me that I needed to get out of Vermont, that I was treading water up in the north woods. But there I stayed, telling myself that I would make the move in 1980 when I was twenty-five. My jogging escalated into a serious obsession, to the point where I ran the 1978 Boston Marathon in four hours and thirty-seven minutes. I shaved two minutes off that time when I did the New York twenty-six-miler the following year. Duncan and Howie were both waiting for me at the finish line as I staggered across it. Duncan's first book – *Through a Glass Weirdly: How American Counterculture Altered American Consciousness* – came out in late '78 to very good reviews and very few sales. But his take on the sixties – the way its unbridled experiments in social and sexual flexibility had chinked the conformist armor of the postwar era – was lucidly argued and written with considerable wit and flair. Certain critics took exception to his belief that a new conservative revolution was coming – and one which was going to be a total refutation of all the progress made from the dawn of JFK onward. In a very interesting op-ed piece he wrote for the *New York Times*, Duncan also asserted that the Iran Hostage Crisis – in which fifty-two American Embassy staff and civilians were held at gunpoint by revolutionary students supporting the Ayatollah Khomeini, beginning in November of 1979 – was going to be the downfall of the Carter presidency and the clarion call for a new conservative movement gathering pace around the country. Duncan again took the flak from his liberal friends for heralding the rise of these new right-wing thinkers. Though Duncan himself was rather centrist in his political thinking, he was nonetheless an increasingly astute and highly regarded observer of what was now being known as the zeitgeist: the tenor of our times. In a piece for *Esquire* he interviewed Norman Podhoretz, Irving Kristol, and Milton Friedman – all of whom were the intellectual boiler room of what became known as the neocon revolution. He pointed out that theirs was a vanguard to be ignored at our peril. Just as Duncan convinced *Esquire* to send him on the road for a month with that third-tier actor turned governor of California, and now someone seriously running for the White House a full eighteen months before the November 1980 election.

'Please don't tell me that Ronald Reagan has a chance against Carter,' Howie said to Duncan as they took me for Chinese food and beer after my marathon.

'In private the guy is distant, reserved, to the point where I sense that even the people closest to Reagan don't really know him. But get him in front of a Middle American crowd and he has a way of connecting, of invoking a Norman Rockwell vision of the country, of reassuring everyone that Carter's brand of national bleakness should be rejected.'

'But it's such a cartoonish view of America – and one that doesn't really exist anymore,' I said.

'All conservatives talk about the past as if it was the best of all possible worlds,' Duncan said. 'Watch what happens when the Brits elect Margaret Thatcher and her party before the end of the year. She's on record as saying that she fully approves of Victorian values.'

'You mean, like hanging children for pickpocketing and keeping poor houses flourishing, and tossing piss and shit out onto the street?' Howie asked.

'My, you have a colorful way with words,' I said.

'I will take that as a compliment,' he said. 'But you do have me worried, Mr Duncan, that we might just have a B-movie actor in the White House in 1981. Maybe he'll make Bob Hope Secretary of State.'

'I think Roy Rogers might get that,' I said.

'And he can negotiate with the Soviets with his loyal dog Bullet by his side,' Howie said.

'One thing about Reagan,' Duncan noted. 'He is a true modern conservative. But he is not an autocrat, a demagogue.'

'We'll elect one of those eventually,' I said.

Duncan had a bit of a minor heartbreak when Andrea left him for a fellow entertainment lawyer. Even though he quietly admitted to me that she was too 'aiming for the social stratosphere' for his tastes, his history with his mother and other women made him particularly sensitive to getting dumped. That was something I found both sad and self-limiting about Duncan: he took the breakups badly ... and then fell in love again quickly thereafter. Duncan himself understood this, telling me:

'I'm a bit of a romantic fool. I always need to be with someone, even if that "someone" isn't totally right for me. I envy you, having your little thing with Mystery Man – and being able to detach.'

'I envy you searching for love, Duncan. But I really hope that you stop trying to marry your mother.'

He laughed.

'Howie told me the same thing a few days ago.'

Howie meanwhile had come into some money. His Auntie Marie left him the entire contents of her estate – which turned out to be, after taxes and death duties and the undertaker and the lawyers, around $40,000. He asked me if my mother would help him buy a bigger apartment. Since leaving my father Mom had reinvented herself as a canny, wildly efficient and super-hardworking business-woman, telling me that by 1979 she was going to be her agency's 'number-one closer'.

She made good on her pledge, turning over almost $1 million in sales her first year and more than doubling it the next year. The fact that she was reaping a 22 percent commission on everything she closed meant that, by the end of her second year, she'd bought herself a lovely two-bedroom 'partial Hudson-view' co-op on 84th Street and Riverside Side Drive. She furnished it in a somewhat overwhelming Masterpiece Theatre/English country-house style.

Mom told me manifold times that the small second bedroom in her Upper West Side pad was mine. She found my insistence on staying at Duncan's to be just a little insulting. Once, when out for dinner with Mom and her new boyfriend, Jerry, a rather flamboyant theatre producer, Mom started in on the 'my only daughter is reject-ing me' routine. Jerry – with his thin dyed jet-black hair and his taste for shiny black three-piece suits and Windsor-knotted check ties said:

'Now, Brenda, you know that this young lady of yours needs her space. Which, from what you told me, you never had from your own mother. In fact, the only time that the old lady finally left you alone was when she had the good taste to die. Surely you're going to show Alice here what a classy, successful broad you are by not visiting on her the same dreck that your own mother buried you in.'

Way to go, Jerry! Even if the feminist in me was thinking that call-ing my mother 'a broad' was a little too 1950s for my taste. Then again, Jerry was sixty-four, which meant he was born when the First World War was just raging and, twenty years later, found himself storming Omaha Beach as an infantryman on D-Day. He was a big

Democrat who, even as the Carter administration was beginning to implode, still vowed support for our morally honorable president and the liberal causes he espoused. As such I had to forgive him for sounding like a Damon Runyon character: a fast-talking, minor-league Broadway hotshot. His ability to curb my mother's excesses also endeared him to me.

Dad, on the other hand, couldn't stand Jerry.

'The guy looks like a cross between an asshole rabbi and the sort of shyster lawyer whom you call after your upstairs neighbor has left the tap running and you've got a Niagara coming down on your bed.'

'He's been pretty nice to me,' I said.

'Because he's gotten you orchestra seats for *A Chorus Line* and brought you to dinner at Sardi's a few times?'

'Because he knows how to handle Mom.'

'No one can tame that crazy.'

'Jerry seems to have found a way.'

Dad looked at me as if I had just spat in his face. He turned away, motioning to the waiter to bring him another Scotch and soda.

'Next thing you're going to tell me is how rich she is.'

'I don't think Mom would describe herself as that.'

'Okay – it's her clients who are rich.'

'My friend Howie just bought a two-bed in Chelsea thanks to Mom and he's hardly rich.'

'He's that fag, right?'

'Don't call him that, Dad.'

'Am I saying something you don't already know? I mean, when I last took you out for dinner in the city and he showed up to whisk you off afterwards and was getting all palsy with me at the table, I felt as if fucking Tiny Tim was trying to hit on me.'

'Jesus Christ, Dad – why say something like that?'

'Because it's the fucking truth.'

'*Your* truth, *your* ignorance, *your* nastiness.'

'Now don't go all self-righteous on me, young lady.'

'I am not your "young lady". I am nobody's "young lady" – and I truly object to the fact that –'

'*What? What?* The fact that, after a few drinks, my tongue gets a little loose? You want to hang out with homosexuals – *there*, I used the right word! – be my guest.'

'You're still bereft, aren't you?'

'Is that why I paid for your fancy education ... so you can use big, fancy words like "bereft"?'

'You paid for my education so I can discern the difference between decency and brutishness – and yeah, there's another big word to chew over. Now if you'll excuse me ... I've actually had enough of your –'

But as I stood up Dad reached out and grabbed my hand.

'Please don't go ... please don't leave me ... '

'Then don't make me leave.'

'I'm sorry. Sorry about so much ... '

He lowered his head. He began to cry. I returned to my seat, pulling my chair closer, my hand still in his.

'I'm an asshole,' he hissed. 'A total jerk who killed it all. I screwed around on your mom all the time. Now she's having her payback.'

I pushed his Scotch and soda toward him. He took a long, steadying sip.

'Now I don't know much about this stuff,' I said, 'but isn't it hard to be faithful to someone when the two of you are fighting all the time?'

Dad looked at me quizzically. 'So when did you start having an open-minded view of all this?'

'All I know is: when it comes to love nothing is simple or straightforward.'

Dad then gulped down the remnants of his Scotch and soda and told me that he'd just been eased out of his job.

'I haven't been fired or anything. The asshole company president – Mortimer S. Gordon, the original fat fuck – called me into his office last week and announced that my work in Chile was finished. The mine was up and running, the privatization complete – and "we now need a younger guy running around the world for us". He wanted me to become Senior Vice President in Charge of Internal Operations – which is a highfalutin way of turning me into the

426

office manager. I asked him what he would give me if I decided to leave the company now: stock, bonds, a payoff, all that golden parachute shit. He told me a year's salary – sixty thousand dollars – and nothing more. Twenty years with that company – and their kiss-off to me is three grand a year for all that work, all that *profit* I brought to them. Naturally I kicked up shit, yelled at that tub of jello, told him he had to give me more. Immediately he said: one hundred thousand, one year of medical, and I was fired on the spot.'

'How do you feel about that?'

'Like a has-been. Called your mom yesterday, told her what happened, she let me know that she didn't want her rightful share of the house or anything else from me. In fact, she wanted nothing to do with me whatsoever. Which made me feel even more like yesterday's guy.'

To his credit he found a new executive position a few weeks later – heading up a trading division that specialized in commodities. He was appointed a senior vice president. He told me he would be making the same sort of money he did before 'but with big opportunities for profit participation'. And he was moving into the city, renting a furnished one-bedroom place in Tudor City, an old 1920s complex way east on 42nd Street. He sold the family house. He gave away all the furniture. He offered his three children the opportunity to take anything we wanted from the place we once called home. Peter and Adam took certain practical things – guitars, skis, a set of exercise weights (for Adam), books (for Peter). But all I asked for was a photograph of my dad in his Marine Corps uniform, and of my maternal grandfather on a field in Flanders during World War I. I also took away with me a picture of Mom when she was working, right out of college, at NBC – standing next to an early antediluvian TV camera, clipboard in hand, looking like the very model of early fifties comeliness and sexual reserve. I wanted nothing else – except certain notebooks and school essays and the remaining LP records from my collection that I hadn't taken with me to Vermont. Dad got just above one hundred thousand for the house. Goodwill Industries stripped it of everything. Adam joined me that Saturday afternoon when the house was emptied, Dad packing up his clothes, a few keepsakes (his honorable discharge from the military, his college degree, photos of us as kids), then piled it all into Adam's car. Adam had agreed to move Dad – and it was Adam who turned all moist-eyed as the last of our old furniture was packed up by the gruff Goodwill men and driven away, leaving us to stare in at the empty, scuffed, dusty shell of the place where we used to live, now devoid of any hint that we once called it home.

'It all can be taken away in a moment, can't it?' Adam said as the vans disappeared into the distance.

'Had you ever gone to war you would know how blindingly obvious that observation is,' Dad said.

'But you'd be more screwed up,' I added.

'You saying I'm screwed up?' Dad asked.

'You tell me,' I said.

I went with Dad and Adam into the city, helping Dad unpack in his new place. The apartment didn't exactly strike me as a happy one. Dad being Dad he'd probably told himself it was a good deal and decided to overlook certain basic facts: it was on the third floor facing the back alley, which meant it didn't have much in the way of natural light and was the sort of furnished place that seemed not to have been updated since the second Eisenhower administration. Besides the ancient kitchen and the moldy bathroom there was its collection of elderly, sad furniture – leaving me and Adam wondering why the hell he hadn't taken a sofa, a bed, a desk with him. Dad answered this question for us, saying:

'Yeah, yeah, I know I could've furnished the dump with all our old stuff. But then I would have been forced to always live with all those reminders of how it was.'

'And how *was* it, Dad?' I asked.

He gave me that grimace which said: do you really think I'm going to answer that?

Dad settled in and got started at his new job, pulling off a real trading coup his first week by betting short on zinc. He soon found himself a new girlfriend: Shirley, a thirty-seven-year-old divorced secretary at his trading company. She didn't want children (which was a relief). And what touched me most about

Shirley was how caring she was toward my father; how she was able to gauge his moods and tamper down his cantankerous tendencies.

I told Dad on several occasions that I considered Shirley good news. He agreed, but there was also a significant part of him that was still mourning the departure of my mother. A strong streak of jealousy was clouding things for him; the very idea that his wife could be having sex with other men while also pulling in the big bucks. But what was he missing? The mutual aggressiveness? The screaming matches? The deep disaffection?

Dad never pried into the reason why I was in New York every other weekend. He knew there was someone and he really didn't want to know anything else – I think he was still uneasy with the idea of me having sex with anyone. The matter of Toby therefore remained under wraps – which is how my father wanted it. As I did too.

Toby. There were moments in his arms, in the middle of the act of love, when I felt that I was giving myself to him profoundly; when I knew that I did feel a deep connection to him, that we were so right for each other. Toby hinted at such feelings as well, especially after Emma got tired of him playing Hamlet on the subject of their future together. One Monday morning he arrived at his office to find a letter informing him that their relationship was over, that over the weekend in the Hamptons she had met a man who worked in high-level finance, that it was '*un coup de foudre*'.

This was the late summer of 1980, around the same time that the unthinkable was now beginning to appear possible: Ronald Reagan seemed likely to become the next president of the United States. After a lackluster Democratic convention, after economic forecasts showing that the grim grind of recession was ongoing and with our people being still held as hostages in Tehran, the Carter presidency was doomed.

Privately, I was delighted that he'd lost that careerist social climber. Was this due to my growing sense that what I had with Toby might transform into something more permanent? Especially as I had finally decided to break ties with Vermont and had found

---

an editorial position in an old-school literary publishing house, commencing right after Labor Day.

It was Howie who set this great personal move in motion by suggesting, when I was next in the city, that I join him for brunch with Jack Cornell, a senior editor at Fowler, Newman and Kaplan – and one of his Fire Island friends. Jack was a seriously elegant man in his late forties; a Princeton graduate who had done the whole husband thing until finally coming out as a gay man two years ago. Jack said nothing about this during our first meeting. It was Howie who supplied all the background information, just as he primed Jack about me. I found him ridiculously smart and literate – someone who spoke fluent German, having spent a year at the American Institute in West Berlin after college. He had fantastic stories about life in that 'free island amidst all that Soviet-dominated oppression'. We talked politics, we talked books, we talked about my time in Ireland (sidestepping the attack). He wanted to know much about my family, having read Peter's book with interest. His world view intrigued me. Even though he was now very much a proud gay man he was very Republican when it came to economics and the Communist threat, his time in Berlin having made him virulently anti-Soviet. He talked on about crossing the Wall on several occasions, the bleakness of life in the East, 'the way that we here in the States take free movement and the right to openly protest against our government for granted, whereas anyone who does that in East Germany risks imprisonment and even having their children taken away from them. So yes, I will be voting for Reagan – because we're in financial chaos right now, and because Brezhnev is a hardliner who still has big imperial ambitions for the Soviet Union, and we need our own hardliner to stand up against him.'

I made the slightly rash decision of arguing against this statement, telling Jack that I worried about Reagan rolling back what few social safety nets this country had, and also finding his blind patriotism to be 'lacking in nuance'.

For the next ten minutes we had a sharp, respectful exchange on our differing notions of the role of government – Jack being a serious supply-sider, while, for me, the neocon 'less state, more personal choice' ideology was a Trojan Horse for a new Gilded Age.

At the end of the brunch Jack handed me his business card, mentioning that Howie had said I was interested in breaking into publishing.

'If you're around next week,' he said, 'maybe we can meet for lunch.'

As the spring semester was over and I was loitering in the city for seven days before returning to teach the summer term, I rang Jack's secretary on Monday and – to my surprise – found myself booked in for lunch that Wednesday. When I was told I would be meeting him at the Four Seasons I went out and bought a simple-but-reasonably-elegant black dress and a nice pair of relatively high-heeled shoes. I made the right sartorial call, as Jack was (I was discovering) quite the fashion statement. Beautiful designer suits, ninety minutes a day in the gym (at a time when jogging was still the exercise of choice – if, that is, you worked out at all), always needing to be immaculate, impeccable. He noted my clothes with approval.

'We would have gotten off to a shaky start if you'd shown up here dressed like you'd just come off a peace march,' he said. 'Yes, I am someone who expects my assistant to dress well. That doesn't mean you have to wear Halston. Think Paris intellectual chic. What you're wearing today is perfect for lunches like this one or the parties we'll be going to. I hope you like parties. Because they are going to be a big part of our work.'

I assured him that I was fine with parties – even if he probably knew that I was just saying that to please him. To my relief we then had a long conversation about books – and what interested me in fiction (when I mentioned writers like Graham Greene, V.S. Naipaul, Thomas Pynchon, Richard Yates, Donald Barthelme he nodded vigorously, saying that he himself also had very eclectic taste). We talked non-fiction, and how I felt that a book like Tom Wolfe's *The Right Stuff* was the very model of narrative new journalism, but that it would be wrong to believe publishing could capitalize on this singular success.

431

'It's a bit like Hollywood. Because *Star Wars* was such a surprise hit now the studios are bringing out half a dozen sci-fi films – almost all of which are destined to flop. I'm still just the outsider looking in – so please excuse my presumptuousness – but it strikes me that, when it comes to books, you must never think that you are onto a trend. A successful book is always atypical.'

'Unless it's the sort of bestselling writer who has established a brand.'

'But a writer can't treat his craft like a tire that he or she keeps retreading. That's where the editor comes in – not to tell the writer what to do, but to try to get the best out of them and make them up their game.'

'You don't want to write yourself?' he asked.

'Not at all. I want to be the midwife, not the mother.'

'Nice analogy.'

By the end of the lunch – a martini each, a bottle of Chablis, many cigarettes, and an eau de vie for my host (I thought I'd do a swan dive if I kept further pace with his booze intake) – I'd been offered the post of Junior Editor.

Toby took the news of my new job with notable unease.

'Not only are you joining our little club, but you're also going to be here full-time.'

'You don't sound pleased.'

'On the contrary, I've been saying for years that you should be in Manhattan.'

'But now that I will be here full-time – your exact words – what …? Are you nervous that I'm going to want more?'

'It will just be … different, that's all.'

Then he changed the subject, asking if I wanted to see the new François Truffaut film, *Love on the Run*, which had just opened in the city.

Strange, isn't it, when you receive in a somewhat offhand manner the signal that the internal logic of a relationship has changed. But when I tried, after the movie, to press the issue over a beer at Chumley's, when I asked out loud if he preferred that I was his Vermont fuck friend safely out of range for all but two afternoons a month, he got very defensive, telling me I was making far too much out of 'the simple fact that I just need to absorb this big new information – and, as I said before, it changes nothing'.

I knew that I could not blurt out what I was thinking – 'So even though I will now just be a subway ride away from you, you still want to keep *us* to twice a month between 5 and 7 p.m.?' But had I said that I would have stood accused of wanting to change the parameters of all this – which, truth be told, I now did. Or, at least, that several years on from Dublin, I finally felt a yearning for something beyond this circumscribed arrangement. Did Toby smell this off me? Was the commitment-phobe in him now terrified that I was about to raise the ante and demand *seriousness*? Was he already working out an exit strategy? If I pressed him further on this issue would he flee?

I knew the answer to that question. Which is why I leaned over and kissed him lightly on the lips and told him that I was happy to continue our thing as it was. To which he replied:

'Now you think I'm a shit.'

What I thought was: *you want everything and nothing, and you can't really decide what is good for you and what is toxic. You know I am not someone who will crowd you or will play high-maintenance games with you. You know that I get you.*

But I simply smiled and shook my head and said:

'Let's just carry on as normal.'

The next night Mom arranged a dinner out with me and my two brothers. We all had news. Mine was announced first and was greeted with raised glasses and Mom insisting she'd help find me an apartment – 'if you don't think I'm crowding you as usual'. I told her that, given her status as NY Realty Queen, I would be delighted to have her help. Then we learned that Peter had been commissioned by a super-cool producer in Hollywood to write a screenplay based on his Chilean book – and though the money was good, he was into the third frustrating draft as the director attached, Brian De Palma, kept changing his mind about the trajectory of the film.

'Naturally my publishers are asking where I am with the novel. I'm telling them I'm halfway done. Which is not the case.'

'How far are you actually?' I asked.

'Maybe fifty pages into the first draft.'

'Peter ... '

'I know, I know. But the script is taking a lot of time. And Samantha has us booked for July and August out in this house in Southampton – which means nonstop socializing.'

'Let me guess,' I said, 'it's costing, what, five or six thousand for the month?'

'That would be a cheap rental,' Mom interjected.

'Seven thousand?' I asked.

'Seven-fifty,' Peter said, almost ashamed to be admitting this.

'Jesus,' Adam said, 'that was more than half a year's salary for me at the school.'

'*Was?*' I asked. 'Why the past tense?'

'Because, like you, I've just resigned.'

'Wow,' Peter said. 'Let me guess: you're joining the French Foreign Legion.'

'I'm marrying Janet.'

There was a shocked silence. I could see Mom trying not to roll her eyes. None of us approved of his choice – but Peter, to his credit, put his hand on his brother's shoulder and said:

'I'm sure I speak for everyone here when I hope the two of you are truly happy.'

'Don't tell me she's pregnant,' Mom said.

Adam flinched, as if slapped.

'Would that be a problem?' he asked.

'Only for you and your future life,' Mom said.

'I'm getting a job in finance.'

'Because Miss Old Age Nurse wants that station wagon of her dreams.'

'No need for that, Mom,' Peter said.

'I'm not speaking with "forked tongue" as they say in westerns.'

'Well, I always knew you were an emotional Apache,' I said, also thinking: when Mom was in her 'take no prisoners' mode she was relentless.

'Do not denigrate our Native American brothers and sisters,' Peter told her.

'It's a metaphor, Mr Novelist,' I said.

'It's stereotyping.'

'Oh please, it was a smartass New York aside. Get rid of the Divinity School sanctimony.'

'Guys . . . ' Adam said.

'Too bad your dad isn't here,' Mom said. 'He'd call the Apaches "redskins" – and really create a riot.'

'*Enough,*' Adam hissed, sounding vehement. 'The baby is due in six months. In four weeks I am putting my MBA back to good use and heading to Wall Street. And the reason I am heading there is because, from what I'm smelling, Reagan's going to win and everything is about to change.'

'You mean, money is about to talk?' I asked.

'Money always talks,' Mom said. 'Especially in this crazed country of ours – where money is the way we keep score.'

'I don't want to settle scores,' Adam said. 'I just want to be rich.'

Peter raised his glass.

'Here's to lofty ambitions.'

Adam grabbed his beer mug and all but crashed it into his brother's, saying:

'Fuck your smug irony. Here's to the brave new world.'

26

ADAM WAS, INDEED, on the money. With the landslide victory of
Ronald Reagan in November of 1980, the entire political and fiscal
landscape of the United States began to tectonically shift. The night
of the election Toby showed up unexpectedly at my new apartment
around one in the morning. He was the wrong side of intoxicated
and depressed. I'd been over at Howie's with Duncan and around
a dozen of his friends, hitting the cheap wine and watching the
wrecking ball of history decimate the Carter presidency.

'If we had to elect an actor,' Howie said right after Reagan
addressed his cheering supporters, 'why couldn't we have chosen a
Redford or a Newman?'

'Because they're too educated and too liberal,' Duncan said. 'But
I warned you both, months ago, that this was on the cards.'

'Should we now kiss the hem of your *shmata*, Monsieur Oracle of
Delphi?' Howie asked.

'You can begin by kissing the 1960s goodbye,' Duncan said.

Toby posited the same sentiments when he rang the buzzer on
my apartment. I had just gotten home, feeling a little tipsy and
politically disoriented. Toby never arrived unannounced – and I was
under strict orders from monsieur not to show up *chez lui* without
first phoning (because, of course, he might be entertaining someone
else at the time). I was just a little surprised to find him standing
outside my door, the whiff of five Manhattans too many on his
breath.

'I needed to get drunk,' he said. 'I succeeded. Am I ruining your
beauty sleep?'

'As I seem to be still fully dressed ...'

'The country has just shot itself in the foot with a machine gun.
Might you allow me in?'

I motioned him inside. He followed me up the three flights of
stairs to my studio apartment.

'This is not a physical activity I should do while loaded,' he said, panting as we reached the second landing. 'You're eventually going to have to move out of here before old age sets in.'

'If I am still living here when I am seventy – and you happen to somehow also be alive – you have my permission to shoot me.'

We reached my front door. Toby staggered in after me, making a beeline for the kitchen cabinet where I kept the bottle of Wild Turkey that he had deposited here for his occasional visitations. He grabbed it and one of my jam-jar glasses. Then he opened the small freezer section of my fifteen-year-old refrigerator (it was a true old-school icebox) and reached for my one tray of ice.

'You've only got two cubes,' he said. 'I did ask you to get some more ice trays.'

'Maybe you can buy me an additional one for Valentine's Day.'

'Very funny. Want a slug?'

'I'm tanked enough,' I said, lighting what seemed to be my eighteenth cigarette of the evening.

'You keep smoking like that you're going to look like an incinerated chimney by the time you're forty.'

'You should show up next time in a gas mask. Anything else you want to criticize this evening? Perhaps the way my magazines are fanned out on the coffee table? But you, sir, are someone whose place would probably be condemned by the Board of Health if it wasn't for that very courageous cleaning lady who braves your mess once a week. When you were with Miss Vogue you kept it reasonably – because, of course, the Divine Emma intimidated you into a modicum of tidiness. But since she left ...'

'Why are you bringing this up?'

'Because you are giving me grief about nothing.'

'I'm being a jerk, right?'

'Indeed you are.'

'All I can say in my defense is: I blame it all on the Triumph of Reaganism. Tonight we are witnessing the beginning of the end of everything Franklin Roosevelt did during the New Deal to advance the cause of social democracy in this country. Trust me, by the time

Reagan and his cronies are out of office, money is going to be the civil religion in these United States.'

'But money here has always been just that,' I said.

He emitted a small burp at the end of my statement, then passed out on top of the hand-stitched Shaker New England bedspread that my colleagues at Keene Academy gave me as a going-away present, and which Peter's lady Samantha singled out as 'so old-lady cute' when they first visited my place.

Unlike my mother, who poured through British *Country Life* magazines to get the look she wanted for her new place, or Samantha, who turned Peter's pad into a Scandinavian shrink's office, I cared little about design, or making a statement with my apartment. Full credit to Mom for not just finding me an airy, L-shaped studio in a brownstone on 88th between West End and Riverside Drive, but also a place that was rent-stabilized and only $270 a month. It had high ceilings, hardwood floors, a working fireplace, and a kitchen and bathroom that were a little out of date but suited me just fine. I'd furnished it with second-hand stuff bought in a warehouse place on West 82nd and Broadway, much of which I'd sanded down and repainted distressed white.

'So this is sort of a budget-Nantucket look,' Samantha said when she sashayed in with my brother, a bottle of champagne in hand.

'It's just thrown together.'

'Well, you clearly like order – which wins points with me. And your library is most impressive,' she said, pointing to the floor-to-ceiling bookshelves left behind by the previous tenant, and which I had filled to brimming point.

'I think it's very "you",' Peter said.

'Define "me"?'

'Stylish in an "I don't give a shit" way.'

I liked my little place. Besides my books I had a growing mountain of records, and a stereo that wasn't high-end but did the job. I had a radio which was always tuned to WNYC and WNCN (twenty-four-hour classical music). I had a tiny television which I only turned on when something major was happening in the world. The building was quiet. Like in my dad's place, two bay windows faced the alley behind me. But I didn't care. I was here, in Manhattan, at last. And I was discovering that I had a certain flair when it came to editing books.

Jack gave me some basic ground rules on my first week under his professional wing:

'Never think you can write for an author.

'Always understand that every writer – no matter how successful and/or accomplished – is a walking bag of insecurities and neuroses.

'As such, your job is to handle all their baggage, and that includes the ongoing self-doubt, the fear of failure, the worry that they will never be able to replicate past successes, or climb out of the mid-list, or get the next chapter written.'

'Never, *ever* sleep with one of your writers – or if you do so, make it a one-night thing, not to be repeated.

'Know when to be lenient and when to be firm – and judge each writer's tolerance for criticism. The ones who believe that every word in a delivered manuscript is writ in stone require special handling. But so too the ones who will show up, looking like they haven't slept for four days, with twenty half-crumpled manuscript pages in hand, begging for an opinion.

'Build up your tolerance for long boozy lunches – and for hearing during these lunches all about the current domestic crisis, the third divorce, the tangled extramarital thing or – most of all – why that son-of-a-bitch one-time friend and fellow colleague in the literary trenches has just won the Pulitzer or landed the big movie sale or is selling far better than the bag of angst in front of you.

'Don't be afraid to suggest serious reworking of a manuscript but know you can only get away with this if you show the writer that you have their best interests at heart – and if you can also impress upon them your intelligence and clarity of editorial vision. Being smart but never smug is the key here.'

Jack was a great mentor. Besides sticking to his enforced dress code, the 'Paris boho in New York look', he let me know on my first day that he was a stickler for punctuality. I had to be at Fowler, Newman and Kaplan by nine-thirty every morning – and I was expected back at my desk even after an epic lunch. He himself was someone who, like Howie, accomplished so much on very little sleep. He was also very much the man around town. He rarely spent an evening in by himself in the very beautiful two-bedroom apartment in the West Village that had been his for the last decade, and to which I was frequently summoned on a weekend afternoon when he needed to throw ideas around about a manuscript or a submission.

I never said no – especially as it was indicated early on that he was looking on my first year as a trial run. 'Editorial boot camp' as he called it.

As such I worked double time those first twelve months. One of my tasks as a junior editor was, along with the other newcomers in the company, to read the slush pile: complete manuscripts, chapters, outlines that were sent in on spec to the company. A few weeks into my time I found myself intrigued by a rather overlong but potentially gripping account of being raised in a family of charismatic snake handlers in the most low-rent, intolerant corner of North Carolina. It was written by a woman named Jesse-Sue Cartwright whose first sexual experience had been with her crazed father. He was a man who not only spoke in tongues and claimed to have direct cognitive contact with the Almighty, but every Sunday wrapped his arms in poisonous pythons and used prayer to ensure that they did not fatally sting him.

I was both fascinated by its primitive narrative style and, more tellingly, the way the writer gave us a window into a world so foreign to most of us, yet also so deeply American. I told my boss that it had potential if she was the sort of writer who would be willing to cut and rethink much of the text. Jack read the first two chapters, and said that, on the proviso that Ms Cartwright was ready and willing to engage in several further drafts, I could work on it. Within twenty-four hours I called Jesse-Sue. She was very soft-spoken to the point of reticence, but we seemed to connect. She explained that, as was detailed in the book, she had managed to escape her monster father and depressed mother by getting into the University of North Carolina at Chapel Hill, and then finding a teaching job in Charlotte. She turned out to have a very dry, but potent sense of humor, and a survivor's ability to discern life's more crucial contours. She was also in overall agreement when it came to grasping what I was going to ask her to reconsider and rewrite in the next draft. I promised her a marked-up manuscript and detailed notes by Christmas.

Since we were now in early December of 1980, I was using every free moment to work on the manuscript, especially as Jack had piled me high with other duties. I wasn't complaining. I loved my work.

So too did Adam. He had joined a small Wall Street trading group called Capital Futures run by a forty-year-old hotshot named Tad Strickland. From the outset Tad was Adam's new-career guru. He was always using epithets like 'financial genius' and 'dynamic vision-ary' to describe him. Not only did Tad fill the big brother role that Peter sidestepped, but also specialized in the sort of motivational blather that spoke to Adam.

He actually told me: 'I have something immense to contribute to the world.'

My bullshit meter went into the deep red zone when Adam espoused this. But I also began to quickly understand that what my brother wanted most of all in life was acceptance. Tad spun an entire narrative around this idea – and essentially presented Capital Futures not just as a place where he could discover 'a forceful new professional path' and 'make a killing' (both Tad-isms), but simultan-eously 'find a financial workplace that will also be your family for decades to come'.

Tad had decided that my brother was 'a natural leader' – because Tad's eldest son from his first marriage, Connor, had been a star player on the Rye Country Day School's hockey team. Adam, of course, was the coach of the team – and one which he had led into their first championship season for almost twenty years. Tad was at the game where they won the regional prep school trophy, and where (in true Hollywood style) Connor had scored the winning goal. Being someone who was also develop-ing a lucrative sideline as a 'success guru' (*The Millionaire Within You* ... that sort of high-capitalist jive) Tad was thrilled with the way that Adam had, over two seasons, turned a scrappy group of players into 'a true winning team'. He invited my brother for lunch down at Lutèce. Adam showed up in his regulation blazer and gray flannels, a button-down Oxford shirt and striped tie. Tad schmoozed him, saying at the age of twenty-nine he needed to understand that he could stay on coaching for the next thirty years, buying himself and his 'bride-to-be' a little ranch house in Port Chester or Mianus or 'some other also-ran suburb. Or he could join Capital Futures' 'forward-charging team' and discover what it meant to 'travel in the upper edges of the financial stratosphere'.

Adam climbed aboard, entering Capital Futures in September of 1980, right after his marriage to Janet. The wedding was not exactly the most joyous afternoon any of us had ever spent, especially as Janet's family was a grumpy bunch from the small upstate town of Geneseo – and who (in my mother's memorable words) 'had all their taste in their mouth'. Peter, sensing what we were going to be witnessing, decided to leave Samantha behind in Brooklyn Heights, as he knew she would find Janet and her family 'beyond déclassé'. Janet's people were Presbyterians who regarded my Irish Catholic father and very Jewish mother with ecclesiastical distrust. Just as they had very big cement blocks on their shoulders about all our New York City credentials. Still, I didn't think Janet to be a nightmare; rather a provincial young woman who had little in the way of worldliness or sophistication, but who recognized a fellow awkward loner in my brother and thought: this could be a match. I did, on several occasions, try to engage her in conversation and even twice suggested that she come in to the city for *a getting to know you* dinner and a Broadway show with me. But she always found an excuse not to meet up with me. Adam, for his part, was susceptible to anyone who played the mothering card, as Janet did most effectively with him. I knew, by the time of the marriage (when she was already five months pregnant and showing), that she was already expressing reservations about him 'going all high finance' on her. Dad told me, after meeting her for the first time just before Adam started at Capital Futures, that he then took his middle child out for lunch and told him he should get out now. 'She is not the woman you should be with – especially as you are now positioned to become a big cheese on the Street.' But dear

Adam was, first and foremost, loyal. The coach in him, the generous good guy, longed for fatherhood. How could he abandon a pregnant woman? Dad offered him several hypothetical ways out. Adam refused to even consider such a plan, telling Dad that he had pledged himself to Janet 'and I am a man of my word'. To his credit Dad said nothing in reply. Except:

'Two, three years from now – when you are making the big bucks – getting out is going to be a lot more expensive, a lot harder.'

'I'm not a quitter.'

As Dad told me later, he had to stop himself from saying:

'You just might want to be.'

The wedding was in a rather glum chapel, with Janet all dressed in pink and all the bridesmaids also in pink and all the ushers in cream tuxedos with frilly shirts and brown velvet bow ties. Tellingly, Adam asked his assistant coach at school to be his best man. Outside the church, seeing all the ushers in those terrible tuxes, Peter turned to me and Mom and said:

'I am so glad he chose someone else to be his best man.'

When Dad showed up minutes before the service started, rushing down the aisle to where we were seated, he hissed at us:

'Got stuck behind some fucking local rube in his fucking rube pickup.'

Then he caught sight of Adam and his cohorts in their wedding suits and looked a little stunned.

'Is Janet's old man in the mob?' he asked us. 'Or do she and her mom favor a Dago Deluxe look?'

'Why don't you say that a little louder?' Mom said.

'I'm just articulating what you're thinking.'

'Let's all count to ten and tell ourselves in a couple of hours we'll be far away from all this,' Peter said.

'But my little boy won't,' Mom said.

'His decision, his call,' Dad said.

'Maybe we could kidnap him before he makes it legal and binding,' I said.

'The rednecks here would never let us out alive,' Dad said.

Mom had to stifle one of her explosive laughs, nudging Dad with her elbow, whispering:

'You can take the boy out of Brooklyn ... '

'So speaks the Flatbush Princess.'

Another of Mom's laughs, somewhat more pronounced this time to the point where she was glared at by Janet's hawk-faced mother seated across the aisle from us.

'I've just been given the evil eye by the Wicked Witch of the West,' Mom hissed, now causing Dad to laugh – which resulted in another ferocious glance from the woman wearing a weirdly over-the-top maroon velvet gown.

'Okay, New Yorkers – we have to call time on the sarcasm now,' Peter said, as our brother marched down the aisle and took his place up in the front row. His nervousness was manifest. So too was his inability to make eye contact with any of us.

'Oh God,' Mom whispered to Dad, 'he doesn't want to go through with this.'

'I can stop this now,' Dad whispered back.

'It's his call, his life,' I said.

'We can't be responsible for the decisions he makes,' Peter said.

'Always the fucking ethicist,' Dad said, but in a manner that made us all stifle more laughs.

Then the off-key organist broke into 'Here Comes the Bride' and we all stood up as Janet's ruddy-faced father led his daughter – her dress all pink satin, the five-month pregnancy bulge just a bit noticeable – down the aisle. As the minister approached the couple and we all sat down, Adam took Janet's hand. At that moment Mom began to sob. To my surprise Dad took her hand and drew her close. She put her head on his shoulder and kept it there until the service was finished. Mom looked sad, Dad looked sadder. Peter took note of this hitherto unseen (for decades) moment of closeness between our two parents and simply raised his eyebrows toward me. Neither of my parents was watching the events unfolding at the altar. Instead they were both staring down at the floor, not daring to look at each other, both together and lost at the same time.

Four months later their divorce came through. It was Mom who passed on this information, calling me at the office (which I had asked her on several occasions not to do), sounding so choked up at first that I feared someone had died.

'What's happened?' I asked.

'I am no longer Mrs Burns,' she said.

'But that's what you wanted.'

'Don't tell me what I do or don't want,' she said.

'If you didn't want it why did you go through with it?'

'Because your father wouldn't stop it.'

'But you were the one pressing for it, weren't you?'

'He still could have stopped it ... though that woman of his would have never have allowed it. She's a very controlling person.'

'Shirley's always struck me as rather good news.'

'Thanks for your loyalty.'

'Mom – what's all this about? Aren't you still with ... ?'

'Nah, got dumped.'

'When did this happen?'

'The night before your brother's fuck-awful wedding. Did you ever eat more depressing food in a more depressing Howard Johnson's banquet hall? Who the hell holds a wedding reception in a plastic shithole motel like that one?'

'People from upstate, I guess. But listen, this is work time for me. Can we continue this tonight when I'm at home?'

'I slept with your father the night of the wedding.'

This statement came out like a cry from the heart – as only Mom, in her best Joan Crawford mode, could deliver it.

'I'm not surprised,' I said.

'What do you mean by that?'

'Peter and I saw how you and Dad were clinging to each other while dancing at the reception.'

'You and your know-it-all brother discussed us?'

'Children do discuss parents, Mom.'

'Thank you, Dr Spock.'

'I think his thing was parents talking to children. Anyway you and Dad got it on. How was it?'

'Stop that now, young lady!'
'Why did your guy drop you?'
'He said I was too needy.'
'I see.'
'He also said I still had a longing for your father.'
'Is that true?'
A pause on the other end of the line.
'Yes and no.'
'Have you discussed this with Dad?'
'That asshole ... '
I stifled a laugh.
'I can see you really want to get back together with him. Now I do have to return to reading this manuscript.'
'What do I do, sweetheart?'
'I just have one simple question for you: why did you push ahead with something you didn't want?'
'Isn't that how life works?'
I had just finished the edit on Jesse-Sue's third draft. As I reported to Jack before heading out, I was very much pleased with her work to date. It still needed one more pass on her part – largely to tighten up some of her still digressive passages on faith and the harsh rural landscape in which she was raised. But together we'd managed to cut two hundred pages and allowed her twangy Southern lyricism to captivate the reader and guide the narrative.
'Can we schedule this for autumn?' Jack asked after I'd updated him on everything.
'Let me get one last draft out of her – because I think a final push will get it to the place I really want it to be, where it will play both the serious and popular sides of the street. We've also folded far more into it about the sexual and emotional brutality of her father, and how difficult it was to flee his domination, the fear he engendered in her.'
Jack thought this over. Then:
'Is this Jesse-Sue woman presentable and reasonably articulate in public?'
'We've only talked – and as I didn't exactly ask her to send a photograph ... '

'She could weigh three hundred pounds and be in serious need of a depilatory.'

'That is a possibility.'

'Does she have a wonderful Southern accent?'

'Hill Country Dixie, modified by a serious desire for serious education.'

'Well, if I really love the next draft, I'll probably send you down to meet Jesse-Sue and size her up. Get her to bring you back to her home village: the scene of the crime. If you feel she would be publicity-friendly – and if she isn't built like a brick outhouse – we might put some muscle behind the publication. But please make certain that the draft is in top-flight shape. This is your first solo passage as an editor. I am expecting something exceptional.'

I related this conversation to Peter as we settled into a booth at Peter Luger's and both ordered vodka martinis. Peter looked tired and somewhat stressed. But he still managed to shake his head when I repeated my boss's pronouncement to me, saying:

'No pressure on you whatsoever,' he said.

'Fuck the pressure on me. Why are you so down?'

Peter shrugged, then reached for his just-arrived cocktail.

'Here's to our insane parents getting it on at that nightmare of a wedding, then proceeding with the divorce, then continuing to meet once a week at Mom's place for sex.'

I nearly choked on my martini.

'They've been having an affair since the wedding?' I asked.

'Well, as they were married until just last week you can't exactly call it an affair.'

'But Dad has Shirley ... '

'Yeah, but monogamy is not one of our father's talents. Nor mine, either – though I have been a very good boy since Samantha and I got together.'

'Do you want a Boy Scout merit badge?'

'So speaks the woman who sees someone twice a week and keeps all the details to herself.'

'I am hardly judging you, Peter.'

'You have judged me. And harshly.'

'You mean after sleeping with that tour guide at Bowdoin? That was a decade ago. I've never brought it up again. You know I'm not puritanical anymore about such things. Which is why I'm more amused and surprised that our parents have got a sexual thing going again.'

He reached for the pack of cigarettes in front of me, fishing one out.

'Mind if I ... ?'

He lit up his cigarette, inhaling awkwardly.

'Samantha read the first hundred pages of my novel three nights ago. She was pretty damn brutal in her verdict about my efforts so far.'

'What exactly did she say?'

'That my characters were one-dimensional, that the narrative never animated into life, that she could care less about the dilemma of a divinity school student caught in the campus mayhem of 1968.'

'I guess you have to credit her for complete directness ... even if it is not what you want to hear from the person who lives with you. But if you want me to read it ... '

'I don't want that. Because you might just hate it – and that would complicate things between us.'

'You really think it's that bad?'

Peter took another sip of his martini.

'Truth be told: I don't know.'

'Why don't you show it to your editor?'

'Because the actual book is due on April 1 – a really bad choice of delivery date – and all I have to show for a year's work is that rather rough one hundred pages. It doesn't bode well.'

'Ask for an extension. Another year for a big novel is nothing.'

'The thing is: I think Samantha might be right. I got lucky with my first book. A lot of fanfare, a lot of noise, and I was feted as the alleged "voice of my generation". But my generation didn't buy my book. Because who really wants to hear about some faux radical mucking about in South America?'

'It was a brilliant book, Peter – and one which spoke volumes about what it means to be American and have a conscience and realizing that it's not enough to want to do good and live ethically in this culture. Because money and power always trump everything.'

'Now I have a big advance which I've already spent, and film option money which I've already spent, and a screenplay which has just been put into turnaround, and –'

'You're feeling sorry for yourself,' I said, an edge in my voice.

He lowered his head.

'Yes I am. I am complaining about things that most mere mortals would consider gifts from the gods.'

'All writers live with a demon – and the demon is doubt.'

'But I am giving in to the demon ... unlike you.'

'I'm not a writer, Peter.'

'But you are the ultimate survivor.'

'Oh fuck off,' I said, the anger leaping out.

'Alice ... '

'Never, *ever*, bring that up again. Calling me a "survivor", telling me how brave and resolute I've been – it's demeaning. Because it's trying to cast me in the role of the heroine, which is a role I don't know how to play. I am someone who puts on a perfectly rational and controlled and focused front to the world, and does her work, and functions reasonably enough to have twice-a-week sex with a man I rather love but who will never commit to me, and I understand that maybe it's better that way, because I cannot fathom ever absorbing another intimate loss again. As such, I am always feeling that a part of me has been damaged beyond repair, yet I still somehow manage to stagger through the day and not show this side to anyone. But you're not anyone, Peter. You're the one person in this insane family with whom I feel an actual proper kinship about all the shit we've been through together. So you, of all people, should know that calling me a "survivor" –'

I broke off, the rant suddenly overwhelming me, blindsided by the grief that had snuck in from that part of my psyche which I had tried to close off for so long. Peter, to his credit, came over to my side of the booth, put both of his arms around me and let me bury my head against him. I lost all track of time, of place. When I was spent I whispered into his shoulder:

'I must think about Ciaran once every hour. I can't get beyond it.'

'Maybe you never will.'

I went off a few minutes later to the bathroom. I threw cold water on my face. I adjusted the little makeup that I wore. I returned to the table to find Peter sucking down another cigarette, all color drained from his face. I slid into my side of the booth and found that my martini had vanished.

Moments later the maître d' was at our booth with a cocktail shaker and a chilled cocktail glass.

'This one's on us, ma'am,' he said.

'I'm so sorry for –'

Before I could finish the sentence he lightly touched my shoulder with his free hand.

'You must never apologize for sadness. *Never.*'

'Thank you,' I said. 'Thank you so much.'

As my lips met the exceedingly cold gin touched with vermouth, Peter reached for another cigarette and said:

'As we speak, Samantha is across town. In bed with Toby Michaelis.'

I shut my eyes.

'That's quite some news,' I said.

'Do you know this Michaelis creep? He's in your world. A big-deal senior editor around town.'

'Never met him,' I said, reaching for my martini and downing most of it in one go.

'I gather he's quite the lady's man, quite the stud.'

'At least she's his problem now,' I said, trying to keep the chaos in my head in check.

'I always knew that, as soon as she thought my star was no longer in the ascendant, she would move on. She told me that Michaelis promised her the child she so desperately wants right now. I did love her. Madly.'

'Then she wasn't worthy of you. Let her make this Michaelis guy's life hell.'

'Being dumped is never nice.'

I wanted to scream and shout. But one breakdown tonight was more than enough. All I said was:

'None of this is, in any way, nice.'

27

I BECAME AN aunt that winter. Rory Thomas Burns was born in White Plains Hospital at 3.48 p.m. on February 24, 1981. His father was absent at his arrival – as that was the day that Capital Futures had 'a high-yield bond thing' happening and Tad let it be known that he needed 'all hands on deck'. This financial event turned into something of a Wall Street sensation – for reasons too technical and above my fiscal knowledge to comprehend. Adam came away with a bonus of $500,000 ... which, as far as he was concerned, made up for the fact that he was elsewhere when his first child arrived in the world. Janet did have her own mother present – and her mother-in-law raced up after closing a sale on a five-story townhouse in Park Slope for a record price of $245,000. Mom was hugely excited by the arrival of her first grandchild, but her Brooklyn deal made the real estate pages of the *New York Times* – especially as the subways were iffy after dark and Park Slope was a still-questionable area ('Let's face facts,' Mom told me, 'Brooklyn is still, for most New Yorkers, the end of the fucking world – and I speak as a girl from Ditmas Avenue'). The fact that a Wall Street wonder boy bought it – and had a very photogenic lawyer wife and twin baby girls – gave the story even more play, as Mom was quoted as saying that her clients were 'early adopters' who would lead the transformation of 'this magically historic corner of Brooklyn with some of the best townhouse stock in the city into one of the most sought-after upscale professional family areas of New York'. Suddenly everyone was buzzing about this newfangled educated and moneyed social unit: the professional family, in which both husband and wife were working highly remunerated jobs with long hours, but also raising children and getting geographically adventurous by rejecting the usual Upper East/Upper West Side family-apartment options. This was news. Mom, showing great shrewdness, had also started courting the younger MBAs out of Harvard and Wharton and Columbia, making her one of the 'go-to realtors'.

On the day of Rory's birth, Dad got off the trading floor at seven and grabbed a commuter train out of Grand Central Station. He was at the hospital at 8 p.m. He called me from there, his voice heavy with emotion.

'Our family name's going to live on,' he said down the line from a hospital payphone. 'And the kid looks exactly like me at birth.'

'You can remember that far back?' I asked.

'Don't be a smartass, Alice. My first grandchild! And a boy!'

Indeed, the fact that the male line was going to continue – that was key here ... not that I was going to mention that.

'How's the mother doing?' I asked.

'Oh, you know Janet – a woman of few words, and those that come out are not exactly worth remembering.'

In the background I heard my mother hiss:

'For God's sake, don't shout that shit out – especially with her dried prune of a mother just down the hall.'

'Want to speak to your mother, sweetheart?' Dad asked.

'Sure.'

'Just think – in years to come, Little Rory is going to remember that he was born on the same day that Prince Charles and Lady Di got engaged. We're heading off now to dinner in the city. You won't be pissed if we don't invite you?'

'I've got a manuscript to finish, Mom.' To which I felt like adding: 'and I know the two of you are going to head back to your place for sex afterwards, so you definitely don't want the kid of the family around.' Instead I said: 'Peter and I plan to go up and meet our nephew tomorrow.'

'Well, he is a cutie,' Mom said, 'because he looks nothing like his mother.'

The next day, on the train up to White Plains, Peter was musing out loud how he should find some really down-and-dirty true-crime story and write the next In Cold Blood.

'Stop panicking. Finish the novel.'

'That's easy for you to say. I opened the New York Times on Sunday and there, on Bill Cunningham's page, was a picture of Samantha and that asshole Toby Michaelis at some black-tie society thing last week.'

'You're still mourning her?'

'She moved into his place. I don't have his number. It's unlisted.'

'I have his number.'

'Really? Why?'

'Because I was his lover for five years.'

Peter's reaction was one of recoil, bemusement, followed by a wry grin.

'Fuck off,' he said, smiling.

'I'm telling you the truth.'

Then, in a quiet, steady voice, I explained all about my years with Toby. Peter almost aged ten years during my recounting of our ... the word eluded me. An 'affair'? An 'arrangement'? It was a lot more than that. But we both denied ourselves a future – and then he had to blow it all up by running off with my brother's love. Not only was that the outer realms of injurious behavior, he didn't have the courage to tell me to my face (or even in a letter), knowing that Peter would be the unsuspecting messenger of this body blow.

I kept quiet when Peter told me, four or so weeks back, that Samantha had dumped him for Toby. I took my brother's late-night phone calls when he was full of despair. I went out with him twice a week and held him when he broke down after hearing a Dexter Gordon set at the Village Vanguard, and the great saxophonist launched into that heartbreak classic, 'How Long Has This Been Going On?'. He apologized for such raw emotion later that night as we walked north on Seventh Avenue at the end of the 1 a.m. set, and wondered out loud if he was just a literary one-shot wonder who had let slip a dazzling woman.

'She was dazzling in her own mind,' I said. 'Yes, very beautiful – and someone who realized early on that she had a considerable amount of control over men. Yes, super-erudite. Yes, she knew everybody. But she was also a girl from Cleveland and had that "born in a third-tier city" thing going. Which meant she had to conquer Manhattan at all costs. That meant grabbing and discarding people to aid her victory campaign. Your moment in the New

York stratosphere didn't last long enough for Samantha. As they say at Yankee Stadium: there's no real depth in the outfield. Because she is all about surface. In time, she would have brought you down.'

'She's done that already.'

'Only if you let her, Peter.'

Now we were on the train to God-awful White Plains and Peter was listening to the tale of my years of afternoons with Toby. He kept shaking his head, finally telling me:

'I'm such an asshole.'

'Why do you say that?'

'Because I've been feeling sorry for myself for weeks, not realizing the pain you were in.'

'But I didn't share that pain with you. I didn't share it with anyone. No one knew.'

I didn't want to hurt my brother by letting him know that I'd confided in Howie. He actually took my call around 1 a.m. on the night that Peter let slip the news, and told me that he was getting in a cab and coming right up to my place. That was so Howie. He arrived with a bottle of vodka – his favorite tipple – under his arm. He gave me a big hug. He threw himself on my sofa and noted that, as I moved up the publishing ladder, I would have to also move on from painted pine furniture. He did make me laugh and did mitigate the anger and the heartache that was coursing through me right then. He heard me out, rolled his eyes, kept my vodka topped up, held my hand, and told me:

'Now, kiddo, you knew full damn well that Mr Michaelis was this way inclined when you got involved with him. He was, to his credit, completely direct with you about this from the start. The problem is: you were in love with him. As he might have been with you. But he knew he could never complete the deal. You knew that too. The fact that he's run off with your brother's lady ... well, good taste is timeless. But you are going to have to tell Peter. You don't just owe him that. You also owe yourself that. He'll be shocked. He'll feel even worse for you – because, from what you've told me, he's a good guy, albeit as mixed up and contradictory as the rest of us.'

Howie got that one right. Sitting there on the train, he did something very big brotherly – he put his arm around my shoulder and said:

'I do understand why you needed to stay shtum about all this. Just as I am truly impressed with how you kept it secret for so long.'

'That's our one great family skill: secrecy.'

To our quiet relief Janet was asleep when we arrived at the hospital. But our brother was there. We both blinked in shock when he greeted us in the hall. It had been over four months since either of us had seen him (not since the wedding, in fact) – and we were both genuinely surprised to see that, sartorially speaking, he had transformed himself. Gone were the prep-school-coach clothes. Gone too was his fitness. Now he was sporting a tailored black suit, a spread-collared shirt with French cuffs and silver-dollar-sign cufflinks, a floral Hermes print tie, highly polished expensive black shoes. He'd put on about twenty pounds ('When you're working twelve-hour days exercise is never possible') but the suit had been tailored in such a way as to minimize his growing belly. More tellingly he emitted an aura of importance that neither of us had seen before. When we congratulated him on yesterday scoring his first big deal he played down its lucrativeness.

'It's a nice start – but the way I see it we're only beginning to watch the absolute transformation of the American attitude to money. Tad says: from the Crash of '29 onward we've looked upon men of capital as flawed and selfish, just as the accruing of money is considered crass.'

'But the Crash of '29 was caused by avarice and an unregulated market,' Peter said. To which I added:

'Even Teddy Roosevelt – *a Republican* – busted up monopolies at the turn of the century. Because as a member of the plutocratic class himself, Roosevelt saw that the super-rich were even more grabby if left unchecked.'

'More capital benefits everyone,' Adam said.

'Oh God, here comes the trickle-down economics stuff,' Peter said. 'Now you and the Reaganites can apply it directly to the daily lives of ordinary Americans with disastrous results.'

'Can we go see our nephew?' I asked, knowing that this was the start of a long and unending argument – and that visiting hours were due to end in around twenty minutes.

Rory Burns was a beautiful baby – and sleeping soundly as we peered in on him in the newborn nursery in the maternity wing of the hospital. Seeing him I didn't have an overwhelming need to have a baby – but I was transfixed by his fresh, angelic countenance; the fact that, just a day or so into his existence, he looked so new-minted, so unscathed by everything that life might throw his way. I wondered if our love of babies comes from the realization that we remember nothing from that new-arrival phase of life, that most of our very young years vanish from our memory. Reaching into the crib with my hand, letting my nephew clutch my pinkie with his tiny fingers, I felt like whispering to him: *do whatever you can to sidestep gloom, and know that your aunt will always be here for you.* Just as I also understood that he would have no control over so much until he was a damaged adult ... like the rest of us.

'You lucky man,' I told Adam. 'He is a wonder.'

'I'm pleased you approve,' he said. 'And by the way you seem captivated by Rory ... '

'No, I am not having the big maternal yearning moment.'

'Sorry if I was sounding a little old-fashioned, a little "all women want babies",' he said.

'You *are* old-fashioned,' Peter said.

'There is nothing wrong with traditional values,' Adam said. 'I am a libertarian. I believe you have the right to do what you want, live how you want, make as much money as you want – and to expect minor interference from the state.'

'Let me guess,' Peter said. 'Your boss Tad probably shoved a copy of Ayn Rand into your hands on the day you joined his firm – along with the silver-dollar cufflinks.'

'What Ayn Rand says about individual destiny is spot on.'

'It's also known as the cult of selfishness,' Peter said.

'Why don't I take us all out for a big dinner?' Adam said. 'A celebration.'

'Only if it's cheap and cheerful,' I said.

'But we don't have to do cheap and cheerful,' Adam said.

'Because you just made half a mil?' Peter asked.

The old Adam would have suddenly become uncomfortable at that comment, absorbing it the way a tired boxer handles an undercut. But Our Brother in the Big Deal Suit just shrugged and favored Peter with a wry, knowing smile, saying:

'Right then, cheap and cheerful. How about that old family favorite, Pete's Tavern? And you, older brother, can pick up the tab.'

Peter tried to do just that around three hours and three bottles of wine later, a juncture when we were all a little more than tipsy. Before that we immediately got talking about our parents' strange, skewed reconnection – and how, as I noted, 'maybe they are back to where they were before any of us showed up and hemmed them in'.

'Children don't hem you in,' Adam said. 'You do it yourself.'

'That's wise,' Peter said. 'But for people born in the late 1920s what choice did they have but to do what society expected of them?'

'Now they have become the first generation to actually divorce without fear,' I said. 'Mom once told me that none of her friends growing up had divorced parents.'

'But the majority of them had hateful marriages,' Peter said, then somewhat boozily grabbed Adam by the shoulder, adding: 'That said, you're a happily married guy, right?'

'At least I've found someone who wants to stick with me.'

Peter was just a little surprised by this verbal slap. Especially as it was so unlike Adam – or, at least, before he put on that suit.

'I suppose I deserve that,' Peter said. Adam leaned over and landed a light playful punch on his older brother's shoulder.

'Never play the Janet card again, okay?'

Peter's reply was a quiet nod of the head. It was a curious, sad moment. The balance of power between my two brothers had changed. The awkward, self-conscious, self-doubting, cosmopolitan-rejecting Adam who had fled to teach hockey was now on his way to becoming a true Prince of the City. Peter knew this. To him, it was further proof of just how much his star had fallen, how he was no longer at the epicenter of things. Adam discerned this, saying:

'No doubt when that novel of yours is the success everyone is expecting it to be Samantha will be knocking on your door, begging forgiveness. But you'll have moved on, right?'

Fuck. That was a low blow. And one which Adam had timed to angry perfection. Was this decades of pent-up frustration finally erupting? Adam once said that 'outside of those years playing hockey I've always been considered the runt of the litter'. Was he taking lessons in channeling his inner aggressor from Tad, bolstered by that big six-figure commission he'd just garnered? Or did he just need to remind Peter: *who's got the power now?*

The check landed. Adam made a play for it, but Peter insisted on picking it up, even though I knew that the hundred or so dollars it amounted to was probably what he was trying to live on a week.

'There's no need to do that,' Adam told him.

'Yes there is,' Peter said, an edge of wine-fueled belligerence to him. Jesus, he too had inherited my father's stubborn streak: the refusal to back down when confronted; to not admit weakness when challenged by another man. Even his brother.

'I may be a struggling writer,' he said, bringing out his American Express card, 'but I can still treat my brother and my sister to dinner on a momentous occasion for our family: the arrival of the next generation. But tell me this, Daddy Warbucks: what exactly is this high-yield bond thing you're doing down on Wall Street?'

Adam ignored the Little Orphan Annie reference, poured out the last of the bottle into our glasses, raised his in the direction of Peter and told him:

'Here's to you leading yourself into a better place. Because, Older Brother, only you can do that. Your attitude determines your altitude.'

'I hear a song coming on,' Peter said. 'Or is that a quote from the Tad Strickland playbook?'

'Does it matter who said it? It's sound advice – and it certainly has helped me reconsider the way I look at myself and my relationship to the world.'

Peter was about to say something, but I jumped in here.

'High-yield bonds, Adam. I want to know all about them.'

Adam drained his wine, put it down decisively on the counter-top, then began to talk. Explaining to us over the next fifteen minutes everything I ever needed to know about high-yield bonds. How they were divided into three categories: non-investment-grade bonds, speculative-grade bonds, junk bonds. How bonds that are rated below investment grade have a higher risk of default or 'other adverse credit events', but typically pay higher yields than better-quality bonds ... which is what makes them attractive to investors who don't veer to the cautious side of the street. How junk bonds function as an IOU from a company – and pay high yields because their credit ratings are less than pristine.

Peter – who had been listening to all this with considerable interest – raised his finger.

'Is it just corporations and fat cats who invest in junk bonds?'

Adam smiled, saying that if either of us wanted, he could easily get us an 11 to 12 percent annual return on investment.

'No investment product is going to give you such a yield: a doubling of your money with a compounded return in about six to seven years. That's why junk-bond investing is strictly for the wealthy. For many individual investors, using a high-yield bond fund makes a lot of sense. Not only do these funds allow you to take advantage of professionals who spend their entire day researching junk bonds, but they also lower your risk by diversifying your investments across different asset types.'

'You're quite the salesman,' Peter said.

'You're quite the shrewd brilliant mind,' I said, trying to counter-act Peter's little sideswipe.

'Now you have an inkling about how high-yield bonds work. And yes, the bond sale I was running for the past few weeks cashed out big for us. Which is why ... '

He reached into his briefcase and pulled out two envelopes, hand-ing one to me and another to Peter. I looked inside and blanched. There was a stack of hundred-dollar bills contained within.

'Both of you should take cabs home tonight, given the crime in this town.'

Peter stared down into that enveloped wad of cash as if he were peering into some sort of abyss.

'How much is all this?' Peter asked.

'Five thousand each,' Adam said. 'And you are going to accept it from me.'

Peter shut his eyes.

'You've just saved my ass,' he said. 'I couldn't pay my mortgage this month.'

'All's well that ends well,' Adam said.

'Thank you,' Peter said. 'I'm overwhelmed.'

'We're family. It's a good moment for me.'

A few minutes later we got Peter into a taxi back to Brooklyn. All the wine had hit him hard, intensifying his moroseness. He gave me a goodbye peck on the cheek then encased Adam in a drunken bear hug, whispering something into his ear. After he'd gone and Adam suggested we share a taxi uptown I asked him what Peter had said to him.

'He asked me to forgive him. Which, of course, I told him I already did.'

'Your gift is far too generous,' I said.

'Do something interesting with it – like redoing your apartment.'

'I'm fine with it the way it is. Maybe I'll put it away for a trip somewhere – not that Jack will ever allow me more than a week off twice a year.'

'That's more than I'll ever get from Tad. Not that I'm even think-ing about vacations. Maybe when I've got ten million in assets.'

'That's the goal?'

'At least. And guess what: I just put a deposit down on a house in Greenwich. Not far from the country club. Very "French chateau" style. A pool. A tennis court. And I've also just bought a co-op in the city: just two beds, on 71st and Lexington. Mom, of course, did the deal.'

'How much?'

'One-forty-five. It's an old doorman building, and the place needs a little work – not that I care about decor. But at least I've got a

New York pad during the week. Considering that I'm putting in fourteen-hour days ... '

'How does Janet feel about all that?'

'Hey, she's about to move into a five-bedroom house with staff.'

'Staff? What do you mean by that?'

'A full-time nanny, a maid.'

'Aren't you getting yourself a little overextended?'

'That 500k I just raked in: it's just the start. This time next year maybe I can even buy you a place. Outright.'

'Don't get ahead of yourself.'

'You're doing well. On your way up, right?'

'Whatever that means. I like what I do. My boss is a bit like yours – totally exacting. Still, he seems pleased with my progress to date and I've got this book I've totally championed myself which will make some noise.'

'And on the guy front?'

'Let's skip that subject,' I said.

'I don't want you to be lonely.'

'I'm not lonely,' I said.

'You sure about that?'

'Adam, please ... '

'Fine, fine. I do wish you'd stop smoking,' he said as I lit up a Viceroy.

'I wish that too.'

'How many a day?'

'A pack to a pack and a half.'

'Jesus, Alice ... '

'Tell you what: if you start reading one book a week I'll quit smoking.'

'One book a week ... me?'

'Don't you want to save my life?' I said with a smile as the taxi pulled up in front of my building.

'That's your job. Do you think Brother Peter will be okay?'

'Eventually, yes ... or, at least, that's what I hope.'

But Peter's block about his novel became monumental. He could not move the narrative forward, could not animate any of his dramatis personae into life. In late April he called me, saying he'd finally decided to show his editor at Little, Brown, Ken Franklin, the 180 pages of the manuscript. A week later Franklin called him into his office and expressed polite dismay at what he'd read so far.

'He basically let me know that he considered it all a misfire, that though there were "brilliant narrative flashes", it was far too discursive and long-winded with "big stretches of dialectic argument about the nature of being American which simply fail to hold the reader".' (Peter had this ferocious memory ability to quote others back verbatim.)

'Okay, this is bad news,' I said. 'But why not take the five grand that Adam gave you and disappear somewhere for a couple of months? Maybe go on a big adventure, come back and write it. A narrative journey through somewhere edgy, important. You're really good at that sort of thing. And –'

'But I told you before: the money's spent.'

'On what?'

'Life. You know that I lived far too fast and high on the advance, and film money. Adam's gift helped me pay off some debts and cover my mortgage.'

'There's only one solution here: show that you're smart and come up with a new idea for a book that will make Ken Franklin forgive the novel. You're also going to have to figure out a way of paying your bills while you write that book.'

'I don't know if I can face the draft-after-draft pressure of a new book.'

'Find a saleable idea first.'

Would that Peter had the appetite for rewriting shown by my Southern literary protégée, Jesse-Sue. She'd delivered a superb further draft – totally nailing all the rewrites and editorial suggestions I'd requested. I spent a very long weekend at home with the manuscript, about 90 percent delighted with what she had accomplished. I still had some quibbles – but the overall shape, rhythm and impact of the book was a world apart from the fascinating, ill-constructed and frequently meandering work that Jack had handed me six months earlier. When I arrived at the office that Monday, I knocked on Jack's door, noting huge crescent moons beneath his eyes and the look of a man who needed twelve hours of urgent sleep. He was shaking out a couple of pills from a plastic prescription bottle.

'Had a good weekend?' I asked.

'Don't go witty on me this morning, Burns.'

'That was a perfectly neutral question, Jack.'

'And I have a particularly un-neutral hangover combined with three nights of sleep deprivation. If you ever need to get through a day on two hours in bed go to your doctor, as I did, and get him to prescribe dextroamphetamine. You can thank our mutual friend Howie for recommending this. From what he tells me he lives off the stuff.'

'Well, after you've caught up on proper sleep maybe you can read this,' I said, putting the manuscript of Jesse-Sue's book on his desk. 'She did everything I told her to do.'

'Which makes it now a masterpiece, eh?'

'I sense, with the right campaign, this could find a huge public. And I've tweaked Jesse-Sue's original working title, *Daddy Snake Bite*, to simply *Daddy Snake*.'

'That might have legs if we give it an atmospheric but explanatory subtitle, along the lines of *Growing Up Backcountry*. I'll have a read and let you know.'

Twelve days later, at an editorial meeting (with me present), Jack made his pitch to the group, telling them that *Daddy Snake* had all the makings of 'an American classic – Southern Gothic meets a terrible coming-of-age story – yet one which has a redemptive ending'.

When I showed him a recent photo of Jesse-Sue (taken at my request the previous week) he could see that she was rather pretty in a long-haired, wistful, 'down-home country girl with smarts' kind of way. As such he okayed a trip by me and the head of publicity to North Carolina to meet with her, and also take a look at the terrain of her story: to see just how we might be able to capitalize on it all, press-wise.

The trip was nothing less than revelatory. Jesse-Sue was even more interesting in real life. Tall, lanky, with waist-length hair and searching, injured-by-so-much eyes, she favored tight blue jeans, blue work shirts and scuffed cowboy boots. She lived in a simple small 1920s arts and crafts house in a quiet corner of Charlotte – a city, she explained, that was a Southern provincial ten years ago, but was now starting to expand its economic base, wanting to emulate its ever-growing neighbor, Atlanta.

'I have a theory about life below the Mason–Dixon,' she said to us in her favorite local 'shit-kicker bar'. 'It wasn't the Civil War and Reconstruction that changed the South. It wasn't the Civil Rights Act of 1964 and federally enforced desegregation – which is never really enforced here. What changed the South is one thing and one thing alone: air conditioning. Before people down in Dixie could work in a cool, climate-controlled environment, the place was an impossible swamp for eight months of the year. Air conditioning has been a civilizing factor in the South – it's why Atlanta is now a boomtown. And why Charlotte is also gunning to become a financial hub, attracting all those northern opportunists looking for a cheap place to set up corporate shop. Trust me – fifteen, twenty years from now this little Southern city will have skyscrapers and a whole class of Yankee dudes in suits running the big insurance and accounting firms which are already sniffing around town. The airport will have direct flights to London, and there will be five-lane highways and far too many new country clubs.'

Wow. The girl could talk. Especially after an Ezra Brooks or two (her preferred bourbon) in that dive bar – the Last Outpost – where she often went for an evening drink with the guy in her life: a still-hippie carpenter from Alabama named Jake who'd studied English at Old Miss, and who had an impressive library in his home office. He'd also done all the amazing work on Jesse-Sue's house and was rather handsome in a ruffled, mustachioed, early-middle-aged-dude sort of way. He'd dodged the draft by heading north to Canada, then returned south when Ford offered that amnesty in '75, drifting around, doing odd jobs, finding carpentry work here and there, deciding to loiter for a spell in Charlotte, where he met Jesse-Sue while helping install a new fence at the high school where she taught. As she told us:

'He saw me coming out of school, having just taught a seminar on Faulkner's *The Sound and the Fury* to five of its brighter kids. I had the book under my arm, and he stopped me and started talking rather convincingly about Faulkner. I thought: this is the smart dude I've been hoping to bump into.'

A year on from our first meeting the story of how my amazing new literary discovery first met her beau was repeated many times in the press when *Daddy Snake* came out to a wave of positive reviews and stayed on the bestseller lists for twelve weeks, reaching as high as number 4. There was an amazing *60 Minutes* segment on Jesse-Sue where she brought the reporter back to the tiny shotgun shack village she'd once called home and convinced the local church elders to let them film the snake-handling ceremony. It caused a small national sensation. I watched it at home with Duncan and Howie – whom I'd invited over for order-in Chinese from my local Upper West Side Szechuan joint, along with several bottles of Prosecco I'd bought to celebrate this big PR coup. I'd visited the same church eight months earlier accompanied by Jesse-Sue and Sarah Richardson, one of our senior publicisits. Jesse-Sue's home village, Banner Elk, was – as she described – a nowhere place. The Apostolic Church – where she spent every Sunday from her infancy until she fled at the age of seventeen – was a tiny rough-hewn wood chapel with five pews, a simple altar, and little more. Banner Elk, population 970, abutted the border with West Virginia, and was as low-rent and socially depressed as anywhere I'd ever been. The rural hinterland I occasionally bisected in Maine during my Bowdoin years was nothing compared to this Other America: dirt poor, under-educated, geographically marooned and intensely religious to the point of superstition. Jesse-Sue's father had long since left the community.

'As soon as I ran away and alerted the authorities, they vanished with my four younger brothers and two sisters,' she told us as we drove toward Banner Elk. 'Last I heard, they settled on the Texas panhandle, near Amarillo. Daddy got a job on the oil rigs there, my siblings all grew up and left. I made it clear to the Feds – because they were involved by this time – that if they could guarantee he'd never come near me again I wasn't going to go through the nightmare of

465

testifying against him in a court of law. Nor could my mama ever contact me – because she went along with everything that Daddy Snake did. The Feds assured me they would make certain neither of them ever bother me in the future. I think they approved of my stance. 'Cause these were North Carolina and Texas Feds – and this was the start of the seventies. They were inclined to think: incest really should remain a family affair.'

When we reached Banner Elk I expected hostility to be pouring out of all its collective pores at the sight of Jesse-Sue. But people were genuinely warm toward her – not in a hugging-kissing sort of way, but pleased that she had decided to pay them a visit.

As it was a Sunday the entire village went to church. There were Baptists, there were Presbyterians, there were Church of Christ fundamentalists, and then there were the Apostolics. When we showed up just prior to the service all eyes in the packed five pews were on us. The Man of God – mid-fifties, barrel-chested, a short-sleeve maroon shirt, a clerical collar, a tattoo of JC on the cross adorning his hairy left bicep – approached us gravely. This was Pastor Jimmy.

'Miss Jesse-Sue, I welcome you home – and I welcome your friends to our house of worship.'

With that he returned to the rough-hewed altar and called everyone to their feet, and he began a screeching prayer to the Almighty: a prayer about having mercy on us sinners who don't deserve mercy, and how the Apocalypse was near at hand and the Four Horsemen would soon be upon us, and all His People would rise straight to Heaven and those not saved ...

He stared, laser-like, at me and Sarah as he said this. But then, as if some strange internal celestial switch had been flipped, he began talking in a crazed, off-the-charts language – or, at least, what sounded like garbled words spewing forth from Pastor Jimmy. As Jesse-Sue explained to us later, this was known as *glossolalia* – or speaking in tongues, a private prayer language that seemed to erupt within Pastor Jimmy and all his parishioners, causing aural chaos to reverberate everywhere in the chapel. Then Pastor Jimmy reached into a closed, low, wicker basket by the altar. Moments later a lethal rattlesnake was wrapping itself around Pastor Jimmy's very bare arms as he continued speaking in tongues, though now his voice was just a notch above a whisper, so as not to perturb this venom-stocked reptile.

60 Minutes also filmed this snake handling ceremony for their segment on Jesse-Sue. Broadcast in prime time on Sunday night when the majority of America was at home, it was a knockout. The moment it was off the air I got a phone call from Jack.

'I may be running a fever of 103 due to this stupid flu I somehow picked up – and I may not be able to get further than from the toilet to my bed – but I did manage to see Jesse-Sue's segment on *60 Minutes* and I am already ordering a second printing tomorrow. This book is going to launch you, Alice. Congratulations, Junior Editor: you've just arrived.'

I accepted such rare and fulsome praise from Jack and offered to come over and play Florence Nightingale.

'Don't you have Howie with you?' he asked.

'My word, sir, you know everything.'

'Keep our friend company ... and hopefully I'll make it to the office tomorrow. Bravo to you.'

When I mentioned to Howie and Duncan that Jack was laid low with a serious flu, Howie noted that 'there's a lot of it going around right now'. But then he insisted on reaching into his shoulder bag and bringing out a still-cold bottle of French champagne to celebrate 'Alice's triumph'. I told him that he shouldn't be so extravagant on my behalf (the label said Bollinger and I knew it was anything but cheap). His reply:

'It is the Year of Our Lord 1982. Ronald Reagan is in the White House; Maggie Thatcher is in Number Ten Downing Street. Business is booming. Money is the lingua franca of our times. So yes, we should be drinking Bollinger to celebrate your big catch.'

'That sounds far too macho and Hemingway,' Duncan said, 'unless you've developed a sideline in chasing Florida marlins.'

'Only if they have cute *derrières*,' Howie said.

'You might get arrested for corrupting marine life,' I said.

'But this is America. We can buy our way out of anything, including an illicit homosexual liaison with a dolphin.'

'We're supposed to be saluting Alice's triumph, not talking trash.' Duncan said. 'I'm calling a friend at the *Atlantic* tomorrow, pitching them an essay I want to write about *Daddy Snake*,' Duncan said. 'Reading the book, seeing that crazed evangelical church just now ... it's got me thinking. Reagan comprehensively kicked Carter's ass in the South because unlike the Peanut Farmer – a thinking Georgia Baptist with a decidedly thoughtful, serious approach to the Christian message – Reagan, a total non-believer, nonetheless glad-handed all those Bible thumpers who decided that they could hook their wagon to his economic conservatism.'

'Oh please,' Howie said, 'the last hurrah of the evangelicals in this country was when they put Scopes on trial for teaching evolution, and they were comprehensively ridiculed by everyone but their fellow rednecks.'

'The difference is,' Duncan said, 'after decades of being ridiculed by the liberal elites, they are now going to have their revenge on us.'

Later that week, there was a party for *Daddy Snake* at the National Arts Club. Though Jesse-Sue knew nobody in New York, Jack and Sarah ensured that the event was packed. So too did Howie and Duncan, who each brought along a coterie of 'around town' media and literary types. My entire family showed up. Dad came alone, leaving Shirley in New Jersey. He was having a good run in the commodities market – but told me after the third Scotch that he missed all the international travel that once defined his life.

'The work is interesting, even challenging. But I've turned into a guy at a desk. Time is moving too fast – and I still want to be out there, roaming the planet. I'm telling you this because I'm proud of you. Proud of what you've accomplished. But take it from your old man – don't get stuck behind a desk.'

Before I could reply – 'But I love the work' – I was pulled away by Howie, telling me that Jack was about to make his speech welcoming us all and saluting Jesse-Sue. Mom, meanwhile, was working the room – seeming to know everyone there, charming all comers in that open, schmoozy way of hers. We were easier with each other now. Her newfound sense of identity and purpose and independence had turned her days into full ones. Mom had broken free of her

boredom. By reconnecting with my father in the form of an affair –
yes, it was still going on – Mom, in turn, found that she didn't need
the hassle of dating some guy and dealing with his wants and needs.

'It's great with your dad. We have an afternoon and one or two
evenings a week. He goes back to his place. We get what we want out
of it. He should really dump Shirley. Not because she's bad news.
From what he's told me she's pretty okay, outside of that Secaucus
accent of hers. But why does he need to clog up his life with another
woman when he's got me on tap several times a week? The sex, by
the way, has been monumental since we divorced.'

I reported this conversation to Peter – who, in the months since
Samantha dumped him, had managed to talk his way into a column on the *Village Voice* entitled 'Left Field View' which allowed
him to 'mouth off on just about everything from a radical political
perspective' (his words). It also paid him three hundred dollars a
week, enough to cover the maintenance of his apartment and live
a modest life around town. Meanwhile, he'd convinced his editor at
Little, Brown to let him abandon the novel – and instead flip it into
a memoir of being a campus firebrand in the sixties. But there was
one proviso. The advance he'd received to date would be his full and
final payment on the book. When he called me, saying that he felt
he had no choice but to accept this offer, I told him:

'That's right. They are offering you a solution which will not
result in professional suicide. Sorry to be blunt here. My advice:
take the deal and write yourself out of trouble by delivering a brilliant book. Here's another small piece of advice: try to make your
avowed radicalism a little more mainstream. You'll find a bigger
audience beyond Village cranks and the few remaining Trotskyites
up in Washington Heights.'

'My sister has become a New York literary operator.'

'At least I'm not fabulous.'

Peter came solo to the launch party. Though I knew there had
been a few women here and there in the past few months, I could
still tell that the Samantha wound had yet to cauterize – and, in
fact, opened up again when she called him just a week earlier to
inform him that she was pregnant. He reluctantly volunteered this

information, knowing it would cut me deeply as well. But I'd already heard that Toby was an expectant father via Howie – who was the Village Explainer when it came to New York book gossip. The fact that I responded to this news with a shrug hinted that, eight months after his departure from my life, the ache had dulled.

I introduced Peter to Jesse-Sue. She was looking radiant, lovely, and brilliantly masking the anxiety that had been coursing through her ever since she got off the plane a few days earlier. She had suddenly bumped into fame – and as I warned her, it was a tricky construct and one which ruined many a literary career. The fact that Hollywood had paid mid-six figures for the book rights also meant that she'd had to hire a smart accountant. Outside of thinking about buying a place on that raw, Atlantic-swept corner of North Carolina known as the Outer Banks, she told me that all she and Jake wanted was to 'drift back into obscurity' once all the furor about the book died down.

'You will never be obscure again,' I told her, 'but you can choose to guard your privacy. You can also do me the biggest favor going: write your next book as soon as possible.'

I could tell that Peter was immediately smitten with Jesse-Sue. Jake had decided to stay south for the New York launch ('He would feel real out of place among all the big-city types,' Jesse-Sue told me). When I saw that a real connection had been made between my author and my elder brother, I was about to step in and say something. But Adam – who'd arrived just before Jack's welcoming speech – put his hand on my shoulder and said:

'Big Brother needs the female attention. Your cutie Southern Belle author is a big girl – and clearly knows how to handle herself with a smart fellow like Peter.'

Adam's suits got more varied and more tailored to his ever-expanding girth. It mirrored his ever-expanding wealth. Along with Tad he was being written up as 'The High-Yield Bond King'. An article in the *Wall Street Journal* let it be known that he'd taken home almost $2 million in salary and bonuses last year. Janet largely remained out of sight – though he religiously spent every weekend with her and Rory in their extravagant Louis XIV Goes Burbs manse. I visited there once and was just a little astonished to see gold bath taps in the master en suite. Janet had taken charge of all this – and had discovered a real talent for spending her husband's serious money in an excessive nouveau riche way. But when I raised a quiet worry about the cost of inlaid marble floors, hand-cut crystal chandeliers, a day *and* night nanny for Rory, and the fact that Janet had convinced my brother to buy her deadbeat biker brother his very own souped-up rock-star-style trailer and a big new Chevy pickup to haul it, Adam told me to stop fretting. He was about to buy a co-op for Dad, had just insisted on thrusting twenty grand on Peter 'to let him stop living like a self-flagellating monk', and was sending Mom and Dad on a 'dream cruise' along the Mediterranean this summer.

'I should also get Mom to find you a nice one-bed place in your choice of neighborhood which I will then buy for you outright.'

I wasn't going to take him up on his largesse – because there was a significant part of me that didn't want to be beholden to anyone. But I was very pleased to see that, in the midst of his hyperactive Wall Street life, he'd found time to make it here tonight.

'Hey, did you think I was going to pass up the opportunity to see my little sis get crowned a New York player?' he said.

I didn't get a chance to answer him with the necessary ironic disdain for being called any sort of 'player', because Howie was suddenly at my side, nodding a hello to Adam and saying:

'Sorry to steal her from you, Mr Big, but I need Alice for a few moments.'

His tone concerned me. So did the fact that he led me out of the main salon where the party was taking place and into a little lounge nearby. As Howie ushered me in my eyes went wide. There was Jack, collapsed in a big overstuffed armchair, his suit jacket off, his tie loosened, his dark blue dress shirt drenched in sweat, his sleeves rolled up and what looked like a virulent rash covering both of his forearms.

'Jesus,' I hissed. 'We need to get you to a hospital.'

'I'll be fine,' Jack said, his voice weak, denuded. 'It's just some sort of virus.'

471

'Which half my friends have,' Howie added, the somberness in his tone hinting he knew whatever had hit Jack was bad. Very bad.

'Do you have it as well?' I asked Howie.

He turned and looked away, gazing through the window at the illuminated wonder of Manhattan after dark.

'Not yet,' he said.

28

THEY WERE STILL calling it GRID: gay-related immune deficiency. That acronym was courtesy of another acronym: the CDC (Center for Disease Control). Some months later, in August of 1982, its acronym was changed to AIDS: acquired immune deficiency syndrome. The recently created Gay Men's Health Crisis forced this modification. It was founded at the start of the year by a ferocious, rabble-rousing writer named Larry Kramer – who made many enemies and eventually changed history by insisting that federal and international attention must be paid to this escalating epidemic. Kramer also argued that it must not be labeled as a 'gay disease', as it threatened heterosexuals as much as homosexuals. When Jack got sick – along with around a dozen of Howie's friends and colleagues – knowledge of AIDS was still very limited. Lesions had cropped up on Jack's arms, and he told me on several occasions that he woke in middle of the night feeling as if he was drowning in his own perspiration. He was still coming to work, doing his absolute best to keep his illness from public view. As summer arrived, he had the air conditioning in his office cranked up to arctic levels to try and counteract his ongoing sweats. He informed me with alarming regularity, 'under pain of being fired', that I was to never mention his illness to anybody. This was another unsettling aspect of his sickness: an increasing paranoia about being found out to be harboring what he called 'the gay cancer'. It also made him frighteningly short-tempered and angry. On three occasions that summer he blew up at me, calling me incompetent and negligent when he thought I'd missed an editorial deadline, or hadn't come over to his apartment immediately as requested. When I quietly told him that (a) the deadline he was insisting I had overlooked was still several weeks off, and (b) my telephone messaging service had no record of any calls made by him on the Sunday morning that he allegedly called, he said I was a liar. Then he looked as if he had just committed the most grievous sin imaginable, and begged my forgiveness.

'You cannot tell anyone about my terrible behavior,' he said.

But he knew I was talking regularly to Howie – who, in turn, was coming by Jack's place on a daily basis, and got him connected with a doctor off Christopher Street; an avuncular, rabbinical fellow named Morgenstern. He had been Howie's own physician ever since he'd moved to New York in 1976.

'At first I was rather suspicious of this somewhat tubby father of four, grandfather of six, who grew up in an Orthodox Jewish household in Williamsburg. But half his practice is made up of gay men. When I came to him with VD or rectal infections, he couldn't have been more "all in a day's work" about it. By which I mean: he was never judgmental, never the stern father warning me to stop being a bad boy. Ever since the outbreak of what seems to be an epidemic, he did tell me I might want to start using condoms just to be on the safe side – because no one has worked out how and why GRID is spreading, but Morgenstern is pretty convinced that it's bodily fluids. The thing is, they still don't know if it's a virus or not. They still don't have a test to detect if you've got it or not. I could be carrying it as well.'

'But you have no symptoms so far.'

'I'm such a screaming hypochondriac. If I get a runny nose now I'm going to think I'm doomed.'

'Jack isn't doomed, is he?'

'Naturally Morgenstern didn't discuss his case with me – doctor/patient confidentiality and all that. But when I came by last week, terrified that my sore throat was the start of something terrible – it was nothing – he told me he'd been talking with some friends of his who were residents at St Vincent's Hospital, which has become the go-to emergency room for men with GRID. What the doctors there told him was terrifying: nothing they throw at this illness medically reverses it. Once you've got it, it isn't like flu or other viruses that respond to antibiotics. All those lesions on Jack's arms ... half my friends have them now. And they pop up everywhere. I know one guy – he has them all around his teeth. Another guy – really chubby in the past – has lost around sixty pounds and now looks like one of those Biafran famine victims. I'm not talking thin, I'm talking skeletal. It's a fucking plague. If Dr Morgenstern is right – that it could be transmitted by blood and sperm – I'm doomed. Especially considering the amount of men I've been with – even in the last few weeks.'

'Use condoms from now on,' I said.

'I'm thinking about taking an oath of chastity.'

'Yeah, right.'

'Allow me the grand sweeping proclamation that you know I will never follow. But I will use – and insist – on rubbers from now on. How many people know about Jack at work?'

'So far no one has mentioned anything directly. But everyone has seen how rattled he is, how much weight he's lost, and how his temper can suddenly erupt out of nowhere.'

'He won't be able to keep it hidden for much longer. Especially if the lesions spread to somewhere he can't keep them covered – like his face.'

That happened in late August. At my urging, Jack accepted an invitation to spend ten days at his friend's beach place on Fire Island – a huge amount of time off in the mind of the workaholics we both were. In fact, he was beginning to listen to me, asking me to deputize for him, taking over an important book he was editing that was a revisionist history of the fifties, while also handling the near-daily phone calls from Cornelius Parker, one of our more venerable and thorny novelists (then again show me a novelist who wasn't tricky). He was a brilliantly tough and unflinching observer of the self-entrapment rituals of American life, most notably the horrors of a marriage turned toxic. He himself was four times married, a professor at Syracuse with huge amounts of resentments about still needing, at fifty-five, the teaching gig to pay the bills and multiple alimonies. He was also a noted alcoholic who turned out a book every three or four years and couldn't understand why he had never been able to gain the same sort of commercial traction as John Updike, his ongoing bête noire. The truth of the matter was: Cornelius was always very well reviewed – even if certain critics found his caustic outlook on everything to do with men and women, and the chaos they made together, to be increasingly dyspeptic. But his sales continued to falter, to the point where his last novel, *Why She Left Me*, only sold 4,300 copies. We feared he was simply retreading his past work. His public had cottoned on to this and were beginning to desert him. Now Cornelius was approaching the end of his long-awaited new novel and was suffering from a massive case of writerly stage fright.

'Why won't my editor speak to me?' Cornelius asked in a phone call during Jack's ten-day furlough off the coast of Long Island.

'He's having a very needed vacation.'

'But he's been letting you take my calls for over a month.'

'He's just been insanely busy.'

'Too busy to talk to *me*? I've only been a Fowler, Newman and Kaplan author for twenty-five years.'

'No one is shunning you, Cornelius. I can say, with all truth, that everyone in the house is very excited about your new novel.'

'If no one's read it how can you be excited by it? I'm sinking commercially – if this book doesn't cut it for all of you ... '

'How far are you off from finishing it?'

'Maybe fifteen thousand words. I don't know if I *can* finish it.'

'Would you let me read what you have?'

'You're not my editor.'

'Jack told me, before he went on vacation, that I was to handle his writers while he's away. If you would like an opinion ... ?'

'I never show anybody my manuscript while it is in progress.'

'Then finish it and get it to us in the next few weeks, even longer if you need the time. The thing is: to get it right.'

'Because if it's wrong ... '

'Cornelius ... '

Another long silence.

'My son Mark is up visiting me for a few days and returning to the city tomorrow. If he were to drop the manuscript off at your office, would you be able to read it over the weekend and call me without fail, this coming Monday?'

'I'll talk to you first about it before speaking to Jack. That's the best I can do.'

What I didn't promise was: not telling Jack about reading it. Had I said nothing to my boss, and he later found out that I'd agreed to peruse Cornelius's manuscript, he would have professionally defenestrated me on the spot. Also: though he was on vacation, Jack did insist on a daily phone call at 6 p.m. so I could fill him in on absolutely everything that went down at the office that day. And by everything ...

'Did you talk to the office supply people about ordering those twelve dozen Blackwing pencils that I've been after them about for weeks?'

'It's all taken care of, Jack.'

'I told that nightmare bitch Sylvia Luxembourg that I can only edit with Blackwing Number 2s. She said that the official house pencil was now the Paper Mate Number 2. I then found out that her brother is the sales rep for Paper Mate.'

'The pencils will be on your desk Monday. How's the beach?'

'Rather fucking wonderful. I think I'm on the mend. That skin thing of mine – it's almost all cleared up. I've been going for long beach walks every day. And I've even been able to start drinking a bit again. A gin and tonic and a glass of white wine most nights. Considering that I couldn't keep any alcohol down before, this is good news. And, fuck, how I've needed to drink these past weeks. The worst of what I have is behind me now.'

I wanted to believe that Jack was the medical exception, the guy who was going to beat it.

'That's just terrific,' I said.

'Maybe I'll even start being civil to you again. I've been such a cunt recently.'

'I haven't taken it personally.'

'I would have.'

'I need to bring something up with you.'

'That sounds ominous.'

'Not really – but it's something I want to clear with you first.'

Then I explained the long conversation I'd just had an hour earlier with Cornelius.

'Alice, by all means read his manuscript. Very smart that you told him you'd call him first. That will keep him marginally less anxious. But as I am not coming back to the city until Wednesday

evening I will expect an extended phone call about the manuscript
Sunday.'

'What time would suit you best?'

'Phone me here at 5 p.m. sharp.'

I did as directed – calling him in a state of controlled excite-
ment, knowing full well that Jack stamped down hard on too much
enthusiasm, distrusting it, telling me that 'an ebullient reaction to
anything usually came from the gut – and the gut could also later
ulcerate. Even if you think what you've read is just wonderful, put
that enthusiasm on a shelf for a few days, then revisit it with a clearer
perspective.'

Which is exactly what I did with Cornelius Parker's novel *The
Next Mistake*. I was a little unsure of the title. Would readers
turn to anything that spoke directly about the manifold errors
we make in our intimate lives? But the novel was a complete
knockout: a history of two people who meet in midlife after both
having been through difficult divorces and the complexities of
children. But what begins as a passionate, intelligent love story –
a true second chance – turns into a tale of a couple who pull
their happiness apart courtesy of their respective pathologies. It
wasn't a long novel – around 80,000 words, with two final chapters still to come – it cut so brilliantly to the heart of the matter:
the way we often destroy that which we desperately want. More
tellingly, it spoke volumes about the hopefulness of love and our
need to undermine it. I was relieved to see that he had moved
away from a college setting and had chosen New York City. Nora
and Matthew leave their respective lives in the burbs and meet
as single people in their late forties in Manhattan. Cornelius got
the details of modern city life absolutely right, one of the quiet
subtexts of the novel being how Manhattan was suddenly being
flooded with young men and women with money, and how Nora
and Matthew – having been born there in the late 1930s and then
raising families in Westchester – found themselves returning to a
city which had lost its raffish, violent edge and become a place
of high financial ambition. Although Cornelius hadn't written
the final two chapters, the last one I read had me in tears – as

everything fell apart for two people who knew they deserved each other and just couldn't bring it off.

'Okay,' I told Jack when I rang him in Fire Ireland at precisely 5 p.m., 'I am going to stamp down on my enthusiasm. But this novel, if properly handled, could be huge for us.'

The next afternoon I was on the phone with Cornelius.

'I've just poured myself a double Scotch,' he said, 'just in case the news is as bad as I suspect.'

'No need for the Scotch,' I said. 'You've written something wonderful.'

That got his attention. Over the next ninety minutes I took him through my many pages of notes on the novel, while constantly reassuring him that it was indeed superb. I discussed certain areas of the manuscript that needed sharpening, but stressing that nothing I was trying to get him to excise or reshape was going to lessen the novel, but would improve its commercial viability.

'I want *The Next Mistake* to be that rare species: a literary novel that truly sells.'

That sealed the deal.

'I'm overwhelmed,' he said. 'What's more – given how busy you say Jack is right now – would he be desperately offended if I asked that you become my editor for this novel?'

'I'll run it by him.'

When Jack returned to the office I saw immediately that all his talk about him being medically new and improved after his ten days at the beach was, at best, wishful thinking. At worst, it was a complete denial of the true gravity of his condition. He'd lost more weight, his face had a gray hue, and a lesion had erupted on his nose. Nonetheless he refused to speak about his illness, barking out orders, spending three hours after lunch speed-reading Cornelius's manuscript. Then he called me in at the end of the afternoon to say that my initial impressions and the four-page report I had written on the novel were spot on. He informed me that, yes, I was to take over all the editorial work on the book. He even called Cornelius while I was in his office, telling him that he had indeed written his 'literary and commercial resurrection'.

Two weeks after Cornelius delivered the final chapters, I rented a car on the company Diner's Card that I had just been entrusted with and drove up to Syracuse, checking into an elderly hotel that Cornelius had recommended near the campus of the university. Cornelius himself was an interesting mixture of arrogance and insecurity – something I had already gauged from our conversations. Physically he wore his many pains and defeats on his rugged face. He was still in reasonable shape for a man who started drinking around midday. He was living alone, and his small bungalow was rigorously tidy. Like my dad, Cornelius had been a Marine. When I mentioned that my father had been in Okinawa, there was instant kinship, as Cornelius had survived another horrendous Pacific battle, at Guadalcanal. His fourth wife – one of his former students – had left him six months earlier.

'Four marriages really is the triumph of optimism over experience,' he said. 'As a smart young woman like yourself well knows – especially given your trade – the last thing you should ever do is marry a writer.'

'Yes, I've worked that one out already.'

When I made a passing comment about him reaching for the Jim Beam at lunchtime, he pushed the bottle away and said:

'Don't expect me to reform on the spot – but I know I have to cut down.'

'Here's the thing, Cornelius. All going well with this draft, Jack and I will push sales and marketing to back your novel to the full. Which will mean a lot of media attention: press interviews, possible television stuff, and a big national tour. If the reps respond to it and sell it as well as we hope, if we get enough advance press interest, you might just find yourself in a bigger spotlight than you've ever been granted before. But that's where the ball lands firmly in your court. If you keep reaching for the bottle as you do now – if you come across as some late-middle-aged wreck who has stumbled into a big, literate bestseller and doesn't know how to handle it – then you are not going to turn this novel into the resurrection you so crave.'

Hearing myself say all this, thinking how I was sounding all too authoritative and brutally direct, I could only wonder if this was

480

the interesting outcome of all that had happened to me over the past five years. Was this newfound ability to take charge – to tell someone the things they didn't want to hear, but to do so in order to bring about a result I wanted – a signal that I had arrived at a somewhat different place within myself?

The evening before I drove up to Syracuse Jack called me into his office and insisted on making us drinks. Pouring Bombay gin over ice, he told me that – although it was now October and summer was way over – 'drinking a G&T reminds me of that barrier beach just fifty miles from Manhattan, which conjures up for me what Bali or some Australian beach must be like. It made me think: I've hardly been anywhere, that I really should see the world before I can't … even though I know that's now impossible for a whole batch of reasons. Just as I must tell you, Alice: my time here among the living is going to be abbreviated.'

I was about to say something reassuring but stopped myself. Jack saw me apply that verbal break and nodded at me with a sly sagacity.

'You're learning, Burns, you're learning. You're handling things impressively.'

Jack still refused to tell anyone else in the house about his illness. When Cornelius visited for a lunch with the sales reps – and saw the evident frailty of the man – he pulled me aside later and asked:

'Why didn't you tell me that he's so sick?'

'I just couldn't, Cornelius,' I said.

Nor did I mention it to anyone else. Even Duncan. Who was pre-occupied with happier matters – as his new book had made a nice splash. Excellent reviews, better than acceptable sales, an immediate new contract with St Martin's for two further books. He also had his freelance contract with *Esquire* extended – and was about to head off to Casablanca, with the idea of spending six months crossing North Africa and eventually ending up in Israel.

Peter, meanwhile, rang me at work, saying he was back in Brooklyn, after subletting his apartment for the past five months and borrowing a friend's cottage on a lake way up in Western Maine. He'd returned to the city looking even more lean than usual (he'd taken to running three miles a day), with a finished manuscript under his arm. I heard, courtesy of Jack and Howie, that his editor at Little, Brown thought the radical memoir was accomplished but had little in the way of great sales prospects in the Age of Reagan – where even the more educated Democrats were veering away from all their sixties idealism. Still, Peter had delivered his second book (even if he wouldn't let me read it) – and had fulfilled his contract. Though he'd been back for a few weeks, outside of that quick call at my office to say hello, he'd sidestepped the offers I'd made to have dinner and maybe even hear some late-night jazz. Then we ran into each other at the launch party for Duncan's book. His bushy hair and even bushier beard made him look like a backwoods man suddenly washed up on Manhattan's shores. He did give me a hug hello, but was noticeably reserved, preoccupied. He noted that Duncan did not attract the sort of upscale media social climbers that we'd seen at so many of these launches (like his own). And he was relieved to see that Toby and Samantha (who'd just given birth to a little boy, Charles) were not present tonight.

'Good for Duncan, getting all this attention,' Peter said. 'He deserves it – given he's quite the stylist as an essayist and has that insane work ethic of his.'

'You'll be having one of these launch parties in a year's time.'

'I doubt Little, Brown will go to much expense.'

'But word has it that they like the book. Are you going to start writing again for the *Village Voice*?'

'They actually offered me back my column – so that will cover basic expenses. And Mr Wall Street slipped me some money the other day – not that I asked for it.'

'You agreed to meet Adam but not me?'

'I needed a loan, a fast-cash injection. I am back to paying the maintenance and the monthly vig on a refinancing thing I had to do last year to keep afloat. The cash which Brother Moneybags just gave me, along with the *Village Voice* column, will just about cover my bills. Now all I need is the subject of a very big book, something that can really speak to the moment.'

'I'm sure you'll find something, Peter. Maybe you'll even find time to have dinner with me.'

'Did you hear that Shirley dumped Dad?'

That was bemusing news.

'I really am out of the loop.'

'I only found out when the old man called me up around ten two nights ago and asked me to meet him for a drink at P.J. Clarke's. I'm a bit worried about him. He told me that he's doing very well heading up that trading division and is also bored to death. Then the girlfriend finally got fed up with him sneaking off to be with his ex-wife, so she walked out last week. The weird thing is, Dad's taking it badly. Because Mom won't let him live with her and will only continue to see him twice a week. Dad suspects Mom is seeing someone else – which I suspect as well. Still, he went all Irish on me the other night, talking about how life never really pans out well for him. He's also smoking almost as much as you are – which is not exactly a good thing.'

Duncan gave me a lecture later on my cigarette intake when I joined him, his editor, and a few of his friends at a post-party at the Nom Wah Tea Parlor in Chinatown. That was so Duncan – wanting to celebrate his new book in a no-frills dim sum joint on Doyers Street. I noticed he was girlfriendless that night. I knew from Howie – who was (of course) at the table – that Duncan had just been dumped by a woman who was the director of a modern dance company down on Wooster Street. Yet another romantic failure. Though out on public show he was his usual erudite, worldly, witty self – telling the table a sharp, learned story about the effusive, hyper-neurotic Gustav Mahler having a conversation with the taciturn, manic-depressive Jean Sibelius on the nature of symphonic writing. The guy knew so much about so much. Duncan: the smartest guy in the room. But also the saddest. And currently flirting with a very intense woman named Paula. She was a deputy at the *Paris Review*, had the ear of its editor George Plimpton, and looked thoroughly taken with my friend's current spiel. I felt a stab of desire. As much as I tried to convince myself otherwise, there was still that deep, unresolved need to truly connect: to have someone there to be my ballast amidst the mess of life, to help make me feel that I was not alone in the dark. How

I longed for Ciaran. How I could see Duncan so wanting this as well – and constantly hooking up with the wrong person as a way of not allowing the light to get in. Was this the ultimate corrosive residue of familial damage: that yearning to make that supreme contact with another sentient solitary soul – and the need to simultaneously push it away?

Paula had very black hair and very rouged lips and round black glasses to go with her tight black dress. The Intellectual Vixen look. I knew that Duncan would go home with her tonight. Just as I knew that he was on a ten-city book tour and then would be hopping a plane to Casablanca – and disappearing into the geographic void for months to come. I watched as Paula began to noticeably touch the top of his right hand, then lean over and whisper something in his ear. Duncan smiled. She smiled back, squeezing his hand. Then she stood up and headed off in the direction of the old dismal bathroom right off the kitchen.

'Looks like you have a new interesting admirer,' I told Duncan.

He just shrugged, then said:

'My father called me this morning. He'd received the copy of the book I had my publishers send him. Know what he told me? "One of the many great things about Reagan is that he's showing you assholes just how transient and stupid the sixties were. Which is also one of the reasons that nobody's going to read your pretentious book." His exact words.'

'Here's a piece of advice: when that mean little man calls you again just put down the phone. He hates you for actually making your way outside of the corporate realm in which he's stuck.'

'To him I'll always be the weird kid with the funny walk who could never live up to his idea of macho-dom.'

'I think the children of every ex-Marine in the United States should be offered free therapy on behalf of the government – because, like my dad and yours, they all came out of the experience twisted beyond belief. And with all these deranged ideas about duty and honor and *Semper Fi* which just don't play in the real world. Especially if their children don't conform to their idea of regimental standards.'

'I should have told him to go fuck himself. Instead I mumbled something about how the *New York Times* was rumored to be giving it a great review this coming Sunday.'

'Go on your book tour, disappear across North Africa, and remember you are living the life he so desperately wants, but could never have – because he lacks the imagination and talent to achieve what you have done. Know this, however – if you get yourself killed somewhere between Casa and Tel Aviv you will break my heart. I don't think I could stand another loss.'

Duncan looked at me with care. Not thrown by what I just said, but certainly intrigued by it. Just as I was caught unawares by what I had just blurted out. Then again, when we talk before thinking aren't we articulating something that we have, until that juncture, kept from view? Before I or Duncan could say anything further, Paula was back at the table, eyeing me with wariness.

'You two look rather deep in thought,' she said.

'Just reminiscing about our Bowdoin days,' Duncan said.

'Ah yes, old-school tie and all that,' she said, then leaned over and again whispered into Duncan's ear, following it up with a light but deliberately placed kiss right on his lips.

'We're going to make a move,' Duncan announced to the table. 'Especially as I am on a train to Boston in the morning.'

It seems that he did manage to get her into bed that night. She even flew out to be with him for the entire Los Angeles-to-Seattle stretch of his book tour. Four weeks later, back in New York, he asked if Howie and I could see him off on his flight to Paris.

'Doesn't Paula want to say goodbye privately?' I asked.

'She did that herself about a week ago.'

'Sorry.'

'Story of my life,' he said.

Howie arranged that we all meet in the bar of the departure lounge at TWA out at Kennedy Airport. You could accompany the departing passenger to the gate, first passing through a perfunctory metal detector. There was a cocktail bar in a corner of this strange 1960s architectural gem: a white concrete terminal shaped like the wings of a plane atop glass.

'I've got three thousand dollars in traveler's checks, my passport, this one small backpack, a shoulder bag with five empty notebooks, a fountain pen, about two dozen blue-black cartridges, and absolutely no contacts.'

'And when you have a torrid affair with some sultry beauty in the Kasbah of Algiers ... ' Howie all but shouted, the effects of the second martini making him arch his voice an octave or two higher and causing heads to turn around. Duncan, to his credit, shook his head and smiled.

'You're such a queen, Howie. Do you really think that 1940s potboiler with Claude Rains and Hedy Lamarr is what I'm about to walk into?'

'Is there anything wrong with life as it was depicted on the Warner Brothers backlot in 1942?'

'Only if you don't mind the slight disappointment of walking into the current Algiers – which, from all accounts, is a Muslim Havana on the Mediterranean: socialist with all the deprivation side effects.'

'Do you see why our friend is a master wordsmith?' Howie said.

'Oh please ... ' Duncan said.

'Howie's right,' I said. 'You've got it when it comes to the manipulation of language.'

'My one and only talent,' Duncan said.

'Cue "What Becomes of the Broken Hearted",' Howie said, breaking into a loud rendition of the first verse.

'How about a final martini?' Duncan said.

'You sound like you're about to face a firing squad,' I said.

'Just the unknown,' Duncan said, 'which is both daunting and wonderful.'

Howie was about to say something, but suddenly turned away, his face awash with tears. Instinctually Duncan reached out and put his arm around his shoulder.

'You get back alive,' Howie said. 'I can't bear another friend dying.'

'I'm not intending to do that,' Duncan said.

'Then watch your ass, Mr Man of the World Daredevil.'

'How's Jack?' Duncan asked.

Howie lowered his head, more tears now flowing.

'We were just at the hospital before we came out here,' I said. 'He's in a very bad place.'

Indeed, Jack had entered St Vincent's just five days ago after one final appearance at the office. On that day I helped him, at his insistence, stagger in. He was being held up by two canes, the Kaposi's sarcomas on his nose and in his mouth now septic. In the days before this, Howie had stayed on the sofa bed in Jack's apartment and acted as his night nurse. Come dawn Howie would then go off back to his own apartment to shower and change for work, keeping himself going through the day on coffee and uppers. At which point I would show up and get Jack somehow into his clothes and load us both into a waiting car. To their infinite credit the board of Fowler, Newman and Kaplan not only let it be known that Jack was welcome at the office for as long as he could continue working, but they also arranged for a car and driver to get him anywhere he needed to go (which meant that we were spared the indignity of taxi drivers frequently passing us by, not wanting to transport such an unwell man). I was privately told by the house's finance man, Mel Morgan, that if Jack needed a night nurse he would take care of the cost. But when I passed this news on to Howie, he informed me that he would continue to be there from dusk to sunrise for Jack.

'At least let me do two nights a week,' I said.

'Offer gratefully acknowledged and refused. I am seeing him through until he can longer remain at home. In other words, until the end.'

That finality was now approaching with tragic certitude. After showing up at the office five days ago, with me and his canes keeping him vertical, Jack collapsed when he reached his desk. An ambulance was called. The medics on duty noted his condition immediately and rushed him down to St Vincent's. I rode with him in the ambulance, telling my assistant to call Howie at work and let him urgently know what was going on. After waiting with Jack in the receiving area – where he was lapsing in and out of consciousness – I watched two orderlies hoist him onto a gurney. He was then wheeled into a big industrial-sized elevator and brought upstairs to the unit dealing with all the victims of this still-untreatable, ferocious pestilence. The orderlies said nothing when I informed them I was accompanying Jack. When the elevator door opened I suddenly saw the controlled chaos in front of us. All the wards were so overcrowded, so overflowing, that there was no room for Jack. He was deposited in the central corridor of this unit. I looked around and saw men and a few women in assorted states of near-death. There were friends, family members and partners trying to comfort their dying or scrambling to get them some sort of medical attention. All the doctors and nurses were dashing from bed to bed, attempting to maintain some sort of order, the cries and frequent shrieks from patients and those caring for them building into an overwhelming cacophony that was having an unsettling effect on everyone, but which could not be stilled.

'Can you please see to my friend?' I said to at least three men in white coats and two nurses in blue scrubs. They all passed me by, saying they'd get to Jack after they dealt with everyone else in front of him. After the fifth brush-off I screamed at one medic:

'How can there be a fucking line for someone in such agony?'

That's when I felt a steadying hand on my shoulder. Howie.

'I'm on to it,' he said to me, all but grabbing a passing nurse and demanding to know if Dr Barry was on duty. She said he was here but overwhelmed.

'Tell him Howard D'Amato is here with one of his closest friends.'

The nurse took this in, nodding gravely, and hurried off.

'When in a war zone it's best to know one of the captains in charge,' Howie said.

Jack was groaning on the gurney. I took his right hand and noticed that the crotch around his suit trousers was drenched. Seeing this Howie scoured this frantic field hospital, stopping a nurse and telling her that Jack would die if he didn't get attended to immediately.

'You'll just have to wait,' she said, her face hard. Howie exploded.

'Listen, Nurse Ratched, don't you dare talk to me, us, as if you're some omnipotent cunt who –'

'That's enough, my friend.'

Dr Norman Barry – late forties, small, balding and with huge bags under his eyes but also deeply alert to everyone and everything – had imposed himself between Howie and the nurse.

'Now before I take charge here, Howard,' he said, 'I want you to apologize immediately and unconditionally to my very good and overworked colleague, Nurse Clancy.'

'I'm a professional asshole,' Howie told her.

'That's not an apology,' Dr Barry said.

'I'm sorry. Truly sorry. I should have never called you that name. I'm just ... '

Nurse Clancy put a hand on his shoulder.

'Understood,' she said. Then she looked over to Dr Barry. 'Should I move him to the alternative ward?'

'It's the only place we have space right now,' Dr Barry said, then looked at me and added: 'It's a room off the morgue which we've set up as a makeshift ward.'

'At least it's a ward,' I said.

'And so conveniently located,' Howie added.

'Sorry to see you here again, Howard,' Dr Barry said.

Howie looked at the floor, shaking his head.

'Too many friends ... ' he said.

'Believe me, I know. It's like the Black Death – with no way so far to stop it.'

'How long do you think he has?' I asked, my voice a choked whisper.

Suddenly from the gurney came Jack's strangled voice.

'I'm living until I'm one fucking hundred,' he hissed.

He managed to somehow raise both hands. Howie and I grabbed one each.

'Indeed you will,' I said.

'Thank you, Pollyanna,' Jack said.

'I like it when you play the tough guy,' Howie said.

'Got it from my dad. A Marine – just like Alice's old man. Only mine despised the son he called a "pansy".'

'But he was the asshole coward,' Howie said. 'People who hate always are. You were always the brave guy in the room. And you're fucking heroic now.'

I let out a sob.

'Don't go all soft of me, Burns,' Jack said. 'There's too much emotion in here already.'

Dr Barry smiled and said:

'I think we'll get Humphrey Bogart down to our other ward.'

Jack managed a smile back.

'I always wanted to be the gay Bogart,' he said.

Howie leaned over and whispered to me, reminding me we had to be at JFK in seventy-five minutes to see Duncan off on his adventures.

'I heard that,' Jack said.

'Duncan will have to miss us,' I said, taking Jack's hand.

'I'm not planning to fucking die tonight or any time soon,' he said. 'Get yourself out to Kennedy – I'm insisting on that – and then come back here and bring me a Bombay martini properly chilled.'

'If we returned at ten tonight,' Howie asked Nurse Clancy, 'could we pay our friend a visit?'

Nurse Clancy looked to Dr Barry for approval. He nodded his okay.

'It's against the rules,' Nurse Clancy said, 'but have them page me and I'll get you up to see him. Without the gin.'

Now we were at the airport, finishing our third martini with Duncan, Howie getting even more emotional, telling us:

'Life is so fucking fragile. And when you see that it's right between two people ... '

'Where's this going, Howie?' Duncan asked.

'The two of you should get married.'

I felt myself breaking out in an on-the-spot blush – and then noticed that Duncan wasn't far off the same facial color.

'Look at the two of you,' Howie said. 'Like a pair of Bambis caught in the headlights. See, I'm right. And now I need to take a huge pee. Too much death, too much gin, too much wishful fucking thinking.'

As soon as he disappeared into the nearby bathroom an announcement came over the terminal loudspeaker: Duncan's flight to Paris was being called. Out of nowhere my friend for the past eight years leaned over and kissed me. A full, deep kiss to which I responded in reciprocal kind. When we finally broke off we gazed at each other with something approaching mutual shock – but the sort of shock that was tinged with the best sort of amazed recognition.

'Our timing is terrible,' I said, clutching his two hands.

'I could miss the plane.'

'No – you have to go.'

'I don't have to go.'

'You have a book to write. The book requires that you make this journey. But you must promise to come back to me.'

'I do promise that.'

When Howie came out of the bathroom he was smart enough to back off from the couple so entwined, so not wanting to let go of each other; we didn't even notice that the final call for Duncan's flight had just been announced. Howie put his hand on my shoulder, saying:

'I hate to be the harbinger of bad news. But ... '

All the way back to Manhattan in the taxi I sat in silence, my head reeling, my face awash with tears. Howie held my hand and said absolutely nothing. Except this:

'Aren't you lucky?'

'He wanted to stay. I told him to go.'

'That's love. I know the boy. He wants this, *you*, more than anything. Which makes you even more lucky. Love both ways. How fucking rare.'

As we approached the hospital Howie asked the driver to pull up in front of a liquor store. He paid him off. Once inside he told the shy Indian fellow – a Sikh wearing a turban and a look that reflected a lifetime of diffidence – that he wanted to buy a cocktail shaker, a bottle of Bombay gin, a small miniature of vermouth, three cocktail glasses, a bottle of olives – 'and can you fill the shaker with ice, please?'

Ten minutes later we asked the woman at the reception of St Vincent's to page Nurse Clancy. Our mobile martini unit was stuffed into my shoulder bag. We agreed that as soon as the nurse

491

was elsewhere we would, without question, make Jack his martini ...
'even if we get arrested for it', as Howie defiantly noted.

It took no time for Nurse Clancy to arrive. She walked out, as
grim-faced as before, but now with a sense of absolute urgency.
Howie and I were immediately on our feet.

'You have to hurry,' Nurse Clancy said. 'He only has minutes left.'

To her immense credit she led us in a near dash up a back flight
of steps and down a series of corridors. When we reached the trolley
cot on which Jack was lying I was relieved to see that his eyes were
still open, even if he was drifting in and out of consciousness. We
raced over to him, myself and Howie each taking one of his hands.
Jack's breathing was hesitant, irregular. I could see fear in his eyes.
He tried to speak. We both leaned forward. He uttered one word,
barely discernible:

'Martini.'

I glanced over to Howie who nodded to me, as if to say *'get on
with it'*.

Immediately I was unpacking the contents of my bag. Nurse
Clancy was standing nearby and said nothing about rules and regulations as I poured gin over the still-cold ice in the shaker, adding
just a dash of vermouth, then covered it and shook it vigorously,
knowing that Jack liked his Bombay martinis super-cold. I emptied
the contents of the shaker into a glass, passing it to Howie – who
still had the fingers of his other hand entwined in Jack's. Howie lowered the glass toward Jack's lips. Our friend smiled ever so briefly as a
tiny amount of the gin and vermouth touched his tongue. Jack shut
his eyes. There were two final tentative breaths. Then he stopped
breathing altogether. Howie lowered his head, choking back a sob. I
blinked and felt tears cascading down my face. Both of us were still
holding one of Jack's hands. Howie lifted the glass, making a cross
of benediction. Then he took a sip of the martini and passed me the
glass. I too drank a mouthful. For the next few minutes the glass
passed back and forth over Jack as we finished his last martini, the
grief intensifying with each sip.

29

ADAM MADE HIS fifth million dollars on the first day of 1984. Working in close cahoots with Tad the Omnipotent (as I began to call him) my brother had helped refinance a major telecommunications player, Horizon, which had what Adam described as 'below investment grade debt'. Through the supreme manipulation of high-yield interest bonds, Adam allowed Horizon to restructure and reinvent itself.

'I'm totally in it for the money,' Adam told me and Peter at a dinner in mid-February. 'This is high-stakes capitalism – and all the players at the table are high rollers.'

Peter's book had come out three weeks earlier. Though *The Radical Years* had received some good reviews – especially in left-leaning publications like the *Nation* and *Mother Jones*, and a short but positive notice in the *New York Times Book Review* – sales weren't looking so good. Little, Brown had basically let Peter know that he could no longer count on being published by them – unless, of course, he delivered a sensational new book. The *Village Voice* was keeping him going – and he'd also managed to talk his way into teaching a course on writing narrative non-fiction at Hunter College. His bills were being met. When Adam had insisted on giving each of us an additional five thousand dollars in cash at Christmas, Peter disappeared for three weeks to Cartagena in Colombia, determined to start what he described as 'a dark V.S. Naipaul-style novel set in Chile during the coup'. He returned to New York in early January, just before the beginning of the term at Hunter, looking tanned but not rested, telling me that – after hammering out two thousand words on his portable Olivetti – he'd given up, deciding that he was writing 'all the usual clichés about a naive idealistic young man over his head in a South American political steam bath. But the good news is that I was able to get to Colombia and live there in a little hotel for over three weeks and only spend nine hundred dollars. I've banked the rest and am planning to live in Paris all summer, back at La Louisiane.'

493

But he knew he needed a book to write – 'something that will help me shake off the loser mantle and show New York publishing that I am still alive and kicking'.

'That's less important than finding a subject which will be serious but also reach a new, larger audience,' I said, as were waiting at the bar of Lutèce for our brother to arrive.

When Adam showed up ten minutes later, he was greeted by the maître d' and the staff as if he were a Medici prince. The fawning and deference, the insistence that we accept, courtesy of the owner, a bottle of Cristal champagne, was more than amusing. But the even bigger *macher* in the room was being treated by all the staff as if he were Pope John Paul II. Spotting Adam, this prince of the city motioned him over. As we approached his table I could hear him telling an anecdote about some brilliant deal he'd just pulled off. He was in his late forties with a double chin, a bush-blond hairpiece, two hyper-leggy Eastern European models on either side of his prime table, several fawning minions in adjacent seats.

'Let's say hi to Donald,' Adam said.

Everyone in eighties New York knew about Donald Trump. He was the perfect skewed icon for our increasingly rapacious times: a property developer raised in Queens (which meant that he had all that outer-borough attitude) who had grabbed much column-inch space – especially in the tabloid press – for his mow-down-the-opposition approach to business, his flaunting of wealth, his clear passionate love affair with power, his crass property developments, his even crasser need for bimbos on both arms, and the stentorian honk of his self-satisfied voice.

'Adam the Bond Baron Burns,' Trump said, not bothering to stand up. He made cursory introductions to the minions at the table, then made a point of telling us that 'this pair of Polish beauties – Grazyna and Agnieska – are about to become big, big stars ... And what are you doing here with these two downtown types?'

'My brother Peter has just had his second book published, and my sister Alice has just been named a senior editor at Fowler, Newman and Kaplan.'

'I'm a writer too,' Trump told Peter, then shifted his gaze toward me, looking me up and down, rating me low on his Babe Meter (which I took to be a compliment). 'In fact I'm writing a book that's going to make a ton of money – because everyone's gonna wanna read how I've made a ton of money. You should offer me a contract on the spot.'

'If your agent would like to call me –' I said.

'Why does Donald Trump need an agent?'

'It's just how things work in publishing,' I said.

'"How things work"? Tell your kid sister, Adam, that is not how Donald Trump works. I rewrite the rulebook every day. Which is why I'm gonna be president someday.'

Then he about faced and returned to his two Polish babes.

'Good seeing you, Donald,' Adam said, trying to end things on a positive note. But Trump was now ignoring him. I saw a flash of the old Adam – the one who was wounded by rejection, who was privately as riddled with doubt as the rest of us. But then, in a nanosecond, I watched his new Wall Street player status supersede all that past doubt.

'Let Lee Kander know that, if you want a taste of the Chrysler restructuring bond we're putting together, we'd be happy to welcome him to the table.'

That got Trump's attention. He gave Adam a papal nod of approval, a thumbs up. As the maître d' escorted us to our table, I could see Adam bolstered by the man's approval.

'Lee Kander is Donald's financial wizard,' he explained to us as we sat down and the complimentary bottle of Cristal arrived.

'And he clearly holds you in great respect,' I said.

Adam smiled.

'Donald's got a reputation as a bit of a loudmouth. But in this noisy town it's the person with the loudest mouth who gets heard over the crowd.'

'Let me guess,' Peter said, 'that's a Tad-ism. And something that he says regularly in those motivational speeches of his.'

'He sold out a conference center in Houston last week. Ten thousand people paying twenty dollars each. Tad has an audience – deservedly so.'

Peter flinched. Was Adam slapping him down with subtext – *at least he has a big public, unlike you?* Or was he just pointing up again that he didn't like his guru criticized? When Adam signaled for the waiter to pour out the champagne, he asked Peter how the writing went in Colombia. I could see Peter turn sheepish while also fighting off an attack of hostility.

'The next book is going to truly make me,' Peter said. 'Thank you again for the money. I'll spend it well.'

'I don't care how you spend it,' Adam said, raising his glass. 'To my brother's next "big" book and to my sister's big promotion. And congrats on that Cornelius guy's big hit.'

'I'm impressed you keep track of such things,' I said, as it had only been announced a few days earlier in the publishing trade press that Fowler, Newman and Kaplan had named me a senior editor, putting me in charge of Jack's entire list.

'Hey, we're family,' Adam said.

'I'm touched, thank you,' I said, reaching into my bag and pulling out *The Next Mistake.* 'Here's my editorial handiwork. You might find it interesting.'

'I'm not much of a reader,' he said, picking up the novel. 'Just don't have the time. But I'll give it to Janet. She's got a lot of time on her hands … though things are about to get kind of busy again at our house as we are expecting Child Number Two in October.'

Naturally Peter and I made all the relevant congratulatory noises, raising our glasses, telling him how pleased we were for them both.

'The last time you guys saw Janet … jeez, it was Christmas '82. Almost fourteen months ago.'

'Well, we did decide to spend the holidays with Mom and Dad this time,' I said.

'You were both invited over for a drink on the 25th. It's only forty-five minutes from New York on the train. You could have made the effort.'

'You're right,' Peter said. 'We could have, *we should have.* Especially as you've been so generous to us.'

'You don't like her. You don't rate her,' Adam said.

'The larger question here is: do *you* rate her?' Peter asked.

Adam's grip tightened so hard around his glass of Cristal that it snapped.

Immediately a waiter was on the scene, apologizing profusely (even though it was hardly his fault), getting Adam another champagne flute while dabbing his Cristal-baptized hand with a linen napkin, acting as if my brother had just been wounded by a sniper. Adam thanked him for his concern, accepted the brimming flute and downed it all in one large gulp. Then he glared at Peter with something approaching fury.

'You can forget about any more cash envelopes, Big Brother.'

'I was just asking a question, Adam. I mean, everyone around town knows about you and the Turkish model.'

Thankfully Peter whispered this last sentence. Adam looked broadsided.

'What the fuck?' he hissed back.

'You're the Bond Baron, Little Brother. There is a colleague on the *Voice* who has made it his beat to follow all the new money boys around town. He told me he's seen you around three times at places like Studio 54 and the Odeon with a certain Ceren Safek – have I got the name right? – who is quite the beauty, not to mention the hot runway model of the season.'

Adam looked like he'd just been told that the IRS were going to super-audit him.

'Who the fuck knows this?'

'Probably every gossip columnist around town.'

'You're not going to tell Janet.'

Adam's declaration was not phrased as a question.

'Of course not,' Peter said. 'If I haven't seen her in fourteen months ... '

'Did you know about this?' Adam demanded of me.

I nodded.

'Why the fuck didn't you say something?'

'What was I supposed to say, Adam? It's not my business, it's not Peter's business. I think I can speak for the two of us when we say we're hardly judging you here. But here's the thing: if the Page Six assholes know about all this, you are in danger of having all revealed in tabloid black-and-white. Which might not play too well at home with Janet, who will try to asset-strip you. You want to carry on with Ms Istanbul get discreet about it or get found out.'

The following week, on the infamous Page Six of the *New York Post*, Adam was pictured with his arm around the waist of 'the ever-effervescent Bosphorus Beauty, Ceren Safek'. Howie called me immediately at the office, telling me that I should get my assistant to run out and buy a copy of that rag – and simultaneously send word to my brother that 'he was playing with tabloid dynamite – and this is a publicist talking'.

But it was Adam who called first, asking me to join him for a drink that evening at the Martini Bar of the St Regis – and he was bringing along with him the infamous Ceren Safek. I was just a little thrown when Adam arrived with this dazzling thin and raven-haired woman in her late twenties, very tall, very much a head-turner, and far smarter than I expected. She was all charm, telling me that she had, at Adam's suggestion, read Cornelius Parker's novel and was very taken 'with its view of the way we actually script our romantic disaster'. Just as she had perused Peter's first book and had very nice, effusive things to say about Adam's 'highly literate and talented siblings'. I found out that she had been studying English literature at Boğaziçi Üniversitesi in Istanbul, where all the instruction was in English, and where she was spotted in a cafe by a Paris fashion photographer named Henri on a shoot in the city.

'I was nineteen, Henri was forty-one. He brought me to Paris and into a career I never imagined.'

Henri was long-ago history, as once in Paris she had taken up with a film director named Olivier Paul and then came to the States courtesy of an agent, Chuck Chandler, with whom she lived in LA for several years. All these personal details were dropped in front of me as if she were reciting her sexual résumé.

'Even when I was living at Chuck's place in Pacific Palisades – and it was clear that I wasn't going to get far in the movies – he did get me plenty of runway work out there. But LA ... it's a lot like what I've seen of New Jersey, but with better clothes.'

'I might steal that line,' I said.

'Please do,' she said, lighting up a Virginia Slims cigarette. 'It's hardly my own.'

I rather liked her clever brashness. Just as I also smelled serious narcissism in the air. Yet she was also canny enough to acknowledge it. When Adam waved to someone he told us was 'George Soros's chief deputy' and the gent (a hyper-serious-looking fellow, with the look of constant severity in his eyes) motioned for him to drop by the table, Ceren told him:

'You have to go schmooze Stan now.'

Which is exactly what my brother did. As soon as he was gone from the table she touched my hand with hers and said:

'You're a cool one, Alice. You keep yourself one distance back from everyone, if you don't mind me saying so. Which makes me feel like you're sizing me up.'

'As you're involved with my brother, and as all I know about you is what I've read in gossip columns, yes … I'm sizing you up.'

'Let me guess what you're thinking: I'm far smarter than the bimbo model you expected me to be … but also clearly far too preoccupied with her little old self and maybe a bit of a gold digger.'

'You really have a neat line there in surmising what others are thinking,' I said.

'Your brother is a very nice guy working in a world peopled by assholes. It kind of makes him a contradiction. He's got a killer instinct when it comes to closing a deal. But he still wants to be liked and validated, which, from what I gather, goes back to his daddy never really rating him and his two brainier siblings –'

'I so appreciate your insights into my brother and his family.'

'I like the guy. Genuinely.'

'Would you like him more if he was an assistant professor of philosophy at Columbia making seventeen thousand a year?'

'We might have more to talk about, but I wouldn't be here tonight at the St Regis.'

'Know this: if you do anything to hurt him, or get yourself pregnant, or try any sort of cash grab, the furies will be unleashed on you.'

She looked just a little thrown by what had come out of my mouth. But her shock morphed into a smile that verged on smugness.

'So much for the docile, bookish, superior-minded editor.'

'I am bookish, I am not docile, and I certainly consider myself superior to anyone who is invested in men with money. But here's the thing: you're clearly bright and know a thing or two about the ways of the world. Have you ever thought about writing a book about fucking your way upward?'

'You don't have to be such a bitch.'

I reached into my jacket pocket and fished out the small discreet leather sleeve in which I kept my business cards.

'I'm actually serious. We could shape your sexual history into feminism meets social Darwinism: how to use the new golden boys to your advantage. It would be the perfect parable for our new age of unapologetic mercantilism.'

Ceren picked up the card I'd slid by her.

'You're serious about this?'

'Indeed I am.'

'Say I can't write?'

'Then we won't work together. I don't do ghosted books. But I sense you have this in you. Write me a chapter about the photographer who picked you up in that Istanbul cafe when you weren't even twenty and got you to Paris. Did he leave his wife and children for you?'

'It was love.'

'Which lasted – what? – twelve months?'

'Six.'

'Perfect. Write it for me – and make it down and dirty and smart. If I like it, we'll talk some more.'

'You don't have a guy, do you?' she asked me after the second martini, that moment when the conversation starts to get even more nudist.

'There might be someone . . . but he's away for a while.'

'And you're just waiting for him?'

'Maybe.'

'Waiting for someone is romantic folly. Then again, I've been in love around twenty times ... which probably means I love being in love. Unlike you. You've known it, haven't you?'

'Did Adam tell you that?'

'Actually no. I'm just surmising again.'

'Yes I've known love.'

'Why did it end?'

'Because his head was blown off in a bomb blast.'

To her credit Ceren didn't flinch, didn't throw her eyes heavenward, didn't say anything inane like: 'You're shitting me.' She just met my gaze, saying nothing. And then Adam showed up, immediately noting the silence between us.

'You gals get into a fight or something?' he asked.

'Hardly,' Ceren said. 'I'm just learning that you have quite the remarkable sister.'

'She's tougher than me,' Adam said, giving my shoulder a gentle locker-room-style shake.

'That she is.'

Ceren did contact me two weeks later, telling me she had a chapter to show me. I told her to drop it by the office and that we'd be in touch.

'Will you read it or give it to one of your minions?' she asked.

'Oh, I'll read it – and I don't have minions. Just a junior editor and a secretary. If I like it I'll take you to lunch.'

'If not ... '

'We won't be meeting – but I will tell you why it didn't work for me.'

'You're very direct.'

'That's my style.'

Jack once noted the same thing, telling me: 'You often offer the pill unsweetened, but you do so in a way that is never cruel or freighted with your own stuff ... even though everything we do in life is completely freighted with our own stuff.'

Jack. There was a framed photo of us on my office wall; the same office which he once occupied. The photo showed me and Jack at a conference table, a manuscript in front of us, Jack indicating a much

notated paragraph filled with his scribbled comments. I showed it
to Cheryl Abeloff on her first day as my junior. Cheryl was a native
Manhattanite, angular and serious, with a boyfriend who taught
public school and Park Avenue parents who couldn't figure out why
she was rejecting their largesse and living in the Siberia that was
Brooklyn (Bushwick – a near slum). Like me she was edgy. And
ambitious. And willing to learn. Pointing to Jack's photo I told her:

'He was truly old school and someone who knew full well that
editing is a skill you pass on – which I would like to do with you.
But you also need to understand: I never expected to be in this job
at such a young point in my life. I am making it up as I go along –
not that you are ever to repeat that comment to anyone.'

'Anything we say to each other stays between us,' Cheryl said.

'That's how Jack and I operated – and one of the many reasons
why it worked.'

Thinking back on my years in school, in college, the time I hid
out in Vermont, I truly never saw myself as someone who aspired to
be a boss. Assertion and command were foreign ideas to me. Just as
having an important executive post in a company – albeit a literary
one – was never an ambition. But here I was in my thirtieth year,
in charge of a list, in charge of a budget, in charge of others, and
accountable to the financial and commercial people whom we liked
to dismiss as numbers obsessed, but who were the key to the amount
of latitude I had (or did not have) as an editor. I did all the parties, all the schmoozing lunches with literary journalists and fellow
members of the publishing tribe, but then I went home to my very
simple apartment and worked most nights on manuscripts until at
least one. I found I could get by quite well on six hours of sleep,
wake by seven, go run in Riverside Park for a half-hour and be at
my desk no later than nine. Every week a letter from Duncan would
arrive, written in his hieroglyphic scrawl, with exotic postmarks
(Casablanca, Ouarzazate, Algiers) and brimming with his traveler's
tales. I learned of his encounters with bureaucracy (he was held for
five hours at the Algerian border because some guard decided that
the first American he had encountered crossing in about a year was
worth hassling). He wrote about riding dusty trains with blocked

toilets, and meeting a French priest in Algiers whose small parish church had recently been attacked by a band of thugs. He spoke of the wonders of Moroccan souks and how he wanted to bring me to the Sahara at some juncture in the future 'because it enforces the solitary nature of human existence and reminds you that the need to truly connect with someone is key to keeping all the encroaching darkness at bay'.

That was another constant theme in his letters – his longing for me. Reading him, so entwining myself in his smart, shrewd narratives, wishing to God he'd traveled with a typewriter (it really was a job deciphering his penmanship), yet simultaneously focusing closely on those phrases where he indicated the seriousness of his feelings for me ... it was indeed wondrous when I came home and found a new Duncan missive in my mailbox. It also augmented my own desperate need to be close to him. That was the 'didn't see this coming' surprise in the aftermath of all those revelations at the airport: the fact that I should have convinced him to stay for a few more days to consummate our connection to each other. I cursed myself regularly for letting that opportunity pass. But when he suggested that I join him in Tunisia for a few weeks in early August I wrote back and said that, as much as I wanted to be there with him, it was just weeks before our fall titles hit the street. As this was the first year the list was under my banner (so to speak) I simply had to be there all summer to plot and plan the best press, publicity and marketing plans for my titles, also fearing that if I was away (even for a week) all would somehow go awry. But could we perhaps think about running off somewhere after Christmas for a week (when he was due back stateside)?

'You are turning into a poster child for Workaholism,' Howie told me when we met in early June for our weekly night out. Cornelius Parker hadn't pulled off the Pulitzer, but he did win the National Book Award – and we had just signed him for another two novels. But a biography of Eleanor Roosevelt – which controversially touched on her lesbianism and FDR's many affairs – got very mixed reviews and simply did not do the business that we all were expecting.

'Honey,' Howie said, 'no one wants to believe that the great social justice First Lady was also a muff diver. No wonder the book stiffed.'

'Why don't you say that a little louder – so the people at the far end of the restaurant can hear us?'

'English is the minority language at this joint. And I'd recommend the blinis and smoked herring with a shot of vodka.'

We were at the Lithuanian Social Club on Second Avenue and 6th Street, a place that my friend had discovered courtesy of the newest guy he was seeing: a professional bodybuilder from Vilnius who was determined to win the Mr America contest this year.

'Nojus is modeling himself on that Schwarzenegger clown who's just broken into the movies after doing the rippled-muscle thing for years, while also hanging out with Warhol and his Factory crowd. Andy's sense of irony must have gone into overdrive when Arnold the Beefcake started becoming a fixture of his vicious little circle.'

'So Nojus is also trying to be a Warhol acolyte?'

'I love the way you're Frenchifying his name. *No-Jeux*. Very charming. But the way to say it is *No-Juice* ... though he has *no* deficiencies in that department.'

'Thanks for sharing that charming detail.'

'Thank you for going all prudish on me. What are you doing for amusement while your beloved is fending off sultry Muslim Jezebels?'

'Whatever Duncan is doing out in the great wide world is his business. We haven't pledged anything to each other just yet.'

'That's very forward-thinking and Bloomsbury Group of you. But you still haven't answered the question: who are you turning to for sex?'

'My manuscripts.'

'You are so dull, Burns.'

'Unlike your hedonist self. I hope you're being careful with Nojus.'

'I'm being careful with everyone. Six more friends have just been diagnosed with it. And I know another dozen or so people who are in varying stages of dying. It's all too relentless.'

'And you? No signs of anything?'

'So far so clear. My doctor tells me that they still have no idea how long the incubation period is, or when it might arise out of nowhere in anyone's immune system. I keep thinking of Jack at the end.'

'I try not to,' I said. 'It's all too hard. I'd rather think of him before AIDS overwhelmed him.'

'I want to think of Jack in Paradise – and that's not just the Catholic boy in me talking. It's also someone who's seen too much death recently and can't abide the idea that all this suffering results in nullity and void. After what he endured at the end he deserves no less.'

'Do you remember his dad at the funeral? That old Marine, all leathery around the face and wheezing after a lifetime of cigarettes...'

'Look who's talking...'

'I plan to quit on New Year's Day.'

'Why don't you wait until Reagan's second coronation?'

'You sound as if it's a foregone conclusion that the old guy's going to win again.'

'Well, I have problems supporting Mondale.'

'Are you serious, Howie?'

'The economy is booming. All the negative energy of the Carter years has vanished. Mondale was Carter's veep. He radiates dreariness.'

'Can you really vote for our current president who is in the pocket of the religious right and whose communications director – that asshole Pat Buchanan – called AIDS "nature's revenge on gay men"?'

'My stocks have never been higher. There is money everywhere. There is more fun out there.'

'When your next friend dies –'

'Please shut up, Alice. Your "voice of conscience" routine is putting me in an edgy mood. Especially as I got this rash between my toes just a few days ago, and my doctor has assured me it's athlete's foot – picked up in the fucking locker room of the Y on West 14th Street.'

'If he tells you it's athlete's foot...'

'I'm still going to be paranoid. My turn is sure to come soon.'

'Not if you've been practicing safe sex.'

'A condom broke last week. A guy I picked up in the Y.'

'Oh Jesus, Howie.'

'At least it was me on top – which lessens the risk. Still ... '

I reached over and took his hand.

'You'll be okay.'

'You really do have this Ms Optimism aspect to you.'

'What else can I do but think positively ... especially when it comes to you?'

'I am going to quickly change the subject and give you a serious piece of advice: get on a plane to Tunis in early August, meet your man, make mad crazy love with him for a week, then get back to New York and launch your list. You need to see him ... and he so wants you to come.'

'I can't afford the time. There is just too much going on.'

'If you lose him ... '

'Then it wasn't meant to be.'

'I hate that way of looking at the world. Especially as it's side-stepping the fact that you have a degree of say in what will or will not happen here. You have a chance here – with a man who is good, interesting, just the right side of complicated, and rather dishy. After all those detached years with Toby you now crave entanglement. Just like the rest of us.'

'Then why haven't you found it?'

'Because I am as scared as you are.'

I did get a letter a week later from Duncan, telling me all about heading deep into the south of Algeria and crossing into Mali and that fabled desert outpost, Timbuktu, and how he was genuinely longing for me.

As I was for him. But with rumors abounding that the house was being targeted for takeover by this Australian media baron named Murdoch (who was already making inroads into Britain but was still an unknown quantity in this country), the powers that be at Fowler, Newman and Kaplan were emphasizing that it was an 'all hands on deck' moment. The ageing chairman of the house, C.C. Fowler, took me to lunch one day at the Century Club – that sclerotic hangout for the New York literati – and remained quite lucid after drinking two very dry gin martinis (not bad for an eighty-two-year-old), telling me:

'I won't lie to you. My money people have been approached by Murdoch's money people. Trust me, I want to remain independent. I think Murdoch is more interested in a bigger house like Harper and Co. than us. Still, the days when publishing was a gentlemanly pursuit are fast drawing to an end. My grandfather would have had an editor drawn and quartered for even suggesting that we publish, let alone rush through, a book like *Sleeping Upward* by your Turkish literary find – and yes, you can hear the irony in my voice. Still, the sales and marketing people think that the Thanksgiving weekend launch date, and the big media blitz we'll be doing on her, should yield results.'

'The book is going to be huge. Because it will speak exactly to the new careerist woman making her way in this new hyper-capitalist world of ours. Anyway, the fact that we can publish Cornelius Parker *and* Ceren … it shows the flexibility and range of our list.'

'One small issue: please reassure me again that the press will not make a big deal about Ceren being your brother's mistress.'

'They will jump all over that. Let them. We'll play it to our advantage. The media will be all over her due to her unapologetic views on using sex as a transactional tool to get where you want, and the fact that she is articulate as hell and seriously beautiful. It's going to be the big "naughty" Christmas book that everyone will be talking about.'

'Meanwhile your brother gets richer all the time. I read about the big bond refinancing thing for US Steel a couple of days back.'

'The fellow does have the golden touch.'

'Just like your realtor mom. I saw that she just closed that big deal for some empty-headed starlet … '

'She's cornered the rich bimbo market, along with plutocrats and all those ambitious women who are going to read Ceren's book.'

'Let's hope the golden touch runs in the family.'

Was that a warning, a veiled threat? It certainly made me focus even harder on the autumn list – and truly build Ceren's book into a zeitgeisty blockbuster.

Just to test the book with an older demographic I gave Mom the manuscript of *Sleeping Upward*. She rang me up the next night, near to midnight, all worried.

'How can Adam fuck such an operator?' she asked.

'He can handle Ceren – because, though lavishing stuff on her, he's not legally spliced to her. Yet.'

'But that's her game plan. You know it. I know it. But your brother's too much of a sexual sucker not to see it. When Janet and her redneck clan find out he's been *shtupping* a far more accomplished and dangerously gorgeous woman they are going to try and ruin him ... especially with the new baby about to arrive in a couple of weeks. He won't listen to me. And your dad gets all Irish Catholic about anything to do with divorce.'

'You still won't let him move in with you?'

'Not in this lifetime. We did that for far too many decades and we did it badly. Why recreate that? The thing is: I do well on my own. Your father is struggling. "You cannot change others; you can only try to change yourself" – as my shrink keeps telling me. He also keeps hammering home the idea that I can't lay all blame at the feet of my yenta mother and emotionally absent father. Or continue to scream and shout that your father forced me to be a housewife in the fucking burbs. I was complicit in all that. I created my own prison. And I victimized you and the boys because of that. I see that now and am actually ashamed of it.'

'I appreciate you saying all that.'

'Adam, of course, can't really connect to any of this. He brought me to one of his big-deal restaurants recently, a mother–son night out. When I tried to bring this up he dodged the subject completely, saying it was a long time ago and all that. Adam still sidesteps all emotion. Whereas your older brother ... he's got me worried.'

'Me too.'

This was true. Peter was becoming increasingly solipsistic and depressed. Though he was getting his columns done for the *Voice* and teaching his classes, a recent romantic disaster with a fellow faculty member at Hunter had knocked him sideways, making him even more preoccupied by his perceived failures.

What I didn't tell Mom was that, just yesterday afternoon at work, Howie had called me, his voice a little more edgy than usual.

'Want to meet for a drink later?'

'I can always tell when something's up with you. You okay?'

'Still not sick or dying since we spoke three days ago.'

'That's good to hear. But you're still troubled by something.'

'Let's do this over a drink later.'

'Howie ... what is eating you?'

'I have a friend at *Esquire*. An editor with whom I've been trying to land a profile on one of my writers. We had lunch. The guy – Matt Nathan – likes to booze. And talks a little too much after the second gimlet. Know what he told me? "Next month we're running this big piece by Peter Burns ... you've heard of the guy, haven't you?" I didn't mention that his sister and I were rather close. I just acknowledged that, yes, I knew of Peter Burns and his two books. "Well, this piece he's written for us is going to be quite the sensation. Because though you start reading it thinking that it's an exposé of high-yield interest bonds and all that big-money stuff, within a couple of paragraphs it changes gear – as he starts to talk about his brother Adam and his boss Tad Strickland, who have essentially become the junk bond kings of Wall Street. And what follows is this complete takedown of his brother and the financial world he operates in."'

I shut my eyes, not believing what I was hearing. I reached for my cigarettes. I lit one up.

'Yeah, I'd light up something too,' Howie said, clearly hearing the snap and crack of my Zippo. 'Because what this *Esquire* editor also told me was: "The revelations that Burns makes in this article are probably going to land his brother in jail."'

30

HOWIE KNEW HOW to twist arms, call in favors, find ways to draw information from walled-in sources. But try as he did he still could not get a copy of Peter's article from *Esquire*.

'It's completely embargoed – at the author's request,' he reported. 'But one thing I have learned from my editor friend there is: the other reason it's embargoed is because their lawyers are all over the piece, and there is talk that it might be leaked before publication to the Securities and Exchange Commission.'

'Fuck,' I said. The financial police meant trouble for Adam. Big trouble.

'Sorry to be the bearer of such bad news,' Howie said. 'From what I can gather the article, besides shopping Adam as a Wall Street crook, also deals with a family and its secrets, and the rivalry between two brothers with a strong undercurrent of dislike for each other, tracing it back to your hard-assed dad.'

'Fuck fuck fuck.'

'The good news is that Matt confirmed you don't feature much in the article – which, by the way, runs an impressive ten thousand words. But he did say one very telling thing: "I sense this is going to get huge play. Because Peter is essentially setting up his brother for a big fall. And he plays, in the article, with the whole moral/ethical issue about whether he should be exposing Adam's criminality or not."'

'But what exactly does he accuse him of?'

'That's what they're refusing to disclose. It's all very hush-hush. My publicist's take on it is: if it's leaked to the SEC in advance – which I sense it will be – the Feds will probably arrest your brother on or around the publication date. Which *Esquire*'s people can turn into a big coup for the magazine. It could get huge press coverage – and the public debate about whether Peter was right or wrong to do this will mean he is going to come out as a man of either immense moral principle or terrible opportunism, depending on what he reveals about Adam.'

I stubbed out my cigarette, lighting another one immediately.

'I have to talk to Peter.'

'If you do – and I don't know if that's a good idea – you simply cannot tell him how you heard about this.'

'I'd never do that. But should I also tell Adam or my parents?'

'Absolutely not,' Howie said. 'This whole story is also *sub judice.* You could be legally crucified if you warned Adam in advance of what was about to descend on him. He'd then have to tell his shifty boss and then say he flees the country? You'd be implicated. Say your brother starts shredding files, documents, to hide his guilt? You could find yourself up on a charge of aiding and abetting. And it definitely would not look good for me if anyone ever knew ... '

'Oh, Howie, I can't thank you enough for giving me the heads-up.'

'I couldn't have lived with myself if I'd said nothing to you. But you now have to be very careful. Telling Peter you know about its imminent publication – it's not going to change anything. But maybe you'll prick his conscience a bit. He will definitely be interviewed by the SEC. Perhaps he can do some advance plea-bargaining for his brother. I'm just riffing here. Try to get the article from Peter. Then sneak it to me – and we'll plot and plan from there.'

As soon as I put down the phone I had to run into an editorial meeting. I somehow forced myself to appear focused and involved throughout, even though my mind was racing. The meeting overran to 6 p.m. After an obligatory drink with an agent, which I kept to the least amount of time possible, I dialed Peter's number from the lobby of the bar. He answered on the eighth ring.

'Hey there,' I said, trying to sound cheerful. 'You up to anything tonight?'

'Kind of buried in stuff here.'

'Can I get you out for a couple hours? I don't feel like being on my own tonight.'

'Anything up?'

'Just loneliness.'

'Tell me about it. But I really don't want to go to Manhattan.'

'Then I'll come to you. Give me an hour tops.'

A summer storm had blown into Manhattan. It was one of those New York summer nights when the air was so glutinous that it almost felt like walking through a vat of fried rice. Tropical rain had just hit. Fifth Avenue was suddenly deluged, making the finding of a taxi beyond impossible. I had no umbrella. After waiting ten minutes under the awning of the Plaza, I had no choice but to dash diagonally to the subway station on the northeastern corner of 60th Street. I raced out into the torrent, jogging through rivulets of rainwater. By the time I reached the subway stairs and jumped a train heading south I was beyond drenched. I fell into a seat. Sitting down was a bit like discovering that I was a sponge being squeezed. Water oozed onto the seat beneath me. Forty minutes and two changes of train later, I walked out into a now-clear night, the heat and humidity diminished by the storm.

Peter's brownstone apartment was on the top floor. When he opened the door, he looked at my doused state with bemusement.

'You take a shower and forget to undress?' he asked.

'Very funny,' I said. 'You mean you didn't notice the downpour?'

'Had the stereo cranked up and was working on my notes.'

He ushered me in. The place looked as if it needed a serious dusting. There were boxes of documents everywhere and many filled legal pads.

'This is just a bit obsessive,' I said.

'That it is,' he said.

I kicked off my shoes, the leather soaked through.

Fifteen minutes later, having been availed of a bathrobe and Peter's shower, I was seated on his sofa, sipping a glass of New Zealand Sauvignon Blanc and smoking a Viceroy.

'So what is all this?' I asked.

'An article that will have everybody talking. It's about the way we live now, and how we are allowing the big-money boys to dictate the agenda.'

'Nice theme,' I said. 'Can you be more specific?'

'I'm going to write a major exposé of Wall Street and its new cupidity. Why it is such a corrupt environment. And how, if allowed, they could morally bankrupt us all.'

'Any specific part of Wall Street you plan to focus on? High-yield bonds?'

Peter drained his glass of wine, putting it down loudly on the coffee table.

'You're a terrible poker player, Alice.'

'I don't play poker.'

'But you do have what's known in poker as "a tell". You show your hand without intending to.'

'And what do I have in my hand?'

'I know that you know.'

'Know what?'

'Don't bullshit me.'

'Okay, I won't,' I said. 'So here it is: I know about the *Esquire* article.'

Even though he knew this was coming he still flinched.

'Who leaked this to you?'

'Like you, I'm protecting my sources.'

'It was Howie, wasn't it?'

'Who gave you all the inside dope on Adam?' I asked.

'I can't disclose that.'

'Then I'm not disclosing my source. But the article really isn't about Wall Street. What exactly has our brother done?'

'Toss me a cigarette, will you?'

I threw over the pack of Viceroys. He lit one up.

'Do we agree that everything I tell you stays in this room?' he asked.

'Fine by me.'

He took two long drags on his cigarette. Not to steady himself, but to build suspense.

'My research and investigative snooping has shown that what Adam is doing with junk bonds is not just morally suspect, it's also criminal.'

He then went into a detailed explanation on why the junk-bond gamesmanship of Capital Futures, when exposed, was going to be the biggest financial scandal of our time. As Peter talked – in a voice both rapid-fire and a little too vehement for my tastes – I could also begin to discern that what Howie hinted was true: my brother Adam was about to walk into a lot of trouble.

'Do you understand how "insider trading" works?' Peter asked.

'Hardly – being someone who can just about balance her checkbook.'

'Ever heard of Michael Milken? The guy is the dubious financial wizard who came up with the name "junk bonds" – to describe the high-yield bonds with which he's raised a huge amount of capital, and has been able to guarantee his investors 100 percent return on any investments in his company. He relocated a few years ago from New York to Beverly Hills. Everybody's calling Milken a genius, but I smell shit ... '

'Then why not go after him?'

'Because his tracks are still well covered. Tad the Crook and his stooge, Brother Adam ... '

'Don't call him that.'

'Why not? He thinks he's one of the junk bond kings, but he's at the beck and call of his master. These guys have bought struggling companies, dumped thousands of employees out into the street, financed restructurings through these bond issues, while turning around vast profits for themselves. Do you know that Tad the Crook paid himself $210 million last year and Brother Adam came out with $18 million gross?'

'Big deal. Why even care about what he makes? Shit, we've both profited from his success, his largesse.'

'We've both profited from his cupidity, his dishonesty. My exposé will right that wrong.'

'The wrong being: he's made so much money?'

'The wrong being: with Tad's encouragement Brother Adam did this big junk-bond refinancing on a giant electronic manufacturing firm based near San Diego, but with subsidiary factories in assorted blue-collar, last-hope towns: Akron, Ohio; Harrisburg, Pennsylvania; Lewiston, Maine. Brother Adam raised a cool 680 million in a bond issue on a company that was privately owned, but which he helped go public and make a nice little splash on the stock market when the IPO was launched in May. The thing was, Adam got insider information from two senior Wall Street fellows to manipulate the initial price of the stock ... and to ensure that it trebled in value for around ten days, during which time he and Tad each put down three million on the stock at the time of the IPO. A clever move, as they sold the stock for nine million apiece ten days later before it fell back to a more realistic pricing level. Add to this the sixty-one million that Capital Futures made from the junk-bond issue, and you have to think: what a pair of super-shrewd guys Tad and Brother Adam are. Except for the fact that getting insider info to manipulate the IPO stock price is the very wrong side of illegal. They've also used a whole web of aliases to disguise stock purchases – which is also against the law. But the most morally reprehensible thing about all this is the fact that Adam did the junk-bond issue knowing full well that he was demanding, from the board of the electronics company, a complete corporate restructuring, which meant closing down all the factories in the States and moving the entire operation to the union-free, one-dollar-an-hour, *screw-the-workers* paradise that is Mexico. Brother Adam not only engaged in serious financial chicanery, but also cost three hard-up blue-collar towns around six thousand jobs.'

I stared into my glass of wine, not only shocked by what Peter had just told me, but also by the fact that he had somehow dug up all this unsettling information. That was my next question.

'I'm asking you again: how did you find all this out?' I asked.

'It's amazing what you discover when you start to burrow into other people's business. I've been working on this story for about three months.'

'In other words the last time that we had dinner with Adam – seven or eight weeks ago – you were already amassing information to destroy his career.'

'I'm not destroying his career. When the article is published you will see that the center of the piece will be a writer discovering that his brother is a high-level crook.'

'In other words: you've fictionalized it?'

'Stop acting like some naive rube, rather than the hard-nosed New York publisher you've become. You know this is going to be a

515

work of non-fiction, part investigative reporting, part memoir, and it is going to talk volumes about families and all the clandestine stuff that goes on within them.'

'So you are going to not just put Adam in severe legal jeopardy, you are also going to reveal all about us as well?'

'I wrote about Dad before in my first book, I wrote about Mom and Dad and their reaction to my radical politics in the last one –'

'But here you are going to be writing something that could land your brother in jail.'

'If that happens because of my article don't blame me. Adam did something illegal, and continues to do so.'

'If that's the case then why haven't the SEC busted him by now?'

'Because they don't have the inside dope that I've found.'

'Again I ask: how did you find it, besides research and investigative reporting legwork?'

'That's my business.'

'It's now *my* business too. Because he's also my brother. And because I don't really know why you're doing this.'

'You mean, you are going to sit there and tell me you condone his avarice?'

Peter's tone had veered into that self-righteous zone of his: a tone that I found grating and just a little smug because he came across as a scold, and one who knew better than me.

I chose my next words with care.

'I don't know all the facts of the case. Can I read the article?'

'It's embargoed until the end of next month, when *Esquire* publishes it. But I can show you the page proofs a few days before the magazine goes to press.'

'I am your sister – and you're telling me I can't see the article that will probably destroy our brother?'

'Before this conversation I'd have shown it to you. But now …'

'Now *what?*'

'Now you are clearly not giving me the response I'd hoped for.'

'And what response is that? "Oh, fantastic, Peter – you get to tell the world about how you discovered that your brother was a Wall

Street crook, and how you decided to raise your literary capital by doing the dirty on your brother"?'

'That's not fair.'

'Not *fair*? You dare talk about *fair*? Adam played fast and loose with the regulatory rules. But he didn't kill anyone, nor was he an accomplice in a murder.'

My brother stared at the floor, saying nothing.

'Adam insisted on the restructuring of a company,' I said. 'That might not win him prizes for social responsibility. But it is, in the end, just business.'

'Since when did you become a cheerleader for the fat cats?'

'I bet your editors at *Esquire* are beside themselves. What a splash this is going to make.'

'Are you going to tell Adam?'

'If I could read the article ... '

'I can't allow that.'

'Then I am telling Adam.'

'Go right ahead.'

That threat didn't throw him.

'If I promise not to tell anyone about the article ... '

'When you read it you will feel obliged to tell everyone about it. From the moment you "just dropped by" tonight, in the pouring rain, talking about feeling all alone in the world, I knew you'd been tipped off and were on the hunt to find out more.'

'I know why you're really doing this: because it will get you all the media attention and press coverage and invites to all the cool parties and maybe even some Hollywood money again – all the glittering prizes that you have so craved ever since Samantha dumped you and your career never matched that one brief shining moment when –'

'Fuck you,' Peter said, his voice just above a vehement hiss. 'I think you should go, Alice.'

'And I think, *Peter*, that you should ponder long and hard the massive implications of your actions. Do you understand you could be putting our brother away for a very long time? The shadow of corruption falls large, especially on other family members. Mom is going to go into deeper lunacy over this. Dad even more so. Please do not forget that Adam has a baby son and another child on the way.'

'Even if he gets locked up for a couple of years and heavily fined he'll still come out with around ten million in the bank.'

My head was reeling. I couldn't believe what I was hearing.

'This is the scorched earth stuff, Peter. Abject destructiveness.'

'My editor feels the vast majority of people, sickened by the greed that is everywhere now – a greed which not only continues to further marginalize the poor, but which has begun to completely undermine the once reasonably comfortable world of the American – are going to applaud my decision to dish the dirt on a sibling who has destroyed lives for his own gain.'

'Your self-righteousness is even more pronounced than your ethical arrogance.'

'Aren't they one and the same?' he said, standing up. 'Yeah, Adam's been generous to us both. In fact, I figure he's given me twenty grand since he came into the big bucks. I'll tell you this: I talk about that in the piece. Just as I also let the reader know: by the time you've read this my brother will have been reimbursed by me fully.'

'But you hardly have a spare twenty Gs, Older Brother. I'd guess *Esquire* pays a dollar, maybe a dollar-fifty a word, which is a nice thirty pieces of silver sum for selling out your brother. Adam does have an essential decency and he does love us – in that very gut way of his. Please don't level his life to get yours back on track.'

Peter walked to the other side of the room, sat down at his desk, reached for a pair of headphones attached to his amplifier and dropped the tone arm on the record awaiting playing. I had been officially switched off.

I wanted to storm over, pull off his headphones and scream at him. But a little rational voice within told me to count to ten and figure out my next move. I realized that showing up here, trying to get him to reveal all about his big Adam exposé, had been a huge error of judgment. Peter's back went right up when confronted. But was he so green-eyed with envy that he was willing to devastate all that Adam had achieved? As this thought arrived so too did the gripping concern: was I siding with the money? I'd watched Adam turn into a financial high roller – but always sensed that, beneath the veneer, he was still the self-conscious, lonely guy who always wanted to belong, and who simultaneously knew he was never comfortable in the macho confines to which he sadly gravitated.

I told myself: *head for the sofa. Pick up your briefcase. If you make eye contact with your brother nod to him, say nothing and go for the door. If he tells you to come back because he wants to talk some more accept his invitation. If it doesn't arise, grab your shoes by the front door, and walk straight through it.*

It didn't arise. I put on my shoes, hesitating for a moment outside the door. But in shutting it, I knew that I was shutting down a conduit to Peter. Why couldn't I go back inside, insist that he talk to me some more, insist that ... ?

What? That was the hard-edge dilemma, the Gordian knot of this situation: the unnerving fact that I had little in the way of bargaining capital here.

As I reached the sidewalk, and walked toward a phone booth down the street, hoping against hope that it hadn't been vandalized in that casual New York way of ours, another thought came to me: the only reason that *Esquire* editor decided to tell Howie was because he knew that Howie would get word spread around quickly that a big article he'd picked up was about to make quite the splash.

The phone was working. I dropped in a quarter and punched in Howie's number. Miraculously, he answered on the second ring.

'I have my jacket on and was about to head to the nearest den of ill repute,' he said.

'Can you take the jacket off and wait for me?'

'Did you speak to Peter?'

'I saw Peter.'

'Oh dear. Get over here now.'

Thirty minutes later I was sitting in one of Howie's overstuffed purple velvet armchairs. I related everything about the confrontation with Peter. He sat there impassively throughout my spiel, saying nothing. When I finished he pointed to the balcony and told me to have a cigarette break. When I came back he got straight to the heart of the matter.

'You need legal advice here. Your analysis of Peter's reasons for doing all this make sense. But I agree with you: confronting him tonight was a bad idea. He's going to build up his defenses even more.'

'Do you think this is going to cause me professional problems?'

'Only if you play it badly. You will definitely have to tell your boss. But before that: drop some money to spend an hour talking to Sal Grech. He's one of the toughest lawyers in New York. He knows how to close down trouble through stealth. But he will also tell you the truth if he thinks you're not going to get away with something. If he thinks Peter has the stronger hand he'll be utterly direct with you about that too. I would never lie to you, Alice. Ergo, here's what I truly think: your brother Adam is going down.'

Sal Grech was not what I expected. Given his name, his family heritage, the way Howie painted him as some sort of Mafia wise guy, I wasn't prepared for the compact, trim, well-dressed and impeccably spoken man who greeted me at his office on Fifth Avenue and 48th Street.

'Miss Burns,' he said, holding out his hand, 'I truly am so sorry to keep you waiting.'

We were only five minutes beyond our agreed appointment time. I saw Salvatore Grech taking me in, sizing me up.

'May we offer you something? My secretary makes a very good espresso.'

'That would be splendid.'

He ushered me into an office with an imposing mahogany presidential desk, a boardroom table, two very rococo armchairs, and a wall filled with photographs of Counselor Grech with the great and the good of the city.

'I took the liberty, in advance of our conversation,' he said, motioning me to sit down, 'of making a few inquiries about your brother's article. Let me give you the difficult news first: there are several significant obstacles to stopping its publication ... Had I known about all this a month or so ago, I might have been able to find ways of blocking it. But we are now three weeks away from publication. *Esquire*'s lawyers and their fact checkers have been all over the piece, trying to see if they could be in any way exposed. They demanded certain rewrites from Mr Burns to tighten up and close down any potential lawsuits. Mr Burns did all that was requested of him. *Esquire* is being highly protective about the article. It is very much under lock and key. If you seriously want to read it before its publication I can, with work, probably achieve that for you. But I must warn you: serious money will have to exchange hands with my contact for this service to be facilitated.'

'By which you mean?'

'I would say: ten thousand dollars.'

I swallowed hard. Counselor Grech saw this.

'My contact did give me a basic rundown on the contents of the article ... or, at least, what he'd been able to discern from within *Esquire* – where only five people have been allowed access to it. It is, according to him, very well written, thoroughly researched and narrated in a tone he described as "sad love for a brother who has embraced the world of big money without considering the price he would pay for his greed". I regret to inform you but your father doesn't come out at all well from the piece: the paternal bad guy. It's also suggested that Adam became attracted to the outer legal limits of high finance as a way of proving himself to Dad.'

I shut my eyes.

'There is something else you should know. Your concern about *Esquire* leaking the article to the SEC ... that ship has sailed, I'm afraid. There are five agents working on the case right now. Adam will be arrested, along with his boss, on the day that the article is published. If I were his lawyer I'd be thinking about a quick plea bargain and turning state's evidence again Tad Strickland as a way of saving himself some serious big-house time. When this happens – and it will happen – if you want to put him on to me I am rather skilled at getting white-collar fellows out of the legal chamber of horrors. But, of course, you cannot say a word to him or anyone else about this ... though I know you will tell our mutual friend Howard, to which I don't object. Being a good Italian American Howard understands the concept of *omertà* by which I operate.'

'What do I tell my parents?'

'You tell them nothing. If you do, you risk prosecution for endangering and interfering with a federal investigation. I have done some asking around about you, as I do with any new client. The fact is, Miss Burns, you cannot endanger your career by trying to protect a brother who is definitely getting the "Go to Jail" card dealt to him.'

'But my mom and dad ... '

'I know all about your mother. Quite the realtor success story. But the advance knowledge that her son is about to be arrested ... why put her through the agony of all that? Even if you feel you can trust your mother with this information, legally speaking you can't tell her. And your father ... I know all about his work in Chile. Though you may not agree, I think that makes your father a patriot. But he is a notorious hothead. Between ourselves he is having problems with the CEO of his firm. I mention all this not simply to let you know that I have been doing my homework, but also to reinforce the fact that you cannot, *must not* under any circumstances tell him what is about to come down the line.'

My reaction to this news was to puff down so hard on my cigarette that I was already at its filter.

'I know how difficult all this is, Miss Burns. My whole law practice is about finding solutions to some of the law's insoluble problems. But finding those solutions is also bound up in timing. And as I said before the timing is now, alas, against us. Here's my advice: go back to your office and understand that there is nothing you can do to stop these events. I advise you again to say absolutely nothing to anybody, bar Howard D'Amato. I would also like to suggest the following scenario: you arrange a family dinner a few days before the *Esquire* piece is published. You make certain that Adam and your parents are there. Then you let me join you – and I will explain all, especially what is about to befall Adam. Trust me, I will let them know that you were powerless to interfere before now.'

'And say that Adam tells you that he doesn't want you as his counsel?'

'Don't underestimate my powers of persuasion, Miss Burns. Especially when facing a man who could lose a decade of his life – and the majority of his fortune – by being behind bars. Give me five minutes with him and your brother will realize he needs me far more than I need him. There is no latitude in this matter. What we are dealing with now is the limitation of damage. Which I can absolutely achieve, as long as I have everyone's complete cooperation.'

'I will do my best to ensure that. One small difficult question. My funds are limited – and I know that you have put in far more time than our hour today. I need to ask: what sort of tab am I running up now?'

Grech put his fingers together in that pensive papal way of his.

'As long as your brother agrees to take me on to handle the case there will be no charge whatsoever. You will not have to convince him of such a decision. Just put me together with him on the night and I will take care of the rest.'

Later that evening, over dinner with Howie at a Chinese place, I asked my friend if Grech always garnered business in this way.

'Two things you need to understand,' Howie said. 'The first is: Sal Grech hardly needs to find clients. They flock to him. The second is: if a Sicilian Maltese tells you there is no way out of this except by staying quiet and following his strategy, you have no choice but to follow his strategy. He will contain the mess.'

'But how am I going to deal with my parents and Adam before then?'

'You are going to bite the fucking bullet and pretend that all is okay in the world. You have no choice, Alice – unless you want this all to explode in your face. One other thing you need to know: Peter's going to be on *Open End* the evening of October 7.'

Oh Jesus, no. *Open End* was a much-watched, much-discussed talk show, hosted by a brainy man-about-town, David Susskind, who, in a cloud of cigarette smoke, loved to create controversy and its attendant buzz. Peter on Susskind was going to be a bottle rocket of combustible revelations. Susskind would love the ethical dubiousness of both brothers. No doubt Dad's stint in the CIA would also come into public play. Dirty linen would be washed in a sophisticated New York television forum that would guarantee much traction in the high and low press. It would also trigger the downfall of Adam.

And there was not a damn thing I could do to steer him out of from the path of this oncoming vehicle. Except to follow Grech's counsel and arrange a dinner on the evening of the broadcast, and have Sal standing by to intervene when everything imploded.

I tried reaching Adam twice during the following week, I'd read in the financial pages of the *New York Times* that he was in the process of negotiating a major new bond issue. When he finally rang back he was very much the financial live wire.

'Saw that you called twice last week. Anything urgent?'

'Just wanted to know how you're doing?'

'Besides the fact that I could use two weeks of sleep ... all is booming.'

'Isn't Janet due imminently?'

'She's a little behind schedule. The new due date is October 10.'

'But wasn't it supposed to be the last week of September?'

'She's late. So what?'

I stopped myself from saying: *you will probably be under indictment by October 10*. Instead:

'Just asking, Adam. And just wondering: how about a family dinner the week before?'

'I doubt Janet will be up for that.'

'I was talking about the five of us. Maybe meet somewhere like Pete's Tavern – our old haunt – on Sunday the 7th?'

'Are you about to make some big announcement?'

'Nothing so dramatic. I just thought: we should all get together.'

The day after my phone call with Adam Dad rang me around 11 p.m. at my apartment, a drink or two over the clarity limit. He often phoned me at home, late in the evening, leaving messages on my answerphone if I was out, knowing that I was always going to return his call.

'Sorry to keep calling you, sweetheart.'

'Never apologize for that, Dad. I always want to hear your voice.'

'I worry you think me a sad guy, an elderly version of Little Boy Lost.'

'You're still a young man, Dad.'

'Now you are talking crap. I'm fifty-seven – and I look it.'

'You look fine,' I said, also knowing that I was more than stretching the truth as he had packed on around thirty pounds over the last year and was having too many late evenings like this with a bottle of J&B Scotch by his elbow.

'I look like shit, sweetheart.'

'Then do something about it. Go on a diet, join a gym, cut down on the booze. And stop crying into your beer.'

'Stop talking back to your father.'

I laughed. As did Dad.

'Any chance I could talk you into a family dinner on October 7?'

'Sounds good.'

Mom agreed to the dinner as well – though she was more preoccupied with why it was so hard to get Peter on the phone.

'He won't return my messages. You in touch with him?'

'I know he's really busy on a new project.'

'But he doesn't have time to call his mother?'

'He is what he is.'

'Thank you for that insight. At least Adam returns my calls – maybe three days later, but he still does it.'

'If we were to meet at Pete's Tavern on the 7th?'

'That old dump? Why there?'

'I have a sentimental attachment to it.'

'I don't,' she said.

The next two weeks were professionally far too charged, as our big autumn books hit the shelves and I watched certain sure-fire titles do moderate business, and one literary novel break out and turn into a rather nice success. I was in regular touch with Sal Grech. He told me the time was right to go to my boss and let him in on all that was about to go down. I used my now weekly meeting with C.C. Fowler to confess all about Peter's article and what it was going to mean for my other brother. He listened silently as I spoke. I explained also about how I had approached Counselor Grech for advice and hoped that Adam would agree to take him on as his lawyer in the wake of his indictment.

'I don't personally know Sal Grech,' C.C. said, 'but his reputation precedes him. When it comes to this sort of case he is among

525

the best – so well done getting him lined up. I hope your brother will see sense and listen to him. And I thank you so much for bringing this to my attention before the publication of the article. I know that this must remain between ourselves until that issue of *Esquire* is out. By the way, do you think your brother's agent might be willing to speak to us about the book that will follow? Yes I am being a little commercially cold-blooded here. And yes I can see how it might cause you some discomfort if we did sign him up for the book. But there are other editors in the house who could handle it.'

'Indeed there are, sir.'

'If it is a great read – and I am already getting its Cain and Abel subtext – why shouldn't we try to profit on it ourselves?'

In the ten days remaining before the scheduled dinner I tried to bury myself in work, while simultaneously falling victim to a creeping insomnia which no amount of over-the-counter sleep aids would cure. When I told Howie that I was now six straight nights without proper rest – three or so hours maximum accompanied by nonstop dread – he insisted I see my doctor and get something 'properly pharmaceutical'. But I feared becoming as dependent again on mood and sleeping pills as I did after Ciaran's death. Just as I kept telling myself: once I have explained all, once Counselor Grech has made his intervention, once he has calmed down my parents and assured Adam he can get him a good legal deal ... once all that's happened I'll finally be able to sleep.

'You are asking for mental trouble,' Howie said when he saw me a few days before the family dinner. 'Don't tell me you've gone Christian Scientist and have sidestepped modern medicine's magic knockout pills?'

'I did that before – at a time of terrible duress. Now I'm nervous about getting hooked.'

'We're talking Valium, not smack. You've done Valium before and you didn't turn into William Burroughs. Here ... ' he said, reaching into his shoulder bag and pulling out a plastic bottle of pills. 'You have to sleep.'

'I'm doing fine.'

'No you are not. And you are refusing to get proper medical help as a way of punishing yourself for the sins of Peter and Adam. No word whatsoever from the treasonous scribe?'

'Radio silence since our confrontation. Counselor Grech called me this morning to go over final details and said that his spies at SEC leaked to him that they have quite the airtight case against Adam and Ted. We also discussed strategy for Sunday evening. He's arriving about nine, will place himself at the bar, and I am to start telling them all as soon as he arrives, so I can signal him to come over once my dad gets hot under the collar.'

'Whatever you do you must promise me that if they turn their anger on you that you will get Sal between you and them. Another promise I am insisting you keep: that you take two Valium tonight before bedtime and another two tomorrow night. You need to be rested before you face the family music.'

That night I didn't touch the pills – because something sad crowded in on me. Returning home after the dinner with Howie I found myself facing, in my mailbox, a letter from Duncan: a letter postmarked Khartoum, this time typed, and full of color and detail. It was toward the end of the letter that the tone suddenly changed – and he wrote, over a long, single-spaced page, a declaration of love, telling me that this extended absence truly did make the longing more intense, but also helped clarify feelings that he had 'submerged' for years.

We still don't know each other intimately, and I regret now not having broken off the trip to come back to New York when work couldn't free you up for a few weeks. But please know that I am longing for you, longing to get back – and it's just another eight weeks which strikes me as an age – and I am going to finish this and not reread it through because I want you to read exactly what is in my heart and how I feel, that what we have comes along once or twice in a lifetime, and yes, call this the ramblings of a lonely man in a shithole sub-Saharan city, but one who knows that our destiny is together, and yes, I have had about four Scotches too many – Indian Scotch, cheap and hardly cheerful, but about the only balm available to me right now.

At the end of the letter he told me that by the time I got this he'd probably be back in Cairo and I could write/telegram him care of American Express. And, besides again telling me that he loved me, he added a PS: *Shall we get married a week or so after I am back? – and no this is not the Mumbai whisky talking.*

Perhaps it was a vertiginous week without sleep. Perhaps it was the specter of impending familial drama in just forty-eight hours – and the sense that the last thing I could or should be thinking about right now was building a future with someone whom I'd yet to even sleep with. Perhaps it was Duncan's heart-on-sleeve, far too effusive, boozy proclamations which made me shed exhausted, overstressed tears and had me immediately thinking:

How dare you say all that to me, you perpetual wanderer? You want me to wait for you, but you will always be a tumbleweed blowing from place to place. Which means that you're certain to eventually break my heart. And I can't afford to know such pain again.

I glanced at my watch. It was almost midnight. I told myself: take the Valium, get some sleep. But that part of me which was now operating on some sleep-deprived autopilot – and which had decided to take serious offense at Duncan's romantic ramblings – convinced myself that I needed to end all this immediately, to stop pretending that there would be a happy ending in a few months' time when he finally showed up in New York; that my instincts about him were right: he was always going to be the vagabond who might talk love, but would always have his eye on the door marked 'Exit'. Best to kill it now before I fall even more in love with him. Before we shared a bed and I longed for the touch of him. Before I convinced myself that we could have a life together.

The four Valium tabs were on my kitchen counter. I glanced at my watch. It was twelve minutes after midnight. The big post office on West 34th Street was open twenty-four hours. Telling myself again – *Get this done now before you have second thoughts –* I grabbed my coat, I headed out toward Broadway, I grabbed a taxi downtown, composing a succinct message along the way. When I reached the post office I went straight to the one counter open and filled out a form. I pushed the form over to the clerk. He read it out loud to me, checking that all was correct.

This is never going to work. I cannot give you what you need, what you want. It's best to end this before it begins. I'm sorry. I'm sad. But I am also definitive about this. Alice.

When he finished reading it to me the clerk ever so slightly raised his eyebrows, as if to ask: *you sure about this?* Seeing this I demanded:

'What do I owe you?'

'When do you want it delivered?'

'Immediately,' I said.

'Then it will cost you eleven dollars and ninety-eight cents, which will get it there within the hour.'

I handed over a twenty. The eight dollars and pennies pushed back to me paid for a cab back uptown. Half an hour later, trying to black out all thoughts of what I had done, I dropped the two Valium, climbed under the covers and surrendered to sleep.

When I awoke, I found myself squinting at the bedside clock and was rather amazed to discover that I had been unconscious for over ten hours. The Valium had left me somewhat fogged in and druggy. But one thought immediately overshadowed the cloud in my head: that telegram was one of the worst mistakes of my life.

I got up. I staggered into the bathroom. I threw water onto my face. It didn't lift the inner murk. I filled the sink with cold water. I dunked my face fully into it. I dried off, changed into gym clothes, made myself a pot of espresso, ate a small tub of yogurt and then downed three straight shots of the high-octane Italian coffee, all the while fighting despair. I went to the gym. An hour and a half of crazed exercise burned off much of the pharmaceutical mist. I returned home, the *New York Times* under my arm. I resisted the temptation to call Howie and confess my self-sabotaging misdeed. I told myself I should get over to the nearest post office and send a second telegram, pleading fear of love and telling him how much I wanted him. But another voice within me said: *as sad as it is, it is easier this way. He might be wonderful, but he's also complex and damaged. And I needed simple and …*

But wasn't I just as complex and damaged? And wasn't 'simple' exactly the sort of banality I would never truly let into my life?

I tried to focus my attention on the newspaper and then burrowed into a manuscript about an account of the early days of the AIDS plague by a San Francisco journalist who himself was dying from the illness. Thoughts of Jack were everywhere around me as I read it. I could not help but wish that I had some sort of faith that assured me of a life beyond this one; that all the people I had lost – Professor Hancock, my beloved Ciaran, Jack – were waiting for me somewhere in the celestial beyond. I knew I could never get my head around any conception of a paradise beyond this one. And yet, by the same measure, how I also embraced all the mysteries – the immense unanswered questions – that life threw into the path of just about everyone, the biggest one being:

What, in the end, did all this amount to – and why was it all so bloody difficult?

I had no answers to any of those questions, just impending dread of the evening ahead. And of more pain for a family that seemed to organically generate so much of it.

I counted down the hours until 8 p.m. I continued ploughing on with the manuscript, thinking how it needed a serious rewrite, that we'd have to get someone to handle the second draft. But, it was a brutal dispatch from the AIDS trenches, a battlefield in which the enemy was still running rampant, leaving those in its path defenseless against its pitiless attack.

At one point I squinted out the window. It was a perfect autumn late afternoon. I could see this peerless impending sunset. I kept my head down, working until 6.30 p.m. Then I grabbed my leather jacket and decided to walk all the way southeast to 18th Street and Irving Place.

The air was calm, an edge of chill undercutting it. I headed south on Broadway, passing by the street where Duncan went to school, telling myself again it wasn't too late to send that telegram and try to limit the damage.

I kept walking, kept quoting that French phrase which Ciaran used to sing out loud: '*C'est le destin, le destin ...*' though he was always highlighting the irony of it. Because he knew that destiny was so often written by yourself. Even when it arrived by chance – or, in our case, when we walked right into its horrible path. Was that sort of accident anything more than the music of chance?

I passed by what used to be Needle Park: junkie headquarters back before New York developed its current moneyed edge. Though I knew that, down around Times Square, there was undoubtedly a Western Union office still open, I stopped myself from sending that second telegram. Because I had too much else crowding in on me to play emotional roulette right now.

I moved to 59th Street, turning east on Central Park South, passing the Hampshire House, now a very exclusive apartment building, but back in the mid-century years a hotel – and the scene, on May 10, 1950, of the marriage between my two parents – and an entire, subsequently troubled trajectory of life that only found a certain, distant equilibrium after the kids had left and divorce cleaned the emotional slate. Could they have ever imagined the place they'd arrived at today – apart, but still somewhat together, with the balance of power between them so radically changed?

I decided to walk all the way down Fifth Avenue – my entire early childhood flooding in: the visits to Santa Claus on the fifth floor of the now-vanished Best and Co. department store: the desperately awkward moments on ice skates at the Rockefeller Center rink; past Sal Grech's office; peering west on 46th Street where my grandfather had his jewelry business, thinking how for years, from afar, this city had seemed imperial, unconquerable.

I thought back to something Dad once told me on a snowy evening in Connecticut, when things were particularly bad in high school and I wondered out loud if I would one day be revealed as the fraud I felt myself to be. Dad smiled, lighting up a cigarette, clinking the ice in his glass of Scotch and growling in that half-boozed-up way of his:

'Sweetheart, the greatest fear in the world – outside of death – is the fear of being found out. We're all afflicted by it.'

Dad. I was glad I wasn't one of his sons. Whatever I felt about those moments when he turned difficult on me, I knew in my heart that I was pleased to be his daughter. Just as walking into Pete's Tavern, seeing him in a rear booth, staring down into his Scotch, a cigarette on the go, a man on the cusp of sixty, brooding, solitary, I felt this immense stab of love for him. How I wanted to help him. How I wanted to see him in a better place. How I knew there was little I could do. How I feared all that was about to transpire.

'How's the star publisher?' he asked, after getting to his feet and enveloping me in a bear hug.

'Happily overworked.'

Adam came in, waving. On seeing him looking so relaxed and pleased to be here, I tried to tamper down the immense guilt and stress rising within. Mom was with him, in a shoulder-padded black pants suit. I could see her immediate disappointment in my black jeans, black western shirt and black leather jacket.

'Hope you don't do the downtown junkie chic look when you're taking clients out to the Four Seasons,' she asked.

'Great to see you, Mom,' I said, accepting her air-kiss on both cheeks.

'Where's Peter?' she asked.

'Unfortunately he got caught up in something at the last minute.'

'But this was supposed to be a proper family get-together,' Mom said.

'Especially as we have some news to announce,' Dad said.

'Not just yet,' Mom said to him, sounding just a bit testy. 'Let's get a drink first.'

'Your news requires that we first have a drink?' Adam said.

'Very funny,' Mom said.

Adam had his hand in the air, snapping his fingers. A waiter was on the scene in moments.

'Champagne,' Adam said, sidestepping the word 'please'. 'The best you have.'

'Mr High Roller,' Mom said.

'Hey, the kid just scored big on that $600 million bond share thing of his,' Dad said.

'Quite some "thing",' I said, wanting to be part of the conversation, but also trying to keep my mounting anxiety under wraps.

The champagne arrived. The cork was popped, glasses filled. Dad insisted on making a toast.

'To the four of us and the absent firstborn. There are none better.'

I blinked and felt tears. I had positioned myself in the side of the booth facing the front door. I glanced at the door, glanced at my watch.

'Expecting someone?' Mom asked.

'Just hoping against hope Peter might somehow show.'

'Looks like we'll just have to drink without him,' Dad said.

'So what's the damn news?' Adam asked.

Mom and Dad exchanged glances. I sensed what was coming next. Especially when Dad reached out and took his ex-wife's hand.

'Your mother let me move back in with her,' Dad said.

'Permission was finally granted,' Mom said.

'She fell for my charms again,' Dad said, allowing himself a smile.

'This is great news,' Adam said.

We ordered food. Mom got talking about some Hollywood producer type who was in town last week, looking to buy a 3,000 square-foot SoHo pied-à-terre and who had to duck away every twenty minutes for a fresh line of cocaine.

'Wall Street's now running on the white powder,' Adam said.

'I hope to hell you're keeping away from it,' Dad said.

'As Tad said: "Coke is God's way of telling you you'll never have enough money." Fear not: the only drug for me is pure capitalism.'

The food arrived. So too did a man in a black Burberry trench coat, a snappy black fedora, a black three-piece suit. He took a seat at the bar and ordered a drink, his back to us. Dad noticed his arrival.

'Now if that guy isn't a Mob lawyer . . . ' he whispered.

'It's Salvatore Grech,' Mom whispered back.

'A friend of yours?' Dad demanded.

'Hardly. One of New York's top lawyers. A real *consigliere* – but of the legitimate variety.'

'You sell him an apartment?' Adam asked.

'Two of his clients were referred to me,' Mom said. 'But I've never met the gent, and I really should say thank you.'

'Let the man have his drink,' Dad said.

'It will just take a minute,' Mom said.

'Jesus Christ, Brenda, you can let the networking shit go for an evening. Especially with your kids here.'

'Let her pay her respects to the man,' Adam said.

'So speaks the other great schmoozer,' I said.

'In my game the bigger the talk, the bigger the payoff.'

Mom was on her feet. But as she stepped away from the booth something stopped her dead in her tracks. I saw what she'd caught sight of: a small portable TV behind the bar, exclusively for the perusal of the guy pouring drinks. And on the screen right now, in full close-up, was Peter.

'Oh my God,' Mom said.

'What?' Adam said.

'Look,' Mom said, pointing to the television.

Now Dad was on his feet.

'He's on Susskind's show,' she said, then turned right on me. 'Did you know about this?'

Oh fuck. Why did I not wonder in advance if there was a television at Pete's Tavern?

'If I can explain ... '

'Explain what?' Dad demanded.

'Let's all sit down again and –'

But I didn't get to complete that sentence, as Adam was marching to the bar, his hand coming out of his pocket holding a big wad of cash encased in a silver money clip. I could see him detaching a twenty from the wad, tossing it down and telling the guy pouring drinks to bring the TV over. Mom and Dad were now by Adam's side as the little Trinitron was placed in front of them, the volume cranked up. I wanted to bolt for the door. I wanted to burst into tears. I did neither. I came over to where they were standing just as I heard Susskind pose the following question to Peter:

'When did you become aware that your brother might be engaged in serious financial fraud?'

The camera now panned to Peter – who was coolness itself.

'When I saw how all that "junk bond" money had gone to his head, and when he hinted once to me that "insider dope" – his exact words – was the way to score big on Wall Street in this new Gilded Age of ours.'

'Oh my fucking God ... '

That was my mother, her voice a near shriek. She turned on me.

'You knew about this, didn't you?'

'If I could explain –'

'Explain?' Dad shouted, all eyes in the restaurant on us. 'Explain *what*? That you knew your asshole brother was going to denounce Adam?'

I could see Adam staggering away, in free fall, heading in the direction of the exit. But Sal Grech was now on his feet, blocking Adam's path.

'Adam, I'm Salvatore Grech. And your sister – who is the innocent party here – asked me to come and –'

My father was now careening toward Grech, crazed.

'She asked you to come here? The fuck you talking about?'

'Dad, please ... ' I shouted, putting myself in front of him. But he shoved me out of the way. Grech – his presence of mind remarkable – caught one of my father's flailing arms and twisted it in a way to cause pain.

'You, sir, are way out of line. Understandable in the circumstances. But your daughter was in a no-win situation and came to me to find a solution to Adam's considerable problems.'

'You let go of my fucking arm ... '

'Dad, let the man speak.'

This was Adam, his hand on Dad's shoulder. When Dad struggled again, Mom was at his side – putting her arms around him.

'Sweetheart, stop ... '

There was a terrible silence. My father hung his head, his face beet-red, his rage only contained by Grech's ferocious police grip on his arm. Behind him, from the television, came Peter's voice:

'The sense of entitled corruption which my brother and his criminal guru Tad Strickland represents ... '

Grech barked to the bartender:

'Turn that off now.' Then he said to my father:

'If I let go of your arm will you go back to the booth and sit down and allow me explain to you and your wife and your son here how this all came about? How Alice did good by seeking me out, and how we can limit the damage to Adam?'

'He's on fucking Susskind, ruining my boy, ruining my family,' Dad said.

'It is a bad business, I agree,' Grech said. 'But let's sit down and have a civilized conversation.'

'Susskind does his show from that studio way over on West 55th Street, right?' Dad said. 'I know that because Shirley once had tickets for one of his broadcasts ... '

He almost sounded as if he was talking to himself.

'Sweetheart, listen to Mr Grech,' Mom said. 'Let's all sit down, please.'

'Fifty-fifth and Tenth,' Dad said.

'Sir,' Grech said, 'I am going to ask only one more time: if I let go of your arm ... '

Dad stared down at the ground, tears running down his face.

'How the fuck did you let this happen, Alice?'

'She let nothing happen,' Grech said. 'You need to answer my question ... '

'Work all your life, do everything you can for your children, then this.'

Grech glanced over at the maître d', who was standing right behind my father with two burly fellows in white dishwasher's uniforms.

'Charlie, I think I'm going to have to turn Mr Burns over to you.'

That got Dad's attention.

'No need,' he whispered. 'I'll behave.'

Grech, nodding to Charlie to be ready in case Dad did not behave, looked directly into my father's tragic eyes.

'I am now going to let you go, Mr Burns. It's three paces back to the booth. We're going to have no trouble now, understood?'

'Understood.'

Grech let go of his arm. Dad stood there, hunched, denuded. Mom immediately had her arms around him, bringing him close to her, saying:

'It's going to be okay.'

Dad just shook his head. Then he allowed her to guide him back to the booth. Grech put a reassuring arm on Adam's shoulder and motioned to him and to me that we should all sit down.

'I need a drink,' Dad said. 'J&B, a double.'

Moments later the drink appeared. Dad threw it back.

'Thank you,' he said to Grech. 'Thank you ... and sorry.'

'Apology accepted. If I can begin by explaining what brought Alice into my office –'

'I need to go to the can,' interrupted Dad. 'Then I will come back and listen to everything Mr Grech wants to tell us.'

'It's in the back,' Adam said. Grech nodded.

He stood up, holding on to the side of the booth for support.

'I can help you get there,' I said, now on my feet.

'Fuck you, Alice,' he hissed.

I fell back into my seat as if slapped.

Dad turned and started moving with care toward the rear of the restaurant, his gait slow, unsteady. Charlie was watching him carefully. I could see my father, with great deliberation, trying to somehow maintain a sense of equilibrium. But then, just as he was about to reach the door marked 'Men', he suddenly veered right and crashed out of sight. I saw a side exit fly open and my dad charge out of it. Charlie was immediately racing toward the back of the restaurant, Mom in pursuit. When Adam jumped up, Grech grabbed his arm and pulled him back down.

'You're staying here and talking with me.'

I heard him say that as I charged down to the emergency exit, finding Charlie and Mom on the street, screaming at a cab that was now speeding down 18th Street. Charlie hailed another cab straightaway, yanked open the door as Mom and I dove into the back seat, and Charlie told the driver:

'That cab ahead of you – catch up to it and follow it.'

He slammed the passenger door shut. The cabbie did as ordered, flooring the accelerator, the huge jump in speed slamming the two of us into the vinyl of the back seat. The taxi up ahead was a full street in front of us. The cabbie was quite the fast driver. Within a minute, as the other cab turned north up Third Avenue, we were nearly behind it.

'There's a big tip for you if you keep up with him,' Mom told him.

'Any idea where he's going?' the cabbie asked.

'Fifty-fifth and Tenth,' I said, scrambling in my bag for a cigarette.

'You're not smoking here,' Mom said. 'You're not steadying your nerves with –'

'Would you let me explain?'

'No. I don't want your explanations.'

'Mom ... '

'Shut up, Alice. Shut up and let me think.'

Mom closed her eyes. A shudder came over her as she began to sob. But when I attempted to put an arm around her she screamed:

'Don't you fucking touch me.'

Silence. The driver glanced back at the two of us, his eyes wide.

'Don't look at us like that,' Mom said. 'Keep your eyes on the other cab.'

Silence. I slid to the far end of the seat, leaning against the door, thinking: *I could just throw it open, throw myself out, hit the sidewalk and – with any luck – black out forever on impact.*

I shut my eyes. I told myself: 'Ciaran would never forgive me for giving up on what was taken away from him.' I let go of the door handle. I knotted my hands together. I kept my gaze glued on the taxi ahead. Our cabbie kept pace, tailing it with speed and dexterity all the way up Third Avenue, then turning left on 57th Street, getting us all the way west to Tenth Avenue and two blocks south.

'Over there,' I said, seeing a crowd by a doorway on the side of the studio. Up ahead the cab in front of us suddenly braked, the door flew open, and Dad fell out.

'Stop now,' I screamed, throwing two tens through the glass, Mom and I both racing out our respective doors. I saw Peter surrounded by people. Dad was barreling his way through this crowd, Mom screaming at him to stop, me charging ahead, determined to get a hold of him. Dad started to roar:

'You fucking, fucking disgrace of a son. You destroyer of everything.'

Peter turned.

'Judas,' Dad shouted – at which moment his gaze met that of his son's, Peter looking as scared and cowed as I had ever seen him, Dad's hand out, ready to hit his eldest boy.

But then, out of nowhere, Dad halted, as if blindsided by something from within. He froze, just feet in from Peter. And then pitched straight forward, hitting the sidewalk face first.

Behind me I heard Mom cry out one word:

'No.'

I fell to my knees beside my father, now motionless, still.

As the coroner later told me:

'His heart exploded.'

31

IRISH CATHOLICS PREFER to bury their dead with haste. A life has ended, last rites administered, the body washed and dressed and prepared for its final send-off, and 'the removal of the remains' scheduled to get the coffin from the undertaker to the chapel, where the Requiem Mass will be celebrated. Then, by midday the following morning, all prayers and words of remembrance having been said by the priest, the coffin is taken to the cemetery and lowered into the earth. Your temporal existence is over. When I asked the priest, Father Meehan, whom Howie had arranged to 'handle all the spiritual arrangements', why there was this rush to get my father into the ground so quickly, he put a reassuring hand on my shoulder and said:

'He's already with God. Putting him back into the soil which Our Creator made for us to grow and nurture the substance of life ... it is the necessary transition we make into Eternity. It is best for those left behind that it all passes quickly. It will allow you and your mother and brothers to get back to the business of living. As your father was a daily communicant, his time in Purgatory will be a swift one. I would not be surprised if he wasn't already in Paradise.'

As your father was a daily communicant ...

That was news to me. Father Meehan was the new priest at St Malachy's (Howie's previous confessor having fallen ill and been sent to an undisclosed location ... 'I'm almost certain he caught the plague as well'). A few hours after Dad died I called Howie at home. He rushed to Columbus Hospital where they had taken the body and stayed with me all night. As light came up over Manhattan, Howie called St Malachy's and raised Father Meehan from his bed. He was with us an hour later, praying by the body, trying his best to comfort me (I was too numb and sleep-deprived to make sense of anything) and dealing with Shirley, whom I'd asked Howie to call to break the news. She came running in from New

Jersey, a morass of guilt and tears. It was Shirley who told Father Meehan that Dad was a regular at the 8 a.m. Mass at Holy Family Church on East 47th Street. Then she burst into tears in front of us.

'He never stopped loving Brenda. It broke my heart, but I could never get him to want me the way he wanted her ... sorry to say this in front of you, Father.'

Father Meehan – a man in his forties, small of stature, thin, with quick eyes and a ferocious cigarette habit (we smoked several times together outside the hospital, the funeral home, the church, and after the burial in the cemetery) – was quick to take over so much. Mom had fallen into a nervous collapse in the immediate aftermath of Dad hitting the sidewalk on West 55th Street – so much so that, when the ambulances arrived on the scene, they found me crouched down by my dead father and simultaneously enveloping my mother in my arms, trying to somehow prevent her from edging into hysteria. I rode with my mother to Columbus Hospital where she was admitted to the psychiatric wing for observation, given a sedative and put to bed. When she came to the next morning, she found her daughter half asleep in the chair next to her bed. Seeing me, Mom began to keen, her crying escalating upward until a nurse came hurrying into the ward, surmised the situation and made her down a paper cupful of tranquilizers. The psychiatrist on call showed up and, after telling my mother that he wanted to keep her here another twenty-four hours for observation, he insisted that I go home, giving me a prescription for a week's supply of Valium 'to make things just a little easier for you'.

'Nothing is easy about any of this.'

'Of course not,' he said. 'But I am urging you to get home and sleep.'

'There is too much to do.'

'Miss Burns, without sleep ... '

'You don't have to tell me,' I snapped. 'I've been through a major fucking bereavement before.'

I immediately apologized. And accepted the Valium. And let Howie help make all the arrangements with Father Meehan for the funeral – which we agreed would take place at St Malachy's, as that was not just Meehan's home parish, but also (according to Howie who'd been to Mass once at Holy Family) an older and more atmospheric church than Dad's local.

'Holy Family has the look of a community prayer hall in the Bible Belt,' Howie said. 'St Malachy is Gothic. I wouldn't want my send-off anywhere else.'

Howie and I visited a Hell's Kitchen undertaker – Flanagan and Sons – recommended to us by Father Meehan. The fellow in charge of things that afternoon, Colum Flanagan Jr, told me he was a recent arrival from Dublin, his uncle being the proprietor of this '112-year-old establishment'.

'I know Dublin,' I said, but from my tone he could tell I didn't want to explain why. To his credit he didn't press me. Nor did he balk when I told him that my father was not in any way a man who cared a toss for life's fineries. 'As such he would be deeply aggrieved to know that I had chosen anything but the simplest coffin for him. I want no debate about that' – knowing full well how funeral directors often tried to talk the bereaved into an over-priced, over-upholstered 'final resting place'. We also found a plot in a cemetery out in Brooklyn that was near to Riis Park, where Dad lifeguarded at the end of the 1930s before the war swept him into its ferocious grasp. As the undertaker showed me a very straightforward varnished pine box with a basic white satin interior I shut my eyes and saw Dad again charging for his errant, treasonous son, his face tomato red, his uncontrollable fury finally ganging up with his overstrained cardiovascular system to throw the punch that snuffed out his life in a moment of paternal impotence; an inability to save his son from fraternal revenge and the long arm of the law.

After I'd chosen a coffin Howie told me that he simply had to go back to work, and if he put me in a taxi uptown to my apartment would I not do something crazy like head to Peter's apartment for a further terrible confrontation?

'The asshole vanished as soon as Dad hit the sidewalk and Mom clawed at Peter and called him an assassin.'

'Don't think about returning to the hospital tonight either. I will check in on your mother later. All going well they might release her tomorrow. But let me worry about all that for the moment. You have to close your eyes now.'

'Adam has to be told.'

'I called Sal Grech late last night, letting him know what had gone down – because Sal is someone who gets very edgy if he learns of important news second-hand. Adam has been informed. You did good work putting Sal into Adam's path. He's hired him. Sal will get him the best deal going. And I know he will ensure that he is there for your father's funeral.'

But as soon as Howie put me in the taxi I told the driver that there was a change of plans. We were going to head to the East Side, then south on Park Avenue. Logic being subsumed by stupor and grief I decided I couldn't be alone at home. As such I simply had to go back to the office and check in on my professional life. Walking in fifteen minutes later I saw the receptionist go wide-eyed at the sight of me, saying:

'Oh, Miss Burns, I am so sorry for your loss.'

I nodded and carried on down the long corridor toward my office. Seeing me in the approaching distance Cheryl was on her feet immediately, gauging my mental state, shocked to see me walk with great purpose toward my desk, descend into the big overstuffed office chair I'd inherited from Jack, and asking her for my call sheet.

'Excuse me if I'm talking out of turn ... but, oh my God, Alice, why are you here?'

'I should have been here hours ago.'

'But ... your father ... I'm so sorry about your father.'

'How did you know about that?'

'It's been everywhere on the news and in the media this morning.'

'I wouldn't know. I've been at the hospital and the funeral home. Why didn't Howie tell me we made the news?'

'Possibly because you were coping with so much already.'

'You saw what happened outside the studio?'

Cheryl nodded.

'So it's ... public knowledge?'

Before Cheryl could answer the door behind her opened. C.C. was there, in his shirtsleeves, his tie loosened, dark polka-dot suspenders keeping his trousers up.

'I have heard of service above and beyond the call of duty,' he said, 'but, Alice, you should not be here right now.'

'Where should I be?'

'You know where: with your family.'

'My family is a little otherwise engaged. Dad is dead. Mom is under sedation in the psych ward. Adam is about to be arrested. And Peter ... I don't know where Peter is.'

C.C. turned to Cheryl.

'I want you to take Alice home to her apartment.'

'I don't want to go home.'

'Where do you want to go?'

'Anywhere I don't have to be by myself.'

'I'll stay with you,' Cheryl said.

'That's a plan,' C.C. said.

'I'd rather get back to work,' I said.

'I'm not allowing that,' C.C. said.

'Please, C.C. – I need to be here.'

'You need sleep. When did you last eat?'

'What time is it now?'

'Just after three,' Cheryl said.

'Dinner last night ... that was the last meal.'

That dinner. How wrong my strategy had been. I should have seen how badly Dad would take all this.

Dad ... Daddy ... my one and only father ...

I put my face in my hands. I stifled a sob. I would not break down in front of my boss. I felt C.C.'s hand on my shoulder.

'You need to get up and let Cheryl take you back to the West Side and to a restaurant of your choice. And if you first need to see a doctor about getting something to help you sleep ... '

'That's taken care of.'

'Then off you go now. I'm insisting you don't come back here for at least a week.'

'I have two books out next Friday ... '

'We will handle it all, and all will proceed smoothly. You are barred from the office until then.'

'You won't fire me, will you?'

'Now you're sounding crazy,' C.C. said.

'I'm sorry,' I said, sounding elsewhere.

'No, it is me who is sorry, Alice,' he said.

I waved my hand, asking him to stop. I stood up, suddenly feeling more tired than I'd even been. Cheryl got me into my coat, then grabbed her own. Tucking her arm into mine she guided me out of the office, out the building, into a taxi. She knew my address. I told her that there was a good Chinese on 67th Street and Columbus Avenue, and that food was now a necessity after almost twenty hours without anything but water. The cab dropped us at the Empire Szechuan, and we sat at a table in the otherwise empty restaurant. The menu swam in front of me. I let Cheryl order for the two of us, and ...

Then I made the mistake of looking up in the direction of the little bar at the front of the restaurant. There was a television there. Illuminated. For the second time in twenty-four hours I had the privilege of seeing a brother of mine on the small screen ... only in this instance Adam was being led away with his hands cuffed behind his back. At his side were several burly Fed types, bundling him out of his office through a phalanx of previously alerted members of the press, all of whom were shouting questions at my brother while his passage from Junk Bond Prince to Under Indictment Felon was recorded in a fireworks of camera flashes.

Seeing me transfixed by something behind her Cheryl swiveled her head and saw what I was watching. Under this carefully stage-managed perp walk was a subtitle. It read:

'ADAM BURNS, WALL STREET WIZARD, ARRESTED FOR INSIDER TRADING.'

I put my head in my hands, wanting the world to disappear. I knew this was coming. But seeing my brother cuffed and being strong-armed and publicly shamed by the Manhattan DA's office ...

At least Mom was momentarily in a place where there were no televisions. When I got home Cheryl insisted on coming upstairs. She sat opposite me, like a social worker dealing with a touch-and-go patient, as I called Janet up at her faux palace in Greenwich. The phone rang out, the answerphone picked up. I left a simple message, telling Janet that I was so sorry for all that had happened to Adam, that I was here for her, especially as the baby was due imminently, and that she must have heard about Dad and how hard everything was right now.

My voice got shaky as I made that comment about my father, the reality of his death again hitting me full-frontal. I checked my watch. The last time I was in bed was Saturday night – and it was now 6.12 p.m. Monday. I told Cheryl she could go. Cheryl demurred, saying she was not going to leave until I was truly asleep.

'I don't need you to play the cop here, Cheryl.'

'I'm just following C.C.'s orders.'

I got undressed. I took the pills. I slid into bed. I buried my head in a pillow and let go, the grief now raw, unbridled. The pills did their work. I woke just after 4 a.m., the trauma rushing straight back in. I went to the kitchen where I made coffee and found a note from Cheryl, telling me she'd left at 8 p.m. when it was clear I was out for the night, that she was at the end of the phone whenever needed, and that *I know you will find your way through this very dark wood.*

There was also a message on the answerphone – the volume of which I had turned right down – from Mom.

'It's 3.30 a.m. I have just checked myself out of the psych ward – despite the concerns of the intern on duty. I am at home. I won't be going back to bed, as I am still recovering from the coma they put me in. Get over here as soon as you're up and listening to this.'

Half an hour later I was at my mother's apartment. She gave me a cursory hug, she was talking rapid-fire, she was all-business.

'Tell me what you have already done in the way of the funeral arrangements.'

Mom heard me out, agreed with my choices, then told me she was taking everything else over.

'This is my show now.'

She was anxious for news about Adam. I told her of a message following hers on my answerphone from Counselor Grech. He said that the bail hearing was in two days and that he'd managed to avoid having Adam temporarily incarcerated in the nightmare that was the prison on Rikers Island. He would ensure that my brother was there at the funeral ... though he would probably be accompanied by plainclothes detectives.

'He also said that he would call you this morning and arrange to pay you a visit at home today.'

'So he can tell me how you're Miss Clean Hands in all this?'

'Mom ... '

'I'm not talking about this now with you. As my own mother used to say – one of the few good things about a death is that there is so much to plan and do for the funeral. Mom loved a good planting. It was one of her preferred entertainments. Because it reinforced her grim view of life. I am following her dark yenta train of thought and just focusing on getting your father sent off to wherever his idiot religion thinks he's heading.'

I was going to say something about the idea of Dad being in some sort of paradise now was better than thinking of him on a cold slab in a hospital mortuary. I also wanted to know how Mom had rebounded so quickly from all the sedation given to her at the hospital. She answered that question for me.

'The intern on duty in the crazy-house ward was pretty insistent that I stay until morning. I complimented him on the drugs they gave me. They did the knockout job and got me through the grand-opera phase of all this, but did so without making me feel like I had been hit over the head with a baseball bat. I also told him that, as I hadn't been committed or forced to wear a straitjacket, I was walking out of here – and just try to stop me.'

'You certainly have mastered the art of bouncing back.'

'Don't be so sure about that. I have just decided to keep my grief to myself until this is all over. One thing I want to make very clear now: there is no way that Peter is coming to the funeral.'

'I don't think you have to worry about that.'

'Why? Because you know his whereabouts now?'

'Like you I've been just a little preoccupied with everything that has happened in the last thirty-six hours. I've no idea where Peter is.'

'Promise me you won't go out to Brooklyn in search of him.'

I was going to ask Howie to do that for me. Just as I was going to get the lowdown from him on all the press coverage. Mom had not been briefed on all that, though no doubt her ultra-efficient secretary, Marge, had cut out every press clipping and even perhaps had used a VCR to tape all television reports on Adam's arrest. Mom was somebody who needed to know everything. Just as I could see that all this full-speed-ahead, all-business approach she was taking this morning was her way of numbing the desperate pain within.

The article by Peter had hit the streets yesterday. When I left my mother's around 7 a.m., I bought a copy from the news guy on the corner of 86th and Broadway, then walked south and sat at the Burger Joint, my favorite greasy spoon in the neighborhood. I ate eggs and toast, drank their reasonable coffee, and read Peter's very manicured and expressive prose. As much as I didn't want to admire the writing I couldn't help but be impressed by his immense readability and the way he drew you right into the web of familial and communal deceit – as he made the point very clearly that the chicanery on Wall Street was a larger reflection of a culture, a society, in thrall 'to money as the ultimate way we keep score with each other'. Peter's skill was to thread these themes into his brother's tale of trying to please Dad and always feeling like 'the reluctant jock with the pressure to conform', and to show how he'd been undermined by that equal need to earn big. The portrait of the hothouse that was our family life in Old Greenwich, the way that Adam suddenly gave up on ice hockey (because, according to Peter's hypothesis, 'he never had the killer instinct'), the years of prep-school coaching, the rebirth as Junk Bond Gunslinger, the way he fell under the spell of a corrupt hotshot guru named Tad Strickland ... it was all rendered with immense urgency and stylistic aplomb. I finished it with a sense of despair – because it ended with Peter directly surmising that the publication of this story would mean Adam's arrest and the certain end of his relationship with his father. 'Dad, being the old Leatherneck Marine that he is, will never forgive me for breaking his deep code of family loyalty at all costs.' To his credit Peter never once tried to defend his decision to reveal all about Adam. He sidestepped all sanctimony or moralizing. Instead he posed many questions about the validity (or not) of denouncing someone you love but who has still done criminal wrong. Not once did he try to get the reader to side with him. The editor in me had to admire the canny way he negotiated all the big ethical issues that the piece raised without once trying to tell us how to think. He wanted us to draw our own conclusions, even if those were against his decision to go public on his brother's crimes and misdemeanors. He was not afraid of being judged badly for his actions even if Peter also hinted that he knew he'd be judged an opportunist by many for opening the door to Adam's arrest.

After reading it I sat quietly for several minutes, staring into the depths of my coffee cup, trying to pull myself together and not tip over into even more sorrow. Damn you, Peter – you nailed us, your flesh and blood, so well. He said little about me – hinting that I had been damaged by the white-bread bullies in Old Greenwich, and always felt outside of the conformist norm (an assessment I liked). But when it came to Mom's crazed dynamic at home, Dad's colossal infidelities, the male imperative that he placed on both sons – causing one to take the radical road and the other to be everything that his father wanted him to be – he was brutal in his lucidity. Mom, I was certain, was going to go ballistic when she read it – though he did show a degree of compassion for her status as a postwar housewife: highly educated, forced into a domestic role she truly despised, especially as she was exiled up in WASPland where her Brooklyn Jewishness was regarded with outward disdain.

But it was the mechanics of the frauds that Adam perpetuated – the detailing of all the insider trading games he played – which formed the bulk of the second half of the piece. Peter's technical recounting of them was devastating in its thoroughness, a clear account of Adam's immense cupidity and corruption. I now knew why Peter and *Esquire* kept the article under such wraps until publication. It read like an indictment.

There was a payphone by the toilets in the Burger Joint – and one which was functioning. I checked my watch. It was coming up to 8 a.m. I called Howie at home. He answered on the fourth ring, sounding in urgent need of caffeine.

'I figured it was you. Coffee awaits you here.'

I walked with speed to the 72nd Street subway station, past a drag queen standing outside the Ansonia Hotel, bawling his/her eyes out, eyeliner and mascara streaking his/her face, the howls emanating from him/her sounding like the greatest woes of the world – which, to him/her, they undoubtedly were.

Howie was dressed in gray silk pajamas and velvet slippers, with a silk paisley bathrobe tied across his thin frame.

'Did you actually do something sane and sleep?' he asked after giving me a hug.

'Valium has its virtues.'

'Valium is pharmaceutical Nirvana.'

'Until you get hooked on it.'

'Nothing wrong with being hooked on Nirvana.'

He pointed the way to the little table by his nook of a kitchen. A pot of French-press coffee was awaiting us. He pushed the plunger down and poured us out two cups.

'May I tempt you into a shot of cognac to accompany it?'

'I am trying to sidestep the larger temptation to fall apart. So ... no to the cognac. And knowing your horror of cigarettes I won't light up in front of you.'

'But you've already had two or three this morning. My nose never lies.'

'Dad might have lived longer had he laid off the smokes.'

'Your father died of anger, if I may say so. It's the most corrosive thing we carry with us. It eats the soul.'

'I'm going to be angry at Peter for a long time to come. But I'm even more angry at myself.'

'Why? Because you couldn't prevent the family implosion?'

'Because I did something beyond fucking stupid three nights ago. Stupid and probably irreparable.'

'Tell me.'

I explained Duncan's letter and my destructive Western Union reply. Howie listened in silence, putting his hand on my own when I felt myself starting to sob, calling myself a total mess-up when it came to matters of the heart.

'You've heard nothing in reply from Duncan?' he asked.

I shook my head.

'I'm a jerk,' I said.

'The more urgent question is: what do you want?'

'What I don't want is to get hurt.'

'Well then, never get involved with anyone again. Live the casual fuck life like yours truly. But that's not you, honey. You have connected with someone. You spent many years mourning him and doing the no-strings thing with the very elegant and emotionally limited Toby. A pity about Duncan – but something in you wanted to kill it before it started. Seventy-two hours later the question remains: what do you want?'

'How can I even think about that when I'm about to bury my father?'

'Then don't think about it. But if you are having regrets about that telegram a simple second one might save things. I'll even dictate it for you: *My dad died. I have not been thinking clearly. I miss you. Can we talk?*

'I've blown it. You know Duncan. He's your best friend.'

'Send him a telegram.'

I shook my head.

'I'll take that cognac now,' I said.

I wanted to go to work. But I knew that C.C. would order me home. I wanted to be at the funeral home when my father's body arrived there – but Howie told me that I should let the undertakers do their stuff, and that my mother would, no doubt, take care of details like choosing the suit he'd be buried in.

'Keeping out of your mother's range of fire might be best right now. As Peter has probably disappeared she is going to turn her guilt and rage on you – even after Sal has a talk with her and explains there was absolutely nothing you could do to save the situation. But you know your mother. Even if she has much improved since fleeing

DOUGLAS KENNEDY

back to the city and becoming the Real Estate Queen, old maternal habits die hard. Especially when there is the opportunity to deflect her own guilt and grief by giving you a supremely hard time. Stay away from her – unless she calls needing you for something practical.'

Mom did call, late the following night, after a lengthy interview with Peter appeared in the Metropolitan pages of the *New York Times*. He gave it the morning after the Susskind interview, in the wake of our father's death. The journalist reported that Mr Burns admitted to be doing this interview on no sleep and with immense remorse. Though he admitted to being devastated by his father's death, he didn't blame himself.

'Dad had been living under self-imposed stress for decades,' Peter told the reporter. 'He was a ticking time bomb. Though he believed in the ideology of "the family" he was always running away from its emotional responsibilities.'

The journalist posed many tough questions, asking directly if Peter would be able to now sleep at night knowing that his father died rushing to castigate him in public. Peter, she reported, admitted that 'this is going to take a very long time to process' and that while he was 'devastated' by Dad's fatal heart attack 'he died trying to defend a son who had, like my father in Chile, lived according to a very flexible code when it came to ethical principles'.

But wasn't he himself now accused of questionable ethics, 'of ruining his brother in an attempt to resuscitate a literary career that, after a blistering start, had come somewhat asunder ... until this journalistic coup which now had everyone talking'?

She noted that Peter shut his eyes when she asked this accusatory question, 'looking like he wanted to be anywhere but here ... yet simultaneously very willing to grant the *Times* an interview the morning after his father died raging at him in front of the assembled public and press on West 55th Street'.

Peter's response was ... very Peter.

'I have a very existential take on all this. We are all responsible for the decisions we make. Just as we are all, in the end, alone in a pitiless universe. I thought long and hard about the implications of this article, about the effects it might have on my brother, on my family. People will call me an opportunist. Others will think I did something brave. Know this: I will be able to live with my choices. Just as I will mourn my father every hour of every day. And now if you'll excuse me I'm going to disappear.'

The journalist finished her article by noting that Peter was indeed leaving the country that evening, that this was his last interview on the subject of his piece. She predicted a total bidding war for his book.

'Do you know where that little shit is hiding?' Mom asked.

'No idea.'

'Liar.'

'Trust you to engage in name calling at a time like this. Did Counselor Grech get in touch with you?'

'Yeah – and he even made a point of coming over to my apartment this morning and telling me that you were as clean and pure as Snow White.'

I said nothing. After several long moments of silence Mom said:

'If you want me to exonerate you ... '

'I'm hanging up.'

'Go on, do that. Walk away as you always do.'

'My biggest mistake was not cutting things off with you years ago. Every time I think we've gotten to a better place –'

'All you had to do was tell *me*, Alice. Just a word of warning – and I would have stepped in and –'

'You have clearly chosen to ignore everything that Counselor Grech told you.'

'No, I heard him all right. He made your case very well. Still, *still*, had you told me I would have brought my negotiating skills to the fore and worked out a solution. Had you told me, your father would still be alive today.'

I slammed down the phone. When it rang again, I didn't pick it up. I grabbed my coat. I walked out into the Manhattan night. It was a clear cool night. I wandered uptown, keeping close to the curb north of 96th Street, avoiding the edgy side streets, thinking I should call Howie and cab it south to his place and break down amidst his velvet opulence, and also telling myself that I couldn't keep running to him at every crisis point.

Instead I kept walking north, passing 106th Street, passing the West End Cafe where Arnold Dorfman and I both discovered jazz as teenagers, while we were discovering so much else. Arnold. I got a note from him when I was promoted at Fowler, Newman and Kaplan; he told me he'd read about my senior editorship in the *New York Times* and was not surprised, 'as I always thought you'd do something bookish and smart'. He'd graduated *summa cum laude* from Cornell, gone on to Yale Law School – 'finally pleasing my unpleasable parents' – and then found himself cruised by a 'big-deal Philadelphia law firm'. He'd made partner in four years. He was married to a woman rabbi named Judah, they were living on the Philadelphia Main Line in Haverford, and already had a two-year-old son named Isaac. 'So I guess I've fallen into the usual life,' he wrote. 'There will be another child, maybe a third. We have just bought a super-WASP large redbrick house. Life is very acceptable. But I should have had that year in Paris. I should have backpacked my way through the Greek Islands. I shouldn't have been so eager to follow the "success path" as laid out by my parents. However, I am enough of an über-rationalist not to blame Mom and Dad – to say in those middle-of-the-night moments, when I start to rue all this responsibility, that I chose this; that I do very much love Judah and Isaac and am a most fortunate man. But I also envy you being unencumbered in the big city, working with writers, having all the latitude that I have denied myself.'

It was certainly an intriguing letter. But I couldn't help but think: *latitude, moi?* Yes, I had no fellow, no children, no mortgage, no loans, and nominal credit card debt which I paid off every month. But I too was just as much a wage slave as everyone else. I too had to balance the books, to turn a profit, to make myself valuable to my bosses and not give them an excuse to turn me out onto the street. That was the realpolitik of my workaday life. Though I genuinely loved the work, though I told myself regularly how fortunate I was to be paid for this professional engagement with the written world, there were moments when I saw the years stretching out before me and wondered 'is this ever going to be enough?' Why was that question one which seemed to haunt everyone I knew? I thought of Dad in his coffin, awaiting his descent into the cold earth, and how we were all alone, even when we were with someone, how fulfillment and satisfaction (as Arnold indicated in his letter) were not a destination – because even when you had all the building blocks of a life in place – were you then actually happy with the edifice that you had constructed for yourself?

I walked right up past the gates of Columbia University, then turned south again and ducked into the West End Cafe. It was now almost 1 a.m. The late set was just starting. I sat at the bar. I ordered a Manhattan. I silently toasted my dad, wishing he was here, wishing that his final words to me weren't 'Fuck you, Alice'. He'd remained true to his rage right to the end. Had we been able to talk, had he not gone ballistic, had he been the sort of man who could have counted to ten ...

Wishful damn thinking. He did love me. I would hold on to that thought as a way of putting his final enraged act in perspective. Sitting there, listening to an ageing tenor saxophonist and his band swing mournfully to 'Someday My Prince Will Come', I told myself:

Guilt was not the answer.

But oh God, how hard it was to dodge its toxic force, the way it functioned as an internecine vortex, with immense gravitational pull, in the life of virtually all families, and how it had just made me slam the door on a man I actually wanted and whose love for me was, I now knew, real.

I was about to light a cigarette as a way of balming the sadness coursing through me. I pushed the pack away, thinking back to Dad just a few weeks earlier wheezing away over brunch, getting into a coughing fit as he touched his Zippo to the tip of his Pall Mall, telling me:

'Well, they always told me it was a dumb habit.'

Could I renounce cigarettes?

Probably not tonight, or tomorrow. But they were a bad friend I needed to divest myself of soon.

Could I renounce guilt?

That was going to make renouncing the smokes seem facile. Because guilt was even more addictive than nicotine.

Raising my glass for a second time I repeated the silent toast to Dad, adding a footnote: 'I hope there is now some peace for you. Just as I want a little more now for myself.' And I am finally going to put some work into stepping back from the belief that I can fix things. Whereas the truth, now hard-learned, was: at best you might just be able to fix a bit of yourself.

Up onstage the quartet now finished a dark-hued rendition of 'Round Midnight'. After the applause of the ten or so of us listening in, the saxophonist approached the microphone. When he spoke, his voice sounded like tobacco-cured ambrosia.

'Now I do have an eye for the ladies. And I have been noticing that beautiful, sad-eyed lady sitting over there by herself at the bar.'

I glanced around, wondering who he was talking about, as the only other person at the bar was a bald man in his fifties in an ill-fitting suit, drinking shots of Jameson's with beer chasers. Then the penny dropped. I turned toward this grizzled gentleman and gave him the slightest of nods. Then feeling just a little self-conscious I turned my gaze downward into the amber waters of my Manhattan. The saxophonist spoke again into the microphone.

'Not only is the lady sad and beautiful, but also beautifully reserved. Well, this next tune is an original composition. And the title ... it kind of sums up the way I look at all the bad stuff that comes all our way; the fact that, as my daddy once told me, misfortune is simply part of the damn deal. Because, as he was also fond of saying: *it is what it is.* A true philosopher, my daddy. And someone who bequeathed so much to me. Like the title of this next song – which I'm going to dedicate to that quiet study in elegant melancholy at the bar. *It is what it is,* my sad lady. *It is what it is.*'

I didn't see my mother again until we were standing by my father's coffin in the Church of St Malachy. Adam arrived, accompanied by Sal Grech and two rather imposing men in suits. I saw them drive up in an unmarked car. I saw them lead my brother out handcuffed.

I saw them exchange quiet words with Adam and Counselor Grech. The handcuffs were removed. But when my mother and I tried to hug him, the two Feds stepped in between us and Adam. Mom was livid.

'I'm his mother.'

'We can't allow that,' one of the Feds said.

'He's here for his father's funeral,' Mom said.

Sal Grech immediately put a steadying hand on Mom's shoulder.

'Brenda, be pleased that your boy is here.'

'They treating you okay?' she asked Adam.

'They're treating me just fine. Counselor Grech tells me I'm being transferred up to a very nice minimum security prison in New York State tomorrow.'

'Why isn't he out on bail?' Mom demanded.

'This is not the time or place, Mom,' I said.

'Don't you dare tell me –'

'Alice is right,' Sal said. 'I will take you through everything to do with Adam's case after this is all finished. Until then ... '

Linking his arm in hers he guided her into the church.

'Hello, sis,' Adam said.

How that hated nickname made me choke up now.

'You're looking okay, under the circumstances,' I said.

'Sleep would be nice. The place they've got me ... '

'That's enough, Burns,' the second Fed said.

'Sorry, sorry,' Adam said, hanging his head.

'How is Janet?'

'Suing me for divorce.'

'That was fast.'

'I guess she figures that she might as well get me while I still have money.'

'I left her a message. No answer.'

'She's gone tribal. She's with her people ... and who can blame her, with the baby due any day now.'

'Have you heard from Ceren?'

'I've been kind of incognito. But hasn't she been in touch with you since this went down?'

No, but her agent certainly had been, as well as the publicity maven she'd hired to ensure big exposure for her book. They both said that she was waiting a few days to see how it all played out with Adam, so they could together devise a strategy to maximize her connection with Adam when it came to media attention for her tome. Her agent actually apologized for 'being a little merciless about this, especially as the guy is your brother. But I'm sure, as you can appreciate, this is just business.'

'Maybe we can talk about this after I bury my father, okay?'

Though the agent was on the other end of a phone line, I could hear her sharp intake of breath, indicating that she knew she had transgressed a certain frontier. When she began to apologize – and to do so profusely – I reassured her that no offense had been taken. But I knew that I now had the upper hand with her the next time we were in negotiation for something. Just as I was not surprised that Ceren – being a very bright opportunist – would milk her intimate association with a big-deal Wall Street felon ... who also happened to be my brother.

'I'm sure Ceren is very concerned with what's been happening to you,' I told Adam, 'and will be in to see you whenever that can be arranged. Any news about bail?'

'I know that Counselor Grech is working on it.'

What Grech was working on, first and foremost, was a plea bargain designed to get Adam reduced time, in return for turning state's evidence against Tad and several other junk bond kings. Tad himself had been arrested the day after Adam, his lawyer telling the press that his client 'wouldn't allow his name to be sullied by the corrupt Adam Burns who was the mastermind behind all that my client has been accused of'. Grech told me not to worry about such proclamations as 'the SEC really want to draw and quarter Tad Strickland and are willing to cut your brother a deal as long as he tells them everything they want to know ... which Adam is now willing to do. Especially as I think I can get him no more than eight years in a Club Fed and preserve around 25 percent of all the money accrued to keep Janet and the kids in a less-opulent, but still reasonable, standard of living. It will also let your brother have a little cushion to soften his return to life when he's paroled in about four to five years.'

Sal Grech sat with my mother in the front row of St Malachy's. I was on the edge of the pew, near my brother who was sandwiched between the two Feds. These guys were clearly packing heat (I could see the bulge beneath their respective jackets). They had also worked out in advance how they were going to ensure that Adam didn't try to slip away from their custody – not that he would ever do something insane like that. But I could see all eyes in the church focusing less on the flag-draped coffin, and more on the fellow whose face had become tabloid fodder over the past few days. Adam smiled and nodded at everyone who made eye contact with him. But the deep fatigue on his face – coupled with his haunted countenance – gave him the air of someone who knew that his life was plunging downward; that things would never be the same for him again.

There was a two-man honor guard standing by Dad's coffin. This turned out to be a de rigueur service by the US Marine Corps for any of their veterans when they left this life. Mom requested them. Dad would have approved. There was also a reasonable crowd in the church, as C.C. and ten of my colleagues showed up along with blessed Howie. Mom's real estate associates were also there. Notably absent from the funeral were anyone from Dad's office, outside of a woman who introduced herself as his secretary and told me:

'The president of the company asked me to be his representative here today. We've sent flowers to the graveside.'

Nor was anyone there from his copper days – even though I made a point of phoning his old company and asked to be put through to the head of personnel, telling the fellow with whom I was connected that Brendan Burns – who created their Iquique mine and was with their company for almost twenty years – had passed on. If anyone wanted to attend the funeral ...

The priest began the Mass. He recited prayers for the dead as he sprinkled the casket with holy water. He gave a brief recounting of my father's life, borrowing a bit from the two pages of notes that I sent him about the highlights of Dad's existence. He talked about how he had survived war. How he had come up from a humble

Brooklyn background. How he'd become a world traveler and someone who felt that, in the mine he had planned in Chile, he'd left behind something of importance. How he loved his wife and children. And how, in true Irish American fashion, he frequently let his emotions get the best on him – and, in the end, collapsed defending a son of his, whom he would still be proud of today.

Across the aisle Adam began to sob loudly at this comment – which I had put in my notes to Father Meehan and which he repeated word for word. When Adam's sobbing escalated, I stood up and crossed over to my brother, wanting to put my arms around him, to make him realize that, in this very dark juncture in his story, he was not alone. But as soon as I attempted to reach him the two Feds stood up, blocking my contact with the man in their custody. Mom was nothing less than outraged, hissing at them:

'Assholes.'

That caught the attention of the priest, whose eyebrows shot northward, as he and a Hispanic altar boy (I liked that Hell's Kitchen touch) prepared to offer communion. Several rows behind me I heard Howie giggle, then hiss at my mother:

'You tell them, girl.'

I shared a limousine out to the cemetery alone with Mom, as the two Feds insisted on taking Adam out there in their own official vehicle. Like me, Mom was dressed in black. Unlike me she wore a small black pillbox hat which looked like something sported by Lana Turner in some 1950s black-and-white melodrama. She wasn't sad, she was outraged.

'My spies around town told me the bidding for Peter's book started with a floor of one hundred thousand. That shit is about to come into serious money again. And you still don't know where he is?'

I shook my head.

'But you have an idea,' Mom said.

'No, I do not.'

'Thank you for being in touch over the last few terrible days.'

'You kind of pushed me away, Mom.'

'Don't blame me. Blame your thin skin.'

'The priest spoke well.'

'I'm surprised you didn't insist on reading a poem over his body.'

'The Catholics have their way of doing such things.'

'You could have called me.'

I met her gaze straight on.

'Not after what you said.'

'So you want an apology?'

'I actually want nothing from you, Mom.'

That comment pushed her back in her seat, tears running down her face.

'One day you might just have children ... and I seriously hope you discover just how ungrateful they can be to the parent who has done everything for them.'

We rode in silence for the rest of the journey.

I stayed calm during the scene at the graveside. More holy water, more prayers, Mom and Adam crying, the priest reminding us of the bleak 'ashes to ashes, dust to dust' nature of our temporality. The coffin was left above ground as we said our final goodbyes. I put my hand on its simple pine veneer. I silently wished my dad some sort of eternal peace. Adam looked beyond shell-shocked as the two Feds tapped him on the shoulder and indicated that he was being brought back to their car and onward to the undisclosed prison where he was being held. I saw Mom whisper something to Counselor Grech who, in turn, approached the Feds and was striking a bargain with them. After a moment he motioned me and Mom over.

'You can give him a hug.'

Mom enveloped Adam in her arms and let go, weeping copiously, telling him that he was going to be all right, that she would get him through this. Adam kept repeating one phrase, 'I'm sorry, I'm sorry, I'm sorry.' After a minute the Fed lightly tapped him on the shoulder, indicating that he should withdraw. Then it was my turn to have a fast embrace.

'You will survive all this,' I said.

'Janet refuses to come see me.'

'Janet is about to have a baby.'

'Her lawyer sent Sal Grech a message yesterday. They are going to try to clean me out – after the US government does that first. All that crazy hard work, all the insane risks I took – and which I'm paying for now – it was all for nothing.'

'Counselor Grech will limit the damage on all fronts. And I will do everything I can to help you get through what's to come.'

'Why did Peter do this? Why?'

'The same reason why you did what you did: he saw an opportunity and seized it.'

The tap came again on Adam's shoulder. I gave him one final hug before he was escorted away, a Fed taking an arm each, to their nearby unmarked car. They insisted on handcuffing him again before opening the back door and doing that head-push that cops always engage in when getting the perp into the car.

As they drove off, Mom shook her head many times then turned to me and said:

'Why didn't you cry once today?'

My response to this question was a simple one:

I walked away, saying nothing.

That night, after the small wake in Mom's apartment – during which I assiduously stayed out of her line of fire – Howie insisted on taking me to a local dive bar, the Tap-a-Keg, on 80th and Broadway for a few cocktails. Over the second Manhattan he told me:

'Another two friends – Fire Island people – died over the weekend. That makes 112 people I personally knew who are no longer here.'

'But you're still with us.'

'There are rumors going around in the community that they'll have a test for it soon.'

'You still feel doomed, don't you?'

'Do you blame me?'

'Of course not. But so far you've dodged it.'

'I still think about that one idiocy a couple of months back. I could be a ticking time bomb.'

'But you've been safe since then?'

Howie nodded. Then:

'I'm not going to ask if you sent the telegram to Duncan.'

'Don't ask.'

'You've answered the question I dared not pose.'

'Maybe I can't do happy.'

'But you did once.'

'When it's all taken away from you "happy" becomes Albania: a closed-off country.'

'I'm sure there are many Albanians who are plotting that moment in the future when they can bring down the authoritarian regime that rules them.'

'Are you following my bad metaphor with one of your own?'

'Unhappiness is authoritarian, because it controls you. As such: it can also be a choice.'

'I didn't choose what happened in Dublin.'

'But you've chosen what happened since then.'

'Unhappiness ... it's the Burns family emblem.'

'Until one of you decides to change the narrative.'

I stared into my cocktail for a very long time.

'This is all too hard.'

'Consider the alternatives. I've been doing so since everyone around me started dying far too young.'

I resisted Howie's attempts to drag me out to dinner. Lack of sleep was overtaking me. I told him we'd catch up tomorrow – and yes, I would accept a Valium from him now to help me make it through the night.

When I got home I decided that I needed to make one phone call before I could try to surrender to sleep. To find the number meant digging around one of five storage boxes I had under my bed where I kept my notebooks from the past. It took around fifteen minutes of rooting around before I discovered the spiral-bound book that I'd bought at Eason's on O'Connell Street and which came with me on my one and only trip to Paris. The number I was looking for was written on the inside cover. I steadied myself – because I was unsure if this call was the best of ideas. But then I reached for the phone, punched in the international access code, then 33 for France, then the rest of the number beginning with 1 for Paris. I checked my watch. 9.08 p.m. – which meant it was six hours further on in the City of Light.

The phone rang and rang and rang. On the twelfth ring someone finally answered. He sounded as if I had just snapped him out of a very deep sleep.

'*Hotel La Louisiane ... oui?*

'*Je veux parler avec Peter Burns,*' I said in my limited French.

'*Qui?*

'Peter Burns.'

'*Qui?*

'Burns. B-U-R-N-S.'

'*Moment.*'

The line went dead. After what seemed like an interminable silence a rumbling ring came down the line. This time the phone was answered on the second ring. My other brother answered.

'Yes ... *désolé ... oui?*

'So you are in Paris,' I said.

There was a long silence. Then:

'Why are you calling me?'

'Because, weirdly, I actually care about you. And I wanted to know where you are in the world.'

'Your tone indicates wild disapproval.'

'Think what you like.'

'I will.'

With a click Peter had ended the conversation.

I was hardly happy after this exchange. But at least I now had, for the moment, an actual geographic point of reference for my older brother (and one which I was certainly not going to share with Mom). And I had communicated an important piece of information to him: despite all that had transpired, despite my better judgment, I was still here for him. Knowing Peter it would take weeks, maybe months, for him to get back in touch. But that moment would come – and I would take the call. Just as when Mom got out of her grief/rage dance and began to distance herself from the narrative she had invented for all this, she too would make a call. In turn I would take it. And try not to show hurt or rancor. There had been five of us. Now there were four, with one about to be locked away from the world for several years. I had spent my life running away from, yet still engaging with, all the familial shit. Now there was a different frame of emotional reference: I would be there for my brothers and my sometime benevolent/ frequently malevolent mother. But from this moment on, I was perfecting that one art so necessary amidst the mess that is family: the art of walking away.

I got out of my black suit. I took a long hot shower. I got into a pair of track bottoms and a T-shirt. I decided to get into bed within the hour with a book and see if I could avoid a sleepless white night without medication. I sat down in one of the uncomfortable armchairs that were a feature of this place. I shut my eyes. All the grief that I had kept under wraps for the past few days – the immense sense of loss coupled with the mess of events that had triggered this loss – finally came flooding forth. I must have cried for a serious ten minutes . . . until I was so spent that I staggered into the bathroom, filled the sink with frigid water and plunged my head into it.

The cold baptism helped. I caught sight of myself in the mirror and didn't like what I saw. But at least I had finally broken down – *I don't have an icicle in my heart, Mom.* And now, I sensed, the long slow process of properly mourning my father's loss could begin.

I resisted the temptation to reach for a cigarette and open a bottle of wine. Bed with just two cocktails in me struck me as a smart approach.

But then, out of nowhere, the intercom began to buzz. I checked my watch. It was 8 p.m. Damn you, Howie. As much as I love you, you are relentless when it comes to dragging me out into the Manhattan night. But though part of me wanted to pick up the intercom and tell him to buzz off and let me have a decent night's sleep for a change, I also could not help but feel so grateful to this profoundly good man who was one of the few stable constants in a profoundly unstable world. Whenever I considered Howie one thought always came to mind: friendship is God's apology for family.

I hit the intercom button, barking into the speaker:

'If you can bear seeing me in my Wicked Witch of the West guise come on up.'

I hit the entry button. I heard footsteps on the three long flights of stairs up to my eyrie. There was a knock on the door. I opened it.

But it wasn't Howie in front of me.

It was a man with a few weeks' growth of beard and a face that showed extended exposure to the sun. He looked disheveled, weary – as if traveling for a very long time. A stuffed backpack was by his side, a leather satchel slung over his shoulder. He looked at me and smiled.

'You don't look a mess. You look as beautiful as ever.'

Duncan.

I blinked and felt tears.

'Howie telegrammed me in Cairo three days ago. I tried to get back in time for the funeral. But the first flight available was this morning via Athens and then –'

'Shut up,' I said. 'You're here.'

He smiled again.

'I'm here.'

He reached out for my hands.

'Can I come in?' he asked.

My fingers intertwined with his.

'As long as you don't leave.'

'I won't leave.'

I pulled him right across my threshold and into my life.

Reagan won big that November. Landslide big. Forty-nine states in his neoconservative pocket. The markets shot ever more northward. Real estate boomed in Manhattan. Everywhere there were articles about a new metropolitan species: the yuppie (young urban professional) with cash to burn. Shopping suddenly became the major cultural activity of our time. Vast amounts of column inches were spent on the culinary wonders of new restaurants, with people clamoring to get a table at certain hot places where the menu read like foodie science fiction: *hydroponic lettuce with crème fraiche and dill.* One-time fishing villages deep in the Hamptons suddenly became the target of plutocrats. Designer labels were now an obsession. Just as there was the belief that all those past concerns about conspicuous consumption were so 1968. The new reality was that money was now the way we kept score. Although it was always an essential component of the internal combustion of American life, it now held everyone – even those of us who turned up our noses at its current excesses – in thrall.

Knowing that we had a real zeitgeist magnet on our hands I decided to bring forward Ceren's book to election week. Many people at the house thought this a big gamble. But C.C. backed me after an editorial meeting when I outlined exactly why we could capitalize on what looked to be a slam-dunk for Reagan and the ethos he embodied ... one which was reflected in Ceren's take on modern sexual gamesmanship and its inherently transactional nature.

Yes, Ceren did also use her boyfriend's imprisonment for insider trading in a most canny manner and to her maximum advantage. In tandem with her publicity maven she did clear everything with me first. And yes, there were certain journalistic questions raised – in the 'Intelligentsia' column of *New York* magazine – about whether I was playing fast and loose by being the editor on a book written by the mistress of My Brother the White Collar Felon. And, of course, there were more mentions of how Peter himself also used family *merde* for his own professional edification.

I gave one, strategically chosen interview, to the *Wall Street Journal* – which our own in-house press people made sure got much play elsewhere – in which I pointed out that, yes, my brother had introduced me to Ceren, but the fact that she had an involvement with Adam did not sway my decision to publish her. My house backed buying Ceren's book on both its commercial merits and the fact that it is such a racy, witty, knowing read – as demonstrated in the fact that it was already number 5 on the bestseller lists and we were already beginning to think that sales of 100,000 in hardcover was more than possible.

When it came to questions about Peter and his new book deal – worth a cool $150,000 – I said that I was not in contact with my brother (the truth). Out of respect for the grief of all of us in the family, I had nothing further to say about all that had transpired. Mom wrote me a short postcard a few days after the interview appeared – we were still not talking – with a two-line message:

Well done with the WSJ.
Exactly the right response and tone.

She signed nothing after this … not even a simple 'Mom'. Still, that was high praise from Brenda Burns. In keeping with the current protocol between us I sent back a postcard:

Glad you approved.
Love – Alice

C.C. was also pleased with the way I'd handled much of the press fallout, noting that:

'You're very adept at saying what seems to be much, while revealing very little at the same time. Then again you also seem to be quite skilled at not being an open book about anything in your life outside of here at the house. So I'm sure I'm not going to get a direct answer if I ask: is the recent lightness that myself and others have sensed in you perhaps due to you being in love?'

I favored my boss with the smallest of smiles.

'Perhaps,' I said.

'Fear not, I will ask no further details. But I'm pleased for you, Burns. You deserve a big dose of happiness after everything else that has come your way.'

On which note …

Sal Grech turned out to be a master at legal deal-making (no surprise there), getting Adam transferred to a minimum-security setup in Hudson County the day after Dad's funeral. Sal called me regularly to keep me informed of all the judicial progress. He explained that his strategy was to not apply for bail so that Adam could get working immediately with the Feds and SEC when it came to giving them what they wanted vis-à-vis Tad and his company's scams.

'Adam has agreed to turn state,' Sal said. 'Which is very smart on his part. Because we're able to fast-track the entire process. He's going to plead guilty straightaway – and we have a deal with the DA's office: eight years, a fine of eight million ... '

'Good God.'

'It's still leaving him with around $3 million. We're also handling his divorce. Janet's getting a clean-break payment of $2 million. The big house is going to be sold, but she'll also get the half-million in equity – which will buy her and the kids something very nice in Rye or Byrum. There will be no alimony, no child support – though Adam has made it clear that, once he's out and on his feet again, he'll want to contribute significantly to their education and well-being. By the time he pays off Janet and the costs of getting him a seriously reduced sentence – he'll be out in five years tops, maybe even a little earlier – he'll probably have around six hundred grand in the bank when he walks free. Not exactly riches beyond avarice. But considering how the courts and angry greedy wives like to asset-strip the big-deal money guy in cases like this – and considering how a fifteen-year sentence is about average for insider trading these days – I sense that Adam has done okay. By the way, he asked me to personally tell you the terms of the deal he made with the government and with the ex.'

'You did brilliantly, Counselor,' I said.

'All part of the service.'

I began to visit Adam weekly in prison. Though he was relieved to have gotten away with a moderate sentence, and to know he would eventually leave prison with some money in the bank, his initial disposition worried me. He was clearly depressed, overeating, lacking in exercise, lacking in focus. I brought him books. I brought him magazines and newspapers. I brought him all the snack food he demanded: M&M's, beef jerky, tortilla chips. When he complained about not sleeping, about feeling listless, about being awash in shame and sadness I suggested that he try to speak to a resident therapist in the prison. There was no such person on staff, only a locum psychiatrist who came in every two weeks. This being a minimum-security place, the

State Correctional people felt they didn't need to be paying too much attention to the mental well-being of their inmates. Which is where the more omnipresent evangelical man of God, the splendidly named Pastor Willie, came in. He'd connected with Adam at the end of his first week inside. By the time the election came around Adam was seriously born again. Which is how, dealing with a hangover and the prospect of four more years of our B-movie actor president, I was not exactly prepared for this out-of-nowhere statement during my morning-after Reagan Victory prison visit:

'Pastor Willie says you can never apologize enough for past sins; that the only way you can redeem yourself is by walking the walk of righteousness and atoning for the past.'

'I'm not sure I want any truth this morning.'

'But this is something that needs to come out.'

'Why today?'

'I need to share it.'

'I hear the voice of Pastor Willie behind this need to *share* . . .'

'He did tell me that until I confessed this transgression –'

'Transgression is a big, loaded word.'

'Will you hear me out, *please?*'

I sat back on the hard metal chair, surprised by the vehemence underscoring that last statement. I could see Adam getting agitated again, so I reached for the bag of Oreos at my feet, offering it to him. He ripped it open, scooped out three of the black-and-white wafers and virtually inhaled them, looking a little calmer after the sugar-rush hit. Then closing his eyes, as if momentarily at prayer, he snapped them open and began to speak.

'Remember when I was in the car accident?'

'The one that happened your senior year at college?'

'January 11, 1970. The same day as the Kansas City Chiefs beat the Minnesota Vikings 23–7 in Super Bowl IV.'

'The things you remember.'

'I will always remember January 11, 1970 – and how it all happened around one in the morning, heading back to college after losing a game to Dartmouth.'

The 'game' in question was ice hockey, which Adam played brilliantly back then. So brilliantly that he won a sports scholarship to a so-so college – St Lawrence – and was being groomed for possible entry into the NHL. My father could not have been prouder; he himself had played hockey at the Catholic prep school to which he'd been sent after he found his mother dead of an embolism in the kitchen of the third-floor walkup apartment in Brooklyn when he was just thirteen years old. Adam was Dad's absolute pride and joy. The happy-go-lucky jock who did everything his father told him to do; who was quite the stud by the age of sixteen; who got the full ticket to college because of his prowess on skates while wielding a stick; and who was being scouted by the New York Rangers and the Philadelphia Flyers ... until the accident happened.

'You weren't badly injured in the accident, right?' I asked my brother, my brain whirring back through the years to the pre-dawn phone call that my dad received from the police near Hanover, New Hampshire; my mother getting hysterical, and Dad jumping into the family station wagon and racing up to be with Adam and sort out matters.

'I had a concussion after the car hit one of the VW microbuses that were popular back then, especially among hippie types. The car killed this young couple and their baby daughter.'

'I remember all that. Just as you were lucky to be alive. Because you were in the front seat. And you weren't wearing a seat belt.'

'Back then seat belts were something for nervous mothers and old ladies. And my car was that big 1965 Buick which Dad gave me as a gift the year before when I was named team captain. It had one of those long front seats in upholstered in beige vinyl.'

'I also remember the car. Just like I remember Mom telling me one of your teammates had been driving it, and that Dad was really furious at you for letting the kid behind the wheel. He was also killed in the accident, right?'

Adam nodded acknowledgment, then fell silent for a moment, his gaze focused on the scuffed linoleum below us.

'The guy behind the wheel was named Fairfax Hackley. He was a Negro scholarship kid from the South Bronx. And something of an anomaly: a dude from the ghetto who played ice hockey. Seems there was some teacher at this big rough public school he went to who got him interested in skating, and he just shot off into the stratosphere when this teacher hooked him up with an amateur team up in Westchester. Here was this guy – whose older brother was doing time in Attica for a succession of armed robberies – playing hockey with all these prep-school assholes in Tarrytown and kicking everyone's ass. Naturally a bunch of colleges were after him, and St Lawrence offered him, like me, the full ticket. Though I was a pretty terrific player I was not in Fairfax's league. Yeah, the NHL scouts were interested in me – but no one was making any immediate bids for my services. Fairfax, on the other hand, was offered a contract by the Bruins for the '69–'70 season. But that would have meant not finishing St Lawrence – and Fairfax had his eye on the bigger prize: being the first person in his family to graduate from college. Back then the NHL maybe paid sixty thousand per year: good money, but not the insane sums they've started to pay recently. The way Fairfax figured it: he'd finish St Lawrence *magna cum laude*, play pro hockey for around eight years, salt away considerable cash, then head to law school, Wall Street, and eventually Washington. The guy was Negro Upward Mobility Personified. And then ... then, after the Dartmouth game ... '

Now Adam got up and started pacing the room again manically.

'He fell asleep behind the wheel, right?' I said. 'After you guys had drunk a bunch of beers. Is that why you're suddenly bringing this up? Did you give him the beers?'

'Fairfax didn't drink or smoke dope. Which everyone else on the team was constantly doing. Back then getting shitfaced and driving was an acceptable norm just about everywhere. Remember Dad having those three martini lunches at the weekend then driving you to the Girl Scouts?'

'What I remember most is hating every minute of the Girl Scouts. But I do recall Dad bringing along a cocktail shaker and a martini glass with him, and smoking around five Lucky Strikes and finishing the martinis by the time our troop meeting was finished ninety minutes later. But why are you mentioning all this now? I mean, if my memory serves me Dad was relieved that he'd taken out an all-party policy on your car, knowing full well that at some juncture during your college years you'd probably allow someone to drive you home. Most of all, Mom and Dad were so grateful that you weren't dead. Explain to me how come this is now a topic of conversation almost fifteen years later?'

Adam suddenly stopped pacing – and put two hands against the far wall. Then staring ahead into the web of cracked plaster, his back completely turned to me, he said:

'I'm telling you all this now, because ... '

A long pause, which I didn't interrupt. Finally:

'Because Fairfax Hackley wasn't driving the car. I was.'

Silence. My first thought was: this is a story I really don't want to hear.

But the confession having been uttered I now had no choice but to ask questions.

'If you were driving, how was it blamed on Fairfax?'

He kept staring into the wall.

'After the accident I changed positions with Fairfax.'

'What?'

'I was driving. Before we got in the car, Fairfax kept telling me to give him the keys; that he was sober, that he would drive. But big stupid macho me ... hey, I wasn't going to let some Negro drive me home. And yeah, that's an ugly thing to admit now. But I've got to admit it all to you. Everything.'

I said nothing, thinking: how often an admission of guilt – especially to a member of your bloodline or your spouse – is also a means by which you can diminish your own sense of culpability by dumping the guilt into their lap. And thereafter making them share it with you.

Adam continued on.

'After we lost the game most of the team went home on the bus. But I convinced Fairfax to keep me company in Hanover. What did we do? End up in some frat house where I threw back too many beers while the Dartmouth Delta Kappa Epsilon assholes made comments about allowing a Negro across their threshold.'

'Did your frat at St Lawrence welcome him with open arms?'

'Of course not. Back then a Negro was considered...'

'I think the proper term now is African Americans.'

'Trust you to play the semantic card. Always the editor. But fine: an *African American*. Anyway, around one that morning I insisted that we started heading back to New York State, as I was in danger of failing a course and had a paper due Monday morning. The way I figured, we could drive all night, get back to college around 6 a.m. I could crash for eight hours, get up, write the paper and avoid flunking out. But by the time we were leaving Hanover I was seriously drunk. So drunk that I wouldn't listen to Fairfax when he tried to tell me: "I can drive, man. I can get us home." I insisted on getting behind the wheel. I always remember how reluctant he was to slide onto the seat next to me. And how things were blurring already for me. So much so that I took a wrong turn, missed the highway and found myself on a back road. Realizing my mistake, I made this insane U-turn, not even looking if anyone was behind me or coming in the opposite direction. That's when I ran head-on into the minibus. There was this almighty crash. I was knocked out cold against the steering wheel. When I came to – it couldn't have been more than a minute – the minibus was already on fire. I saw the couple and their baby crushed inside. And next to me ... there was Fairfax. His head had slammed up against the dashboard, his neck broken.'

'And you?'

'Me? Someone clearly wanted me to live, as I hit the windshield with my head, but didn't smash through the glass. My ribcage was all banged up by being thrown against the steering wheel. But as concussed and traumatized as I was I had the fucked-up presence of mind to throw open the door. I stumbled out, then reached back in and grabbed Fairfax's dead body. I dragged him across the seat. I placed him behind the steering wheel, getting his limp hands around it. Then I slammed the door, staggered around to the other side of the car, and threw open the passenger door to make it seem like I escaped out that way. After that I fell toward the other side of the road and collapsed. When I came to again I was half frozen, surrounded by cops and ambulance people. Two fire engines were there, trying to douse the inferno that was now engulfing the mini-bus and my car. On the way to the hospital one of the paramedics told me:

"'Had some truck driver not come upon the scene fifteen minutes earlier and driven like hell to the nearest telephone and dialed 911, you might have frozen to death. Lucky man. You escaped so much tonight."

'But at that juncture all I wanted to do was die.'

He reached for another Oreo, gulping it down.

'When they brought me to the ER I could hear the doctors dis-cussing all the bruising around my ribcage, wondering how it hap-pened as I was in the passenger seat. But my head was so concussed that they drugged me up for around seventy-two hours in an attempt to help the brain heal. They had me on a drip to keep me hydrated. When I came to again Dad was by my bed. After the nurse made sure I was conscious and functioning he asked if he could have a few moments alone with his son. Once she left the room he turned to me and whispered:

"'You did the smart thing. Because of your rib injuries both the doctors and the cops suspect you were behind the wheel. But because the two vehicles were so badly burned, and because the kid was colored, and because he was seemingly behind the wheel, and because I got Walter Bernstein, a smart Jew lawyer from New York, up here immediately ... well, the case is already closed. Your team-mate was driving the car. You were asleep on the seat next to him. He lost control. It plowed into the bus, killing him and the hippie parents and their baby. You were knocked out cold. You came to when the car was about to burst into flames. You managed to stag-ger out just before both vehicles exploded. You passed out in the snow. You were found by some trucker. End of story. Do you get that? The story as I've just told it is *the story*. Never to be challenged, never to be changed. We have smoothed things out with the doc-tors, the cops, the insurance company. Everyone has agreed on what went down, and an official version has been rubber-stamped. Con-sider yourself lucky. Very fucking lucky. Know this: you owe me big time. But one last thing: we're never talking about this again." And the fact is: we never did.'

Silence. A very long silence. Adam kept his back to me, his gaze fixed on the wall. Finally, I spoke:

'So ... fifteen years after the event ... you decide to lay it all on me. In doing so you're insisting that I share your secret – and keep it just that: a secret.'

'You can tell the world if you want.'

'I'm telling no one. You've brought enough trouble down upon yourself over the past few years. But I have to ask you: who, besides Pastor Willie, knows about this?'

'No one.'

'You're absolutely sure you never mentioned it to Janet?'

'Never.'

My eyes scanned all four corners of this grim little room, checking to see if there were any cameras or microphones in sight. None on view. But I still dropped my voice down to a choked whisper as I said:

'Keep it that way. Don't listen to that evangelist about sharing this story with anyone – unless you want the case reopened and to find yourself on trial again. Only this time not only will you be charged with negligent homicide and corrupting the course of justice, but Fairfax's family will bring the sort of civil case that will have you wishing you were truly dead. Do you think Pastor Willie can keep his mouth shut?'

'He's always telling me that everything we talk about is confidential; that he is a great keeper of "eternal secrets".'

And I bet, like so many men of hyper-piety, he has more than a few dark secrets of his own.

'Well, your secrets are profoundly *temporal*, and could seriously see you never leaving prison. So from this point on ... I am going to forget that I heard this story.'

'You're sounding like Dad now.'

'I am anything but our father.'

'Then why are you conspiring with me, the way he did all those years ago?'

'Because, alas, we are family. And one of the truths accompanying that statement is the fact that: I am going to have to live with the knowledge of what you just told me.'

'Even though, a moment ago, you said you were going to forget that you ever heard it.'

'That was me being far too facile. I'm never going to forget that story. I'm also never going to talk about it again. Just as, unless you never want to leave these penitentiary walls, you won't repeat it again to a single soul.'

'You had to know. Because it's so about us. Because it's what we are.'

But then, after casting his eyes up toward the cracked ceiling tiles and fluorescent lights above us, his gaze turned to me, eyeing me like a sniper who'd just found his target.

'And now you're implicated,' he said.

Indeed I was. But on my way back to the city, as my head swam with the knowledge of everything just revealed, another thought struck me: this was a secret I would not ever repeat to anyone. Not to my mother. Certainly not to Peter. Not to Howie – because even though I trusted him implicitly, a secret shared is no longer a secret. But as my train arrived at Grand Central and I switched to the Lexington Avenue subway, I revised that vow not to tell anyone.

I left the subway at Astor Place, then walked two blocks east to Second Avenue and 11th Street, and into the venerable 1920s apartment building into which Duncan had just moved. I rode the elevator up to the eleventh floor and into his place.

While traveling across North Africa, a close academic friend of Duncan's who didn't get tenure at NYU was offered an associate professorship at the University of Wisconsin. Through a bit of negotiation and some money under the table Duncan was able to take over this rent-controlled two-bedroom place, facing east toward Alphabet City. A week after arriving on my doorstep he handed me a set of keys and told me his place was mine. In turn I searched a set of keys from one of my overcrowded desk drawers and told him my place was his.

A life together began – but with the agreement that we would maintain separate residences for at least a year, so we could find our way with each other and have necessary space. As it turned out, we were spending virtually every night together. Just as the moment one of us walked into the other's apartment, we were almost instantly in bed.

'Do you think it was this way for your parents?' I asked Duncan that evening, curled up in his arms, sharing a bottle of St Pauli Girl beer that he had found in the fridge.

'There had to be some sort of passion there at the start,' he said. 'But when it went wrong – and God did it go wrong – I sense they didn't touch each other for decades. Which is why my dad was like your dad – someone always looking for the refuge of another woman's arms, while never being able to leave my mother.'

'That won't be us,' I said, immediately regretting this comment. Duncan smiled.

'No need to reassure me, let alone yourself. That definitely won't be us.'

'Forgive me for sounding anxious.'

'Your family, my family – it would make anyone anxious. We'll do better.'

'That is my hope.'

'And mine.'

'And no secrets.'

Duncan leaned over and kissed me.

'There will always be secrets,' he said. 'It's the nature of the human condition to hide stuff – especially from oneself.'

'No big secrets then,' I said.

'That sounds reasonable. I have none. No hidden ex-wives or children born out of wedlock to a crazy Mormon widow. And no addiction to porn or cockfighting. And you?'

I reached for the bottle of beer and took a long hit. Then said:

'My brother revealed today that he killed four people in a car accident when he was drunk, that he put the blame on the dead friend in the passenger seat, and that our father helped him cover everything up with the police.'

Duncan was looking at me, wide-eyed.

'That's some revelation. I'm surprised you kept it to yourself until now.'

'I wanted you to take me to bed first.'

Over the next few minutes I repeated all that Adam told me – and how, when I told him he mustn't go public on this – as his pastor was suggesting he do – he then informed me: *now you're implicated.*

'By the time I left this afternoon I did get a promise from Adam not to do anything before talking to me again. He agreed to that.'

'Wouldn't it be best to place a call to Sal Grech? Tell him you have something important to report to him and get him up to Otisville to enforce the "you're never going to mention this again to anyone" law. And also get him to strong-arm the asshole Man of God.'

'That's a very smart strategy.'

'All part of the service.'

I had Sal Grech's home number – 'If it's urgent you call Sal whenever,' he had told me on several occasions, his use of the third person in talking about himself very Sal. I felt this was urgent and picked up the phone by the bed and rang his home number. It was a Manhattan area code. I had no idea where he lived. Park Avenue in the Seventies? Central Park West in one of those Gilded Age apartment houses? Certainly not down here in the funky East Village with a panoramic eastern view of the junkies shooting up in Tompkins Square Park, or up near me where the working girls lined my corner of Amsterdam Avenue, looking for a trick. The city might have been infused with a new hyper-capitalism ethos, but the place remained gritty, out there, not at all conforming to the clean, safe norm preferred elsewhere. Which is why I so hoped that the increasing, gentrifying menace of yuppiedom might be halted by some market correction.

Sal's housekeeper answered on the second ring. When I explained that I was a client's sister and it was urgent, she told me to hold on. A minute later Counselor Grech was on the line.

'Is this life or death, Alice?' he asked.

'Adam told me some serious things today in prison that could have major implications on his –'

'We'll stop right there, as we don't discuss such matters on the phone. Your brother is an important client. As such, can you meet me in the bar of the Carlyle Hotel in an hour?'

'I'll be there, sir.'

Duncan told me that I should jump a cab, and then he'd meet me later at Sweet Basil where the great jazz pianist Marian McPartland was playing tonight. I quickly showered, changed back into my suit (you have to show up well attired for Counselor Grech and the bar at the Carlyle) and actually raced over to Astor Place and caught a subway north. Walking quickly west from the 77th Street stop I made it to the hotel just at the appointed hour. Grech was a stickler about punctuality, and I knew he was interrupting his evening to see me, so there was no chance I was going to be late. He was waiting for me in a discreet side booth, dressed as always in an immaculate three-piece suit. He stood up as I approached the table. A waiter was on the scene immediately. Drinks were ordered. He began by asking me:

'Did you hear our friend Howard's very good news?'

'About the test?'

'Exactly.'

'You were so wonderful to set that up for him.'

'Howard is a man who would never break a confidence, never show disloyalty to a friend. I'd heard of a rather brilliant fellow in the medical school at Johns Hopkins who was masterminding a test for HIV. I made a call. I said that I had a close friend who needed his understandable fears put to rest, and who would volunteer to be one of the trial tests.'

I knew all this already because Howie, during our weekly lunch last Monday, revealed all about giving blood twice in a lab at NY Medical which then got shipped down to Johns Hopkins in Baltimore. That was fourteen days before our lunch.

'The first test came back negative, the second – six days later – also negative. It looks like I have somehow managed to dodge it.'

I wanted to jump up and down. Instead I just hugged my great and good friend and said:

'Stay safe. I want to grow old with you.'

'Sal Grech told me the same. Sal – who set this all up for me. Sal – who can fix just about everything except death.'

Back in the Carlyle bar I told Counselor Grech:

'You did a splendid thing for our mutual friend.'

'That is most kind of you to say so. But enough of good news ... tell me all.'

I recounted everything that Adam had told me. Grech raised his finger once when the cocktails arrived, indicating I should stop talking while the waiter was nearby (he was obsessed with secrecy), then lowered his finger when he was gone. After I finished he told me that he would easily ensure that Pastor Willie conveniently forgot that he ever heard this story. Just as he said he would be paying Adam a visit tomorrow and laying down the law about never repeating this tale to anyone again.

'As to your boyfriend ... ' Grech said.

'He can be totally trusted. And it was he who suggested that I call you straightaway.'

'I am liking him even more. But let me impart one simple life lesson to you – one which I am sure you have already figured out, but which is worth repeating. Everyone is hiding something. Everyone, in their own way, lies. Everyone has secrets. Transparency is a myth, a fairy tale. Especially in a marriage – and even more so in a family. No one is completely telling the truth. Nor can they. Nor should they. Because the vast majority of us are simultaneously trying to figure out the biggest mystery going: ourselves.'

He lifted his gin martini and clicked his glass against mine.

'You did the right thing coming to me tonight with such critical information. Your instincts are good ones. Keep them honed. You're going to need them for as long as you can still take a breath. And in the future keep this one thought in mind: If you want to keep a secret, you must also hide it from yourself.'

It gets cold at night in the desert. That was an intriguing discovery. So too the sight of snow when you were above its blood-red sands.

It was below zero at the Grand Canyon. There was a whiteout on the journey back to Flagstaff, forcing us to crash at a dive motel where a couple next door was having drunken verbal fisticuffs and – courtesy of 'the communion-wafer thin walls' (Duncan's comment) – very audible, fast sex punctuated by some loud post-coital burping.

'Let's now break into a rendition of that Rodgers and Hart favorite, "Isn't It Romantic",' Duncan said.

'Keep your voice down,' I said. 'They might hear you and think: we've been eavesdropped on by a New York cultural snob.'

'Me: a New York cultural snob? I think you might just have uttered a tautology. Anyway we've listened to enough of their Neanderthal idea of carnality. Now they can have a dose of our metropolitan smart talk.'

'I approve of your smart talk,' I said, leaning over to kiss him. 'Thank you for finally getting me out to the Wild West.'

'All part of the service,' he said, kissing me back.

It was his Christmas gift to me, this trip to Arizona. He managed to convince me to walk away from work for ten days and see why this corner of America remained so mythic. We'd flown into Vegas – an absurd place – spending two nights on the Strip, reveling in its gimcrackery, its neon-tangled, bad-taste excesses. Then we got into our rented car and headed southeast, winding our way toward that emblematic canyon. When first glimpsed not only does it reinforce a Darwinian view of time, but also reminds you that there was a place called the prehistoric many millennia before we started to emerge from caves. As such the vast majority of human striving and endeavor vanishes from view as soon as you and the people intertwined with you are no more.

I looked out at that vast metaphysical crevasse. It cleaved the earth clear to the horizon. I could not help but think of my father, now part of that limitless community of vanished souls. All that he wanted and never found. All that he railed against. All the secrets he accumulated. All the sadness that didn't have to be. All gone now. He was part of a past as vast as this canyon, a place to which we all travel, and which cannot be sidestepped by anyone who has ever walked this earth. Every one of us is ephemeral. Which is why life is both preposterous yet absolutely priceless. We are all heading toward the unknown. Along the way we are all going to make a mess of a great deal of our time here. We will talk ourselves into situations, involvements we don't want. Dodge the activation of dreams. Stand still when we should be moving forward. Shortchange ourselves of so much.

As if reading my thoughts Duncan said:

'Are you having an existential moment? Are you humbled in the face of such stark, primitive beauty?'

'Something like that. But also marveling at the way you sure do know how to talk beautifully, Mr Kendall.'

'It hides all the anxiety within. And the fact that, for all the outward confidence, I feel such a lost mess inside.'

I put my arm around him.

'Consider yourself found,' I said.

The next morning, after a sub-zero start on the gritty streets of Flagstaff, we headed south, taking a two-lane blacktop that cascaded its way through a vertiginous alpine terrain. Then the sky returned, the grandeur widened. Before us was a crimson desert defined by craggy peaks, rocky and eruptive amidst this nowhere terrain.

'Let's pull over,' I told Duncan. He stopped the car, killed the engine. We got out, the blacktop beneath our feet hot and molten, the air drained of moisture, ash-dry. We stepped off the road into the red sand, our feet crunching its crust. The silence was cavernous, encompassing.

'Imagine what the first settlers who came west thought when they saw this,' Duncan finally said.

'They had no idea what lay beyond here.'

'They'd reached the end of the world ... or the beginning of it.'

'The Great Wide Open. That's what they called it. The big possibility of life as expressed in these vast empty spaces. Also known as: the future.'

'What else do we have but the future?' he asked, reaching out to take my hand.

There was much I wanted to say in reply, many reflections bouncing around that head of mine about all matters past, present, and in time to come. But all I could think was:

You can never really see the future. You can never know what is coming your way. You can make plans, embrace hopes. But the music of chance is always there – life's ever-incessant variations reminding you that the capacity for the interesting, the good, the wondrous will always be counterbalanced by the bad, the tragic, the downright terrible. It's the price we pay for this extraordinary, crazed gift that is our narrative: the recognition that nothing can be predicted ... except that your time in the Great Wide Open will one day come to an end. That moment when you reach the true end of the road.

But for those of us still here, still traveling, what else can you say about that which lies before us? What is that one succinct statement which sums up the story ahead?

To be continued.